# ENDANGERED SPECIES

# BAEN BOOKS by CHARLES E. GANNON

### THE TERRAN REPUBLIC SERIES
*Fire with Fire*
*Trial by Fire*
*Raising Caine*
*Caine's Mutiny*
*Marque of Caine*
*Mission Critical* (with Griffin Barber,
Chris Kennedy & Mike Massa)
*Endangered Species*
*Protected Species* (forthcoming)

### THE VORTEX OF WORLDS SERIES
*This Broken World*
*Into the Vortex*
*Toward the Maw* (forthcoming)

### THE RING OF FIRE SERIES (WITH ERIC FLINT)
*1635: The Papal Stakes*
*1636: Commander Cantrell in the West Indies*
*1636: The Vatican Sanction*
*1637: No Peace Beyond the Line*
*1636: Calabar's War* (with Robert E. Waters)

### JOHN RINGO'S BLACK TIDE RISING SERIES
*At the End of the World*
*At the End of the Journey*

### THE STARFIRE SERIES (WITH STEVE WHITE)
*Extremis*
*Imperative*
*Oblivion*

To purchase any of these titles in e-book form,
please go to www.baen.com.

# ENDANGERED SPECIES

## CHARLES E. GANNON

ENDANGERED SPECIES

This is a work of fiction. All the characters and events portrayed in this book are fictional, and any resemblance to real people or incidents is purely coincidental.

Copyright © 2023 by Charles E. Gannon

A Baen Books Original

Baen Publishing Enterprises
P.O. Box 1403
Riverdale, NY 10471
www.baen.com

ISBN: 978-1-9821-9271-6

Cover art by Kurt Miller

First printing, August 2023

Distributed by Simon & Schuster
1230 Avenue of the Americas
New York, NY 10020

Library of Congress Cataloging-in-Publication Data

Names: Gannon, Charles E., author.
Title: Endangered species / Charles E. Gannon.
Description: Riverdale, NY : Baen Publishing Enterprises, [2023] | Series: The Terran Republic ; 6
Identifiers: LCCN 2023019642 (print) | LCCN 2023019643 (ebook) | ISBN 9781982192716 (hardcover) | ISBN 9781625799227 (ebook)
Subjects: LCGFT: Science fiction. | Novels.
Classification: LCC PS3607.A556 E53 2023  (print) | LCC PS3607.A556 (ebook) | DDC 813/.6—dc23/eng/20230501
LC record available at https://lccn.loc.gov/2023019642
LC ebook record available at https://lccn.loc.gov/2023019643868

Printed in the United States of America
10  9  8  7  6  5  4  3  2  1

## A DEDICATION AND AN ACKNOWLEDGMENT

This book is dedicated to you,
the readers and fans of the Caine Riordan series
or, as many of you have dubbed it, the Caineverse.

I may have written it. Baen may have published it.
But *you* are the reason this book is in your hands
right now...as well as all those to come.

And with thanks to: Mark, also Mark, Jeff, Tom, and John.
—Because if you know, you know.

# CONTENTS

# ENDANGERED SPECIES

# PART ONE

# Too Far from Home

*Unknown World*
*March 2125*

# Chapter One

Caine Riordan felt as much as heard the rough crackle that came through his damaged EVA tether: the only signal still reaching him from the ship. Throat dry, he swallowed and muttered the mantra he revised every half minute: "One hundred twenty seconds. Then fifteen more."

Words to live by. Literally. Because if he wasn't back inside the air lock before then, he'd be dead.

Or as good as dead, anyway. In two minutes, the inbound solar storm's bow wave would spike. The fifteen additional seconds were an estimate on how long it would take for the soaring REM rate to impart a lethal whole-body dose. So every remaining moment had to be spent surveying the blue-and-tan planet beneath him.

The river he needed to study one last time began to emerge from the ink-black crescent that divided night from day. To the south of that meandering line he saw the start of vast flatlands: the only feasible landing zone. He was only partially aware of the other planetary details rotating into view: multiple hurricanes upon the blue seas; masses of churning charcoal clouds creeping across wastes; curtains of ochre haze marking where sandstorms spun away from the equator. Of the many words with which he and his crew had described the world, "hospitable" had never been used.

But strangely, the most frequent label had been "fortunate," since the presence of the planet defied all logic. After multiple

3

mis-shifts, the ship should have re-expressed as a diffuse spray of high-energy particles in deep space. Instead, it had not only emerged intact and near a star, but above a world with broad oceans and quite possibly a breathable atmosphere. Pandora Veriden, who was typically more rough-mannered than religious, had proclaimed it a miracle. Riordan suspected their deliverance was not due to a deity, but rather some forgotten rescue system left by the ancient and inscrutable intelligences that had preceded the Dornaani themselves.

Finally, the landing zone edged beyond the terminator. Riordan folded his left pinky against his palm and blinked twice, hoping the Dornaani vacc suit was still responding to that command sequence. He sighed in relief as the middle of the helmet's HUD zoomed in and showed the flatlands at ten-times magnification. But the precise area he needed—the point where the river he'd been tracking met an even larger one—was not quite centered. Focusing his eyes on that confluence, he used the same finger-and-blink combination. The view became murky as it swam inward, then resharpened. Now at an adjusted altitude of thirty kilometers, the image was more grainy but much more useful.

The new, larger river entered from the upper left edge of the magnified view—the northwest—and ran almost straight down to where it exited at the southeast. The tributary he'd seen first ran eastward to meet it. There he saw what he'd first presumed to be a circle of faintly bleached terrain. But thanks to the magnification, this time Caine confirmed it was not a circle after all, but a thick ring around a small, greenish dot. And at that dot's center was an irregularly striated grey speck.

Time as a defense analyst had taught Riordan what those colors and patterns signified. The bleached terrain was typically flattened and compacted land, whereas the light green band was almost certainly vegetation. But only one known feature produced the striated pattern of the small grey speck: buildings and streets. In this case, a city just over a kilometer wide, most of it snugged up against the southern bank of the tributary.

Riordan expelled his breath in a long, ragged sigh. Since arriving thirty-eight hours ago, everyone had been fixated upon one question: was the world habitable? With only two days of life support, the answer would decide their future: making planetfall or asphyxiating in space.

However, survival was still far from a surety. Just because there was a city—

The tether squawked.

Riordan gritted his teeth—"Ninety seconds, then fifteen more"—and resumed tempering his hopes. There were plenty of reasons why a city might be present on a completely lethal planet. It had probably been built by locals who either evolved on the world or spent eons adapting to its possibly deadly atmosphere. Also, since Caine and his self-styled "Crewe" hadn't detected any activity or signals, a long-past global cataclysm could have not only withered its surface, but left it uninhabitable. He was tempted to spend a few more seconds seeking further clues, but with just over a minute remaining, he kept his eyes on the landing zone.

Three hundred kilometers long and half as wide, the flatland south of the tributary gave them lots of room for error. Which they were likely to need. Badly. Without power to run a planetary survey, there was only one way to gather data for the automated descent software: suit sensors. The tether had piped the measurements to the ship's only functioning computer: a personal unit powered by the emergency batteries. Crunching numbers nonstop, it raced to define and refine two crucial datapoints: the hull's angle of incidence to the equator and the atmosphere's density.

It was still interpolating atmospheric friction, braking values, and descent vectors when the tether failed. Riordan had rerouted the sensor feed to his suit's computer, but within seconds, the data crystal warned of impending overload. The one remaining option—to use the processor's memory to capture the overflow—required shutting down almost every other system. As he complied, a sharp stab of trepidation cut deeper because of uncertainty: the data might still be insufficient or fried like the tether. And there was no way to tell until the suit was back aboard.

The one positive side effect of the tether failure was that, with nothing else to do, Riordan was free to devote all his attention to the one task that only a human could complete: a nuanced assessment of the terrain. A recently resurrected saying—"there's no substitute for the Mark One Eyeball"—was particularly pertinent when it came to detecting subtle clues associated with unpromising landing conditions.

However, it was also the kind of task that required sustained, myopic focus. And that allowed one's thoughts to wander—in

Caine's case, toward Elena and their son Connor. The irony was especially dark: that the monotony of the task was why his thoughts strayed...and with them, his attention. Just when he needed it most.

Ever since the mis-shift, it was tempting to imagine that the universe was taking sardonic delight in reminding them that one of the universal realities of human existence was haplessness. And of all the examples, the tether's failure had been the most ironic. As was so often the case with disasters, the first sign of trouble was not a bright warning light, but an apparently unrelated and harmless anomaly.

It began when Eku, the Dornaani-educated human running the computer, paged him via the tether. "Commodore Riordan," he'd begun with customary formality, "Ms. Veriden and Ms. Tagawa are standing by with me. I didn't want to distract you, but—"

"Hey, Boss," Dora Veriden broke in, "this ship is going *loco*."

"Say again?"

Ayana Tagawa explained calmly. "The ship's alarm sounded. Eku tells us that this klaxon warns against engaging the shift-drive."

"See?" Dora exclaimed. "The ship *is* crazy! We don't have power, the drive is burned out, and it still thinks we are going to *shift*?"

Eku's voice was as mild as Dora's was excited. "The alarm does not indicate that the ship is *unable* to shift. Only that it is unsafe to do so."

Caine frowned. "So, what's the hazard?"

"Without diagnostics, there is no way to tell, Commodore."

Ayana's tone was introspective. "I doubt the ship itself is the cause. Its systems are inert, and Colonel Rulaine and Chief O'Garran found no damage during their hull survey."

Caine felt his frown lines stiffening. "As we near the atmospheric insertion point, we go deeper into the planet's gravity well. Could that be the cause?"

Riordan could almost hear Eku's slow headshake. "No, sir. That would not compromise the shift navigation of a Dornaani ship."

"However," Ayana murmured as if discovering her insight as she spoke, "shift activation involves delicate management of matter and energy states. And solar emissions are increasing."

Riordan checked his then-functioning dosimeter. "Nothing consistent with flare activity, though."

Eku's correction was as sharp as a starter's pistol. "Not yet."

Ayana's voice was less calm than usual. "Please explain."

"Certain stellar emission patterns are highly predictive of increased activity. That said, a flare does not constitute a shift hazard."

Veriden sounded exasperated. "But then why are you worried about—?"

"Dora," Ayana interrupted, a marked break from her normal manners. "Eku only excluded a *flare*."

Riordan understood and swallowed. "But an incoming coronal mass ejection might set off the alarm."

"Most assuredly, Commodore," Eku agreed.

"*Madre de Dios*," Dora whispered.

Caine took a deep breath. "What's my revised mission duration?"

Ayana's answer was crisp. "Twenty minutes remaining, sir. No more."

Riordan bit his lip; they'd counted on having more time to take sensor measurements. "Eku, Ayana, do we need to reprioritize the sensor tasks?" When no answer came, Caine repeated the query, then noticed the absence of a carrier wave, looked up, and saw that the tether's comm icon was no longer green but flashing yellow. Still connected but not even reliable enough for Morse code. Riordan cut all redundant functions to free more memory . . . and saw the REM detector and dosimeter freeze: both serious losses.

He was still reprioritizing the suit's few active systems when the tether's comm line emitted a grumble of static. Random noise from the fried audio links, Caine guessed. But when it happened a third time, he realized the incidents were occurring with unusual regularity.

*A signal? Maybe . . . a time hack?*

But with every clock function shut down, he couldn't measure the interval.

*Unless . . .*

When the next growl of static arrived, Riordan shut off life support. The HUD painted a yellow symbol just above his eyes: first warning. He waited and, sure enough, just as the icon began flashing its thirty-second emergency warning, another burst of tether static arrived. Caine ran the math: there'd been five signals since the tether had failed, meaning just over two and a half minutes had passed since Ayana told him he had twenty left.

He reactivated life support and recited his first countdown mantra: "Seventeen minutes and thirty seconds." And because Ayana's estimates always erred to the side of caution, Riordan added, "And fifteen seconds more."

As if summoned by the end of that memory, the next crackle announced that he was almost out of time. Which Riordan reminded himself by reciting, "Sixty seconds. Then fifteen more."

He scanned the landing zone again, zoomed in on the only suspicious pattern he'd noticed. A systems expert would have identified it as ridge shadows cast from just outside the footprint. But his human eye saw another possibility: a combination of low rills and dry wadis just *inside* the zone.

He finger-blinked to get a maximum-magnification snapshot then waved his right arm through a slow, careful swimming stroke. Now slowly rotating to face the ship, he allowed himself to rotate into alignment with the distant air lock until tapping a control on his belt.

One of the thrusters in his EVA pack emitted a counter-puff. His rotation stopped and, after confirming that the tether was relatively straight, he used the same finger to activate its return reel.

A gentle tug on his belt started him moving slowly toward the elongated arrowhead shape of the ship. Because the retraction rate was preset to bring him to the air lock at a safe velocity, there was nothing to control or adjust.

But when the gentle tug of the tether stopped abruptly, a foreboding chill raced out along his limbs. *If the tether's motor has failed—*

The retraction reel started again, but with a jerk: not something it was supposed to do. Frowning, Riordan killed his automated helmet recorder to free up power for its laser range finder—

Just as the pull from the reel cut out again.

It tried to restart: a stuttering sequence of sharp jerks and then—

Nothing.

# Chapter Two

Riordan didn't have time to panic, even if he'd had the tendency to do so.

The laser range finder reinitialized. The distance to the ship was ticking down by only two meters per second and there were still two hundred and twelve left to go. Which meant he hadn't noticed drifting a further one hundred meters from the hull during his EVA. That small a number normally wouldn't have mattered at all. But now, with lethal rads sleeting in...

Caine glanced up at the tether's data-flow icon: red. Zero connection. And therefore, zero chance that the reel's retraction motor would reengage.

But that wasn't Riordan's biggest worry. With the tether now fully fried, he wouldn't receive the burst of static that would have been his final warning: thirty seconds left. And—*maybe*—fifteen more.

Riordan pulled the tether's slack toward him. His mental calm started spreading into his body: a familiar response to situations where foresight and preparation had been overtaken by events. As he coiled the drifting loops around his left arm, he double-blinked through two screens to bring up the HUD's target-tracking mode. He double-blinked again to designate his target: a featureless part of the hull flanked by the air lock on one side and the tether well on the other.

With the last loop secured, he unfolded a small manual grip from the integrated control unit on the EVA pack's belt. He expelled all the air from his lungs, and as he squeezed the grip's activation trigger, he whispered, "One-one-thousand."

Riordan had never pushed the Dornaani EVA pack's thrusters to their rumored limit and was suddenly glad he'd prepared himself for the results. The kick was sharp and hard. All at once, the ship seemed to be rushing toward him.

"Two-one-thousand."

The tether between him and the hull tried to curl and trail behind, but he kept circling his left arm to gather it in. The motion rolled him off his vector. He double-blinked at the crosshairs already painted near the air lock, attempting to force the system to realign him more rapidly.

"Three-one-thousand."

He was now coming in too fast, but the danger of doing so was less than that of coming in too slow. The hull seemed ready to engulf him, looming in all directions at the same time like an impossibly burgeoning monster. He snatched the coils of tether close to his chest and released the thrust trigger.

As he did, he double-blinked on the crosshairs—the pulsing box around the target point vanished—and then blinked at the automatic deceleration icon as he kicked slightly upward.

Two klaxons began whining in his helmet. The first indicated there wasn't enough distance for the EVA pack to counter-boost to a safe contact velocity. The second warned him that his current feet-forward attitude reduced his maximum counterthrust; the nozzles couldn't gimbal far enough while his body was perpendicular to the side of the ship.

Riordan glanced down between his feet. The hull leaped up at him as he forced himself not to brace his knees. He wrapped the last length of tether around his left wrist, and tried not to anticipate—

The impact slammed his organs downward. His knees and hips felt as if a hammer had been swung up against each one separately. Caine hadn't expected a perfectly squared landing, but he was already veering to one side.

Vision greying, he bounced off the hull, spinning to his right—until his left arm was almost wrenched out of its socket, wrist strangled by the tether he'd snugged around it. But that searing pain meant it was doing its job: keeping him close to the hull by limiting the slack in the line. It also brought Caine swinging back in toward the ship. He purged his lungs just before he hit again.

The suit's automatic kinetic resistance helped soften the impact; it was merely stunning instead of incapacitating. Riordan came off the hull much more slowly, and as the rapid decrease in motion put some slack back into the tether, he slipped the coils off his wrist.

Head ringing, Caine pushed back against the grey haze crowding the edges of his vision and fixed on a single thought: to keep clutching the larger loops of the tether close to his chest. When the peripheral dimness began fading, he reached over, got his right glove around the line, and began hauling himself hand over hand to the air lock coaming, just three meters away.

Caine toggled the manual air lock release, watched as the unpowered iris valve dilated with maddening slowness. He swam through the widening aperture as soon as it was large enough, intending to shelter in the lee of the bulkhead's heavy shielding.

But a slim, space-suited figure was already in the air lock. It caught him as he entered and pushed him swiftly into the corner he was already heading toward. The figure reached over to ratchet the iris valve's priming mechanism, and finally triggered the manual seal. The pie-slice sections reversed into a slightly faster contraction as the circle of stars peeking through its center shrank.

The figure leaned its helmet against his: it was Pandora Veriden. She was smiling. "You still had eleven seconds, boss," she shouted through their abutted faceplates.

He smiled up at her. "And then fifteen more. Let's get inside. We've got lots to do."

As Riordan drifted out of the air lock, he removed his helmet . . . and Dora switched into her favorite mode for caring interaction: remonstration. "Damn you for cutting it so close, Captain Courageous!" She looked away. "Sir," she added.

Caine smiled at her. "Well, I didn't cut it *that* close."

She managed not to smile back. "You got a strange definition of 'close,' Boss."

Ayana Tagawa was waiting just outside the small EVA support locker in the corridor. "Luckily, the CME surges are building more slowly than Eku first projected."

"Meaning?" Dora asked testily.

"The total REM dose was lower than anticipated." Ayana smiled at Riordan. "You remain under the hazard limit, Commodore."

Riordan heard a hanging tone at the end of her reassurance. "But...?"

Ayana shook her tightly cropped bangs: a sign of her reculturist "Neo-Edo" upbringing. "Because surges have slowed, the CME's peak will not pass before our descent window opens, but during."

"So we'll have to start as soon as we arrive in the deorbit envelope."

She nodded. "Which occurs in four hours."

Duncan Solsohn's voice came out of the open equipment locker behind her. "It's either no news or bad news, these days!" He floated into the corridor. "Good to see you all in one piece, sir." He cocked an eyebrow. "Assuming you are, that is."

"What do you mean?"

"Your, eh, unorthodox return to the ship: we heard it through the hull." Duncan grinned at his own wild exaggeration, but also scanned Riordan for signs of injury.

"The spy lies again!" Dora exclaimed, even as her own eyes roved across Riordan.

Duncan shook his head. "Dora, *all* of us are spies, according to our detractors back home. But for now"—he carefully removed the helmet from Caine's hands—"Eku needs this...well, an hour ago."

As Duncan started drift-walking toward the bow, Caine called after him: "Inventory done yet?"

"Taking it to Colonel Rulaine right now."

"Is he still on the bridge with Eku?"

Duncan grinned. "Just went back. He was wringing his hands back here with the rest of us until Dora got you inside."

Veriden made to move forward as well. "And I'm bringing Dr. Baruch back here." She stared defiantly at Caine's quizzical look. "You need to be checked out. Right now."

"As Ayana said, I'm fine."

"I'm not worried about the rads, boss. Like Spy-Guy said, you hit the hull hard. Too hard."

Riordan shook his head firmly. "No; don't take Newton away from rousing our three cryo-sleeping beauties. But I give you my word I'll go to *him*. Assuming you give me a sitrep on the way."

"Deal!" Dora launched herself toward the bow with a smile that could have been relief, victory, or both. "Just keep up, yeh?"

✧　　✧　　✧

Bannor Rulaine swam around the coaming of the bridge's double-sized entry. Jammed half open during their seizure of the ship, it was going to stay that way until the power came on again—if it ever did. He followed along the curve of the interior bulkhead, gliding from handhold to handhold until he reached a much narrower hatchway leading off the bridge: access to the captain's ready room.

However, their abductor Hsontlosh had transformed it into his private stateroom, probably because he wanted the bridge's bulkhead-rated doors between himself and the passengers he was secretly betraying. A loji cocoon-hammock floated at the far end of the compartment, which had been outfitted with a bewildering array of electronic devices; in places, they almost touched the overhead. Bannor understood the function of roughly half of them. Well, almost half. "How's it coming, Eku?" he called ahead.

Eku's head rose, eyes cresting the back of a large control screen slaved to the compartment's stand-alone computer. The human factotum sounded as frustrated as he appeared. "It is coming very slowly," he sighed, then sank back out of sight.

Bannor released a sigh of his own as he pushed himself into the ready room. In his twenty-three years in the Special Forces—most as an officer—he'd frequently worked with civilian insurgents and collaborators. Most of them eventually embraced the military need for quick, concise, and pertinent communication. Eku had not; he seemed temperamentally incapable of it.

As Rulaine drew abreast of the screen, he finally discovered how Eku had managed to power Hsontlosh's computing suite. The housing of the closest emergency light was open and a power cable snaked out of it to connect to the multi-plug supplying current to the active machines. *Well, if Eku can hotwire a computer, maybe there's hope for him yet.* "Caine is back aboard. Not a lethal REM dose. It's unlikely he'll even feel any effects, given the Dornaani prophylactics."

Eku paused for a moment; his shoulders slumped in what looked very much like nerveless relief. "I am very glad to hear that." He expelled a long sigh, straightened to readdress the computer controls—and winced; the movement had jostled his splinted arm. As he shifted it to a more comfortable position, various data streams on the immense semi-holographic screen swirled, reconfigured, and began sorting themselves into serried ranks. "Do you have the data crystal from the commodore's suit?"

"It's on the way, I imagine."

Eku's spine stiffened. "So someone else is coming here?"

Bannor frowned. "Yes. Why?"

"I have something to show you, Colonel. Just you." Eku's fingers and eyes moved rapidly across the input controls. "It took a long time to access the deepest level of Hsontlosh's private data. It is taking almost as long to copy it all."

Bannor peered over the factotum's shoulder, understood exactly none of the swirling objects, symbols, and sigils. "How much are you trying to download?"

"As much as possible."

"That's not very precise."

The factotum's tone was sharp, focused, even tense. "There is no way to ascertain which files might be important. Many are clearly written in a cypher. Others might be."

"Okay, but that still doesn't tell me why you're trying to download 'as much as you can.'"

Eku sounded like he was shooing away a gnat. "That is the implicit requirement of the commodore's instructions."

Bannor frowned again. "I thought he only needed you to collect information about the ship's transit path up to our mis-shift." *For all the good it will do us, with a dead ship and completely unfamiliar starfield.*

"Yes, and that has been accomplished. But he also tasked me to download everything I could find that might pertain to Hsontlosh's betrayal: specifically, his plans and any coconspirators or accomplices." He continued working, then added, "That required scanning through the readable parts of Hsontlosh's log."

"And?"

"And it contains... other important information."

Bannor frowned. "Will it affect our mission?"

"Eventually, yes."

*Damn it, Eku!* "I'm asking about the *immediate* mission: making and surviving planetfall."

Eku hesitated. "No, but the commodore might want to be apprised of this information, even so." He turned just enough to glance at Rulaine from the corner of his eye. "It concerns the fate of his wife."

"Firstly, Elena is not Caine's wife. Secondly, we don't have the time to—"

Eku sighed, toggled a control.

The diagrams on the screen were abruptly replaced by mad waves of curlicues and spots: a document in Dornaani script. "I don't read Dor—" Rulaine started.

Eku tapped another key. English was superimposed over the alien characters in bright red. Before Bannor was aware of doing so, he had read the first line:

The human female's subsequent demise has not altered our—

Rulaine looked away, but not before his much-vaunted peripheral vision registered a few words and phrases that were even more grim. As if it might help unsee them, he half-covered his eyes.

"There is more," Eku murmured after a terrible silence. "I can only conclude—"

Bannor looked up sharply, found and held Eku's surprised stare with his own. "No. Don't tell me."

"But—?"

"Eku, you need to wake up and understand exactly where we are, right now."

"Our position—"

"Eku, stop. You need to listen—no; you need to *hear* me. We are in a dead ship above a barren planet. In four hours, we have to get down to it or die trying. Keep hammering that into your head until it hurts, until you can focus your mind on that and *only* that." Rulaine leaned back, crossed his arms. "Now, what you've learned about Elena: is there anything we can do about it?"

"I cannot be sure, yet." Then he shook his head. "But certainly not from here."

Bannor nodded. "Then you'll have plenty of time to tell me—to tell us all—if we survive. And if we don't, it won't matter."

"What won't matter?" Duncan's voice asked from out on the bridge.

"Anything other than getting down to the planet," Bannor answered casually.

"No argument there!" Solsohn agreed as he worked his way into Hsontlosh's lair. He whistled appreciatively. "Damn. Looks like a mad scientist's laboratory." He handed Caine's helmet to Rulaine, who passed it off to Eku. The factotum's fingers were immediately busy extracting its data crystal and accessing its processor.

Duncan inspected the tangle of wires and interfaces that had previously powered the charging frame for one of Hsontlosh's two very deadly proxy robots. "So the proxrov recharging rig was removable, after all?"

"With some 'persuasion' from Yaargraukh," Rulaine smiled, glancing at Eku: the factotum was already scanning data from the helmet's crystal.

Solsohn huffed out an ironic laugh. "Yeah, Hkh'Rkh can be pretty persuasive when they want to be. All three meters of 'em."

"They're only a little over two," Bannor corrected.

"Guess you and I met very different ones on Turkh'saar." Duncan looked around. "So was it difficult to get into the evil mastermind's sanctum sanctorum?"

Rulaine shrugged. "Since he kept everyone off the bridge, he left it unlocked."

"Cocky bastard," Duncan sneered.

"More likely he was simply contemptuous," Eku muttered with a hint of asperity, "and therefore, incautious." He gestured toward the screen; four rotating images of the planet were draped with aqua lines connecting different strings of white or yellow guidons. "The suit's data was not corrupted. The automated descent package is calculating optimal vectors. Final planetary values are being compiled now."

Bannor clapped Eku carefully on his good shoulder; he started anyway. In response to the factotum's concerned surprise, the commando muttered, "That's just a gesture of approval. Carry on." He pushed himself away from the firm-chair he'd been using as a zero-gee anchor. "Is Caine still back at the air lock?"

Duncan shrugged. "Might be. More likely he's with Newton and the sleepers by now. At least that's where Dora made him promise to go next."

"You coming?" Rulaine asked as he drifted toward the hatchway.

"Nah, I'm going to stay here for a minute and watch the pretty pictures." He nodded at the descent trajectories. "Helps me believe we'll get down in one piece."

Bannor nodded, swam out of the ready room, and made sure neither of the other men could see his face as he silently replied:

*Wish I was as optimistic as you are, Duncan.*

# Chapter Three

Caine trailed two fingertips along the bulkhead as, up ahead, Dora slowed her forward drift in a similar fashion. She glanced into the commons room, then gestured for Caine and Ayana to follow her in. Caine had come to a halt as he reached the opening; hand on the hatch's coaming, he pivoted into the ship's largest compartment.

For months, it had been where he and the Crewe had eaten, groused, laughed, and ultimately held coded confabs as they plotted to take the bridge. Now, everything that could be removed had been: a necessary precursor for its coming transformation into a combined assembly and equipment-inspection area.

Dora's shrug indicated she had nothing to add to the sitrep she'd given as she led the other two forward from the air lock. "That's the state of our preparations for descent, boss."

"Sounds like it's well in hand."

"Huh: sounds *boring*, more like. Particularly compared to your news! A city on the surface!" She shook her head ruefully. "You gotta stop this first-contact stuff. Earth has more than it can handle, as it is."

Riordan drifted to a handhold. "This time it might be first contact with a graveyard. And even if it's not, there's no way of knowing if they'd ever see us as anything other than hideous otherworld invaders."

Veriden rolled her eyes but smiled. "Always the optimist, hey?"

17

"Always the realist," Caine replied with a shrug as Ayana completed her flawless zero-gee entry with a balletlike pirouette. It gave her just enough impetus to snag the first handhold beyond the hatch.

"Realist or not," Dora persisted, "sometimes you worry too much—boss or no boss."

Caine replied with a grin. "Guilty as charged." He couldn't resist adding a semiserious coda: "And if you hadn't followed me into Dornaani space, you'd not only be safer right now; you'd be less annoyed."

"Hah!" she laughed, her chin rising. "For once, you're right!" She shook her head. "You're a funny guy, boss . . . particularly when you don't mean to be. And hey: you're not the only one with big news!" She glanced at Ayana.

Tagawa nodded. "Shortly after you commenced your EVA, we detected a visual anomaly just beyond geosynchronous orbit: a bright object with an irregular signature."

Riordan leaned forward. "A structure of some kind?"

Tagawa nodded. "A structure of the most *interesting* kind. Using the targeting scope on Hsontlosh's coil gun, we were able to confirm that it is a slowly tumbling spacecraft, at least a kilometer long. The resolution was insufficient to observe any details beyond its general configuration: large engine section at the stern, a radiation shield just forward of it, then a long keel trusswork leading to a large bow section. Almost certainly an STL ship."

Caine had to keep his mind from racing out along the spider web of possible implications. "You're sure it doesn't have a supraluminal drive?"

She nodded. "The engine decks are too small, even if the shift drive was as compact as Dornaani models." She smiled knowingly, anticipating Riordan's next question. "And no evidence that it was disabled in battle: no gross damage nor the typical debris cloud."

Riordan shook his head. "Damn, if we'd seen it before committing to descent—"

"And get to it with what thrust?" Dora exclaimed, then shook her head at her own outburst. "Sorry, boss. I'm just frustrated. If we *could* get to it, we might be able to salvage everything we need."

"Even if we had thrust, our life support would have run out before we could make intercept," Ayana corrected calmly. "And there is no assurance that any of that ship's components or contents are in usable condition, nor that they would be compatible with ours."

Riordan nodded reluctant agreement. "And what about the thrust we *do* have left? Are you happy with the burn you've plotted?"

"Judging from all the preliminary data, I am as happy as I am going to be. Between the fuel in the restart tanks and the other five missiles currently rigged to provide an auxiliary boost, we have just enough delta-v for the necessary maneuvers." Although her report was crisp and assured, Ayana's eternally youthful eyes and perfect skin were slightly haggard; it had been a brutal thirty-six hours. Sleeping in shifts, and using pills to do so, the Crewe couldn't risk using any of their limited supply of stimulants to help stay alert. They had to be saved for whatever might follow, either during or after the descent.

Riordan's reflection upon the need for peak performance triggered another concern. "Dora, is Bannor favoring the side injured by Hsontlosh's first proxrov?"

"Can't get him to stand still long enough to find out," Veriden answered with a futile flap of her free hand. "Green Beanie let Newton examine him for twenty seconds. Maybe thirty. No broken ribs, but the doc doesn't have a way to detect hairline fractures. He's watching for signs of a damaged spleen, too."

As if on cue, Rulaine appeared glide-walking past the compartment's hatchway, attention fixed aft. "Bannor!" Caine called after him.

Startled, his friend turned abruptly—and his face underwent a sudden and baffling transformation: from complete surprise to grey-faced dread. "I thought you were with the sleepers," Rulaine muttered, looking away. He did not enter the compartment.

And suddenly, Riordan understood Bannor's reaction: because he hadn't expected to encounter Caine yet, he hadn't groomed his tone and his face into easy affability. Into an easy, casual demeanor behind which he could have concealed what Caine now realized with grim certainty: "Eku found something. About Elena."

Bannor still could not meet his gaze. "Yeah."

Caine could only ask the obvious: "It's not good news, is it?"

Bannor's silence seemed to press inward on him, toward implosion—until he shook it off. "Eku's got more digging to do.

There are too many files, too many cyphers." He looked down. "But Hsontlosh's last report is . . . well, it's not promising."

Riordan repeated the awful euphemism before he could stop himself: "'Not promising'?" His tone had said, "utterly hopeless."

Bannor's eyes rose. They were as hollow and anguished as any Caine had ever seen. Rulaine's mouth started moving, but it was several seconds before two words came out: "I'm sorry."

"You've no reason to be." Riordan leaned toward his friend. "Hsontlosh was always finding another way to locate or save Elena, always dangling another improbable hope in front of us, keeping us on the hook." He shook his head. "He never intended to deliver her. He just needed to keep us believing it was possible."

Ayana shuttered her eyes in Dora's direction and drifted smoothly out of the compartment; somehow she managed to keep it from looking like a hasty withdrawal. Dora stopped in the hatchway a moment, hand against the coaming as she looked back at Caine. Her eyes still large and sad, she followed Tagawa with long, gliding strides.

Head almost hanging, Bannor looked up at Caine. "You okay?"

Caine did what a commanding officer was supposed to do; he nodded and resolved to ignore the ball of ice where his stomach had been. He pushed away from the bulkhead, gave his best imitation of purposeful vigor. "I'm heading back to check on the sleepers. Tag along?"

"Sure," Bannor said miserably.

Caine heard Newton Baruch's clipped diction well before he entered the storage room in which three of the Crewe were recuperating from their rapid reanimation out of cold sleep. The tall, taciturn, IRIS agent was also a physician and, in that role, was quietly yet savagely chastising his charges for poor compliance with his recovery regimens. He straightened when Caine and Bannor drifted in; the movement set him floating slowly toward the overhead.

"I am happy to see you are safely back from your EVA, Commodore. I am also relieved that you have taken the time to visit this sorry lot of soldiers." The glare he sent across them became histrionically agitated as it finished upon his old friend Peter Wu: a fellow IRIS agent who was anything but a "sorry soldier."

Liebman, one of the two so-called Lost Soldiers who'd

accompanied the Crewe, sat up, struggling to keep himself from floating off the thin mattress lashed to the deck. "Now wait a minute, sir—"

Baruch turned sharply. "Sergeant Liebman, did I ask you a question? Or give you leave to speak freely?"

"Well, no, sir. But what gives? It's no fair, you accusing us of—"

As Liebman fell silent before Newton's withering stare, Riordan tried to recollect the expression, "what gives?" Like Liebman, it was well over a century and a half old and had largely fallen out of use before half of those years had elapsed.

Baruch, however, didn't react to the bygone idiom, probably because he hadn't even listened to Liebman. "Sergeant, if you do not exercise when and as I instruct, and then rest when you are told to, you will not be fit for duty when we descend in six hours."

"Four hours," Bannor added, leaning against the coaming.

Newton raised one long, thin eyebrow.

Caine shook his head. "Solar weather isn't behaving as predicted. The worst of it is coming later, now."

Baruch nodded. "And we cannot wait it out, given the vector to which we are committed." He pushed himself toward a small container moored near the translucent lockers lining the wall opposite the entry. "I will have to give these three another dose of the emergency revival cocktail."

Katie Somers, the third person who had been in cryostasis when they commandeered the ship, rose to her elbows. "What do you mean by *another* dose, Lieutenant? How many have we had?"

"Two," Newton replied as he sorted through the vials in his makeshift drug kit. "Administered within the first hour of your reanimation. Eku shared the protocols for its use. In desperate need, the basic dose can be doubled if a subject must be conscious within twelve hours, and mobile in twelve more. But a third dose?" He stared at the three mismatched vials he had selected. "It should not be harmful, but you may experience difficulty focusing for several hours." He glanced at Caine. "They should be fully recovered by the time we commence descent."

Caine nodded, frowning. "What about the preliminary briefing? They've got a lot of catching up to do."

Newton sighed. "I cannot assure you that all the side effects will have worn off by then." He gestured to the open-lidded Dornaani container which held the vials. "The revival compound is typically infused while a subject is still in a cryocell. But since these three are already being revived faster than protocols allow, the effect of a third dose is uncertain."

"In that case, Commodore," Peter Wu said calmly from the third mattress, "perhaps it is best to tell us what happened while we were asleep. Before Newton administers the third dose, that is."

Bannor glanced at Newton. "You haven't told them?"

Baruch shook his head. "Their ability to retain new memories only returned twenty minutes ago. An update would have been pointless."

A new voice—that of the other Lost Soldier, Craig Girten—came from the corridor behind Bannor. "Colonel Rulaine, Chief O'Garran is asking if you could lend a hand rigging for the descent."

"Coming," Bannor answered. He turned toward Caine as he pushed back from the entrance. "I'll make sure they've got the new time-hack for planetfall."

Girten's exclamation made it clear he hadn't. "What'd you say . . . er, sir?"

Rulaine's chuckle was sardonic as he drifted out of sight. "I'll explain on the way."

Caine didn't glide toward Peter until Newton was secured to a handhold alongside Katie, syringe in hand.

Wu sat up slowly. "I presume our circumstances have changed."

Caine smiled. "You clearly retain your gift for irony."

"When that is gone, you may pronounce me dead. I presume we were correct in our suspicions regarding Hsontlosh?"

"And then some. He wasn't just lying to us; he was going to sell us to the Ktor."

"So you took the ship."

Riordan nodded. "No choice, even though the drive was already ticking down toward a fail-safed shift. If we had tried to stop it, the drive chamber's magnetic containment would have shut down."

Wu nodded back. "And the antimatter would have vaporized us. Very thorough," Peter concluded. "And very foresightful."

"Not entirely," Caine corrected. "He assumed that if he stood in front of the navigation controls, we'd back down for fear of a stray bullet hitting them and causing a mis-shift."

"A serious miscalculation," Peter agreed, then looked around meaningfully. "Of course, mis-shifts are fatal." His statement ended on the rising tone of a query.

Caine shrugged. "Well, that's always been the theory, since no one's ever returned to report otherwise."

Wu folded his hands. "So: where are we, and how did we get here?"

"No idea, and no idea." Caine indulged in a rueful grin. "The first mis-shift triggered a cascade of other ones as the ship tried to return to its initial coordinates. In the process, it burned its drives and all the antimatter."

"What a great outcome," groused Liebman.

"Better than the alternative," Katie snapped as Newton's needle entered her arm.

The G.I. put up his hands in surrender.

Peter's nod of agreement was slow, philosophical. "Well, I suppose things could be worse."

Liebman turned back sharply. "How so?"

"We could all be very, very dead."

"That," Newton muttered darkly, "is not yet beyond the realm of possibility."

Peter smiled toward his saturnine friend. "So I gather." His gaze returned to Caine. "Skipping over any details and caveats, Commodore, what is our current situation?"

"We have four hours to get down to the planet beneath us. If we don't, we're dead."

Peter's eyes widened slightly. "I take it back; a few more details and caveats would be welcome. Starting with what Sergeant Girten meant about 'rigging for the descent.' I assume that without power, our landing is likely to damage the hull, and us, quite badly?"

Riordan shook his head. "He wasn't talking about rigging the hull; he was referring to rigging the parachutes."

"The what?"

"We are not using the ship to make planetfall. We are using emergency descent frames. The Dornaani use them to drop supplies on worlds where they cannot land."

"We are . . . are *parachuting* down? From orbit?" Peter tried, but failed, to prevent the last word from emerging as an incredulous squawk.

Caine nodded. "It's the only option. Without power, there's no way to generate the thrust and vector control needed to keep from tumbling and burning up. The descent frames, on the other hand, each have an automated descent package; they're being fed

the necessary data now. Each one is rated for five metric tonnes and has thrusters to make vector and attitude adjustments. Since none of them will need to carry a full tonne, that leaves plenty of extra thrust potential, which means a greater margin for error."

Peter's eyes were wide. "Commodore, you will forgive me if I do not find any of this information especially . . . reassuring."

Caine nodded, patted the smaller man's shoulder. "It hit us the same way." He didn't mention the initial nausea. "Frankly, we were lucky there wasn't much time to think about it. We had to complete a lot of tasks if this plan was going to have any chance of working." *If it does.*

The other two sleepers had overheard. Liebman was staring at the overhead, swallowing rapidly. Katie, on the other hand, frowned. "So, Commodore, where were these, eh, descent frames?" She skipped to the logical conjecture: "Did you get into engineering, somehow?"

He smiled at her. "If we'd found a way to do that, we would have been able to restore power."

She grinned back, chortled. "Och, don't mind me; I'm a dullard."

"No, you're just coming out of cryodaze. Actually, the frames were in this compartment." He pointed at the lockers lining the rear bulkhead. "They were stuffed underneath the emergency packs."

"How many?"

Riordan glanced at the dozen Dornaani cryocells, stacked against the wall facing them. "Twelve. One for each of the ancient human factotums in those 'pods."

Katie frowned, her speech slowing. "Who are they? 'Zon'losh's crew?"

"No," Newton answered as he prepared to inject Liebman, "they were his cargo. For the Ktor."

"Whatta *sleekit bodach*," Katie hissed unsteadily, yet venomously.

"So there are only twelve frames," Liebman muttered tensely. "But there are thirteen of us."

"Fortunately, Hsontlosh had a personal kit secreted in his quarters."

"Okay, but what about space suits?" Liebman pressed, cheeks taut. "We've only got ten: eight Dornaani-made and the two we brought with us from Zeta Tucanae. What will happen to the three who—?"

Newton's interruption was a terse grumble. "All of us, including Yaargraukh, brought duty suits with EVA shells."

In answer to Peter's stare, Caine added, "We won't go space-side until the ship dips under one hundred kilometers altitude. So we'll spend less than ten minutes in hard vacuum. And there's plenty of Dornaani 'magic tape' to reinforce the seals."

Peter frowned. "Why not have the ship take us deeper into the atmosphere?"

Caine shook his head. "Same reason we can't land it: not enough thrust. Any lower and we'll lose it and everything we've left aboard."

Peter's eyebrows elevated as Caine uttered the words "left aboard." "Wait: you mean to *save* the ship? Why bother, with all its systems burnt out?"

"The only systems we lost were those carrying current when we mis-shifted," Riordan amended. "The fusion engine and its dedicated capacitor were off-line. Part of Eku's wizardry was going through Hsontlosh's personal computer to send timed commands to the engine through its test-fire circuits." In response to Peter's quizzical expression, Riordan expanded. "Some Dornaani ships spend centuries in depot storage. So they have a separate set of test circuits that don't require much power and a stand-alone tank with just enough fuel to cycle through reactivation."

Peter's face was expressionless. "Still, igniting a fusion thruster requires somewhat more electricity than emergency lights."

Caine smiled. "There's also an isolated battery for powering short tests. Typically, would expend its full charge in a few seconds, but Eku rerouted the power conduits so that the auxiliary capacitor will recharge the battery until the engine burns through the fuel in the cold-start tank."

"And that will return the ship to a safe orbit?"

"For a while, yes, but—"

"But?"

"But the numbers are derived from data gathered by suit sensors," Newton answered. He pushed away from Liebman's mattress toward Peter's. "The values pertaining to local orbital mechanics are woefully imprecise."

Riordan wondered how long it had been since he had heard someone use the word "woefully." If he ever had.

Peter settled back as Baruch slid the needle slowly into the Taipeian's very round bicep. "I think I will rest, now, Commodore."

"About time you did, you stubborn old mule," Newton grumbled.

"I am two years younger than you," Wu observed.

Riordan pushed off the deck with a smile. "Will he at least be ready to sit in for the final debrief?"

"I suppose he has to be, Commodore," Baruch muttered.

Peter nodded over his friend's shoulder. "I shall be there, Commodore."

"Good. You're one of our few Low Orbit High Opening jumpers, so we need your experience front and center."

"I understand, sir. You can count on me."

Riordan nodded, pushed toward the hatchway and thought: *Now, if only I could count on myself.*

# Chapter Four

Survival pack slung around his neck to keep his mass centered, Riordan drifted out of his stateroom and angled forward toward the assembly room. Bannor was already approaching it from the opposite side with the longer, easier glide-and-touch movements that came from extensive experience in weightless environments.

Caine finger-dragged himself to a halt. Rulaine closed the distance, slipping silently past the assembly room. A distracted buzz of conversation was already coming out of its open hatchway.

Riordan made sure he was the first to speak. "Before we throw ourselves out of a perfectly good spacecraft, I want you to know that I'm glad it was you who told me about Elena."

Rulaine shook his head as he slowed his approach. "Yeah—even though I was trying *not* to. Great job on my part."

Caine shrugged. "Damn, I'm not sure there's any way to do a 'great job' under these circumstances. I'd probably have been following the same strategy: no additional distractions for a CO who's already got too much on his plate. And had no way to know that I'd already come to the same conclusions on my own."

"That's kind of you, but still, crappy timing or not, you learned about it. Not my objective."

Caine shrugged. "Not like there will be any time to think about it, or anything else, until we're on the ground. And even then—"

"Yeah: 'and even then.'" Bannor shook his head. "Because

dirtside is where the fun might *really* start." He glanced at his wrist comp. "We are officially late for our own brief." An almost genuine smile pushed one side of his mouth upward. "Of course, rank hath its privileges."

"Pretty lousy compensation for the headaches."

Bannor sighed. "No argument, there"—and then he straightened, face suddenly expressionless. "Ready for final review, Commodore." He said it as if he was presenting a formation on a parade ground.

Caine almost started at the abrupt formality, but a second look at his friend's rigid posture made its purpose clear. The mission didn't start when they went into the assembly area; it started *before* that. They had to enter the compartment not as Caine and Bannor but as CO and XO. The sharp return of custom and rank announced that the operation was already underway and the countdown clock was ticking. And those formalities would remain in place until such time as the mission was over—or at least, until they were out of immediate danger.

Wondering just how long that might be, Riordan nodded at his granite-faced friend and pushed himself briskly through the hatchway.

All the gear was laid out and all the time hacks had been reviewed three times. Caine leaned out from the bulkhead, making sure his hand remained wrapped around the nearest handhold. "Section heads will report by operational sequence. Ms. Tagawa?"

Ayana pushed herself forward, trailed a toe to stop herself. "We will soon perform a manual attitude correction for optimal insertion. All subsequent maneuver operations will occur after we have left the ship and so, are necessarily automated." Liebman's hand shot up, lifting him slightly from the deck. She nodded.

But instead of addressing his query to her, Liebman turned to look around the ring of faces. "Am I the only one who feels uncomfortable being downrange when the computer lights up the five ship-killer missiles mounted at the back of the ship?"

When Craig Girten raised his hand, Caine kept his face expressionless. He'd had similar misgivings, at first; igniting missiles pointed straight into the hull wasn't just a leap of faith, but a wild pole vault of desperation.

But Girten was not alone: the large, hulking shape in the far corner of the compartment raised its distinctly alien hand: four quadrilateral fingers arranged as opposed pairs.

Liebman stared at the big Hkh'Rkh, apparently trying to meet the black-marble eyes that poked out from beneath the bony ridge of its seamless head-neck structure. "Damn, Yaargraukh, I thought your kind isn't scared of anything."

"You are mistaken," the Hkh'Rkh replied, the consonants made sharp and crisp by its leathery palate. "Fear is not merely known to us, but a carefully cultivated companion. Its presence encourages prudence, just as mastering it allows one to distinguish courage from recklessness."

"Uh, yeah, sure...but you still fear the missiles?"

Yaargraukh's neck circled lazily; his species' equivalent of a slight shrug. "I took your words literally, Sergeant Liebman. You did not ask about 'fear.' You asked if anyone else felt 'uncomfortable.' I am, but no more than with any other dangerous device being used in an unforeseen and unintended manner. However, I am also fully satisfied that the benefits of doing so far outweigh the risks."

"Besides," Bannor added, bringing Liebman's gaze back to the front of the compartment, "Chief O'Garran and I started by removing the warheads. All that's left are the engines, and the centerline engineering air lock is holding them like a vise, with their front ends buffered by high-impact packing all the way to the bulkhead."

Girten looked from Bannor to Miles; fixing the missiles in place had required significant REM exposure. "Why take all the risk for just a little extra kick?"

"To increase the odds that this ship will survive."

Girten sighed. "Permission to speak freely, ma'am?" She nodded. "Why does the ship even matter, once we're down on the planet?"

Ayana glanced at Caine; the discussion had shifted from technical to strategic.

Riordan drifted forward. "Sergeant Girten, one of the few facts we possess about our current situation is that this craft's shift drives are our only reasonable hope for ever leaving the system. Given the complexity of supraluminal travel, any civilization on the world below—past or present—is far more likely to have achieved *local* spaceflight. So however low the odds are of getting back up here, they're a whole lot better than the chance of finding another starship."

Liebman's voice was careful. "But it's not like we have any reasonable hopes for getting back up here to use them, sir."

"At present, no. But we're going to remain alert for any opportunities that might make it possible."

Ayana drifted forward to float alongside Riordan. "To return to your initial question about the missiles, Sergeant: there is another reason we converted them into boosters. If the fusion thrusters fail within the first fifteen seconds of operation, the ship will not merely reenter and break up in the atmosphere; it will fall through our descent vector. The speed and spread of the debris would give us only seconds to react, and the descent frames' thrust packages are too weak for quick evasive maneuvers."

Liebman's gulp was a bone-grating sound. "Oh. Well. When ya put it that way..."

Dora folded her arms. "*Coño*," she muttered. "Liebman: *grano en el culo.*"[1]

"Huh?" asked Liebman.

Ayana smiled. "She said you always ask good questions." She raised her chin and looked around the circle. "Our last discretionary maneuver—brief thrust from the ACS—will optimize our position for insertion and ensure that the ship maintains positive pitch, even as it dips down into the upper reaches of the atmosphere."

"Wait: *into* the atmosphere?" interrupted Girten. "But everyone keeps saying we have to keep the ship *out* of the atmosphere!"

Ayana nodded. "And, except for the time it takes for us to insert, it shall be." Girten's increasingly bewildered look drew further explanation from her. "As the ship reaches the end of our insertion vector, it will also be at the perigee of our current orbital track. After we have commenced EVA, but before the bow can dip too far, the ACS will automatically discharge to maximize positive pitch. Shortly afterward, all five missiles will ignite. This will cause the ship to rise. Once clear of the upper atmosphere, its fusion thrusters will fire until their fuel is expended. That will put the ship into a higher, less elliptical orbit with a longer period."

---

[1] "[you] pain in the ass."

Liebman was shaking his head as if a gnat were stuck in his ear. "Okay, no insult intended, Miss Tagawa, but I'm not Buck Rogers. You're going to have to explain that in words I understand. Or pictures, if you've got 'em."

Ayana frowned, glanced toward Bannor: he'd had a lot of experience explaining things to the frequently bewildered Lost Soldiers.

The colonel pushed himself away from the bulkhead. "Okay, Liebman: here's a picture for you." He put his hand in a palm-down flying position. "The ship will be grazing the atmosphere, but with its nose up." He moved his hand forward, fingertips raised, then started lowering it. "At the point where the atmosphere starts to drag on it, we exit the ship in the descent frames. As soon as we're out, it lifts its nose higher"—his fingertips tilted upward—"and lights the missiles jammed up its butt." Even Liebman chortled as Bannor's hand suddenly angled upward.

Bannor put his hand through the same motions, but in one smooth pass. "So if you put it all together, it's a lot like skipping a flat rock across a pond. First it goes down, but because it hits the water at an acute angle, it bounces back up. And finally, when that's over, the fusion thrusters kick in and—" He sent his wedged hand shooting toward the overhead.

"Wait a minute," Girten exclaimed, "the commodore just said we will try to get back to the ship. But now you're sending it out into space?"

Ayana nodded her thanks to Bannor. "There is not enough fusion fuel to break the ship out of orbit. So we are attempting to put it in a rounder, higher orbit that will decay more gradually. But we cannot predict how long it will remain there."

Riordan nodded toward her, shifted his gaze to the person sitting just to her right. "Give us the final planetary data, Mr. Eku."

The factotum nodded and slowly straightened at the waist. "The planet has a diameter of approximately 12,550 kilometers. Gravity is 0.916 gees. Magnetic fields are slightly weaker than Earth's. It completes a full rotation in just under thirty hours. That is unusually slow given its other characteristics; it is likely to be a consequence of its large satellite. We lack detailed data on it but, although it is more distant than your moon, its gravity is far greater. Indeed, it was a significant factor in Ms. Tagawa's navigational computations."

Newton frowned. "Then how does the planet remain stable?"

Eku nodded. "It isn't, not entirely. There is intense volcanic activity all along the equator, consistent with sustained pressure on the planetary crust. There are also many archipelagos clustered near what appear to be ocean trenches: a common feature on worlds with highly energetic tectonic plates."

"Speaking of islands," Girten said, glancing at Dora, "didn't Ms. Veriden see one with some green on it?" She nodded. "Then why aren't we landing *there*?"

Chief O'Garran leaned forward. "That island has a maximum width—or for our purposes, longitudinal landing footprint—of one hundred and eighty kilometers."

"So?"

"*So*, we're coming down from the edge of outer space with only fifty percent trained jumpers. Of those, only two have genuine LOHO experience. More amusing still, none of us has any experience with the descent frames—which, by the way, were designed for dropping supplies, not people. *So*, even assuming the gods of wind and weather smile on our sorry selves, just how close do you think we're gonna be landing to each other?" Girten's eyes widened as O'Garran's words sunk in. "That's why our intended landing zone is five hundred klicks long and two hundred wide. And we've got twice that amount of open area around it if we overshoot."

Newton's voice was respectful. "And what if we *under*shoot?"

O'Garran shook his head. "Don't. Or you'll come down on the other side of that big north-south river we've shown you. So if you have to make an error, land long, not short." He glanced at Eku. "Back to you, wizard."

The factotum started. "'Wizard'?"

"Well, do you see anyone else here who can work miracles with a personal computer and coarse data?"

When Eku still looked uncertain how to reply, Peter leaned in his direction, "Despite the gruff tone, it is a compliment."

Eku's nod was appreciative but still puzzled. "The planet's present axial tilt is approximately fifteen percent. But we have only two days' worth of measurement, so its maximum could be much greater."

Girten's tone was now one of desperation. "And that matters how?"

"Axial tilt determines the season. If the present tilt is the planet's maximum, then the southern hemisphere is just entering winter. If it is not, then any season between early autumn and late spring is possible. So we must be prepared for extreme temperature variations, made even greater by the longer days and nights."

Girten was glancing around the group, eyes a little too wide. "Hey, but at least we know we can breathe down there, right?" When no one reassured him, he put out his hands in dismay. "C'mon! What about the green places you've seen?"

Eku's expression was as neutral as his tone. "Green does suggest that there is exoflora which utilizes the same light wavelengths as chlorophyll. That in turn implies the production of oxygen. But very little green has been detected and it is quite faint. Consequently, the amount of oxygen could be very limited."

"You mean the air could be thin, like in the Himalayas?"

"No, the sensor data suggests the atmospheric pressure is very similar to Earth's, which is the best news of all; the descent frames' parachutes should deploy and function as expected. As long as there is any significant amount of oxygen present, our suits' compressors will allow us to breathe."

Dora shook her head. "But even then, we won't *really* know until we pop our helmets."

Girten blinked. "Huh? Why?"

Newton's voice had a gallows tone to it. "Most air contains microorganisms."

"You mean like—like pollen?" Craig sputtered. "What? You're expecting killer hay fever?"

Dora shrugged, cocked her head toward Riordan. "Something like that almost killed him a few years ago."

Girten turned a horrified stare upon Caine, who shrugged, checked his wrist comp, and glanced into the far corner of the compartment. "Yaargraukh, a quick review of our loadout, please. Before we suit up."

# Chapter Five

The Hkh'Rkh did not float upward; he stood slowly, one arm raised until his hand made contact with the ceiling. His digitigrade stance and thin, round tail formed a tripod which, with steady downward pressure, kept him steady and stable upon the deck. "Since almost all our equipment remains locked behind the bulkhead doors separating the crew and engineering sections, there is little for us to carry. Our primary loads are the survival packs found in the lockers of the cryogenically suspended factotums. It was unimportant that there was not one for me; because Hsontlosh had no supplies for a Hkh'Rkh I retained access to my own supplies. Only my weapons are in aft storage. Including additional gear, pressure suits, and EVA packs, the average personal load is thirty-four kilograms."

"Everywhere you go," Miles quipped, "it's a forty-kilo pack. 'Or near as dammit,' as my meemaw used to say."

Caine managed not to react to the revelation that Miles O'Garran had a "meemaw" back on Earth.

"I have adjusted loads to address differences in capability," Yaargraukh continued. "Notably, Mister Eku's pack is significantly lighter due to his broken arm."

Dora's suspicion had transformed into a frown. "I've seen you, Craig, and Miles making piles. I divide that by the thirteen of us. No way we'd be carrying thirty-four kilos on the average... unless *someone* is going to hump a lot more." She crossed her arms. "So how much are *you* carrying, Yaargraukh?"

34

The big exosapient's pebbled hide twitched. "Slightly over the average."

Caine shook his head. "I want to know precisely; *how much* over the average?"

The Hkh'Rkh lifted his head, his voice simultaneously entreating and defiant. "Eight-seven kilograms."

"Yaargraukh, that is—!"

"Commodore, that is comparable to the loads with which I trained. I shall have no problem maintaining any pace you might set." He glanced almost furtively at Newton. "Frankly, my greatest concern is for Dr. Baruch. Given his greater size, I was compelled to increase his load to thirty-eight kilograms."

"I have carried more," Newton replied at the same moment that Caine silently congratulated Yaargraukh on shifting the focus away from his own load.

Yaargraukh's response—a stuttering grunt—signified grudging acceptance. "However, Sergeant Girten and I did discover several problems when we conducted inventories of the survival packs themselves."

"*Coño!*" Dora spat, "why is it that every time someone says the words, 'survival pack,' the next thing out of their mouth is, 'but there are some problems...'"

Eku's comment sounded slightly defensive. "The equipment is quite good, actually."

"Just as long as it's better than the crap we had when we crashed on Disparity," Dora muttered.

Caine's wave for silence almost set him twirling. "What are the problems, Yaargraukh?"

"In three packs, the original contents are gone. They've been replaced by various human and Dornaani personal items."

"So instead of a dozen packs, there are only nine."

"Correct. None of those nine contain the orbital uplink set indicated on the packing list. Two lack the smart blade, sampler, monoscope, and standard issue firearm. One of which does not function."

Dora gestured toward the Hkh'Rkh, eyes appealing to Caine. "See? Why do they even *make* survival packs?"

Yaargraukh's eyes had swiveled toward Liebman, who was frowning deeply. "Sergeant, you appear concerned."

"You could say that."

"I just did. What are your concerns?"

"We were counting on twelve survival rifles, but now we're down to six. And last I counted, there are thirteen of us."

The Hkh'Rkh's eyes retracted slightly. "Correct, but we also have replacements for most of the missing weapons."

"Such as?"

"The extremely powerful coil gun with which Hsontlosh's primary proxrov was equipped. There is also Mr. Eku's keepsake antique—the Ruger nine millimeter—and there are two grapple guns from the EVA locker."

Liebman shrugged, apparently mollified.

Duncan, however, had caught his frown. "So, are any of these weapons something *you* can use?" Caine had begun wondering the same thing: the size and structure of Hkh'Rkh hands made most human-scaled weapons too small and awkward to operate. During the final, desperate day of the Battle of Jakarta, they'd cut away trigger guards to use the firearms of the slain insurgents.

Yaargraukh pony-nodded. "The grapple guns have grips designed for use with your EVA gloves. They will be adequate."

"Yaargraukh, you know as well as I do that those aren't really weapons. Your targets will have to get damned close before you can engage."

"Then that will be most unfortunate for them." The tip of the Hkh'Rkh's tongue wiggled out for a moment: ironic amusement. "If enemies are within five meters, I assure you, the grapple guns will prove quite effective... more so than the survival rifles, depending upon the target."

Liebman spoke without looking up; his voice had become hollow. "That's four replacement weapons and six working survival rifles. That's only ten weapons for thirteen people."

Ayana sat slightly straighter. "I have always traveled with a family katana. It is with me aboard this ship. It will suffice."

"And," Miles said brightly, "I made sure to get one of the packs with a Dornaani smart knife in it. That will suit me just fine."

"No," said Yaargraukh.

"What?" Miles' laugh had perplexity behind it. "You won't even let me have a knife?"

"No, Chief O'Garran. You will have the knife. But you will also have the second grapple gun."

The SEAL seemed to grow two inches. "For your information, I happen to be quite good with knives. And I like them. A lot."

But Caine was studying Yaargraukh, who had assured him that the armament shortage had been solved. *But apparently not to everyone's satisfaction.* Riordan folded his arms, gave the situation a chance to play out as the Hkh'Rkh intended.

"Chief O'Garran, I mean no insult. We are comrades; my honor is tied to yours."

"Then what are you going on about, Yaargraukh? You think I can't get by with a knife?"

"Chief O'Garran, you are a redoubtable warrior and an excellent comrade. I doubt few humans could match your ability to survive armed only with a knife." The Hkh'Rkh's pony-pangolin neck swayed and then sank slightly. "I also know how hard and well you have trained for such a challenge. But I have *lived* that challenge, from earliest youth. It is part of my peoples' upbringing." The two did not so much stare at, but study, each other for several long seconds before the Hkh'Rkh bowed slightly. "As one comrade to another, I request you let me do this," the Hkh'Rkh finished, using a tone in which Caine heard hints of...a plea? *From Yaargraukh?*

Miles stared at the other for a moment, then shook his head and looked away with a surprised grin. "You get points for style, I'll give you that. Okay, I'll pack the grapple gun." He pushed off the bulkhead, faced the room. "I'm sure it will surprise and delight you to hear that my report is the last *and* that I am not going to repeat every step of the descent profile. I'll do that again, but just before we insert. However, this *is* your last chance to ask questions about the drop or your gear. Who's first?"

Caine felt sorry to see Craig Girten's hand raise, dragging with the weight of embarrassment. "So when the ship is done with its maneuvers, we'll get into the descent frames."

O'Garran nodded.

Girten looked reassured. "And then we jump out once we reach the drop zone."

Miles shook his head—a bit sadly, Caine thought. "Well, not immediately. And it's not jumping. And the term isn't drop zone; it's optimal insertion vector."

"But, uh, isn't 'insertion vector' just another way of saying drop zone?" Girten sounded lost all over again.

"Nope. They're related—call 'em cousins—but they're not twins, not by a long shot."

O'Garran leaned forward. "Think about jumping from an airplane. You lose your forward momentum really quickly. Mostly, you fall downward into a pretty tight footprint; usually a long oval.

"But in a LOHO drop, you are in near vacuum, so your vector will match the ship's: more forward than downward. Only when the descent frames' automated descent systems are synced will they fire their thrusters. That's what pushes you deeper into the atmosphere. But even when you come out of the frame on your personal 'chute, you'll still be going forward as much as you're going downward."

O'Garran scanned the faces in the compartment. "No more questions?"

"Just one," Liebman said quietly. "If the drop does put us all over the map, that means that all of us might start out alone. Craig, me, maybe others, have never had to survive in a place that is totally, well, alien. But half of you have, so I figured you'd talk us through what we don't know. But we still haven't been told anything about radio range, discipline, or...well, or anything."

O'Garran shook his head. "That question is above my pay grade," he explained as he pushed himself back toward the bulkhead.

Faces rotated toward Riordan. Half were puzzled, half wore tightening frowns of consternation. Caine nodded at them. "The answer is that until an hour ago, we couldn't really answer those questions. We had to wait."

"Wait?" Katie Somers asked. "For what?"

But it was Duncan, finger pointing beyond the limit of the hull, who answered before Caine could. "For the STL ship that's hanging out there."

Craig's head snapped erect. "You all said it was a wreck!"

Caine raised his hands for calm. "We know that now, but we had to wait to see if it, or anything in the system, was sending signals. And nothing is."

"So then it's not a problem," Girten concluded. "Is it?"

Riordan sighed. "The problem isn't the ship itself; it's what it signifies. Specifically, its structure closely resembles that of our own long-duration STL craft: so much so that it is probably a human design."

"But it *can't* be one of ours!" Craig exclaimed. "You said Earth can't get to, well, wherever we are."

"You are correct," Ayana said quietly. "But so long as we are within a thousand light-years of Earth—and for a variety of reasons, I suspect we are—then we are not the only polity that might have constructed it."

Katie nodded, admirably calm. "The Ktor."

Ayana returned her nod. "The Ktoran Sphere has been expelling defeated families for thousands of years. The region of space they reserve for such exiles—the Scatters—extends away from their borders and the rest of known space."

"How far?" Craig asked.

Ayana was very still as she answered. "There is no way to know."

Duncan nodded. "We could be near, or even in, those Scatters right now."

Even Chief O'Garran was frowning now. "Okay, but if we haven't heard any radio chatter, why all the worry?"

Ayana's reply was low and careful, as if she feared summoning the entities she named. "Death Fathers." The compartment fell silent. "During my captivity among the Ktor, they demanded I show them how best to operate my ship, threatening to execute the crew if I refused. Eventually, I became so invisible to some of them that they began engaging in conversations about the Sphere. Some of these concerned how the hegemons dealt with exiles like themselves.

"In short, the leaders of the great Houses—the Death Fathers—unleash their 'unblooded' lordlings to destroy any world where exiles no longer observe the two restrictions to which all of them must agree: no long-range radio transmissions and no supraluminal travel. So if the wreck out there"—now it was she who pointed through the hull—"brought such exiles to this place, their descendants might still listen carefully, fearfully, for radios. It is also possible that the long arms of the Death Fathers might have already smitten the world beneath us, or simply visited it preemptively. Either way, they would likely have left listening devices."

Liebman sounded as though he was speaking through a drunken stupor. "So we can't use radios at all."

Caine shook his head. "We can, but we'll be restricted to low-power squelch breaks. From orbit, or beyond one hundred fifty kilometers on the surface, they'll be indistinguishable from static."

He surveyed the now-solemn group. "Anything else?" When there was no response other than a few headshakes, he shifted into a crisper command tone. "Yaargraukh: you will, with Colonel Rulaine's assistance, commence assembling your frame. Everyone else: you have ninety minutes to double-check your gear. You will then present your rig to Chief O'Garran for inspection and sign-off. We will then gather to deploy. If you have other concerns regarding safe descent or survival on the ground, you will bring them up at that time. Any questions?" After two silent seconds, he turned to Ayana. "Are you ready to execute final hands-on maneuvers?"

"Aye, sir. Automated commands are synced to begin when we commence the pre-deployment countdown."

"Very well, Ms. Tagawa. Take us in."

# Chapter Six

Riordan surveyed the group gathered at the intersection of the corridors outside the air lock. Within, they could hear Bannor and Miles preparing the special materials for Yaargraukh's descent frame. He nodded at Newton. "Doctor, administer the stimulants, please." The autoinjector hissed three times; Peter, Katie, and Liebman seemed to have shaken off the cryodaze, but better safe than sorry.

Caine raised and sharpened his voice. "Once you're dirtside, where do you head?

The response was a loud chorus. "Toward the city at the river fork."

"And if you can't view the landing map?"

The rote-learned reply was a flat, syncopated singsong: "Head north to the tributary, then east to the fork."

Riordan nodded and spoke normally. "If your equipment fails, that's where you go. If there are locals, observe but avoid if possible. I have the Dornaani translator, but if that's lost"—*which is to say, if I crash and burn*—"you'll need to introduce yourself the old-fashioned way: at arm's—or spear's—length. If you have to hole up, keep your helmet powered so we can locate you. But so long as you can, keep moving toward the rendezvous."

Girten swallowed before asking, "And what if heading toward the rendezvous requires shedding some weight—like the musette bag?"

Riordan smiled at the term: once Craig had described the musette bag strapped to his leg when he dropped into Normandy, the term stuck. "Do what you have to, but just remember: the gear in those sacks is crucial group equipment. So hang on to them however you can."

Girten nodded but was also frowning. "Yeah, but why not put all the additional payload on a single frame and drop it separately? We'd move faster, rendezvous quicker, and then double back to get the load."

Liebman shook his head. "Ya think that's really such a good idea?"

"Why not?"

"I seem to remember reading about how some of your gear was dropped that way at Normandy. And was lost."

Girten sighed. "Yeah. The heavy weapons and the radios."

"Right. So this way, even if we lose some of the extra gear, we won't lose it *all*."

Caine nodded at Liebman's conclusion, noticed Eku wiping at a smear on the leg of his vacc suit. "Try not to lean against the musette bag."

Eku looked up. "Why is it coated with grease?"

"To make sure it comes off the frame with you when your 'chute opens." Caine waved off Eku's puzzled frown. "Chief O'Garran will explain it in a minute. Final systems check. If your HUD indicates your radio has received the coded freekset, raise your hand." Everyone did, although Girten lagged a moment behind the others.

Riordan leaned toward the air lock. "Chief: you ready?"

"Been waiting on you, sir." O'Garran emerged, face flushed and shiny with sweat. He pointed behind him, beyond the hull. "The emergency descent frames are strung outside the air lock. After you slip into the cargo harness, activate the frame as we've practiced. The harness will tighten and pull you a few centimeters into the foam that has started expanding behind you. When it's hardened, you'll see a blue—well, aqua—ready light on the facing side of the thrust unit."

Miles took a sharp step toward them. "Eyes and ears! This is the last review of the descent profile, so listen to every word as if your life depends on it"—his grin was evil—"because it does.

"Our mass-to-surface ratio is low, so the foam aerobrake may try to skip off the atmosphere. If it does, the automated descent package will change your attitude, make your entry angle more steep. The aerobrake will experience greater atmospheric resistance. That will increase heat and ablation. But once the sensors confirm that the frame is back in the optimal reentry corridor, it will adjust you back to normal attitude."

Ayana crossed her arms. "I examined the frames as you were inspecting them. I did not see any sensors."

O'Garran grinned. "More Dornaani magic. The sensors are nanites, embedded in the foam of the aerobrake. Individually, they monitor thermal levels and structural integrity. Collectively, they work like a gyroscope, only better. And if there is a problem with the shell, they'll show you how to fix it."

Duncan smiled broadly. "Problems? Surely there won't be any *problems*."

O'Garran matched Solsohn's facetious smile with one of his own. "Well, of course... because nothing ever goes wrong on *our* ops! But"—the banter bled out of his tone—"if the rate or pattern of ablation becomes uneven, the nanites will show you where you need to compensate and how much."

Ayana frowned. "How long do we have to effect correction?"

"Not long," O'Garran admitted. "Uneven ablation burns away one part of the aerobrake much faster than the others; it can go from a slight wobble to an ass-over-ears tumble in less than ten seconds. Normally, only a shipside operator would see and correct that, but Dora found a way to jack our suits directly into the automated descent package and project the operator interface onto HUDs."

Dora surveyed the faces that had turned toward her. "It's just like all the other Dornaani controls. Stare at the problem, fold your pinky, and blink twice. The system will do the rest."

"And if it doesn't?" Liebman sounded like he regretted having to be the one to ask.

Little Guy shrugged. "Then you break out of the shell early. But all that mass will accelerate your fall. So the higher you are when the final 'chute deploys, the further you'll drift away from our target point. Frankly, given our angle and rate of descent, some of us may miss the drop zone by a hundred klicks."

"Or by *hundreds* of klicks," Newton amended grimly.

Miles continued with a brittle smile. "But since everything is going to go *perfectly*, the aerobrake's ablation will slow you and carry away the reentry heat until you're just above the strato-sphere. At that point, the smart foam will release you. That's what triggers the first drogue 'chute, which will pull you away as the shell evaporates into dust.

"Now, remember how the frame wasn't designed for a live operator? Well, neither were its parachutes. Even experienced jump-ers will have very limited control over the final phase of descent. Those with no prior experience—Eku and the commodore—will have none. That's why two of us old hands will be paralleling them closely, all the way down."

Caine nodded in approval as he thought, *Yes, I'm such an outstanding asset to the mission.*

O'Garran waved toward the air lock. "Group one: with me."

As the chief closed the hatch behind the first six jumpers, Riordan discovered that Eku was once again wiping absent-mindedly at another oily stain on his vacc suit. "Eku?"

"Oh, yes: the grease."

Riordan nodded, then pointed at what he was clutching tightly in his other hand. "I think I need my helmet, now."

Eku handed it over hastily. "I am sorry, Caine. I am . . . dis-tracted."

*Couldn't tell.* "We're all anxious, Eku. By the way, did you get all the data stored on the crystal?"

He nodded tightly. "I also made a copy for my own helmet." He glanced at Riordan. "If something happens to this ship, those will be the only remaining records regarding Elena. Or of Hsontlosh's treason." The hatch's red-orange warning light flashed; the air lock was open to vacuum. "How long will we have to wait, do you think?"

Riordan shrugged, put a hand on Eku's shoulder, could feel it quivering through the suit. "Not long now."

Despite being no stranger to EVAs, Eku's fist was tight on the lead line as Bannor finished the final inspection and gestured toward the slowly rolling starfield on the other side of the iris valve. But instead of exiting immediately, the factotum rubbed at yet another stripe of grease as he held the musette bag awkwardly away from him with his splinted arm.

Riordan frowned, pointed, toggled the command channel. "Colonel Rulaine, that concerns me."

Bannor, who'd already started inspecting Caine's rig, turned.

"Damn, how could I have missed that? Eku, you're going to have to keep hold of the bag with your good arm when the frame dissembles."

"Why?"

"Because if the musette works free of its bindings during separation, it could yank that arm something fierce."

"But if I need my good hand to—?"

"Then loop your arm through the strap before you use it. Just don't re-break that arm. The pain—and possibly, unconsciousness—could make your landing, eh, more hazardous." Riordan knew an understatement when he heard one.

Eku nodded and, bag still held feebly, he used the other hand to tow himself to his frame. Bannor had half-completed inspecting Riordan by the time the factotum reached its basketlike cargo harness. "Quite a job he did with those," Rulaine commented.

Caine watched as Eku slid into it and adjusted the straps; it was entirely too reminiscent of an open-work iron maiden. "I thought it was you who'd performed the necessary miracles."

His friend shook his head. "There wasn't enough time for me to learn about Dornaani smart materials." He jerked his chin at the grey framework. "Just as well. At the start, that thing looked pretty much like every other pallet I've pushed, dropped, or loaded. Thirty minutes later, and Eku had it in a human-friendly configuration."

Riordan nodded. The descent frames had been given the same string of commands and transmogrified themselves within a few minutes. All but one of the dozen were moored at ten-meter intervals along a rigidized tether: the one that had been fried during Caine's EVA. Three baskets remained empty: his, Bannor's, and Miles'. "Where's O'Garran?"

Bannor gestured toward the tumbling cosmos. "C'mon: I'll show you."

Even before Riordan was through the opening, he detected movement to his right, turned—and was so surprised by what he saw that he almost lost hold of the tether.

Miles O'Garran was glide-crawling all over an irregular, lozenge-shaped object that Riordan couldn't identify until he recognized the side that was mostly turned away from him: a fully deployed and hardened foam aerobrake. But the other side of that teardrop shape was an irregular, partly nacreous mass that seemed to have accreted atop a rough cocoon at its center...

"Yaargraukh?" Caine breathed.

"Yes," came the Hkh'Rkh's decided morose reply. "It is I."

Riordan turned to Bannor, who was smiling broadly. "It looks like hell, but it does the job."

"That remains to be seen," Yaargraukh grumbled sourly.

"Ah, don't be a big, leathery baby," O'Garran muttered as he liberally applied Dornaani smart paint to an exposed flap of equally magic Dornaani tape.

Riordan resisted the urge to shake his head; partly because it would be disorienting, partly because every fraction of a second was increasing his whole-body REM dose. "I saw the parts list for this contraption, but...what am I looking at?"

"A marvel of ingenuity," Bannor chuckled, but there was pride behind the ironic self-deprecation. "The biggest challenge was to create a pressure-tight whole-body capsule around him."

"Yeah," Miles added as he checked whether the paint had set. "Hkh'Rkh duty suits—sorry, but it's the truth, Yaargraukh—have piss-poor EVA duration, pressure integrity, and radiation protection. Nothing we could do about the rads."

"But," Bannor resumed, "we solved the other two by encysting him under three pressure-rated tarps."

"Okay, but won't the airflow tear them off long before his frame reaches the stratosphere?"

Bannor pointed at the base of the third and outermost of the tarps. "Might have, if we hadn't sunk all of them into the foam. They're cemented into it just like everything else."

"But that foam sets in less than a minute."

"Don't remind us," groused Little Guy. "That was the hardest part of the job: getting our lovable snork fixed in the foam in a few seconds, along with a pony tank of air and his escape tools. Only then could we layer the tarps over him and get their edges down into the foam before it set. Oh, and did I mention we had to evacuate the air from the space between each of them? If we hadn't, the pressure changes would have popped them like balloons, or made them sag and shred." He floated back from Yaargraukh's surreal reentry capsule, inspecting his handiwork. "Tell you what, though: if Ayana hadn't lent a hand, we'd never have finished in sixty seconds."

But Caine's focus had snagged on a different detail. "You said something about 'escape tools'?"

"Actually," Yaargraukh grunted, "that is my favorite part of the design."

Bannor rolled his eyes. "It also happens to be the most dangerous part." His gaze went sideways toward Caine. "You may have noticed that he is completely encapsulated?"

"You mean, he...he can't see outside?"

Rulaine shook his head. "No way to achieve that without compromising pressure integrity. Now, if everything goes according to plan—"

—Little Guy emitted a single incredulous guffaw—

"—his descent profile will be almost identical to ours."

Caine frowned. "And if something goes wrong with his automated descent package?"

"Then he has to go to manual control. Which means cutting himself out of the cocoon."

"Yeah," Miles added, "which is why we had to keep his arms out of the foam but with just enough room to use the escape tools in his hands. To hack his way out."

"Thanks, Chief; I kind of foresaw that part. But why does he have to go to manual control?"

"Sir, you remember what I said about the Hkh'Rkh duty suit? Well, the helmet is the worst part: no HUD. So we had to rig a manual control stick."

Riordan shook his head. "But how will he know when and where he needs to steer? Or change thrust?"

Bannor pointed at the mummified mass that was Yaargraukh. "The helmet does have a small panel for video feed. The descent package can superimpose navigational guidons on that image."

"Except, just like the rest of us, he's facing away from his direction of travel."

Miles shrugged. "Between some hot-wiring and a few mystic passes, Eku rigged it so that if Yaargraukh keeps the frame within the limit of the guidons, the software will translate his steering choices into matching maneuvers for the descent. Like I said, Eku's a wizard—even if he is a frog-pet."

"Chief," Riordan snapped, "jettison that last term. Right now."

O'Garran sounded injured. "But, sir—"

"Right now. We need everyone in the group to feel like a full member of the team. 'Frog-pet' is a nonstarter nickname."

"Aye, aye, sir. Any other questions?"

"Yes. While no one has more confidence"—*or personal experience*—"regarding the physical prowess of Hkh'Rkh, I'm worried if Yaargraukh hits a snag, he might not be able to clear the tarps fast enough."

"Already solved, sir." The chief pointed to a protrusion at the approximate top of the swaddled cyst. "Drogue 'chute. Yaargraukh can pull it from inside the cocoon. When it deploys, it will either pull the cocoon off entirely, or at least stretch it out away from him. He'll have plenty of room to hack at it."

Bannor nodded down at the awkward agglomeration. "Well, Yaargraukh, to borrow the idiom of the Lost Soldiers, you are definitely the biggest badass of all badasses."

"You exaggerate the risk," came the basso-profundo reply. "You and Chief O'Garran have ensured my safety. The only unfortunate aspect is that the process has been . . . most undignified."

"How?"

"I have been fretted over like a whelp."

"Well," Miles sneered, "if you'd brought a real space suit, we wouldn't have to do any of this."

"As you may recall, Chief O'Garran, I did not leave Turkh'saar with anything other than my life and the assured enmity of the Patrijuridicate's Old Families."

Riordan could hear Bannor's grin: "Well, yes, there's that."

The Hkh'Rkh let air wheeze out his three equilaterally arranged nostrils: sardonic amusement. "I am ready."

"Time to deploy," Bannor agreed. "Commodore, whenever you give the word."

Riordan nodded and moved toward his own descent frame, third out along the tether. "The word is given."

# Chapter Seven

After the foam had finished billowing out to fill the almost invisible filaments of each aerobrake's shaping mesh, Caine started a timer: one minute until it hardened. "Eku, are our descent packages synced?"

"Just now, Commodore. And biomonitors are functioning."

Riordan toggled for the open channel. "Systems check. Sound off."

By the numbers, each of the other dozen jumpers confirmed that their frames, and they, were ready.

Riordan looked down the length of the mooring tether: the teardrop bulges of the frames' hardened aerobrakes were lined up like misshapen white birds perched on a power line. He eye-toggled his private channel to Bannor. "I've got to say it one last time: it is insane that I'm in charge of this when you've actually managed LOHO drops."

His friend's answer began with a chuckle. "No, I *commanded* them. The person who actually managed them was the senior NCO. This time, that's my job: down in the weeds, dogging the details. Even more than usual, we need our CO to be watching, and adapting to, the big picture."

Riordan found he was smiling. "How's it feel to be a sergeant again...Colonel?"

Bannor's reply was genuinely bright. "Feels great. Liked my life better before I went green to gold."

"Before you what?"

"I'll explain when we're on the ground."

"Speaking of which"—Riordan looked at the world looming beneath and beyond his toes—"time to head downstairs."

"Yep," Bannor agreed. "But watch the first step; it's a doozy."

Caine stared at the archaic Lost Soldier colloquialism. "Bannor, what is a 'doozy'?"

"Damned if I know, Commodore. Ready to count us down?"

*Hell, no.* But Riordan said, "Yes," and switched back to the open channel. "All hands, prepare for automated insertion. Eku, you will commence release sequence on my mark. Three, two, one...mark."

The descent frames did not detach all at once, but in three staggered groups, the result being that both of the first two tiers were separated from the one immediately behind it by a kilometer. Their movement would have been imperceptible had it not been for the one reference object that was already moving well ahead of them: the ship, sunlight picking out the edges of its lifting surfaces.

"The automated descent package will fire briefly," Eku warned them, "to widen our lateral intervals."

"Yeah, tight traffic conditions up here," quipped Duncan. Riordan hoped his jocular tone kept Girten and Liebman from realizing the actual reason for the maneuver; in the event a descent frame experienced a catastrophic failure, it minimized the chance that the resulting debris would crash into any others.

Slight puffs from Riordan's thruster—perched just within arm's reach atop a low tripod—imparted a brief sensation of side-slipping to the right and slightly downward. Shortly after, an equivalent puff pushed to the left, canceling the lateral drift. Riordan waited a moment before asking, "Eku, confirm successful evolution."

"Confirmed, sir: optimal formation achieved. Descent velocity is nominal. Sending a visual."

From Eku's position at the center of the first wave, his helmet camera showed two slow, stately lines of inverted white teardrops: the reentry side of the frames' aerobrakes. Four in each rank, their matched vectors would have made them appear motionless but for the rising rim of the world.

The view moved to the right and then the left as Eku turned

his head from side to side. Two more frames, seen in profile, flanked him. Sharing the images wasn't operationally necessary but, at the outset, it helped orient those who had been unable to adequately visualize the process.

As the image disappeared, Bannor asked the group to sound off and report their status: more a means of diminishing the sense of isolation typical of EVA operations than a strict necessity. As Rulaine ran slowly down the roster, Riordan had enough time to bring up the dynamic mission profile on his HUD.

The diagram showed the curve of the world on the bottom, with the arc of their deorbit track descending toward it from left to right. It crossed through three faintly colored layers before reaching the planet: the mesosphere, the stratosphere, and finally, a narrow band just above the surface: the troposphere. The blinking dot indicating Riordan's frame had sunk a third of the way from the top of the mesosphere to the beginning of the stratosphere.

He checked his slowly increasing rate of descent, compared it to the ideal mission time hack: they'd be halfway through the mesosphere in about four minutes. Right on schedule. That would also be when the reentry heat began building in earnest: a unique situation, in Riordan's limited experience.

As a passenger—and twice, the second seat—on deorbiting craft, Caine had grown accustomed to the first part of a typical deorbit profile: shedding a lot of velocity early in the descent. But here, a lot of the normal physics were reversed. Their ship had re-expressed from shift in a comparatively static relationship to the planet, meaning a minimal difference in momentum. So, since they were not entering the upper mesosphere with a lot of excess energy, shedding excess velocity would not become necessary until the planet's own gravity had dramatically accelerated their rate of descent.

As if underscoring the difference, the frame jostled him slightly from below.

Craig Girten was on the open channel instantly. "Is that... is that us skipping off the surface of the pond?"

"Correct, Sergeant Girten." Eku's voice was almost too calm. "The atmosphere is now thick enough to offer noticeable resistance. The automated descent package will soon make small changes to the attitude of your individual frames in order to keep them within the reentry corridor."

Sure enough, the thruster just a meter away from Riordan's face angled, puffed, reangled slightly, puffed again, then recentered. A moment later, the irregular jolts subsided...but now a faint vibration was persistently drumming against his back, as if he were lying upon a giant tuning fork.

Eku reported that change with a hint of panic in his voice. "My frame is...it may be coming apart—!"

"Stay calm, all of you." Rulaine's voice mixed firmness with boredom: a surprisingly reassuring blend. "Constant vibration is normal, even at this altitude. Any object digging down through an atmosphere generates friction. That's all you're feeling, and it's going to increase as we drop further. As long as the vibration is smooth and steady, there's no reason to be concerned. Same if the thruster fires a burst or two; it's just keeping you five-by-five in the reentry corridor."

"Five-by—?" began Girten and Eku simultaneously.

"Centered," Bannor interrupted, then paused. "Any problems? Any questions?"

After a few faint demurrals, the line was silent.

The icon for a page on the command channel illuminated. *Shit: a problem already?* Riordan muted the main channel, opened the other. "Riordan. Go."

"Damn, Commodore!" Miles exclaimed at his hard tone. "We're not calling with bad news, promise!"

Bannor sounded bemused. "Just touching base, CO. Enjoying the ride?"

Riordan snorted. "It's overrated."

"Well, enjoy the boring part while it lasts."

Caine glanced at the descent tracker. "Yeah, looks like there's still three minutes before things get 'interesting.'"

O'Garran sounded philosophical. "So, any plans for all that downtime, sir? Mixing some cocktails? Napping?"

"Worrying. I'll be monitoring the open channel. Anything else to report?"

"No, sir," they chorused.

"Well, no news is good news. Riordan out."

After two quiet minutes, Duncan Solsohn confirmed Caine's implicit assertion that most news was a harbinger of woe. The IRIS operative's soft mutter shattered the silence of the open channel like a hammer going through glass: "Got a little problem, here, Mission Control."

By the time Caine had placed the reference, he was responding on the main channel while opening the command line as well. "What's your problem, Duncan?"

"Well...my automated descent package is glitching."

Riordan kept his voice calm, wished he could boost the temperature in his suit to drive off the sudden chill running down his limbs. "Eku, can you diagnose from your suit?"

"I cannot, Commodore. Also, I am noting increased interference on all channels and data links." A pause. "I believe the solar weather event is beginning. Duncan, describe what is happening."

"The interfaces for the different programs on my HUD are, well, mashed together. They either overlap or are superimposed on each other. None are responding to commands."

Eku's response was confident. "The problem is not in your HUD. It is in the feed from your automated descent package. You must reinitialize it. Immediately."

"What?"

Riordan muted the open channel, muttered to Miles and Bannor, "Do you agree?"

Miles' response was immediate. "I'm out of my depth, sir."

"Bannor?"

"Sorry, CO, I'm not much better off than Miles. We're not familiar with the system and we can't even read Dornaani. My guess? After traveling in the Collective for months, you're the only one who might be able to help."

*Well, then heaven help us all.* Riordan unmuted the open channel. "Eku, what happens if the reboot doesn't work?"

"Then Major Solsohn will have to finish his descent using the manual assist software, which runs as a separate system."

Riordan pondered, asked, "What is the probability that only the interface is corrupted and that the descent controller itself is still functioning?"

Eku sighed. "No way to know, sir."

Riordan suppressed a sigh of his own. "*Major* Solsohn, prepare to reboot." He muted the channel. "You two heard?"

"We heard," Miles muttered. "It's really the only choice he's got."

"What if he punches out now?"

Bannor exhaled sharply. "Even though the drogue 'chutes are made from smart fabric, Eku didn't know if they'd work in the mesosphere, so opening them here could be useless. On the other hand, if they *do* work, then the main might also deploy in the upper stratosphere—and he'd land God knows where."

"On a planet that is eighty percent ocean," O'Garran muttered darkly.

"Right. Stand by." Riordan unmuted the open channel. "Major Solsohn. Here are your instructions. You will reinitialize the automated descent package as per Mr. Eku's recommendation. Mr. Eku: if the system fails to reinitialize, what are the consequences of Major Solsohn overriding the descent profile and jettisoning the frame?"

"Jettisoning the frame? Sir, that would—!"

"Mr. Eku. Just. Answer. The. Question."

"He should be able to assume direct control, including jettisoning the frame, through the manual assist program. But he might not—"

Riordan didn't wait for the factotum to finish. "Major Solsohn, if the system does not reinitialize, you will jettison the frame if it becomes dangerously unstable. Be warned: your drogues and main are not rated for the mesosphere, so the lower you punch out, the better."

"I understand, sir. I'm ready to turn out the lights."

Riordan couldn't help smiling. "Godspeed, Major."

"Reinitializing. Stand by."

Riordan muted the line so he could take a deep breath and release it slowly as he waited. The vibration against his back was increasing but still regular. Mostly.

"And..." Duncan murmured, drawing out the word before he announced: "Eureka! System is up again!" Relieved sighs and exhalations almost drowned out his question: "What do you think caused the glitch, Eku?"

"Possibly the interface between your Terran helmet and Dornaani software, but more likely it is due to the CME. The energy in the atmosphere has already pushed its resistance coefficients past projections, and comms may begin to lose clarity. Other failures are likely."

Riordan frowned. "Eku, go back: how is the solar weather increasing atmospheric friction?"

It was Ayana who answered. "Energetic particles create various forms of resistance and disruption, Commodore. In this case, it requires more effort—and generates more heat—for the aerobrakes to push them out of the way."

Riordan nodded to no one, cleared his mind, and carefully prioritized his orders: any second might be the last in which he could send them. "All hands: if your automated descent package fails, activate manual assist as per the protocols just given to Major Solsohn. For those of you in Terran pressure suits: your electronics are three times as susceptible to EMP and radiation damage as Dornaani gear. Yaargraukh, your risk is at least double that.

"Warning lights may also malfunction, so watch your altimeters closely. If you pass the altitude benchmark for an automated descent evolution, jettison your frame as soon as practicable. Or sooner. Acknowledge receipt of these orders by voice."

After all twelve confirmations were received, Riordan breathed deeply. "Mr. Eku, we could lose comms at any time. So walk us through what will happen from here to the ground. Concisely and clearly."

"Yes, sir. Each frame will start experiencing individual variations in friction, temperature, and wind. Continuing to synchronize them would be difficult and dangerous. Each is now being shifted to autonomous control. This optimizes safety, but the formation will degrade."

The vibration had become similar to riding in a car without shock absorbers. The stars were becoming less visible, and in their place, faint vapor trails were now reaching back along each frame's trajectory.

"Your HUDs should now be displaying a graphical representation of your aerobrake's integrity and performance. Do not become alarmed if one of the edges glows red for a moment. That indicates the nanites detected uneven ablation there. When your automated descent package has adjusted your frame's vector to correct it, the red disappears."

Liebman's voice was tight. "What if the red doesn't go away?"

"You may need to wait a moment."

"I did. The red is still there. And growing."

Caine was about to break in, but Bannor beat him to it. "Liebman, use the Dornaani command override and blink at the red part! That will correct—"

"Correction isn't working; it's getting worse. Wait...shit! I did it backwards! How do I—?"

"Liebman: punch out!" Caine shouted.

Liebman's connection flared into static, then died. At the far right edge of Riordan's vision, a bright orange flame flickered against the blue black of the mesosphere, like a suddenly lit candle falling sideways. The incandescent tongue brightened, rolled, and with a final sharp flash, winked out—before reappearing as a shower of orange and red sparks, plummeting planetside.

# Chapter Eight

The open channel was utterly silent—except for labored breathing. Losing Liebman was bad enough; the abruptness was terrifying, almost paralyzing.

Which Riordan could not allow to take hold. "Who was alongside Liebman?" he asked, keeping his voice low and steady.

"I was," Katie replied thickly.

"What did you see leading up to his...to the frame failure?"

"I saw—not much, sir. By the time I looked over, his aerobrake was already trailing vapor, leading edge white-hot. Then it rolled, tumbled like a mad thing, and was gone."

Riordan clenched his teeth. Of course Katie hadn't seen anything; her faint slurring meant she was still fighting the cryodaze. She had to sacrifice some situational awareness to stay focused on her own actions. *But if* I'd *warned him, just a second sooner—*

"He never had a chance to jettison the frame," Bannor explained, as if reading Caine's mind. "In that kind of rapid onset, almost everyone blacks out. But what the hell did Liebman mean by saying he 'did it backward'?"

Girten's voice was mournful. "It means he was too smart for his own good."

"What?"

"The chief explained how, when the heat burns too much off one side of the aerobrake, the machine turns it to the opposite side to even it out. When Liebman heard that, he snapped his fingers and said, 'hey, like the tiller on a boat; always turn away from where you want to go!' And he couldn't get that image out of his head. He was like that."

"And how did *that* kill him?" Dora almost shouted.

"Because," Miles answered as he sucked in a sharp breath of realization, "Dornaani controls work by aiming your eyes *at* the problem. But during our one drill, Liebman stared at the *opposite* side."

"But red means danger!" Eku gasped through chattering teeth. "And green means safety. Surely he knew to correct the red?"

Girten may have choked back a sob. "Maybe...except he was color-blind."

For a moment, Riordan saw the disaster through Liebman's eyes. He had to fix one of two illuminated areas, but couldn't tell them apart. But he *could* sense the pitch of the frame, so he reacted—before remembering that he had to stare toward, not away from, the failing side. In an instant, the ablation redoubled, aerodynamic stability was lost, the frame rolled...and he was gone in two seconds.

Riordan exhaled silently, then realized Eku's teeth were still chattering. *Damn it.* "Mr. Eku, we're coming up on the stratosphere. Talk us through what happens next." Not only was repetition prudent, but it might help focus any shock-blanked minds in the group. And having a task to perform might calm the factotum.

Eku's voice started faint but gathered strength. "The frame will provide controlled descent to the lower half of the stratosphere unless it detects an imminent catastrophic failure or the operator elects to jettison it. No matter how the frame is jettisoned—as part of regular operations or in an emergency—the process is the same. The nanites in the foam dissolve it as the first drogue 'chute deploys and pulls you clear. Subsequent drogue 'chutes will reduce your speed of descent. When the last detaches, it deploys the main parachute. Remember to scan for other canopies and take bearings on them, if possible. If you pass through fifteen kilometers altitude and the frame has still not self-jettisoned, you must do so manually."

As Eku finished, Riordan watched his own frame's vapor trail thicken into a smoky, spark-flecked plume. An orange-yellow glow rose up around the edges of the aerobrake. Just as well that he couldn't see it from the same perspective that he was now viewing the others: inverted teardrops of fire falling at increasingly steep and divergent angles. "Chief O'Garran, we seem to be drifting apart. How's our formation?"

"About what we expected, but that doesn't predict much about our actual landing pattern. That will be determined by where individual frames start losing stability or integrity, because that's when they'll cut us loose. The higher that begins to happen, and the greater the variation among the altitudes at which it does, the more scattered we'll be."

O'Garran's voice changed. "Heads up, Eku. Three frames are not increasing their angle of attack: Wu, Somers, and you. Why?"

"I am not certain. But I suspect—"

"Lower mass," O'Garran interrupted. "Damn it. Those were the three loads we lightened."

Caine frowned, as much at the angry orange halo rising around the rim of his aerobrake as Miles' assertion. *Hard to believe ten kilograms more or less could cause such a difference, but—*"I need alternate guesses—and solutions—now. Or we go with the chief's."

Bannor replied instantly. "It's the frames' software, CO."

"Explain."

"All of us are under the frame's minimum-rated drop mass. Every kilogram is just confusing the descent package that much more."

Caine bit his lip. "Eku: comment. Quickly."

"Yes, that's possible," agreed Eku, "or it could be that the frames' current actions may only make sense later."

"Or never," Miles amended, "if they're trying to chew on numbers they can't digest. CO, we need a fast decision, or all three will overshoot the target."

Caine's frown returned. "How far?"

"Unknown, sir, but they are still going downrange a lot faster than they're going down*ward*."

Caine switched to the command channel. "Recommendations?"

"They've got to jettison the frames," Bannor shot back. "There's no other fix."

"How soon?"

Miles' diction was clipped. "Estimating now, sir. Trying to make sure they come down on the west side of the big river."

Riordan unmuted the open channel. "Peter, Katie, and Eku: prepare to jettison your frames."

"But, sir—!"

"That's an order, Mr. Eku. Chief O'Garran's first priority is to keep you on the same side of the big river. But punching out early means you'll spend more time in the stratosphere's higher, stronger winds."

"Jumpmaster," Peter began, tactfully putting his question to Bannor, "how steerable is the main 'chute?"

"Not much: it's a round cargo canopy. And the smart fabrics are designed to be controlled from the ship. However, look for a yellow stud on the front of your harness: that's an emergency motion sensor. Push it sharply in the direction you want to go; that might work."

"*Might* work?" Girten gasped.

Bannor spoke over the Lost Soldier's dismay. "No way to change rate of descent, though."

O'Garran paged in on the command channel. "I have a number, Commodore."

"Do the honors, Mr. O'Garran."

The little SEAL returned to the main channel with a big voice. "Wu, Somers, Eku: you will punch out in thirty seconds. I will begin counting you down in five-second intervals. I will start at twenty and finish with five-to-zero. Understood?"

Katie's and Peter's confirmations of "Aye, chief" came a moment before Eku's breathless, "Yes."

Riordan spent the next twenty seconds craning his neck to visually locate the three frames. Peter's was relatively close, Eku's was at the edge of his vision, and Katie's was nowhere to be seen.

As O'Garran passed "five," his voice became successively louder with each step of the countdown: "four, three, two, one!"

Caine watched as Peter's frame dissolved like sugar in boiling water—in the same instant that he was yanked backward, away from what was now only a flame-flecked puff of dust. But Wu's rearward direction was illusionary; he had simply been pulled away by the drogue 'chute billowing out behind him. But the envelope did not become swollen with air.

Riordan glanced toward Eku, saw the factotum's own drogue struggling to find enough air in the same moment that Miles shouted, "Eku, what's—are you *spinning*?"

"I...I am! The bag was stuck and I—"

"Eku, do you still have the bag?"

"Y-yes."

"Is it still attached to you?"

"Only by the, the D-clip."

Riordan felt his scalp pull back. Once the musette bag came off Eku's leg, it had swung out to the end of its strap, pulling the factotum into a spin. Which meant—

O'Garran's order was sharp and loud. "Cut it away, Eku! Now!"

Riordan held his breath as the first drogue 'chute detached lazily but still with enough force to deploy the second one. Eku emitted a sharp grunt of pain: the jerk had probably ground his broken bones together. "I have my knife out...but I can't hold the strap."

O'Garran was shouting. "Then just slice at it, damn it! Right at the D-clip!" Even as he was howling instructions, the chief's frame banked in Eku's direction, its nose rising slightly. As its angle of descent decreased, its fuming aerobrake brightened.

*What the hell—?* "Chief—!"

"Sir, I can talk him out of that, but I need to see what's happening," Miles interrupted sharply.

For what felt like the tenth time in as many minutes, Caine suppressed another sigh. "Your discretion, Chief."

"Aye, aye; back soon."

Riordan hoped that would be the case.

O'Garran was already coaching Eku again. "You need to cut that strap!"

"I'm trying, but—"

The chief's frame straightened, paralleling Eku's. "What the—? Eku, cut the strap from the *bottom*! And hold it against you with your bad arm. That will—"

"Yes! It's working! I can—ohh!"

Eku audibly vomited as the second drogue 'chute was tugged sideways by an invisible force: the suddenly decreased drag as the musette bag flew free. The envelope appeared to be on the verge of collapsing instead of filling, but was then pulled out straight by the airflow. A moment later, it detached, releasing a third drogue that deployed clean and firm.

"Okay, Eku," the chief said calmly, "now we're going to correct what's left of that spin..."

Riordan didn't hear what followed. He had a new worry: Peter's and Katie's drogues also looked weak. And for the first time, he had the presence of mind to notice how frequently his own thruster was spinning and firing in different directions. Beyond it, looking over the rear of the frame, Caine saw that his and the other descent plumes were diffusing rapidly: more wind than they'd bargained for, even in the stratosphere. Not surprisingly, the few frames he could still see—less than half—were now widely scattered at different altitudes.

Caine shifted his attention to the HUD and increased the display size of the tracking grid. Peter's and Katie's frames had slowed, but as the first drogues pulled away, the second ones emerged sluggishly. Frowning, he opened the command channel. "Bannor, what's going on with our 'chutes?"

"Not sure, CO. It almost looks as if—"

"I'll tell you what's going on," Miles interrupted, voice tight with suppressed anger. "We're not just under the automated descent package's lowest programmed load; we're under the 'chutes' minimum suspended mass requirement."

It took Riordan a moment to remember that term: that was the load a 'chute needed to ensure it was being pulled down firmly enough to fill the canopy. "What's the minimum?"

"Damned if I know...sir," the chief snapped. "When I asked Eku back on the ship, he'd never heard that they had any minimum limit. Stupid me: I thought that meant 'no limit.'"

Bannor made a *tsk*ing sound. "Made worse by the thin air. It could also give us problems when the main 'chute deploys. I'll ask Eku about that on a private channel."

"Be my guest. Sir." As Bannor's carrier wave dropped out of the command channel, the chief took a deep breath. "Commodore, Eku's dangerous: not just to himself, but all of us."

Riordan didn't disagree, but—"You have a specific failure in mind, Chief O'Garran?"

"Sir, I do. Soon as I got him straightened out, he says, 'maybe I rubbed too much grease off the musette bag?'"

Riordan fought against the urge to groan, or perhaps laugh, or possibly both. "I'm betting you told him to stop, just like I did."

"Yes, sir. And told him why. Three or four times." O'Garran's tone grew careful. "Sir, I...well, I don't think he sees how all the moving pieces of a mission fit together."

Riordan, surprised that Miles would pursue such a topic during an operation, checked the frame tracker. "He's drifting north."

"Yes, sir. Winds are pretty changeable. The three that punched out early are pretty much going to go wherever those gusts take them."

"Do you think Eku will land north of the tributary?"

"Too early to say, sir. But I wouldn't be surprised."

Riordan saw a comm icon illuminate: Dora. Paging on a private channel. "Chief, check in on everyone. See how they're doing."

"Aye, sir."

As that channel closed, Riordan opened Dora's. "Eku is fine, Ms. Veriden."

"Like hell... sir! He's going to land far away from any of us. Maybe north of the tributary, if someone doesn't guide him down."

"And how do you propose to do that?"

"I'd override the descent package. Use glide and attitude control to keep up with him. Make sure he uses the emergency motion detector the way he should."

"Once you disable the descent package, the frame can't steer you back to the landing point, Dora. Worse, you'll be flying on makeshift controls while facing the wrong way."

Veriden's response was every bit as flippant as Riordan expected. "*Ai!* This mission is so boring, I'm going to sleep. Need a challenge to wake me up!" But before Caine could object, her tone became serious. "Boss, you said it flat out; we need Frog-pet alive. And well." A beat, then: "You think he'll stay that way on his own?"

Riordan wanted to object... but grumbled, "Damnit, Dora—go ahead. But be careful."

"I always am."

*Bravado and a lie, all in one.* "Ms. Veriden, if you die... I'm going to kill you."

She barked a laugh. "See? You *are* funny. I'll catch up with you dirtside, boss."

As Dora's private channel closed, the command channel paged. "Riordan."

"CO," Bannor said calmly, "we've got a major decision to make."

*I live for those words.* "Go."

"The chief and I have gathered data from across the drop. It shows we're facing variables we didn't expect, mostly because we followed a terrestrial wind model. We expected strong tailwinds in the stratosphere, but not at a constant of one hundred kph or more. That's put us downrange too fast, so the automated descent packages are going to jettison the frames sooner: to get us to slow down and fall faster.

"One little problem; judging from cloud movement, the winds in the troposphere are also higher—a lot higher—than those on Earth. And they're westbound."

*Just like us.* Riordan gritted his teeth. "So when the frames see that, they'll either keep the aerobrake too long in order to pitch down and bore through those winds, or they'll decide that maneuver is too dangerous and will jettison early."

"Yes, sir," O'Garran muttered. "And either way, that leaves us with a hard choice: stay together or stay on target."

"Explain."

Bannor almost sounded apologetic. "At a guess, anyone still in a frame now will overshoot the target point by fifty to two hundred kilometers, minimum. The three who've already punched out will be pushed twice as far. Maybe more."

Riordan closed his eyes. "So the choice is between keeping the present drop point or shifting it further west in the hope that we'll all land in a tighter footprint."

"Yes, sir."

"We keep the established drop target."

O'Garran was clearly surprised. "Sir—!"

"Chief, I hate the idea even more than you do. But if we clear our target settings and then lose comms before we get new ones plugged in, we will have *zero* control over where we land. Our best chance is to keep the target so that most of us can quickly regroup and rescue the more distant ones who should be heading our way. Comments, XO?"

Bannor's tone was heavy with regret. "That would be my call, too, sir."

O'Garran's tone was formal. "Roger all that, sirs. Commodore, request permission to assist Corporal Somers."

"Chief, you've already—"

"My drop, my responsibility, sir. And Katie's response time is—well, she's still cryodazed."

Riordan clenched his teeth. Newton had worried that given her elfin build and low body mass, Somers would have the longest recovery period. *And if there's aggressive local wildlife*—"How's she doing using the motion sensor to steer?"

"She's not, sir. Her arms aren't long enough to reach it reliably, and to listen to her, she's being bounced around like a cat in a clothes dryer."

Riordan swallowed back yet another sigh. "Request granted, Chief. No heroics. Find a safe place and hunker down."

"Will if I find one. Safe landings, sirs." His circuit closed.

Riordan scanned the frame tracker. "Peter, you're about to overtake Craig."

"I see it, sir. Orders?"

"Just that you two should try to keep each other in sight."

"You want I should punch out now, sir?" Girten asked.

"No." Then, replaying Girten's voice in his head, Caine realized that Girten had put unusual emphasis on "now." "Sergeant, what is your altitude?"

"Uh—just under nine kilometers, sir."

*Nine kilometers?* "Girten, your frame's descent package is corrupt. Minimum jettison altitude was fifteen kilometers. Execute and confirm manual jettison on my mark...and—mark!"

"Confi—urgh!—rm, sir. Jettisoned and good drogue release. I have Lieutenant Wu's frame in sight above m—" A momentary wash of static forced a reinitialization of comms links.

*And here comes the CME.* Riordan continued down the status list. "Yaargraukh?"

"Yes, Commodore?"

"You seem to be doing better than any of us."

"The irony of that is not lost on me, given the irregular composition of my frame. A further irony may reside in *why* my descent is more nominal."

Bannor understood first. "Both he and his load are twice as heavy. Add in all the tarps and smart paint and he's probably within the frame's rated mass."

*More of the universe's black humor,* Riordan reflected with a shake of his head—which showed him a flash far to the left. A fast glance at the tracker indicated the frame had dissolved and that its passenger's comm channel was still active. "Newton, are you—?"

"Quite well, Commodore. Automated jettison was nominal. Winds are quite strong. And"—a thump and a grunt—"and there goes the first drogue."

Riordan would have replied, but a hiss was rising behind the comms. "Eku, weather report?"

The factotum still sounded shaken, or in pain, or both. "As you surmise, Commodore: the CME is likely striking the upper atmosphere now. I would—"

"Thank you, Riordan out." *No time for chitchat.* He reverse-paged Dora as he checked her position on the tracker, which was now refreshing irregularly.

"What's up, boss?" Her *esses* trailed sibilant static.

"New orders. You will—"

"Boss. Please. I can get to Frog-pet. In a few more minutes, I'll—"

"Dora: listen. You. Will. Abort. Immediately."

"But, boss, he—"

"You are more likely to die than survive. We're more likely to rescue him if we gather quickly. That means staying on the same side of the tributary. So, unless you've seen a bridge that I missed—"

"Damn you, boss. That isn't funny."

"Probably because I was trying."

"Probably," she muttered, punctuated by what could have been either static or a sniffle. "Aborting," she acknowledged through a tight throat.

Caine nodded to no one: so he'd saved one person, probably at the cost of another. *Just like I did almost every day in Indonesia. Shit: what a lousy job this is.*

Two more frames jettisoned their passengers: Ayana and Duncan. Blinking dots indicated they, too, were still alive, but then stopped blinking. After a moment of dread, Caine realized the reason: the screen had frozen. He tried to refresh it, but after two tries, the system reported that the other signals were too erratic.

Riordan studied the positions on the tracker: probably the last reliable data he'd have for the foreseeable future.

Newton, Bannor, and Duncan were all on track to be in roughly the right position: just south-east of the city at the river juncture. Yaargraukh had been part of their cluster, but was moving further downrange: odd, since he had reported the most normative descent. Miles was now pulling even further downrange than Katie. It was probably due to the wind, but it was equally likely that he'd decided to use it to make sure he overshot, rather than undershot her landing point. Peter and Girten weren't as far west as those two but were farther south. Eku had been caught in a northwest air current;

Riordan's revised worry was that instead of coming down north of the river, he might come down *in* it. Dora had cheated back south, away from the river, but now, any wind that pushed Eku safely north of the river might push her into it. Ayana was about fifty kilometers south of her, but in terms of being able to provide assistance, she might as well have been halfway around the world.

Riordan looked around. None of his crew were in sight: no still-glowing aeroshells or canopies. The carefully planned drop formation wasn't merely compromised; it was nonexistent.

A blow—as if in punishment for his failure—jarred his torso and spine. The aeroshell beneath him was gone; his drogue 'chute snapped out full. He swung on the harness, feet angling down toward the ground. When he got air back in his lungs, he was mildly surprised to discover that, even from fifteen kilometers, the curve of the planet had become a flat, if distant, horizon. There was only one problem: he was still falling. And accelerating rapidly.

As if to punish him again, the first drogue tore away and yanked out the second. The sudden jerk was akin to being in a low-speed car crash. He had the presence of mind to confirm that all his gear was firmly secured—just in time to be hammered by the third drogue's release.

As he began accelerating yet again, a comm icon flickered: a weak connection to Bannor. He toggled the channel. "Glad to see you're still alive, Bannor." He gasped as the next drogue popped out.

Bannor's voice was dubious. "Likewise, but...are you all right?"

"Yeah; that's just the drogues proving that I should never doubt them. Can you see anyone?"

"No. You?"

"Nothing." Riordan waited for another drogue to deploy, but this time it was not so much a brutal impact as a longer, slower crush. Caine looked up. The main 'chute had deployed. He looked around again: still no 'chutes. "Not exactly what we planned."

"Not exactly."

"Hey: what's that Lost Soldier acronym you like so much?"

"You mean SNAFU?"

"Yes. That one. What's it mean, again?"

"Situation Normal, All Fucked Up."

Caine exhaled, studied the barren flatlands beneath him. "Yeah. That. See you dirtside."

Bannor started to respond, but his voice was swallowed by a sound like crackling bacon: the coronal mass ejection had finally caught up to them.

Riordan's radio went out, then reinitialized, but there was no carrier signal. No one was talking to each other because no one could.

But there was no time to care as the ground came rushing up.

# INTERLUDE ONE

# Too Close to Home

*March 2125*
*Dustbelt (Zeta Tucanae III)*

# Interlude One

When Melissa Sleeman entered the small comms room, the tall, broad-shouldered man didn't turn away from the panel in front of him. However, his head shifted just enough to confirm that he had obviously heard her.

She closed the door. Which stuck, as usual. Not much worked properly at the deserted airstrip in the region that had given the Zeta Tucanae III its name: Dustbelt. But at least the price and location had been right; the only cost had been assuming the debt on the failed interface facility. And, in the years they'd been there, their only visitors had been the long-legged, eyeless herbivores that often sheltered in the lee of the facility's single hangar. However, they were reminders of just how far from home she and the rest of the scant group were; they were a perpetually alien sight as their flowerlike full-spectrum sensor clusters swept the smaller structures and plains beyond to ensure that nothing was approaching.

Sleeman smoothly slipped an arm around the man's waist, rested her hand on his left oblique; it was as taut as rope stretched to breaking. It wasn't unusual—Christopher Robin had never relaxed into the role of the base's CO—but the tension was always greatest when it was his turn to keep the lonely vigil in the comm "shack." It had been forty months since they'd arrived on Dustbelt, and six months since Bannor and the rest of the Crewe had departed with Alnduul. And there'd been no word of them, or Caine Riordan, since.

Melissa stood on her toes to whisper one of many in-jokes into her husband's ear. "Darling, shall I light a candle?"

Christopher "Tygg" Robin's answering smile was strained. "You might, luv." When she looked up at him, curious, he shrugged. "After they disappeared into the Dornaani Collective, I told myself it would be half a year, tops. After all, how long would a crowd of primitive humans be welcome there?" He sighed. "Now, that half year has run its course. But still, here we are... and they're not."

Melissa nodded, rubbed her other hand along Tygg's arm. "At least our turn in the walkabout rota is coming up." That was the slang label for the rotating week-long leaves that gave those few who stood watch a change of scenery: much needed after a month squatting in the featureless dry prairie. Travel to the marginally more pleasant northern regions was a risk, but with nonmetallic microsats watching the planetary approaches and almost no traffic anywhere on the surface, it had been deemed acceptable... especially since the alternative would have been going slowly, quietly stir-crazy.

But whereas the mention of escaping the tight quarters and unwelcome pressures of command usually brought a twinkle to Tygg's eyes, all he could manage this time was a wan smile and faint nod.

She turned her closeness into a tight hug: always a bit comic, since the top of her head didn't even come close to reaching his collarbone. "Talk to me, my love."

He tensed, then sighed. She could feel his body loosen, but not relax, exactly: just surrender to gravity a bit. "When we left Turkh'saar, everything was uncertain. If we weren't working hard, we were playing hard. And trying our damnedest not to panic by staying too busy to remember that people from our own planet would happily string us up for refusing to turn over the Lost Soldiers.

"And then, when we finally stopped running and consolidated here, it was like one long sigh of relief, yeh? Just glad to be alive, to be together, to see some hope for the future. But after all this time, I wonder: will we ever get off this bloody backwater? And if we do, will we ever get to see our family, and our friends, on Earth?" He sighed. "I'd accepted that possibility, but as I did, I came to rely more and more on others, the rest of the Crewe."

"They're your mates," Melissa said simply.

"Yeh . . . or more like my family, now." He shook his head. "We've been together for almost six years. Since before I had these." He reached up, touched the silver hairs that had recently started appearing at his temples. "The only people to witness our vows, too."

Melissa nodded. She'd had, and expressed, similar feelings, but much sooner. She'd grappled with them less than a year after arriving on Dustbelt. But the twenty-odd people who kept watch over more than three hundred cold sleepers found ways to live and love and keep their spirits up. Whether it was completing projects that Duncan Solsohn had called "optimizing activities" or long-running tournaments of outdated board games that their intermediaries on Rainbow brought back, they'd remained busy, sane, and increasingly tight-knit. Early on, there had been a poker group, but without anything of value to wager or buy with winnings, it had quickly proven to be more depressing than exciting.

It had also been helpful that a third of the watchers were already romantically involved pairs: Tina Melah and Phil Friel, Dora Veriden and Karam Tsaami, Peter Wu and Sue Philips, and of course, Tygg and her. But the team that accompanied Bannor into Dornaani space had not only split up half of those couples, but had halved the population, too. Although it hadn't affected Melissa as profoundly as it had Tygg, it sometimes felt as though the walls were closing in, even though the complex itself felt desperately empty.

As if reading her mind, Tygg added, "But at least we're still together," along with a bear hug. But she felt the tension returning to his body even as his arms tightened around her.

"It's hard to wait," she sighed, "but right now, there's little else we can do except to stay hidden and be ready to respond. With any luck, our biggest problem will be boredom."

The traffic control bunker's comm panel paged once, then emitted a rapid series of tones: a secure vox-only comm from Susan Philips. Unscheduled.

Sleeman rolled her eyes: *Thank you so very much, Susan, for helping me soothe my darling's frayed nerves.*

Tygg had already toggled the circuit, waited for the automated authentication handshake to complete its back-and-forth confirmations. "'Petrel' online."

"'Starling' here," Susan Philip's voice announced. "We have boarders without reservations."

Sleeman discovered that now, she too was tensed. "Boarders without reservations" was code for unexpected contact made by persons of undetermined intentions. The same code which had announced the arrival of Ayana Tagawa six months ago.

"Do they have good credit?" Tygg asked: the coded query for whether or not Susan thought they should be vetted.

"They have cash in hand," was her reply.

Which caused Melissa to exchange a surprised glance with her husband. That reply was not code.

"Say again, 'Petrel,'" Tygg requested.

"We know these boarders," Susan replied.

"Do we like them?"

"Maybe. Could be old chums. Could also be a major problem. Need to make special arrangements."

"Special arrangements": that was the code they'd never yet heard, and the contingency they had never yet had to activate. It meant bringing people up to Dustbelt without vetting them first because they represented a security emergency of the highest order. And if they did not check out, it meant terminating them.

Melissa Sleeman closed her eyes. *So much for boredom being our biggest problem.*

Missy Katano stood alongside engineer Phil Friel as they watched the atmo-interface craft bring its nose up just before its leading wheels touched the dust-strewn runway. The flaps on the back of its delta wings flicked down a few times before its fuselage straightened out and its speed began to diminish.

Phil exhaled slowly; Missy hadn't noticed him holding his breath. "Problem with the shuttle, Phil?"

"No, Missy, and Karam is the best pilot we have. But I'll admit that I'm a bit nervous, what with Ms. Philips herself on that shuttle."

So, it was true: they'd pulled Susan Philips off her duty station on Rainbow. Which meant that, whatever message she'd sent was more urgent than Tygg and Melissa had let on—or anyone had guessed.

In retrospect, the writing had been on the wall. The base's one, third-hand shuttle launched a mere hour after Philips had called in. As the group's only available—which was to say, unburied—spacecraft, the shuttle was typically coddled and fussed over before every launch. But four days ago, it had been sent aloft with the bare minimum of preflight checks, took on just enough fuel at the automated low-orbit tankage facility, and crowded gees to reach Rainbow. There, a similarly brisk timetable had been observed; if it hadn't, the craft wouldn't have returned for another day or two. At least.

But here it was, with almost the full waking staff waiting within the warehouse that they used as the shuttle's hangar, its big doors open and the sand swirling inside. Karam Tsaami had requested a direct roll-in. According to scuttlebutt among people in the know, that meant whatever or whoever was on board warranted full concealment protocols, despite the absence of any CTR observations platform overhead.

The dual-phase thrust nacelles throttled back and shut down as the craft's nose entered the cavernous building, just in time to keep the roar from rebounding between the thin walls. There was no way to dissipate the heat from the engines, though; it kept washing over them like a perpetually opening oven door.

As the vehicle drifted to a halt and the warehouse doors began closing, the light over the combination air lock and ingress/egress hatch brightened; it had been unlocked. Standing alongside Doc Sleeman, Tygg Robin crossed his arms in impatience; apparently even he didn't know much more than anyone else.

The hatch opened and the access ramp unfolded. Sue Philips emerged, trailed by two of her station chiefs: Joseph Capdepon and Vincent Rodriguez. Capdepon, a Lost Soldier who'd been an NCO in the Vietnam War, was her security lead. Missy had never seen him in action but, according to all reports, he'd proven profoundly unflappable in the face of just about everything, including an especially dangerous river crossing and counterattack during the battle on Turkh'saar.

The other, larger man was Philips' technical chief and Missy's pal from over a century ago, Vincent Rodriguez. Abducted minutes after her, Vincent had started out as a tech on jet fighters but his unnerving facility with all things mechanical had made him Philips' first choice. He was the one person who had a chance of understanding the new technology but did not have a face that security cameras would be looking for.

The next person who exited the shuttle wasn't immediately recognizable to Missy. But by the time he began descending the ramp, she had recalled his face from her initial briefings. And so, also understood the murmurs rising and why Philips' precautions had exceeded even her ferocious opsec SOPs.

Richard Downing trotted down toward the dirt floor of the warehouse. Seemingly oblivious to the guarded reception he smiled crookedly and, using a softly ironic tone that had evidently been patented in Britain, observed, "I understand we're just in time."

Melissa Sleeman forced herself to exhale, to shake off the paralyzing pulse of dread that persisted even after she looked away from Downing. But her initial reaction persisted: *He's lied to us in the past. What keeps him from doing so again?*

Another man appeared behind Downing, just as tall but almost twice as broad. His face was familiar, but Sleeman could not immediately place it.

"Trevor!" Tygg said it so loudly it was almost a shout. He started forward, hand out—

Susan Philips held up one of her own. "A moment if you please, Captain." She frowned, gestured to another two men who had appeared at the top of the ramp, helping a third in a wheelchair. "We can't yet be entirely confid—"

Tygg shook his head at Philips. "Captain, I fought alongside Trevor Corcoran in Java. Whoever he trusts, I trust." He crossed the gap and grasped Corcoran's hand. "Bloody hell; how are you, mate?"

Melissa noticed that Trevor had his famous father's movie-star smile. "I'm alive. And reasonably hopeful I'll stay that way, now." He waved toward the three men who remained back near the shuttle's starboard wing. "I'd like to introduce you to the Three Wise Men who got us here: Larry Southard, Angus Smith, and Ryan Zimmerman."

Tygg nodded, turned to Downing with the start of a salute.

But the Englishman waved it off. "We never stood on such formalities before, Captain. I'm not about to start now. Besides, I am no longer the Director of IRIS." He smiled brokenly. "I'm no longer the director of anything. Including my own fate. I am here seeking asylum. And offering assistance, if I can be of any use."

Melissa Sleeman approached, making sure her face was neutral as she met Downing's gaze. Cautiously. "You'll forgive me if I am a little less effusive in my greeting, Mr. Downing, but... how did you know where to find us?"

Downing's answering smile was convincing. Then again, it always had been. "Mr. Southard is the one to answer that. Bannor's messages to Caine contained locational clues, which, when subjected to numerous regression analyses, revealed how and where you must have moved after a number of you spearheaded the anti-piracy campaign in Epsilon Indi."

Southard tilted his head at the fellow in the wheelchair. "The real wizard was Ryan. I just came up with the model. He came up with the program to sort it all out."

Susan Philips frowned. "Not to underestimate your credentials, gentlemen, but I cannot help but wonder: if three of you could do this while you were jumping around known space, why have legions of analysts on Earth not been able to perform the same feat?"

Trevor smiled at Philips. "Because, Captain, those legions of researchers didn't have a crucial data point: the starting coordinates that were embedded in Bannor's earliest communiqués to Caine. And for which I was the cutout, the go-between."

Southard nodded. "That was the cornerstone of our regression analyses. Once we knew where at least two groupings of the Lost Soldiers had been initially deposited, we were able to start working. It's dull stuff, really. How many carriers were operating between which systems at which times, further modified by traffic in and out of Epsilon Indi in the six months following the completion of Colonel Rulaine's operations. And we also knew that he had detected 'enemy' agents sniffing around one of your hiding places, which evidently triggered the reconsolidation that brought you here to Zeta Tucanae."

Tygg frowned. "Wait a minute: so how long have you known we were in Zeta Tucanae?"

Ryan shook his head. "Only a few months, now. At first, we didn't have much more intel than the opposition: when and where you dropped off the grid and when the colonel popped up at EpsIndi. With that, we could start eliminating places you couldn't have been. But narrowing the places you *could* have been was slowgoing. We probably weren't far ahead of the opposition.

"But then Captain Corcoran caught up with us at Delta Pavonis. He gave us all the seemingly casual locational data Colonel Rulaine had embedded in his messages to Caine, as well as two other systems where he *knew* you'd been and when. The computer chewed on the timing restrictions of the shift-carrier schedules both before and after, and in less than a day showed there was only one place you could have reconsolidated: Zeta Tucanae."

Philips laughed: a musical sound. "Two centuries on, and the game is still played the same way. No way around it, of course. But I understand you made the journey out here in just twenty-four weeks? That's less than half of the sixty it took just a few years ago."

Trevor smiled. "It would have been a lot longer than sixty if we weren't living in the brave new world of reverse-engineered exosapient technology. The shell game that Mr. Downing and his Wise Men were playing with the cryocells was like taking two steps forward and one step back, but the data from Bannor changed all that. And with the best carriers now making nine-point-four-light-year shifts with only three weeks of pre-acceleration"—Corcoran made an expansive gesture that took in all the arrivals—"here we are."

"Still," Melissa objected, "even if you were not tracked here, that doesn't mean we are safe. Once the Developing World Coalition finds your trail—which is only a matter of time—their agents will follow it here."

The quietest of the Three Wise Men, Angus, nodded. "That's why, if we hadn't found you, we'd have had to keep running, beyond the borders. Mix into the land grab."

Tina Melah, the Crewe's other engineer, shook her head. "Naw, if you never found us, what could anyone charge you with? You could just give up. But we can't, not if we want to stay alive."

Angus shook his head. "Nope. We're in the same boat. Worse, actually."

In response to Tina's frown, Downing shrugged apologetically. "If our pursuers find us, they will learn about the intelligence cell that these three men were working for prior to running. That would lead to its termination. And that, in turn, would leave the CTR deaf, dumb, and blind to the threats that are being missed by its other intelligence organizations. Its very *compromised* other intelligence organizations."

Angus turned his palms upwards in resignation. "So we've got to run as fast and as far as we can. We were figuring you'd been working on that yourself, had maybe found a way to get over the border, into the frontier?"

Melissa heard Angus' coy concluding tone, discovered her suspicions were abating. Angus wasn't much of an actor: if Downing had anything to hide, he wouldn't have let this fellow talk so much and so openly. She folded her arms. "So it seems Captain Philips told you about Alnduul's visit and his intent to extract us from CTR space."

"Nah, that was me," Karam drawled from the hatchway. "Breaking rules again. And Doc, I never thought I'd say this, but we've gotta give Downing all our situational data ASAP. I'm not a fan"—Tsaami and the former director traded assessing looks—"but I know a first-class spook-chief when I see and hear one. If there's a way to head off into some other sunset, he'll find it."

"Yeah, but which sun?" muttered Tina Melah. "All this talking is fine, but we need action." She cut her eyes at the newcomers. "I'm not gonna bet the farm that Alnduul comes back, so how about it? Any ideas for getting us to someplace safe?"

Downing shook his head. "I'm afraid not, Ms. Melah. And I must say that the one plan I have learned that some of you are considering is... well, it's bloody near suicide."

Melissa suppressed a sigh of relief. "I take it you mean the notion of seizing a shift-carrier to cross over into the frontier."

Downing nodded. "Madness. Although I understand the reason many of you may have fixed your hopes upon that scheme."

"Yeah!" Tina yelled indignantly. "It's called necessity. Like the doc said, it's only a matter of time before they find us here. So we've got to go someplace they can't find us. That means not just another system, but over the border—and there's no way to do that legally. Or on the sly."

Her chin came out in response to the gathering frowns. "The one thing on our side is that there are almost twice as many shift-carriers runnin' as there were before the war. Upwards of one hundred twenty, last I heard. So the odds are better that we'd be able to grab one from its berth, shift to a good hideout in the frontier, and then send the ship into the star." She folded her arms. "No path to follow, no traces to find."

Ryan Zimmerman leaned so far forward that Sleeman feared he might topple out of his wheelchair. "Almost half of all shift hulls are CTR naval assets, so that plan means you might as well hoist the Jolly Roger and paint a bull's-eye on our backs."

"Besides," Southard added, "they'd know where it was taken. That gives them a fixed position from which to start a search."

Vincent Rodriguez spoke up from behind Philips. "Don't mean to dogpile on you, Tina, but we couldn't even run the ship. We've got only five qualified personnel, six, if you count me."

Tina's nod was grudging but genuine. "You'd do in a pinch. I guess."

"Thanks, but I'm not so sure. And even the most advanced shift-carriers still require a skeleton crew of thirty. You'd need a lot more if you're crewing an older, less automated class. And the more shorthanded you run, the more dangerous and slower your operations become."

Tina's chin came out even further as she launched a stubborn riposte. "Maybe all that's true. But if we have to get out of this system and over the border, what other options do we have?"

"That, Ms. Melah," Downing conceded with a somber nod, "is what we have to figure out, and these Three Wise Men are specialists at coming up with solutions to that kind of problem."

Melah humphed. "So that's why you said your arrival was 'just in time'?"

Downing's smile was lopsided. "Actually, I was hoping that Alnduul might have sent a message indicating he would soon be extracting everyone here. But since he hasn't, we've no choice but to take matters into our own hands."

"Never thought I'd say this," Karam muttered, "but I'm with you, Mr. Downing. As long as you don't piss off Tygg."

Tygg shook his head. "I'm not the bloke in charge anymore." He nodded toward Downing. "We have the head of an intel organization here."

Downing's smile was faint. "I repeat, Major Robin: I am the *ex*-director. Not part of any command structure, here or there."

Tygg frowned. "Well, then command falls upon Trevor—er, Captain Corcoran."

Grinning evilly, Trevor snapped a salute at him. "Major Robin, you are incorrect, sir!"

It looked as though Tygg was starting to sweat. "With all due respect, *sir*, that's bollocks. I'm not even a real major; I was breveted to fill in for Bannor. Last I heard, you were an O5, and that was five years ago."

Trevor's grin widened. "That would mean something if I was

still active duty and if this was a regular unit. But I'm not and it's not. But I'll sign on as a private contractor. Pro bono, of course. Hell, I'll even agree to be your XO, if you'll have me."

Robin nodded. "You're hired, mate, on one condition: if you're still employed after three months, you replace me"—he grinned—"and I get my life back. So, XO, ready to head up the troops?" Sleeman saw the hesitation on Corcoran's face a moment before her husband did. "Now, sir, don't play coy; I remember you in Java."

Trevor's grin became both painful and fond. "I remember Java, too, Tygg, but given current needs, I think I might do most good overseeing your spaceside assets. And from what I've heard, Mr. Tsaami is the natural choice for lead officer on flight ops."

Karam nodded. "I'm your guy."

Sleeman touched Tygg's arm, discovered it was less tense than it had been in . . . well, a very long time. It relaxed further as he glanced toward Downing. "Sir"—*old habits die hard, apparently*—"you are hereby appointed as our ops coordinator. Recommendations?"

The tall Englishman's faint smile returned. "Intelligence stays with the supremely competent Captain Philips. I strongly urge that these Three Wise Men be detailed to her for data analysis and operational projection. We will also need a staff coordinator and chief of training."

Tygg glanced at Missy Katano. "Ready for a new challenge?"

"Always, sir!" Katano answered with a big, bright smile.

Downing inclined his head slightly. "Mind you, Miss Katano, the job will be almost nonexistent as long as the Lost Soldiers remain in cryogenic suspension. But if that should change, you may very well be the most overworked and under-slept of the lot of us."

"That pretty much describes my whole work history, Mr. Downing."

"Hey!" a new voice called from the doorway.

All faces turned in that direction: Dr. Ike Franklin, ghostly grey with dust, was leaning into the hangar. "Guess who I've got on the tight-beam?"

Melissa was the first to break the tense, fearfully hopeful silence. "Alnduul?"

"The one and only."

Tygg cleared his throat: a sure sign that he was ensuring his voice would sound fully composed and resolute. "Any word regarding his . . . status?"

"Well, he was more interested in ours."

Tygg frowned. "*Our* status?"

Ike grinned broadly. "Yeah: he wants to know if we are 'still resolved to leave Terran space.'"

PART TWO

# Hostile Territory

*Unknown World*
*March 2125*

# Chapter Nine

Riordan grunted as he tried rolling up from his landing fall, but stumbled sideways instead. The Dornaani smart fabric had thickened its weave thickness and reduced its air permissibility to slow him more rapidly during the final hundred meters. But now, on the ground, the brisk wind was entering the canopy from a new angle and tugging him in that direction.

Caine kicked back to get his feet faced toward the flapping 'chute. But he didn't dig his heels in, remembering O'Garran's warning: "You're not stronger than the wind, so don't resist it directly. If the canopy fills, it'll pull you off your feet and drag you behind: headfirst and facedown. This is not just embarrassing and painful but, in an unknown landing zone, dangerous."

It was good advice: the round 'chute was filling with wind and Riordan had to use every moment it slacked to swivel his feet toward it. Fortunately, the Dornaani fabric was becoming "smart" again: even as it stiffened against expansion, it also became more air permissive, allowing much of the wind's force to pass right through it. Between that and O'Garran's advice, Caine managed to maintain enough control to release the rig's right-hand toggle. With only one side of the 'chute still secured to him, it was no longer able to catch the breeze; it simply unfurled and rolled listlessly downwind.

Riordan finally staggered up to his feet, began reeling in the risers and suspension lines, and discovered that his scuffing feet were raising clouds that obscured everything beneath his knees.

That, along with the sharp impact of his landing, confirmed what he'd come to suspect during his descent: the wastes of the landing zone weren't dirt, or even sand, but a featureless expanse of hard-packed dust.

With half the suspension lines looped around his still-sore left arm, Caine quickly swept the horizon: nothing except a few low rock outcroppings. He blinked through to one of his HUD's few available options: the visual motion detector. He turned slowly; the only object that the sensor limned with its faint orange indicator was the fitfully flapping canopy. Riordan exhaled: the lack of contacts was hardly a guarantee of safety, but it was a whole lot better than irate beings converging from all sides.

He began the more involved process of gathering and saving the canopy, a priority task for which there was no set strategy: Eku had lacked detailed knowledge of the frames and Miles could only draw flawed comparisons to Terran analogs. The full measure of those flaws had become evident when the parachutes deployed: the bags holding them did not open, but simply tore away. Every part of the system had been engineered toward expendability.

Riordan spent a few minutes folding the highly cooperative fabric into a still-sizeable trapezoid. After rolling and securing it to the side of his survival pack, he retrieved the musette bag he'd dropped just before landing and checked the icons in his HUD. Most were still blinking: not full system failures, but too long to be a simple reinitialization. The CME had caused a full reboot.

Caine had hoped that at least the compass and atmosphere analyzer would function before he had to move, but he couldn't afford to wait for them. The only direction in which there was any promise of shelter was to the south, where distant irregularities hinted at slopes or hills. Unfortunately, his destination—the tributary that led to the city—was to the north. So if he were to have any chance of finding cover there, he'd need to get beyond the present horizon by nightfall.

After fixing the musette bag across the top of the survival pack, Riordan slipped back into its harness and tested the balance of the load. Ignoring his still-sealed vacc suit, he was carrying twenty-eight kilos: the approximate mass of a soldier's full kit ever since such things had been recorded. He'd intended to walk with the survival rifle—well, puny carbine—at the ready, but had settled for stowing it just under the pack's top flap. The suit would alert him to anything approaching over the flats, and if something jumped up out of the dust as he passed, he'd rather have a sturdy stick to block it. So, with a fully extended EVA gaff stick serving as a staff, he put the sun over his left shoulder and started north.

Shortly after a set of low ridges finally edged tortuously above the ruler-flat northwest horizon, Riordan's HUD lit up with bright green-blue icons: the suit's various systems had returned to life. But he only had eyes for one of them: the transponder tracking system. He held his breath as he called it up.

Miraculously, no one else had died. But as Newton had portentously intoned before they had left the ship, the day was still young—and the scattering of the group did not augur a happy outcome.

No two of the color-coded transponder markers were closer than seventy kilometers, but it was the broader pattern—or lack of it—that was truly arresting. Including his own, the twelve blinking dots south of the tributary were liberally scattered along a fan-shaped dispersal footprint eight hundred kilometers in length and just over four hundred wide at its terminus. Which, if memory served, was a patch of ground slightly larger than the state of Montana.

Eku's transponder was about halfway along the east-west axis, but offset three hundred and fifty kilometers north: on the other side of the tributary. Worse still, his marker was ringed in yellow: a biomonitor warning. Whether they were simply reporting his already broken arm or new injuries was impossible to determine without contacting him.

That yellow ring was one of the few events that called for a contact outside the daily squelch breaks, the timing of which also served as a status code. However, when he brought up the subscreen that monitored the strength and fidelity of the various comm channels, he discovered that the network was still laboring to establish itself. Parts were intact, particularly among transponders that were close to anyone wearing a Dornaani suit; they'd been programmed to self-assemble into a network of repeaters. But those nodes had not yet bridged the greater distances. Whether that was because they'd been degraded by the solar weather or were still trying to restore connections was, again, impossible to determine.

Fortunately, no one other than Eku was terribly isolated. Whether by chance or effort, almost everyone had landed in roughly proximal pairs. Newton was the one exception, but he'd come down barely a hundred kilometers from the river juncture, and so would probably remain there to let others collapse inward on his position. The pair closest to him were Bannor and Duncan, just over two hundred kilometers to the south. Two other pairs were located about the same distance, one to the west, the other to the southwest: Ayana and Dora, and—happily—Yaargraukh and himself.

But beyond that cluster, the separation beyond the remaining pairs increased markedly. Peter and Craig were almost seven hundred klicks southwest of the rendezvous point. Miles and Katie were at the same distance, but due west. More troublesome still, if those two pairs followed the post-landing protocols—to link up with those closest rather than each individual heading directly for the river juncture—their meeting point would put them slightly further away.

The moment Caine's focus drifted away from the revelations thrown up upon his HUD, he became aware of aches and pains all along his back: reminders of the survival pack and the musette bag atop it. The urge to rest was strong, but the notional safety of the distant ridge line called more powerfully. He had yet to encounter a single terrain feature that provided some benefit of elevation, flank protection, or concealment. And while that hadn't been a concern so far, once the sun went down...

Riordan smiled, glanced to the west: that's where Yaargraukh was, probably moving toward the same ridges, if they ran far enough in his direction. The temptation to rest arose again; if he did, he could move longer, into the night if necessary. But it had been Yaargraukh himself who had recommended against doing so.

In doing so, he'd put himself with Miles, who'd loudly asserted that, with their HUDs and thermal vision, they would "rule the night." In response, Yaargraukh's neck had circled lazily: a slight shrug. "It has not always been the case for us Hkh'Rkh. Perhaps because our sensors are more rudimentary, we had unfortunate experiences during early exploration of worlds. Not only did various exobiota possess superior night vision, but we encountered several with other senses—hearing, echolocation, smell—that enabled them to surprise us in various, costly ways. So until one knows an environment, unwarranted confidence can prove to be as great a danger as the exobiota one might encounter."

Caine remembered the truculent set to Miles' jaw—the little SEAL had never met an argument he didn't like—but Bannor defused the debate with a single shake of his head. "We should learn from Hkh'Rkh experiences. This situation is likely to resemble the ones that shaped their approach: a lash-up of tech and old-school caution. And with the exception of long-range visual acuity, our senses are a lot worse." When the chief frowned and started to open his mouth, Bannor added, "Trust me: I know."

Little Guy looked back and forth between the Special Forces colonel and the Hkh'Rkh. Under the aegis of a letter of marque, the two of them had led a post-war security mission in the pirate-plagued Epsilon Indi system. Whatever occurred there had forged a strong bond between them and brought in enough ecus to relocate, hide, and support the Lost Soldiers and the renegades who watched over them.

Riordan shook off the memory and resumed moving, but more westward. With any luck, he'd still have enough time to find a safe place before nightfall.

Riordan's morning alarm did not employ the same strident alert that announced suit malfunctions or dangerous REM levels. Reminiscent of persistent wind chimes, the sound roused him so slowly that Caine's first waking image was of diffuse brightness: sunlight filtering through his eyelids. Annoyed that he'd misgauged his intended wake-up—daybreak—he opened his eyes.

And saw the belly of a large insect, crawling across his face.

He swatted at it—before remembering that his sealed visor separated him from the intruder. His hand clunked into the side of his helmet, only grazing the bug. It fluttered off in a drumming of wings.

Caine sat up sharply—and almost pitched himself into the shallow, dry wadi beneath him. He paused, drew in a deep breath and released it slowly.

Not an auspicious start to his first full day on the planet. He'd misgauged the sunrise by almost an hour and the motion sensor had not detected the insect. A malfunction, perhaps? He glanced at the helmet icons.

The day was already improving: every system was now active

and running a green light. Which meant, that in addition to everything else, he could run an air sample. As he pinky-flexed and blinked his way through the screens and commands, he had to suppress a surge of optimism. Yes, the insect had scared the hell out of him, but it was a living creature, so the odds of some oxygen in the atmosphere were now quite high.

But as Caine navigated to the HUD's transponder tracker, he frowned as a second realization imposed itself atop the first: it was *recognizably* an insect. Most green worlds did have crude analogs; small, physically simple creatures were the typical foundation of any xenofauna pyramid. But this was so similar to terrestrial insects that he'd reflexively thought of it as a palm-sized palmetto bug. Perhaps the prior civilization the Dornaani called the Elders hadn't just left behind an unfathomable shift-beacon near this planet; maybe they'd seeded it with primitive life-forms, as well.

The transponder tracker winked on and showed Riordan what he'd hoped to see; all the pairs he'd spotted yesterday had pulled closer together and Eku's signal had at least changed position, although it still had a yellow ring. Newton's marker had moved incrementally closer to the confluence of the rivers; he was probably within forty kilometers, now.

The faintly pulsing icon of the air test blinked off...and returned as a steady green glow of hope. Caine scanned the report that scrolled alongside it: a long list of unrecognized microbial taints. Hardly a surprise: if a planet had life, some of it invariably mixed into the air. There was a marginally higher sulfur content, but both the atmosphere and oxygen pressure were, as predicted, a near match for sea level on Earth. Fortuitous, yes, but so improbably optimal for humans that Riordan had to wonder if this was yet another hint of influence—or terraforming—by an earlier civilization.

Riordan stood carefully, keeping his heels against the small nub of rock that had sheltered him during the night. The slopes he'd spotted the day before had proven to be nothing more than low, useless rises. But just beyond them, the land dipped and was grooved by a shallow wadi, marked by a solitary tooth of stone protruding from its lip before disappearing into the crack-veined plaque of the dry course two meters below. He'd spent the night in a leeward notch between the stone and that lip: probably cut by runoff from rains and melting ice. Although the suit's internal temperature remained twenty degrees centigrade while sealed, he'd also broken out the Dornaani shelter half and draped it over his body. Cocooning into it would have even been more effective at preserving the suit's power, but that would have left him looking like a foil-wrapped appetizer to passing creatures.

The temperatures had not been as extreme as projected, the environmental monitor recording an overnight low of minus nine C after yesterday's midday high of fourteen. But had he been exposed to the nighttime wind that had occasionally whistled around the rock, he suspected it would have been closer to minus twenty.

Riordan rose, stretched stiff limbs and a stiffer back. He wanted to shoulder his pack—better to have that misery over as soon as possible—but food and water had to come first, beginning with an assessment of the latter. Locating the controls for the water-recapture gauge took the better part of a minute; there hadn't been the time to master the suit's many functions. The result was reassuring; the baffled storage bladders had rebuilt to sixty percent. Happily, a sizable portion was pulled from the air; as amphibians, Dornaani required higher humidity and their suits were designed to provide it. Even those built for their factotums.

In anticipation of a long day's march, Riordan bled half of the stored water into a valved container and began to unpack his breakfast. He was determined to spend a minute or two enjoying it because, once he'd gone through the six-day supply from the ship's galley, eating might become a grim task. Dornaani emergency rations were likely to be even worse than those prepared by humans. But before he could begin, there was one final, fateful test required.

He popped the helmet's visor and sniffed the air.

Odorless: oddly so, even for a barren world. Drawing in a cautious breath, he imagined he detected a faint, flinty aroma... but the dust that began to tickle his nostrils was all too real. Particularly if too much got into his lungs.

Caine dug out the survival kit's combo-mask—it could both filter and compress air—and as he snugged it over his nose and mouth, decided to put off eating until he'd unfurled the solar panel and hooked it into his suit. He considered doing the same with the smaller and impossibly thin "solar tissues" but decided against it; the intermittent breeze might carry some off, a risk he could not afford. Between maintaining temperature, reclaiming wastes, running the HUD, and every other suit function, regularly recharging its battery was literally a matter of life and death.

Once the suit signaled it was getting current from the solar panel, Riordan removed the combo mask to finally begin his breakfast: a Dornaani rendition of an egg salad sandwich.

*Damn*, he decided as he chewed the first mouthful, *it almost tastes like one.*

Almost.

Meal finished and survival pack secured, Riordan checked the HUD's compass/Coriolis detector. Aligning it to the heading that would take him directly toward Yaargraukh's transponder marker, he started out.

But as he completed the first step, his helmet painted a query alongside the compass:

Heavy load detected: do you wish to engage the support-frame mode?

Riordan read it again, blinked on the icon for a detailed description.

Evidently, the suit's "smart hardening" feature that provided resistance to impacts could be retasked to function as the equivalent of a light cargo exoframe. However, the typically obtuse Dornaani technobabble explained that it was not a load-*bearing*, but rather a load-*sharing* system. Its ancillary calculator indicated that it would reduce Caine's perceived load by approximately 9.4 kilograms.

He almost laughed out loud, but only because that was better than fantasizing about throttling Eku. Yes, the support-frame option had been buried beneath one of the many dark icons which had only finished rebuilding and returning to function as he'd slept. But to think that Eku had never even thought to mention it?

Caine shook his head. It was possible that the factotum himself hadn't known about the system. But either way, as Miles had observed during planetfall, Eku needed to improve his personal initiative and situational awareness. Assuming he survived.

Before activating the support-frame mode, Caine tried to discover its projected power consumption, but either that data did not exist or was buried still deeper. It was a tough choice: risk running low on power or settle for a slower pace and greater exhaustion.

Riordan shook his head: *No, not a hard choice at all.* The sooner he rendezvoused with Yaargraukh, the better. Together, they would have twice the recharging capability, would be safer, and because of that, would move more easily and rapidly.

Caine engaged the support-frame mode, snugged his combo mask tighter, overrode the suit's automatic life support for just enough overpressure to keep out the dust, and began marching hard on a west-northwest heading.

To the south, thunderheads continued to edge higher up into the dome of deepening twilight, a black tide streaked by lightning that shot upward almost as often as it flashed down. Riordan shook dust out of his shelter half, glanced at Yaargraukh's transponder marker. Now directly atop his own, both of them had stopped blinking. But that had been thirty minutes ago and there was still no sign of his Hkh'Rkh friend.

Caine glanced at the flare he had removed from the survival pack. If something had happened to the big exosapient—a fall, even an ambush by some local creature—maybe he was unable to move and his radio had been damaged. And since he had only a crude handheld tracker instead of a HUD, he might not know Riordan was in range to see his own flares. If so, then Caine might need to launch one first.

Picking up the flare, Riordan sealed his visor. The HUD's night vision setting—a combination of thermal imaging and light intensification—showed nothing upon the flatlands to the north or the south. He looked back along the spine of the low ridge he'd followed from out of the east: empty. He turned to the west...

A murky speck glimmered for a moment, then disappeared. Riordan blinked for magnification. As he did, a faint wash of light reached over a dip in the ridge, then grew as the source ascended back into view: the foggy outline of a biped with a digitigrade stance. Just what one would expect to see if looking for a Hkh'Rkh in a duty suit running with thermal suppression.

Riordan swapped the flare for his hand light, set it to UV pulse, and aimed it at the oncoming figure.

Which stopped and, a moment later, replied in kind.

Riordan exhaled, and, allowing himself one inattentive moment, laid back in an abandon of relief. Then he rose and resumed showing his friend the way to the camp he'd made near the crest of the ridge.

✧　　✧　　✧

Yaargraukh was moving—skillfully—on all fours as he made his final approach to the small, rock-sided declivity which Caine had chosen both for the shelter it offered against the elements and searching, hungry eyes. "It is good to see you, Caine Riordan. I believe the hurricane will pass very close to us."

"Hurricane?" Riordan echoed in surprise.

The Hkh'Rkh crawled over to shelter under the edge of the small dip. "Yes. We passed over it during the most unfortunate moments of our descent."

Caine admired the effortless tact with which the exosapient ambassador-soldier managed to avoid referring to Liebman's death and the utter debacle that followed. "Still, I can't believe I didn't even see it."

"You would have been fortunate to notice it; it was very far away at the time."

Riordan frowned, made some crude guesses at its initial distance, compared that to the elapsed time. "To get to us already, it would have to be moving at least one hundred kilometers per hour."

"Significantly more, I suspect." Noting his companion's alarmed stare, Yaargraukh circled his neck diffidently. "As you observed during your EVA, this planet's weather is quite...dramatic."

Riordan sighed. "Thanks for reminding me." He smiled. "Speaking of reminders: I thought you said it was unwise to move at night?"

The Hkh'Rkh pony-nodded. "I did."

"And yet—?" Caine gestured back along the path of his approach.

"It was not yet night." In response to Riordan's raised eyebrow, Yaargraukh allowed a garbled fluting to escape his three equilaterally arranged nostrils. "Caine Riordan, there is a saying among my people: 'He who gives advice is typically the one least likely to follow it.'"

Riordan had to stifle what would have been a loud laugh. "Sometimes, if I close my eyes, it's difficult to remember that you're not human."

Yaargraukh's garter-snake tongue wiggled out briefly. "I am well chastened by that insult." But in the next moment, his neck curved downward. "I fear that by rushing to join you and be of assistance, I may have failed in a more serious particular."

Riordan shook his head. "I don't see how that could be. Now that we're together, we're much safer."

"Yes," Yaargraukh allowed, "but in my haste, I may also have brought even greater difficulties."

"What do you mean?"

"I cannot be certain, Caine Riordan, but I believe I have been followed."

# Chapter Ten

Chief Miles O'Garran did his best to snarl rather than speak as he ordered his suit, "No: *monitor* freekset channels. Do *not* send again!"

Already annoyed at the Terran vacc suit's comparatively clunky comms management, he indulged his growing annoyance. *Of course* he hadn't been given one of the fancy Dornaani suits where you didn't even have to give vocal commands; you just batted your lashes and curled your pinky to get it to do your bidding. And so what if it had been *him* who insisted that others get those suits because they'd benefit the most from Dornaani automation? And why not, since Miles O'Garran was so expert with bog-standard Terran gear that it actually gave him the best odds of survival?

No reason why a few pesky facts should be allowed to disrupt a perfectly good rant.

And it was just his luck to be first in the daily squelch-break rota, he fumed while checking that he was still on course toward Katie Somers. After all, wasn't there some unwritten law that a SEAL had to be the first to send a signal in the clear? To make himself the most attractive target for opponents just waiting to triangulate and rain hell down on someone's head?

Which was, once again, the sheerest crap, but inasmuch as griping was an art form and Miles was a particularly gifted practitioner, he wasn't about to ignore an opportunity to exercise his God-given talent. Besides, he took especial pride in not being one bit bothered by the illogic of his umbrage or the fact that he was, in fact, an atheist. Well, an agnostic really, but since God was clearly a foul-tempered old bastard, the chief enjoyed calling himself an atheist, just on the chance it might piss off the Big Guy.

And *of course* Eku hadn't broken squelch last night. Hell, if his transponder wasn't still moving and circled in yellow, Miles would have written the factotum off as deader than dead. God above—bastard that He is!—knew that if anyone was going to buy the farm right out of the gate, it was going to be Frog-pet. And He also knew—and did not care—that Chief Miles O'Garran had done everything possible to keep that genius simp alive and so, had no reason to feel any guilt over his fate. Absolutely no reason, Miles repeated forcefully as he stole a look at the transponder marker and then at his HUD's chrono. It was Eku's turn in the freekset rota—had been for over a minute, now—and still no squeal-hissing that signified a sitrep or that Frog-pet was still taxing the universe with his infuriating existence.

Miles would have spit in annoyance, but *of course*, water was in short supply for *him*; Terran suits only had urine recapture. And it didn't matter that he was far better off than Newton, Dora, and Yaargraukh, whose duty suits had no fluid recapture at all. Hell, the first two had come down within fifty or sixty kilometers of the tributary. And the Hkh'Rkh were harder to kill than tardigrades. So long-suffering Chief O'Garran had *every* reason to resent *everyone* else.

But of all of the sorry souls that Fate had shackled him to, none was more deserving of his ire than Corporal Katie Somers, who clearly was not pushing hard enough to close the distance between them. Which was particularly ironic, since the SEAL whom everyone called "Little Guy" had been tasked to carry one of the millstones—oh, right: "batteries"—they'd yanked out of the guts of the dead Dornaani robots. It was six extra kilos dragging his already dragging ass that much lower and slower, all because Commodore-Pretend Riordan had pointed out that "Everything we have is just so much dead weight without electricity."

Well, that dead weight was now doing its level best to kill one Chief Miles O'Garran, who didn't care about the blunt truth of his CO's words any more than he did about the appeals of

the idiot who'd insisted that said-same CO should not carry
one of the batteries. He was the very same idiot who'd not only
volunteered to carry the battery himself but who, more the pity,
insisted on breaking out of a perfectly good descent pattern to
caretake that snot-nosed waif Somers. Yes, the very same idiot
that was said to bear a striking resemblance to a small-bodied but
big-hearted SEAL chief who, by all rights, should be drinking a
drink with an umbrella in it, surrounded by an adoring harem.

Miles looked at the lengthening late-day shadow stalking angrily
beside him. "Am I right, or am I right?" he asked it. When it didn't
reply, he nodded, satisfied that in the case of shadows, as was the
case in law, "silence grants consent."

He pushed on, heading south toward Katie...and that much
farther away from the river.

Of course.

O'Garran's UCAS-manufactured HUD chimed; he glanced at
the small transponder tracker tucked in its upper left-hand corner. His transponder and Katie's were now superimposed and no
longer blinking. Well, shit. After forty-plus hours of humping a
ruck toward her, the bell finally rings...but there's no one home.

He stared at the wastes around him, flat and empty except
for some uneven ground to the south, which also lay directly
on the heading he'd been following for the past two hours. He
activated the helmet's laser range finder just long enough to get
a distance to the rumpled spot on the horizon: four kilometers.

He swung the pack off his back. Time to take a rest and take
stock of the situation.

Eku had eventually broken squelch but after the hour in which
he was supposed to. Not good. On the positive side, three of the
transponder pairs had merged into single markers: Riordan and
Yaargraukh last night, Dora and Ayana today and, a few hours
later, Bannor and Duncan. Judging from the overhead, the pair
closest to Miles—Peter and Craig—would make contact either
tonight or early tomorrow.

He stared at the uneven ground where Katie should be. If
he'd had a Dornaani helmet, or one of the kits that still had
a monocular scope, he'd at least have been able to make out
enough details to assess the best angle of approach. But once
again, Chief O'Garran was the sad sack who got the dirty and

deficient end of every stick with which Fate poked him. Instead, he tugged open one of the side pouches and pulled out a flare.

The chief figured there were three possible outcomes if he used it. Katie would signal back with one of her own or shine a light in his direction! The second would be that she might come out to him. The third could involve drawing whatever was pinning her down—or had devoured her—out to O'Garran, who'd be waiting with his grapple gun in one hand and his molecular-edged machete in the other.

Once he'd laid out the various tools that might be required for the various scenarios, Miles aimed the flare upward at a steep angle and discharged it. Instead of launching like a roman candle, it functioned more like a miniature missile launcher; a small clearing charge sent it five meters up before the solid rocket kicked in and sent it soaring—really *soaring*—high into the darkening sky. He stood back in grumpy awe at the Dornaani engineering which could launch a payload over a kilometer into the air from a handheld tube no bigger than an outsized pistol barrel.

The flare descended slowly, bright against the sky but floating much farther south than O'Garran had intended. *If Dornaani are going to make flares that act like sounding rockets, they ought to put a warning on the package.* On the other hand, there was no reasonable chance that Katie could miss such a high, bright object.

But instead of one of the three outcomes Miles had foreseen, he got a fourth and more worrisome one:

Nothing.

No answering flare, no light, no running Katie, no charging enemies.

"Well, shit," O'Garran muttered. In order to slip an arm back through the straps on his pack, he laid aside the grapple gun. He'd practiced with it a few times since landing, but only used one grapple; best to preserve as many of the full, boosted loads as possible. Either way, the kick was extremely even and the barrel had jets that seemed to compensate for muzzle rise: a nice feature that would ensure minimum destabilization for zero-gee operations. But when fired with a "fresh" grapple, it became another example of Dornaani technomagic in action. The one-hundred-gram "warhead" was only half of the package; the other half was a booster that only ignited once the composite projectile was clear of the barrel. It provided a great deal more range and, significantly, velocity.

O'Garran finished shouldering his arms through the straps, scooped up the gun, made sure the telescoping gaff stick was handy, and double-checked that the fast-release toggle on the survival pack was unobstructed. Reflecting on how many times he'd needed it in situations that began just this way, he eased into a trot toward his objective.

The uneven ground was an odd collection of bumps and lumps, some simply hard-packed dust mounds, others naked, wind-smoothed stone. At the outer edge, he dropped his musette bag and kit, lowered into a crouch and began sliding along the surfaces, machete out, pistol held close and ready for a pivot to the rear.

The mounds were akin to an open maze, but even if it had been tighter and more challenging, he would have had no problem staying on course; he just kept heading toward the intermittent sounds near its center. They alternated between snuffling, growling, and annoyed squeals that were not like animal noises so much as wooden surfaces grinding against each other. Restricting his movement to the first moments of each new outburst, he crept closer to the center.

The mounds there were larger, a bit taller, and more frequently made solely of rock. As he started around one of the largest, the area ahead widened and the sounds became more clear, enough so that he could hear pattering of what sounded like broad feet or paws. Muting all helmet alerts and turning off its internal lights, he opened the visor carefully and leaned his head forward to look further around the curve of the stone he'd been following.

Ten meters away, two bipeds, no larger than preadolescents, were circling around a tall rock at the center of the open space O'Garran had expected to find. However, there was nothing young about their lean bodies, their strange heads that were broader than they were high, or the tapering claws on both their rude hands and wide feet—which were all routinely in contact with the ground. On all fours, they prowled around the pillar of rock that was the source of their frustration. Or rather, what was atop it:

A Dornaani device. Specifically, one of the reusable flash-bang grenades that came in every survival kit. As O'Garran watched, it blinked, and then did so again three seconds later.

Miles scanned the rocks that had vantage points on the pillar, noted two that resembled smooth, lopsided domes. He was aware of a possible third, similar shape but because it was close to the rock behind which he was hiding, O'Garran would have had to lean out too far to confirm it. As it was, he ducked back just in time to avoid being detected by the smaller of the two, which stalked away from the pillar as if disgusted—before turning and running back at it, preparing to leap.

But as it stretched into its final stride, the flash-bang emitted a yowl that ascended into extremely high frequencies, strobing as it did.

Shaking its head sharply, the creature aborted its leap and swerved away, snarling and snapping—which was when Miles noticed that its wide jaws were full of wildly barbed and cluttered teeth, rather like the sand tigers he'd seen during practice dives for the counterattack into Indonesia.

But the next moment, he was as riveted to the flash-bang as the two creatures...because it had started ticking.

Except, as O'Garran listened, he realized that the pattern was quite uneven. Well, not *completely* uneven, but—

*God's balls! That's Morse code!*

"—then break squelch," the flash-bang clicked out, before pausing two seconds and resuming with "Chief, if you are there, break squelch. Chief, if you are—"

The chief not only broke squelch, but did so in a pattern that spelled out "Here."

The flash-bang went silent, then resumed with, "Stand by. Break squelch when you are prepared for attack. I will count down to zero."

*Girl after my own heart!* O'Garran closed his visor, hefted his weapons, and broke squelch.

The two creatures were already reapproaching the now silent grenade. But when they reached the two-meter mark, it quickly tapped out, "Three, two, one—"

O'Garran cut his helmet's audio pickup, turned his head sideways to reduce the burden on his HUD's filters...and stepped out, grapple gun raised as the grenade clicked "zero."

A wild cascade of strobing colors painted itself on the facing rocks. He couldn't hear the accompanying cacophony, but could feel vibrations through his suit; since the reusable grenade couldn't generate a concussive blast, it compensated with ear-rending frequency clashes and overpowering volume.

The instant the light show ended, O'Garran turned back toward the creatures.

They had staggered back but were still facing the pillar: blinking, shaking their heads, and screeching in undiluted rage. Their bodies were already pitched forward in an attack posture: futile, since they couldn't reach the offending device.

*So: prone to mindless fury. Good to know,* O'Garran thought as he extended the grapple gun toward the closest one, sight settling on its spine. He squeezed the trigger.

The grapple's booster ignited halfway across the ten meters and drove the flaring projectile into the creature's spine with a meaty crunch. It went down, but was still thrashing and immediately tried to regain its feet.

*Well, fugg me,* O'Garran thought, wishing he had the time to finish that one before reloading to shoot the other—which had already swung around and was sprinting at him.

Sprinting faster than a cheetah.

*Well, fugg me again; new plan!* Miles stepped back, dropped the grapple gun—no time to reload—while switching the machete to his right hand. He grabbed for the club-sized gaff stick—

—And drew it just in time to deflect the little monster's raking claws and immediately stepped toward it, bringing down the machete.

Instead of splitting the creature in two, the molecular blade only left a gash—the kind a regular machete might have made by slicing into regular flesh. And barely that.

O'Garran leaped backward—*what the* hell *are you made of?*— and brought up the gaff stick.

Again, just in time: the insanely swift monster came up in a smooth leap, claws extended to pierce and hold flesh for its wide jaws to tear away. It batted past the gaff stick but that delayed it just enough for Miles to lean out of the range of its jaws.

But not its claws. O'Garran's suit resisted the talons, but they left three parallel marks on it, partly because he didn't take another rearward step. This time, he stood his ground as the creature's rage and hunger almost tumbled after him, jaws snapping as they reached toward his leg—

Miles waited until the head was stretched out as far as the neck would allow and then cut down *hard* with the machete, trying to compensate for its light heft. The blade sheared away the left side of the creature's face, a twisted ear hanging by a thread and part of the skull exposed and seamed. It staggered back, shrilling insanely, but not so much at the pain as the frustration of not being able to orient itself.

Before it could, O'Garran stepped slightly past its injured side, turned and, from the rear flank, finished the creature with a blow across the back of its bent neck. With a screech, its head sagged obscenely to one side and it fell its length.

A similar screech rose up behind the chief, who spun in that direction, machete and gaff stick raised.

Back at the pillar, Katie was standing over the first one, a fresh gash in its neck feeding a widening pool of dark mauve fluid. The smoking grapple still protruded from its back. But more surprising still was what Katie had slung across her back:

Her survival rifle.

O'Garran popped his visor, gaping. "Didja ever think to use *that*?" he shouted, pointing with the gaff stick.

She rolled her eyes. "Didja ever think it might be *broken*, ya daft man?"

Chief Miles O'Garran stared, opened his mouth, and was startled by his own reply:

Confounded silence.

"You should have sent a message in the clear," O'Garran muttered as he discovered the fault with the survival rifle: one of the battery's leads had joggled loose within the sleeve that shielded its connection to the acceleration coils. "That's protocol if any of us are attacked."

Katie Somers was still trying to get the grapple out of the first creature's back. "Wasn't being attacked, but would have been if I'd tried sending. Their hearing is not to be underestimated. *Might* have been safe if I'd sealed my visor, but if not"—she glanced up toward the top of one of the rock domes—"I think they might have torn their claws out trying to climb up to me."

O'Garran frowned. "Yeah. As angry as the flash-bang made them, they went truly nuts when they saw *me*."

She nodded. "On Earth, yeh dunna see that extreme predator reflex in any but the simplest species." She stared at the corpses and shuddered. "But these . . . they were advanced enough to get frustrated, angry. Not that I could understand what they were saying."

O'Garran forgot the survival rifle was about to reseal. "What they were *saying*?" He glanced back at the bodies. "They're intelligent?"

She nodded tightly. "Enough to have something that sounds like language. That's why I didn't want to make any sound until you arrived. Saw your transponder approaching, then your flare. Knew you'd wander in here. And if they didn't give up on the blinky light I left on top of the rock, I could be sure they hadn't heard or smelled you coming."

"Smell?"

She shrugged. "It's how they found me to begin with, I think. I had to unload the suit's waste desiccator. They came along about an hour later, nasty little noses up in the air. When they wandered off to search the rest of these lumps, I...er, dumped some more scent in the area. Kept them plenty interested...that and the grenade."

O'Garran nodded. "Gotta hand it to you, it was a pretty good setup. Kept 'em distracted and looking in the other direction. I can't ask for better than that." He handed the survival rifle out to her. "And you can't ask for better than this: good as new."

She stared at it then shook her head. "No. You should have it."

He frowned. "That's nonsense. And stupid, Corporal. Now you take—"

"No, Chief. This is not the time for chivalry, which you'd deny, anyway. It's time for plain facts. Aye, I'm CTR infantry, but my specialty is cyberweapons, drones, and proxies. Sometimes networking target designators with heavy weapons. Maybe even regional or orbital support fire. Aye, I qualify with my weapon; I have to. I'm not half bad. But I'm barely half good.

"But you?" Elfin Katie Somers snorted like a grizzled sailor. "You're the Crewe's CQC expert. What's more, I've heard you and Duncan trade stories about marksmanship. So don't patronize me; it's best for both of us if you carry the gun."

"If you can really call it that," O'Garran muttered. "There were two versions. The others actually pack some punch and have decent batteries. This model? One hard shot—which is no greater than an old brass-cartridge pocket pistol—will damn near drain the battery."

She folded her arms. "Dinna talk pish, Chief. It may not stop much with a single shot, but it shoots straight as a ruler for two, maybe three hundred meters. Plenty as might attack us will be leaking by the time they get close enough. Probably a few leaked dry, as well."

Miles grumbled without bothering to turn the sounds into any particular words. "Well, then you take the grapple gun."

She considered it solemnly. "Aye, I think I'll do that." She picked it up, held her hand out for the remaining grapples. "You saw that Peter and Craig linked up?"

The chief stood, nodding. "Just before I got started winding in among these lumps. The two of them are the only ones within five hundred klicks." He hooked the weapon's battery to the one he'd been carrying.

"And only because instead of moving toward the rendezvous point, they moved closer to us." She frowned. "Why do you think they did that?"

O'Garran shrugged, glancing at the moon rising in the east. "Mutual support. They started almost four hundred klicks away from the nearest group to the east. By the time they linked up, the gap had widened to five hundred. So it was march alone half a thousand klicks to the rendezvous or link up with us and double their—well, our—resources to make that journey." Katie had finished gathering the bodies, and her improvised scent baits, into a single heap. "I see you've got the mess gathered."

She nodded back. "I'll take it beyond the lumps."

"*We'll* take it beyond the lumps," O'Garran corrected, the Dornaani survival rifle light in the crook of his arm. "And keep that grapple gun handy."

# Chapter Eleven

Peter Wu rubbed dust off his hands as he connected Craig's suit to the battery that had originally powered Hsontlosh's gun-toting proxrov. The paratrooper had arrived just before dark, face grey with exhaustion and fear; his suit had almost run out of power. If that hadn't been bad enough, his helmet's alarm system had spent the last two hours issuing increasingly urgent warnings to that effect.

Wu smiled encouragingly at the miserable sergeant, resisted the urge to go to the other side of their shelter and pat him on the shoulder. Girten had done his best, but he'd been unable to manage the bewildering array of devices and controls required to keep the suit powered, diminish needless drains on its batteries, and make use of a variety of key features. As a result, his greatest problem was not his profound exhaustion or lack of sleep; it was his certainty that he could not survive in this new world and that he was nothing more than a burden to the rest of the Crewe.

Granted, Girten had ample reason to be disappointed. He'd not understood how to take an air sample, and so had remained buttoned up ever since landing. Consequently, he'd spent the first two days existing solely on the protein compound available through the tube in the helmet, and then spent the entirety of this day without any nourishment at all. The hasty shipside instruction on setting up and connecting the solar cell had been confusing to start with, and he'd been unable to navigate the Dornaani HUD well enough to locate the instructions. Had the suit not had a limited kinetic energy recapture system built into it, he'd never have made it through the third day. And if he hadn't used the frame-tracking grid on the way down, Peter doubted he'd have known how to bring up the fortuitously similar transponder tracker after he'd landed. And if he hadn't figured *that* out...

Wu sat next to Craig's musette bag and inspected the rest of his rations while, finally freed of his helmet, the GI was able to eat a whole day's worth of solid food. Peter was satisfied the food was still edible, thanks to the generally low temperatures, but they'd need to increase their intake to ensure it was used before it spoiled.

Girten looked up, cheeks still full. "I could probably eat another," he ventured. His tone said there was no "probably" about it.

Wu shook his head. "I recommend against it. Best to let your stomach process this before adding more."

Girten nodded, crestfallen. He looked at the low tent that they'd made from their shelter halves. "Nice being out of that suit," he sighed.

Wu nodded. "And you got here just in time for us to set this up." Girten nodded, a hint of gratitude in his eyes. He'd been glad—desperately so—to actually be useful; whatever else had changed in one hundred seventy-five years, military tent halves remained largely the same in shape and construction. And when Peter had shown him how to connect the temperature-exchange module that came with it, Craig had only required one thorough explanation, followed by a quick review, to begin setting it up himself.

Wu nodded at the small, humming unit that was cycling cold air out of their shelter. "It is running just as it should, Craig. Well done."

Girten nodded but looked away.

Had he been alone, Peter would have closed his eyes in self-remonstration. *That sounded like praise for a childishly simple task... because it* was, *you fool. You are not a social worker; you are a soldier and an operative. Speak directly.* "Every meal, we will go over another piece of knowledge you must have for survival. The first will be the suit's ability to help you carry your load."

"It's *what*?"

"Think of the suit as having a robot built into it. That robot will bear some of the weight. But it uses a great deal of energy."

Girten nodded. "So, at lunch, we'll go over the solar panel, right?"

Peter's pleased smile surprised even him. "Yes. That is correct." *So he can get this. Meaning...* "We should have reviewed more systems like these when we were still waiting back on Rainbow."

Girten shrugged. "Oh, I was plenty busy. Had to dig hidey-holes for the corvette and the coldcells, had to learn all about your radios and computers and—damn, it's hard to remember all the new stuff there was to qualify on. I'm just sorry I wasn't better at it."

Peter suppressed a frown. Now that he thought about it, Girten's name had never come up as being a poor learner.

"And you know," Craig blurted out, "I was a pretty damned good paratrooper, back in Fran—well, back in my day." His face crumpled. "But here—sheesh."

Peter stared at him. "Sergeant Girten. Without any prior experience, you jumped out of a spaceship and landed—alive and uninjured—on a planet it was just barely orbiting. By any definition, that is a resounding success."

Craig's frown modulated into a broken smile. "I guess that's true enough. I—"

The wind rose quickly; it produced a low moan as it went over the lip of the wadi just a meter above them.

"Damn," he said with a sympathetic shudder, "this place is damned cold at night. It's like I could feel it through the suit. And when I went out to, er, unload the waste desiccator, I swear it reminded me of the Ardennes. Without the trees." He glanced at Peter. "Must be below zero out there, yeah?"

Peter frowned before he understood. "Ah. You are thinking in terms of Fahrenheit?"

"Well...yeah."

"Four below. But it usually gets lower."

"Sounds like the Ardennes, all right."

Peter nodded, remembering what Bannor had shared about Girten before they'd departed Zeta Tucanae for Collective space. It was the kind of crucial information that never made it into a file, that only existed as scuttlebutt. And in the case of Craig Girten, it was that as likeable as he was, he was considered a "black rabbit's foot": the fellow who attracts disasters to the unit he's in ... and is the only one to survive.

It had started when he jumped into Normandy, then again during action in Holland. And then twice more in the Ardennes: first when his original squad had been chopped to pieces by a troop of Panthers, the next time as part of a pickup platoon from various units that got overrun on the perimeter at Bastogne. Each time, he had been out in front of the main body, either in an observation post or as a forward observer. Each time, he had been overlooked, or the only survivor in his hole, as the onrushing Nazis bypassed him in their push to breach the line. And when he woke up in this century, the pattern had repeated on Turkh'saar; he was the only one to survive in his hole when the Hkh'Rkh steamrolled most of the defenses at the River Kakaagsukh's northern ford.

Ironically, he'd originally been considered a good-luck charm, protected by an invisible halo of divine favor or any of its various permutations; soldiers are a notoriously superstitious lot. But that began to invert when it became clear that Craig's good luck never rubbed off on anyone else: time after time, he was the *only* survivor in his unit. That variety of luck had become a source of shunning and, in some cases, thinly veiled suspicions of craven self-preservation that no one had survived to report. By the time Bannor and the rest of the Crewe met him on Turkh'saar, he had already become a pariah among the Lost Soldiers. The final tragedy at the northern ford simply ensured that the black legends surrounding Craig Girten were urgently passed on to anyone who had not already met him.

But despite that, or maybe because of that, Liebman had befriended him. It might have been simply because Murray Liebman was innately and unrepentantly contrarian. But Caine and Bannor had shared their suspicion that Liebman's friendship might have been rooted in the strange sympathy for outcasts which often lurks beneath the crablike shells of iconoclasts and pessimists. Perhaps, therefore, he'd warmed to Girten because the paratrooper seemed a fellow victim of a universe that used both of them as the dupes in ever-blacker comedies of error.

And now, if any were foolish enough, it would be whispered that the curse of Craig Girten had also reached out and touched Liebman through the very hands with which he'd checked Murray's rig, just before their fateful planetfall.

Girten's voice pulled Peter out of his assessment of the many threads that had woven a thick tapestry of despair into the skein of his life. "Lieutenant Wu, I know how to use the freekset okay. I just don't understand how it works."

Peter suppressed the logical reflex: to ask the GI why he just hadn't asked to have it explained again during the admittedly hurried training.

But Craig's eyes revealed that he'd already read the reaction in Wu's. "Look, a guy like me gets tired of always asking to have everything explained a second or even a third time. But Liebman? Hell, Murray was just the opposite. He was the smart one. Wherever he went, from the sound of it; A's in everything, right down the line. And fer sure the smartest in our unit on Turkh'saar.

"But me? I worked hard to get B's and C's in high school. And living and working around folks like you... well, it can get pretty embarrassing, sometimes."

Peter nodded. "I understand." Because, suddenly, he did.

Girten frowned. "Frankly, I kinda doubt you *could* understand... sir."

Wu shook his head. "I am not saying I know what it is like to live through what you have. What I mean is that, starting in the later years of your century, we began to identify various differences in people that make it difficult, if not impossible, to thrive in the educational models of your time, Sergeant. We know a great deal more about that, now. And from my observation, I suspect you might still benefit from some of the different approaches used today."

"Not sure about that, sir. Like my Aunt Tilda used to say, you can fix ignorance, but stupid goes right down to the bone."

Hoping that Aunt Tilda was now burning in the mythological hell she'd no doubt believed in, Peter smiled patiently. "Sergeant, allow me to ask you one, maybe two questions."

"Sure."

"Did you have a hard time with both math and reading?"

Girten snorted. "Sure did. I just couldn't keep things straight. Not in either subject."

"You 'couldn't keep things straight.' That's an interesting turn of phrase. Tell me: did letters and numbers seem to change?"

Craig's eyes widened. "Yeah, every time I tried to fix a word

or a math problem, it was like playing hide-and-seek with a...
well, a chameleon. I'd think I saw one thing, then I'd go back,
and *bam*, it was something else." He shrugged. "Often as not,
the teacher would tell me I just didn't have enough confidence in
myself, that the first thing I'd seen was correct. But sometimes,
it really *was* the second thing that was right. And I never knew
which it was going to be. And everybody just thought I wasn't
paying enough attention or that I wasn't trying hard enough."

Peter smiled sadly. "I am quite sure you were paying attention
and trying very, very hard, Sergeant Girten. Just as I'm relatively
sure I know why you had such a hard time learning."

Girten's taut lips relaxed slightly. "You do?"

"Later on, I will tell you about a condition called dyslexia.
In the meantime, allow me to explain how a freekset works..."

It became very clear very quickly that Craig Girten was not
"slow" or "dim" as he'd been told since childhood. The concept of
a freekset—quickly changing frequencies for radio transmissions—
was not always a self-evident concept even to persons of average
intelligence. But Girten immediately saw the cypher value implicit
in it: that messages sent using the rapid frequency changes could
not be intercepted unless one possessed both the wavelength and
duration values of the signal.

A further surprise was his rapid grasp of how the changes
to their present freekset were being generated: fractal evolutions
of a set of number seeds. Craig snagged on the terms, but not
on the basic concept. And he immediately intuited how it was
being combined with their current, timed transmissions: that each
of the Crewe broke squelch during a different hour of the day
and the minute in which a transmission was matched to one of
thirty blind codes for different statuses or events. Furthermore,
the first thirty minutes indicated that the sender was safe, the
last thirty indicating that they were not. All of which he grasped
with marked ease.

Although Craig was armed with a grapple gun, the next item
on his retraining agenda was the operation of Peter's survival
rifle. No matter whose kit it had been in and no matter who was
more proficient with it, it was the default weapon for whoever was
standing watch at night. Girten side-eyed the device ruefully; he
admitted that when Chief O'Garran had picked it up to review its

operation, he hadn't even recognized it as a gun. And given the differences from those on which he'd been trained—the M1 Garand, the Thompson, and the M1 carbine—Wu could understand why.

Almost every aspect of its operation was radically different. Gunpowder had been replaced by magnetic coils pulsing the projectile down a barrel that was little more than a tube of self-realigning smart material. Instead of a box- or drum-shaped magazine in front of the trigger guard, the bullets (well, projectiles) were fed into the firing (well, launching) chamber from a rotary cassette where they were not stacked, but stored in a helical pattern. Craig was not alone in finding this a particularly baffling arrangement, but slowly warmed to it as Wu demonstrated how, with the magazine lying flat against the weapon, it not only improved ergonomics but eliminated the awkwardness of having a part of the weapon sticking out at a right angle.

His skepticism about the bullpup design was particularly short-lived: having taken buildings in over a dozen French and Belgian towns, he deeply appreciated that without diminishing performance, the shorter barrel made the weapon infinitely more handy in close quarters. For the same reason, he notionally approved of the extendable stock but eyed its construction warily. "Looks flimsy," he muttered. Peter left the more esoteric features for a later lesson. The sights that could be jacked into the Dornaani HUD, the reusable sabot carriers, the scalable muzzle velocity: these were grace notes, easily added now that Girten possessed basic operational competency.

By the time they'd finished, Peter suggested a further half ration. Craig devoured it and soon became drowsy. More importantly, he was far less demoralized than when he'd arrived out of the dusk four hours earlier. Wu assured the paratrooper that he would wake him for the second watch. It was the only falsehood he'd uttered, and he did not regret it. Unsure of how to manage or recharge the suit, Girten had neither slept long nor soundly since landing, and he wouldn't be a reliable soldier without it.

"Sir, don't do that again. Please."

Wu turned, frowned back at Girten. "I will change our watch rota as I see fit, Sergeant. I do note that your objection seems to be motivated by concern for me. That is commendable—however misguided it might be."

Craig looked like he was ready to object, then saw Wu's stare, and nodded. "Yes, sir."

Peter nodded back, turned, and resumed paralleling the wadi before the paratrooper could see the grin on his face. Although with both their visors down, he might have missed it anyway.

After using their two solar panels to recharge Girten's suit, Wu decided that although the wadi seemed to be leading slightly north of the shortest route to O'Garran and Somers, it would allow faster travel.

But remaining down upon its dry bed had one significant drawback; it made them blind to whatever might be approaching across the wastes. Peter had ultimately decided upon a compromise: for every three kilometers they moved along the bottom of the wadi, they would walk one along its lip. That routine opportunity to scan their surroundings at ten-times magnification, aided by both motion detection and thermal discrimination, would almost certainly give them ample warning of an approaching threat. And if it didn't—if anything could close all the way from the horizon during their interval in the wadi—well, he and Girten probably wouldn't have much chance against it, anyway.

After making one last visual sweep of their surroundings, Wu motioned down into the wadi. Craig, who reached the bottom first, once again tried to caretake his superior, albeit using a more indirect approach. "Sir, you just let me know when you want to stop."

*As if I wouldn't?* But Wu only said, "Why should I want to stop?

"Well, uh...to rest a bit."

"I feel fine and am quite alert. I do not need any—"

"Sir, behind us!"

It was a full two seconds before the speakers in Peter's helmet conveyed what Girten had heard; distant shouts, channeled by the sides of the wadi. The paratrooper preferred traveling with his visor up, but that hadn't been why Wu ordered him to do so: even Dornaani audio pickups were unacceptable surrogates for uncovered ears. "Up, over the lip," Peter muttered. "Slowly," he amended when Craig almost leaped to comply.

"Slowly?"

Peter nodded as he checked the spider-veined course behind them. "Take a few more seconds. We do not want to leave raised dust or tracks behind us." By the time he'd finished the explanation, they were out of the wadi and on their bellies.

They barely ducked down in time. Two bipeds—*humans?*—came running along the wadi from behind them. But they were not the ones shouting; they kept looking over their shoulders as they ran past. Raising one eye to the lip that concealed him, Peter risked a better look.

They were shaped like humans—two arms and legs—but seemed asymmetrical, misshapen, as if they'd been built from parts of multiple species. Wu didn't dare study them long enough to make out any more—the shouting of their pursuers was growing much louder—but they were certainly not Homo sapiens. As Wu ducked down, he caught a short glimpse of the ones chasing them.

So did Girten, who was about to lift his head even higher before Peter pulled him down. "Humans?" he whispered.

"Not quite," Peter murmured as the next group—three, he thought—pounded past two meters beneath them. Not unless humans on this planet looked like some nightmare version of Neanderthals. Or worse.

A savage cry from the now-passed group brought up their heads—just in time to see one of the pursuers hurl a bone-tipped spear into the back of the slower of their malformed quarry. Its gait, already uneven, broke as the weapon went into its back. With an almost animal cry, it fell facedown. Wondering what had become of the other, Peter craned his neck.

Twenty meters further along the wadi, the second creature had come up short against a chest-high barrier of dust, dirt, and rocks. Either the edges of both sides had fallen inward at the same time or the pursuers had set a trap. Wu suspected the latter when they turned the bend and were completely unsurprised by the obstruction. Instead they laughed—a hauntingly human sound—and approached the unwounded creature with weapons held casually, hair kirtles swaying beneath what looked like tunics made of cured hide.

All except the one who'd thrown the spear. He turned back and approached the wounded being that Wu now realized was indeed disfigured; its mismatched legs flexed and kicked as it struggled to rise, despite the spear lodged in its back.

The nightmare Neanderthal put a broad foot next to the bloody entry wound and pushed down.

The creature howled; the sound was more like a dog's cry than a human's.

Girten's eyes were wide as they turned toward Wu. "What the hell are—?"

Wu shook his head, needing one crucial moment of silence to decide upon their course of action. By all appearances, the one who'd thrown the spear would soon torture or kill the malformed being struggling beneath his almost spatulate foot. But the planetfall protocols were clear: avoid detection by locals, and above all, avoid hostile contact. Also, just because one side was cruel didn't mean the other was morally superior. If the tables were turned, the misshapen creatures might behave the same way.

Except, Wu realized, whereas the pursuers had crude armor and sizable weapons, the creatures they'd chased had neither.

Peter was already rising as he made his decision, activating the HUD targeting interface and tracking the survival rifle toward the one standing over the wounded creature.

"Sir?" Girten whispered far too loudly.

"Cover me," Peter muttered as the HUD's smart targeting guidon led the superimposed crosshairs onto the jeering semi-human—just as he leaned into the spear so that it went clear through his victim's body.

Peter squeezed the trigger twice, didn't stop to watch the attacker fall; he had already moved the virtual reticle to rest upon the larger of the other two. Hearing the spear thrower cry out, they'd turned and froze upon seeing the strange figure perched on the lip of the wadi, twenty meters to their rear.

Peter squeezed the trigger, drifted the reticle to the left, cheated it a hair more to be sure he wouldn't hit the creature behind the second one. He fired again.

The first, larger one had fallen, whereas the second only lurched when hit. Peter kept the guidon between the two; how to get them to surrender? How to communicate at all? There was no easy—

"Down, sir!" Craig shouted.

Peter ducked even as he turned. Which was why the arrow flew over his helmet rather than hitting its visor.

Girten, grapple gun held firmly, fired at the bowman who'd appeared around the bend in the wadi just ten meters behind them.

The grapple didn't hit the new Neanderthal anywhere near the center of mass; it caught him low and to the right, but plunged deeply into that corner of his abdomen. He fell back, shrieking as the still-flaring booster both burned into him and drove the grapple deeper.

Peter spun back toward the two he'd wounded. The one who'd fallen seemed barely alive, but the other was moving up the side of the wadi.

*Trying to escape, not attack—*

Peter shook his head, both at survivor's action and his own necessary response. He kept the guidon in front of the scrambling nightmare-man, leading him before tracking back toward his body. The reticle met the target's torso; the HUD outlined the silhouette: locked. Wu squeezed the trigger twice.

The figure only jerked at the first hit, but the second produced a gout of blood from what was likely its suprascapular artery. The heavy-limbed humanoid pitched backward and hit the bottom of the gully as limp as a bag of sand.

For a moment, none of those who could still move did. Then, crouching, the being they'd rescued began inching forward, eyes cast up at them. If Peter was willing to see human expression in those eyes—a profoundly unlikely projection—they seemed both wary and hopeful.

On its approach, Peter slowly allowed the survival rifle to tilt down until its muzzle was pointed at the ground. As he did, he examined the being more closely by shifting the HUD back to high magnification.

He suppressed a start at the shocking combination of facial features. Although most of the features were human—more or less—the bone structure left him with the impression of a flat-faced reptile, possibly because of the faint scales encroaching downward from its hairline and upward from where a beard would be, if it could grow one. The most pronounced difference was the broad fleshy nose that descended directly from the brow and was vaguely reminiscent of a turtle's. The arms and legs were even and seemed essentially human, enough so that Wu reflexively perceived of its shape as male, but without any confidence in that label.

The being reached its wounded fellow and, a moment later, its head sunk heavily. Peter had already presumed it was dead; the widening pool of reddish blood left little room for doubt.

The being's next action—so casual and natural that it took Peter and Craig a moment to realize it had happened—was simply a long, mournful sigh. Then it moved toward the dead nightmare Neanderthal. But rather than defiling or raging at it, the turtle-nosed being lifted a bag from around its neck and what appeared to be a flint knife from its belt, and held them out to Peter.

Peter wondered if it was a gesture of gratitude, but then noticed that the being's legs were taut, the tendons in high relief; it was ready to flee at a moment's notice. Which made the proffered goods some cross between tribute, supplication, and placation. Until now, Peter had been glad the visor concealed his own reactions and expressions, but now...

Wu slowly released the visor and, hoping it would be recognized as a calming gesture, he let his one open palm sink downward.

The being moved quickly: to kneel.

Peter almost rolled his eyes, but at himself. *Of course that gesture could mean other things, you dolt! If I had half a brain—*

Before he was even aware of the movement, Girten was past him, moving down the side of the wadi, his left hand extended, his right touching his mouth.

*Damn it, Girten—!*

But instead of fleeing, the being cocked its head, face softening into an expression that, on a human, would have been one of perplexity, possibly curiosity.

*Promising,* Wu had to admit.

As he reached the bottom of the wadi, Craig slowly opened his left hand... and Peter finally realized the paratrooper's intent, just a moment before the malformed humanoid did. Girten was offering the being food: what the Dornaani called a sandwich wrap and the Crewe had renamed "mystery meat in a tasteless tortilla."

Wu's first thought was, *That "meal" might kill it!* His second was, *The taste might scare it off!* He almost chuckled... except this was first contact and it was quite possible that the next five minutes would shape how, and if, they survived on this planet. Either way, the being would only get confused and chary if Peter tried to call back Girten's offer. So Wu turned his hand over and lifted his palm.

The being's startlingly human eyes went rapidly from Craig to Peter and back to Craig: or rather, what Craig held in his hand. Girten extended it even further, his steps small and slow. The being matched the approach and, rather than snatching the food away like an animal would, removed it slowly and carefully from the GI's fingers with a finely scaled and faintly greenish hand that was otherwise as human as theirs.

It sniffed the dreaded mystery meat and tasteless tortilla and delicately nibbled at a corner. Its eyes widened—Peter had a vision of it vomiting green goo in reaction—but instead it bowed its head deeply, took a very sizable bite...and looked up and smiled.

Craig glanced back at Peter with a smile of his own. Peter returned it along with a sigh of relief: both at the strange local's response and the renewed purpose he read in Girten's eyes.

# Chapter Twelve

Bannor Rulaine and Duncan Solsohn both stared, arms akimbo, at the mechanism that had once recharged Hsontlosh's personal proxrov assistant, and finally, enforcer. "Think this crazy setup will actually work?" Bannor muttered.

Duncan looked at the two solar cells hooked to it. He shrugged. "We won't know if we don't try."

Bannor stared at the juncture between the battery that powered the anthrobot's coil gun and the charging grid they'd extracted from its storage booth. "There's no way to be sure that what recharged the proxrov will recharge its gun."

Duncan scratched his chin. "I'm not worried about that so much. We know the grid was built to recharge the battery that was in the proxrov. And we know that, in a pinch, the proxrov itself was able to power the coil gun. And although a direct hookup between the grid and the gun's battery wasn't part of the design, the leads *did* adapt to each other immediately."

Bannor nodded his head cautiously. Over time, he'd become the voice of caution and skepticism that tempered Duncan's innate enthusiasm and optimism. But this time, Rulaine wondered if maybe he was being too pessimistic. Despite the staggering diversity of devices and designs that the Dornaani had freely developed and retained over millennia, the Collective had mandated at least one universal technological requirement: that every lead for both control and power conduits had to be able to detect and adapt to all others.

Frankly, it was an amazing accomplishment, even for the Dornaani. But it was also the kind of thing that was far too subtle and *far* too dull to ever attract the kind of attention and inspire the kind of wonder that their other, flashier achievements elicited.

And, Bannor allowed, he was also dragging his heels because of how much was at stake. The solar panels did charge the gun's battery, but there was only one point of attachment for them, and they were extremely inefficient in both time and energy loss. The grid, on the other hand, was built to both relay and store charges from multiple sources. So instead of hooking the gun's battery up to a single solar cell, all the Crewe's cells could be lined up to charge the grid, which could then pass the power to the gun's battery in a few minutes. And if the group was able to top up that hand cannon's battery every day, well . . . God help anyone who tried cases with them.

Bannor set his jaw. "Turn it on."

Duncan complied. Lights on the battery and the frame started winking and flashing . . . and then all of them glowed a harmonious aqua.

"Well, waddya know?" Duncan drawled, before his face grew somber. "Sucks not having Eku."

"On so many levels," Bannor agreed. Technical expertise aside, the factotum had become a member of the Crewe, of its family. A frequently annoying family member, to be sure, but family is family.

Duncan nodded, glanced sideways at Rulaine. "Fourth time he broke squelch in the second half of the hour."

*As if I didn't notice that?* "Not a good sign," Bannor murmured.

"Working on our understatement muscles today, I see."

Rulaine couldn't suppress a rueful smile. "Okay, get it off your chest."

"Do I really have to?" Solsohn sighed. "Four days. Four squelch breaks. Always in the latter, 'negative sitrep' half of his signaling period, but never at the same minute." He shrugged. "The only constant to his message is that he's in some kind of trouble."

Bannor didn't disagree but as much for himself as Duncan, he played the devil's advocate. "Okay, it looks bad, but then why not send at the same minute, relay a consistent code?"

"Because maybe he can't. Look: as of last night, two of our pairs have reported 'encountering' locals. And Peter and Craig used the code for 'locals contacted.'"

Bannor glanced at him. "Oh, judging from their codes, I'd say Miles and Katie 'made contact' as well."

"Hah hah. As my grandad would have said, that's comedy gold, right there. Seriously, I'm sure there will be plenty more 'kinetic' contact. But Peter and Craig—they struck *real* gold."

Bannor nodded. "I don't disagree. As you know. But how does this connect to Eku?"

"Well, what if he's not sending the same code because he can't? If he's either being observed or held prisoner, he'd have limited freedom of action, would have to signal whenever he could. Doing so in the thirty-minute 'distress' window might be the most control he has."

Rulaine knew what was coming, but asked anyway. "So what do you propose we do?"

"Break protocol to contact Eku, Colonel." Duncan continued before Bannor could reply. "We've only been dirtside four days and we've already answered most of the big questions. There's breathable air. Potable water. There's flora and fauna. And given the local sapients, I'm gonna bet there's food we can eat, too. But now one of us is almost certainly signaling distress."

He stared at Bannor. "The only reason we're not in contact with him right now is because we're worried that our signals could be intercepted. Except it turns out there are no more radio transmissions down than there were in orbit. The air is dead except for us and sferics."

"Doesn't mean there isn't something listening for signals. Or something that will wake up if we send one."

Duncan nodded. "I can't and won't argue against that. What Ayana said about how Ktoran 'Death Fathers' might set traps, automatic listening stations: that stuff is scary enough to make my eyeballs sweat." He extended an open hand: an appeal to reason. "But we're never going to *know*, are we? The only difference between proving something exists versus proving it doesn't is that, if you try poking it and it *does* exist, it will come at you. And then you know. But if you *don't* poke at it, then you'll never know if it's actually out there. You'll just live in fear of it. Forever."

"And you're willing to pay the price of finding out?"

"To get in contact with Eku and find out how best to help him? You bet I am." Solsohn paused. "And from the look on your face, I think you're willing to take that risk, too. At least this one time."

Bannor felt his stomach knotting. He'd been one of the strongest advocates of the squelch-only signals protocol. But perhaps, just this once—

His comms pager didn't just ping; it issued a priority alert. An incoming voice comm...from Eku.

*Well,* Rulaine thought as he opened the channel, *that settles that.* "Eku, what is your—?"

"I must be swift, Colonel," the factotum interrupted breathlessly as the rest of the Crewe's active comms icons lit up Bannor's helmet like a Christmas tree. "I have little time. I landed badly. I cannot move my arm. I was taken captive two days ago by humanoids that seem related to humans. They have not harmed me, but I suspect that is because they think I am valuable. We are moving south. I am free now but cannot outrun them. I fear that—"

Shouting by harsh voices speaking a harsh language. An impact—either with the ground or from a weapon—cut through the bedlam. Eku cried out—

Silence. The circuit had either closed or the helmet radio had been broken.

"Resume comms protocol," Rulaine heard himself say; his voice was hollow. The rest of the Crewe's comm activity icons blinked off, but not all at once.

"Now what?" Duncan muttered.

Rulaine sealed his visor, used the HUD to sweep the horizon. Nothing visible. "Well, since there is no imminent contact and we've already got a protocol break, we might as well make use of it."

"You're sending to Riorda—the commodore?"

Bannor nodded. "Over the alternate freekset. Caine will want to—" The command channel pinged. *Well, speak of the devil.* Bannor opened the circuit. "Beat me to it. You heard the whole send?"

"I did," Riordan confirmed. "First, how are you two?"

"In good shape. Grid recharge works for the coil gun. We'll be moving toward Newton within the hour. Unless..."

"Yes?"

"Unless you've got different orders." When Caine didn't reply, Rulaine added, "To rescue Eku, CO."

✧     ✧     ✧

Caine leaned his forehead against his hand. He wanted to shout "yes!" but the sheer impulsivity of that urge told him what his answer had to be. "No, XO; we stick to the plan."

He heard Rulaine's sharp intake of breath, interrupted before his friend could argue. "We can't reconfigure without extensive coordination. That means extensive transmissions. Maybe there's nothing out there listening. Or maybe we just got lucky this time... assuming we did." *Guess we'll know that soon enough.* "Moreover, we are in no shape to mount a rescue operation. We're still scattered to hell and gone. It would take weeks—and for most of us, a lot of backtracking—to collapse on Eku's current position. Assuming we could get over the river."

"So... no change in protocols." Rulaine sounded gut-shot.

"No change to *comm* protocols, no. But I'm changing contact protocols. If we're going to find a way to get to Eku, and get some advance intel on the region, and who or what might be holding him, locals are our only option. Given the contacts of the last thirty hours, the odds are a lot better that the city at the river fork is inhabited. Keeping that as our rendezvous is likely the fastest path to saving Eku, too."

"Roger all, sir." Bannor's voice had regained most of its calm buoyancy. "Shall I spread the word? Prerecord, compress and fast-squeak?"

"Smallest comm footprint, so yes. Riordan out."

Yaargraukh's pupilless black eyes were fixed on his face. "That was a difficult decision."

Riordan nodded. "Made similar ones in Indonesia. Never got used to them."

"One never does. But in this case, your hand held two fates, not one." When Caine looked questioningly at him, the Hkh'Rkh explained, "Saving the factotum and securing justice for your mate Elena. I am aware that without Eku, it is unlikely that any evidence left by Hsontlosh, either of his personal crimes or those of the conspiracy he was abetting, can be accessed, let alone decoded."

*Well, that news certainly made the rounds quickly.* "And we don't even dare to open his emergency bag," Riordan added, nodding toward its perch atop the rest of Yaargraukh's various packs and sacks.

"It would certainly be imprudent."

Riordan waited for Yaargraukh's tongue to flick out, signifying humorous irony. But the Hkh'Rkh only began unpacking his dinner.

Caine put aside his own rations. "We need to talk."

The black eyes rotated toward him. "We do?"

"Yes. Since the mis-shift, you've avoided all but essential contact or conversation with others. Do you need us to change the way we interact with you?"

The Hkh'Rkh's pony neck shook slightly. "The problem is not in you; it is in me."

Riordan frowned. "I don't understand."

"That is because you do not see the burden."

More confused than ever, Riordan glanced at the pile of packs again. "Don't see it? I repeatedly asked you reduce it, but you—"

"Commodore, you misperceive. I am not speaking of the physical burden—it is well within my carrying limits—but of being a burden to the group. It is a source of . . . profound shame."

Riordan was not sure whether or not he blinked in surprise. "You're a burden to *us*? How?"

The Hkh'Rkh emitted a phlegmy rattle through his nose. "Caine Riordan, a Hkh'Rkh can endure ten times the radiation a human can. And yet I was the only one who could not take on my fair share of the EVA operations, despite having better skills than anyone other than Ms. Tagawa. And perhaps Chief O'Garran."

Riordan hardly knew how to respond. "B-but, without a vacc suit, how could you perform an EVA?"

"Exactly. And it was that same lack which necessitated humans to both fashion and secure me within a makeshift pressure cocoon on the descent frame. I was not even able to assist Ms. Tagawa with the astrogation calculations because these"—he held up his quadrilaterally arranged hands—"cannot operate human computers. Or Dornaani. And when it came to their tools, I was once again unable to use them, since they seem to be designed for thin-boned avians."

Yaargraukh rose abruptly, stalked around the periphery of their camp as if he meant to outrun himself. Then he stopped and turned back toward his friend. "Caine Riordan, in all the years since my whelping, I have never been so constantly and completely shamed. At present, we Hkh'Rkh do not have the science or technology of other races, nor the art, nor the philosophy. Our one clear advantage is this"—he gestured angrily at his body—"our ability to absorb damage, to survive in many temperatures and atmospheres, to bear heavy loads, to strike mighty blows, and to persevere in the face of all adversity." His conclusion was a self-deprecatory snort punctuated by a gobbet of far-flying phlegm: "My ancestors would turn their faces from me."

Caine considered. "Far be it from me to criticize anyone else's family...but I thought the Greatsires also encouraged shrewdness."

Yaargraukh turned. "I do not see the connection between that and my current failures."

"Well, don't they teach that shrewdness is what tempers reckless courage? Ensures that Warriors do not simply run headlong at every foe to prove themselves?"

The Hkh'Rkh's eyestalks extended slightly. "Yes, but—"

"But *that's* the direct parallel to this situation. Yes, you were physically unable to help prepare for planetfall, but once here, the situation reversed. Now it is *we* who must count upon *you*. If our suits fail or our tools are lost or taken, *you* would be the one to thrive, and help us survive, on this planet." Riordan paused to give his conclusion more weight. "I am sure that your ancestors would also agree that a shrewd Warrior realizes that patience, even acceptance, may sometimes be essential to achieve final victory. So it was in space, for you."

The Hkh'Rkh stared at Riordan for what seemed like a very long time. "Have you read the Axioms of the Ghostsires, the core wisdom of the Patrijuridicate?" Caine shook his head. "Well, I suspect you do not need to. You all but quoted several passages from it." He raised his neck so he could peer over the low ridge behind which they were sheltering; during the day's travels, the land had become more varied in its topography. He maintained his focus on the horizon for several seconds. He looked away with a low interjection:"*Yrrgrrm.*" Evidently, it was the Hkh'Rkh equivalent of "hmmm."

"We're still being followed?" Riordan asked.

Yaargraukh bobbed his neck. "I could probably discern what they are—for there is more than one—if I was able to use a human HUD. You would probably do the same if you'd been raised a hunter and knew what to look for."

Caine smiled. "I think you just proved the point I was making."

Yaargraukh turned. "Commodore, to use the phrasing of your armed services, do I have your permission to speak freely?"

Riordan nodded.

"I find it baffling that at the moments when you are most annoying, you also prove to be most agreeable."

Caine laughed.

Yaargraukh's black-worm tongue wiggled out momentarily before he straightened. "Commodore, I wish to suggest I stand both watches tonight."

"Why?"

The Hkh'Rkh nodded at Riordan's pack. "Although you have already demonstrated reasonable facility with the Dornaani translator, it may prove wise to hone your skills tonight. I suspect we will have need of them tomorrow."

# Chapter Thirteen

Riordan stifled a yawn as he reached behind with his right hand for the fifth time in the past fifteen minutes; his survival rifle was still slung out of sight, yet in the handiest possible position. But he was more concerned with the rounded mechanical object upon his left hip: the Dornaani translator.

Yaargraukh was looking through the monocular telescope which could also serve as the rifle's smart sight. The Hkh'Rkh held it at a considerable distance from his eyes; they were not well adapted to human optics. "The bipeds have discovered the end of our false trail. They will either flee because they realize they've been duped, or double back. If the latter, they are either highly confident or highly curious."

Riordan nodded at the latter. If they did retrace their steps to determine where their quarry's actual path deviated from the false one they'd followed, it meant one of two things. A fight, or a hasty first contact situation that could prove even more difficult. Caine would need to establish a common vocabulary to learn their intents and, if they were hostile, to incline them toward an outcome other than mutual slaughter. *Sure, all in a day's work.*

Initially, Riordan had suggested that Eku should be the one to carry the translator, but the factotum had objected. "Commodore," he'd said as he and several other Crewe-members were adjusting individual drop loads prior to planetfall, "your prior expertise argues otherwise. You are the only one of our group who has made amicable contact with new species."

"He's the only *human* who's done it. Period," Dora had muttered.

Riordan laughed. "You make it sound like I knew what I was doing."

"And you make it sound like a great way to get eaten," was Miles' sotto voce quip.

Riordan grinned. "I've thought the same thing, Chief. And if what we find down there decides to make a snack of us without chatting first, I might not be able to get the translator to convince it otherwise. At least, not in time."

Dora leaned forward from her seat between Ayana and Bannor. "Boss, permission to speak freely?"

*When don't you?* Caine had thought as he nodded and managed not to smile.

"With all due respect, boss—that's crazy talk! I mean, why do you think you're in charge, here?"

Eyes had widened at the presumption behind that question, but Dora's tone told Caine it arose from exasperation not insolence.

"No offense," Dora continued, aware she'd stepped over the line, "but you're not in charge for how well you fight. You're in charge because of how you think and talk, particularly when meeting aliens."

She jutted her chin at Rulaine. "There's the guy for a fight— and that's why he's the one who'll be landing with that Dornaani hand cannon. You? You need to have that translator. Maybe that way, we won't have to use his hand cannon so often, yeh?"

Eku nodded. "She is correct, Commodore. If we are all separated, your familiarity with Dornaani devices and language makes you best qualified to operate the translator. But importantly, your success at prior first contacts predicts you will have more success using it than I would."

Yaargraukh's calm report startled him out of the memory. "They have detected where we mounted the long rock spine to backtrack without leaving prints." He lowered the monoscope. "At least two of them are skilled trackers. They will be here within ten minutes."

The five humanoids managed to close to within one hundred meters without exposing themselves again. Almost certainly, they also knew where Caine and Yaargraukh were located as well; it

wasn't serendipity which had unerringly put them behind inter-
vening rocks and rises as they approached.

They had no doubt realized that they were not the only
skilled scouts playing this game of hide-and-seek. Yaargraukh
had chosen a significantly higher position with only one avenue
of approach: a slowly rising apron of scree that culminated at
the crest of the razorback ridge behind which they stood. The
bipeds would certainly expect it to be difficult to attack but had
no way of anticipating the full cost of charging upslope against
Caine's smart-scoped rifle.

After five minutes of preparing or arguing, one of their
number came around the corner of the hump of dirt and dust
behind which they were sheltering. After sending a reproachful
glare at the ones still under cover, it advanced slowly, hands
down and open.

But Caine was hardly aware of its posture or garments or
weapons or tools or anything else, except for the impossible
appearance of the being ascending toward them.

It was mostly orang, but there was clearly some gorilla in the
mix. The proportion of the limbs suggested at least some Homo
sapiens, as well. Or maybe Australopithecus, but that's where
Caine's knowledge of prehistoric hominids ran out. Something
else in its genetic code had sharpened its features, made the chin
slightly more prominent, the ears slightly longer and more erect.

"I believe I have seen such creatures before," Yaargraukh muttered sideways. "Prior to landing in Indonesia, we were shown
images of various indigenous animals."

Riordan nodded, struggling to speak around a hard, dry swallow. "Orangutans. But these are not just orangs; they're polge."

The Hkh'Rkh's eyes remained on the approaching being as
he asked, "I do not know this word, 'polge.'"

"Short for polygenetic. An artificial combination of different
species."

The orang—*no, it's a* being, *damn it!*—had stopped midway
up the slope and spread its empty, very long-fingered hands
to either side. It glanced from Yaargraukh to Caine: although
hardly a human face, the expression was unmistakable: a blend
of quizzical and wary.

Riordan turned on the translator. It could not establish correspondences immediately, but the more it heard, the sooner it

would begin doing so. He called down the slope. "Hello. We mean you no harm."

The being's perplexity doubled. After a slight bow of its head, it replied with a long stream of utterances. Occasionally, at the end of a rising tone, it paused for a response: almost certainly a question.

The Dornaani translator's processing light glowed serenely, but nothing emerged from the speaker.

The lack of reply increased the being's wariness; its back foot began edging down the slope.

*Well, it's got hands, so maybe this gesture will be universal.* Moving slowly, Riordan raised his own empty hand and waved that the being should approach.

More unintelligible queries, but it was no longer preparing to edge away. However, its gaze was now fixed solely upon Yaargraukh.

Riordan glanced at the two molecular machetes the Hkh'Rkh was holding, one in either hand. "Are you comfortable laying those down where our visitor can see them?"

Yaargraukh did so with a light snort, the kind that a professional boxer might have made if confronted by a grade-school bully. Ignoring the advanced ballistic cloth of his duty suit, he had nearly a full meter of height advantage, and the humanoid's hide armor and stone mace would do little to offset the Hkh'Rkh's speed and claws.

Before it could respond, a helmeted head peered around the dirt hump concealing the being's comrades. A few words were exchanged. The orang hybrid turned back toward Caine and made a hands-downward gesture with both palms, then backed away slightly.

*Stay there? Wait a moment?* Riordan guessed, since the translator had yet to establish any correspondences.

Another of the humanoids emerged, wearing armor that resembled boiled leather. One hand was open and stretched to the side; the other held a spear, but far away from the body and with the point toward the ground. Caine noted variations in its facial features—they had a hint of chimp or gorilla—as it moved gingerly up the slope. It was also larger, and as it drew alongside the first, Riordan noticed that the spear was tipped with a dark metal: bronze, from the look of it. *So, not strictly paleolithic.*

The first one was clearly watching for some reaction, but when neither Caine nor Yaargraukh gave one, it called toward those who remained under cover.

As the remaining three stepped out, the leader was immediately obvious: larger still, armor more finished, and a sheathed sword. The one closest to him had a shorter blade and a self-bow. Although none were holding their weapons at the ready, they could correct that in a moment. They stopped at the base of the slope, arrayed three abreast.

Riordan extended a hand in greeting. But before he could change that into a gesture inviting their approach, the humanoids shrank back from the raised hand. A rapid exchange of looks between the upslope and downslope groups, and then they were all sinking to their knees, eyes resentful beneath lowered brows.

"That," Yaargraukh murmured, "is a novel response."

Caine frowned, but tried another hopefully universal gesture: he turned his palm toward the sky and raised it. Several times in quick succession.

Again, cautious looks were exchanged between the two groups, but some of the fear and resentment was fading away. As Riordan had expected, the leader was the first to stand, albeit slowly and warily.

Riordan kept gesturing upward with his palm. As the others followed their leader's example, he waved them forward. When all five stood together, Yaargraukh asked without turning, "And now?"

"And now, we start naming things."

First-contact missions had taught Caine that the easiest part of establishing a common vocabulary was to exchange words for the same objects. But there was an equally important and completely nonlinguistic factor: simply becoming familiar with each other's appearance, motions, gestures. As they worked through sharing labels for all the weapons, tools, garments, limbs, appendages, and facial features, there was a great deal of side conversation among the humanoids. There were chortled observations, sudden remonstrations, mutters of perplexity...all of which the Dornaani transponder recorded and assessed, watching for lexical repetitions and patterns to build context.

Its first independent correspondence between nouns was also the first time the humanoids heard its synthetic, sexless voice. As they looked about in panic and then curiosity, Riordan held up the translator as it finished speaking. The orang-hybrids' exchanges resumed in tones that were more awed than fearful. The one who had first ascended the slope, the youngest of the group and assistant to the leader, was pointing at the translator's blinking light when it threw out its first modifier: "*Ator.* 'Big.' Confidence: high," it announced.

The groups' reactions transitioned from awe to near-terrified amazement. Again, it took a few moments before conversation resumed among them.

As it did and the name-swapping of nouns finally exhausted the available objects, Yaargraukh leaned over and spoke in his other Terran language: German. "It is surprising how rapidly they grew comfortable with us."

Caine's German was much rustier. He winced at the errors in his reply. "First lesson of first contact: shared tasks reduce perceptions of difference and increase appreciation of similarities."

"They also reduce tensed muscles," the Hkh'Rkh replied. "Except for the leader and the archer, I think they have forgotten their weapons exist." He paused, scanning for any objects that might not have been named. "What next?"

Of all concepts, the "yes/no" binary opposition was the most fundamental and, when one party had no codified mathematics, it was also one of the hardest to establish. That certainly proved to be the case with the orang-hybrids. Try as they might, neither they nor Riordan could break through that barrier.

And at the rate they were going, they were not going to achieve it before they ran out of energy. To say nothing of daylight: Riordan had noticed their leader sneak occasional appraising glances at the sun, measuring its inexorable progress.

*Wait: the sun!*

Lifting his arm slowly, Caine extended his hand and then his index finger to point directly at the sun. "Sun," he said.

The apparent assistant to the leader stared, then pointed similarly. "Asír."

Caine picked up a pebble with his other hand. He held it up for them to study before raising it so that it was next to the sun. He pointed at the sun again. "Sun. Asír." Then he presented the pebble prominently. "Sun. Asír," he repeated.

The beings exchanged long looks, several glancing dubiously toward the leader. Probably wondering if the being in the strange armor was suffering from the heat of the very object he was now confusing with a pebble. The frowning leader's answering gesture needed no translation: *Not now, damn it!*

Using the finger with which he was indicating the actual sun, Caine slowly traced its arc across the sky, finishing where it would set on the western horizon. He then returned both hands to his lap for a moment, and repeated the movement. But this time, he kept the pebble tracking right along with his pointing finger. "Sun. A*sír*," he repeated.

The five pairs of simian eyes followed the strange progress with a new expression: intense interest.

Riordan drew a deep breath; *Now the hard part.* He repeated the track across the sky, but when he finished, he said, "Day."

Two of the five increasingly less-alien faces brightened. "Ladsír!" the assistant exclaimed. The translator confirmed the match: "Ladsír. Day." The assistant's rapid commentary to his fellows was genuinely excited.

After repeating it several times to ensure that the concept was firm in their minds, Riordan drew a deep breath and started with his pointing finger and pebble not at the place where the sun rose, but to where it set in the west. *Here goes.*

Moving both his finger and the pebble slowly, deliberately, Caine reversed the passage of the sun "False," he said.

The three who were perplexed became more so; the leader and his assistant frowned. Their respective expressions intensified as Riordan repeated the motion.

Caine exhaled and once again, rested his hands in his lap for a long moment. *Moment of truth.* He brought both his pointing finger and pebble over to the eastern horizon and repeated the motion that had been established as "day." But this time, when the passing of the sun ended on the horizon, he said, "true." He repeated it. The brow of the assistant began rising.

Seeing that tip toward a crucial cognitive inflection point, Riordan put his hands back in his lap, then brought them back to the western horizon and repeated the impossible progress of the sun from west to east: "False." He repeated it. Then he switched back to the proper day cycle for two additional repetitions; he punctuated each conclusion with "true."

The assistant leaped to his feet, excitedly shouting "Urgh! Urgh!" as he stared around at the others. A rapid combination of debate and explanation, during which the leader's frown began to melt away. He nodded at his assistant and muttered something that sounded like permission.

The assistant picked up a pebble of his own and followed Riordan's motions, completing the anti-day with "*Urgh.* False."

"False," Caine agreed.

The other then completed the correct circuit. "*Iish.* True."

Riordan sighed in relief: the gateway to every conceptual term was now open. "True," he agreed with a nod.

And almost laughed aloud when the assistant nodded back in an eminently human motion of agreement.

"Well," Yaargraukh commented in a sly tone as all the orang heads began nodding, "your extraordinary labors to establish 'yes' versus 'no' may have been somewhat redundant."

This time Riordan did smile and laugh.

And as if to further prove the further truth of Yaargraukh's suggestion that common gestures seemed a vastly superior translational tool, the leader of the five beings returned Riordan's smile.

*This,* thought Caine, *might not be so hard after all.*

The shadows were leaning markedly to the east when the leader, Arashk, leaned back, shaking his head. "Us want rest. Want food." He began rummaging in his hide shoulder sack.

Riordan reached into his musette bag and produced one of his last Dornaani egg salad sandwich imitations. He held it up, took a bite, swallowed, cut off the part his mouth had touched, and passed it to the leader.

Arashk stared at the unfamiliar food, then produced a blackish tuber from his bag. He held it out in exchange.

They both studied the unfamiliar foods, then each other, and smiled. Ruefully. Riordan extricated the Dornaani food and blood sampler from his survival pack and held it up for Arashk's consideration. "Tool see good food. Speaks yes, no."

Arashk responded with a nod and slightly narrowed eyes. Caine was merely determining if he could safely eat the tuber, but the other appeared to be interpreting the device as a means of detecting intentional poisoning. However, whatever Arashk's reservations might have been, he smiled and replied, "Here *my* tool for see if food good." He clapped his assistant on the shoulder and handed over the Dornaani sandwich.

The humanoids, who called themselves *h'achgai*, roared with laughter: all except the assistant. As Riordan fed a thin slice of the tuber into the Dornaani sampler, that worthy eyed the sandwich warily before steeling himself to put his lipless mouth near the unfamiliar food.

The Dornaani sampler glowed green aqua: the chirality of the proteins was a match and the cellulose analogs were not toxic. There was an unsurprising array of unknown exobiotic microbes, but none were toxic or carrying parasites. Riordan took a bite: the texture was similar to an unripe pear and the flavor was both musky and salty. It reminded him of a cross between a turnip and soursop and would not take much getting used to. At all.

Meanwhile, the hapless assistant had finally nibbled at the edge of the sandwich. His first reaction was unpromising: a facial contraction that Riordan would have expected from biting into a lemon. But a moment later the young h'achgai's face began unpuckering; interest quickly became enjoyment. Arashk patted him on the shoulder, removed the sandwich from hands that were now clearly reluctant to return it, and glanced at Caine. He pointed, mimicked the human's chewing, and asked, "Good?"

Riordan smiled, replied "Good!" and gave a thumbs-up.

The h'achgai stared at that gesture. Their gazes eventually collected upon Arashk, whose frown was not one of displeasure but more as if he were puzzling out a conundrum.

Yaargraukh offered a muted observation. "They respond to hand gestures...unusually."

Caine nodded, recalling how what he'd intended as a hand raised in greeting had been mistaken as a call for supplication. Unfortunately, they were still at such an early stage of understanding that any attempt to understand the difference could risk a disruptive, or even dangerous, gaffe.

Evidently, he was not alone in that concern. Arashk had mimicked and held the thumbs-up gesture. "This be good?" he questioned.

"Good," Caine affirmed with a nod.

Arashk glanced at his assistant. "Hresh make question at you."

Caine nodded toward the young h'achga. Hresh nodded his respect toward Arashk, then toward Caine. "Why you start hand up?"

It sounded as though the h'achgai were trying to puzzle out their side of that first, unsettling exchange. Caine slowly raised his hand. "This?"

Hresh shook his head. "Not same."

Riordan looked at his hand. "Not same how?"

Hresh held his hand out to the side, spread his fingers, then pointed at Caine's; his fingers were together.

Yaargraukh made a rumbling noise. "Slowly, Commodore. And start with your hand tilted toward the side." The Hkh'Rkh's tone was not so much one of understanding as recollection.

Riordan followed his friend's advice, turning his hand sideways before spreading his fingers.

Hresh nodded at the gesture. "That no bad."

Caine took a risk. "This bad?" he asked, and rotated his wrist until the spread fingers pointed directly at the sky.

The h'achgai not only became silent, but glum. "Bad," Hresh agreed.

"Many bad," Arashk grunted. "*X'qai dregdo* do that hand. They all bad."

Riordan switched the translator to the interactive mode for the first time in over an hour. "*X'qai dregdo*: analysis."

"Definitions: unknown," the translator replied. "Structural analysis: *x'qai* is a plural noun. *Dregdo* is an adjective, modifier, or attribute."

Riordan turned to the grim-faced h'achgai. "*X'qai* bad?"

Nods, grunts, and one sardonic laugh.

"I think we need to learn more about x'qai," Yaargraukh murmured.

"I see your sense of humor has returned," Riordan muttered sideways.

The Yaargraukh's tongue whipped out before zipping back into the top nostril, as if that might undo his species' equivalent of a chuckle.

Riordan would have smiled, but for the seriousness of his next question: "*Dregdo* bad?"

That elicited sighs of frustration: not with Caine but at the lack of language which kept them from explaining something they clearly felt to be very important.

Hresh stood, gesturing for Caine and Yaargraukh to remain

seated before he made a respectful request of Arashk, who shrugged and stood. The leader stared and asked a sharp question; his assistant's answer brought a slow smile to his face.

Arashk walked a few steps down the slope. Hresh prompted the others, who rose and made a row three abreast behind Arashk. Hresh turned toward Caine and pointed to Arashk. "Dreg*do*," he said, placing peculiar emphasis on the last syllable.

"A leader?" Caine mused.

The translator confirmed. "Dregdo. Leader."

But Hresh was not finished. He had all the other h'achgai sit in a circle, after which Arashk put aside his sword and helmet. "Dreg*dir*," Hresh announced, making a circular gesture to indicate the entire group.

"A...a council?" Caine wondered. He glanced at Yaargraukh as he waited for the translator to say something. Anything.

The Hkh'Rkh's neck rose and fell slowly. "Equals, at the very least."

Once the h'achgai had returned to their original places, Arashk pointed cautiously at Yaargraukh. "Dregdo?" he asked. Then, indicating Caine: "Dregdo?" When neither of them replied, he pointed at the two of them with a hesitant query: "Dreg*dir*?"

It felt anticlimactic when the translator provided the now-obvious translation: "Dregdir. Equals."

But still, Arashk gestured uncertainly between the human and the Hkh'Rkh. "Dregdo? Dregdir?"

Yaargraukh spoke before Riordan could respond. "Caution, here, Commodore. I suspect that, at this particular moment, my cultural background may be more helpful than yours. With your permission?"

Riordan nodded.

The Hkh'Rkh faced Arashk and pointed at Caine. "On fight day, he dregdo. Good dregdo." Yaargraukh's next gesture indicated both of them. "On no fight day, we two dregdir."

The translator started spitting out equivalences—"war," "peace," "leader," "commander"—mere seconds after a relieved babble arose from the h'achgai. Arashk nodded vigorously. "Yes. We, too." He pointed to himself. "Fight day, I dregdo. No fight day, I dregdir." The others were producing more food from their packs, even as they thumped Hresh in what looked like joyful hazing.

Caine nodded, hated to utter the word that might dampen the lighter spirits, but it had to be done. He cleared his throat. "Arashk, Hresh: bad word comes."

Arashk's face became sober.

"X'qai leaders make you bow to high hand, all fingers wide?"

Arashk's nod was even more savage than those of the other four.

Riordan sighed, shrugged apologetically. "You tell me x'qai? Tell me all?"

With a feral smile at the two strangers' weapons, armor, and gear, Arashk's answer was a feral growl: "Yes. I tell you x'qai—all day, all night."

# Chapter Fourteen

Newton Baruch raised an eyebrow when Yaargraukh's daily freekset squelch occurred two seconds into the minute reserved for "strategic advantage attained." Following Riordan's earlier "contact made" send, and given that both had been sent during the first thirty minutes of their respective hours, it seemed that despite the very rough start to the Crewe's arrival on-planet, conditions were improving.

Newton glanced at the sun: three hours to sunset. He'd set his duty suit's helmet chronometer to the local time—unlike the vacc suits, it could not be tasked to do so automatically—but was resolved to train his eyes and other senses to the realities of this environment. After all, they might one day find themselves without the use of all their impressive survival toys. But he was not hesitant about putting those toys to use; without them, it would have been far more work to shape his current perch upon the rocky rise at the end of a deep wadi.

He'd spent last night nearby, lacking enough daylight to make a full survey of the high ground that had been his destination. But this day, by rising before dawn, Baruch had finished assessing the surrounding terrain just before noon. Midway through, he discovered his current eyrie and had correctly projected that he would not find a more suitable spot.

It was a remarkably lucky find, he allowed, as he used the Dornaani multitool to expand the footholds he'd carved out of the hard-packed sand into legitimate steps. The wadi he'd followed ended, but also widened into a small box canyon, where it met the rocky roots of the east-west ridge he was perched upon. Near its crest, Newton had discovered a runoff channel that followed the rock to the floor of the wadi. In effect, he'd stumbled across a small, naturally created trench system that looked down upon the canyon and through its narrow entry to the wadi beyond. Happily, the view in the other direction had proven almost as advantageous.

Baruch leaned back from the rough riser he'd just finished: time to scan north again. He stood and turned, looking over the lip of stone and sand behind him.

Even from ten kilometers, the city at the confluence of the two rivers was readily visible, even if its details were not. Almost three kilometers across, a surrounding sprawl of low, rounded structures became more dense as it neared the cluster of thin, uneven spikes at its approximate center. Fanning out from its margins, the color of the ground was slightly darker and mottled by patches of what appeared to be ground-hugging growth of some kind. Earlier in the day, hazy wisps had appeared radiating out from the city, but always close to the ground. A quick look through Newton's Dornaani monoscope discovered the cause: dust raised by clusters of indistinct figures moving into the periphery of exoflora or possibly beyond.

But at present, there was no hint of change or movement about the city, only a few scattered tendrils of what he presumed to be fires. Every day so far had started with snow or frost on the ground. But God only knew what they were burning.

Changing the multitool over to the telescoping and rotating awl, he wondered if there would be lights at night. Measuring out a span of trench equal to the distance between the grommets on the Dornaani shelter half, he set to boring mooring points into the rock lip on both sides of its highest stretch. The work would be long, sweaty, and dull, but he welcomed the almost meditative relaxation that a properly disciplined mind could achieve while the body labored at a simple task. And at the end, he would have the comfort of knowing that if rain fell, the shelter overhead would send the runoff to the down-sloping ground on either side.

With one mooring point carved out, he paused to drink from the dwindling supply of rain and meltwater he collected each night in a Dornaani container which was either plastic or a translucent composite. He lifted the duty suit's helmet with his free hand, activated the transponder tracker.

The paired icons of Bannor and Duncan were closest and approaching from the south. About a day behind them were Ayana and Dora, approaching from the west, who, two nights ago, had used flares to locate each other. Like Newton, Dora wore a duty suit and had to contend with its limited ability to separate signals within five kilometers of each other. It had been pure chance that Baruch had noticed their signaling. Scanning the heavens for any recognizable constellations, he'd seen what he first thought was a shooting star, but soon realized it was a Dornaani flare fired high into the night sky.

He frowned. It was not wise, moving at night, even less so launching flares that could attract hostile exofauna. Still, if either his friends or creatures did approach in the dark...

Newton unpacked the Dornaani EVA hand light and secured it on a natural shelf in the rock. At its brightest, narrowest setting, the beam would be excellent for signaling. Set slightly wider and shined in the eyes of an enemy, it was likely to cause profound afterimages, possibly temporary blindness.

But, Baruch temporized, all things being equal, if he had to use it at all, he'd rather the former than the latter application. As he set to boring the second mooring point, he hoped that the others would stop traveling at night. But if they insisted on doing so, it gave him comfort to know that, like a lighthouse keeper poised above treacherous oceans of darkness, he could guide them home to safety.

Ayana Tagawa shook her head. "Dora, there is no reason to risk drinking groundwater. I am happy to share from my supply."

Dora Veriden looked away from a crevice in the rock formation that they'd been following. "You mean the supply from your suit?"

"It is all I have."

"Yeah, and it all comes from your pee. No thanks." Dora extended the gaff stick, dialed around until she found the setting for the EVA momentum brake, locked it, and toggled the tension release. The desired tip emerged from the slot at the top of the gaff stick and rapidly unfolded into four equilateral prongs or "feet."

"Hah!" she exclaimed. "Just like Yaargraukh's paws!"

Ayana sighed, resisting her reflex to point out that despite a superficial similarity, it didn't work like Hkh'Rkh hands at all. "What do you mean to do with it?"

"You'll see," Dora chuckled. She picked up the plastic cup with which she'd been trying to scoop water out of the hole and held its lip so that two of the tongs were to one side, two on the other. She reversed the tension release and the "feet" began folding back into the body of the gaff stick. Halfway in, the collapsing tongs met the cup's lip, pinning it from either side.

Ayana raised an eyebrow. "That is a very inventive idea," she commented, "but it is not designed to stay in that position. You could easily lose the cup in—"

But Dora had already poked the stick into the hole. A soft splash indicated the cup had made contact with the water. She looked up at Ayana with a rakish smile. "You were saying something, yeah?"

Tagawa exhaled slowly and resisted the urge to sit on her stacked pack and musette bag. *Insufferable.* But she only said, "Just so long as you can get it out."

"And if I can't, then I fish it out. Not too hard with the feet extended, I bet. Hey, why they call this grabby thing a . . . a moment's brake?"

"EVA momentum brake," Ayana corrected. "During EVA, if you approach an object too rapidly, you can deploy the brake and hold it out in front of you. The feet have smart resistance; they start fairly flexible but become less so as more pressure is exerted from behind."

"Huh," Dora observed, drawing the gaff stick slowly out of the crevice. "Sounds handy. But not as handy as tongs!" She triumphantly recovered the mostly filled cup, made to drink it—and laughed when Ayana started forward with outstretched hands. *"Ai, Madre!* I'm not gon' hurt myself!" Still grinning, she shifted her fingers to reveal the purification tab she'd been hiding in her palm. "I'm not stupid, you know!"

Ayana nodded. *I am unconvinced.* Aloud: "Is there any dust in the water?"

Dora was pouring it carefully into her almost empty container, studying the stream closely. "Nah. There's probably some at the bottom of the hole, but it's deep and I was careful not to stir it up." She went back for another cupful. "It would have been nice for the others to give us at least one of those Froggie-made water and food testers, though."

Ayana shrugged. "There was no way to know where each of us would land, let alone who would be closest to whom."

Dora's wordless reply—a low grumble—was one that Ayana had heard often enough since they'd departed Zeta Tucanae. It was the sound of Dora Veriden pushing back against logic that threatened to undermine her unfettered enjoyment of a good, cathartic gripe.

She finished pouring off the second cup and immediately dunked it back into the hole. "Must be a pain getting the tongs back into the gaff stick after they get bent up."

"They return to their original shape, eventually. That is another way in which the material is 'smart.'"

Another grumble. "The Frogaanis needed to make the knife bigger. And the spike longer."

"Neither were intended as weapons; they're EVA tools."

"To do what?"

"Cut away cables and circuitry. Or moor oneself to an asteroid. Respectively."

Dora's grumble was diminished yet dogged. "Wouldn't be hard to make them real weapons, too, if the Frogaani bothered to think that way." As the fourth and final cup added to the water sloshing around in her container, Dora's tone changed from gruff disappointment to eager animation. "*Ai!* I know what! I'll find a way to put a spear tip on this thing." When Ayana didn't reply, she raised her voice, "What? No warning against that, Mommy?" She looked over.

Ayana had almost forgotten about her, and had heard her last words as if from a very great distance. "Dora," she said calmly, "stand slowly and keep your hand near your weapon."

Dora, for all her anti-authority insouciance, always dropped it when serious circumstances arose. Now a focused professional, she did not glance about to look for the source of Ayana's concern. "What and where's the problem?"

Ayana struggled to keep her eyes on the object. "One hundred meters to the north. Flying object. Shaped like an insect. Following along the course of the wadi we passed."

Dora's voice was low and slow. "You mean the big wadi? The one that runs down to the river?" It left a visible cleft all the way to the horizon.

Ayana nodded, realized that Dora was probably no longer looking at her. "That is the one. The insect must be flying beneath its rim, now. I cannot—"

Either the creature was familiar with the area, or serendipity had fated it to approach along a narrow gap that neither of the humans had noted when passing the wadi. The insect abruptly popped above the northern edge of the stony spine they'd been following.

There was no way it could be a dragonfly, Ayana told herself, but her eyes insisted otherwise. The only caveat was its impossible size; over a meter long and its wings a blur, it seemed to levitate as it inspected them. And although Ayana had only taken one college course on entomology, she noted that the creature's head was far more reminiscent of a mantis. A head built for killing.

Dora freed one hand from her gaff stick, moved it slowly toward her holstered Ruger.

Ayana was careful not to move her head as she spoke. "No. Keep the stick."

"But I can—"

"If it comes at you first, threaten it with the gaff."

"You mean these *estúpida* prongs? I—"

"It does not matter," Ayana murmured as the insect started angling toward Dora. "Just keep it off."

"Like I need you to tell me that when—?"

Perhaps it was her louder, sharper tone; perhaps it was the indignant raise of her chin—but the insect's wings brightened and hummed as it drove at Dora.

She was instantly focused and calm, gaff stick at the ready. Motionless, she waited until the insect had sped to within two meters...and did not just jab, but lunged, at it.

The insect halted abruptly, dodged slightly to the side, seemed to regard the suddenly effective opponent...even as Ayana moved her hand toward the scabbard on her left hip.

The mantis head rotated slightly in that direction—and the immense dragonfly was suddenly flashing toward her, mandibles clattering like shrill castanets.

Pandora Veriden gasped, leaped forward. "No! You'll—!"

But Tagawa's statue-still pose, legs slightly bent and weight on the rearward right, spun into motion like a forcefully uncoiling spring. The creature arrowed at her—but like a mirror-slash of reflected sunlight, Ayana's katana was through, its two halves tumbling away before Dora could even blink.

For a moment the head and the thorax struggled to move, the still-attached wings a whirring counterpoint to the ferocious grinding buzz emanating from beyond the mandibles—

And then all was silence.

Dora almost shook her head in surprise. "You're okay with that thing," she muttered, nodding toward the sword.

Ayana's tone was not one of false humility but frank, even irritated, appraisal. "I was adequate, but I did no justice to my training." She tossed back the flap of the small sack she carried on the outside of her musette bag, carefully removed the most soiled of her sanitary cloths. She ran its last clean fold along the blade, squeezing the creature's black-amber ichor off. "With prey so scarce, I suspect many local creatures have a keen sense of smell," she said as she made a more careful pass with the rag. "We must move quickly."

# Chapter Fifteen

Duncan Solsohn stopped the instant he secured his helmet's faceplate.

Bannor turned to stare at him, unlimbered the Dornaani coil gun as he did. "A contact?"

Duncan shook his head as he popped the faceplate. "Tell me what you see. Azimuth is about one o'clock."

Bannor shrugged, sealed his own helmet. A moment later he opened it again. "UV dye marks. Three, I think. Only one is facing us directly."

Duncan nodded. It was exactly what they were looking for, right down to the placement and the wavelength-hopping algorithm. The marks were set at south, southwest, and west: the directions from which any other jumpers would approach. And if an observer didn't have the right algorithm, they wouldn't see a steady UV signal: just random flashes as the wavelength crossed back and forth across their detection span. "Think that's the first one?"

Bannor shrugged. "Sure looks like it. The transponder tracker indicates we're between fifteen to twenty klicks from Newton. That's the range band he chose for the first marking."

Duncan closed his mask again, brought up the HUD's spectral filter, focused on the dye marks, tagged them with the range finder: seven klicks. The rendezvous point was almost certainly within thirty kilometers. He glanced at the locally adjusted chronometer as he popped open his faceplate again. "I think we can make it today, if we push."

Bannor's hazel eyes were squinting in the same direction. "We'd be coming in at dusk, or a bit later." His jaw worked slightly. "But it's absolutely worth the risk."

Duncan held in a relieved sigh, imagining the unprecedented luxuries of linking up with Newton. Night watch split three ways instead of two. Three firearms. And no more sleeping without reasonable—or any—cover. Judging from the slow, methodical movement of his transponder Newton had spent a day and a half surveying the rendezvous zone before settling upon a campsite.

Duncan hitched the combination pack and musette bag slightly higher on his shoulders; after consuming almost six days of rations, the latter was noticeably lighter. "Then let's get going."

Two klicks past the marker, Bannor stopped to make a perimeter sweep with the HUD, the way they did every three kilometers. Normally, that would have been a hazardously long interval, but on this billiard-table wasteland, it was reasonably safe. He closed his visor, powered it up . . . and stopped.

"Contact. West-northwest. Aerial. I make range as six klicks. Confirm."

Duncan finished the sweep of the opposite compass point that he'd begun the moment Bannor reported the bearing. "No contacts visible to the rear." He turned to check Rulaine's spot. "Confirm bearing and range. But . . . multiple contacts."

Bannor double-checked. "Good catch. Confirm your correction. Increasing gain." Bannor increased the HUD's magnification and centered the field on the contacts. "Thermal is slightly above background. Their movement is abrupt, fast."

"Like insects," Duncan added with a nod.

"Very big insects," Bannor amended. "And I don't think they're all the same type."

"I noticed that, too. Their outlines and even their patterns of movement vary. Kind of odd, a heterogeneous group of insects moving together."

Rulaine shrugged. "Odd on Earth, perhaps, but maybe not so strange here. We saw stranger, when we were in Slaasriithi space." He measured the range again. "Not closing, although they're a little higher now."

Duncan nodded. "Maybe looking us over."

Bannor nodded back. "Let's check on them every two kilometers."

"Sounds like a plan." He started marching.

Bannor took one last look at the tightly swarming contacts and followed.

Duncan increased the magnification on his HUD, then pointed. "Second set of dye markers. Range: five klicks."

Bannor sealed up to confirm. "Yep," he muttered. "We should be within ten kilometers." He turned to glance toward the maybe-insects. "They're gone."

Duncan opened his own faceplate. "Yeah, they were just dipping under the horizon a few moments ago. Guess we're not that interesting."

"Assuming they ever saw us."

Solsohn was careful to make his grunt more deferential than disputatious. "Sir, I—"

"Just 'Bannor,' here."

"Uh . . . okay. Bannor, I did a lot of hunting as a kid. Rockies, mostly. Sometimes critters stay in sight because they're busy doing something at that location. Like vultures waiting for a wounded animal to exhaust itself."

"But?"

"But we've walked two klicks since we first saw the insects. And I saw them just a few seconds ago. That's an awful long time for *all* of them to stay in the same place."

"So you think they *did* see us but decided we weren't worth the trouble? Or risk?"

"Probably. But like you said, Col— er, Bannor, maybe things work differently on this planet."

Rulaine glanced to the west. "So we keep checking every two klicks."

"That will delay us a bit."

The colonel's grin was rueful. "That's why we're going to pick up the pace."

When they'd stopped after the first two-klick interval, Rulaine hadn't seen anything, so Duncan expected the same thing when his turn came. Indeed, the horizon to the west was empty. Exhaling, he turned slowly, sweeping south.

He froze, both in terms of his motion and the icy chill that ran down through his core. "They're back."

Rulaine turned to look. "They're close. Just under three klicks."

Duncan nodded. "And spread out."

"Following us, trying to tire us out?"

Duncan frowned. "I don't know. Looks more like they're trying to herd us. If they were trying to run us to ground, I'd expect them to press us more." He shook his head. "They're just trying to keep us going north."

Rulaine turned slowly to the west, faced that way for several seconds before he grunted.

"See something, si—Bannor?"

The compact Special Forces colonel sighed. "Yeah. Dust plumes, probably seven kilometers out. Heading this way."

Duncan glanced back at the insects that lay across the trail they'd left coming up from the south. "They're hunting us, all right."

"Then why not press us?" Rulaine sounded uncertain.

Duncan hitched his load higher on his shoulder. "Because they know the terrain. They know that there's a river to the east of us and another to the north."

Bannor nodded. "So they mean to box us into an area that we can't move beyond: the juncture of the rivers." The light was fading, so his lopsided grin wasn't immediately obvious. "Good thing we're going in that direction, anyway."

"And bringing trouble right behind us," Duncan added. *Assuming it doesn't overtake us first.* "Should we radio Newton, sir?"

Rulaine was quiet for two long seconds before answering, "No. Let's wait until we've got a better idea of what's coming and just how fast." He pointed to the west. "If they don't mean to attack until they've pinned us against the rivers, let's not give them any reason to speed up. Better to face them after rendezvousing with Newton."

"Roger that. Maybe we should button up, though."

Bannor studied the ground ahead. He nodded, pointing to a shallow wadi lying across their path, about a kilometer to the north. "We'll zip up once we reach the wadi's bed, kick on the thermaflage setting—"

"—and come out the other side without a heat signature." Duncan nodded vigorously. "Even if they're visual light hunters, it's still going to make us harder to see. They might have to spend time finding our physical tracks to get back on our trail."

"My thinking exactly. Lead the way."

✦　　✦　　✦

Bannor stopped to let Duncan catch his wind. Months on a spacecraft, even a Dornaani model with tethered spin pods for exercise, hadn't been kind to any of them, but the IRIS analyst had been mostly at a desk for the year before he'd been attached to the Crewe at Delta Pavonis. The decreased aerobic activity was making its consequences felt now.

"Three kilometers...to...rendezvous?" he panted.

"Closer to four," Bannor corrected.

"And the...pursuit?"

"Just under three kilometers, but not heading directly for us." And that was about all they knew about the two creatures that had come out of the west, the taller, leaner one speeding ahead of the other for the past half hour. Storm clouds had come up from the south, hugging the western horizon and largely blotting out the sun. They were in the equivalent of late dusk an hour ahead of time.

They had only one other, tentative data point on their pursuers: that one or both of them could see in the UV spectrum. Instead of heading directly for the two fleeing humans, the creatures were veering more toward Newton's final set of dye markers about a kilometer further north. But that wasn't any kind of help; both groups' paths were set to converge on that point.

Duncan straightened up, gulping in breaths so great that Bannor could see his chest heaving through the Dornaani suit. "And the insects? Still holding their distance?"

Bannor nodded. "But their intervals are wider."

"Expanding the dragnet as they get closer," Solsohn wheezed. "Hope they're not more aggressive than vultures."

"You and me both."

"Sorry to slow us down, Bannor. I'm ready."

Rulaine very much doubted that but nodded and set off toward the high ground ahead: apparently the location of Newton's campsite.

"Think it's about time to radio him?" Duncan asked, as if reading his thoughts.

Rulaine frowned. Under other circumstances, he might have done so two kilometers earlier. But Newton had drawn one of the weaker survival rifles and was in a duty suit. So he was comparatively lightly armed, lightly armored, and unable to engage from longer range. He was also a bit too courageous for his own good when it came to helping others. Rulaine and Riordan had both noted and discussed how Newton's self-sacrificing stubbornness came very close to compromising military prudence at times. And if that happened now...

"I'll radio him as soon as we get past the last marker," Bannor muttered between breaths. He glanced northeast at the high ground again, searching—

"Damn it!" Duncan swore, stumbling as he looked over his shoulder. He dug his feet into the sand to stop abruptly, popping the straps on the survival pack's harness as he did; its remaining momentum sent it rolling away from him.

Rulaine turned to look in the same direction and discovered what he'd missed in the moment he'd turned his attention to the northern ridgeline.

The tall, thin creature was now approaching so swiftly that its thermal outline was slightly blurred. Furthermore, at this range— seven hundred meters and closing with ghastly speed—Bannor noticed that most of its heat was coming out of its mouth and eyes; its hide was preventing any significant loss of body heat.

It had closed another hundred meters in the seconds Rulaine had spent studying it. He unlimbered the Dornaani coil gun and glanced at Duncan.

Solsohn was busy sealing his helmet and readying his survival rifle.

Bannor raised the Dornaani weapon—it hardly looked like a gun at all—and blinked the HUD into smart-targeting mode. A guidon winked into existence near the creature, which had closed to four hundred and twenty-four meters. Its motions did not appear real, looked more like a hologram being played at three-times speed.

Rulaine raised the weapon to his shoulder, the tracking guidon prompting the necessary adjustment to put it on target.

Three hundred thirty meters. The creature had hands, but its strangely thin fingers tapered into long, wickedly pointed claws.

Rulaine activated the Dornaani weapon; it responded by vibrating like a perturbed tuning fork.

Two hundred and sixty meters.

The targeting guidon flicked from yellow to aqua; the weapon was now able to compensate for any correction required by the object's size and speed.

Two hundred meters.

As Rulaine squeezed the trigger, his HUD's compass spun wildly.

There was no report—just a loud, flat crack—as the supersonic projectile left the gun, which did not recoil but *quaked* in his hands. For an instant, the round marked its path with a flitter of flame—

It did not merely hit the onrushing creature, but went straight through, blowing a wide chunk out of its abdomen. Hot fluid sprayed, glowing in the HUD like gobbets of phosphorescent paint. The nearly bisected body bent obscenely at the waist, the upper half trying to fall in a different direction than the bottom.

But its shrill scream was solely one of rage.

"Holy shit," Duncan breathed as he struggled to fit the mono-scope onto the top of his survival rifle.

Bannor nodded, but was too busy, and concerned, to reply. The Dornaani weapon was not only emitting a steady wave of heat, but the HUD indicated it was not yet ready to be fired again.

"Problem?" Solsohn inquired.

"Waiting for this cannon to come back online." Rulaine eyed the second bipedal creature—*being?*—approaching. Its only reaction to the gruesome death of the first was to launch into a headlong charge across the remaining eight hundred meters. "You ready yet?" He glanced back.

Duncan was lowering himself to the ground.

"What are you—?"

"Can't shoot at range with my heart hammering like this. While I'm setting up, you might want to—"

A duller, attenuated report interrupted him: the downrange sound of a supersonic projectile. The second creature twitched, slapped at itself, but kept on coming.

"Well," Solsohn amended, "seems like Newton doesn't need to be alerted."

Bannor was studying the oncoming creature as he carefully detached the battery that was connected to the Dornaani weapon and laid it aside.

"What are you doing?" Duncan asked, glancing away from the survival rifle's data panel for a moment.

"Not counting on that cannon reloading in time." He moved to the other's pack. "Where do you keep your machete?"

Duncan shrugged. "Top of the musette bag." *Wouldn't do me much good buried at the bottom!* He tapped the charge-consumption indicator, studied the results.

Bannor reappeared beside him, his own machete in his right hand, Duncan's in his left. "We're running out of time."

"I'm aware."

Rulaine's grip tightened on both machetes. "Five hundred meters with that smart monoscope should be an easy shot."

"Not worried about hitting."

"What do you—?"

"Sir, you learned about your weapon. I did the same with mine. This pop-gun's battery will power one shot at maximum charge and deliver just over six hundred joules. Five shots at four hundred joules." As Duncan extended the sliding stock, he saw Bannor glance at the Dornaani hand cannon: the orange indicator had changed to blinking white. Nearly ready.

Solsohn snugged the survival rifle close. Probably not much recoil, but having never fired it... "Engaging at two hundred meters," he said and squeezed the trigger when the guidon glowed steady upon the upper chest.

There was no discernible recoil. The impact of the four-gram projectile staggered the creature, a thermal crease blooming at the base of its neck.

Bannor hesitantly put one machete aside and picked up the Dornaani hand cannon as he took on the spotter's role: "Hit at center of sniper's triangle. Minimal effect."

"Yep," Duncan confirmed as he changed the helical magazine feed to tungsten penetrators and increased the charge to maximum. He re-snugged the weapon.

"One hundred meters," Bannor muttered. Duncan's HUD showed the range, of course, but calling the marks was SOP.

"Holding to fifty," Solsohn muttered back, just before the range indicator ticked down to that number. He fired again.

The charging figure—hulking, bipedal, vaguely boarlike—broke stride as a thermal bloom erupted underneath its left eye. It squeal-roared, shrugged off the impact, resumed charging—and then fell headlong.

The light on the big Dornaani weapon glowed aqua. "Cover me," Bannor muttered, fastening the battery back on his harness.

"Just a second," Duncan murmured, as he swapped a power cable into the back of the survival rifle. "Try not to get in trouble."

"Didn't know you cared, Duncan."

"Naw, just might blow out the battery," Duncan chuckled

after Rulaine as the colonel trotted toward the intermittently flailing creature.

As Bannor jogged back, Solsohn was no longer covering him. The rifle—a misnomer, but too ubiquitous to overcome—was now hanging over his neck and one shoulder; his hands were busy with the hand light from his survival kit. "Newton signaled?"

Duncan nodded. "Confirming we received. He'll send us UV signals every minute from the waypoints on the best route to his camp."

"How far did he come out to help us?"

Solsohn shook his head. "Didn't say. But judging from the range of his light, way too far."

Rulaine suppressed a sigh. *Of course he did.* "Let's get going then."

As Duncan stowed his light, he looked over. "So what were we fighting?"

"Monsters. About which I've got more questions than answers." He started toward the ridgeline. "The after-action report will wait until we're safe." He glanced at the insects which had slowed their approach. "They could still be after us."

"Or waiting," Duncan added.

"For what?"

The IRIS analyst nodded his jog-bobbing head toward the two slain creatures. "Safe carrion."

# Chapter Sixteen

Without glancing over, O'Garran saw Peter Wu's worried expression relax and a silent sigh escape his unpursing lips. Smiling, Miles drawled, "Ta'rel is heading back, I'm guessing?"

Peter just nodded, eye affixed to Katie's monoscope as he tracked the approaching figure returning from the south.

Miles managed not to grumble *About time*. Now that the IRIS agent no longer felt the need to keep watch like a mother hen, maybe he could focus on a few questions that couldn't be asked in front of their local guide. "So, what does he call his people?"

Wu still seemed only partially attentive. "The Mangled. At least, that's my best guess at the term. I still don't understand half of what he says."

"Well, the half you *do* understand has probably saved us all." The compliment was a subtle ploy to keep Peter's attention on the conversation, but it was also inarguably true. Without the linguistic bridge Wu had built with Ta'rel, it was unlikely they'd have arrived at so ideal a destination and in such excellent time. Besides, mangled or not, the local moved quickly, was proficient at finding concealment and shelter, knew the region and its inhabitants, and was familiar with the habits of its predators. The latter was why he'd ranged south at daybreak: an attempt to ensure that they would not be detected or trailed as they made their final approach to the river just three kilometers to the north.

In fact, the only problem with Ta'rel was how damned sociable he was. And they needed his various expertises so frequently that so far, there hadn't been any reasonable excuse to have a quick side conversation that excluded him. Miles went straight to the key issue. "So these trogs that you saved him from—"

"Praakht," Wu corrected with a hint of a sigh.

"—what have you learned about them? Are all of them hostile?"

Peter thought before answering. "I don't think it's that simple. Many of them live in cities and towns. Like the one along the river." He gestured over his shoulder. "A good number live in what he calls 'free tribes.' I think. They make their homes in caves or barrows: earthen shelters of one kind or another. Those were the kind we ran into. Except for the one who brought up the rear. His kind are from deep subterranean communities and are extremely aggressive and predatory. He has a separate name for those, but I haven't been able to translate it."

"So: the ones underground are 'extra-bad' trogs," Miles allowed, eager to get on with more questions. "All of their gear looks pretty primitive. More so than Ta'rel's."

Peter shrugged. "The Mangled don't have more advanced materials: they're barely Copper Age. But they're better artisans because they're more patient. More clever, too. Since they're not fighters, they favor missile weapons."

Miles had admired Ta'rel's sturdy recurve composite bow. "So it seems. But then why the hell wasn't he carrying his bow when the trogs came after him?"

"I cannot say. Whenever he tries to describe what he and his dead companion were doing when the praakht attacked, he starts using too many words I don't understand. But he'd left almost everything of value in their hidey-hole: implements, food, waterskins, and what looks like dried moss."

"Dried moss? And it's not food?"

"Apparently not. It's barely a handful, but Ta'rel keeps it in a separate pouch and handles it very carefully. He acts as though it's more valuable than all his other possessions put together. And I think the praakht valued it even more than he does."

"Guess these trogs aren't too bright then, killing the only ones who could lead them to it."

Peter raised an eyebrow at O'Garran's dogged insistence on calling the praakht "trogs." "Ta'rel hasn't said it directly, but they seemed to know he was the only one they needed to keep alive."

"Why?"

"I think it's because of what he *was* carrying: tinder, flint, tools. They knew he was the more skilled, and probably smarter, of the two. His companion's equipment wasn't any more advanced than that carried by the trogs—*praakht*." Peter corrected, then looked away irritated.

*Ha ha!* O'Garran rejoiced behind carefully indifferent eyes. *The simpler name triumphs!* But to his mind, it was also more accurate. He'd used Katie's monoscope to watch one of the "praakht" hunting parties as it approached the riverside town. The first thought that had come to mind was: *They're troglodytes.* Because their features left him with the powerful impression that they weren't just primitive; they were, well, brutish.

His first glimpse at lower magnification showed beings that were built, and stooped, like Neanderthals. But then he zoomed in and saw the differences Peter had mentioned.

Whereas most hominids before Homo sapiens were sort of blunt- or round-featured, there was a sharper cast to a few of the trogs' faces. But not the kind he associated with Cro-Magnon; it was more like some troll from a fairy tale had found its way into the local gene pool. So, no, they weren't Neanderthals but something more arresting. In a word, they were trogs.

Craig Girten had come up with a different label after the encounter with them in the wadi: morlocks. He'd had to explain the reference—devolved beings straight out of the pages of H. G. Wells' *The Time Machine*—but it made sense. Hell, maybe it made more sense than "trog."

But O'Garran's term had the advantage of being both short and familiar and so, it was increasingly the one used by the group. About which Miles nursed an inordinate swelling of pride. Just think; Miles O'Garran naming a species! Hardly one of the activities that his meemaw had foreseen in his future: a topic upon which she always ruminated with a despairing shake of her greying locks. "Ta'rel tell you anything else about 'em?"

"No, but I noticed something he did not mention: their smell."

"You mean...worse than *him*?" A faint odor of ketosis wafted after the mangle wherever he went.

"Much worse," Peter affirmed. "I suspect it is because their diet is almost entirely protein." He paused, reflecting. "Oddly, the cave dweller's smell was different. Not the chemical reek of ketosis, but more like an animal musk."

"Why, do you think?"

Peter sighed, let the survival rifle in his right hand sag slightly as he lowered the monoscope in his left. "That is a question for Newton, if anyone. My guess? The subterranean subspecies digestive system has become fully adapted to an all-meat diet."

O'Garran nodded, surveying the barren flatlands; they'd become sandy closer to the river, but there was still no sign of exoflora. "Yeah, doesn't seem like they do a lot of farming around these parts."

"Still," Peter commented, welcoming Ta'rel with a raised hand, "the Mangled evidently grow a good portion of their food. Like the tubers and lichen he shared when Craig and I first met him."

Ta'rel came over the lip of the small notch they'd used for shelter, formed where a low rise from the southeast met a slightly higher one that ran in from the northeast. They'd follow the latter down to the river, staying in its lee as long as possible.

The mangle and Peter settled behind the rise; Katie rose up just high enough so that her eyes could see out to the southern horizon. "No sign that he was followed."

Ta'rel made a sound very like chuckling as he smiled, revealing spatulate teeth. He dusted his feet off carefully with hands that were unusually shiny: a consequence of subtle scales that only yielded to flesh as they reached the palm. Miles pointedly avoided looking at the "feet"; they were more like a sloth's than a human's, and were, to his mind, the mangle's most arresting feature.

"What's so funny?" Katie asked Peter.

But Ta'rel, who'd made far more progress with the humans' language than they had with his, released a stream of words that were mostly hard consonants and indifferently distinct vowels.

Peter smiled. "He says you can be sure he did not attract any attention."

"Why?"

Peter's smile widened. "Because he would either have run all the way back or be half eaten by now."

Miles had a career-NCO's attitude toward locals, particularly helpful ones: not distrust, exactly, but a constant awareness that any such relationships were inherently provisional on both sides. One day, both would have to go back to their own homes, so any amity that might develop could not be allowed to complicate that return. Still, this mangle had proven a good guide and an easy fellow-traveler. And that was clearly how he perceived himself: as an equal, not a subordinate. He gladly shared what he had and just as gladly accepted what he was given, but without any of the suppressed resentment or exaggerated fawning that O'Garran had seen in every occupied human land.

*Which is exactly why you have to be extra careful with him. It would be too easy to start reacting to him the way he seems to be reacting to you.* "Ta'rel," Miles said in a carefully flat tone, "how long?" When the strange eyes regarded him uncertainly, the SEAL pointed south. "The bait bag: how long until it is smelled?"

The raised brow—perplexity—straightened and he nodded. "Hour. Or half."

Miles wasn't fast enough to keep one of his own rather bushy eyebrows from raising in response. That was a more precise answer than he'd expected. And a much shorter estimate than he'd been hoping for.

Craig came off his watch point on the northern lip of the notch, carrying tattered rags: the last remains of the dead trogs' garments. "Replacements," he murmured handing them out.

Katie's nose wrinkled at her new sanitary rag which was sanitary in name only. But there had been no way to wash the old ones, which was what Ta'rel had carried three kilometers south. Peter had hesitantly approved to seal the small hide bag with a few small strips of Dornaani smart tape. Only Craig had understood the intent, having hunted from boyhood: if the bait bag's scent was open to the air on the way out, then it could be followed back to its point of origin. But if the hide sack wasn't opened until deposited at the bait point, it would attract any nearby predators *without* leaving a further scent trail back toward the group.

*But still . . .* "Do you really think our shit will attract that much, well, interest?" O'Garran asked the group in general, ignoring Katie's stare that translated as, *Yer jokin', right?*

Craig was nodding as Peter replied. "Ta'rel assures me it will." He gestured at the wastes. "Any biological scent is so rare that it is the most common way that predators first detect prey out here."

Craig's final nod was like a decisive period to Wu's statement. "Trust me, sir. Any critter that poops is some other critter's prey."

*Ah, the glorious cycle of life . . . and shit.* "I'm presuming your predawn stroll to the river was equally successful?" He looked between Ta'rel and Peter, the latter of whom had simply stood profiled on the bluff nearest to the water, making sure that his silhouette included the distinctive outline of his survival rifle.

Peter nodded, leaned forward. "Now that Ta'rel is back, we can all hear the details together."

Craig started. "You haven't heard them yet, sir?"

Wu shook his head. "There wasn't time. We had to move back here with all speed to get the bait bag prepared and placed so we can get to the river before noon." He turned. "Ta'rel, what did you find out?"

"We can get boat here. It go where we need."

O'Garran leaned forward. "And what if someone asks us where we're from? Or where we're going?"

Ta'rel looked sidelong at Miles. "You will not know if they ask. I am speak very slowly. I make all sounds, eh, more different. So you hear them better. Others will speak fast and rough."

"Okay, so if they ask, what are you going to tell them about us?"

Ta'rel shrugged. "I tell the true. I meet you. You tell me little. You are strong and give food. I help you to the place you go. That you mean to trade at that place."

Katie was staring at the mangle. "Aye, an' what if something happens to *you*? Then what do we do?"

Ta'rel's brow raised very high and he turned to Peter, speaking rapidly in a mix of his own language and theirs.

At the end, Ta'rel nodded and leaned back as Peter leaned forward. "If we no longer have him to speak for us, we have the following challenges. We must explain why we do not know the local language, which is a mix of lingua franca and trade argot called Low Praakht. And the only humans who do not know how to speak it are from places he says we should not claim as our home."

"Why?"

"He emphasizes that it would be...most unhealthy. Instead, we should act, eh, proud"—Ta'rel leaned over with a brief comment—"ah: no, we should act haughty and answer in single words. And only if absolutely necessary. Our 'story' is that we are journeying to bear a message to a great, um, lord in the city at the fork of the rivers, and are sworn not to divulge the identity of the recipient, the sender, or the message."

Katie frowned. "And they're just going to gie us leave to travel as we will? Because we're haughty?"

"That and because we have guns. And vacc suits, which he calls magical armor. I think."

O'Garran squinted at that. "I guess it's not so strange that they recognize humans. But I'd feel a lot better if we understood how they know about guns."

Wu nodded. "I agree, but we don't yet share the words necessary to have that conversation. However, we *should* say we are recently from the city we saw upriver."

"The one that trades salt brought overland from the western coast?"

"Yes, and which Ta'rel urged us to avoid once he learned our final destination."

"And because this upriver city was yet another place that isn't healthy for humans," Craig added.

Katie nodded. "He called it ... er, Gurmugdu, aye?" When Ta'rel smiled and nodded, she asked, "And since every name is a description here, what's it mean?"

Ta'rel answered. "Gurmugdu mean 'blood and salt.'"

"Well, that's certainly reassuring," Miles sighed in his best sardonic tone. "So I guess he was right about this being a place to get a barge downriver to the city at the river fork?"

Ta'rel nodded. "Yes. Most good here. More than town."

"Let me guess: because the town wouldn't be healthy for us either?" *Sure is starting to sound like* everyplace *around here is outside the wire.*

Ta'rel conferred briefly with Peter, who explained, "The town is not healthy either, but that wasn't the major reason he directed us here. This is just a rock landing that juts out into the river. It's not a good location for a town, but has long been used as a safe mooring for boats. So we can get aboard without attracting any attention. Secondly, he believes it is where Eku's beacon touched the river, not further downriver in the town."

"So, he means to put us on Eku's trail?" Katie said brightly, straightening.

"More than that; we may be able to talk to some ... persons who saw him. According to the vavasor at the jetty—"

"The vava-what?" Craig asked.

"A vavasor is, ah ... a vassal of a vassal, and that's who's in charge of the rock mooring or jetty. Ta'rel says that a barge would normally have been waiting there for another few days. But a large group of trog—eh, praakht arrived on the north bank from out of the wastes, eager to unload some equipment of a warrior-lord that was apparently stolen by a frail and injured human—"

"Shit!" O'Garran exclaimed, on his feet before he'd known he was in motion. "Eku?"

Peter smiled. "The description certainly fits, right down to the magic armor. The praakht were so eager to get underway that they paid for all the remaining cargo space on the barge to set out to Forkus immediately." Ta'rel leaned over with another suggestion.

"What's he say?" Craig asked.

Ta'rel turned to him. "When we go to boat, armor is closed. When boat stop at town, we stay on. You hide."

"Why?" Katie asked with a frown.

Ta'rel shook his head: a very human gesture for a being whose face resembled that of a fleshy turtle. "Bosses and big leader at river town. *They* bad to you. Very."

"And who's this leader we have to hide from?" O'Garran asked, barely suppressing a sneer.

Ta'rel's voice became quiet. "He x'qao."

"Who's X'qao?"

Wu shook his head. "Not who: *what* is an x'qao."

"Fine: what's an x'qao?"

"You met little x'qa, Cheef-Ogarrn," Ta'rel said with a respectful nod. "When you find Katy-Sumurz."

Miles almost laughed. "Those little runts? They couldn't even—"

"No. They most little of all x'qa. They name is 'qo. But at town, boat-place: each boss is vavasor, a big x'qao."

Even if Ta'rel hadn't had such human eyes and expressions, Miles was sure he'd still have read the terror in them. "Okay, we'll stay on the boat then, Ta'rel. And we'll follow your lead. Now tell me about the barge." O'Garran smiled. "I've a bit of skill with them." SEALs were increasingly oriented for EVA ops, but a high level of nautical skill remained practical. Besides, it was the root of the service's identity, tradition, and pride.

But Ta'rel stared in confusion. "Barge…is barge."

*Oh, fer the love of—*"Yes, I'm aware of that. How big is it?"

"Eh…eh…it carry ten dustkine. Maybe twelve."

*Well, if I knew what dustkine are, maybe that would be useful information. But since I don't—*"What's it made of?"

Ta'rel brightened immediately. "Bone," he said proudly.

Miles stared. When that did not elicit any further explanation, he repeated, "Bone?"

Ta'rel looked confused, checked the four human faces. "Yes. Bone. What else?"

O'Garran sat back and laughed. *Bone. Well, of course: "what else?" Not like there are any trees here, so sure: bone.* "And what do you call the city to which we're heading, the one where the rivers meet?"

"That is Forkus."

This time Miles did chortle. *Forkus: the city at—surprise, surprise!—the fork in the rivers. Well, at least that name made sense.*

And against all odds, it was beginning to look like they might all get to the rendezvous. Late on drop-day plus five, the fused transponder signals of Bannor and Duncan had blended into Newton's. A day after, that growing cluster grew larger when Ayana's and Dora's had merged with it. And very late on drop-day plus seven, the now pregnant icon had been joined by those of Caine and Yaargraukh.

The only exception was, of course, Eku's. But now it was all but certain he'd been heading in that very direction for two days, and O'Garran began to see a slim chance that, despite much bad fortune and worse timing, the whole Crewe might be converging on the same point in space and time. Which might very well provide an opportunity to rescue Frog-pet and so, face this mad, hostile world together. It was almost enough to make him smile.

Far to the south, a faint cacophony of growling and squealing arose. Ta'rel nodded in satisfaction. So more than one creature had found the bait bag.

Katie Somers shook her head. "An' ye mean to tell me that the beasts out there are fighting over . . . shite?"

Now that was worth a smile, in which Miles happily indulged. "Well, it might have started that way, but I'm guessing that now some of the contenders have started in after each other." Miles picked up his pack and musette. "And we get a carefree walk down to the river, so everyone wins. Well . . . except whoever winds up as breakfast, back there. I've got point, LT."

# Chapter Seventeen

Caine injected water into the rehydration port of the three-hundred-gram Dornaani ration and watched the packet balloon as though it might explode.

The others stared as their own meal packs underwent similar transformations. When the seams were taut and expansion tapered, Dora muttered, "How long do we wait? I'm hungry."

Newton's reply was flat. "Three minutes. Be careful when you open it."

"Why?"

Duncan answered as he poked his ration tentatively. "The exothermic heating core makes it pretty hot."

Yaargraukh, the only one without a ration in front of him, reached into his musette bag. "I prefer the local food." He produced a thick, almost conical tuber that Caine had sampled on the march to Newton's camp and had mentally nicknamed "the bitter potato."

Bannor stared sidelong at him. "I only finished mine yesterday because I didn't want to insult our friends." He shifted his eyes momentarily toward the five h'achgai busy with their own supper, ten meters further down what they all called "the trench line" of Newton's camp.

Yaargraukh's wormlike tongue flitted out for a moment. "Then clearly you have not tried their sea leaves, yet."

Bannor shuddered; several others had similar, involuntary motions. "Makes the tubers taste great, by comparison."

Caine shrugged but could not disagree. The freshwater weeds had to be soaked in brine for days to leach out chemicals that made them painfully indigestible. However, they remained edible even longer than the tubers and were—reportedly—far more palatable when combined with other foodstuffs. "We're lucky we can eat anything on this planet," he observed. "Ten days ago, we didn't even know we'd be able to breathe."

"Yeah," Dora replied, "but that doesn't make dinner taste any better!" She frowned mightily at the faces around her...before smiling through a sharp laugh.

Riordan smiled. It was never entirely clear when Pandora Veriden was being genuinely crabby or when it was an act. He suspected that she wasn't always sure herself. "I'm just glad that we haven't needed to use the emergency rations until now."

"For which I will be the expendable taster," Duncan announced as he opened his swollen ration packet. A puff of steam burst out. The aroma was not like any that Riordan knew from terrestrial kitchens but was still moderately appetizing. The others did the same and there was relative silence as they sampled the contents. The only reactions were a few relieved sighs; it wasn't home cooking, but it was entirely acceptable. Unfortunately, they were too useful to consume except at need. "Hopefully, we won't need to use many more of these," Caine added.

Ayana nodded as new sighs—this time, of regret—answered Riordan's reminder. "Once we enter the city, acquiring local food must be the first order of business," she agreed. "As soon as we have found safe lodgings, of course." She glanced sideways at Caine. "Arashk has made a suitable recommendation, I understand?"

"He has. He's confident that we'll be welcome there."

"Then why won't he come with us?" Dora asked suspiciously. "And why are all the h'achgai sitting over there, having their own private conversation?"

Riordan shrugged. "Because they've got to make the same decision we do: whether it's best to enter the city together with us or on their own. And, like us, that could involve considerations that might be confidential. Or unflattering."

Bannor frowned. "As in, they don't really trust us?"

Caine shook his head. "They're past that, now, I think. But it could mean trouble for them if we arrive together. Given our gear, the local assumption will be that they are our servitors. If so, then they could get targeted along with us, if any of the local lords believe us to be a bunch of roving harrows or scythes."

Duncan held up a pausing palm. "Sir, can we back up? That's the second time you've used those two terms. Maybe other folks know what they mean, but I haven't heard them before." Heads in the circle nodded.

Riordan did not try to keep the rue out of his answering smile. "Sorry, all: I'm losing track of what Yaargraukh and I have relayed and what we haven't. Scythes are shock troops and personal guards of the local lords. Harrows are their commanders. They're collectively referred to as reapers, sometimes. But they are *always* furnished with the best weapons and armor."

"And evidently other technologically sophisticated devices," Yaargraukh added, "but we cannot be sure what kinds. The h'achgai still use many words for which the translator has not been able to assign equivalents."

Bannor nodded. "So Arashk and Company took one look at your kits and figured that's what you were: harrows or scythes."

"Yes, but it was not merely our equipment which led them to that conclusion. Both our respective species are common in reaper groups."

Bannor stared at Yaargraukh. "The locals: they know about Hkh'Rkh?"

Caine nodded. "Either that, or Hkh'Rkh look very much like this world's apex predators: the x'qai."

Dora's brow furrowed. "You mean those things you guys"—she gestured toward Bannor and Duncan—"killed just south of here? He doesn't look a bit like either of them."

Yaargraukh pony-nodded. "Apparently, there are many different kinds of x'qai. Apparently, I resemble one of the more fearsome, if rare, varieties. Which further confused the h'achgai."

"You mean, that you were out in the wastes alone except for the commodore?"

"No, I mean they initially assumed that I was the leader." Good-natured grins sprung up around the group until it dawned upon them that Yaargraukh was speaking in earnest. "That was why they did not make a closer approach when they first detected me. Apparently this variety of x'qai is not only very dangerous, but frequently, very influential. The h'achgai became even more intrigued, and cautious, after discovering that I had met and begun traveling with a lone human. Journeying alone in the wastes is considered extremely hazardous. Even the most powerful harrows are unlikely to do so without a sizable detachment of servitors."

"So," Ayana mused, "they deemed you the stronger, and so, the leader."

"The h'achgai are refreshing in their perspicacity," Yaargraukh agreed blithely. The tip of his black garter-snake tongue poked out so briefly that a fast blink would have missed it.

Caine stopped grinning to add, "So when we arrived here, and they saw all of you in roughly the same equipment, they became even more certain that we were harrows and scythes. Despite the apparent contradictions."

"Such as the way we treat them as equals?" Ayana ventured.

"That and our lack of a standard or symbol." Riordan paused. "At least, until they saw those," he added, pointing at the vacc and duty suits worn by Newton, Duncan, and Dora. All were Terran, the four-pointed star of the CTR emblazoned over the heart.

"Oops," Dora murmured.

Caine laughed. "Actually, I think it put them at ease. They were unnerved by the idea of this many 'lordless' harrows and scythes wandering around the wastes."

Bannor frowned. "Still, I think we need to cover those insignias when we enter town. They could lead to some difficult questions, particularly if the Ktor are here or drop by. For now, I say we stay under the radar as much as possible."

"Concur," Caine said. "Although, I think they're realizing that, symbol or no, we're not anyone's household troops. At the same time, we're not a bunch of loose cannons. But that makes us even more dangerous."

Duncan nodded. "Because we're a complete unknown. Even rogue reapers fit into a pattern, of sorts."

"Which is why," Caine concluded, "I think the smartest move is for the h'achgai to enter the city a day or two after us and from a different direction. In the meantime, Arashk used my mono-scope to point out the place he recommended to us. It's pretty formidable. Built up from the remains of an old ruin, I think."

"And who is this potential benefactor?" Newton asked dubiously.

"His title, as best I can translate it, is the Advocate or Defender or Legate. Arashk believes we'll be allowed into his citadel with minimal difficulty."

Ayana's voice sounded almost as doubtful as Newton's. "How can Arashk be so certain?"

"Because, like him, we are humans who do not serve x'qai."

Duncan was frowning. "Okay, but even if we can get in, how can we be sure this Legate won't betray us?"

Caine shrugged. "Arashk swore to it in front of Hresh, who has dedicated himself to the path of a chogrun: a h'achgai oathkeeper."

Duncan rubbed his nose. "Sir, that still adds up to the h'achgai saying, 'You can trust us because we told you so ourselves'... doesn't it?"

"No," Yaargraukh answered in a quiet voice. "It does not. Not among beings who must live out on such wastes." His black-marble eyes swiveled on their stalks, shifting from one face to the next. "Oaths are crucial for groups to continue to exist in such dangerous places and with such perilous foes. They are not easily made or given, which is why the rest of the h'achgai were visibly surprised when Arashk pledged the truth of his words by formally asking Hresh to witness them. It was not a scene crafted to deceive us."

Bannor nodded. "I agree. I'm sure they could be crafty if they wanted, but that's not the way they've been acting. Besides, I've noticed that they never speak of having lords over them. Arashk may be their leader—dregdo, is it?—but every time they speak of their tribes, or clans, or whatever, the word they keep using is dregdir: a group or council." He frowned. "Every other power center they mention—except humans—seems to be organized as hierarchies. With pretty brutal pecking orders, I might add."

Ayana nodded. "I think this is true." She turned to Riordan. "So, if we are asked about our business when in the city, what shall we say?"

"Firstly," he answered with a smile, "it's best if you let me and Yaargraukh do the talking. We've had five days with the translator and tutors. Secondly, Arashk recommends that if we're asked, we just say we're going to meet the Advocate or Legate. It's the most logical destination for a group of humans who are not showing an allegiance symbol, have no servitors, but still have harrow-level equipment."

"And what if we're stopped by x'qai?" Dora asked, arms crossed. "They sound like their motto is 'kill first, talk later.' Assuming they talk."

"And not all of them do," Yaargraukh replied with a slow rotation of his neck. "But according to the h'achgai, their impatience and combativeness means that they are rarely given the duties of sentries, guards, or patrols. If we see them in the streets at all, we should treat them as we would any other warriors moving from one location to another: give them a wide berth. Even if they desire a confrontation, their leaders will not permit it."

Dora nodded. "Fair enough. But how do we even know which beings are x'qai? The two you showed us out there"—she waved toward the site of Bannor and Duncan's engagement—"don't look anything alike. *Madre de Dios*, one of them looked like it was half warthog! And now you say that there are ones that look like you? If we don't know all the kinds, then how do we know to avoid them?"

Caine put aside his meal. "Most of them shed very little IR through their skin, probably because it's so thick. And no, let's not try to puzzle through the metabolic implications just now. The other thing is that if a creature has sex organs—I'm not talking about sex characteristics but actual *organs*—it is not a x'qao."

"Then how do they reproduce?" Duncan asked.

"By depositing their young, or eggs, or whatever, in live hosts," Newton answered in a very calm voice. "I suspect this is why the h'achgai's own word for them translates as 'killspawn.'

"I had little opportunity to examine the remains of the two you killed, but in place of gonads, they had what looked like ovipositors. The one with the resemblance to an entelodont was already being consumed by other, smaller insects that had apparently lived on or in its body. Symbiotic and, or, parasitic, interactions may be fundamental among the xenobiota of this world."

The other humans in the group looked mildly revolted or nauseated by Baruch's conjecture. Yaargraukh, however, tilted his head in curiosity. "I have never heard the word entelodont. What is it?"

"It is a pre-Pleistocene megafauna species that is the ancestor of modern swine."

Even Yaargraukh stared at Newton, now.

He stared back. "I was captivated by prehistoric animals when I was young." His stare became a glare. "Is that so unusual?"

"Not at all," Caine assured him, but failed to add, *It's just hard to imagine that you were ever a little kid who loved dinosaurs and mastodons.*

Duncan broke the silence before it went from being uncomfortable to embarrassing. "So what have the h'achgai told you about—uh, they call it Forkus?" He gestured to the sprawl that clung low to the northern horizon.

Caine nodded. "They say it's typical of most cities here; everything is orchestrated around food. Growing it, moving it, distributing it, storing it. It sounds like a barter economy where a single day's worth of food is the coin of the realm."

Bannor stared at the sere lands around them. "I can see why."

Caine nodded. "There are some seasonal caravans, funded by lords, that haul finished goods and high-value items. But the majority of the trade—food, hides, basic resources—is carried by smaller trade groups which depend on porters and smaller draft animals. The h'achgai don't live in the cities, but move smaller volumes of rarer goods between them. They're also prospectors."

Dora looked up quickly. "You mean, they look for ore?"

"That or things left behind in ruins. I didn't understand most of what they were trying to explain, but one look at the city through the monoscope shows this planet had at least an industrial-era civilization."

"So they might be salvaging metal, too."

Riordan nodded. "You've seen the city: a core of larger buildings built up from or atop advanced ruins, surrounded by what looks like a single-story adobe sprawl. Arashk said that, the taller the building, the more powerful the lord, particularly if the upper stories have been turned into water towers."

"Okay," Dora continued, "so let's say this Advocate or Legate is willing to take us in. That doesn't mean we get to stay for free. So how do we pay him? What do we have to trade?"

Duncan rubbed his nose again. "That's what the commodore tasked me to determine. Bottom line: we've been using damn near everything we dropped with. The only things we haven't touched are the emergency rebreathers, the spare filters, and the backup Dornaani air tanks. Unless you want to trade away your spare boots? Or maybe your kits' dietary and performance supplements, along with the broad-spectrum antibiotics and antivirals?" The reactions were as emphatic as they were negative.

"So, in point of fact," Newton summarized drily, "we are simply very dangerous paupers." He seemed gratified by the answering chuckles. "Duncan, it sounds to me like you have done this before."

"You mean being a bean counter?" Solsohn sighed. "Yeah, logistics and supply always fell to me on operations. Partly because I can remember the stats without taking notes, but also because that's the kind of job you get when you're not on an entry team."

Yaargraukh's eyes swiveled toward him. "What was your role?"

Duncan's tone was muted, evasive. "Standoff support."

Dora almost sneered. "He was a sniper. Didn't you know?"

"I did not." The Hkh'Rkh sounded perplexed. "Why did you not volunteer that information? It is a great asset."

Solsohn didn't meet any of the human eyes in the supper circle. "Well, there's a lot of prejudice against that specialization." He glanced at Dora. "Hell, even assassins hate you."

Veriden's eyes narrowed even as they brightened. Her mouth worked for a moment. Then she looked away, unable to deny the frank truth of his statement.

Bannor nodded. "Yeah, a lot of soldiers even have mixed feelings about their own snipers. At least until someone, or maybe the whole unit, owes their life to that guardian angel looking down a scope a klick or more away."

Riordan shrugged. "And now, such nice distinctions are as far behind us as Earth and all its civilized attitudes. As Yaargraukh said, every skill, every asset is a gift."

Duncan glanced at Caine. "So, speaking about assets: since we don't have any goods to trade, what about services?"

Veriden sat bolt upright. "And get embroiled in turf wars before we even know who's who?"

Duncan returned her wide-eyed stare with a gaze of exaggerated patience. "Information and education are services, too, you know."

Caine put up his palm. "Let's cross those bridges when we come to them. Knowledge may prove to be our best trade option, but until we know more about what locals would want and what they might do with it, we can't determine what's safe to share and what isn't." He looked around the group; everyone had finished their meal. "Anything else before we break into watches?"

The silence that answered was tense, rather than settled.

Dora sighed. "Well, someone has to say it, so it might as well be me: this is our last chance to change our plans and go after Frog-pe—uh, Eku. Once we show our faces in the city, we'll be known and probably followed."

Riordan nodded and understood Veriden's searching gaze. Only four hours earlier, Eku's biosigns had gone dark. Losing him was unacceptable. So was losing all the evidence against Hsontlosh, since he was the only one who had any hope of getting through the traitorous loji's firewalls.

But the importance of those records was part of some unforeseeable—and likely unattainable—future in which they returned home. Right now, all that mattered was the Crewe: keeping it alive, unified, and together. Which is why the answer Caine had to give was also the hardest: "No. We keep to the plan." Dora's and Newton's mouths were both opening to protest as he added, "For the past two days, Eku's transponder has been moving east on the river: not beside it, but *on* it. It's the only way his transponder could move seventy kilometers during every twelve hours of daylight, particularly when you consider his injuries."

"To which he might have succumbed," Newton murmured.

"Doctor Baruch, like me, you saw his biosigns before they winked out. Tell us what you observed."

Newton didn't look away, but his eyes wavered. "They were fundamentally normative. Frankly, they'd been improving. Probably because he was no longer moving on foot."

"So what might lead to the sudden loss of signs?"

"Removing the suit or death."

"Let's stay on that second alternative. What kind of death would terminate the biosigns so suddenly?"

Newton shrugged. "Decapitation. Perhaps."

Bannor leaned forward. "What do you mean, 'perhaps'?"

Baruch sighed reluctantly. "Even decapitation does not cause an immediate termination of biosigns. What's more, the first few moments after a terminal trauma such as beheading would precipitate dire and profoundly erratic readings."

Dora looked at Caine, eyes wide. "So you believe that Eku is—?"

Caine dropped his hand like a headsman's axe. "I don't believe *anything* at this point, because we don't have any real information beyond the fact that his suit's transponder is still working and moving.

"But it is highly *unlikely* that, after finally getting him on a boat, Eku's captors would then kill him out of hand after

expending all the effort and resources it took to keep him alive.
Hell: they never made more than twenty klicks a day overland.
But now that they're getting close to the first market where they
could trade him, they decide to get rid of him? No: that doesn't
make sense."

Dora was nodding slowly. "The market where they might
trade him: you mean Forkus?"

Riordan nodded, let the information sink in as he looked
into every pair of eyes in the circle, human or otherwise. "Since
Peter's group has working suits, and is already a day into the
same downstream trip that Eku's taking, they surely see what
we are: that he's coming to the very point upon which our two
groups are converging."

"It'll be a wait," Duncan pointed out. "Peter and Company
still have a long stretch of river ahead of them."

"That, also, is to our advantage," Yaargraukh rumbled in a
satisfied tone. "We are not yet in readiness. By the time they
arrive, we shall be."

Riordan nodded, pointed toward the faint firelight flickering
around the greater structures in the distant city. "Everything we'll
need to rescue him—information, supplies, contacts—is in there."

"Contacts?" Ayana repeated. "Do you feel it safe to include
indigenous beings in such an operation?"

Caine shrugged. "If we can surreptitiously reestablish communications with Arashk once we're in the city, then yes, it might
be safe if he's willing to vet those contacts for us. Or maybe the
Advocate or Legate can help with them. Either way, I like that
option more than trying to find and rescue him without local
intel."

Duncan nodded. "Whether Eku's captors mean to trade him
in Forkus or beyond, we won't be able to make a move without
being seen a mile away. So if we don't have locals fronting for us,
the opposition will either move Eku or be waiting to slaughter us."

Bannor was nodding agreement. "That raises a good question:
What are the odds that Eku's captors actually stop here?"

Riordan leaned forward. "I put that same question to Arashk
just before we sat down to dinner. He thinks it's a near certainty,
even if it this city is only a transfer point on the way to a farther
destination."

"Why?"

"Because, given his gear, Eku is either a scythe himself, a minion, or a thief who made off with the equipment. Whoever found him knew that right away, and a second later, realized that merely keeping him around was a high-risk, high-gain proposition. What if his harrow caught up to him? What if the scythes or x'qai of a rival lord hear and get to him first? Besides, anyone who sees his gear will know he's worth his weight in guns. Or gold. Or blood. So if he's too dangerous to keep for long, his captors would be fools not to make best speed to a place where they can trade him out quickly."

"Forkus," Duncan finished.

Dora nodded. "And you can bet that since the bastards holding Eku headed straight for the river, they already have a buyer, or at least a market, in mind. And one they can deal with at arm's length."

Newton frowned. "Why?"

Dora smiled. "Because if you aren't strong enough to hang on to a black-market diamond yourself, you can't risk setting up a trade with the final client. Like as not, all they'd give you is a sincere 'thank you'...just after they take it from your dead hand. That's why smaller gangs can't sell direct to big bosses. They have to use a fence or go through a boss that's stronger than them, but not so strong that they could hold on to the diamond, either."

Riordan smiled. "Sounds like you just finished answering your own question about mounting a direct rescue mission, Dora."

She shook her head. "Never said it was my preference. Just that we had to settle the matter before we go to Forkus. Because once we're in there, who knows what will happen?"

Riordan nodded. "True enough. So let's be ready for it. First watch up. Everybody else, grab as much sleep as you can. Tomorrow's going to be full of unknowns, so it's likely to be a long day."

*Or possibly,* Riordan worried as he smiled fondly at the others, *our last.*

# Chapter Eighteen

Caine paused, shielded his eyes as the sun finished separating itself from the horizon. It painted a bridge of glittering jewels from the far bank to the near one, just a few klicks to the east. There, mote-sized silhouettes led larger, longer ones out into the shining sand flat that lined the water.

"What are they doing?" Dora wondered aloud.

Faces turned toward Caine and Yaargraukh; their time with the h'achgai had given them some advance knowledge of what they would encounter on their way into Forkus. The Hkh'Rkh looked over. Riordan nodded; he'd been fielding most of the questions since they'd set out before dawn.

Yaargraukh lifted his head slightly. "The figures are those of workers; I do not know if you would deem them serfs or slaves. After the height of the backflow, they gather alluvial soils before the flats become dry. They are much richer than the soils of the wastes and are crucial to crop production."

Ayana was frowning. "How is it that the river's backflow reaches these flats? We are almost three thousand kilometers from the ocean."

Yaargraukh's neck circled lazily. "We asked the same question, but the h'achgai lacked relevant knowledge. It may be a combination of the profound gravitic pull of the moon and the extreme weather we observed from orbit. But whatever the cause, the tidal reach on this river exceeds the greatest on my homeworld or yours.

"As far as river rising to run across these flats, I suspect it may be caused by the long bend you can see in the river, just before it reaches the city. That seems to impede the backflow and causes the excess to flood the lowlands at those times when it cannot move through that meander swiftly enough."

Newton nodded. "I have seen that occur. But what creatures are the workers leading?"

"They are domesticated examples of ubiquitous, and danger-ous, herd animals known as dustkine. They drag the soils back to the city's agricultural zones."

Duncan shielded his eyes. "Which look to be just two klicks ahead."

"That is correct. As we approach it, we may have melee weap-ons at the ready, but not firearms. Arashk indicated that they would likely be presumed to signify hostile intent."

"I detect no patrols or watch posts," Newton replied, scanning the thinly vegetated margin ahead.

"Indeed. There are none at the outskirts," Yaargraukh confirmed.

Dora nodded. "But there could still be eyes watching us approach, eh?"

Yaargraukh stared meaningfully at her. "I suspect there are *always* eyes watching."

The brownish-green patches that marked Forkus' agricultural limit hardly looked like vegetation. "Don't tell me they actually eat that," Bannor muttered, his tone as much one of disbelief as disgust.

Caine laughed. "You're looking at the staple crop, I'm afraid. And it's just as unappetizing as you'd expect."

"It stinks, too," Duncan observed, nose wrinkly.

"That is the ordure of wild dustkine," Yaargraukh added.

"They just let them roam in here? Don't they eat the, the...?" He looked at the almost scabrous growth.

"It is lichen. And yes, they do eat it, but in doing so and tarrying here, they, er, enrich the soil even more."

Dora spat. "Well, this just gets better and better. Do they at least hunt some of these dirt cows?"

"Some," Caine answered, "but it's a major undertaking for both the praakht who serve the local lords. Usually, they have nothing better than stone weapons. Yet, dustkine are almost twice as large as their domesticated cousins and almost as tough-hided as an x'qao. So it's a long hunt, which depends on separating the most vulnerable while threatening the others' rear flanks."

"Heh. Then why don't the lords send x'qai to hunt them?"

Yaargraukh's neck wobbled again. "Because when they do, there is nothing left for anyone else."

As they drew abreast of the first mud-brick constructions at the outskirts of the city, Riordan realized that having spent days conceiving of them as "adobe" had put a very specific image in his head: the even, orderly buildings associated with the pueblos of the American Southwest.

What he encountered now was anything but. Leaning, awkward lumps—you couldn't really call them domes—dotted the skirts of the city. Ahead, they became more densely packed and grew larger, but not in the form of more massive single structures. The buildings ahead were simply chaotic agglomerations of the same sad heaps that were greeting them on the edge of town. Colored and shaped like dung piles that had failed multiple attempts at mitosis, each one's entrance was guarded by an armed praakh or two. Or sometimes, in the case of the bigger dung heaps, three. And the smell—

Bannor's question echoed Riordan's metaphoric musings: "Are they actually made from dung?"

"No." Dora's reply was as certain as it was grim. "Dung is what they're *burning*."

Duncan frowned toward the already warm sun. "For heat?"

"For everything," she said. "Think there aren't places still doing it on Earth? Tag along with me, next time we get back."

As they advanced deeper into the thickening wilderness of cob huts, eyes followed them, some long after they'd passed: they were among the very few heading toward the tall, ancient structures near the river juncture. The tighter the quarters became, the more Riordan noticed the ammonic reek of ketosis. A growing portion of the faces were so haggard and empty that they hardly seemed self-aware. The most malnourished barely moved, and those that did were chased away from even the most dismal hovels.

In addition to the ketosis, another stink grew as they approached the core of Forkus: that of tanneries and equally odiferous bone-works. The h'achgai had shown Riordan examples of that craft:

finely turned arrow shafts, spear hafts, tools, even a collapsible drying rack. When he'd asked about the process, the Dornaani translator became useless: too many words for which there were no equivalents. Not that any of the Crewe was presently concerned with those gaps in their nascent command of "Low Praakht"; they were too busy adapting to the overpowering mix of odors that was a daily reality for the inhabitants of Forkus. Most of whom were a species they'd not seen yet, but were instantly recognizable from Arashk's painstaking descriptions:

Praakht. Their complexions recalled the evolving norm of Earth itself: not so dark as Newton's (who was equal parts African and Samoan) or as light as Dora's olive-bronze. There was little discernible variation in their hair color—dark to very dark—but here and there, hazel and green eyes stared out from beneath the heavy bone brow ridge that Newton had predicted they might see.

The h'achgai's descriptions had led Baruch to expect many characteristics associated with Neanderthals, so he'd familiarized the group with the most likely differences. Some of the Crewe had nearly—or actually—rolled their eyes at his forensic precision, but Lieutenant Baruch's conjectures were proving impressively proleptic. Caine half-turned to mutter as much back at their hulking doctor.

Newton grunted. "They are not just Neanderthal, though. And there is a great deal of variance in the ratios of limb length."

"Malnutrition?" Ayana wondered.

Baruch shook his head. "Unlikely. A diet so deficient that it will cause gross skeletal stunting would have other health effects." He glanced sideways at a particularly short-legged yet broad fellow hefting a stone axe as they passed. "His role, musculature, and weight suggest he has always been strong and well fed, meaning his limb ratios are not genetically remarkable."

"Then what would cause such dysmorphia?"

Newton's tone was polite if a bit impatient. "It is not dysmorphia if it is a normal variation within a species, as I suspect. As to the cause it..." He stole a glance at another male whose proportions were more akin to their own, but whose features were narrower, sharper, even elongated in places. "The regularity of the variations suggests hybridization. But with what, I cannot begin to guess."

Dora eyed a female warrior whose features were so absolutely like those of a Neanderthal that she could have walked out of a life-size diorama in a museum. "Y'know what we haven't seen, yet?"

Yaargraukh glanced at her. "A market."

She nodded. "I've seen some bartering for a few items, but nothing more than that."

Caine heard her hanging tone. "But—?"

"But I've been listening to what's going on in those hovels, looking when I can see inside. They're making their own clothes and tools, I think. At least the basics."

Bannor nodded as he slowly tuned his focus from one compass heading to another. "You're right. Which is damned strange."

Duncan frowned. "Why? Maybe that's all they can afford."

Bannor's answering nod was tighter. "Exactly, but you tend to see that in smaller, not larger communities."

"Green Beanie is right," Dora muttered. "Little town means little trade. People make do or make their own. Big town or city? Big money means less barter. Even in the poorest parts." She stuck her chin at the path before them. "We're not passing through a slum; this is how Forkus is, for the most part. Make do or make it yourself."

Ayana shrugged. "Actually, all the pieces fit."

"Meaning?"

"There is almost no plant life. The wastes are vast and dangerous. The only trade arteries seem to be rivers. Resources are scarce. Dried dung is the primary fuel." She seemed surprised by their still-questioning glances. "What we call industry cannot grow here. Food is the basic currency, goods after that." She frowned. "It is not the praakht that are stunted; it is their world."

"Assuming it's really their world at all," Riordan amended. "Looks like we're coming to the better part of town."

Duncan leaned forward, trying to look between him and Yaargraukh. "How can you tell?"

Riordan opened the gap a little. "Look up ahead, right along our path."

"Huh," Solsohn huffed, "I guess it was only a matter of time before we ran into a welcoming committee."

"That is a strange expression," Yaargraukh commented, "since brandished firearms are rarely a sign of welcome."

By the time they'd closed to within speaking distance, the armed contingent before them had almost doubled in number. Whether that was out of precaution or curiosity was unclear.

Riordan allowed that his orders might have amplified both. He'd had the whole group seal up and lower their visors as they approached, and those with Dornaani vacc suits had initialized what Duncan had dubbed "armor mode." Bannor had his hand cannon ready within a sack; Caine wondered if these guards would even know what it was, but there was no reason to take that chance.

Yaargraukh was, by necessity, the one exception. Having neither suit nor helmet of any kind, he approached without any additional, impressive gear. But he and Caine had already considered this problem and had strategized a way to turn it into an advantage.

Hopefully.

With the Dornaani translator running and patched into its own tactical channel, Riordan took a moment to scan the eight individuals blocking their path. Almost half of them were clearly Homo sapiens, without any visible trace of hybridity. But whereas the h'achgai had indicated that the "original" humans of this world were dark complected—"much darker than him," Arashk had explained, pointing to Newton—all of these were considerably lighter. One would have struck Caine as extremely fair even if he'd seen him in Stockholm's Old Town.

The leader took a step forward from the center of their inverted wedge formation. As he raised a hand for the newcomers to halt, Riordan quickly scanned the remaining, nonhuman members of the city watch.

Two were cadaverously lean, skin taut over facial bones that had probably been human at some point. Or maybe still were. Another was almost as tall as Yaargraukh and either wearing an ornate suit of armor or had a body segmented like an armadillo's, but which had sprouted hard, uneven flanges. Caine mentally doubled the time he'd need to review the video he'd been recording since arriving.

The watch's equipment was even stranger and more varied than they themselves. Their firearms ranged from handguns to heavy rifles, no two the same design. The largest was either some form of cassette- or belt-fed weapon with a bore so large that it could even have been a micro-missile launcher.

Their armor was an even more eclectic—not to say bizarre— mix. Only three of them were wearing complete suits of a single manufacture, none of which were the same, and one of which could have started out in the Tower of London. The other guards boasted protective gear that ranged from chain mail to ballistic composites to random parts of plastic combat armor, sometimes all on a single warrior. Indeed, everything about them—from their highly personalized equipment to their loose formation— underscored that they were, in fact, *warriors*, not soldiers.

The medium-sized leader, who was both fully armored and nearly motionless, nodded to the most idiosyncratically outfit- ted of the others, who strutted forward and emitted a stream of gibberish.

The Dornaani translator tossed out a few equivalences: pro- nouns and articles that probably had their origins in Low Praakht. Or vice versa. Once again, Arashk had allowed them to prepare for this eventuality: that they'd be addressed in one of several more formal or respectful cants, particularly if they attracted the attention of harrows and scythes. And it very much appeared that they had.

Yaargraukh responded to the indecipherable address as they'd planned. "We shall speak in the low tongue."

The spokesman was suddenly less expressive, more collected. *So: his flamboyance is an act. To invite underestimation.*

His demeanor now wholly at odds with his outlandish garb, the human spoke with subtle menace rather than excited rancor. "Do you mean to insult us with this speech?"

"What is amiss with our speech?" Yaargraukh made his pronunciation so harsh that it was almost indecipherable and decidedly unpleasant to the ear. Hkh'Rkh had many sounds that the human mouth was incapable of duplicating. According to Arashk, the speech of the x'qao had many that were similar... which was now proving useful.

As he and Yaargraukh had hoped, that gave the spokesman further pause. When he resumed, it was in a tone of an equal or even a servant, not a master. "How should I call you, *Arurkré*?"

The Dornaani translator buzzed uselessly at the last word. But whatever it meant, the change in tone and posture suggested it was one of careful respect.

"With all due respect to your masters," Yaargraukh replied, "if I wished to announce myself by name, I would have been preceded by a herald."

The spokesman glanced back at his motionless, grey-draped superior, who made a casual gesture.

The liaison nodded, turned back to ask a different question. "Where are you from?"

"I would have my own question answered first, which I ask again: Why do you take offense at our speech?"

"You speak Low Praakht. Poorly."

Yaargraukh released a stream of an almost forgotten tongue of the Hkh'Rkh. It sounded like a rockslide killing a herd of angry cattle. "Do you find this tongue more seemly?"

Another one of the watch's number—one of the near-cadaverous humanoids—responded to a gesture from the leader, whose thoroughly modern combat helmet remained sealed. "I have not heard that tongue before." He turned toward Yaargraukh. "And it is hard for us to understand you, Arurkré."

Riordan waited for the translator to identify that term or title... but to no avail. "Nothing," he whispered on the tactical channel to Yaargraukh, who would continue to simply ignore the word. So far, that strategy—avoiding any requests for clarification—was working well enough. Instead, he simply gestured to Caine.

Riordan eye-triggered his visor; it opened slowly. "We have no knowledge of any other languages in this land." He kept his voice calm, indifferent.

"'In this land'?" was the new speaker's gravelly repetition-as-question.

Riordan shrugged, gestured to the six impassive figures behind, all in sealed suits. "We chose to have them educated in this tongue, that they might not become too proud."

That statement caused a mix of puzzlement and consternation, and Riordan was pretty sure why: they were wondering, *would ten apparent scythes tolerate such treatment?* The only logical answer would be that the two who were speaking were so fearsome and powerful that they did not dare do otherwise. Riordan waited patiently as the welcoming committee completed that calculus.

The first spokesmen resumed, this time with a hint of actual deference. "Do you know whose domain you enter?"

"We know enough to wonder if that question is a trap. Is not Forkus a domain shared by many great ones?" The startled reaction proved the value of Arashk's knowledge once again. Before the speaker could recover, Caine followed with, "As far as the names of the great, we cannot know that the names we have been given are current. Besides, any we fail to name might perceive that as a slight." He made sure his smile was utterly humorless. "It would be imprudent to give offense and make enemies before we have even entered into the city proper."

Several small smiles were the only answer to Riordan's observation...until a broad-chested animal with jaws like a predatory hippopotamus rumbled out from behind one of the highest, humpbacked fusion of numerous adobe hovels. Its rider was of the same species as the other extremely lean warriors in the group, who bowed slightly as she prompted her savage-looking mount toward Riordan. She had a lance in her free hand, tipped with a long, chromatically bright sliver of metal and fixed with a red pennant. A brace of varied flintlock and percussion-cap pistols were snugged in saddle holsters in front of either of her thighs.

She reined in the growling, drooling beast a meter in front of Riordan and looked him up and down. She did the same with Yaargraukh, then glanced back at the perimeter guards. It was not exactly a provocative glance, but Riordan saw the warning in it: *Contradict what I'm about to say...if you dare.*

She turned back abruptly. "In this city, you make final answer to my Liege Shvarkh'khag, sworn suppliant of Brazhglu'u, for any offenses you may give or laws you may break. Although there are few restrictions upon such as you, show the restraint that you yourself would expect, Arurkré"—she leaned toward Yaargraukh—"or that harrows would show any lord, in any land. Including your own."

She was about to tug her mount away, paused. "With respect, *X'qagrat'r*," she said to Yaargraukh in a voice that sounded disapproving rather than deferential, "it does you no honor to have servitors that sound like hawkers in a 'vansary paddock."

She started at the voice in which he answered her: sharp with authority and the clashing of a horn-hard split palate. "And now that they know my discipline, I will allow my servitors to learn the languages appropriate to their station." He paused before adding. "In my own time." He was very still for a long moment. Everyone, including the Crewe, was visibly motionless, eager, and possibly fearful, at what he might say next. Caine found himself beginning to worry as well until the Hkh'Rkh asked, first of the rider and then of the liaison, "Have you other questions?"

The thin rider simply shrugged and returned behind the cover of the tumorous pile of rammed earth structures from which she'd emerged.

The liaison swallowed. "No, Arurkré," he murmured. "You and your scythes—"

Yaargraukh gestured toward Caine and then Bannor as he lifted his head.

"—and your *harrows* may pass," the human corrected hastily.

Without acknowledging the speaker's permission or deference, Yaargraukh led them past the guards, and into the shadows cast by the tall ruins at the center of Forkus.

"Report," ordered Riordan as soon as he'd resealed his visor and checked that his radio was sending the weakest possible signal.

Bannor and Dora offered similar assessments: there had been no observable reaction force supporting the guards, and no one was following them. "Of course," she added, "there's no telling what's possible in this crazy place."

Riordan was inclined to agree with her. "Newton: species?"

The doctor began with a heavy sigh. "Before planetfall, we knew of two human varieties: Ktor and terrestrial. After landing, we found what appear to be two more: h'achgai and praakht. Now, we see yet another—the thin ones—and a biped that might be partly human but is certainly mixed with something else, judging from its . . . er, hide? Skin? Perhaps it is part x'qao. Which are themselves yet *another* new form of intelligent life."

"For some values of 'intelligent,'" Bannor grumbled.

Newton was undeterred. "In short, we have doubled the number of known sapient species and subspecies since we dropped. And all are humanoid. I hardly know what else to say."

*Well, I* do: *"and we discovered* all *of them on the very first planet we found beyond the Dornaani's self-imposed survey perimeter." What the hell was going on here twenty millennia ago? Or more?* But that was a discussion for later: much later. Instead, Riordan wanted Duncan's feedback on—"Technical?"

Solsohn exhaled. "Also crazy. You saw that whacky mix of firearms and armor. No weapon matched any other, and only a few parts of the protective gear did. Even the age and usage defied any pattern."

"What do you mean?"

"I mean the rider's pistols were probably local manufacture. Visor zoom-in showed crude casting, bone furniture. Some of the watch's guns looked completely rebuilt; every part had different levels of craftsmanship and probably different alloys. But then there are other guns that aren't rebuilt at all. And I don't mean they look as if they were preserved under some local version of Tutankhamun's tomb; I mean they are *factory*-new. Which makes no sense: not one of our thermal scans showed anything large or hot enough for industrial-era production."

Dora's voice was haunted. "Maybe rogue Ktor traders *do* come out here?"

Bannor *tsk*ed. "If so, why would they leave that wreck hanging in far orbit? It's good salvage. And that begs yet another question: Why would they come *here*? Hardly looks like this world is a trove of valuable resources."

"There is another possibility," Duncan realized in a hushed voice. "Remember what we saw on Turkh'saar? Everything the Ktor swiped from the twentieth century was in that super-cosmolene. Nothing had decayed or aged."

Before anyone could agree or demur, Ayana murmured, "My linguistic report may bear on that observation."

"Go ahead," Riordan muttered, slowing as they neared the first of the ancient ruins. X'qai of different types were ranging between them. "And please, make it fast."

"I did not get consistent directional audio of the conversation among the patrol that met us, but the fragments confirm that whatever language they speak among themselves has more than coincidental similarities to older Ktoran dialects."

"Wait," Dora objected, "I know you heard the Perekmeres bastards talking in Ktoran all the time, but are you saying they made you learn their version of Shakespeare?"

"More their equivalent of *Beowulf*. And no, they did not teach me, but they have many sayings, and the ones they attribute to the Progenitors are still rendered in that ancient tongue."

"How much did you understand?"

"Nothing, Commodore. I cannot translate it. It is more akin to hearing cadences and phonetic similarities that are still shared by languages as far removed as ancient Icelandic and modern English."

Riordan frowned. "Could the Ktoran influence be as old as these ruins?"

"Sir, I doubt that terrestrial models of linguistic drift and shift obtain on this world. Earth was inherently more conducive to travel and migration. We also devoted many of our plentiful resources to shorten those travel times and remove obstructions."

"So you are saying—?"

"The introduction of Ktoran speech could be as recent as a few dozen decades ago or a few dozen millennia."

"No matter which, it is hardly welcome news," Newton grumbled.

"Indeed not," Riordan agreed, suppressing a shudder. "Is everyone's destination guidon still showing? Good." He glanced at the direction his own was indicating. Two tall, reclaimed ruins stood on that northeast heading, each capped by a bowl-shaped cistern. Looking between them, Caine could just make out a low but massive stone structure near the river. Its Paleolithic construction recalled what he had seen at Machu Pichu and Malta. "Only four hundred meters to the ferry. Arashk says the river should be at its highest in an hour. Close ranks. Brisk pace but unhurried. Let's go."

# Chapter Nineteen

The wait to board the ferry—which, remarkably, was made of bone and cured hides—was almost too short. As they waited to cross to the narrow fringe of buildings on the far bank, the wind out of the north pushed the odors of the city further behind, leaving them in fresh, brisk air. The only drawback: the same wind also carried more of the dust from the wastes beyond the less imposing ruins scattered among the far shore's profusion of primitive windmills.

The humanoids who presided over the ferry's operation were of the same type as the one whose body had recalled the segmented surfaces of a pangolin, albeit without the bizarre, horn-like extrusions. Although the Crewe had witnessed them moving freely among the x'qai on their approach to the jetty, they evinced none of the perpetually simmering aggression of the "killspawn."

The stevedores and crew were all praakht, although Caine had begun to notice further distinctions among them. Those with the elongated, narrow features spent more time arguing and shouting; they were disproportionately represented among those loading the boat. Obversely, its far less disputatious crew generally looked more akin to Neanderthals, albeit somewhat more lithe.

Halfway across the swollen, yet strangely currentless river, the weather once again proved that, at least in this region, it could not be reliably predicted even thirty minutes ahead of time. Thunderheads appeared on the eastern horizon, apparently rearing up high into the sky. However, that proved to be an optical illusion; in actuality, they were approaching at over twenty knots.

The last few hundred yards of the crossing were hastened by attaching the ferry's far shore guideline to a stone-sunk windlass turned by three dirtkine. They were even smaller than those they had seen dragging alluvial soils, more suited to turning machines in the workhouses and mills of the city. Had it not been for the speed with which they pulled the barge to the north shore, it might have foundered in the deluge that sped out of the east and ran hard along the course of the tributary, driven by a howling gale. As it was, the boat's drainage flaps had to be opened as soon as it was safe ashore; it was so filled with rainwater that it would have foundered if launched again.

Five steps ashore taught Caine and the others that they would have to rethink their comfortable assumption of being able to move through the rain with their visors down. Only the Dornaani suits had overpressure sufficient to keep the helmet visor from becoming opaque with condensation. But no suit or technology could rescue them as the dusty sand rapidly transformed into a thick sludge so treacherous that they couldn't keep their footing without the help of their unobstructed senses. So the visors stayed up.

By the time they reached the Legate's stronghold—an almost windowless three-story building with an immense footprint—they were thoroughly drenched. The wind had driven the surging torrents into their faces and so, washed down into their vacc suits. They'd acquired an escort shortly after debarkation: a mix of Neanderthals and modern humans. Almost a third of the latter were armed with crude muzzle-loaders and wearing cured hide armor, cunningly segmented to allow great freedom of movement. Sheathed swords and hatchets rode at their hips and while they guided the group to the Legate's reinforced concrete fastness, they did not come close enough to engage in conversation. There was no telling whether that was the result of pure chance, personal choice, or explicit instruction.

However, this much was clear: they had arrived at an important destination, and probably pivotal meeting, looking like a pack of drowned rats in high-tech wrappers. Their escort faded back to shelter in hovels or beneath narrow underhangs of ancient buildings that had been reclaimed with sunbaked bricks.

The guards on either side of the door were equipped much like the others, except one was wearing chain mail, and the other held a great axe at the ready. Their eyes were patient and unread-able, except for the tendency to flit briefly toward Yaargraukh, not in trepidation so much as curiosity.

"We have been told—" Riordan began.

"You are expected," the one in the chain mail said calmly. "Keep your hands empty and where they may be seen."

When the group had complied, he rapped his fist in a com-plicated pattern against a bone clapper mounted alongside the entrance. Above it hung an almost heraldic pennant depicting a sword crossed over a...stick? Riordan squinted. *Wait; is that a—?*

Duncan was pointing at the same emblem. "What is that? Some kind of pen? Here?"

Wu sounded pleased. "Apparently, even here, there are places where the pen is mightier than the sword. Or of comparable strength."

The bone clapper answered the guard in a very different pattern of clacks and clicks. He stepped aside, adding, "Your escort is on the way. You are welcome guests, but you are watched. At all times."

Over the hammering of the rain, O'Garran's half-hushed exclamation was almost inaudible. "We're *expected*?"

"Not sure I like this, boss," Dora added.

"The lack of questions is suspicious," Ayana agreed.

"Particularly the lack of questions about my resemblance to an x'qao," Yaargraukh added regretfully.

Riordan waited for other comments. "I didn't expect this either," he eventually said in English. "But it's what Arashk predicted: we were likely to be admitted easily because we're human and have advanced equipment." Riordan stared at the dark opening; the wall just beyond the threshold bent in what looked like the start of a defensive dogleg. "And if this is a trap, then they're pretty inept by *not* asking questions."

There was a long pause. Then Bannor laughed.

Ayana sounded satisfied. "Of course. If the Legate was attempt-ing to mislead us, detailed inquiries would be a necessary cha-rade. Otherwise, we might begin to suspect that we were being admitted *too* easily."

"Could it be a double-fake?" Duncan asked warily.

"I'd ask the same thing," Riordan said with a nod, "except that since the Legate clearly *is* expecting us, he's probably aware of *why* we've come, too. If not, he wouldn't have let us get this close."

Bannor smiled. "So maybe we just passed the *real* test: to reason that out."

Riordan could hear the grin behind Duncan's words as they started forward. "Well then, what are we waiting for?"

Riordan, not Yaargraukh, was invited to sit at the center of the shallow arc of stone seats in the room to which they'd been led. The overpowering odor of camphor which hit them as they had exited the dogleg was somewhat fainter here. Not that it had been unpleasant—compared to the reek of the streets, it was wonderful—but Caine was reminded of an old axiom: no matter how fine the perfume, you wouldn't want to live in the bottle.

As the last to be ushered into this room, Riordan had a few moments to run a surveying glance around the cavernous outer chamber. The large empty spaces—two stories in many places—were reminiscent of those found in old armories, power plants, utility stations, or smelting factories. But he could only guess at the thickness of the walls, because they were almost completely hidden. Dozens of catwalks linked ground-to-ceiling stone silos, keeps, even towers. It was as if someone had built a castle inside out.

The guards who'd escorted them to their seats nodded respectfully, exited, and returned with two hide-covered chairs of bone, as well as a woman in chain mail. Nodding to the Crewe, she dismissed the guards before sitting.

After a quick survey of their faces, she began studying each of them at length, a small smile growing as she did. When none of them offered more than a wan imitation of her smile, she laughed. "Well, I can see that you are not new to this!"

Riordan smiled back. "New to what?" With any luck, his casual irony would show her that the game was over: that they understood very well that, during potentially dangerous encounters, untrained persons usually filled silences with nervous chatter. But they had silently mirrored their host.

Happily, she did not miss his meaning. She looked round the group with a slow, appreciative nod. Which allowed Caine to concentrate on what his peripheral vision showed him of the walls: particularly, any darker lines that might mark observation or murder slits in their deeply shadowed grooves.

"I suspect," she mused, "that if I offered refreshments, you would not touch them."

"Perhaps later," Caine replied. "At present, I'm still enjoying the scented air. What do you call the plant that produces it?"

"*Ursheve*," she answered, lingering on the phonemes as if to underscore that they had not come from Low Praakht. "You are not familiar with the aroma?"

Caine's aversion to lying was all that informed his response this time. Arashk had told him—repeatedly—that above all else, they must not lie when meeting the Legate, that his servitors had a mystic ability to detect prevarication. Riordan had simply nodded politely, but now—psychic phenomena aside—he was acutely aware that they were not being met so much as they were being observed. "I know the scent," Caine replied, "but did not expect to encounter it here." All true.

The woman's interest was markedly keen. "Truly? So you have smelled it in the wild?"

"I don't remember where I first encountered it." Which was also true. "I was simply wondering why you have concentrated the odor near the entry."

"To repel the insects, of course."

Riordan folded his hands: the prearranged sign that he considered it safe for the rest of the Crewe to join the conversation. "We have been fortunate not to encounter so many pests as must trouble you here."

"Pests?" she repeated, unable to fully suppress her surprise and . . . incredulity?

"Is the use of cam—*ursheve*—common among the, uh, lords of Forkus?" Bannor asked.

She almost managed to keep a puzzled frown from bending her brow. "Almost none of the other lieges or their vassals make use of it."

"Is it expensive?" Ayana wondered.

"It is. But it is worth every groat to us."

"*Groat*"? *Really, translator?* "When you say 'us,' do you mean the Legate?"

Her brows no longer resisted the frown. "No, I mean any humans who can afford it. Without ursheve, the x'qao vassals would be able to wear down our guards with constant attacks."

Duncan understood what she meant by "attacks" a moment before the rest of them. "You mean, they could send *large* insects?" He indicated their size with his hands.

"Yes," she confirmed.

Yaargraukh's neck circled slightly. "As we entered, I saw no apertures large enough for such creatures to exploit."

She seemed more fixed upon his voice than his words. "Danger comes in all shapes and sizes." Her smile returned. "Have you any other questions?"

"Yes," Dora almost shouted. "Your guard said we were expected, but he didn't tell us *how*. And neither have you!" When the woman did nothing but continue to smile and watch her, Dora slapped the side of her chair. "*Coño!* Your guard wouldn't have said it unless you expected us to ask!"

The woman's smile and gaze remained untroubled...which is how Caine realized what she was actually doing: assessing the group's dynamics. In this case, identifying the individual with the lowest tolerance for delays, frustrations, or constraints. In this world where humans had little power and even fewer alternatives, such impatience could prove to be a lethal liability.

Riordan leaned forward, drawing the woman's eyes off Dora. "I'm sure you will understand that although it is very gratifying that we were expected, it is also a somewhat unsettling mystery. We are, as you must also know, new to this city." She nodded. "It would be easier to understand your knowledge of us if only we had any connections among the praakht." He paused. "Or even the h'achgai."

At the last word, her smile broadened slightly. "Yes. If only. Did you have any trouble on the way?" Her eyes flicked toward Yaargraukh for an instant.

"There was a welcoming committee," drawled Duncan, glancing at Caine.

"Ah. Reapers."

Riordan nodded. "There was also a herald of, er..."

"Of Shvarkh'khag." She nodded. "It is not typical to be confronted by a herald of the greatest liege, but nor is it particularly unusual." She smiled openly at Yaargraukh. "It is probably because you were along."

He glanced toward Caine; her question put them at a crossroads they had foreseen. The Hkh'Rkh's answer was slow, allowing him to emphasize his flawless articulation of human phonemes. "I am not an x'qao."

She simply nodded. "Nor are you a *grat'r*, clearly. Given your skill at speech and implements, the herald probably concluded that you are a unique arurkré. To my knowledge, no one has ever seen nor heard of an *x'qagrat'r*." She smiled, nodding toward him. "And apparently, I still have not." When he did not immediately reply, her smile became satisfied. And knowing.

He glanced at Riordan. Until now, they had managed to conceal their most dangerous vulnerability: their near-complete ignorance of the world. But now... *Well,* Caine thought, leaning back with a crooked smile, *it was an accomplishment to get this far.*

The woman was no longer merely smiling. She was openly amused, but not in a disparaging or superior fashion. "Shall I tell you what those words mean?"

Riordan nodded.

Yaargraukh's rattling exhale was his species' version of a defeated sigh. "Please."

Abruptly, she was no longer watching and observing, but explaining with the animation of a born teacher. "You," she said, gesturing toward the Hkh'Rkh, "resemble a slightly larger, and vastly more intelligent and composed, specimen of a species known as grat'r."

"Is that what they call themselves in their own tongue?"

She blinked at the question. "I...I do not believe the grat'r have a language of their own."

"Then what does that name mean?"

"It is from the Deviltongue words *gra* and *tur.* Colloquially: 'does-not-die.'"

A new voice spoke from just beyond the entry. "However, in formal x'qajo, it is a phrase that signifies an unusual property that is innate to some creatures." A man strolled through the doorway: he wore a loose robe draped over a combination of plastic and cured hide armor. "The closest meaning in Low Praakht would be 'intrinsic rebirth.'"

Two guards appeared at the doorway as he sat; they turned and faced outward.

"I am Tasvar," the man explained. "I speak for the Legate and will ask several questions on his behalf."

Caine nodded. "I understand...but we may not be at liberty to answer all of them,"

Tasvar nodded. "In which case, you must leave. Immediately."

# Chapter Twenty

Tasvar gestured to the group. "Please be assured that we—Yasla and I—appreciate your patience with our safety measures. The greatest danger to us is not attack, but infiltration. That is why I did not greet you personally. It was necessary to assess if you posed any immediate threat."

"And we just proved ourselves trustworthy...how?" Bannor asked.

He smiled. "By not attacking when your ignorance was conclusively revealed. Frankly, I had no expectation that you would do so. Every other aspect of your behavior and speech was reassuring. But it was also quite odd."

"In what way?" Ayana asked quietly.

"We shall return to that presently," Tasvar said with a casual wave of his hand. "For now, let us define the other terms you seemed not to recognize: *arurkré* and *x'qagrat'r*."

"That last one," Dora grumbled, "it's a modification of grat'r, yes?"

Yasla's smile was almost rueful. "More literally than you can know. It refers to x'qao spawn resulting from the infesting of a grat'r." She checked herself. "Well, it *would* mean that, if such a thing had ever happened."

Yaargraukh's eyes pushed slightly beyond their protective bony ridges. "Grat'r cannot be hosts for x'qai?"

She shrugged. "Hosts? Yes, but the resulting spawn are never more than q'akh."

Riordan nodded, remembering Arashk's tutoring. "They're stunted, unable to speak or even use weapons."

Tasvar nodded. "There are other differences, but those are the important ones."

Ayana straightened. "The last word, *arurkré*: the herald spoke it with a formal, even deferential, inflection."

"That's because it is the term for the intrinsic aristocracy of the x'qao: those that can transform themselves."

Newton leaned away as if the concept alone was worthy of avoidance. "What do you mean by 'transform'?"

Yasla steepled her fingers. "Over time—decades, maybe centuries—arurkré can progressively alter their physical form. They can also compel increasingly slavish obedience from, and alter the behavior of, lesser killspawn."

Duncan was hoarse with revulsion. "Then...then why haven't the arurkré overrun everything? What keeps them in check?"

Tasvar sighed. "I wish I could claim it was due to the resistance of other species, but we are little more than an annoyance. We continue to exist only because, collectively, we are a *necessary* annoyance." His face became grim. "The only check on their spread is each other. They are intemperate, voracious, and self-seeking. We survive only because they cannot unite in any meaningful fashion, or for any extended period of time."

"So," Yaargraukh said slowly, "the reapers allowed us to pass because they thought I was a...variety of self-transforming x'qao they had never seen before."

"Well," Yasla temporized, "I am sure that accelerated the process, but I cannot envision them denying the rest of you entry to Forkus. Many of you are too fair to be anything but reaper burntskins." She saw their confused glances. "Burntskins are..." She paused as if choosing her next words with particular care. "They are any humans who are not descended from the original population."

"And they can tell that by complexion alone?"

"The original humans' skin is always very dark in color. *Very* dark."

*Not surprising*, Riordan thought, *given an F-class sun.*

Yasla had not paused. "And even though you were not a typical group of harrows and scythes, there would be no other way to explain seven persons carrying equipment such as yours.

I suspect that may have made them particularly cautious in questioning you."

"Because of what we might have done to them?" Dora asked, her tone indicating she already doubted Yasla had intended that meaning.

"No: because your equipment looks quite new, a great deal of it is similar, and you are traveling without servitors. So, yes, you appear quite formidable. But that was further complicated by their inability to ascertain who your liege or even suzerain might be. Meaning that they had no way to gauge how much retribution they might incur if they obstructed you."

"But logically," Duncan muttered, "that also means they're going to be watching us. Really closely."

"That, too, is true. Which is why your next steps, and even ours, must be settled in advance and taken with great care."

"I appreciate your concern," Riordan said with a nod, "but you still have not shared how you knew of us."

Tasvar smiled. "Is it truly so mysterious?"

*Damn, do we have to agree to tell the same secret on the count of three?* Riordan shook his head. "I presume that Arashk notified an ally soon after we started out. I suspect he sent Hresh, since he's an oathkeeper. We conjectured they had contacts in Forkus, or they wouldn't have known so much about it. Hresh probably went further east before he entered the city proper, thereby ensuring that our paths would not cross. Assuming that his route allowed him to remain within the precincts of those contacts and their allies, he probably got ahead of us pretty easily."

Tasvar's smile had broadened.

Caine smiled back. "But here's the part we don't understand."

Tasvar's smile dimmed.

"Getting into Forkus before us is easy to explain. But how he got word to you before we arrived? That isn't as obvious. Maybe he managed to pass something to the crew of the ferry, but we kept a close watch on them: if anyone meant to set up an ambush on the north bank of the river, that was how they'd have to send word."

Tasvar's smile was faltering.

*I won't make you sweat, although I could. And maybe I should. But we're guests and prospective allies, so—*"Here's what I propose, Tasvar. Since you knew we were coming on the advice of the h'achgai, you must also know *why* we were heading to you in the first place. I'm guessing that's why you vetted us this way: not because we simply wished to meet you, but because it was likely that we would wish to *stay with* you or your allies." Riordan shrugged. "As you said, infiltration is your greatest danger.

"We appreciate how much trust accepting guests requires, even after putting us through these paces and watching how we reacted. So we shall trust that you will *eventually* reveal how you received advance word of us, once you've decided that we will be sufficiently cautious and responsible with that knowledge."

Tasvar nodded slowly. "That seems reasonable to me. But there is one last question I must put to you. And quite bluntly."

Riordan noticed the slight shift in Yasla's posture and the direction of her gaze, but only because he'd been watching for it. *Okay, Tasvar; you just gave her a cue.* Caine did not react to it, but instead, sent a questioning glance around the hemicircle of his companions. None looked doubtful or hesitant. He met Tasvar's eyes again and nodded. "Ask your question."

Tasvar was a good actor, but not accomplished enough to hide that he was almost as nervous to ask the question as Caine was to hear it. "Your arrival"—he gestured to the whole Crewe—"is not, by any chance, related to the appearance of the new star...is it?"

Caine managed not to react externally. But, internally... *Shit: the* one *thing we decided we wouldn't reveal under any circumstances. But maybe—*

Newton spoke before Riordan could consult the surrounding faces again. "What new star?" Baruch asked.

Caine hoped his rueful smile concealed the full measure of his surprise and dismay. *Newton, for the love of God: really?* He watched as Tasvar's darting eyes noted all of the Crewe's reactions, particularly their surprise when the answer to that *particular* question came from someone other than Caine, as well as their bafflement that it had come from Newton.

Tasvar folded his hands. "Assuming you intend to revisit that answer"—Newton's expression was both angry and aghast—"I will tell you what we have seen over the past ten days or so. First a star shows up, the kind that moves in the heavens, which we call an *asíkrerk*."

In his earbud, Riordan heard the constantly running translator declare: "Asíkrerk. Comet."

"However," Tasvar continued, "this one moved erratically, distinctly changing direction on two different occasions. Then, after a few days, it flared suddenly and headed away on a consistent course. We supposed that this heavenly body had split or fragmented. Clearly, a sizable remainder was now heading away. We presumed that the rest had probably fallen, as do shooting stars. And so we thought the matter ended.

"But then we received word from an ally—a small but independent h'achgan liege here in Forkus—that we shall soon have visitors of a most unusual nature. We had few details, but when you arrived, we noticed the same unique and puzzling details that the reapers did. And many more, besides. And so, here you sit, highly intelligent and yet startlingly ignorant."

He paused, lowering his hands to rest on the arms of his chair. "It is my observation that when highly intelligent creatures enter a new environment, they attempt to reduce their ignorance as swiftly and completely as possible. Which leads me to conclude that you have not yet had ample time to do so." Tasvar shrugged. "It is still entirely possible your arrival here is merely an event of perverse serendipity, and that your appearance so soon after that of the erratic star is mere coincidence." He paused, looked around the group. "But that would be a very strange coincidence, indeed."

Riordan smiled. "I quite agree. But it is *so* strange that we should speak about it directly with the Legate himself."

Now it was Tasvar's turn to look uncomfortable. "Unfortunately, no one sees the Legate personally.

"Why?"

"If they did, they would be killed. All specific information pertaining to the Legate is closely guarded." Tasvar frowned. "Perhaps you would be more at ease if I asked my question in reverse: Can you tell me that you are *not* from the star?"

Riordan took a moment to check the Crewe's faces as he'd meant to before Newton had blurted out his well-intentioned lie. Several of the group looked sanguine; several others looked panicked. Ayana and Yaargraukh were equally unreadable.

He turned to Tasvar. "Would it trouble you if we took a moment to discuss this in a different language?"

Their hosts exchanged glances. "That is acceptable," Tasvar said hesitantly. Riordan noticed that the guards who'd been posted to either side of the door were no longer facing *directly* away.

Caine turned to the others, who leaned in to form a hemicir-cular huddle. "Quick reactions: now," he muttered in English.

Dora and Bannor started at the same moment:

"Boss, I don't like this one damn—"

"Sir, this may be the best chance of—"

"STOP!" shouted Tasvar.

He had jumped to his feet, eyes wide. But his expression—was it shock, rage, awe, or something closer to rapture? "Do you test us?" he shouted. "Do you think us fools?"

Riordan stood slowly. "We mean no—"

"Explain yourselves! Immediately!"

"Explain what? We hadn't even started our discussion."

Tasvar waved his hand irritably; Riordan saw that it was hor-ribly scarred. "I do not care what you were about to say. It is *how* you were saying it." His anger, and possibly fear, dimmed in response to the uniformly stunned faces wondering at him. "Your speech. That is one of the many tongues revealed by the Legate."

Riordan swallowed. *Holy shit.* Others said the same two words aloud. "Tasvar, this...this is our most common language. Half of us grew up speaking it." Riordan realized he'd put his hands out in the fashion of those who are too blindsided, too shocked to tell anything but the truth.

Now it was Yasla and Tasvar who were stunned. Tasvar recovered a split second before she did. "And do you know the Legate's battle tongue, too?"

"Uh..." Dora muttered, "since we didn't know this was the Legate's special language, how would we even know that he *had* a battle language, let alone what it might be?"

*Wait a minute. What if—?* "Tasvar," Caine said quickly, "if the Legate's battle language is another one from Ea—from his homeland, we might have a way to translate it."

"You mean, by using the magic talking machine?"

*Seems your h'achgan friend gave you a pretty detailed report.* "Yes: the talking machine. If you speak some words, it will be able to—"

"No. The battle tongue is only useful if it is secret. Discover-ing whether you speak it is not important enough to risk that."

Riordan nodded. "I'd make the same decision. So I shall make you a further promise: we will not use the translator without informing you first. That way, you can be certain that it shall never be operating in a place where you might be speaking in your battle language. Is this acceptable?"

Tasvar swallowed heavily. "It is." His eyes were still wide, his expression such a strange mix of emotions that Caine could not tell if the other man wanted to kill him or embrace him or both. "I shall send word of your arrival. This changes much."

But the way he said "this changes much" made it sound more like "this changes *everything.*"

Yasla stood. "I have a further question. Have any of you been given any baubles or gifts? Objects that the tribes might have claimed to be charms?"

Caine shook his head. "No." She stared hard at him. "The only thing we shared was food."

She continued staring at him, then glanced at Tasvar in evident frustration, and finally looked away with a sigh.

*What the hell was* that *abou—?*

This time it was Dora who leaped up from her seat. "*Coño!* I know the evil eye when I see it! We show you trust, and this is how you repay—?"

Tasvar raised a hand as he shook his head, his face serious. "It was a precaution only. Please understand: what you claim is... unique. And if there was anything on your persons that could relay what you see or hear to others—"

"*Ai!* Okay, then." Dora was still frowning, but moved back toward her seat.

Caine glanced at her; she shook her head with a look that said, *I'll explain later.*

Ayana had reengaged their hosts. "Concerning our 'unique claims': are you referring to our origins"—she glanced up beyond the roof toward the new star—"or our language?"

Tasvar and Yasla exchanged glances. "Both."

"Yet, they are not entirely unexpected?"

Yasla thought for a moment. "Let us say there is reason for us to think that such things might be possible." She stood. "Hard travel is plain upon your faces, your equipment. Please: we would offer you food, drink, and a place to bathe."

Riordan nodded around him; the Crewe stood. "We would be honored." He smiled. "And probably much more pleasant to the senses, afterward." However miraculous Dornaani suits were, they still didn't have built-in showers or deodorizers.

Yasla and Tasvar smiled. "I look forward to continuing our conversation in the days to come." He gestured to the guards beyond the door. "Please: they shall show you to your quarters." The two tall warriors moved out into the great hall, pointing to a dark doorway across the much-repaired expanse of concrete flooring.

Duncan caught up to Caine as they exited the room. "Damn, how lucky can we get?" he murmured.

"That they speak English?" whispered Ayana from behind.

"Sure, and assuming that someone from Earth taught them, we should be able to get acculturated really quickly."

"They do seem like natural allies," Bannor added quietly.

Riordan was about to respond when the guards reached the top of the stairs. The first three risers had been cut through the concrete; the rest were carved from the native rock. "Do not be concerned," one said, gesturing into the stygian darkness below. "Your accommodations are in the most secure part of this citadel. We shall answer any questions you have once we arrive there."

But Riordan hardly heard the words or Ayana's suppressed gasp; he was too surprised by their appearance.

Both guards' features were chiseled from skin that was not so much swarthy as tawny. And their gaze was so easy, so steady, that Caine could not fail to notice that their eyes were bright amber.

Ktoran eyes.

Not trusting his voice, Riordan nodded and motioned that they should lead the way down the stairs.

As they turned to comply, he looked over his shoulder into the stunned faces of his companions. "Here's hoping we *have* found natural allies," muttered Caine, "because otherwise, we've just delivered ourselves to our worst enemies."

# INTERLUDE TWO

# **Uncertain Territory**

*March 2125*
*Zeta Tucanae VI, Far Orbit*

# Interlude Two

As the turbulent striped-agate dot of Zeta Tucanae VI faded in the aft viewer, Melissa Sleeman leaned against Tygg Robin's arm to watch it disappear. The sizable bicep of that arm was still tense. "Relax, Christopher," she murmured. "A standing-shift is the best strategy, the best way to avoid detection."

"Odd thing to say about a terawatt-level discharge of energy," her husband muttered. "If any of the newly arrived ships on the other side of the star move to a point where they're no longer blinded by the corona, they'll see our shift clear as day. And then we're all just meat pies on the roo-bar."

Melissa pushed closer. "Alnduul's disposable microsats have been watching that approach for days. There has been no new traffic since the last shift-carrier came in almost five weeks ago. The only sensors that are in a position to see it are the ones around Dustbelt, but Alnduul has kept the gas giant between us.

"But, if he had chosen a standard shift, *Olsloov* would have been running her fusion thrusters for at least a week of pre-acceleration, leaving a particle trail as well. And in the end, that shift would have been almost as noticeable as the one we'll make in a few hours. This way, once the shift's radiant signature is gone, there will be nothing left to detect."

Tygg put an arm around her waist, smiled sideways. "How is it you always manage to explain things in a way that makes me feel less anxious?"

She hugged him. "Because I love you."

He stared down at her. "No, that's *why* you do it. I asked *how*?"

Her smile became mischievous. "Well, three doctorates in the sciences and forty more points of IQ *probably* has something to do with that."

He sighed and hugged her back. "Yeh, probably does."

When Richard Downing emerged from his shared stateroom, Alnduul was waiting just beyond the iris valve, three of his new Dornaani crew arrayed behind him. "The last of your equipment will soon be secured. Are you ready to inspect it?"

Downing nodded and they began drift-walking toward the dorsal half-bay that was the only access to the cargo module stuffed with the materiel from Dustbelt.

After a dozen steps, Alnduul added, "We are also ready to commence final boost to deorbit the impactor."

Again, Downing nodded.

Two more steps. "Are you certain that destroying your group's facility on the third planet will convince pursuers that all of you have met a violent end?"

Downing wondered if, at any point in their evolution, the Dornaani had rubbed their hands in anxiety, because Alnduul made it sound like it must—or at least, should—have been one of their most common activities. Richard smiled. "Certainty is a commodity in perpetually short supply. But whoever finds the ruins of our base is unlikely to be accompanied by a forensics team, so their discoveries will be limited to debris. Accordingly, we left just enough useless Lost Soldier equipment so that a determined investigation would find some rubbish that they *might* be able to date back to twentieth-century Earth, but no more than that.

"They will *certainly* determine that the site was destroyed by the small asteroid you're ready to deorbit. And in sweeping the impact zone, they are likely to discover that it had been meticulously swept for any other, incriminating objects before it struck."

As Alnduul preceded Downing up the vertical tube that led to the expanded storage area, his voice was one of carefully controlled perplexity. "But whichever of your adversaries finds the aftermath will know that they did not conduct the attack. So will they not then seek those who are responsible for it? For logically, they will suspect Earth's other blocs, and seek to discover whose operatives were responsible, and so seek and accuse those who possess the evidence that was removed."

"They would certainly be tempted to do exactly that, but they will be reluctant to do so."

"Why?"

"Because they fear uncovering a plot that would be quite counterproductive to their own ends."

"Propose such an outcome."

They reached the top of the tube as Downing explained. "The worst-case scenario would be if they discovered that the Ktor took matters into their own hands. Specifically, that the Sphere still has agents in the megacorporations, which located the Lost Soldiers and passed that intel back to their masters. Whose ships then came over the border and steered a small asteroid into a fiery descent that burned away all their worries, right down to the bedrock. Perhaps they sanitized the site beforehand, or perhaps the impact really did wipe away almost all the evidence.

"Second scenario: that the destruction of the Lost Soldier base *was* carried out by one of the other blocs, but as a black flag operation. Yes, the Developing World Coalition is the most likely, but other culprits are possible. After all, every bloc is worried about what will occur if it is openly revealed that the Lost Soldiers were hijacked by the Ktor: public outrage that pushes Earth into a war it cannot win. So it is conceivable that even those blocs sympathetic to the Lost Soldiers might decide to eliminate them, but then point fingers at the DWC. It's almost comical to think of it: the consuls sitting around the table, all looking surprised . . . because all of them are. Essentially, *we're* the ones behind the false flag operation."

Alnduul waited for his three new crew members to catch up before moving toward the entry to the cargo access bulkhead. "I see how the ripples run even further, Richard Downing. If the Developing World Coalition mounts an investigation to prove themselves innocent and succeeds, they cannot know in advance that the evidence which exonerates them will not also ineluctably implicate the Ktor. And so, that is yet another pathway to war and another reason for them not to investigate what happened on Zeta Tucanae III."

Alnduul's mouth twisted. "So, your opponents will logically strive to deflect any discovery or focus upon what transpired here, lest public fears and suspicions lead to the outcome they are trying to prevent: war with the Ktor."

Downing nodded. "That's our hope: to achieve what is effectively a stalemate. Which, for us, is a strategic victory."

Alnduul had stopped at the access doors. "You speak as if you are intimately familiar with the plight of your adversaries."

"Nature of intelligence work, old boy," Downing muttered with a smile.

After one lid nictated in response to being called 'old boy,' Alnduul's fingers drooped. "I am not speaking in generalities or in relation to our current circumstances. I refer to the conundrums which, from the outset, undermined your ability to effect a just outcome for the Lost Soldiers."

Downing frowned. "Not sure I know what you're getting at."

"Truly? I see this parallel: you must have been tempted to ask either me or the Custodians in general to provide asylum for the Lost Soldiers so long as they remained in cryogenic stasis. But on reflection, you realized that you could not do so, not only because they are undeniable evidence of the Ktoran violations of your planet's autonomy, but stark proof that the Custodians themselves failed to prevent those violations and then, failed to make good their assurances to protect Earth against invasion.

"Perhaps if that had been the limit of the quandaries, you might still have made your request. However, by then you knew or had reasoned that doing so would initiate a cascade of events which would preclude the very outcome you desired."

In response to Downing's blank stare, the Dornaani explicated. "Your request for us to conceal the Lost Soldiers would have led to questions about how and why the Custodians failed. The insufficiency of those answers would in turn have revealed that it was the Arbiters who forbade us the Custodians to act as they had not only promised, but were obliged to by the Accords. So, it would have been revealed that the very core of the Collective had actively undermined the very order it had brought about.

"We Dornaani would be shown to have violated the Accord by obstructing the Custodians. So the Collective had only one ethical path: to vote for its own suspension from the Accord. Which, if it did, would have left only one full member in good standing: the Slaasriithi, the most ineffectual of all the species. And so, division and war would follow among the races." All his fingers trailed limply. "Or as would have been more likely, the Collective would have worked to suppress all evidence and accusations against it, showing itself to be so corrupt that the Accord would lose all respect and validity. And again, division and war would follow among the races."

Alnduul's sad eyes regarded Richard. "So, you eschewed action because your initial intent—to secure legal asylum for the Lost Soldiers—would have led to the dissolution of all order and any hope of peace. And still, the Lost Soldiers would have remained literally and figuratively frozen in place: hostages to the endless debates and eventual unraveling of the Accord itself."

He blinked, as if that were sufficient to both initiate and complete a dramatic change of subject. "Are you ready to see the cargo's lading, now?"

Downing was too stunned to speak for a moment. "Y-yes, I am."

Alnduul was gesturing one of his crew forward to lead the way into the cavernous hold when Trevor Corcoran's voice called up from the bottom of the access tube. "There's a new wrinkle before we can put the new cargo module in deep freeze, Uncle Richard. Seems some of the Lost Soldiers are requesting that particular representatives address their various concerns to 'the brass.'" Trevor emerged from the tube. "Problem is, those representatives are still in cold sleep."

"Then why have you come to me, lad? I am hardly—"

"Richard."

Downing stopped; Trevor was giving him "the stare." The stare that meant he wasn't in the mood for any of his godfather's evasions or ingenuous protestations. Tygg Robin was still the de jure CO, but with Downing and Trevor soon to be joined by the recently reanimated Three Colonels of the Lost Soldiers, the two-dozen conscious Lost Soldiers now considered those five officers to be "the brass." Or they would be as soon as the colonels had fully recovered. "And what does Captain Robin have to say about this?"

"To quote him: 'That's brilliant, mate!'"

Hardly a surprise; Tygg Robin was—by aptitude, inclination, and preference—an in-the-muck type of soldier. Probably the only reason he'd ever been willing to become an officer was because the only thing he liked less than being in charge was being subordinate to "bleeding whackers." "Very well, we'll get to it after the tour."

"Tour?"

By way of answer, one of Alnduul's new crew opened the cargo doors.

Century-old vehicles, conexes, and crates were stacked and lashed from deck to overhead. And at the far end was a gridwork holding what Downing still thought of as high-tech sarcophagi: coldcells. Except not all of them operated on the principles of cryogenic stasis; there were Ktoran symbiopods in that mix, most of which defied ready analysis or understanding. Only one thing was certain: a lot of the units had newly illuminated warning lights. What that meant, and what they should do, was unknown, even to the Dornaani: the Ktor hadn't included instruction manuals.

Trevor came to stand next to his uncle, released a low whistle. "That is a hell of a lot of gear. Thank God for your loaders, Alnduul." He glanced back at *Olsloov's* new crew members, two of whom had controlled the cargobots that had worked the miracle of loading and securing all the gear in forty-eight hours. "Your crew certainly can get jobs done, Alnduul. Which, I'll admit, is a relief."

"A relief, Captain Corcoran? Did you have reason to suspect that my crew is incompetent?"

"No! Not at all! But, well, Tygg and others had the impression that you might be shorthanded on *Olsloov*."

"They are correct. I was. But on the way here, I stopped in a system to which I shall not soon return. It is overseen by a very old friend, who happened to have quite a number of retired Custodians on hand, most of whom were growing restless. As was he. It was a very congenial coincidence."

"Which system is that?"

"You know it as BD +66 582. We call it Rooaioo'q. While there, I received permission to requisition the shift-barge in which to carry your personnel and equipment."

Trevor squinted. "A shift barge? What's that?"

"You are standing in it."

"This is a ship?"

"Not as you mean it, Captain. It has one significant distinction from typical cargo barges: it is fitted with a system that interfaces with the shift-grid of a starship. Together, they expand

and modulate the expression of the incipient event horizon to accommodate the combined shape of the ship and barge."

Trevor's eyebrows had raised throughout the explanation. "That's a pretty neat trick."

Downing nodded, smiled knowingly. "It is. It's even better that Alnduul was able to trick the Collective into parting with it."

Trevor glanced between his uncle and the Dornaani. "And when was someone going to read me in on this?"

Alnduul's eyes widened in distress. "Be assured: there was no intent to exclude you, Captain Corcoran."

Downing cleared his throat softly. "Alnduul?"

"Yes?"

"Trevor was joking."

The Dornaani's lamprey-mouth rotated slightly: ironic amusement. "It is often difficult to discern the cues that distinguish your species' sarcasm from ironic levity. I will happily share the story of how I came into possession of the shift-barge." He gestured that they should venture into it, pointing to the hex-grid securing system built into the deck.

"After assuring the officials at my board of inquiry that I would bring you over the border, I subsequently asserted that extracting the Lost Soldiers themselves was not sufficient. Safety required that all traces of the Lost Soldiers had to disappear. Therefore, it was necessary to remove all their gear as well.

"Although the board agreed, there was some negotiation required in order to get the barge. The negotiation became an annoyance, in which I perceived a strange opportunity.

"I became increasingly adamant in all my efforts to secure it. I harried depot administrators, sent daily updates to the board, repeatedly sent communiqués to all concerned. All to underscore that, without the barge, I might not be able to accomplish a full exfiltration. Not only did I make myself enough of a nuisance to have my request for this craft swiftly approved, but the board is now thoroughly exasperated by—and therefore, convinced of—my ardor to complete the task."

Trevor frowned. "I get everything except why it was necessary to exasperate the board to get them to trust you."

Downing glanced at Alnduul, who was already looking at him. Downing nodded. Trevor frowned, looked between them suspiciously. Richard smiled. *Well, he had the scent of it now, anyway.*

"The importance of that point," Alnduul explained slowly, "is that the board and their ostensibly discreet watchers now expect nothing other than eager compliance. If the ships that no doubt shadowed me to the border notice that I am somewhat late returning, they will not immediately be alarmed. Therefore, we have more time before I am deemed missing and the board's judgment on me reverses. Ferociously."

Trevor stopped in the middle of the deck. "Hold on: what's this about your going missing?"

Alnduul folded one hand of sticklike fingers over the other. "Captain Corcoran, although the Collective is eager for me to retrieve you and the Lost Soldiers, that does not ensure that they will be equally eager to defend you from the Ktor."

"Are you saying the Ktor would invade the Collective? Just to get to *us*?"

"No. I am speaking of whether the Collective has the political fortitude to resist pressure from the Ktoran Sphere to provide them with proof—living proof—that you have in fact been removed from the CTR and are firmly under our control. Note the word: our *control*."

Trevor's frown was now studied, serious. "Duly noted. Go on."

"It is not out of the realm of possibility that they would hand your group over, in part or whole, to the Ktor to satisfy the Sphere's demands for verification. Some of the Arbiters would wish that. Some would fight against it. But given the apathy I have witnessed recently, and the erosion of the Senior Assembly's sense of duty and justice, I will not balance your lives upon that uncertain inflection point."

"So what do you propose we do?"

"We chart our own course."

Trevor blinked. "You mean, go rogue?"

Alnduul folded his hands. "I would frame my answer in the form of your own group's innovative responses to the current scenario. Unless I am mistaken, when Bannor Rulaine's group returned to the Collective with me, he carried a transferrable letter of marque to confer upon Caine Riordan. Is that correct?"

Downing nodded. "It is."

"I found this action not only informative, but inspiring." Alnduul crossed his hands "A letter of marque is a fascinating convention. We Dornaani have no analog for it. As I understand it, the letter grants the holder extraordinary freedom of action, which can entail both significant risk and opportunity.

"This seems particularly true when the polity that issued the letter of marque is in the throes of either political or military internecine strife. In such conditions, the holders could easily find themselves carrying out actions ordered by one side, but decried by the other. They could thus become a convenient scapegoat.

"On the other hand, if the holder is judicious and foresightful, he or she may undertake independent operations that the restored nation might retroactively recognize as extremely beneficial. Indeed, the privateer's deeds might even help ensure that domestic power remains in legitimate hands. In such cases, the victorious faction is often eager to validate those actions, retroactively declaring them as having been in compliance with their orders.

"I suspect Caine Riordan understood this dimension of a letter of marque when he demanded your group receive one when presented with the initial quandary of how best to ensure the safety of the Lost Soldiers." Alnduul turned his unblinking eyes upon Trevor. "In recent weeks, I have found myself frequently reflecting upon the enviable flexibility afforded by such letters of marque, particularly as conditions in the Collective continue to change and become more...factious."

Trevor nodded slowly. "Just as the CTR is too divided to enforce its promises to us, your Collective is too divided to live up to theirs."

Alnduul's eyelids nictated very slowly. "In times such as these, it is difficult to retain freedom of action as well as a reasonable hope of avoiding the stigmatic label of 'traitor.' In the long run, I see only one possibility whereby I may hope to achieve both: to chart an independent course."

Trevor's smile was wondering, wide, and very bright. "Alnduul, you are one ballsy bastard."

"If I understand your idiom, I think the appropriate response is, 'thank you.'" He put his hand to his control circlet. "My trainees tell me we are nearing the point where we will engage the shift drive." Before turning to lead them out, he glanced back at the wall of cryosleeping soldiers who'd been stolen from Earth's twentieth century. "Those are my greatest worry."

"You mean, how much power the cryocells require?"

"No, that they could fail any month or week, possibly any day, and we may have no warning." He regarded the two of them with wide, unblinking, pupilless eyes. "I believe it wise that you have agreed to reanimate those whom the others consider important representatives of their interests, persons they trust regardless of station or rank."

"Why?" asked Downing.

His nephew turned and pointed at the wall of coldcells behind them. "Because even though we're saving them from Earth doesn't change the fact that if they don't have a voice, we're just hijacking them."

"To bring them to where they can live," Downing protested.

Trevor shrugged. "Or to send them to a different death. Me? If I couldn't speak for myself, I'd want someone to do it for me." He looked at Downing. "How about you?"

For the first time in a very long time, Richard Downing did not stop to weigh the consequences of a decision. "Right," he said, chin up. "That's what we'll do, just as soon as the Three Colonels are recovered. Now, Alnduul, I believe you have a ship to shift."

# PART THREE

# Into the Wastes

*"Bactradgaria"*
*March 2125*

# Chapter Twenty-One

Miles O'Garran leaned back, swallowed his last mouthful of edible lichen. "Jesus," he muttered, "how do they eat this shit, day in, day out?"

"Guess we're going to find out," Craig Girten observed, still chewing his own helping of the fibrous strips.

"Sorry there isn't a better welcome dinner." Caine was pretty sure his smile was crooked. "Unfortunately, it's pretty much the staple everywhere, from what we've been told."

Katie stopped eating to clean her hands for what might have been the tenth time: not because the food was messy—it was anything but—but because Peter's team had all arrived at the Legate's fortress caked in mud. Despite being in their suits. "So," she complained, "is it always glawr to yer bum here?"

"What'd she say?" Duncan whispered quietly.

Not quietly enough, apparently: "Mud up to your arse," she translated.

"No," Dora answered with facetious enthusiasm. "Sometimes, it floods. Just for a change. Like yesterday."

"From the rain?" Peter asked. Half the ration of lichen was still on his clay plate.

"That's part of it," Bannor nodded. "But according to Erset, the commander of the guard, the flood was also caused by the lunar cycle: at the shortest interval between high tides, there are overlapping backflows. That pushes the river to its highest level.

Add heavy rains for the two preceding days, and half the city was knee-deep in water."

"If only it was *just* water," Newton amended gruffly.

Peter looked around at the walls. "This seems to be a very secure place," he observed, scratching under his neck with two fingers. The motion was code for *is it safe to talk here?*

"Very," Riordan answered, nodding three times, the first one starting from a chin-down position. Which signified: *uncertain.* They'd first come up with the system after Hsontlosh proved untrustworthy. It was probable they'd continue to have regular use for it in their new home.

"So what have you been doing other than lazing around, eating prime rib?" Miles asked.

"Increasing our knowledge of this world," Ayana replied.

"Such as?"

She folded her hands. "This is the eighth day of spring. Hence, the weather. There are one hundred and four local days per season. This continent, which the locals call Brazhgarag, is one of the two most populous, and clearly the most important."

"Well, lucky us!"

"Perhaps," she answered calmly.

Peter folded his arms and glanced around the group. "So you deem landing here a mixed blessing?"

Duncan swallowed the last of his meal with the aid of a long gulp of water. "Too early to say either way, but that's part of the problem. The only reason this continent is called the most populous is because it has the most cities. Which is a logical correlation, but there's no guess about the number and size of towns or tribes living in the wastes." He shook his head. "I'm an intelligence analyst. Or was. But there's no real intel here. No countries, no alliances, no standing armies. Hell, there aren't any routine trade arrangements."

"Fits what we saw, too," O'Garran nodded. "Just warlords, with the big ones controlling the food production directly through vassals and...uh..."

"Vavasors," Yaargraukh supplied. "Vassals of vassals. The Hkh'Rkh Patrijuridicate retains a similar structure. The difference is that among my people, the rules governing those relationships are matter of record, as are the histories of the nations that arose from them. Here, nothing is centralized. Beyond rituals of obeisance, there are no laws or even traditions."

"So what have you been doing *besides*?" Katie asked, looking around the group that had been in Forkus for five days. "Learning that didn't take up all your time, certainly."

*It took less than an hour,* Caine thought as he answered, "Actually, we spent most of our time learning about Tasvar's fortress. Well, 'facility' is a better word. And we spent almost as many hours helping him and his scribes learn more about this world. Or, more properly, its past."

"And how did you do that, seeing as how we've nae knowing of it?"

"Using this," Riordan answered, patting the Dornaani translator. "The war, or whatever devastated this planet, left a lot of gear and records for prospectors to salvage, and sometimes, to excavate. The problem with the records is that they were written in several different languages, none of which are spoken today except by scholar-scribes. With some work, the translator was able to identify almost half of the unknown words from context."

"How?"

Riordan shrugged. "We started by uploading images of the records themselves. Then, we tagged each word as Tasvar's chief scribe read it aloud."

Peter was frowning. "I do not see how that would help."

Newton nodded at his friend. "The Dornaani translator analyzes language at a very deep level and with real-time cross-referencing. It frequently deciphered a word by identifying a previously undetected etymological root it shared with known words. Then it refined the meaning through the context of the sentence or passage in which it appeared."

O'Garran whistled. "Wow. That *does* sound like magic."

Riordan smiled. "When it came to context, we had a pretty sizeable advantage over the locals, though."

"How so?"

"The records were written by a society that was at roughly the same state of technological sophistication as our own." Riordan leaned back. "The locals here had no chance deciphering words pertaining to most machines, or science, or processes that have been forgotten. But since both our language and Dornaani is rich in such terms, the translator proposed likely equivalents. And the more that was read out, the more those initial guesses were refined."

Bannor smiled. "But there was one class of words that eluded everyone until *I* stepped in."

Ayana smiled at him. "Your humility is an inspiration, Colonel."

He smiled back. "As it should be! And don't call me 'colonel,' at least not here. Anyhow, leave it to a career soldier to realize that the words we couldn't figure out were not actually words. They were acronyms."

Miles' laugh was louder than Bannor's had been. "Typical! But, damn: how did you untangle them?"

Riordan shrugged. "Simple phonetics. Once the translator knew what to look for, it spat out literally hundreds of decoded acronyms. With instant cross-indexing, we could see the kind of content and context in which they appeared. After that, a little inspired guesswork solved all but a few of them. Hell, that's how we learned that this world's name is just a bastardized remainder of the planet's post-war classification."

"Come again?" Katie asked.

Yaargraukh's head rose slightly. "One of the few constants across the various local languages is the name for this world: Garya. But scholars have always been aware that it had a much longer name in the oldest records. What the Dornaani translator revealed is that 'He't' is the first syllable of the ancient word for 'bacteriological,' and 'fal' is a similar fragment of the word for 'radiological.'"

He continued when he saw that his explanation had not driven off even one of the four frowns of uncertainty. "He't-fal-garya was an official string of abbreviations which identified the world and why it was to be avoided: bacteriologically and radiologically compromised Garya."

"So it would be like us calling it, uh, Bact-Rad-Garia?" O'Garran chortled. "Really?"

"Really," Ayana answered.

"Well then, Bactradgaria it is!" Miles laughed. "Home planet of the trogs!"

Caine managed not to roll his eyes along with those of the Crewe that did. Chief O'Garran's penchant for concocting sardonic nicknames was already evolving into a group tradition. Unfortunately, just like the jokes of a sharp-tongued court jester, his labels were usually as uncomfortable as they were apt.

But Riordan saw a utility in letting Miles fill that role. His taunt-laced labels were also creating a unique set of codenames that the Crewe could insert into everyday speech if they wanted to frustrate ready understanding by eavesdroppers. Just as important, by giving the chief free rein as namer-in-chief, it made it easier for him to accept Caine's occasional vetoes. Such as referring to Eku as Frog-pet; that could not be allowed. Assuming they managed to get the factotum back alive.

Craig Girten was still smiling as he asked, "So since you guys got here, did you do anything *besides* finding more words?"

"*Gracias a Dios*, yes. We hit each other with bones."

"No, Dora: seriously."

"I am being serious! We sparred. A lot." She rubbed an arm. "And some people don't know their own strength." She shot an exaggerated glare at Newton.

"I had no prior training with archaic weapons," he muttered. "I lack the skill to adequately control my blows."

"Well, see that you learn!" Dora said sternly, then laughed. "You are too serious, always. I am teasing. Maybe you lack skill at that, too?"

Baruch's expression was glum. "You are not the first to suggest it."

Which Riordan did not find hard to believe. He stood. "We'll show you the training hall. We all need to brush up on our skills with 'archaic' weapons."

Girten frowned. "We *do* have guns, sir."

"We do, but the more often we show them, the more often we'll be noticed. And that's not healthy for us. Whereas training is: let's go."

Despite grumbling, the new arrivals immediately began taking turns with practice weapons in the mostly empty training hall. It was an easy transition; it had become a tradition on Hsontlosh's ship, one which fused agility and aerobic training with weapons drills.

However, it offered an additional benefit here; the training room was one of the few places in Tasvar's citadel where they could speak privately. Multiple passes with Dornaani suit sensors at max resolution detected no apertures or hidey-holes for hidden observers. Probably the Legate's nod to the futility of hearing quiet conversations in a noisy, echoing chamber.

Peter and Miles, the first pair to train, came off the floor to watch Katie and Dora circle each other with dummy shortswords. "That's some fine bone-shaping work," the chief commented, eyeing the practice weapons. "How do they get the weight, though?"

"Sand," Bannor answered, "inside a central tube. Not perfect, but gives about the right heft. Welcome to the big city."

As O'Garran snickered, Peter muttered sideways, "So, I am presuming you mean to tell us about the unusual eye color we noted among some of Tasvar's personal guards?"

"No," Riordan said quietly. "We can't risk that here. Tomorrow, when we are on the streets." He was glad that Peter simply nodded and let the burning issue of a possible Ktoran presence slide away.

Instead, Wu merely crossed his arms and asked, "So, what do you wish to tell us now?"

"The deal we made with Tasvar."

O'Garran angled his head toward them. "I'm all ears," he said pleasantly.

Bannor picked up the thread. "You've seen the local firearms."

"Sure have," Miles muttered, then let a few moments pass as they watched Katie's parries. "Black powder. Mostly flintlocks."

"Correct," Ayana murmured. "Have you seen the more advanced weapons, also?"

Peter nodded approvingly at Katie's improving speed at attacking and then recovering to a defensive stance. "Didn't see any until we got here. High-prestige items, apparently. I am surprised they can produce them."

"They don't," Duncan mumbled. "They unearth some every once in a while."

"Still," Peter objected, "they are evidently producing ammunition for them. I saw a scythe loading a magazine. Old-style brass."

"Yep, but filled with black powder."

In response to Wu's raised eyebrow, Bannor expanded on Duncan's overview. "It means their modern weapons are just glorified bolt actions. The black powder doesn't cycle the action reliably."

"But at least they have primers?"

Riordan nodded. "Various compounds, but all based on fulminate of mercury."

"Ouch," hissed O'Garran.

"Yep," Rulaine agreed. "Testy and corrosive."

Peter nodded faintly. "How does this bear upon the arrangement you have made with Tasvar?"

Yaargraukh rumbled from behind and above. "He has been provided with the knowledge necessary for formulating what you call smokeless powder."

O'Garran almost turned to look over his shoulder in surprise. "And how the hell did we do that?" He stared at Bannor. "Are you playing 'equip the rebels,' again, Colonel?" Insurgency support was still one the Special Forces' primary missions.

"Wish I could take credit for it," Rulaine answered with a grin. "But you'll need to ask the commodore about the specifics."

"The commodore?" The chief's incredulous tone was a bit too loud. Caine suspected he'd come close to blurting out, "What? *Him?*"

But Peter was smiling and nodding. "This is the result of what you learned during your time in Dornaani Virtua, I presume."

Riordan shook his head. "A lot of it is what I learned while I was recovering afterward." He waved aside frustrating memories. "The rebels in virtua needed any military edge they could get. So I helped them develop better explosives. But it took so long." He shook his head. "I only remembered the basics of nitroglycerine, and could barely recall anything about the evolution of smokeless powder." He sighed. "My ignorance cost them months of trial and error, and dozens—maybe hundreds—of lives."

"*Virtual* lives," Bannor stressed.

Riordan nodded reluctantly. *Yeah, they were virtual. But try telling yourself that when you live and fight alongside them every day for months, years. And when they die in your arms.*

Peter was scrutinizing Katie's footwork. "What I do not understand is what you discovered here that makes the knowledge useful. The relevant resources seem quite scarce."

Riordan tilted his head toward the fragrant dogleg passage that communicated with the fortress' main entry. "They have camphor."

After a long, perplexed silence, Wu murmured, "But...but camphor is not an explosive."

"No, it's not." Caine chased away enough of the virtual ghosts to manage a smile. "The problem isn't a lack of ingredients. The two explosives in smokeless powder—nitroglycerine and guncotton—can be generated in sufficient quantities on this planet."

Newton nodded. "Nitrites are produced in many mammalian

intestines. They can also be generated from nitrates by treating them with sulfuric acid, which the locals acquire by leaching low molarity output from seaweeds."

Riordan nodded. "You could use the Ostwald process on copper nitrate, too. The point is, it wasn't the explosives that were lacking. It was the stabilizing ingredients."

"You mean the cotton?" Craig asked dubiously. "Because I don't think it's likely to grow well around here, sir."

Riordan smiled at the paratrooper. "Cotton was just a convenient source of the right kind of cellulose. Here, you can get it from lichens and fungi; they use it instead of straw when making adobe. It's very inferior, but with enough refinement, it can serve the same role as cotton."

Miles crossed his arms. "So if it's easy to make all the stuff that goes bang, why do you need the camphor?"

"Because," Riordan replied, "the stuff that goes bang does it *too fast*. It's good for bombs, which is why it's also good at blowing firearms apart. That's where the camphor comes in. It's both a fixative for nitrite-based explosives and it slows the speed with which they release their energy."

O'Garran sounded slightly chagrined as he looked around the group. "So how come I never heard of this?"

Riordan shrugged. "Because unless you're digging into the history of smokeless powder, it would never come up. Camphor was only used for a few years. It wasn't as efficient as later fixatives and it broke down faster. But here? As long as they're making preindustrial batches, they'll use up the ammunition faster than it can become unstable."

Craig Girten was looking from face to face, perplexed.

"Question?" Bannor asked him.

"Sir, yes, sir. I don't know much about chemistry, but I do know this: we didn't bring a laboratory with us. So how the heck did you get all this information about the local plants and such?"

The black tip of Yaargraukh's tongue poked out. "Actually, Sergeant, we *did* bring a lab with us. Several, in fact."

Girten frowned, then blinked. "The food testers."

Bannor nodded as Katie and Dora walked out of their sparring circle. "Took us a day to collect all the samples. Seaweed was the hardest to get this far from the coast, but there's always some being shipped upriver. Locals use it in their poultices."

"And the camphor?" Peter asked. "I was told that is quite expensive."

Riordan nodded. "Camphor is the sticking point. Not because it's rare, but because it only grows on a distant island."

Dora nodded toward Wu as she wiped sweat from her brow. "Remember the little island I saw just after we came out of shift? With the green on it?"

"Oh," Miles drawled, "you must mean the one you wanted as our drop target? The one that isn't one twentieth the size of the landing footprint we actually used?"

Dora looked like she might stick her tongue out. "Yes, that one. That's where the camphor comes from. It's also the home of the planet's original population."

"Or their final refuge," Ayana amended. "Neither Tasvar nor his subordinates were particularly explicit in their responses. Possibly, because they are not sure themselves. Ironically, a considerable number of Tasvar's soldiers believe Newton is from that place."

Baruch shrugged. "Almost no one in this citadel has met anyone from there. All they know about the place—it is called Zrik Whir—is that its inhabitants have very dark complexions. Those few of Tasvar's retainers who *have* encountered a Zrik Whiran point out that they are actually much darker than I am."

As Duncan turned back toward Peter, his enthusiasm bordered on vengeful glee. "So, all those assault rifles the locals are using like bolt actions? Well, we've just handed the Legate the ability to turn those weapons back into semiautomatics and automatics. Bad times a'comin' for the x'qai."

Miles raised an eyebrow. "Assuming that decades, or more, of metal fatigue will stand up to the new ammunition."

"Yeah, well, you haven't seen the maintenance here."

"That bad?" Craig asked.

Duncan shook his head. "No: that *good*. Anything more modern than a bronze-age implement is regularly assessed. In detail. Anything judged close to failure is put aside and scheduled for replacement." He smiled. "Which gives us yet another trading chit."

Bannor folded his arms. "In what way?"

Duncan rubbed his hands in actual glee. "So, there are only three energy sources here, right? Dung, alcohol, and oil rendered from fats. The last two are extremely expensive, which is why they're usually reserved for their vehicles—"

"They have vehicles?" Craig interrupted through a loud gulp of surprise.

"Yep. Only internal combustion, but that just increases the value of this other trading chit. As I was saying, they replace every piece that fails. *Every piece.* They insist on each new part being a precision fit and made from materials with similar tolerances. And that's where our opportunity lies."

Katie nodded. "Their furnaces aren't hot enough."

O'Garran raised his eyebrows. "I thought you were a...a sociologist, originally."

"I was a sociology *student.* More money in information management for engineering, which is why I got tapped for fire control and heavy weapons. Including maintenance reviews. But back to what matters: How do we help them make hotter fires?" She looked expectantly at Bannor and Duncan.

Who looked at Caine with a smile.

Katie couldn't stop herself from blinking. "Sorry, sir, don't mean to suggest you're dim or anything, but..." She stopped lamely, having realized that she'd only dug a deeper hole.

Caine waved it off. "I was indeed 'dim' about furnaces, until I started researching it four days ago.

Katie frowned. "You researched it here? On this planet? They have libraries?"

"No," he answered, "but *we* do. Well, anyone with a Dornaani vacc suit."

Miles nodded, beaming. "So that's why Eku was so tied up with downloading files. He was pulling records. On everything."

Riordan nodded. "Given Dornaani data compression, we have a very extensive codex of Earth's printed materials. At least, those that existed before 2100."

Ayana folded her hands. "We owe a great debt to Eku. We must retrieve him as quickly as possible."

Miles frowned. "Yeah, and time may be running out. According to the transponder grid, he got to Forkus three days ago."

Ayana nodded. "But where? His suit indicates that basic comms have failed, and the regional grid is too imprecise. At highest resolution, it only shows that he is in the northern half of the city."

"Well, *that's* frustrating," Craig muttered.

"Just like everything having to do with information on this

damned planet," Duncan groused. "No one keeps records. The maps are laughable. Well, the ones that exist. And it's no wonder they don't have any historical record, since they don't have a unified dating system."

"Speaking of records," Craig asked, "what's the story on our hosts?"

Caine nodded cautiously. "That's a very interesting topic. We'll start with it tomorrow, assuming we have enough time."

"Tomorrow's going to be that busy? Why?"

Duncan stretched. "We're going to see the sights and do some shopping."

"Shopping?" Katie echoed, incredulous.

"'To market, to market!'" Miles chanted in a nursery-rhyme singsong. "Or what passes for one, hereabouts."

Riordan smiled. "We need to be on our best behavior." *To say nothing of being on our toes.* "Could be another long day. Time to get some sleep."

# Chapter Twenty-Two

"Why do you call the market a vansary?" Katie asked as the Crewe disembarked under the watchful eyes of a mixed group of warriors cadred by two human "troops." The pennant atop the dock's bone-lading scaffold showed the colors of its owner: a liege known as Vissakash.

Bannor was scanning the weapons of the watchers as he answered. "It's called a vansary because the closest term Low Praakht has for 'market' translates as 'caravansary.' They just shorten it."

"Not that it's really a market," Duncan added. "It's more like an occasional suq hosted on the premises of a major trader: Kosvak, a h'achga. He's the first vassal of Vranadoc."

"Who is...?"

"A human liege," Yaargraukh rumbled, "and independent. As the commodore implied last night, it is best to conclude such conversations before we reach the vansary. Once there, we must assume any exchanges will be overheard."

Dora looked around casually. "And are we really sure the *streets* are any better?"

"'Sure'?" repeated Duncan; he'd overseen counterintelligence and security since the Crewe had boarded Hsontlosh's ship. "Every day, I become *less* sure of anything in this place. But since there's no sign of refractive audio analyzers or old-fashioned parabolic mics, yeah, this is probably our best opportunity. Particularly for topics that we haven't been able to discuss yet."

228

He was answered by knowing nods: oblique and coded conversations on simple matters were safe enough in the Legate's precincts, but not the bigger issues. Particularly not the one that loomed above all others: whether or not Tasvar and the Legate were, knowingly or otherwise, proxies of the Ktor.

Whereas Riordan usually put aside formal titles, they were on the winding streets of a broadly hostile city; operational standards applied. "Sergeant Girten, last night you asked what we know about the Legate. The answer is: not as much as we'd like. His personnel have unusual gaps in their education and technological capabilities. I suspect that's because they have their hands full preserving the machines and knowledge that is most crucial to their survival.

"However, what is harder to explain, and mystifying, is the equally strange silences that dominate what few records seem to exist about the nature and history of their organization."

"Silences such as?" Wu asked slowly.

Bannor shrugged. "The Legate, whoever that is or was, is a name that has been around for a very long time, possibly centuries. Over time, it was thought it was just a title, something from a lost legend and that it had never been attached to an actual person."

"But now he is known to exist? Or at least, someone claiming to be him?"

Bannor nodded.

"Well, where is he, then?" O'Garran asked irritably. "On that island...er, Zrik Whir?"

Bannor shook his head. "That's the one place his followers know he *isn't* located. Although it's also possible that he might have started out there."

Ayana nodded, adding, "And more recently, there are rumors that he has at least visited that island again in the past several decades. During the same period, the Legate's bases began their continuing ascendance: they are far more widespread and effective than they were even fifty years ago."

"So," Katie mused, "whoever first wore the mantle of the Legate had humbler beginnings."

"Much humbler," Duncan emphasized. "Apparently, the original Legate wasn't really a power-holder like the lieges. He built and then sponsored a growing network dedicated to helping escaped humans avoid recapture by their owners."

"Owners?" Dora hissed.

Duncan glanced at her sideways. "Do you think our kind serve x'qai willingly?"

"How do they hold on to us, then?"

"The oldest of methods," Bannor replied. "Hostages."

Dora frowned mightily. "I thought human servitors weren't allowed to have families."

Bannor's tone and eyes were grim. "Just enough to keep them in line."

"Bastards," Girten grumbled.

"Won't get any argument from me," Duncan muttered. "Nor from the Legate's people. The one piece of history that all of Tasvar's people know is that the organization started out as a cross between an underground railroad and a string of well-defended safe houses. Over time, it grew, and sites in the toughest cities had to evolve into full-on strongholds like the one here. But in the past thirty years, its numbers and holdings tripled in size."

"Any idea why?"

"Tasvar and his troops may be cordial, and even friendly, but they don't share much information about themselves. Which I guess I can understand."

Katie nodded. "You mean, because they still don't trust us."

"I mean they can't trust anyone. Even themselves." Duncan shrugged in response to the questioning looks. "No one can stand up to pain forever, and the x'qai enjoy torture almost as much as killing. At least, that's what the Legate's people say."

"As do the h'achgai," Yaargraukh rumbled.

"And the Mangled," Wu added.

"Yeah," Solsohn sighed, "that seems to be one of the few things that everyone can agree on." He shrugged. "There's really not much more than that. I get the feeling they don't have much real history for the reason they don't have any real science; there's just no time for it." He shook his head. "But I'd give a lot to learn how the hell Tasvar learned English."

Riordan heard the rising tone on which Duncan had ended; he had a theory. "So, what are your thoughts?"

"Not so much thoughts, sir. More an interesting coincidence."

"Go on."

"Well, it was just about thirty years ago that trouble started brewing back in our neck of the woods. Specifically, that was when the Accord started having serious problems, mostly because your pal Nolan Corcoran discovered that the Doomsday Rock wasn't a random asteroid but an alien attack.

"Fast forward through first contact, invasion, and the discovery of the Lost Soldiers. Back in the Ktoran Sphere, the big Houses go on a witch hunt for the rogue operators who were behind all those disasters. They kill most of them and exile the rest to the Scatters."

Newton shook his head. "Those exiles cannot be here yet. The earliest they began their journey was five years ago . . . on an STL ship. This system is hundreds of light-years distant. At least."

Duncan nodded. "Absolutely right. But now, let's turn the clock back oh, say, almost two centuries. The big players in House Perekmeres have just decided to go rogue. Some of the other hegemons think they're nuts but don't dare say so. So that group comes up with a contingency plan: establish a hidden colony out beyond the Scatters. That way, if the crazy schemes fail and they're exiled, they'll have a place already waiting." He gestured at the world around them.

Chief O'Garran looked like he'd bitten into a rancid lemon. "So you think the Legate is actually—what? A front for Ktor renegades who set up a safe haven?"

Duncan shrugged. "I'm not married to the scenario: just trying to find one that explains both the amber eyes and the English language."

Riordan raised his hand, as much to steer them around a congested cluster of huts as end the debate. "We won't settle this without more information. But Duncan's scenario tracks with something we've all felt: that even if there are some Ktor genes in the population here, the Ktor *culture* itself doesn't seem to be. For instance, there's no trace of their various social rankings and titles. Similarly, there's no apparent knowledge of the Sphere itself or the Accord, let alone any recent events in either.

"It's possible that a bunch of Ktor colonists brought knowledge of English with them. It's also possible that we're not the first ship to ever mis-shift into this system. But here's a final fact to consider: if the Ktor or their descendants are still in charge here, then why haven't they *concealed* everyone with amber eyes? And why would Tasvar admit to understanding English? We have to remain watchful, yes, but so far, I don't feel that we're being duped."

Katie sighed. "But from whut ye're sayin', it's still not safe to ask more about this world for fear that it might set them to asking more questions about *us*. And maybe themselves."

"Unfortunately, that ignorance is much more likely to kill us than Ktor who might not even exist on this planet," Newton added.

Riordan paused long enough to be sure he was heard loud and clear. "We are in a world where the greatest danger is to appear weak, and that is precisely how we will be seen if we start asking about its most common pitfalls and dangers. Better to be silent and presumed dangerous than to show everyone that you're an easy mark because you're not from Bactradgaria."

"But boss," mumbled Dora, "Tasvar knows that already."

"Yes, he does. And we'll discuss it when we return from the vansary."

Miles' voice was tense. "Yeah, but where? I swear to God, if Tasvar hasn't already realized we're using the practice chamber for conversations we don't want him to hear, then he's a low-grade moron."

Bannor smiled. "That's not a problem any more. We approached him on that and he's agreed to give us access to a place we chose: outside, on the roof of one of the towers." There was a general chorus of approving mutters and grunts.

"We need a second language, too," Dora said a bit more loudly than she should have. "Our own battle language, like Tasvar."

"I suppose you have a suggestion?" Ayana asked with a rise at the end of her question; it made her sound almost impish.

Veriden grinned at her friend. "I do. Spanish is best. Over half of us already speak some. And I could teach the rest of you, so you'd catch up fast. Yes?"

Riordan kept his voice low. "Spanish is great because most of us at least speak a little of it. Unfortunately, that's also why it might be the worst language: because it's so widely used on Earth. And if Ktor colonists are how Tasvar got his knowledge of English..."

After a long frowning silence, Dora shrugged. "Yeah, you're right. So what's our next choice?"

Riordan managed to hide his surprise at Veriden's easy compliance. "On the other hand, we've got a number of folks who speak a fair amount of German."

"Who, other than you and Yaargraukh?"

Craig shrugged. "I grew up with Yiddish in my ear. When we landed in France, that made me the closest thing we had to a translator."

"And me," Solsohn added. "My ex-wife was Danish, from a town that straddled the German border. Her mother was from just south of it."

"And just to make life harder for eavesdroppers," O'Garran added, "we're already coming up with our own words. Like 'trog.'" He smiled triumphantly in response to several pairs of rolled eyes. "Before long, between that and German, whatever patchwork language we're speaking isn't going to make sense to anyone outside the Crewe. Now where's this damn, eh, vansary?"

"Yeah," Girten followed, "and how are we going to buy anything, if we don't have money—or what passes for it—around here?"

Riordan smiled. "Tasvar implied we would be furnished with an expense account, for lack of a better term."

Craig became eager. "Really? So what are we getting? Local weapons? Supplies?"

"All that," Bannor answered, "and, hopefully, a business opportunity."

"A what?"

"A way," Riordan answered, "of making our own way in the world. That's part of what Tasvar is providing in exchange for the smokeless powder."

"You mean he's set up a meet?" Dora asked, at once eager and wary. "How do we know we can trust him?"

"We don't need to," Bannor smiled.

"What? Why?"

"Because Arashk is our go-between," Riordan answered. "But better still, Hresh is vouching for us."

Wu nodded, understanding. "Because as an oathkeeper, if he attests to our trustworthiness, he is committing his own oath and honor in place of ours. Ta'rel mentioned this."

"There is a similar convention among the praakht," Yaar-graukh added.

"Yeah," Miles agreed. "There are lots of trogs in the Legate's ranks, but none can join until they've sworn an oath of loyalty in front of an oathkeeper."

Riordan increased the pace. "We won't actually meet with Arashk's group. They can't risk being seen with us. But once we locate our contact, Hresh will send them a prearranged signal that we are the ones who can be trusted."

"And how do we locate this contact?" Katie wondered.

Bannor smiled. "They will be the only ones selling oars."

"Oars?" Miles laughed. "Really?"

Riordan nodded. "I suspect it's an attempt to sow seeds of misdirection."

"It encourages any one observing us to presume that our next mode of travel will be by boat," Yaargraukh expanded.

Up ahead, the haze of dung fires thinned, revealing fitted stone structures and tall, smooth outlines of reclaimed ruins beyond them.

"Are we headed in there?" asked Peter, a bit reluctantly.

Bannor shook his head. "We'll be skirting it, staying just inside the edge of Vranadoc's area of control."

"More like 'turf,'" Dora muttered, glancing at the buildings and ubiquitous armed bravos standing at their entrances. All wore a distinctive symbol or color, sometimes both. "A lot more like gangs than 'domains.'"

"You're not far off," Miles chuckled. "That's the Low Praakht term for their own groups. They call themselves 'tribes' in the wastes, but here they're gangs. Or great gangs, if they've got more than a few dozen mouths to feed."

Riordan nodded ahead. "There's the vansary. One o'clock. Low ruin expanded by a slightly lower, fitted-stone wall."

"Not the mad rush of merchants I was expecting," Newton admitted as a steady flow of persons both entered and exited the wide opening.

"Probably because there aren't enough excess goods to support general trade," Duncan said with a frown. "Even when it's almost all barter."

Veriden smiled sideways at him. "Much as I hate agreeing with Mister Suit, he's right. I was born in a place almost as bad. You watch: almost everything will be items most people can't afford and wouldn't be able to use."

Riordan nodded toward the opening, where a human—or was it a trog?—was stopping individuals intermittently. Two guards who were clearly trogs stood behind him, silent and watchful. "Wrap the robes tightly, now."

Dora snickered. "Okay, boss, but you know it's not gonna fool anyone, right?"

"Not up close, no. But it makes our gear less visible from further away. And that's helpful enough."

As they neared the opening, the troggish human took a step toward them. The outline of a circle had been tattooed on the center of his forehead. "I speak with my Liege Vranadoc's voice in this place. You are expected at the vansary."

"We are honored," Riordan said. Yaargraukh nodded diffidently.

But the gatekeeper's eyes had fixed on Newton. "I did not know . . . eh, was not told that there would be . . ." He leaned closer to Newton. "If you are from Zrik Whir, you must know this place is not safe for your kind." He glanced at a rammed-earth platform that was pushed up against the marshalling yard's north wall. Riordan turned his head just enough to bring it into his peripheral vision.

Reapers. At least a dozen of them, but standing in four different groups. Some were watching the entry, but most were disinterestedly scanning the crowd winding through the hides and tents of the vansary.

In the meantime, Baruch had drawn up to his full, impressive height. He stared down at the gatekeeper. "I *am* from an island, but it is very unlikely you have heard of it. If you wish to question me further, I shall comply."

Riordan turned his head just enough to ensure that neither of the guards could see his small smile. Newton had responded just as they'd rehearsed it: a truth that not only evaded the question, but did not deny being from Zrik Whir, either.

"Questions will not be required," said the gatekeeper. "You are free to enter with your friends." He moved aside, already preparing to intercept another approaching group.

Veriden's tone was pure preen as they strolled through the opening. "I see you took my advice about *mal de ojo*," she said, glancing sideways at Caine.

"No reason why I shouldn't," Riordan answered. If it made Dora happy to feel that her beliefs—not to say superstitions—were being acknowledged, then that was fine with him. But beyond that, Caine had to admit that, although there was no evidence that Yasla possessed parapsychological gifts, there had certainly been times when Ktor actions or knowledge defied reason. It went far beyond their prowess and extraordinary control over their bodies. There had been too many occasions when they had apparently exchanged or acquired knowledge more rapidly than should have been possible over the distances involved. And if they had indeed left some mark on Bactradgaria...well, better safe than sorry.

"I didn't know you were actually from Samoa," Duncan was murmuring as they surveyed the wilderness of blankets and tents before them.

"My father was a professor and a naval reserve officer on Guam when he met my Samoan mother. From there, we lived in Okinawa, Hawaii, and ultimately returned to Samoa." He may have smiled. "I am in no danger of running out of islands with which to mislead interviewers, trog or human."

"Or in his case," Miles added, jerking a thumb back at the gatekeeper, "a trogan."

"A...a what?" Craig stammered.

Yaargraukh's tone was that of dogged, even grim, patience. "Just this morning, Chief O'Garran assigned that label to Legate troop leaders who are trog-human hybrids."

"Trogan," Miles repeated. "Kind of catchy, I think. And not racist, like their own words for mixed-species folk."

Riordan hadn't heard those. "Which are?"

Wu glanced sideways at him. "You don't want to know, sir. Really."

They had to form a tight column as they entered the wilderness of ware-loaded blankets scattered on the vansary's dusty marshalling ground. At the far end was a paddock, apparently for dirtkine. To the left were the ancient walls which anchored a larger stronghold that had been built out from them. It was fronted by a portico of rude columns which, judging from the troughs of stone in front of them, doubled as hitching posts. And to the right—

Riordan was careful as he let his gaze return to the platform upon which the bored scythes and harrows stood. Behind them hung bleached hides bearing the sigil of their host: Kosvak, first vassal of Vranadoc and one of the few h'achgai who held such a high position.

But despite that reminder of whose domain they were visiting, the reapers did not comport themselves as guests: their swagger and behavior was anything but respectful. As had been the group encountered at the edge of the city, they were a polyglot group of many races. This time, however, when Caine's glance passed over the humans among them, he noticed a few eyes that glittered a distinctive amber, visible despite the distance and dust being raised by both sellers and buyers.

Several larger and decidedly metallic gleams caught Riordan's attention: not only did each group hold a bone staff topped with the banner of their liege, but surmounting each was a gold disk, shining like a small sun in the early morning light.

"Hey, boss," Dora muttered, "are you actually going to look at what's on offer, here?" She smiled mischievously. "Or are you just going to gawk like a tourist?"

"I figure I can just gawk, since I have such a supremely capable tour guide."

She snorted a short laugh as they continued to wend their way through the vendors.

"No stalls," Ayana murmured, "but many have low tents."

Duncan nodded toward the portico to the left. "Or not so low." That end of the marshalling ground seemed to be where the larger, or preferred, merchants were clustered. Many had pitched tents large enough to hold several persons.

"Good way to endure a long day in the sun," Newton observed.

"An even better way to make deals in private," Duncan added. "And given some of what's on offer, I could see that being a major consideration."

Riordan was inclined to agree. As Dora had predicted, none of the core resources of Bactradgaria were present. The closest was what appeared to be specially treated animal sinew and a variety of products fashioned from them: ropes, heavy nets, and thick bowstrings.

Also as Dora had foreseen, the rest of the goods would only have been of interest to those who held, or aspired to, considerable power. Expertly crafted obsidian weapons were displayed alongside scalpels and other surgical tools, not all of which were familiar to Riordan. Nearby, several of the very thin humanoids were negotiating commissions for crafting several mystifying implements. Trogs, or probably trogans, were doing much the same with flint knapping, most of their projects involving knives or arrowheads.

But the mainstay of the vansary was a wide array of more costly—and rare—resources and the finished goods made from them. Ingots of copper, tin, bronze, and iron lay alongside metal weapons, armor, and tools, many of which were repaired salvage. Fluids in crude glass tubes, some quite noxious, were the predominant chemicals, although the pride of place was given to more esoteric compounds: salves, unguents, and what appeared to be machine lubricants. Newton shrugged helplessly when Caine asked what he thought the various substances might be; the translator did no better.

Then there were the salt merchants—a whole row of them—who were the most contentious in the vansary, busily undercutting each other's prices while disparaging the purity of competitors' supplies. By comparison, those who dealt in mined substances—coal, sulfur, talc, limestone, and possibly phosphorus—were taciturn and not disposed to haggle at all: their wares seemed so intrinsically valuable and rare that they were assured of selling out their stock by day's end.

The most enigmatic of the merchants were two who remained fully robed and had no wares on display, but, after brief conversations with customers, retired into their tent and always reemerged with a small hide pouch. The contents were light and irregularly shaped, and the hushed nature of their exchanges led Veriden to chuckle, "Wonder if they're drug dealers." Riordan had to admit they certainly acted that way.

But Peter murmured. "No. They are not."

"How do you know?"

"Look at the hand of the one who is receiving the payment."

Riordan did. "Yes?" Although dust-covered, it looked almost greenish.

"That hand is Ta'rel's."

Dora's eyes went wide. "He's a drug dealer?"

"He most certainly is *not*," Peter hissed. "He deals in moss—a curative, of some sort. And very valuable." Instead of heading in that direction, Peter turned away.

"What? Don't you—we—want to meet him?"

"It is *he* who doesn't want to meet."

"How do you know? He didn't even see us!"

Wu let a very small smile escape. "Oh, I'm quite sure he did. But just like Arashk and his group, he cannot risk being seen with us. If he wishes to make contact, I am sure he will. Let us move on."

"Not so fast, Peter," Duncan muttered. "Turn around."

They all did.

Two hides further along the winding path between the display hides of the vendors, the white edge of an oar-blade was visible around haggling praakht.

# Chapter Twenty-Three

Riordan stopped in front of the oar; the others remained nearby, but not clustered around him. "I am in need of oars," he said.

The h'achga sitting on the other side of the display hide looked up from keeping accounts on a piece of slate. "How many?" The chalk in his long, orang fingers had not stopped, only slowed.

"At least four."

"So many?"

"Yes."

"You must be traveling in rough waters or in a large boat."

Riordan stared at the merchant: if anyone was watching, it would hopefully appear to be a moment of forced patience. "How much?"

The chalk in the h'achga's hand became still. It was more than slightly disorienting to watch a creature that was at least as much simian as human wield it so deftly when most of the trogs around were clearly incapable of reading or writing a single symbol. "I have not seen you here before."

*You're really playing the part, aren't you?* "And you may not see me here again, if you continue to touch on personal topics."

The other's heavy, receding brow rose. "I am merely being friendly." He glanced toward, but not directly at, the mound where the scythes ostensibly watched the marshalling ground. "Unlike some others." His gaze moved back toward Caine but it lingered on the feed silos behind the paddock for a moment.

Then Ulchakh's eyes reconnected with Riordan's. He smiled again. Knowingly.

*So Hresh just gave his thumbs-up.* Riordan let his own glance wander toward the platform where standards of four x'qai lieges flapped fitfully in a faint river breeze that had struggled into the center of the city. "It can be so difficult to tell when unfriendly people will act on their feelings."

The trader waved away a fly as he glanced down at the hem of Caine's robe... and the vacc boot soles that were visible beneath. "Yes, but today, they appear uninterested. At least, so far."

Riordan played along. "Perhaps they are simply blind."

The greying h'achga huffed. "They are certainly able to see through or around anything less than a complete disguise." He returned to making more marks on his slate, but his attention was clearly still on Caine. "But if they already know to expect unusual visitors, they would not be unduly concerned. Or even interested. Unless those visitors had failed to take the step of concealing their status from those less alert." His eyes briefly ran the length of Caine's robe.

"And if the visitors hadn't taken that precaution?"

The human-orang shrugged. "It might well injure their pride, prompt them to confront such persons... even if they had orders not to." The h'achga looked up again. "Grievances are easy to manufacture in a vansary where there is much shoving and jostling."

Riordan nodded. *And while we're on the topic...* "I am unfamiliar with the gold disk with which our watchers adorn their standards."

The merchant regarded him with a look that Caine read as, *Congratulations: you just told everyone standing close enough to hear that you know absolutely* nothing *about life in this, or any other, city.* "I doubt the vansary here is too different from the ones you've seen before. It is one of the few places that such watchers may mix safely. Indeed, they enforce the truce that makes such trade possible. The bond-gold disk signifies not only the wealth of those whom they serve, but that they are sworn to uphold the peace."

"And if a power wishes to send such watchers but hasn't enough gold to craft such a disk?"

The h'achga shrugged. "Then that power hasn't enough wealth to warrant sending watchers, and so, has no voice or business here." He glanced up. "But clearly you do, bond-gold or not." He put his slate aside. "You asked how much. I asked why you are interested in purchasing an oar because your answer may influence the price I quote."

Riordan nodded. "Ask your question plainly, then."

"If you are heading downstream, then I might reduce the price. I have a message that must be relayed to my partner in the port of Atagurkhu. So, if you are traveling that far, we should have a private meeting to discuss the cost of the oars *if* you are willing to deliver my message."

"Then let us have that discussion," Riordan replied, suppressing a smile. He'd dealt with senior interstellar diplomats, human and otherwise, who could learn a thing or three from the paleolithic orang hybrid in front of him. Who'd purposely spoken loud enough to be heard. Who'd made sure the conversation proceeded as contentious haggling, rather than as a suspiciously smooth agreement. Who had used an implied reduction in price to pry Riordan's travel plans out of him, which would mislead anyone who might intend to follow the Crewe. And of course, whose need to both share his message and settle on the price made it essential that they retire to the privacy of his "office."

The h'achga rose, brushing chalk dust off his hide armor. He held open the flap of his tepee-shaped tent just as Duncan joined Caine. "My name is Ulchakh. On my oath and honor, I bid you enter as guests."

Ulchakh's "office" only had room for three, but most of the others were listening on an open channel. Outside, Yaargraukh was already reprising the role he'd played upon entering Forkus: diffidently monitoring his "human servitors."

"I would offer you water and salt," Ulchakh said in an apologetic tone, "but we should not spend much time within."

Riordan nodded. "Wise. So: our mutual friends are of the opinion we might help each other."

"I agree. You have noticed that I am the only vendor who is alone in the vansary?"

"We have," Duncan answered. Which was good, because Riordan had not.

"That is because my assistants have abandoned me or are dead, and I have no way to return home safely."

"And where is your home?" Riordan asked.

"We shall return to that in a moment. So you may know that helping me will not bring the anger of any lieges upon you, here is the tale of how I come to be alone.

"Twenty days ago, I arrived in Forkus with my trade goods. I had started out with three warriors from my home and five others who helped bear the loads to the nearest town on the northern river: Khorkrag. Once there, the five bearers returned to their hearths and I hired five more guards from among the many unattached praakht of that region.

"The journey down the river was swift, for we had brought the sections of a boat both for travel and, upon reaching Forkus, sale. Once we had assembled it, we started south, staying close to the west bank, which is safer. However, camping ashore as one must, we were twice set upon by beasts of the wastes. One of my kinsmen and two of the praakht were lost.

"It was our good fortune to draw abreast of a caravan that had set out from Fragkork, a city north of Khorkrag, shortly after half our journey was complete. Unable to control the boat adequately with so few hands, we agreed to parallel them during travel and camp with them at night. We also rowed slightly ahead of the caravan twice a day, to report back any dangers visible from the shallows. It was a useful agreement and only one more of my praakht guards was wounded.

"Upon arriving in Forkus, we parted ways with the caravan. The praakh's wound did not heal on its own. So, I acted as I had promised when hiring them: I found a shaman to heal him. The praakht were grateful at first, but less so when their share was reduced—as were all of ours, in equal measure—to pay for the shaman's help.

"We were sheltering with my kin on the north bank of this city, but after I had secured a buyer for the cargo—hides, salt-meat, waterskins, bonework, and the boat itself—I still had to deliver them. This required hiring porters to bear the goods on the ferry that took the boat in tow. Unfortunately, one of the winter-end storms swept in and, although the trade was completed, I was unable to board a returning ferry until the next day.

"The night I was gone, an argument arose between my kinsmen and the two healthy praakht, who claimed that they had never been told that their shares would be equally reduced in order to heal one of their number. They insisted that the salt I had been given as an advance against full payment should be their compensation. My kinsmen disagreed and physically prevented them from taking the salt.

"During the night, the praakht slew my two friends and fled with the salt. Untended, the wounded praakht was dead by morning. So I returned to find myself alone and stranded in Forkus."

He rested his long, flat hands on his knees. "That is the sum of my tale. I am now wealthy but friendless. That can quickly change to 'poor and dead,' unless I travel in the company of strong and trustworthy friends. Which Arashk and Hresh say you are. My cargo is light: more salt, iron warheads, several bows, several ingots of bronze and one of iron. There is also a suit of scale mail, also bronze. I have angered no lieges or vassals. I know these lands well and shall teach you of them and the creatures that call them home. Will you have me travel with you?"

Duncan was rubbing his nose. "We are honored by your trust, but it is not certain if we will be traveling in the direction you wish. It could—"

"However," Riordan interrupted, "let us hear more of what you propose. It may convince us to travel in the direction you require." If they moved an eight-man boat overland to a town and then assembled it there, they not only had impressive skills; their understanding of planning and precision made them natural allies. That alone might make the trip worthwhile. And Ulchakh had yet to put his part of the deal on the table.

He wasted no time doing so. "That we may be quick, I hope you will forgive any assumptions I make, based on what I have been told and now, have witnessed."

Riordan nodded.

"You are new in this, eh, region, and so, are ignorant of it. That is a great danger, whether you remain within Forkus or depart. You do not know what you might encounter, or whose anger you might incur and why.

"There is but one remedy for this: to have friends who will answer your questions and show you safe paths. And to have a safe place in which to learn those lessons and from which to make your first forays to achieve whatever goals may shape your actions. Do I speak correctly?"

Riordan smiled. "Please continue."

Ulchakh smiled back. "My home is such a place. It is a stronghold of the h'achgai, called Achgabab. This is the place to which I must return. I can assure that you will be gladly received there, treated as guests, and, by the time we reach it, you will have completed most of the learning you must have to move safely about these lands."

Solsohn nodded. "How far is the journey?"

"It would be in two parts. The first is to follow the river from Forkus north to Khorkrag. Then from there to Achgabab. The journey beside the river is long; I do not know how you measure such things."

"Go ahead," Riordan reassured him, "we understand your distances."

Duncan nodded at the two values Ulchakh shared. "So," he said glancing at Riordan, "I make that about seven hundred eighty kilometers to Khorkrag, and another one hundred eighty to Achgabab." In German he added, "That's quite a trek."

Riordan frowned. "I am aware," he said in English. Then, turning to Ulchakh: "My friend slipped into one of our native languages. He observed that this is a very great distance." He smiled. "However, I expected no less. How long might the journey be?"

"No less than forty-five days, perhaps somewhat more. The weather is often difficult in early spring."

About twenty klicks for every fifteen hours of daylight. Over level ground. *Doable, but add local footwear to the shopping list.* "And we would be responsible not merely for your safety, but meals and other needs during that journey?"

The greying h'achga smiled. "You have bartered before."

"Some," Riordan said, remembering doing so in countless downtrodden towns he'd passed through during his time in virtua.

Ulchakh laughed. "Hresh was right. You will be good companions. You are not easily fooled, and you have a sense of humor."

Riordan smiled. "I presume that we shall work out the details through our mutual friends, so I shall restrict myself to one more question that cannot be asked or answered except directly." He leaned forward. "Why us?"

"Well, it is as I have said: you are strong, have been vouched for by an oathkeeper, and—"

"No, there is something else. As valuable as the education and safe haven of your home might be, you risk none of your wealth and ask us to put all ours to work in ensuring your safety. You must have something else to offer." He smiled. "This was your final test, of course."

"Of course," Ulchakh agreed and unveiled a delighted smile that showed his very simian teeth in a broad arc. "Beyond becoming known to my people and perhaps finding advantageous trade with them, my home is near a terrain anomaly that is likely to be of great interest to you."

"Which is?"

"This winter just past brought hard weather. Terrible wind and rain. There were even two *matjvalkar*."

"Matjvalkar?" Riordan repeated uncertainly.

"A spinning wind that destroys whatever it touches."

*Well, now we know the word for "tornado."* "Go on."

"It changed the land in places, particularly the lay of the dunes where the dust gives way to nothing but sand. We might not have learned how great those changes were for a whole season, had not one of our young males—Djubaran—made his *cho'urz* into it."

"Explain cho'urz," asked Duncan. After Ulchakh had complied, adding many cultural details, Solsohn exchanged nods with Caine. "A walkabout." Turning back to Ulchakh, he explained, "Some of our peoples have a similar tradition."

Riordan leaned forward. "And one has *exactly* this tradition."

"Ah, the x'qagrat'r lord. His people are wise. Better that those who cannot survive life upon the wastes perish early. If not, their frailty can bring death to companions who are honor sworn not to abandon them, even when they should."

Not only did Duncan nod meaningfully, but all the military personnel listening in on the channel grunted approvingly.

Riordan was fairly sure where the young h'achga's story was headed. "And what did Djubaran find in the reshaped dunes?"

"The reappearance of what we call the 'flat tops.' It has been generations since they were last seen, and many doubted that they were anything other than tales. But Djubaran saw them."

"What are they?"

"We do not know, except that they are from the time of ruins. Their tops are flat, their sides are sloped. Their stone surfaces are like those of several liege-forts in Forkus, like the Legate's: one piece, smooth as if poured into that shape rather than built from pieces."

Riordan heard the ripple of murmurs Ulchakh's description sent through the Crewe: surprised and hopeful. Even if he did not react audibly, Duncan's eyes showed the same reaction. Which, for purposes of negotiation, was about as helpful as a poker player who gasped in joy every time a choice card came their way.

Ulchakh smiled. "Be at ease, friends-of-Arashk. We intend fair dealing. We value your friendship more than your strength of arms. Whatever your past, your present shows you to be a clan of powerful humans who are their own masters. Presently, this is very dangerous to you, because it is dangerous to the x'qai.

"But what is dangerous to the x'qai is *very* valuable to us. So, if you are as honorable as Arashk has judged, and we treat you as friends now, it is to be hoped that you will treat us as friends when you come into your greater power. For we have no doubt that you shall do just that."

Riordan nodded so deeply that he was almost in a sitting bow. "You do us honor."

Ulchakh returned the gesture. "As you do us." His reply and movement had the fluidity of a ritual. When he straightened, he waved northward. "The flat tops are legend not because of their shape, but because it is said that in times past, there was much salvage to be found in such structures. Many lieges grew strong by sending their humans to extract wonders from those ruins. But some structures were beyond their ability to enter, there being no gaps or cracks through which they could enter the otherwise sealed vaults of the past."

He gestured to the vacc suit collar peeking out above the folds of the robe which had gapped since Riordan entered the tent. "Arashk told us of your numbers and equipment. It matches what we heard of a similar number and type of unsworn reapers who had just recently entered Forkus through the precincts that answer to the Adbruz Consortium. And I thought, above all others, they will know how to enter the flat tops if it is at all possible. They will also be more likely to understand and fix whatever wonders might lie within them. And if we have reason to believe that they will thus become our true friends, then we would be fools not to be theirs now: that their growth might amplify our own."

Riordan nodded. Bactradgaria was a backward and savage planet, but the concept of mutual enlightened benefit had some-how survived. He began to stand.

But Ulchakh held up his long, grey hand. "Do you not wish some details of the deed that you must yet perform?"

Riordan managed to resist narrowing his eyes. *And here's the small print.* "So there's another part to this agreement?"

Ulchakh nodded somberly. "Yes. I presumed something might have been mentioned to you. We have a mutual friend who often aids Kosvak and who, within reason, shall fund your purchases here. Through that friend's peer Vranadoc, he learned that one of Kosvak's h'achgai bands on the north bank are in imminent danger of attack by a nearby gang of praakht. If someone does not intercede very soon, my kinfolk will be killed."

Riordan remained calm. *Tasvar, I told you that we are not executioners.* But all he said was. "You seem very certain of that sad outcome."

"I am. The praakht gang leader has recently acquired a very valuable asset which he means to trade in exchange for many warriors and weapons. Once he has done so, he will be too powerful for Kosvak's h'achgai to resist." He folded his hands and waited.

*Great.* "Ulchakh, I fear there may have been a misunderstanding. With all respect, we wish to help you and your friends, but our swords are not for sale to the highest bidder."

"And we are not asking that they be so."

"But you said—"

"My apologies. I failed to explain adequately. Kosvak does not propose to pay you for attacking. He is, through me, suggesting that eliminating this threat will also achieve a goal that is very important to you."

"Which is?"

"Why, rescuing the other stranger who's dressed as you are. The first one who arrived on a boat."

Duncan jerked forward. "Wait: is *he* the valuable asset?"

"Most certainly. He is your friend, is he not?"

Riordan looked at Duncan, heard the tense, eager mutters of the Crewe. "He is indeed our friend, Ulchakh. Very much so."

"Excellent. Then I shall acquaint you with what I know of his circumstances..."

# Chapter Twenty-Four

The senior reaper—Harrow Bazakan, a human who hailed from Beyond—stepped from the cluster of his fellows, took the gold hammer proffered by their liege's arurkré lieutenant, and struck the iron-coated thigh bone of their lord's greatest kill. The reverberations sounded through the audience chamber and out into the mustering hall of the immense, ancient-crafted stronghold. "Behold, he comes wreathed in triumphant horror," Bazakan shouted, "Liege Hwe'tsara: suppliant of the dread suzerain Ormalg, and his word and hand in this place!"

Fezhmorbal shifted so that his chain mail did not bunch as he rose with the rest of what Hwe'tsara liked to call his "court." As if the collection of beasts and brutes in the rude chamber could be considered anything other than a squalid lair of rabid monsters. *But, in service to the race, I rise and comply.*

The liege did not enter for several seconds. It was his wont to remind his inner circle that they waited upon his will and whims. Far too many of the latter, for Fezhmorbal's taste, but after all, Hwe'tsara was an x'qao. He wasn't beast-spawned, true, but he still had his species' innate tendency toward impatience and caprice.

*If anything,* Fezhmorbal thought as the three-meter x'qao made a slow progress to his granite throne, *it is his limited prospects that make him so particularly suited for our purposes.* Hwe'tsara was immense, but was neither true-blooded nor had he sprouted

248

a second pair of arms, so it was by now a near surety that he was not an arurkré. Fezhmorbal managed not to smirk. Hence the x'qao's pitiful efforts to impress: his slow stride, the even slower roll of his immense shoulders, and his pointed disregard of those gathered in his great hall.

Upon reaching the seat, Hwe'tsara stopped, faced outward, and raised both his hands. His fingers were spread wide.

Snarling and whining, all the lesser x'qa—the q'akh who had malformed hands and the 'qo who had none—sank to the floor, kneeling or prostrating themselves according to their station. They were joined by all those praakht who were not *kajh*—warriors— but had skills or crafts which had led them to foreswear bearing weapons except in defense of the fortress.

Hwe'tsara held them in their postures of supplication for a ten-count, then lowered his hands. But he did nod toward Bazakan to release him from further attending him until seated and settled upon the throne. *The human will remember that,* Fezhmorbal thought with grim pleasure as the liege gestured to his left without even looking. The newest kajh in the hall, a tribal praakh who had recently distinguished himself in battle, approached the throne. Lowering his eyes, he raised the tribute bowl until its rim was almost touching Hwe'tsara's seventh—and so, smallest—finger.

The moment the x'qao touched it, the typical annoying buzz began. All the insects that were bound to any x'qai in the fortress answered the blood-call of their master—or the master of their master, in most cases—and began gathering just within the entrance. In a few moments, the air just inside and outside the broad opening was thick with their bodies and their noise.

Disinterested, or at least feigning it, Hwe'tsara bade them approach.

A thin stream of the largest insects emerged from the mid-air tornado of their smaller fellows, reaching toward him like a tentative tendril. One by one, they began landing on the rim of the bowl, dropping small chunks of flesh or insect carcasses into it. Each waited a moment and when Hwe'tsara did not react, they alighted briefly on his torso or legs, then flew madly off, a flake of his shedding skin hanging from their mandibles. A few paused before doing so, uncertain if their offering was acceptable: whether it did, in fact, weigh at least half what they did.

When the bowl was full, Hwe'tsara paused the rest of the swarm with a gesture. When they had quieted, he tipped its contents into his mouth.

Just behind Fezhmorbal's shoulder, he heard his new lieutenant Gasdashrag retching. "You have not seen that before?"

Gasdashrag shook his head, swallowing forcibly: to vomit would be a dangerous sign of weakness.

"Good. You have passed."

"Passed...what?" Gasdashrag said, voice thick.

"The test of seeing an x'qao liege consume tribute."

"And if I had failed?"

"Hwe'tsara might have banned you from returning or being a part of any mission we undertake on his behalf. Or he might have had you devoured right here."

Gasdashrag started. "Surely, you are not serious."

Fezhmorbal turned and stared at him. "You have bile on your lip. Lick it off and attend." He turned back to face the throne directly.

The smaller insects were clustering around the bowl now, but always careful to land and drop their tribute separately. When one did so and attempted to fly off in the same instant, Hwe'tsara raised a finger of his other hand. The insect, as large as Fezhmorbal's wizened thumb, stopped abruptly, hovering. The hum of its wings was suddenly loud and irregular, as if it were struggling to fly out of a snare. Then, inch by inch, still buzzing wildly, it flew slowly back toward the liege, rising as it did.

Hwe'tsara's jaws parted in a smile as the insect came closer. He extended his long, serrated tongue.

"What is happening?" Gasdashrag whispered.

"The liege is compelling it by a blood bond...and demonstrating what happens to those whose tribute is less than half their own weight."

The insect, wings working steadily even as its legs struggled wildly, alit on the tip of the x'qao's tongue.

For a moment, all the other insects hovered and the various onlooking humanoids and x'qa watched, silent. Then, with a sound like a muddy knife slipping into a leather sheath, Hwe'tsara's tongue retracted abruptly. The insect emitted a shrill, desperate sound and was gone.

The liege sent a glance around the room, then held forth the bowl again. The ritual of tribute resumed.

Gasdashrag managed to keep his shuddering exhalation almost entirely silent. Fezhmorbal suppressed a sigh. Disappointing, that one of his own race was so easily distressed by the behavior of an x'qao. One should expect monstrous deeds from monsters, after all. But Gasdashrag, being highly intelligent, learned rapidly because of how intently he observed others' failures. In time, he would be able to do so without also imagining himself in the place of the one whom he observed.

The smaller insects filled three bowls' worth for Hwe'tsara. Empty, he held it toward a final humming cluster of insects near the opening. As they advanced, Gasdashrag murmured, "Why have they held back?"

"Because they are not like the others, not mere kiksla," Fezhmorbal explained.

Gasdashrag frowned. "Kiksla? But I was told the word for insect is 'kik.'"

*I hope you are worth the trouble of training you, neophyte.* "It is. Kiksla are those insects with which higher x'qao can forge a blood bond, and so, be influenced. This last group of insects are more special still; they are kiktzo. Through that blood bond, x'qao can not only command their actions, but see and hear what they witness."

Gasdashrag was nodding thoughtfully, almost flinched when one of the kiktzo was consumed at a snap by an irritated Hwe'tsara. "It is strange, that so useful an insect—a kiktzo?—is destroyed for so small a failure."

"If they do not have sufficient tribute, there is no mercy. It is the way of the x'qai. And not just with insects." *But so horribly wasteful,* Fezhmorbal added silently. Such a consideration would only elicit scorn from an x'qao, no matter how evolved or intelligent. To them, losing a single set of eyes and ears was not only acceptable but desirable, if it improved the breeds that could become kiktzo. *And that luxury of loss reminds their subjects—and they themselves—why they can afford it: their control of the world is absolute.* Whereas every other race, including Fezhmorbal's own *deciqadi*, perpetually fretted over every resource, every asset, as they struggled to keep what small margin of power they possessed.

The ritual was concluded, the bowl passed back to the waiting kajh, and Hwe'tsara surveyed the room. His eyes lingered on the small contingent of troops beside his throne: the harrows and scythes who had been picked as this day's bodyguard. Like most lieges, he trusted them more than his closest vassals or most faithful lieutenants. Several different races were present in mix, and half their number had red eyes: those that had altered their bodies to become absolute instruments of war, often at the expense of longevity and comfort.

Fezhmorbal met the red eyes of the most senior deciqad among them: Udremgaj. Both allowed their leathery eyelids to droop for a moment: the equivalent of a secret nod.

"Gasdashrag," Fezhmorbal whispered, barely moving his lips, "follow my lead. Do not speak if you are not required to. Watch and learn." Without waiting for a reply, he straightened.

A moment later, Hwe'tsara turned toward him, eyes narrowing. "So, my deciqadi counselor, I take it you have heard the news?"

"Which news, Your Horror? There has been much, since the flood."

"Yes, and it has all been like the rest of the dung left behind when the waters receded: foul and messy. Especially Nawgd's further failures. He has indeed lost two of his most capable x'qao: an x'qiigh and a young true-blood. Apparently, the tale told by the third of their hunting party—an x'qao of weak origins—is true."

"That they were attacked by spirits?" Fezhmorbal labored to keep the scorn and incredulity out of his tone.

"Who knows if such a thing is possible? Or why such a fate should befall a pair of hapless x'qao in the service of a nearly witless liege? What matters is that our ally is made weaker and less useful because of it. And it can no longer be discerned if this was the work of a subtle rival: the remains are too few and too old. And any tracks have been erased by the weather."

"So is it the x'qai's q'akh coursers who returned with this latest report?"

Hwe'tsara grunted. "They wisely chose not to appear before their master again. The more 'Liege' Nawgd's schemes fail, the less safe it is to bring him bad news."

*As if that isn't a universal trait among x'qa.* "Inconvenient," Fezhmorbal nodded. "But if not them, Your Horror, then what witness confirmed the story of the surviving x'qao? The x'qiigh's kiktzo, perhaps?"

"Yes, though most did not return. Only a few still felt enough of Nawgd's will calling to their blood. Who, being displeased with their reports, ate them like the fool he is."

*Fool, indeed.* "And what did their memories hold?"

"Does it matter?

*And here sits yet another fool!* "It might, Your Horror."

Hwe'tsara's shoulders shone as he shrugged. "Different forms of madness, further distorted by their infinitesimal minds. As they perceived it, the two x'qai fell dead as if by touched by the anger of a distant suzerain. Or that they fought against unseen spirits of the air. Or were struck by fits and lightning." Hwe'tsara glanced sideways at his deciqadi advisor. "What do you make of that?"

"There is one common sinew throughout: that what the kiktzo saw, they could not understand."

"As I said, they are insects."

"Yes, but even insects understand physical combat, just as they can report the species they detect, their locations, and their movements. In this case, their confusion might not simply be a consequence of their miniscule minds. They may also have witnessed events beyond the limit of their experience. For it is as you say, Wise Hwe'tsara: they cannot recognize that which they do not already know."

The x'qao liege shifted restlessly on his stone throne. "This conversation would almost be amusing, if it were not worrisome."

"How so, Your Horror?"

"Here I inform you that an ally, Nawgd, has made himself less useful to me through his stupidity, and you are fretting over the perceptions of *bugs*?"

"I only fret over them insofar as they bear upon the disturbing mystery of how two strong x'qao were killed."

"The specifics hardly matter: they were roaming when and where they should not have been allowed to. They met foes and perished, thereby weakening the idiot Nawgd and reducing his value to me. That is tangible; that is what you should be worried about."

"I am," Fezhmorbal answered. "But he remains a useful tool, who may be used to apply pressure when and where it would be inconvenient for you."

Still focused on his deciqadi counselor, Hwe'tsara waved away the praakht and other non-x'qa, save the harrows and scythes. The dismissed bowed and exited. The q'akh appeared bored; the 'qo simply eyed the two deciqadi hungrily.

Hwe'tsara waited until the sounds of his withdrawing "court" had faded. "You have proven relatively useful, Counselor. How long have you been advising me, now?"

Fezhmorbal wondered if that was just a test of his tact, or the x'qao had truly forgotten. *With them, you never know.* "Two seasons, Your Horror."

The impossibly broad x'qao adopted a posture that almost left him lounging across the arms of his throne. "Thus far, your species' minds and facility with devices has not disappointed me. Deciqadi may indeed prove to be an adequate addition to my forces."

*More than adequate.* But Fezhmorbal's only response was, "Which we shall continue to prove as often as you wish."

He pointedly did not glance at Harrow Udremgaj. It would be disastrous if any x'qao liege learned just how closely all deciqadi were bound into their race's slow schemes to not only gain more, but controlling, power. The first targets of their plans, the humans, had vulnerabilities that could eventually be leveraged against them, quickly and decisively. The x'qai would require a much longer and incremental strategy. *But just as water wears down rock, so too shall we—*

Hwe'tsara's voice was annoyed, harsh. "Your attention is still required, Fezhmorbal." He sat more formally in his chair. "That habit is your one annoying similarity to humans."

"Do you refer to my distraction, Your Horror?"

"No: I refer to how your thoughts become so deep that, although your eyes are still open, you are no longer looking out of them."

"I shall endeavor to refrain from doing so in your presence."

Hwe'tsara looked away, his throat releasing a palate-grinding *grrrkhhh'k'k!*: the x'qao equivalent of *harumph.* "It would please me more if you would cease doing it altogether. But if that is your breed's only flaw, I suppose I can live with it."

*That will prove an ironic turn of phrase if you are not careful, monster.* "No being may change its given nature," Fezhmorbal answered truthfully, "except arurkré. Such as you shall prove to be, Your Horror."

Hwe'tsara sat straighter, became stern. "It is wise that you remember, and honor, that difference between my kind and yours, deciqad."

Fezhmorbal respectfully inclined his head, thereby hiding his eyes lest they reveal his thoughts: *How easy you are to manipulate, merely by flattering your forlorn hope of transcendence.* "You mentioned other troubling news, Your Horror. What concerns you?"

"The coming exchange with the irksome independents on the north bank."

"You are referring to the praakht gang leader who has been in contact with your vassals?"

"The same. They will not relent on their price. The nerve of them! They ask much when the value of what they offer is not yet proven. Their only inducement was that huge rag they sent and which you pored over for hours!"

"The fabric is most unusual, Dread Liege. Extremely light, yet extremely strong. And surely the agents who received it inspected the rest of what they are offering in trade?"

Hwe'tsara's gaze was steady but his tone was evasive. "Of course!"

"And were those goods as unique as claimed?" It was frustrating but necessary to address the pending exchange obliquely; any fault in evaluating the strange captive and his gear lay with Hwe'tsara's hasty instructions to his own agents.

"Is it not you who will tell me if the condition of the material was as claimed...or not?"

"I can certainly do so, Your Horror. But is it not...problematic to be uncertain of its final value until after the exchange has taken place? Had I, or one of my lieutenants been allowed to accompany your agents—"

"That could not, and cannot, be done. It is essential that both you and I keep our connection to this trade unrevealed. At least for now. But if this upstart has misrepresented what he offers"— Hwe'tsara's smile was eager and mirthless—"then I shall make an example of him by feeding him to my q'akh and taking his kajh, urldi, and goods for my own. As recompense for my troubles."

"Of course," Fezhmorbal observed, "if he *does* deliver what he has promised, he may prove to be of further use, particularly if he parlays what he has gained in trade to strengthen himself. His gang might grow to become a great-gang, which could be recruited to bring increased pressure against those which defend the flanks of the Legate's fortress."

The x'qao liege smiled. "Yes. The gang leader is miserable because he is clever and bold, but those same traits would make him a formidable minion."

Fezhmorbal shrugged. "This is true, presuming it is the gang leader who is so formidable."

Hwe'tsara's eyes narrowed in suspicion. "What do you mean?"

"Earlier reports of him are not consistent with the caution and foresight that the other side has evinced during these negotiations. However, those same reports *do* mention that his truthteller is known for just such intelligence and prudence."

Hwe'tsara waved away the distinction. "It is no matter. If I have leverage over the gang leader, then I have leverage over his truthteller. Who, if more worthy, will become *my* asset." The x'qao sighed heavily. "There are always more able bodies, but never enough careful minds."

Fezhmorbal managed not to blink or guffaw. *Can even he be oblivious to the self-parody of that "lament"?*

The liege shared more wisdom in the same vein. "If good commanders and planners did not increase the power of a force manyfold, no liege would keep stables of humans. They are frail and troublesome, but it is easy to breed them for cleverness." There was a sly look on the would-be arurkré's face. "Indeed, they are so proficient and well proven in that regard, that I am always of half a mind to reconsider my agreement with you."

*Trying to see if I will flinch and fawn. Yet, if I am too proud...* Fezhmorbal bowed. "It has always been understood that you may decide against using my kind to replace your humans." In fact, it was likely. Humans were easily controlled thralls, whereas deciqadi—who could always return to their hidden hotside communities—were allies. Fezhmorbal straightened. "In time, your suzerains may even learn to breed humans who are not only more amenable to the yoke, but almost as durable as my people."

Hwe'tsara's eyes narrowed sharply. "Be careful who you bait with *your* cleverness, deciqad. You know that such breeding is not so simple. If it were, we would have done so long ago."

*Dung and spittle, I overstepped. Careful, now.* "I meant only to be agreeable, Your Horror," he lied. "I have no knowledge of the intricacies of how you and other x'qai breed your human slaves." Which was partially true: the details were one of the lieges' few well-guarded secrets, betrayal of which would invite the swift and lethal wrath of the suzerains.

Hwe'tsara's eyes were still narrowed, but not so fiercely. "Then attend; it is necessary that you understand how x'qao manage their human stables." Fezhmorbal glanced at the human reapers; they appeared to be either bored or moderately amused. "They are not concerned with such things," Hwe'tsara snapped. "No harrow or scythe comes from a stable. They cannot have any attachments which could be used to compromise their loyalty."

Fezhmorbal found it easy to believe that Hwe'tsara's reapers had never known a family. The eyes staring out of their faces had no trace of emotion, only a detached curiosity that was as cruel as it was clinical. And suddenly, he understood: "So, *all* harrows are from Beyond?"

"And scythes as well," Hwe'tsara snarled impatiently. "Do not distract me again. Understand: we cannot allow the humans to track their ancestry. This is why no breeding is allowed between those in the same stable. This not only avoids physical and mental defects, but eliminates the complication of relatives fighting alongside each other.

"This is also why the females are cloistered: that they may not know the identity of those who sire their young. For the same reason, infants are immediately taken from their mothers and put in the care of praakht wet nurses." Hwe'tsara stopped, waited for Fezhmorbal to comment, grew impatient and pressed: "Well? You question everything else but not this?"

Fezhmorbal was still working to imagine an existence without family bonds or even knowledge of one's ancestors. "How ... why do they stand for such ... such conditions?"

"Who? The humans? They stand for it because they have no choice. Not if they wish to live. If a sire reveals his home stable to his mate, he is killed. If a female attempts to discover the whereabouts of her infant, she loses a finger and her praakht accomplices lose their lives." Misinterpreting Fezhmorbal's head-shake as a critique rather than baffled revulsion, Hwe'tsara expli-cated. "Of course, there are many who console themselves that they tolerate the arrangement because they must survive long enough to change it, to live to 'fight another day.'"

"You recite that as if it is a common utterance among them."

The liege shrugged. "It is. But never openly."

"And you tolerate it?"

The x'qao shrugged. "Why not? Bitterness and resentment of those above one's station are common at every level of the pyramid of power. A first liege feels savage envy toward his suzerain, just as senior war leaders do toward the vavasor they are pledged to serve."

Fezhmorbal nodded, even as he thought: *But there is a difference. The humans do not hate you because you thwart their ambition. They hate you because of the yoke you keep upon them. And you cannot perceive that because you have no loves, no families, no drives beyond your dreams of supremacy. Because, quite literally, you* are *monsters. And if you are not very, very careful—*

Fezhmorbal snapped himself straight, breaking up through thoughts that were not only unprofitable but dangerous in the lair of an x'qao liege. "Was there other news that discomfited you, Your Horror?"

"It appears that the humans and the apparent x'qagrat'r who arrived several days ago are lodging with the Legate. If they are additions to his force, that more than offsets any advantage I hoped to gain through Nawgd's support."

"I heard report that they reemerged today and did business at the vansary."

Hwe'tsara nodded. "They did."

"And so your scythes were watching."

Hwe'tsara shifted slightly. "Mostly."

*Which means you forgot to keep your reapers alert to the new humans and their doings. But today, when you asked what they observed at the vansary, only Udremgaj provided you with information... because I tasked him to.* "What did they see?"

"Why? What battle-useful knowledge do you think to gain from a shopping list?"

"Perhaps none, but perhaps a great deal. Who may tell me what they purchased?"

Hwe'tsara gestured irritably toward the scythes. However, Udremgaj did not step forward, but bade a more junior human scythe to do so. "Tell us what they were given, Litatraj."

The scythe held a slate in front of him, hand trembling as he shouted in his best herald's voice. "Iron and bronze knives and swords. Half a dozen crossbows, one much larger than the rest. A bow of bone and horn. Arrows and quarrels pointed with many metals. Many small shields and much armor of cured hide. Waterskins, packs, sandals, sleeping furs, all of good quality." He stepped back... but then, eyes widening at a sudden recollection, he stepped hastily forward to add, "And poison. And ink and styluses." His brow shiny with nervous sweat, he stepped back.

Hwe'tsara watched Fezhmorbal digest this information as he tapped his clawed foot impatiently. "And so," the x'qao asked in angry exasperation, "what do you discern from this? Do they mean to bring about the downfall of the suzerains with a handful of crossbows?"

"No. But also, they do not mean to stay in Forkus."

Hwe'tsara sat forward sharply. "Explain."

"Your Horror, if they meant to join the Legate, they would not be purchasing weapons that their employer could supply at need. Besides, they would rely upon their own advanced equipment, which is the envy of many reapers, I am told.

"Instead, the items they acquired are necessary for long travels or to equip kajh impressed to their service. But I noticed something else of interest, Your Horror. When describing their transactions, Harrow Udremgaj said the items were *given*, not *purchased*. Is that distinction intended?"

"It is. The scythes saw no goods exchanged for the ones they received. Nor coin, either."

Fezhmorbal rubbed his lean, leathery chin. "Being newcomers, these humans could not have a balance with merchants. So, they must have been drawing against an account already set aside for them."

"By whom? The money-grubbing h'achga who runs the vansary? Or maybe his liege Vranadoc?"

Fezhmorbal shrugged. "Or the Legate. Whichever it is, we may safely assume this much: the funds they used were for a service they performed elsewhere, or one which they have yet to perform here. Which is very unlikely to be of moment to you or your plans." *Indeed, it is more likely to be significant to my plans. Given the speed with which these arrangements were made, they may already know someone in Forkus. Which may not be of immediate concern, but—*

"Fezhmorbal!" Hwe'tsara roared. "You are indulging in that nasty human habit again! Return your attention to the matter at hand and tell me: are you convinced that these humans and the x'qagrat'r shall not remain long enough to influence our plans?"

"Pardon my distraction, Your Horror. And, no: I predict they will be gone within ten days, twenty at the outside."

"Well, that is welcome news." Hwe'tsara frowned mightily. "Still: harrows and scythes who came in without the banner of a lord? What do you think them? Rogues? Rebels? Traitors?"

Fezhmorbal shrugged. "They were dusty from long travel in the wastes, without a single rad or servitor to carry their supplies. Of this much, we may be sure: they are not in the service of a suzerain."

Hwe'tsara nodded. "Keep an ear turned toward word of their doings and their speech."

"Indeed, Liege, I shall." *For my own purposes as much as yours.*

"But mind you, Fezhmorbal, do not be distracted from your primary purpose."

The deciqad bent his head slightly. "All shall be in readiness by the time the caravan from Fragkork approaches, come midspring. And assuming all goes well, we shall be well prepared to arrange a proper greeting for the more important one that shall approach in midsummer."

Hwe'tsara nodded in satisfaction. "You know your responsibilities. Discharge them well, and I shall think more favorably upon the prospect of replacing my humans with your people." When Fezhmorbal offered no bow of departure, he frowned. "You have an expectant look, Counselor."

"About the splitting star, Your Horror. You intimated that your interest was sufficiently piqued to ask the Suzerain's opinion on—"

"No. It was *your* interest that led me to assure you I would disturb Great Ormalg himself with such utter nonsense." The x'qao sighed. "I shall do so when next my mind touches his. Remember: I have given you my word."

*Which is as valueless as the dust in my sandals,* Fezhmorbal thought as he nodded at Gasdashrag to copy his deep bow of farewell.

# Chapter Twenty-Five

The wind was fresh atop one of the crenellated towers that guarded the northern approaches to the Legate's fortress. Had he closed his eyes, Caine might have been able to imagine himself on the edge of some desert back home: the Mojave or Sahara, maybe.

But then roars of a praakht turf war erupted from the adobe heaps clustered within twenty meters of the walls ... and he was back in the squalid reality of Forkus. "So," he said with a final look to ensure that the nearby parapets were empty, "do we take Tasvar's deal or not?" He saw the uncertain glances bouncing around the gathered faces of the Crewe. "There is no rank in this meeting."

The Crewe sat staring at each other, as each of them was daring someone—anyone—else to become the devil's advocate for what had roundly been accepted as a good deal. Tasvar's aid had already been substantial; not only had he provided them with a great deal of excellent local equipment but had brokered the exchanges with Ulchakh and Kosvak. However, that was secondary compared to the deal he had put before them yesterday: to provide all transport and sales for whatever salvage they might find at the flat tops north of Achgabab. His price: a third of the goods and proceeds realized therefrom.

A few of the group had expressed some dismay at such a high percentage ... until Dora pointed out what black marketeers *usually* charged. "And here," she concluded, "everything is a black-market deal."

And while no one doubted the value of surveying the recently exposed "dunes that do not move," Caine had pointed out a benefit beyond any immediate salvage—and almost certainly what Tasvar was actually investing in. If these structures were indeed sealed, then anything inside them was likely to be extremely well preserved. That did not just mean fragmentary clues about the apocalypse that had ended Bactradgaria's industrial era, but documents and maps that might reveal undiscovered salvage sites that would have remained indecipherable to prospectors that didn't happen to have a Dornaani translator.

After a long silence, it was Newton who sighed and said, "I have no reservations regarding the arrangement with Tasvar."

"But...?" prompted Peter.

Newton's smile said what he did not: *You know me too well.* "But I do not how much we may trust the man himself." There were a few nods at that.

Riordan looked around the group; he didn't want to become Tasvar's sole defender. He leaned back when Bannor cocked his head meditatively.

"Let's go back to basics," suggested the Green Beret. "Tasvar could have killed us any time over the last seven days. Either by assassinating us inside his own walls or by abandoning us on the streets. Different approaches but the same outcome."

Duncan frowned. "He could be setting us up as pawns in some scheme of his own." He shrugged. "Doesn't feel like that to me, but as the commodore said, this is the time to put all the possibilities on the table."

Bannor nodded. "It is. And there's no way to be sure that's not exactly what Tasvar is doing. you may be right. But again, I remember what it's like to sit in his chair, and I can't see how I would—or *could*—do any different, no matter his motivations. Even if he likes us, we are still unproven and largely unknown allies. He'd be a fool to be more forthcoming, or generous, than he has."

Riordan measured the tentative nods answering Bannor's arguments; it was time to drive home the most decisive fact of all. "And remember: we need Tasvar a whole hell of a lot more than he needs us. I'm not talking about acquiring the equipment and contacts we need to survive—although that would be reason enough." He looked around the group. "He speaks *English*, damn it. And not some pre-Chaucerian dialect; he understood the dominant form of the language for the last three centuries or so. That is the *one* connection we've found between our world and this one. So right now, any plan for getting home starts with discovering how he learned our language."

Dora rolled her eyes. "Well, we could just, y'know...ask him."

Riordan smiled. "Now just imagine how *that* conversation would evolve. Who learns more about who: us about him, or him about *us*? And what's more, since English is his secret battle language, we'd be backing him into a corner."

Duncan nodded. "Given the way he reacted, he's probably taken an oath to protect its secrecy. So he'd probably have to lie about it."

Riordan nodded at Dora. "It's like almost all the other questions we really want, even need, to ask. If we do it too soon, it could backfire. So right now, we ask only the questions necessary to survive, become stronger, and remain Tasvar's peers."

Miles folded his arms. "Yeah, because if he makes a hard play to recruit us, he's going to be very disappointed when we refuse. And if his own troops get wind of that, he might feel he's got to show us the door. Just to save face."

"Which is pretty much our worst-case scenario," Bannor agreed. "Once we've traveled that road together for a while, maybe then he'll be willing, or get the permission, to tell us how and where he learned English."

Veriden shrugged. "So: there's lots of information we want that we can't afford to get. But what about the reverse? How do we make sure that we don't reveal the information that we can't afford to share?"

Riordan nodded. "That's a really good question. Thanks to Miles, we've already started to acquire a very...er, unique list of terms. But, to Dora's point, there are items for which we probably need code words."

Dora shrugged. "Well, among ourselves, we're the Crewe. And it should stay that way: just among us. But then what should we call ourselves when dealing with locals?"

Riordan smiled. "I think Arashk gave us the answer to that." He gestured around at the Crewe. "From the start, he assumed we were lordless scythes and harrows. Maybe we should go with that. But it would be better to use a word that he hasn't heard, that no one else is likely to understand." He glanced at Ayana with a sly smile. "Any ideas?"

She smiled and her nod almost became a bow. "We are *ronin*. But be aware: it does not mean lordless, at least not as you think of it."

Bannor, already smiling at her, asked, "How would *you* define it?"

Riordan nodded general agreement instead of telling his friend what his eyes and face had been telling the rest of the world: that Colonel Rulaine was hopelessly smitten.

Ayana returned Rulaine's smile. "Ronin means a wanderer, one who is adrift. Transliterated, the root of it is 'a person of, or upon, waves.'"

"So we are masterless warriors riding the seas of fate," Bannor summarized, smiling broadly. "That's us."

Ayana turned toward Caine and murmured, "Are you sure you wish this title for us, Commodore? In both history and myth, the stories of ronin typically end in failure. Or tragedy."

Riordan smiled. "So we'll rewrite the legend, Ayana. Or at least be the exception that proves the rule."

She bowed in her seat. "*Hai.*"

Riordan turned back to the group. "There's one other code word we need: a way to signal that we're talking about space, whether it's getting to orbit, the ship, or anything else. We've done a good job keeping those topics private, but at some point, the eavesdroppers are going to win. Any ideas?"

"Actually," Bannor mused, "I've been thinking about that. There's a term from an old book that you still hear sometimes, but most people don't even know what it refers to."

"Colonel," Miles said with exaggerated patience, "I'd give you a drum roll if we had a snare handy, but..."

Bannor shrugged. "Shangri-La."

Newton emitted an approving grunt. "A high-altitude promised land that only a select few know how to reach. Quite apt."

Girten's eyes had been growing wide and were now moving from one face to another. "Jesus, am I the only one who's going to say it?" he blurted out desperately.

"Say what?" Miles asked.

"Why, that we don't have a rat's ass chance of getting back to the ship! And even if we did, how would we fix it?"

Riordan regretted having to push back—Girten needed to be built up, not shut down—but defeatism had to be nipped in the bud. "Sergeant, I share your concerns about the feasibility of getting back aboard the ship. That's why the 'flat tops' are a major priority. What we find inside them could answer all those questions, including where we might be able to get our hands on the necessary equipment.

"But at this moment, our only objective is to retrieve Eku. And afterward, to ensure his safety." Riordan saw imminent frowns on half the faces. "He hasn't the skills to be at the front of a fight. But what's more, he's got to teach us everything he knows."

O'Garran nodded. "You mean in case he buys the farm, anyway?"

Riordan paused. "I was thinking about how he has to be able to share what he knows about mounting an orbital mission. Frankly, he hasn't demonstrated the necessary calm or adaptability to be part of such a team. But whoever *does* go will need him to share everything he knows about the ship and space operations."

Caine sighed. "I hope that, in the course of learning to survive on this planet, Eku might still develop the needed focus and flexibility. But I agree with our career soldiers: 'hope is not a strategy.'"

"Hooyah," intoned resident cynic Miles O'Garran. "Is that all, sir?"

Riordan nodded. "Time to meet with Tasvar."

# Chapter Twenty-Six

The clearest indicator that Tasvar felt increasingly secure with, and friendly toward, the group was that he chose to meet in a semiprivate dining space, his guards markedly more relaxed.

"I am glad you have agreed to the arrangement I proposed," he said, his tone and expression suggesting he was far more pleased than his words conveyed. "And I am very interested in continuing our conversation about the mathematical codices I saw in your magi—er, electronic helmet." Because of their vehicles' ignition systems, the humans of Bactradgaria had retained a rudimentary understanding of electricity. Otherwise, explaining the operation of the translator would have been impossible, as well as the HUD on which Tasvar had viewed various useful formulae and mathematical tables.

Riordan nodded. "I look forward to discussing those codices, just as soon as we return."

Tasvar shrugged after a short pause. He had no doubt hoped to finalize that additional trade before the Crewe departed. On the other hand, he now had even more reason to ensure that they survived.

His reply underscored the growing value he placed on them as both allies and a source of new opportunities. "Well, since you must depart, I am resolved to make sure that you get back in one piece. So heed this piece of advice above all others: The rescue of your friend will be reported swiftly, and various powers will commit resources to determine who effected it."

Miles O'Garran crossed the arms that had prompted the Lost Soldiers to give him the mysterious nickname "Popeye." "Everyone—including you—tells us that hovels change hands all the time in Forkus. So why the special interest in this case?"

Tasvar leaned forward. "Because almost all those attacks are made *by* praakht *against* praakht. They are noisy, bloody battles, usually preceded by friction between two gangs where the attacker perceives a clear advantage."

He shook his head. "No one will mistake you for praakht, my friend. Rather, if you use the equipment I have seen, you will be presumed to be reapers."

Riordan leaned forward. "So in addition to completing the rescue as swiftly as possible, how do we avoid being intercepted before completing our escape? Or to prevent being followed, once we have?"

Tasvar speared a sliver of unfamiliar meat and chewed it thoroughly before answering. "I believe I may be able to help with that. The praakht gang leader who holds your friend had no contacts with any power that could afford such an 'asset.' Consequently, he spread word through the black market. And because many praakht are led by *whakt*, those who are part human, we often hear black-market whispers before the x'qai.

"That is how I learned who held your friend and that only one secretive bidder made an offer, probably because he threatened all others. It is also certain that he will be quite angry when you free your companion before his trade is completed. Accordingly, you need a guide to help you exit Forkus with all possible speed. So I took the liberty of retaining someone who is familiar with those routes and is already known to you: Ulchakh."

Dora nodded, eyes narrowed. "I see how everyone else is making a profit from all this 'cooperation,' Tasvar. But what about you?"

It was a mark of his growing familiarity with the various personalities of the Crewe that, rather than taking umbrage at Dora's blunt question, he merely smiled. "A greater bond has been created between the Legate and Vranadoc, whose forces and influence in Forkus are far greater than ours. And Ulchakh assures us that not only will trade with Achgabab become more frequent, but very favorably priced."

"So you're being paid in political and economic capital," Duncan summarized with a smile.

"A very tactful expression. Yes, that is correct."

Riordan nodded. "But you still haven't told us who we'll be angering by rescuing our friend. Or how, once we're out of Forkus, you're going to foil any pursuers."

Tasvar moved his empty plate-bowl to the side. "The exchange is being conducted through an intermediary that is a known vassal of Ormalg's liege in Forkus: Hwe'tsara. The liege and vassal are similar in one regard: both have the subtlety of a battle-ax."

"Great," Craig Girten sighed as he pushed a few remaining morsels around his plate. "So we'll be pissing off some x'qai kingpin."

Tasvar nodded at the paratrooper's idiom; apparently, "pissing off" was yet another colloquialism where little if anything was lost in translation. "Yes. He and his vassals are the ones most likely to mount a pursuit *if* they can find your trail in time. So, facilitating your immediate escape is the first of the ways I mean to help you. I have arranged all your new goods to be positioned just north of the hovel that is your target. Ulchakh will be waiting with them."

"Alone?" Katie asked, startled.

"No," Tasvar answered with a slow smile.

Bannor was shaking his head. "If this Hwe'tsara gets word within a few hours, his forces will still find our tracks. The dust and sand doesn't shift that quickly. And if any of us are wounded, that means slower movement, a blood trail, or both."

"That brings me to the second way in which I shall aid your escape," Tasvar answered. "I am dispatching a small caravan just before you attack. We can be sure that it will be detected: Legate compounds are always being monitored, wherever we are. Eleven of the individuals traveling with the caravan shall be attired in the very robes you wore to the vansary. Their length and weight are both distinctive and will no doubt be reported by those watching. Hwe'tsara's forces have little means or inclination for precise reporting, so no matter the order in which their alerts reach him, he will presume that you attacked the hovel first and that the predawn caravan is your means of escape.

"I am also certain that Hwe'tsara will not put human troops in charge of the force he sends after the caravan: our fellow-feeling has taught x'qai not to pit us one against the other. So he will rely on x'qao or praakht leaders, who will be slow to discover that they are shadowing a decoy. By the time they realize, your actual trail should have been erased by wind and rain." He raised an index finger in warning. "But, as you head north, be careful not to leave spoor. Even if it means slower movement, at first."

Newton crossed his arms. "And if there are wounded among us who cannot help but leave 'spoor'? What then?"

"Then," Tasvar said gravely, "you have very difficult decisions to make." He shook his head. "But you are not merely warriors; you are soldiers. These quandaries are not new to you. You will face them as you have in the past. Now I wish to touch upon one further item of mutual interest and impart one final piece of advice."

Riordan nodded. "What is this item of mutual interest?"

"Camphor," Tasvar replied flatly. "From our conversations, you know Zrik Whir is the only significant source of it. But we cannot secure it. For us to manufacture smokeless powder in meaningful quantities, we must ask you to be our agents—our *very* handsomely compensated agents—to Zrik Whir."

Riordan smiled even as he frowned. "Why do you not do it yourselves? Surely you have infinitely superior resources and ready contacts."

"We do, but they are of no help in the case of Zrik Whir. We do not travel there except at very great need."

"Why?" asked Duncan.

Tasvar folded his hands. "When the Legate's standard is seen anywhere upon or near Zrik Whir, it causes unprecedented worry among the x'qai suzerains. Nothing else has ever caused them to put aside their competition long enough to take unified action."

His tone became grim. "Our visits proved very costly, both to us and the people of Zrik Whir. They rightly insisted that while we must remain friends, it must be from a distance." His voice and eyes brightened. "You, however, would not be traveling under the Legate's sigil or with our assistance. And you alone know why the camphor is required and the form in which we need it."

*So, yet another reason you won't co-opt us.* "Apparently, we would be useful as liaisons."

"Very much so. I only wish I had information that would make it easier to find your way there and to the right persons." He frowned. "Had you arrived just a few days earlier, I could have introduced you to a native of those islands. A fellow by the name of Tirolane."

"When will he return?"

"I do not know if he shall. He was journeying here to meet and discuss the possibility of joint ventures here, rather than upon Zrik Whir. However, the small caravan with which he was traveling was attacked while he was scouting the path ahead. When he returned to it, there were but a few wounded left. They reported that two of his companions had been taken captive."

Ayana's nod was approving. "And now he is attempting to rescue those he calls 'friend.' Just as we are."

Tasvar nodded. "You are much the same in many ways, your people and his. You would have liked each other, I think."

Caine put his own empty plate aside. "You also mentioned advice. We would be grateful to hear it."

Tasvar nodded, but looked away until he was able to push a frown off his face. When he turned back, his gaze fixed upon Dora. "Pandora Veriden, when Yasla was attempting to, eh, assess your group, you cried out that she was using the 'evil eye.'"

"I did," Dora muttered suspiciously, eyes hard on Tasvar.

"Although what Yasla did is not malign, you are not entirely wrong. And your reaction put an important matter before us: that you and your friends are convinced that what we deem significant powers are nothing more than superstition or delusion."

Caine had no reply. Nor did anyone else.

"I have watched carefully while you were our guests," Tasvar explained. "You place all your faith in machines. I suspect that wherever you come from, they are the only power you know. And so, you have no reason to believe that other powers exist.

"So my advice takes the form of a question. First, for the sake of argument, let us suppose that there are powers which are neither detectable by, nor conform to the laws of, the science you worship. Let us further suppose that this place—of which you know very little—is amenable to the projection of such powers. My question is this: By what means may you establish, with absolute certainty, that such powers are impossible?" He ended looking directly at Riordan.

Caine shrugged. "No one can know that a thing they have not observed isn't, in fact, possible. That it might only have been extant in times or places where they were not present."

Tasvar's eyes became slightly less pinched, as if he were trying to conceal that Caine's answer came as a relief. "Then I put this to you, as the logical extension of what you have just said: Is it prudent to dismiss such possibilities as you make plans here? Particularly those which may involve combat?"

He rose, smiled apologetically. "I must attend to other matters. If you have need of me, you may pass word through your escorts. I shall assist if time and duty allow." He glanced at the room's hourglass. "You have much to plan and little time to do it. I shall not delay you further."

# Chapter Twenty-Seven

Duncan Solsohn rested the heavy crossbow atop the Crewe's single tower shield: the only suitable armor they'd found for Yaargraukh. Screening Solsohn—which was to say, blocking him— was the second-in-command, or "first hunter," of the hovel. His cooperation was almost too energetic and eager, but it was easy to understand why. By allowing the humans to use a tunnel that connected the hovel to the fastness of a Legate vassal, his band leader had not only received a promise of protection from that power, but had been made a vavasor of Kosvak.

Duncan peered around the edge of the entry's dogleg until he could see a similar but slightly larger hovel just twenty meters away: the one in which Eku was being held. It was actually an amalgam of two hovels: a large round lump from which a smaller one protruded. The two kajh guarding the entrance did not appear to be aware that they were under any unusual scrutiny, and Solsohn doubted that either had any talent for dissembling.

"Looks good," he muttered into the darkness behind.

"Have them drag me out," Bannor's muffled voice ordered. Two of the resident h'achgai muttered assent and set about dragging out the piled travois upon which the vacc-suited Rulaine was concealed.

"Hope you don't have to scratch an itch," Solsohn quipped.

"I hate you," was the dull mutter that answered him from the travois as the two warriors dragged it past his overwatch position.

❖     ❖     ❖

272

After the two h'achgai perched the travois upon a low pile of bricks, the late-afternoon sunlight sent a few narrow beams through the rents in its covering: the kind of well-worn hide locals used in lieu of tarps. Bannor, who was under a loosely bound heap of rags and hide scraps, leaned his head to peek out the aperture that had been cut specifically for that purpose: he could see almost the entirety of the target hovel.

Rulaine started with the basics: getting precise measurements. He called up the HUD's 3D laser topography graphing function. The beam's characteristics required a bit of initial tweaking, though. Based on what he and Duncan had observed during the engagement with the two x'qai, they had guesstimated the UV frequencies that had most attracted the creatures' attention. So, to minimize the chance that some passing x'qa would detect the helmet's scanning laser, they'd created a special frequency-hopping algorithm designed to avoid those parts of the spectrums. But invoking it meant getting permission from the computer driving the whole suit, and that required a deep dive into the guts of settings written only in Dornaani.

Despite tutoring from both Caine and the translator, he still had trepidations. Riordan had noticed and was prepared to perform the target survey himself until Bannor and the others, in a rare display of instant unanimity, respectfully told him, "Sir, no, sir. Please." In an officer, leaning into personal action was a better trait than the opposite, but in Caine's case, some tempering might be required.

The HUD pinged: surface mapping completed. Rulaine activated the thermal imaging overlay.

The TI's first pass was to measure general radiance coming off the structure, but adobe was a challenging substance. It was comparatively "muddy"—no crisp thermal differentiation—and Bannor had only one measurement perspective. Within the first few moments he discovered another wrinkle. The radiance patterns were being disrupted by curved interior walls: the remains of the first, smaller structure to which the larger one had been added. But the Dornaani sensors had already shown themselves to be both remarkably sensitive and adept at filtering out surrounding radiance, particularly given enough time for multiple passes.

With the suit's computer constantly refining its baseline measures of both average radiance levels and variation patterns, he recalibrated the sensors to focus on a much thinner cross section of the walls in the hope it would indicate density and thickness. Rulaine considered it a long shot. Eku had only mentioned using the setting in passing, implying that when the materials and their shape was adequately defined, the TI could analyze the spectral distribution and decay to interpolate the kind of heat source from which they'd come. Kind of like reverse-engineering a Dopplering echo to arrive at the original sound that produced it.

To Bannor's pleased surprise, the TI did just that. And because the setting worked partly by assessing radiant variations along the walls, it also showed where they were thickest and thinnest. A pity he couldn't get a read of the other side of the structure, but this would certainly be sufficient for their purposes.

However, getting a count on the numbers of trogs inside was almost impossible. In addition to the muddying effect of adobe, there was insufficient distinction between the temperature of the air, the walls, and the bodies.

Rulaine sighed. He'd have to stay hidden on the travois until Bactradgaria's rapid dusk cooling produced better contrasts. Even then, the images were going to lack detail, and if there was a lot of movement, counting occupants could become problematic. At least the suit's own thermal reprocessing system ensured that he'd remain neutral against the background, so no need to worry about being discovered.

Bannor instantly repented tempting fate... but fate proved faster than the speed of human regret. From beyond the right side of the h'achgai hovel arose a screeching, then an approaching skitter of clawed feet. Lying on his side, he couldn't see what was essentially above his head without giving away his position, so he could only wait and wonder as the scrabblings became more confused and the screaming resumed. One voice was shrill: desperate and angry. The others were excited and, very possibly, hungry.

A pack of 'qo swarmed into his limited field of vision, a wounded one keeping just ahead of a half dozen others. Their only similarity was that they all had two legs and two arms. Except for the one they were chasing. He had only one and a half arms; a hand was missing and the forearm flesh was hanging in shreds. Which wouldn't have concerned Rulaine except that he was also heading for the travois.

Duncan had no firing angle for his crossbow; they were too

close to the curved wall of the hovel to be seen from its entrance. And it certainly didn't look like they were going to race past; the wounded one had already started clambering up the pile of shattered adobe bricks upon which the travois' top was propped. *Probably to fight off the others from a higher position. Not that it will change the outcome.*

But if it did try to make its last stand near or atop Bannor's head, that meant all the other 'qo would soon be swarming around and up the travois. *Which will cause it to fall over. A when it does and I roll out—*

Rulaine finger-flexed the HUD to a different screen: the one that controlled the exterior surface and systems of the suit.

The wounded 'qo began repelling attackers, raking savagely with the claws of its remaining hand and equally dexterous feet. More eager pursuers flashed past within half a meter of Bannor's eyes as they flanked their prey, preparing to ascend toward their quarry from the wider base of the travois. Which meant they'd be using Rulaine's body as a ramp.

He increased the volume of the external speakers to maximum and, hoping that 'qo ears were as sensitive as reported, pushed the frequency controls to emit the highest pitch possible.

The predatory patter around the travois became chaotic scrambling as the pursuers leaped off in an attempt to escape the twenty-thousand-hertz tone exploding straight into their faces, yet unheard by the humanoids around them. However, the wounded one was still clinging to his perch and, judging from the bitter gnashing of fangs, the others were apparently trying to force themselves back to the attack.

Rulaine hastily shifted to a new control screen that was both unfamiliar and unreadable and attempted to add a variable cycle to the audio output. At least that's what he'd meant to do. He returned the HUD to the normal audio controls and, hoping Caine's lessons in Dornaani had been sufficient, cut loose with the revised sound profile.

The 'qo were suddenly jumping off the travois. The defender's leap away was a soaring four- meter arc that ended just beyond the reach of the startled h'achga that remained on watch. Desperate to escape the ear-splitting ultrasonic sine wave that cycled from fifteen thousand to twenty thousand hertz, it ignored the startled warrior and charged for the entry—

A very audible slap of shaped bone seemed to propel the hapless creature backward into the dust, a heavy quarrel protruding straight up from its chest.

Bannor exhaled in relief: *Good call, Duncan.* The others would have been sure to follow the wounded one inside, possibly inviting an opportunistic follow-up attack from a local rival.

Surprisingly, the twice-wounded 'qo began to rise but disappeared beneath its swarming pursuers. But they couldn't withstand the unrelenting sound. Pawing frantically at their ears, some took a bit, others grabbed whatever else came away easily, and they all streaked off, howling as they went.

The tactical channel squawked: a momentary squelch break. Bannor responded in kind, signaling to Duncan that he was neither hurt nor required extraction. The only possible concern might have been the two praakht standing watch at the target hovel, but rather than showing any inclination to investigate the events, their unblinking eyes were now focused on the dark entry to the hovel just behind. They appeared suitably impressed, and perhaps a bit intimidated, by the swift response to the wounded 'qo's attempt to escape into it.

Rulaine sighed, turned off the sound system, was careful not to shift position. The 'qo were light and hadn't made much progress up the travois, but any movement might collapse the frame and reveal him. Who, from the perspective of the target structure's guards, would appear to be a harrow that had been secretly observing the entry through which any rescue attempt for their harrow-equipped captive would have to be mounted.

So rather than get comfortable, Bannor had to remain motionless. Which wouldn't have been too bad if it weren't for the most common irritation that arose when wearing any suit for a long-duration mission. An irritation that had clearly stymied Dornaani engineers.

Apparently, even *they* couldn't make a comfortable catheter.

# Chapter Twenty-Eight

"So," Bannor concluded, finishing the breakfast the Crewe had brought to their rooftop conference site, "our best guess is that the target gang is comprised of fifteen to twenty adults. It's hard to guess gender, but based on size, I doubt more than a quarter are females.

"The original structure is the smaller hovel with the entry. The one they expanded from its rear has much more floor space, and is partially screened by remains of the walls left behind when they broke through the first hovel's wall and joined the two spaces."

"And there's still only the one entry?"

"Correct, Chief. It's a short dogleg passage, like most of the structures around here."

O'Garran was scratching the back of his head. "Where do they sleep?"

Bannor shrugged. "All over, in heaps. At least that's what it looked like in the HUD."

Peter nodded. "That agrees with what Ta'rel told me. City praakht sleep in clusters to share body warmth, whether in hovels or out on the wastes."

Newton shrugged. "Not surprising. A dried dung fire is a poor heat source, and most of it will rise up through the vent hole."

Miles scratched the rear of his skull even harder. "How many were on watch?"

"Two or three," Bannor replied, "but there were others sleeping nearby. In armor."

Dora was dubious. "You got that through the walls?"

"No: I got that from how restlessly they were sleeping. Also, when one of them rose to stand his watch, he didn't have to gear up."

"I wish we had more intel," Miles groused.

Duncan nodded somberly. "Me, too. But what I saw in even a well-ordered h'achgai hovel tells me there's just not a lot of intel to be had. Their life is really basic, mostly because it's impermanent."

"What do you mean?" Ayana asked, frowning.

"I mean because there's a constant threat of being attacked and having to flee, they only invest time in things necessary to their survival. Or which are easily portable."

Riordan nodded and leaned forward. "Speaking of time, there's an update from Tasvar. One of his contacts in the black market reports that Eku is going to be exchanged in two days, three at most. So to be sure of rescuing him, we have to act tomorrow. As early as possible."

Peter sighed. "Well, if we must be prepared by first dark tomorrow, we have much planning to finish in the next thirty-six hours."

Caine shook his head. "No. When I say we have to launch the operation as early as we can tomorrow, I mean shortly after 2950 hours *today*."

Duncan started. "Wait: you mean just after midnight? Sir, we need more time!"

"I agree. Problem is, we don't have it."

"With respect sir," Craig mumbled, "why not wait until the night after? That still gets the job done before the first trade date."

But Duncan had already recalibrated and was shaking his head. "But what if the black-market intel is wrong? Or is intentional misinformation? And there's also Tasvar's warning that the OPFOR might start watching the target area a day early."

Craig frowned. "Why?"

"This trade is big enough that it might require the actual presence of a real big shot; someone with enough authority to negotiate the price. And he's going to want to be sure the trade site is clean. So, they'll have observers in place *before* any threat force shows up."

Girten nodded. "So we have to hit the hovel before they start watching it."

Riordan nodded. "And even if the purchaser doesn't think of that, Tasvar suspects the gang leader, or whoever is advising him, will."

"Tasvar thinks he, or his advisor, is that bright?" Dora asked, frowning.

"According to Tasvar, trades between gangs only take place between trusted allies or groups that serve the same vassal. Rarely, a neutral vavasor might host them for a fee.

"But whoever planned Eku's exchange required that the buyer come get him. The leader's gang is too small to fend off a determined ambush, and anyone who heard about the offer on the black market could also hear about the trade date. Just as Tasvar did."

Riordan allowed the following silence to stretch into several long seconds: enough time to digest that they had only eighteen hours left to plan and prepare. Then: "Before we settle on a final plan, any questions about the basics?"

Craig put up a hand. Riordan waved it away and smiled. "Just speak your mind, Sergeant."

"Sir, I don't see the logic of entering with the new crossbows out, instead of the guns."

Riordan glanced at the operation's CQC lead. "Chief?"

O'Garran nodded. "Girten, in the rush of combat that is almost certainly going to be at hand-to-hand distances, we'll never have the chance to reload the crossbows. So they're 'one and done' weapons, this time. Besides, we need their lethality to get a fast foothold inside the hovel."

"They're more lethal than the guns?"

Miles smiled at Solsohn. "Your turn, Major."

Duncan, the default weapons specialist, shrugged. "If we fire the survival rifles at the charge level required to match the power of the crossbows, they'll be single-shot weapons, too. You've seen how fast their batteries drain, Craig: they're built for survival needs, not sustained combat. The older one has zero charges after just three shots that *might* be incapacitating. The newer models have better batteries and more efficient acceleration coils. But still, they're drained after five shots that *should* be incapacitating, and possibly lethal.

"We've also learned how to get their helical magazines to hold and feed four different kinds of projectiles. We'll be loaded with standard, expanding, penetrator, and snake shot."

"Snake shot?" Ayana echoed.

"It's essentially a combination cannister and sabot that carries a small payload out the barrel before falling away. Can be anything from a precision dart to a bunch of small pebbles."

"And what good will that do?"

Solsohn shrugged. "Maybe nothing, but it hardly requires any charge and sprays objects at—in this case, very ignorant—targets. Might make 'em duck for cover. Might be useless. But it's a cheap option."

Dora sighed. "At least ex-Captain Treefrog's hand cannon has lots of charge."

Duncan frowned. "It might, depending on how we use it. Which may have an outsize impact on our final plan."

Peter raised an eyebrow. "In what way?"

"Well, firstly, it is intended to be a real weapon. Which means that it doesn't have all the different projectiles that a survival situation might require. But it does have a special one that we've been studying very carefully. For lack of a better term, it is a high-power smart expander."

Craig goggled. "I'd like that in English, please."

Duncan smiled. "The back of the projectile is made of a frangible superdense material: when it encounters a hard enough surface, it shatters into a cone of really heavy granules. The first third of the round is made of a much lighter smart compound that 'pancakes.'"

Dora rolled her eyes. "Such a big name for a fancy hollow point."

Duncan raised one eyebrow. "A very, very powerful hollow point which you can control by telling the smart compound how big a pancake you want."

Craig nodded. "So with all the granules whacking into the back of it, you can dump all the energy on, or near the surface of, whatever you hit."

"Which," Bannor added ruefully, "would have been very helpful the last time we used it against the x'qao."

Duncan shrugged. "Spilt milk, Colonel. We just knew the basics, then."

"And barely those," Rulaine added with a somber nod. "I think we might have fared just as well with Ms. Tagawa's katana, that time." He glanced at her. Very briefly.

She returned a sly smile. "Possibly . . . although that, too, requires adequate training, Colonel." As her eyes left Bannor to fix on Riordan, they lost their hint of mischief. "Commodore, I have a question. No: I misspoke. I have a reservation."

"With what?"

"Our reliance upon short melee weapons, sir."

Riordan nodded. Although not expert in all of them, Ayana's training had encompassed the majority of her samurai ancestors' weaponry. "The floor is yours."

She glanced wryly around the stone roof upon which they were sitting before allowing a concerned frown to bend her features. "I fully realize the training and skill of Chief O'Garran and Ms. Veriden in weapons with short blades. I am not personally familiar with Lieutenant Wu's classical Chinese short-sword form, but he seems quite proficient with it. However—"

"Here it comes," muttered O'Garran with a lopsided grin.

"*However*," Ayana persisted, "our enemy has a demonstrated preference for axes and bludgeons of many kinds. This gives them considerable advantages in reach and striking power. I am . . . concerned at that imbalance."

Riordan saw that Miles and Dora were, as usual, ready to offer spirited rebuttals . . . which is why he nodded toward Peter. "Lieutenant Wu, do you have similar concerns?"

"I do," he admitted quietly, "but I also perceive advantages that adequately compensate for them. Firstly, the most crucial part of this combat will be the entry: a very tight dogleg designed to constrain the free passage of attackers. In such a space, I believe it is they who will be at a disadvantage. The greater the length of a weapon, the more difficult it will be to wield, especially if it must be swung with force. We enjoy the ability of agility and are largely unaffected by the tight quarters."

Miles and Dora had initially been leaning forward into Peter's argument, as if worried that he wouldn't be an effective advocate. Now, they were sitting back, beaming at each other.

"Furthermore," Wu continued, "we have agreed that we should keep our weapons on lanyards. I consider a shortsword enough of a bother dangling along beside me, if I am forced to drop it. A longer weapon is not only cumbersome but potentially dangerous. And if, as Chief O'Garran projects, we must shift between melee weapons and firearms more than once, the smaller the former, the more swiftly we may bring the latter to bear."

Riordan glanced toward Ayana.

She was smiling. "As I said, it was only a reservation. But it warranted mention before we finalized our plan of attack. My only other counsel is to keep moving and parry when you can."

Girten shrugged. "It would sure be handy if any of us knew how to use a shield. Like the locals."

Yaargraukh leaned forward. "I must disagree. I do not think wearing a shield works well with our extant skills. Unlike our adversaries in the coming battle, we have many options for attack and defense. But to employ them, we must be able to free our hands quickly, as Lieutenant Wu just observed. The small bucklers we procured will prove useful for parrying, but your species' wrists are not sufficiently... structured to remain unharmed by a heavy blow."

"If the buckler takes a hard hit, let it fly away," Dora agreed emphatically. "Better to lose them than break a wrist trying to hold on." She glanced at Yaargraukh. "Me? I'm worried about Grendel, here." She added comic emphasis to the name.

Yaargraukh's eyes protruded in surprise, but his tongue whipped out briefly. "It is a strange human tradition, turning a personal insult into a comrade's nickname. But I suppose I must make certain allowances for such a weak-wristed species." His black tongue jetted in and out again.

Dora's surprised smile was big and very bright. "Seriously, though: the only armor he has is that Hkh'Rkh duty suit." She shook her head. "Not great stuff, and it took a beating after he punched out of his homemade 'pod.'"

Yaargraukh's neck circled. "What you call the tower shield is quite adequate, and since I cannot readily manipulate most of your devices, it is an excellent alternative."

Riordan couldn't be sure if his exosapient friend's assessment was simple truth or a purposely misleading reassurance. Either way, there wasn't much that could be done to improve his level of protection. Which reminded him: "Protect your suits, everyone. Make sure you run the smart resistance setting at maximum. But their functions and features are what have kept us alive so far, so dodge or parry instead of counting on them as armor." *And without them, we can forget about any attempt to return to orbit and repair the ship.*

"And the comms?" Bannor asked.

Riordan sighed. He'd hoped that, by the time he had to make this decision, they'd have more information on whether or not Ktor might be monitoring for radio traffic, either in person or through surrogate satellites. But since they remained as uncertain as they'd started, he had no alternative but to choose the lesser of two evils.

"For this operation, the restriction on voice-comms is suspended. Immediate coordination and control is arguably our greatest advantage in the coming fight, and I'm not about to risk any of our lives because of an enemy who might not even be there. If they are and they hear"—Riordan shrugged—"then we'll all cross that bridge together. Any other questions?"

There were none.

Riordan nodded. "That's all. Take thirty. Then we start finalizing at the sand table. Start hydrating. A lot." It always felt awkward saying it to people he thought of as his friends, but he finished with, "Dismissed."

Bannor did not stand until the others were starting down the spiral staircase that ran from the roof to the basement. He turned toward Caine. "Minute of your time, Commodore?"

Caine nodded.

Rulaine waited a beat as the last of the group sank from sight. "Permission to talk freely, sir?"

Riordan appeared ready to deflect that formality, but to his credit, he controlled that reflex. "Of course," he answered.

Bannor blew out a sigh. "You've been pushing yourself awfully hard these last three days. Something on your mind?" *Like Elena?*

It was as if Caine had heard the voice in Bannor's head. "I'm not going to lie. Getting Eku back means it won't be long before he determines if Hsontlosh's logs are as authentic as they seem."

Bannor frowned. "So that's why you've been training so hard? You've been first in the practice chamber every morning. Last at night, too."

"And I'd be there all day, if I could." Riordan's tone became sardonic. "They say the best therapy is work. If so, then I need as much work as I can get. Particularly since I'm about to lead a rescue that isn't just a CQC operation; it will be hand-to-hand."

"I understand the worry, Caine, but you *have* done it before. Boarding the Arat Kur courier in Barney Deucy, leading insurgents in Jakarta, taking Hsontlosh's ship, nonstop combat in Virtua—"

Riordan shook his head. "It's different when everyone on your team is a personal friend. Who could die if you make a mistake. Relying upon a plan based on almost no intel. And where you're more likely to be a liability than an asset."

Bannor almost started at Caine's concluding worry. "Granted that you're not a trained soldier, but—"

"My timing is off," Riordan interrupted, eyes pinching.

Bannor leaned forward. "Say again?"

"My timing is off. Virtua changed my muscle memory." Caine exhaled a bitter laugh. "Almost everything I learned about fighting I learned there, in a body that didn't exist. And doesn't exist here, either."

Rulaine hardly knew what to say. "But you've recovered from the inactivity of—"

Caine shook his head. "I had seven kilos more muscle mass than I do now. And that's after getting some back while I was dragging us around the stars. So the problem goes beyond reflexes; my proprioception has been rewritten. It's not synced to this body any longer, but the one I left in Virtua. The one I never really had. And despite all the exercise and training with practice weapons, those skills are still off."

Bannor's jaw tightened: *Tread carefully, here.* "Firstly, you are far more capable than you were before Virtua. But besides that, you're the CO. You shouldn't be a skirmisher at all. So if we just—"

Riordan's hand dropped like an axe. "No. My job is to come up with the plan and fit into it, not create a plan that fits *me*. And here's why: Look me in the eye and tell me that you expect that after the first thirty seconds, the rescue will still be going 'according to plan.'" He waited.

Bannor could only shake his head.

"Which means," Caine concluded in a brutal tone, "that I could become engaged, screw up a simple parry, and leave an opening that gets one of you killed."

Bannor waited, then: "Sounds like you needed to say all that out loud."

Riordan nodded. "Yeah, I guess I did."

Bannor waited another few seconds. "Must be tough."

Caine frowned. "What do you mean?"

Rulaine shrugged. "Must be tough being the only human who's got to be perfect. All the time."

Caine's momentary surprise became the precursor of a broken smile. "Low blow."

"My specialty. And: you're welcome." Bannor rose. "Ready to finalize that plan?"

"Yeah," Caine answered, standing slowly. "Yeah, I guess I am."

# Chapter Twenty-Nine

In Riordan's HUD, the view relayed from Bannor's helmet showed the approaching cluster of figures begin to separate. The two that were almost invisible—Tagawa and Wu in Dornaani suits—angled away from the three that still showed up faintly on thermal imaging: Duncan, Dora, and especially Yaargraukh.

"Ronin prime, this is Knife One," Ayana's voice murmured. "Will advise when we are in position."

"Acknowledged," Riordan answered. "Ronin prime, standing by."

Just ahead, Bannor snugged down over the same heavy crossbow that had been fired from the same position two days earlier. Speaking off comms, he reported, "No sign that the OPFOR has posted anyone to watch the approaches."

"Not on these streets," O'Garran grumbled, bringing up his own smaller, crossbow. "Anyone outside at night is a Judas goat. Or might as well be."

"Probably spooked by the earthquake this afternoon," Girten offered from behind Caine. "That's what? The third since we landed?"

Riordan nodded. "That outsized moon makes Bactradgaria pretty lively." He glanced up at the mottled satellite. Despite its distance, it was still quite bright. Hardly ideal for a stealthy nighttime approach.

The feed from Bannor's helmet changed slightly as he opened the visor and peered along the length of the big crossbow's tiller. He'd shown the best ability with the weapon, in part because Special

Forces teams still taught and employed unconventional weapons and tactics. "Duncan's team is almost at jump-off."

Riordan glanced up the street. The three thermal outlines were now less than twenty meters from the rear flank of the target hovel. Along with Peter and Ayana, they'd deployed early, moving into the lichen tracts to silence the ubiquitous crop watchman. Lacking nonlethal means sure enough to prevent him from raising an alarm, they'd resorted to the only sure solution: one low-power, subsonic projectile from the Dornaani hand cannon. With the perimeter cleared of roving eyes, Ulchakh and his Legate escorts had swept past and were now hidden in a wadi several kilometers north of Forkus' fringe.

The other concern, that the five of them might be challenged as they reentered the city, proved unfounded. Whether it was their casual advance or the fully robed Yaargraukh's hulking outline, the guards of the few hovels they passed remained still or retreated into the imagined safety of their dark entrances.

"Ronin prime," Ayana murmured, "Knife is in position."

"Ronin prime," Duncan's voice added, "Hammer is in position."

"Time to start the music, sir?" O'Garran's question was eager.

Riordan shifted his HUD to targeting. He lifted his survival rifle to cover the two guards flanking the entrance of the target hovel, drifted the cross hairs across the bigger one, blinked to confirm that was the target. The crosshairs were instantly surrounded by guidons that would keep him on target. Just in case. "Unit check."

"Knife, standing by."

"Hammer, standing by."

"Splint, standing by," Newton added from behind.

"Bolt, standing by," Bannor muttered.

"Ronin Prime, counting down to zero. Three, two, one—"

On "zero," four crossbow strings—one much louder than the others—slapped forward against their prods. The guard hit by Bannor's bolt staggered heavily, then fell when hit again from the side: either Wu or Tagawa had found the mark. One of the other two bolts hit the second watchman high in the shoulder; the other missed narrowly.

Bannor and Miles dropped their bows, took a moment to unsling their survival rifles. By the time they—Bolt Team—were charging across toward the hovel, Knife had appeared from the right, Peter slightly ahead of Ayana, shortsword in his right hand, stun grenade in the other.

Further in that direction, the three figures of Hammer had arrived at the appointed, and weakest, section of the hovel's wall and were already at work. Duncan and Dora, both holding grapple guns, flanked the section. Making sure their weapons were at the same height, they fired fully charged blunt-head bolts directly into the adobe: two soil-and-gravel grunts answered. As Duncan passed his grapple gun to Dora and unlimbered the Dornaani hand cannon, Yaargraukh swept a two-handed maul from under his cloak. In one smooth motion, he had it raised over his shoulder and swung it around to slam into the wall just a meter above where Solsohn's grapple had punched into it.

Survival rifles at the ready, Bannor and Miles charged for the entry, leaving a wide space between them.

Riordan jogged his crosshairs into that gap, stopped when it touched the remaining guard. He blinked on the target outline as soon as the HUD painted one on the wounded kajh, double-checked that the vector was clear, and squeezed the trigger.

The already-struggling guard clutched a sudden thermal bloom on his diaphragm and tumbled to the side, still moving feebly.

A moment later, Peter plunged into the entry, heaving the grenade as he did. Ayana was right behind him, her katana a cold sheen in the moonlight.

Behind Riordan, Craig asked anxiously, "Our turn, sir?"

"Not yet," Caine muttered, legs tensed to sprint behind Bolt Team, "not yet."

The image in Peter Wu's HUD, dominated by an axe-wielding trog, flickered for a moment as the stun grenade activated. When the image returned, the kajh was covering his eyes and swinging his weapon wildly.

There was something almost dishonorable about their attack, Peter reflected as he slipped outside the cut of the axe. With the grenade's flash pattern synced to the HUD's filter, his view was unobstructed. Similarly, the helmet's noise-canceling program was matching the screeching and cross-frequency warble shrieks, leaving Wu in a world of intermittent silence as he slid a meter along the wall of the dogleg. He plunged his shortsword—twice, in rapid succession—into the blind and deaf trog's right lung.

The kajh's howls of pain were not, however, removed by the Dornaani sound processing.

"Dogleg clear," Peter called. "Knife Two going in."

He felt, more than saw, Ayana flit past him and over the fallen trog like a spectre responding to his summons.

Duncan Solsohn made sure the cables from the salvaged proxrov's battery were handy and stepped back toward the target section of the wall as Dora punched her second grapple into, but hopefully not through, it. Hammer Team's objective, and the entire plan, depended on minimizing penetration, thereby ensuring that each projectile and blow deposited maximum energy at each of the five points they'd selected.

As Solsohn brought the hand cannon up to his hip and braced it, Yaargraukh swung the maul into the second of his two target points; a bit of the adobe sagged inward.

*Perfect!* "Hammer Team: clear!" Duncan shouted, confirming that all the weapon's operating lights were teal: the Dornaani equivalent of "green is go."

Ayana Tagawa reversed her katana in mid-strike, avoiding the second trog's clumsy parry and slashing the blade across its face. Its lower nose wholly separated from the upper, it howled . . . but gurgled to silence when the katana reversed yet again and swept through its windpipe.

Peter arrived alongside her, glancing at the two trogs she'd cut down before noticing the half dozen approaching from the further reaches of the smaller lobe of the hovel. Over a dozen more were fastening their armor while readying to advance from the larger chamber beyond. And behind them were the sounds of others either approaching or scrambling to their feet.

"I think," Wu muttered, "that there are more than we thought."

"I think," Ayana answered, slipping into a rear-balanced defensive stance as three charged at them with either war cries or yowls of inarticulate rage, "that you should throw another grenade."

Miles was first in behind Peter, confirmed that both members of Knife were unharmed, then saw the pack of kajh streaming toward them.

"Shit!" He swept up his survival rifle and put a pair of snap shots into the sniper's triangle of the two closest trogs. Without waiting to see the results, he let the survival rifle swing on its lanyard and cross-drew his melee weapons: his proven molecular machete for his right, and a new iron shortsword for his left. "Boss?" he almost shouted into the helmet mic.

"Yes?" Bannor and Caine chorused.

"Can't wait to call 'clear.' Ronin is needed. Right now!"

Riordan's voice: "Say again, Bolt Two?"

Bannor answered as Miles jumped to cover Peter's flank. "He's busy, sir." A sharp snap from the Green Beret's survival rifle punctuated each word.

O'Garran parried a trog club and shouted, "Time to join the party, Commodore!"

"Ronin moving," Caine replied, already running and sweating.

"Sir? I didn't hear—"

"Girten, we're not waiting for the 'clear.'" Riordan checked his rifle's battery, turned.

Craig was wide-eyed but ready behind him. Over his shoulder, Newton and Katie were already in an assault file. "Craig, you stay on me like glue. Splint Team, you are going to the entry. Somers, you have rear security; Baruch, you support Bolt. We move. Now."

Duncan took a wide stance, braced himself, and squeezed the hand cannon's trigger.

The device spasmed like a bottled earthquake; Solsohn's HUD fuzzed and the direction finder had the electronic equivalent of a grand mal seizure.

The perforated section of the hovel's wall flew inward, the connecting edges disintegrating as if being sucked in the same direction. At the center of that cyclone, a cone of widening visibility trailed behind the expanding warhead—now the size of a large plate—as the remainder of its thirty thousand joules carved a path of ruin into the room beyond.

Even the Dornaani suit couldn't fully disperse the weapon's heat pulse; the thermionic rims on the acceleration rings could only convert half of it into electricity. But even though he was half afraid to look down for fear of seeing a hole burned through both the suit and him, that didn't stop Duncan from shouting, "Hammer One, here. The door is open!"

✧　　✧　　✧

Halfway across the street, Riordan saw the side of the hovel rush inward even before he heard Solsohn's shout. He swerved in that direction.

"Sir—?"

"Girten on me. Splint to the entry."

Miles jumped on the channel. "Ronin? What are you—?"

"Exploiting the new doorway, Knife Two. Watch for our flanking fire."

As the hand cannon started cooling, Duncan plugged the leads from the proxrov battery into its auxiliary power jack. "Dora, cover the breach! Yaargraukh—"

But the Hkh'Rkh was already moving. Cloak gone, he swung the tower shield off his back, and, facing Solsohn, drew the iron longsword they'd bought at the vansary. "We should attack. Now."

Solsohn nodded, remembered to say, "Go! Dora, cover him."

Close to the Hkh'Rkh's side and already muttering something impatient, Veriden followed him into the screen of swirling dust: she low and careful, he striding like a grim colossus.

Bannor swore; another spoiled shot.

Not that it was Ayana's fault. Hell, she was the one really holding the line; she had four bodies in front of her already. But her sudden movements were, by intent, unpredictable. If it hadn't been for warnings as the HUDs analyzed her momentum and center of balance, Rulaine might have shot her twice by now.

But it also prevented him from using his survival rifle to best effect. Gritting his teeth, he exercised an option he'd wanted to avoid. "Splint Two in. Support Knife One."

"Sir?" Katie answered. "The commodore said—"

"Enter and support Knife One. Now!"

Katie Somers sprinted out of the dogleg, weapon ready. Her visor was down like the rest of them, but her momentary pause left Bannor with little doubt about her expression: wide-eyed horror at the mass of trogs pressing forward.

"Supporting fire," Rulaine ordered, taking two steps to the left. No longer forced to cover both ends of the rough skirmish line, he'd now be able to angle fire at trogs which tried to turn Miles' flank. Katie saw his movement and rolled out to the other end of the line, giving the same protection to Peter. More trogs started going down.

But not enough.

Yaargraukh stepped out of the swirling dust into the hovel— and immediately blocked a battle-ax with his tall shield.

It had been a respectable blow; the trog confronting him was heavily built and wielding the obsidian weapon with both hands. But the momentum made it impossible to bring around rapidly, either to parry or strike again. Yaargraukh stepped forward, cut down with the longsword.

And almost missed. Sized for humans, the sword was slightly shorter than the practice weapons the Hkh'Rkh had used both on the ship and in the Legate's fortress. But the force of the blow compensated for striking with only four inches at the tip of the blade: the trog's straining right deltoid was severed to the bone. He staggered back with a howl, barely hanging on to the axe.

Yaargraukh took a moment to survey the area. Another trog, apparently close to the section of wall when it blew inward, lay either dead or senseless. In the smaller lobe of the hovel, the humans of both Knife and Bolt teams were holding back over a dozen trogs, some of which were surprisingly well armed and well armored. Lieutenant Wu, attempting to fend off three with his shortswords, was unable to fully evade a cut with a hatchet. The Dornaani vacc suit resisted the partially deflected blow, but Wu stumbled back from the impact. One of the other trogs tried moving in to follow with another attack, but Sergeant Somers fired her lighter survival rifle. The trog tilted but did not go down. She fired again and her target fell, but that flank of the Crewe's skirmish line had been pushed two steps further back. Two more times and the humans would have their backs to the wall. Not acceptable.

Turning his eyes toward the larger space at the rear of the hovel, he saw why the entry teams were barely holding their line; a dozen trogs were rushing forward from there. Most of them were kajh, several of whom were female. And unless his eyes deceived him, both warriors and urldi were emerging from the very floor. No: from a hole near its center.

So: a subterranean complex which the Dornaani sensors could not have detected. From which two larger shapes were now looming upward to join the battle. They were hulking, brutish, and almost as tall as himself. Which, on second glance, made complete and horrifying sense:

Both bodies were shaped just like his.

Riordan knew, just hearing Yaargraukh's grim tone, that his plan of attack had just gone sideways. "Two grat'r," the Hkh'Rkh announced on the open channel, "coming up from an underground area in the larger part of the hovel."

For about the tenth time in as many seconds, Caine bitterly regretted that not all the team had Dornaani suits so he could see what they did. But in this case, Yaargraukh's report was all he needed.

Arriving at the breach, he gave orders that owed more to instinct and training than thought. "Duncan, hit the back of the trogs pushing up against the entry teams. Dora, cover Yaargraukh's flanks."

She was already doing so; her Ruger barked and a charging trog fell and slid to a halt at the Hkh'Rkh's feet. "And what are *you* doing, boss?" she asked, almost annoyed.

"This." Riordan straddled the breach on Yaargraukh's other flank and began firing into the mass of trogs rushing through the opening between the two parts of the hovel.

Glancing at the battery gauge: about seven more shots at the current power level. Beside him, Duncan raised the battery-linked hand cannon and engaged the trogs that were trying to squeeze forward from the back of the skirmish line. Two went down before others realized what was happening. A third was turning to shout a warning as Solsohn's third shot struck just above the base of its neck: immediately lethal, inasmuch as the muzzle energy—*well, "exit force"*—was twenty-seven hundred joules.

Riordan brought his HUD's cross hairs in line with another trog moving through the opening and squeezed the trigger. It clutched at its abdomen; probably a mortal wound, but at three hundred fifty joules, it only slowed the kajh. But in order to keep firing, Caine couldn't increase the charge, even if his shots were dangerously anemic.

Caine lined up another charging trog . . .

Bannor was the first to spot that, between the dwindling number of new kajh and the clutter of bodies in front of the Crewe, their skirmish line stopped retracting. A few more shots from Solsohn could fully turn the tide. "Keep it up, Hammer One!"

"Gonna be harder, now," Duncan muttered over the channel. "'Cause the kajh are starting to peel off the back of the line."

"Where are they headed?"

"Straight at me."

Which, if it put a stop to Solsohn's decisive flanking fire, might allow the mass of kajh enough time to hold back Hammer, resume pushing back Knife, or maybe both. If they could buy Duncan just a few more seconds... "Katie: grenade behind enemy in contact! Miles—"

"Ah, shit," spat the chief. He stepped back, parrying with the shortsword in his left hand, his right ready to cover the visor of his Terran vacc helmet.

Which couldn't sync with the grenades, only dim or black them out.

The first grat'r had finally pushed aside enough trogs to close with Yaargraukh. *This,* he thought, *will be interesting.*

Instead, it was disappointing and a bit depressing, given that the grat'r was a modified example of a primordial ancestor of his own race. It demonstrated shockingly low intelligence, rushing in without even an attempt at feinting or working toward a flank. Its immense two-handed cudgel landed solidly on Yaargraukh's shield but rebounded, surprising the attacker. It had not anticipated, or possibly hadn't encountered, so much resistance to its attacks.

That moment of disorientation was far more than Yaargraukh required. With an almost leisurely step forward, he ran the longsword through his attacker's forward thigh, tore the blade out sideways through the muscle, then arrested its momentum to thrust the point into the unprotected abdomen.

The grat'r emitted a piteous hooting—*Fathers of my Fathers, it sounds like us, though!*—before it toppled backward. The oncoming trogs broke stride. So did the second grat'r, which stared at the blood-spattered Yaargraukh as if discovering an apparition.

For a long moment, neither side moved... until Dora, seeing a golden opportunity in all those motionless targets, unleashed a lethal barrage into the clustered trogs.

✧　　✧　　✧

Duncan's HUD winked as Katie's flash-bang went off. The image was only gone for an instant, but it returned showing an entirely different scene.

The waiting rank of kajh skirmishers were trying to cover their eyes and ears at the same time. And because most wore shields on one arm and wielded weapons with the other, they were doing a very poor job.

The front rank of trogs had turned to discover the source of the sound and were instantly blinded by the flashing that the HUD filtered out. They began an even more desperate dance of dismay, realizing that if they remained in contact with their foes, they might be cut down.

Their attempt to stumble away came a moment too late. Tagawa and Wu, both in Dornaani suits, were now one-eyed kings in the land of the blind. They rushed out into the midst of the closest kajh. Where Peter's shortsword made swift, abrupt stabs, Ayana's attacks were one, long dance macabre: every movement sent the katana's edge through another hapless trog's flesh.

Dora and Miles cursed as they covered their visors; not wanting to be completely blind, they'd apparently only dimmed the incoming light. But at least their Terran helmets were able to block the grenade's explosive screams and roars.

Yaargraukh, whose Hkh'Rkh duty suit offered much poorer protection of his senses, did not move. Instead, hand shielding his eyes, he stared down as the grat'r and the kajh behind it writhed and reversed away from him.

Solsohn sighed as he shifted his aim to those trogs safely distant from his friends. Killing enemies who were trying to kill you was one thing, but this was too much like his days as a sniper. More like assassination than combat. He squeezed the trigger and, before he could see that body fall, moved his aim-point down the line to the next unfortunate victim...

Bannor followed behind Ayana and Peter as they advanced beyond what had been the skirmish line. Their focus was upon killing enemies: as many as possible before the surprise, effects, and battery of the stun grenade wore out. That meant there were stragglers, though: kajh that neither of them struck because they hadn't enough time to coordinate their attacks.

Rulaine strode forward, survival rifle held firmly. He reached the first of the trogs they'd missed, waited until its motion brought it into the right position, and discharged his weapon directly into its head. The trog quaked and fell its length, as limp as wet rags.

Bannor gritted his teeth and stalked toward the next enemy Knife Team had bypassed.

From the corner of his eye, Riordan saw that Duncan was already walking his fire back from the trogs that hadn't been able to reach the skirmish line and toward the others who had just entered the smaller chamber. Caine shifted his targeting, saving his few remaining rounds for those who tried to join them from the larger room.

Two doubled over, staggered. A third went down.

Riordan checked his weapon: one charge left, and still over a dozen trogs. Not to mention the grat'r.

Which, it seemed, was coming forward again, albeit very slowly.

Dora, still shielding her eyes, swung the Ruger in its direction.

"Hold," Yaargraukh said, raising his longsword as if to block her aim.

Muttering oaths, she checked fire, but kept the pistol on her target.

The leader of the remaining trogs—now mostly urldi rather than warriors—had turned to watch the same strange scene. Another female kajh gestured for the remaining forces to pause.

But two other kajh shifted restlessly and raised their weapons, ready to move forward again—

Riordan glanced at the weapon-charge data in his HUD: either one full charge or four lesser ones. His choice was pure instinct.

Caine switched the magazine's feed from solid projectile to cannister, swung it toward the restive male kajh and fired four fast rounds...at their feet.

The three- and four-millimeter pebbles kicked up an impressive flurry of dust just before Riordan pushed the suit's external audio to maximum and shouted: "*Ir-nek!*"

The two kajh jumped back; more than half the other trogs cowered.

Riordan raised his chargeless weapon menacingly.

The two kajh lowered their weapons, glanced at the female leader. The rest of the trogs followed their gaze, began turning toward her.

Frowning, she turned to stare at Caine.

Who opened his visor and nodded. *"Ir-nek,"* he repeated, before adding: *"Gruz'k jorgna."*

"'Enough killing,' indeed," breathed Ayana, who, panting, surveyed the carnage.

The female kajh cocked her head. Without looking away from Riordan, she waved downward with the hand closest to the remaining trogs. The survivors slowly sank to their knees.

Craig came up close behind Riordan. That had been his post throughout the fight: the CO's dedicated bodyguard. "'Gruz'k jorgna'?" Craig repeated uncertainly.

Caine shrugged. "'Submit,'" he translated. "It's a combination of 'stop' and 'surrender.'"

Yaargraukh's head pitched slightly. "As always, the commodore is very tactful. The actual words are 'be still or be meat.'"

Riordan shrugged, but without taking his eyes off the female kajh, who, in turn, had not taken her eyes off him. In all that tableau, the only source of movement was the grat'r. Unable to kneel because of the digitigrade nature of its legs, it inched toward Yaargraukh. Stopping just beyond the reach of the Hkh'Rkh's sword, it bent lower and grunted a single word. Even that simple utterance was halting and roughly articulated.

"Eh? What'd it say?" Dora complained.

"*He* said, 'Lord,'" Yaargraukh translated, lowering his sword.

Newton, still at his rearguard post within the entrance, jumped on the open comm channel. "Someone tell me what is happening! Have we won?"

"Yes," Riordan muttered. "Katie, relieve Newton. Doctor, there are wounded for you to assess."

"Wounded? Who?"

Riordan let his eyes travel over the bleeding trog warriors, both those on the ground and those standing.

Above the sounds of his hurried movement, Newton's voice was increasingly anxious. "Who has been injured? Someone on the skirmish line?"

"No," sighed Caine. "Our enemies."

# Chapter Thirty

"All clear, sir!" Craig Girten called up from the base of the stairs. "And Eku is right where they said he'd be."

Riordan gestured for the female kajh to precede him, which she did without any surprise or resistance. He followed her down, Pandora Veriden right behind him, a shortsword in one hand, her Ruger in the other.

Instead of the single large subterranean chamber that Caine had envisioned, the hovel's underground turned out to be a narrow tunnel with small chambers sprouting off to either side.

The second one they passed had several female trogs within, weeping. The HUD showed smaller bodies among them, some bright with life, others cooling into death. Riordan forced himself to continue on: *Eku first, then we find out whatever happened in* there.

Girten was standing guard outside the next chamber. "He's ready to go, sir!"

Riordan rounded the rough opening and decided that Girten's reports truly did tend to err to the side of optimism; Eku was barely standing and might not have been without the nearest wall's support.

"Caine," the factotum mumbled through a smile. One eye was almost swollen shut, he had numerous cuts and scrapes, and his widening smile revealed that he was missing a tooth.

Riordan turned to the female kajh, who shook her head. "It was unavoidable," she muttered, nodding toward Eku's injuries.

"You did this?"

She stared at Caine as if he'd slapped her across the face. "*Me?* Who do you think—?" She stopped herself abruptly, forced the indignance out of her suddenly very careful voice. "Your scythe was very crafty, lord. Some of what you see was inflicted before he came to us. Some is very recent."

"Jzhadakh is very violent," Eku mumbled through his daze.

Riordan glanced at him. "Who is Jzhadakh?"

But the factotum's attention had wandered, was now fixed on his entwined index fingers.

It was the female who answered. "Jzhadakh is—was—our leader. He is above us, among the dead."

Her tone was serious, but if there was any regret in it, Riordan could not detect it. *So: you disapproved of his methods. And maybe more.* "My friend appears to be drugged."

She nodded. "I instructed that his food be prepared with a fungus that distracts the mind. At first, it was to dull the pain of both his prior wounds and the ones inflicted shortly after he arrived."

"And now?"

She shrugged. "They keep his wits slow. He was very clever. The fungus made him much less so."

"Where is his equipment?"

She gestured toward what looked like a hide-swaddled mummy against the far wall. Riordan nodded toward Girten. As the sergeant moved to examine it, Dora moved very close to the kajh, the point of her new iron knife barely two inches from the other's kidney.

Without turning, the leader muttered, "I surrendered freely. I will not break the parole you have given me. Also, I am not eager to die."

Caine managed not to nod at her wisdom and, possibly, her honesty. "Craig?"

"Except for the 'chute, it's all here, sir. Suit, helmet, weapon, pack. Some of it's in pretty rough shape, though."

Riordan nodded. "Secure it and give Eku a shoulder to lean on. Join us down the corridor."

His buoyant "Yes, sir!" followed Riordan into the passage, where, puzzled, he paused to take his bearings before turning to the kajh. "This tunnel: it seems to head toward the h'achgai hovel just across from your own."

She nodded as they returned to the chamber where he'd heard the weeping. "It does. It was part of Jzhadakh's plan to become the leader of a great gang. Once the trade for your comrade was complete, he would have used those additional forces to strike it from both underneath and across the ground. Within days, the digging would have brought this tunnel to within an arm's length of a chamber we know to be beneath it."

Riordan glanced at the debris-cluttered floor underfoot. "That sounds optimistic."

"Before today's shaking of the ground, it was quite reasonable. Since then, we were busy removing and repairing the areas that collapsed. In consequence, many of us remained down here to work overnight. Many more were already weary from the day's labors."

They came to the threshold of the room where the weeping continued, although it was softer, more resigned. When Riordan made to enter, she held up a hand...and he noticed that her fingers were comparatively long and slender: far more like a human hand than a trog's. She nodded back toward Girten. "Your scythe has checked this room. Let the mothers grieve, I ask you."

Riordan frowned. "Who killed their children? It was certainly not any of us."

She looked at him as if his words might be some kind of test. "We know this. But it was done *because* of you."

Riordan heard echoes of his own warnings against questions that reveal ignorance, but his instinct told him that he needed to understand this. "Explain."

She raised an eyebrow, but complied. "It is merely as it seems. Five of the eight young were killed by their mothers. Or their mothers' rivals." Her shrug was sad, but without any particular surprise.

*By their* own *mothers? Or rival mothers? What the*—? "Again, explain."

The kajh appeared resigned to what she presumed to be a pointless exercise in obedience. "Their own mothers would wish to save them from the horrors of what might await if they fell into the hands of x'qao. Many rival mothers slay the young of others to ensure that their own offspring have less competition."

"*Madre de Dios,*" Dora breathed, glancing at the rough walls and stygian dark around them, "we are in hell."

"You sound disapproving of the rival mothers," Riordan remarked.

"Does that disturb you?" The kajh asked, with a hint of defiance in her voice.

"On the contrary, your disapproval reassures me." Both of the trog's heavy, straight eyebrows rose. "Tell me; what is your name?"

"I am Bey, Fearsome Harrow," she replied formally.

*Time to take a risk.* "I am neither of those things, Bey. Now: I need your counsel."

Each sentence caused a start of surprise. "Of course. I am your prisoner."

"Let us put that aside, for the moment. I ask not as your captor but as a...a leader that wishes no harm to come to the children that remain."

Her degree of surprise grew until it threatened to become a parody of itself. Until he uttered the word "children." A shrewd look narrowed her eyes, but only for an instant. "This would be my wish, as well, Fearso— Honored One."

"We may not leave with these children. How might we best preserve them?"

"It depends, Honored One. How far do you mean to travel?"

*Shrewd. I use the word "leave" and you try to get intelligence.* "Several days' journey. At least."

She frowned. "My best answer may also become my death sentence."

"I shall not harm you. And particularly not if you honestly try to preserve these children."

She shook her head as if she might have misheard Riordan or suspected herself to be hallucinating. "That is...is hard to believe, Honored One, but as you command it, I shall. To answer, I must ask a question which would also seal my fate, but for your assurances."

"Ask it."

She drew a deep breath as her decidedly human teeth came down on her lip. "Did you have the assistance of the band in the hovel toward which we were tunneling?"

*Ah. Of course.* If he confirmed that they'd been helped by the h'achgai, a cautious attacker would likely kill her to prevent that knowledge from spreading. "Yes," he answered. "We had their cooperation."

She nodded. "Then you must send word to them, with the children. They can be given a small meal with the same fungus I used on your friend. Even if some monster decides to question those too young to remember much of value, their memories will be too mingled with fungus-dreams to be useful."

Dora's voice was sharp. "And why would your neighbors take the children of the gang that tried to kill them?"

"In general, h'achgai are reasonable creatures. And I suspect that the ones of whom you speak are now the servitors of a vassal sworn to a great power." She thought for a moment. "It would also be prudent, and a sign of our fair dealing, to collapse the tunnel."

"How?"

Bey shrugged. "Jzhadakh was intemperate, but not so much that he failed to include a series of props which, when struck away, will cause that part of the roof to collapse. After all, a tunnel leading to a rival's hovel is also a tunnel that leads from his to your own."

Riordan's slow nod bought him a second to think. *So: Jzhadakh was "intemperate"? If so, maybe you're the counsel, or even the architect, of his scheme to trade Eku and his equipment.* "We shall do as you suggest, Bey." He paused on her name: its phonemes and her pronunciation of it was markedly dissimilar from those of other trogs. "Are you from Forkus, Bey?"

She stared at him again; this time there was a hint of umbrage in it. "I am not. I am from what you call the Wild Tribes."

"And what do *you* call them?"

"The Free Tribes." She lifted her chin. "If I was not born of the Tribes, I could not have become a truthteller."

*A truthteller? Something like an oathkeeper?* "So does one have to be from the Free Tribes to be a truthteller?"

She shrugged. "No, but females born in cities are usually forced to be an urld." Her ending tone added, *of course.* "It is not my place, Honored One, but I would ask you a question, if I am permitted."

"You are."

"Do you mean to take me and the others with you when you leave?"

*Damn: we never really considered that but—*"If you prove reliable, then, yes, I suppose we might."

Bey did a very capable job of not looking or sounding as relieved as her more relaxed shoulders suggested. "Very well, then let us go up. I shall help you prepare for our departure."

Yaargraukh nodded to two of the cooperative female urldi who had just finished tying the ankles of all the surviving kajh, wounded and otherwise. Other than the three kajh who had volunteered to help the victors, he had ordered all others that remained ambulatory to be laid out in a ring, facing away from the center. Or, more to the point, away from each other. As with many species, individuals unable to see the eyes of their comrades find it almost impossible to assess the group's mood. Among sapients, this kept planning an isolated rather than collective activity. His warrior culture had long experience and proof of that: mutinies and revolts were rarely attempted by individuals.

The grat'r was only able to understand a limited number of one-word commands, but had already collected its belongings and laid them before its new "lord." The pitiable creature probably presumed Yaargraukh intended to take all or most of them, but his inspection of them was to better assess the grat'r's mind by discovering what possessions it deemed valuable.

What he saw was sobering. The limits of its worldly possessions were a crude flint knife, a skull bowl, and leather wrappings for wounds or protection: he could not tell. However, the grat'r had kept a small hide pouch in its palm; checking to see if they were being observed, it furtively held it out toward the Hkh'Rkh.

Yaargraukh's neck retracted, signaling wary uncertainty.

The grat'r's own neck bowed lower. "I follow. Lord." It proffered the pouch.

Yaargraukh stared at it, relatively certain that if he took it, he was also acknowledging some kind of formal supplication. In essence, he would be accepting tribute from a servitor...and all the responsibilities that came with it.

He opened the pouch: a length of bone, probably varnished, and tarred shut at both ends. A single sigil was carved into it.

He looked up at the grat'r, his eyes describing the small, slow circles with which his species signaled an invitation to explain or display.

Despite being the Hkh'Rkh equivalent of Australopithecus,

the grat'r understood and pony-nodded. It pointed at the right side of Yaargraukh's torso.

Who felt a pulse of concern; the grat'r had seen the wound he meant to conceal. It was not serious: a graze from a dagger thrown as he emerged from the dust of the breach. Still, it was an inconvenient location, located along a muscle that flexed during most movement. Even if it did not open further, it would leave a clear trail for any that might try to follow.

The grat'r waited a moment, then mimicked breaking off one tarred end of the bone and rubbing it against the wounded area. With difficulty, it uttered a word so badly garbled that Yaargraukh gestured for him to repeat it. On the third attempt, he realized what the grat'r was trying to say: "physick."

The Hkh'Rkh fluted a sigh through his primary nostril. Still more shamanic nonsense. But the creature believed in it and was willing to give his intended lord his greatest treasure: the only way he could communicate both his respect and his request. Which, if accepted, made his welfare Yaargraukh's concern. But if rejected, he would not only be lordless, but quite likely to help those who might try to follow. Meaning he could not be left behind: not alive, at any rate.

Wondering if the grat'r would understand the meaning of a fealty gesture inherited from the times before history, from Rkh'yaa's first mythic Ghostsires, Yaargraukh held out the long-sword, edges horizontal.

Without hesitation, the grat'r moved so that the flat of the blade lay along the top of its smooth head-neck combination.

Yaargraukh warble-sighed again. *Just what we needed: another complication.*

No sooner had Riordan's head cleared the top of the stairs than Solsohn was jogging over to make his report. With the combat operations concluded, the radios were off; it was back to personal reports. "How's it coming, Major?"

Although Duncan sometimes groused about becoming the group's de facto quartermaster, he seemed quite comfortable in the role. "Almost done sorting it out, sir. We've finished policing Dora's brass."

"And the Dornaani projectiles and cannisters?"

"Already dug most of the projectiles out of the walls, but some of my misses went straight through. The cannisters you popped off were the easiest, actually." Duncan stopped as Bey came to stand alongside Riordan, looking very much like an adjutant.

Caine nodded for Solsohn to continue.

"So it seems the cannisters are made of a material that emits a faint signal; they show up in the HUD clear as day."

From where he was kneeling on the triage line, Baruch lifted his head. "Is it truly worth our time to find the projectiles?"

Duncan nodded vigorously. "They're optimized for magnetic acceleration, and nothing they hit in here would deform them. So a little dusting off and they're good to go." He turned back to Riordan. "I also have rough totals for the, er, forcibly arrogated equipment, sir."

Despite the grim surroundings, Caine couldn't stop a chuckle before it escaped. "'Forcibly arrogated equipment'? Is that what they call seized enemy gear at Langley?"

"They did, sir. But I haven't been an analyst for years now, sir, and you know how fast the jargon changes inside the Beltway."

"Indeed I do." Riordan pushed back against a rueful grin. "But we don't have the time or need for a tally right now. Just get everything worthwhile ready to move. And Duncan?"

"Sir?"

"Find the least useful ten percent of that gear by weight. Pack that separately."

"So we can drop it if we have to run like hell?"

Riordan smiled. "Or in case your scrounging instincts have us hauling more than we can carry. I want to be able to cut our load without any debates over what needs to go."

Solsohn replied with a histrionic sigh. "I hate being so obvious."

"I'm sure you do. You have twenty minutes to finish the sorting and packing. Get the urldi to help you."

"Sir, that will mean having them strip the bodies of their own gang."

"Get it done, Mr. Solsohn, whatever it takes."

"Sir, yes, sir."

Bey put out a hand. "If you wish it, Honored One, I can assist."

Duncan turned an expression toward Caine that asked half a dozen questions all at once.

Riordan simply nodded. "Yes, that would help. Major Solsohn, tell, uh, Bey what you're trying to accomplish. Including sorting out the survivors we can trust as bearers." Bey nodded and walked into the array of corpses, moaning wounded, and bound individuals that covered most of the composite hovel's floor.

Duncan held back for a moment. "Sir...do we trust her?"

"I don't know if *we* trust her, Major, but right now, *I* have to. Besides, I think she could single-handedly correct the worst of our ignorance. And I suspect she's done this kind of sorting and salvage"—Riordan nodded at the bloody aftermath around them—"quite a few times. Tell me what you learn from working with her."

"Sir, yes, sir!" Solsohn arrested a half-raised salute and turned to follow Bey.

"Commodore," Newton's voice called quietly, "a word, please."

Riordan started to approach him, but Baruch rose from the end of the triage line and intercepted him in an open space. "I did not mean to eavesdrop, sir—"

"No secrets, here, Lieutenant." Then noting the tall man's solemn look back at the wounded, he shifted to what was probably the more immediately pertinent title. "You seem troubled, Doctor."

Baruch nodded. "I heard you mention using some of the captives as porters."

Riordan nodded.

"There are...potential complications, sir."

"Go on."

"There are fourteen nonambulatory wounded. A third of those will not survive until dawn. Another third are almost sure to die within five days, given the severity of their injuries and the lack of sterile facilities. And the last third, while in no imminent danger, will collapse if they attempt to move within the next few days." He paused. "You see the problem, I'm sure, sir."

Riordan did, with a suddenness and horror that sent a hot flash down his spine and along every extremity. *With all the focus on* surviving *this rescue—on getting all our people out—I never once thought about* enemy *prisoners. And now, if we take some...*

Bannor was already crossing toward them, hazel eyes somber: he probably knew the topic just from the looks on their faces.

His first words confirmed it. "Yes, we've got a problem, sir. My apologies."

"*Your* apologies?"

"Commodore, you're the CO. You're responsible for the big

plan and making the big choices. Which you did. Managing captives is part of an XO's remit. Sorry I've created this steaming mess, sir."

Caine shook his head: not only to dismiss Rulaine's apologies, but because rules of engagement, including prisoners, were the CO's call. But that debate would only matter if they lived to have it.

Riordan looked around the combined hovels, not seeing any of it. *Where to start? What happens to prisoners on Bactradgaria? Are there traditions? And can we even afford to—? Wait!* "Bey!"

She cleared the distance in three, long steps: longer than most trogs could take. Just as he was realizing that she was also taller and less compact than the others, she called, "Honored One, how may I help?"

Newton and Bannor both raised their eyebrows at the salutation "honored one." *Gotta fix that: but again, later.* "Bey, we have much experience with combat." *True.* "But we are rarely present when a battlefield is . . . is cleared." *Also true.* "And I suspect that our traditions may be different." *So very true.*

Bey nodded. "I have the experience you require. A great deal of it. What do you wish done?"

*Everything, damn it.* But Caine said, "Start by telling us what you would do, in this situation?"

She nodded, glanced at Baruch. "Great Healer, I have not made a count of the living, yet. It seems you have. With respect, in order to make a reply to the Honored One, I must know the numbers and conditions of the survivors."

Newton raised an eyebrow at her address and repeated the casualty report he had just shared with Caine. He concluded with a summary of those who remained fit or were likely to survive. "Excepting yourself, there are fourteen wounded who cannot be moved. There are two wounded kajh who can move and should recover. There are eleven other kajh and seven urldi that are unharmed."

Bey nodded, thought, then shrugged. "The nineteen who can still move must be reliable. I shall assess them."

"And the badly wounded?" Bannor asked.

Bey blinked. "If we must move as the Honored One says, there is no alternative: the mercy knife."

# Chapter Thirty-One

Caine barely noticed the surprise Newton and Bannor could not keep off their faces. He was too busy trying to do the same while suppressing yet another wave of horror.

Maybe it had been the comparative civility of the Legate, or the basic decency of the h'achgai, or maybe he'd just been too preoccupied with the rescue... but he hadn't foreseen this. Despite the savagery and brutality that seemed to flow as freely and routinely as floods through the streets of Forkus, the part of his mind that *should* have anticipated this possibility had either been blinded by other concerns or blissfully asleep. Or, maybe, *conveniently* asleep: deep in a protective slumber because his conscious mind wasn't ready to envision a moment like this one.

It wasn't as if he hadn't faced and made grim choices over the past five years, but those had been split-second decisions, with enemies close at hand and determined to kill the rest of his team by any means available. There had been two occasions in Indonesia when there wasn't enough time to pull a mortally wounded insurgent to safety, and Caine had followed the terrible tradition of leaving behind a pistol with a single bullet. But he'd never had to order the cold-blooded murder of nearly a score of wounded captives. There had always been another alternative—

"Honored One?"

Bey's voice called him back to the task at hand and the limited

308

time they had in which to complete it. He nodded at her. "D-Do you have special traditions...rites, that we should—?"

She looked at him as if he might be ill. "Honored One, it is probably best if we do it."

"We?"

"Zaatkhur and I. He is my oldest friend, reliable, and only wounded in one hand. We have special knives for such times, if we may fetch them from our kits. We shall follow your parole strictly: no attempt to escape, no treachery. I give my word as a truthteller."

Riordan glanced at his two companions. Newton was looking away; probably his Hippocratic oath was at war with the grim necessities of the situation. Bannor simply dipped his chin: the shallowest of nods. Riordan met Bey's searching eyes, noticed they were very light brown. "Sergeant Girten shall accompany you to ensure that...that you come to no harm as you undertake this task."

Her nod became a shallow bow. Summoning the oldest of the wounded kajh, presumably Zaatkhur, she moved toward the far end of the triage line.

"Caine?" Rulaine prompted in a tone usually used when awakening children.

Riordan nodded. "Right. We still have nineteen captives who can move." He closed his eyes, found the thread of the problem. "Too many. They'd be able to track us with their eyes closed. But if we leave them here...same result. No, worse: the trackers would have reports from survivors who saw our weapons, our tactics." Bannor nodded at his conclusion. "Recommendations?"

Newton answered quickly. "Yaargraukh has kept eight warriors apart who did not give their parole as willingly as the others. They could be marched to the h'achgai hovel, which could send a runner to the Legate. He might be able to recruit these kajh, give them—"

Bannor shook his head. "Can't, Doc. The parole can't just be reassigned, not without the kajhs' permission and the Legate's assurance he would honor its transfer."

Newton folded his arms. "Then what do we do?"

Riordan experienced a sensation he had not known in a long time: flailing after the faintest shreds of a solution. "I agree with Bannor. That won't work, not with the kajh. But what about the female urldi? If we can leave them behind, that saves them from a march that might kill them and cuts the numbers by a third."

Bannor nodded. "It would help. Nineteen captives would not only be hell to police, but they'd be malnourished in ten days, fifteen at the outside. But if we can reduce that number...Okay: what's your idea for the trog women?"

*As if I have one.* "Release them. Bring them a few kilometers north with us, then tell them to head east and south: to reenter the city in Tasvar's territory."

Bannor crossed his arms. "Okay, sir. I see how that's better than trying to pawn off the kajh. But what if they decide not to risk going to Tasvar but decide to sell their story to whoever takes them in. They won't stick together because one is more likely to get a deal than three, and that would spread our story of what happened here all over Forkus. Unless predators wipe them out on the way.

"But let's say some did get to Tasvar. Given the way he's distanced himself from this operation, I suspect that's the last thing he wants. Like he said, the black-market grapevine always runs in both directions, so tales told inside his fort will get out and give him more trouble than any of this—including us—was worth."

Riordan had to nod. "Worst case? It could ignite a war with Hwe'tsara."

A whimper brought them out of their head-bowed huddle. The trog that Bey called Zaatkhur had laid his age-seamed hand on the shoulder of his last charge. Bey, walking past him, cleaned a very small obsidian knife as she glanced toward the outfacing circle of eight bound kajh. Several stared at her, then looked away.

Bey gave them a wide berth and settled gently next to the last of the incapacitated: a young female, barely into her adult years. Newton stepped slowly in her direction.

"So," Bannor whispered, "I don't see how we can cut the females loose at all. If we could get a couple of days north along the river, then maybe we could. But—"

"But those are the very days that we have to leave minimal tracks and move as quickly as possible, or get hunted down in the wastes." Riordan shook his head. "I just don't see what else—"

This time, the sound that stopped them was not a whimper, but soft weeping. They turned to find the source.

Bey's head had fallen until her sharp chin touched the hide armor over her clavicle.

Newton edged closer. "Did she call you 'sister'?"

Bey sucked in a deep breath, then: "Yes. She was born just after I arrived. I . . . I protected her after her mother was killed."

Bannor looked away. His mutter was almost inaudible: "Shit."

Bey stood stiffly, but instead of continuing forward toward Caine, she turned and strode toward Yaargraukh and the grat'r which now followed him with the posture of a bodyguard.

Bannor frowned, moved to intercept her—

Riordan put out his hand. "No. Wait." Yaargraukh was watching them; Caine nodded.

Bey drew near the Hkh'Rkh with a respectful nod, came closer when he gestured that she might do so. Their quiet exchange was brief—no more than five seconds—after which she turned sharply and strode back toward Caine and Bannor. As she did, Yaargraukh moved away from his post near the breach, the grat'r following him but also moving further out to his flank.

"Honored One—" Bey began.

"Call me Ca . . . Leader Caine," Riordan said. "You have something to report?"

She took a deep breath. "I do. I have assessed the reliability of the unwounded warriors."

"And?"

Bey glanced over her shoulder; Yaargraukh had gestured Ayana to come away from her position at the dogleg. Miles, left alone at that post, was about to call out to the Hkh'Rkh, then read the room and jerked a head at Peter, who also drifted closer to the prisoners.

"The eight bound kajh are not reliable."

One of them must have heard a fragment of her report. "Liar!" he shouted. "Dread Lord and Victor!" he cried toward Riordan. "She lies to get your favor! She—!"

"Silence." Yaargraukh's booming voice was entirely too much like an x'qao's, his hard palate rasping and grating just like theirs. The grat'r moved with him, approaching the eight bound trogs; although only armed with its claws, they were evolved for both digging and killing and were quite formidable.

Bey's reaction was difficult to read: her eyes closed and her jaw clenched so tightly that the joints on either side protruded sharply. When she opened her eyes again, they were pained. "I do not say this gladly about my own people, even less about those alongside whom I have fought, eaten, and slept. But the terms of your parole and my oath as a truthteller give me no choice: They plot your death, Leader Caine. You, and all your companions."

"You dead-wombed seductress!" shouted another. "It is plain now that you plotted with these murderers, hoped to be allowed to lead! You are mad with lust for power, since that is the only lust you know!"

She turned her head far enough to shout over her shoulder. "You heard the terms of Leader Caine's parole as plainly as I did. We receive fair treatment because we each gave our word not to flee nor plot treachery. Tell me: what were you whispering as I walked past?"

"You mean as you drained the blood from your own kin?"

"I have no kin in this place, though I have loved those in it better than you ever did. But to the point: As I walked past, you were plotting how and when it would be best to attack. Or if that was even the best way to achieve your betrayal."

Another screamed, furious. "It is not a betrayal to keep our vows to Jzhadakh! We act to keep our word to him!"

She turned on them, heat rising in her voice. "If you meant to keep those oaths of loyalty-past-death, then you could not accept Leader Caine's parole. It required that you forsake vengeance if you accepted its guarantee of safety." She surveyed them solemnly. "Your acceptance of the parole was not just a lie; it was an oath broken in the very act of promising to keep it."

"Liar! No oath to humans is greater than an oath to one of our own!"

"An oath is an oath," she retorted before pointing to a faint sideways oval tattooed on her forehead. "This is the eye that witnesses and must testify."

"Yes! If you are *asked*, traitor!"

"To be silent would have made me your accomplice. I would have violated my first oath: that of a truthteller."

"You wilds-whelped word lover! Jzhadakh should never have—!"

Riordan raised his hand abruptly. "Enough." Projected from his diaphragm, the word was loud without becoming a shout. "Bey, tell me more about these oaths of loyalty-past-death."

She raised an eyebrow. "They swore to kill Jzhadakh's killers. To see his final revenge completed, though he was unable to effect it himself."

"Savages." Newton's mutter was almost a snarl.

"Perhaps, but it is not uncommon on Ear—where we come from," Peter commented.

"In many cultures," Ayana added, katana hovering in her hand as if weightless, "it was a great honor."

"And in the Patrijuridicate," Yaargraukh rumbled, "it breeds fear and reluctance in those who might otherwise murder an adversary."

One of the bound trogs who had remained silent spoke almost quietly. "But now we must foreswear our oath to Jzhadakh. Being discovered, we are unable to accomplish it. We appeal to your mercy, Leader Caine." Several others agreed. Loud and hastily.

Riordan formed his own opinion on that request in the second it took for him to face Bey. "Can we trust them?"

Her eyes did not waver. "You can only trust that, in this moment, they fear you."

One of the loudest of the kajh howled, "I will kill you, x'qa-meat! Our vow to Jzhadakh requires that we slay she who has betrayed it!"

Eyes still on Caine's, she didn't bother to turn as she rebutted, "I never swore any vow to Jzhadakh. You did. Yet not half a minute ago, you assured Leader Caine that you had completely foresworn it. Now you mean to kill me to keep faith with it. You cannot both keep and foreswear an oath."

As the one who had suggested forsaking their vow railed at his intemperate comrade, Yaargraukh crossed to Caine and muttered, "If they are so utterly faithless here, you may well anticipate how they would repay us on a long journey into lands with which they are familiar and we are not."

Bey nodded. "Your fellow Lord speaks wisely. In a coffle, they will work to slow us so badly that we would be caught in a day. If we leave them unbound, there are too many for us to catch or slay, and so, they would bring word to Forkus. But it would be no different even if we took them with us and made good speed."

Riordan glanced from the increasingly quiet circle of bound kajh. "Why?"

She shrugged. "Because they will leave spoor. They are too many to watch and they will leave subtle traces cautiously. Besides, pursuers will find it more swiftly than they might in other circumstances."

Bannor raised an eyebrow. "What do you mean?"

Bey shrugged. "Tomorrow, the purchaser's representative will arrive here to assess the objects we meant to trade. Others who swear allegiance to the same liege will be nearby, watching to ensure that what just happened here could not surprise the actual trading party that will come a day later. Now, all will be unified to hunt you and they will find you within the day, if these eight are with us."

"So," Newton muttered hollowly, "if we cannot bring them and cannot release them—?"

Bey raised her hand; her interruption had the cadence of a formal recitation. "Any who attempt to slay those whose parole they have taken earn death." She turned toward Yaargraukh. "I see the largest lord has already arrayed them to ensure control as the sentence is carried out. I respectfully request that I not be included in the rota; I am still of their band."

Riordan nodded, numb, barely hearing the other words she spoke. *My God, we have to kill them. And, no surprise: for this they* do *have a tradition.* "Bey," he said hoarsely, "the others that can move. Get them outfitted. Loaded. You and Duncan. Now."

Bey seemed to disappear. Bannor seemed to reappear in her place. "Did she say a rota?"

Miles joined the huddle with a shrug. "I've seen this on Earth. Extremist militias make sure that everyone shares the guilt of execution. Although they usually call it a 'privilege.'"

Newton spat. "It might be, in this place."

Riordan knew what he had to do, said it aloud before he could recoil from it. "I ... I have to set the standard. Personally."

"Sir," Miles said, starting forward quickly, "this is not your responsibility."

"The hell it isn't."

"Sir, in combat officers give all sorts of orders that they don't—"

"This isn't combat, Chief. Yes, officers give combat orders they don't take part in. Can't be otherwise. But this is not a combat necessity. This is a crossroads. It's where we show who we are. To ourselves and those we expect to follow us."

He jerked his head toward the other trog captives. "Look at them. This is what they understand. Hell, it's what they *expect*. So if I don't take a hand in this, I've shown that our leaders don't have to get their hands dirty. And I'm not going to set that precedent."

He leaned back. "So I'm not going to just be part of the rota; I'm going *first*. I have to."

He looked at Miles for a long second; he wasn't sure he'd ever seen that much compassion in O'Garran's eyes. "So I need one thing, Chief."

"Name it, sir."

"I've never ... done anything like this. Show me how to do it quickly. Where and how to strike.

"No worries, sir. But actually"—and because Riordan was alert for manipulation, he didn't miss O'Garran's shift into a subtly cajoling tone—"if you're not, er, adequately skilled, that's another reason to let others do it. Those with some prior experience."

"No. I *have* to take the lead on this. But I need you to ... to help me. To make sure that I don't miss." *And then throw up.*

O'Garran inhaled sharply. "You sure about this, sir? Maybe if you allowed me to just start it off, I could show you—"

"Chief O'Garran, my request is now an order. Will you or will you not instruct me in effecting a sure and swift execution?"

"Sir, yes, sir!" When Caine relaxed, Miles sighed. "Okay, boss, sad to say, but you've come to the right guy."

Riordan nodded tightly. "Everything I've ever heard is that it's not the killing that's hard. It's doing it quickly enough." Bey rejoined the group, scanning their faces.

The chief, nodding at Riordan's concern, adopted a soothing tone. Which only made what he said more horrible: "Not to worry, sir. It's going to be easy, with the right ... tool."

"Like this one?" Bey proffered a knife which, at the point, was more like a flat, double-edged ice pick. It broadened as it neared the hilt.

O'Garran stared at her then at the pithing knife. "That's a fine ... tool. But we have one that won't take anywhere near as much skill." He held up his own molecular machete. "You've seen how this slides through damn near everything. Materials a lot harder than flesh or bone. So you just cut right here, beneath the base of the skull. That severs the brain from the spinal cord. No pain. Instant unconsciousness."

Riordan remembered nodding, setting the order of the rota. He remembered confirming the security protocols, ensuring that while one person carried out the execution, a second held the prisoner steady. And each of those assistants became the next executioner. And so forth until the task was complete.

Then he was standing behind the first of the bound kajh,

simultaneously very focused and yet grasping after memories of other times and places: anything, not to be completely and utterly rooted in this horrific moment.

Then, sometime later, he saw O'Garran's face, looking up from where he was holding the prisoner. "Sir?" he murmured. "Whenever you're ready."

Without thinking, Riordan pressed the machete down. He felt a spurt of unexpected blood as the impossibly sharp edge over-penetrated, was proud he didn't vomit, and passed the machete to Miles. He walked stiff-legged to the entry, replaced Katie at her rear security post, fixed his eyes upon the street, and, weapon at the ready, hoped—and tried—to vomit. But couldn't.

All he could do or see was the back of the neck he'd partially severed, the broad head hinging forward as it tipped away from him.

# Chapter Thirty-Two

As the Crewe's strange procession finally cleared the lichen tracts, Peter looked back along its moonlit length. Seen from the low rise that marked the beginning of the wastes, it was part marching order, part prisoner escort. And it would remain so until Bey and the other trog survivors from the hovel—thirteen in all—had their status determined: captives or allies.

For now, that meant Peter on point, a primary reaction force fifteen meters back, then the kajh, followed by the main van. The urldi followed close behind with most of the goods from the hovel, watched over by the rearguard. Between their numbers, the extended formation, and the slower pace of the wounded, they had only covered two thirds of the distance they had planned. Still, by staying close to the river, bright in the glow of the moon, they had managed to put almost ten kilometers between themselves and Forkus.

But false dawn was already starting to tint the eastern sky, and if they did not manage to increase their—

A whistle rose from the rough ground ahead and then warbled as it faded.

Wu brought up his fist. Creaks of creased leather and tucked gear told him that his signal had brought the formation to a crouching halt. "Truth," he announced into the darkness to the north.

"Dare," came the countersign . . . but the voice was not Ulchakh's. Still, it was familiar.

The silhouette of a head rose up from behind the long low ridge ahead. From the shape alone, Peter knew whose it was. "Ta'rel!"

The mangle rose, spatulate teeth shining in the moonlight. "Your Low Praakht is much improved, Friend Wu. I see you have brought many new friends." The mangle paused as he stood on the low spine of the rise. "They are friends, are they not?"

"That remains to be seen. As does the rest of your group."

Ulchakh rose into view. "Well met. Ta'rel and I are the only two in this place. Those who were sent along from our mutual friend have watched over us and your goods and kits. I suspect they are departing even now."

Wu didn't need his HUD to detect Tasvar's overwatch group departing, their outlines moving beneath the crest of the next ridgeline toward the sheltering bulk of the next. They were a covey of dark shadows, slipping into even darker shadows...and were gone in an instant.

Ulchakh gestured to Wu. "Come. There is much to carry." He scanned the column, crouching behind Peter. "But I see you planned for that."

Unwilling to point out they'd had no such foresight, Peter waved the formation to its feet and led the way toward the slope behind which their gear and goods were hidden.

Bey had gradually increased her pace until she reached the head of the kajh marching between the small group that the harrows called their "reaction force" and the main van. She glanced sideways. "How do you fare, Zaatkhur?"

The maimed kajh started. Realizing who had brought him out of his daze, he smiled crookedly, "I am alive, Little Bey. And after such a night, that *is* something."

"It is indeed, old friend." Uncertain if their captors would see danger in two trogs walking close together, she kept her distance from the protector who'd kept her warm and fed after her mother's death. "These harrows are puzzling," she muttered.

"If harrows they are."

"I have wondered the same thing." She reminded herself to speak quietly. None of the harrows were in easy earshot, but they had strange abilities, particularly when their helmets' mirror-visors were closed. "But if not harrows, what are they?"

"That is a question for which I have no answer. But they are almost certainly the ones we heard rumors about, the ones that visited Kosvak's vansary several days ago. Like that group, they do not show nor claim themselves sworn to any liege, for certainly, with so much magic kit, they would not serve any lesser lord."

Bey nodded. "Yet that merely makes their origins mysterious. What I find most interesting is that this group does not *act* like harrows."

"In what way?"

"The one who gives orders—Leader Caine—must be the group's First Harrow, and so, should have the hardest heart. No liege, x'qao or otherwise, would allow any less. Yet, his questions about punishing the oathbreakers and about the young in the underground are not those that come from a hard heart."

"Ah, Little Bey is curious." Zaatkhur smiled despite his savaged hand. "Which means she is about to get into trouble. Again."

Bey would have liked to punch his arm. "Sometimes, curiosity is necessary, you old thickhead. As it is now. City trogs live or die by understanding the intents and ways of those who hold them in thrall. But this group, these harrows-who-are-not, are unknown. Leader Caine, and the others who counseled him, spoke of us as if they were determining the fate of their own kind. Even among independent humans, such as Vranadoc and the Legate, that is not often the case."

"Unless they are speaking of a whakt," Zaatkhur muttered with a mischievous side glance at Bey.

"True, but in this case, it does not seem to matter how much human blood was in our veins. They did not even seem to be aware of the differences."

"Yes, that was strange. As was the leader's insistence on executing the first oathbreaker with his own hand. I thought it would be out of rage. What else would motivate one so powerful as he to act so far beneath his station? But I saw no anger. Only . . . regret?"

Bey shook her head. "Far more than regret. Did you see how pale he became, even for a burntskin? Yet he insisted on doing so. As if it was a terrible duty."

"Ah," Zaatkhur hummed, "so your curiosity is personal, too."

Bey would have liked to buffet her avuncular tormentor about the ears, but even if he had not been wounded, she could not have brought herself to indulge in one of their fond traditions.

Because he was right. The more she reflected on Leader Caine's strange questions, and what at times seemed like his solicitude, the more she recognized that his reactions were much as her own had been when she and her mother had first arrived in Forkus.

Not that life among the Free Tribes had been easier: the dangers of the wastes were more profound than those of the city. Indeed, that was why the bonds of family and clan were their sacred sources of comfort, support and survival. Which was why lieges, but particularly x'qai, did not permit them to exist, let alone flourish. It had been a hard lesson, learning to conceal her hatred for life as it was lived in Forkus. But she'd had to keep that loathing from showing on her face...and now she saw something very similar in the expressions of Leader Caine and his group. The same kind of surprised horror and revulsion that it had taken her years to learn how to suppress in order to be deemed worthy of the titles "counselor" and "truthteller."

Water glimmered to the east. They were finally nearing the river that flowed down from Khorkrag and, further north, from Fragkork. Once the column could simply parallel its high-water bank, they would travel more swiftly: partly because the way ahead became obvious, but mostly because their right flank would be safe against the western bank.

Anticipating that the formation would push harder to reach that better path, Bey shifted her load: a dead kajh's pack in addition to her own. The not-harrows showed no enjoyment in the wealth they gathered from the slain, but had nonetheless been efficient and swift in deciding what to keep and how to distribute it among their captives. And although they had not shared their final destination, the rendezvous with a mangle and a h'achgan trader of repute made it easy to guess: one of those species' communities in the wadi country east of Khorkrag.

Bey allowed herself a small smile. If she was correct about those destinations, that made it just that much more likely that by the time they got there, they would have become servitors, rather than corpses left to rot upon the dust.

When the formation reached the river, Yaargraukh guided his rearguard through the same tactical evolution that the other parts had carried out before. Bringing his detachment forward, he arrayed them in a long column that paralleled the landward flank of the bearers. They, too, had been reformed into a column, protected on the other side by the river itself.

Waving the grat'r ahead, the Hkh'Rkh took a moment to rearrange his cloak against the draft which had been blowing cold upon his right side, and over his wound in particular.

He released the handle of his tower shield, shifted the long-sword into that hand, and used his now-freed right to probe the place where the trog throwing knife had found the one gap in his previously damaged duty suit. Surprisingly, he felt almost no pain despite the steady marching. Indeed, he could barely trace the wound itself, which his fingers now registered more as a swollen ridge.

But as he brought his hand away, he felt it grow suddenly cool as the night air found and attacked a moist spot upon it. Puzzled, raised his fingers up into the fading moonlight.

A black smear, maybe with a taint of dark maroon in this light. Sticky. Blood.

Yaargraukh's eyes reflexively retracted as the chill of realization hit him; he was bleeding again. He returned his hand to the rent in his duty suit. He had to probe the injury carefully but thoroughly, had to find the gash in order to assess the amount of blood loss.

Except he could not locate the gash at all.

Checking the rest of the formation to make sure that his actions were not attracting any attention, he dropped back slightly, released the side-seam clasps of his duty suit and felt around more carefully. When he still couldn't locate anything other than the small ridge—which did not feel swollen so much as hard—he stopped, raised the flap of ballistic armor and looked.

The blood he'd found with his fingers was already thickening where it had run down his flank. But there was no longer any around the long welt that marked the knife's passage along his flesh. Which meant that the gash that had been there two hours ago was gone. Not obscured or covered by swollen skin: it had disappeared.

Yaargraukh's mind recoiled like a sand snake caught out of its lair in one of Rkh'yaa's freak equatorial blizzards. It was not possible. The grat'r's superstitious mummery about a mystic "physick" defied sense, did not warrant a shred of credence.

Yet there was no opening in his flesh, and the welt looked as if it had already formed and shed a scab.

Impossible. The last time the Hkh'Rkh had labeled something "magic" was when parahistorical soothsayers claimed to hear the words of the Ghostsires in every crash of thunder that had been heralded by a blue-white flash.

But as impossible as it might seem, the wound was gone.

*Still,* he thought as he resealed his duty suit with uncertain fingers, *simply seeing something we do not understand does not mean it is evidence of "magic," however miraculous it may appear. The grat'r explains it according to his limited understanding of the universe. I must share this with the others and, together, seek the actual agency at work.*

Yaargraukh hurried to catch up to the rear of the formation, looked ahead to where Bannor was preparing to relieve Caine as the officer in charge of the main reaction force. They were the two humans who would most wish to know about this strange phenomenon. They were also the two people least likely to question the accuracy of his account. But this was not the time for yet another surprise, another unprecedented novelty to assess.

It would wait, he decided.

At least until tomorrow.

Bannor drew alongside Caine, who hadn't spoken more than twenty words since they'd quit the hovel. Although not garrulous, Riordan had never been reluctant to talk, either. "Anything suspicious up ahead?"

"All clear. Behind?"

"Yaargraukh seemed to be having some trouble with his shield or his duty suit. Couldn't really tell which. But he seems to have squared it away, now."

Riordan nodded, slacked his pace to begin dropping back to the van.

"Caine, are you all right?"

Another nod. "I have to be. So I will be."

Bannor shrugged. "I suppose that's one advantage of the long walk ahead of us: a lot of time to sort things out."

"To the extent they can be." Rulaine looked at his friend, who waved away his concern. "I'm not talking about what happened tonight. I'm talking about how we got into it."

"You mean, that we didn't ask the right questions?"

"No: that we had no way to know what the right questions

were. Because even Tasvar thought we were ready for what we had to do tonight. Remember what he said when Newton pointed out that we might have wounded leaving spoor that our enemies could follow?"

Bannor sighed, beginning to understand. "Yes: that we weren't just warriors. We were soldiers, and so had experience making the difficult decisions called for in those situations."

Riordan nodded. "But we don't, do we? Yes, some of you have been in places where things like parole were provisional, or just a pleasant-sounding idea that most combatants ignored. But here? At best, those are just idealistic and ignored notions. The local traffic in life and death is no different than the trade in lichen or flint or dung. Everything and every life is just a resource. There isn't even any concept of good or evil behind the choices made about them. The only criterion is utility and the only objective is survival."

Somehow, hearing that come out of Caine's mouth was more disturbing—and demoralizing—than the possibility that the deeds of the past night were tipping him into a fugue state. Bannor shook his head. "Well, at least some communities have values beyond survival of the fittest. They have enough conscience to be concerned with survival of their group, maybe even their allies. That's something."

Riordan shrugged. "I suppose so. But I think Dora is the one who's done the best job of defining the basic nature of this place."

Bannor raised an eyebrow. "Huh. She's not usually the philosophical type."

"She's not. Maybe that's why she saw, and articulated, the truth so clearly."

"Which is?"

"That we really are in hell. You've got the lead. I'm falling back, now."

# Into the Black

*System GJ 1128, the Dornaani Collective*
*March 2125*

# Interlude Three

Alnduul nodded Downing toward the entry to the shift barge. "I believe your men are already waiting for you."

Trevor frowned. "How long have they been in there?"

"Almost an hour, I believe."

"No riots, yet?"

Alnduul's fingertips drifted downward. "No..."

*Thank God.*

"...but" the Dornaani concluded, "I believe the group is too small to generate that level of disturbance."

*How bloody reassuring.* "Do you have any better estimate regarding failure rate of the coldcells?"

A Dornaani who was exiting the barge, and who appeared significantly older than Alnduul, answered. "Despite having to learn the stasis technologies of three different species, we have gathered sufficient data, I believe. I just completed the last noninvasive examinations of the Ktor coldcells and symbiopods. Unfortunately, the equipment aboard *Olsloov* is not optimal for such tests and measurements. We will commence analyses as soon as we have completed our next shift. However, we must expect that, within a few shifts, there will be some complete malfunctions. After that, they could become quite frequent." He made to walk off.

Trevor called after him. "You said there were coldcells from a third species, sir?"

The wiry Dornaani turned; its eyelids nictated slowly at

the word "sir." "I did. You brought aboard a small number of Hkh'Rkh hibernacula, as well. Asylum seekers who fled Turkh'saar, as requested by their leader Yaargraukh and which was granted by your leader, Caine Riordan. The technology is primitive, but sound. I cannot tell how long it will function, but I see no signs of failure at this time." With a sharp blink of his eyes, he turned to resume his departure.

"Thank you," Downing called after him. "I apologize that we don't know how to call you."

"How could you? We have not met."

Alnduul's lamprey mouth was slightly twisted around its axis: amusement. "The oversight is mine. Thlunroolt, this is Mr. Richard Downing, formerly of—"

"Yes, I know *who* he is. And I daresay"—the grainy-skinned lids of the Dornaani's large eyes puckered slightly—"I know *what* he is, as well."

Downing refused to be flustered at encountering a Dornaani that was not only unwelcoming but irascible. "It is a pleasure to make your acquaintance," he offered.

"A most optimistic greeting," Thlunroolt burbled: the Dornaani equivalent of a distempered mutter. "I advise you to defer judgment until you know me better, Richard Downing." Without wishing anyone enlightenment, he continued on his way into the ship.

"Well," Trevor almost drawled, "isn't *he* a ray of sunshine? Or is it 'she'?"

"Thlunroolt is male, according to your figuration of reproductory roles. As far as his disposition, he is always thus with strangers."

Downing thought he detected both irony and fondness in Alnduul's explanation. "It sounds as though you have known him a long time."

Alnduul's inner eyelids nictated once, sharply. "He was my mentor when I became a Custodian. He was no different then."

"Even toward you?"

"Especially toward me. Gentlemen, your personnel are growing restless."

"So there's no way for more than a few dozen of us to be awake at the same time?" one of the Lost Soldiers was asking. From the slow, careful articulation of the question, Downing knew it was Joe Capdepon, even though all he could see from the entrance were the backs of a score of heads.

Ike Franklin nodded. "*Olsloov* isn't built to haul people or cargo. With everyone hot-bunking, you could maybe—*maybe*—cram in fifty or sixty. But space isn't the real limitation. It doesn't have the facilities, life-support capacity, or consumables to provide for more than a few dozen."

Vincent Rodriguez waved at the cavernous bulkheads around them. "Well, what about housing people in this barge?"

"Lots of space, sure. But it doesn't even have integral life support."

"Well, we're breathing, aren't we, Lieutenant?"

"That's because there are air tanks in the hull. But those are for providing a shirt-sleeve environment when people need to load or unload it. More importantly, it can be pumped back into those tanks...which is what they'll be doing before we shift again."

"Why?"

"Because they're gonna turn this place into a big deep freeze," engineer Phil Friel muttered resentfully.

His partner and fellow engineer, Tina Melah, snorted derisively. "And here I was thinking we were all gonna be camping out on the deck, singing songs and roasting marshmallows."

Franklin crossed his arms. "Are all of you done, now?" Between the respect they had for the doctor who might have to patch them up and the grim stare he'd acquired over the course of too many jumps into enemy territory, the group fell silent. "Pumping the atmosphere out is necessary to get this barge to cool and match the background, which is really important since it's about as stealthy as a neon circus tent. And if something *does* put a hole in it, the last thing anyone wants—particularly the folks in the cryocells behind me—is explosive decompression, which will do its damnedest to pull anything in this hold outside into space, straps and lashings notwithstanding."

Downing saw Trevor trying to restrain himself from adding to the list of reasons for keeping the barge cold and airless. He moved restlessly as he mastered the impulse.

A head turned at the sound: Tina's. Her eyes opened wide, and then her mouth. From which came the cry, "Commander on deck!"

"At ease!" Trevor added hastily.

Slouching torsos that had been halfway to ramrod straight finished by easing into parade rest, crossed arms tucked low behind tense backs.

Downing led the way to the front, where Franklin saluted before retiring gratefully to the nearest bulkhead. "At ease," Richard said, finally in a position to witness the informal standoff taking place at the front of the gathered personnel.

On one side, the so-called Three Colonels from the twentieth century—Paulsen, Rodermund, and Zhigarev—were planted with arms crossed, their grizzled naval peer Carlisle Hansell standing nearby. On the other side were most of the two dozen Lost Soldiers and Cold Guard who had been reanimated. Between the two groups was a far more casual cluster: those who'd been part of Riordan's original crew, as well as Sue Philips and "her" Three Wise Men: Larry Southard, Angus Smith, and Ryan Zimmerman.

Downing peripherally assessed the crew members: their stances were not exactly disrespectful, but it was clear that Richard hadn't made many friends or instilled much trust among them. "Mr. Tsaami, as pilot during the rescue of the Lost Soldiers, I suspect you may have one of the least biased perspectives upon the difference of their opinions in this compartment."

Senior pilot Karam Tsaami nodded. "I probably do, yeah."

"And what is the primary object of contention?"

Karam's sideways smile was more than a bit ironic. "Freedom of choice, Mr. Downing."

"That answer is admirably brief but insufficient. Whose choice and about what?"

The unofficial chaplain of the rank-and-file Lost Soldiers, a backwoods Arkansas preacher who'd been a submariner in the Pacific, stepped forward and gestured at those behind him. "I don't aim nor claim to speak for these men—and ladies—sir, but I probl'y do have the biggest mouth. My name is Seaman Ronald Purcett, sir, and I—"

"Yes, Mr. Purcett, I remember meeting you. I appreciate and applaud the spiritual support you have provided to those who seek it. Carry on."

"Yessir. Them of us as have misgivings, sir... well, like Mr. Karam said, it's about choice. The most basic choice that ever' man should have: of what to do and where to be. Thar's nowt but a few of us Lost Soldiers awake. But the Colonels here, they're askin' us to stand for all the rest of the fellers 'n gals when it comes to leavin' what y'all call 'Terran space.'

"Well, sir, that's as big a leavin' as can be: turnin' our back on Earth and goin' only God knows where." His dingy white service cap was crumpled in his seamed hands. "It's not a thing as can be decided fer anuther feller: to take him so far from home, even if all that's left is the plots where his kin're buried."

Downing nodded, let the small, sad smile he felt inside rise up to his face. "I sympathize with you, Ronald. And with all of you who share his feelings. But the brutal truth of the matter is that we must keep those still in cold sleep right where they are, at least until we have sufficient resources to provide for them. To say nothing of the *time* to wake them safely."

"I hear yer words, Mr. Downing, and I 'speck I unnerstan the problems well enough, but that don't make it right or just, sir."

Trevor walked toward the Lost Soldiers. "I agree with you, Purcett. This situation isn't right and it isn't just. And if we were the ones responsible for the situation, I'd probably be asking the same questions you are.

"But we didn't make this situation, which is about as basic as it gets: the people searching for us will kill us if they find us. And the politicos who should be stopping them are blocked by other politicos who will tear the CTR apart if they don't get their way."

"Everything in the world has changed," Vincent Rodriguez drawled, "except politicians."

The answering laughter was grim but genuine.

Trevor acknowledged it with a smile of his own. "I'd argue if I could, but Chief Rodriguez has the right of it. Because just like in your day, the politicians make the decisions, but we're the ones who carry them out. And pay the price for their mistakes.

"But this time, you won't just be losing your lives because of their mistakes, but because of their moral cowardice. At least on this side of the border, you can choose whether or not you're willing to accept that. Whether you'd rather go back to Terran space to stay and die, or leave and live out here.

"But the only—the *only*—way any of us are going to live is by traveling light and moving fast. Ike," Trevor called, raising his voice, "where are you?"

Franklin put up a hand. He was squatting with his back

propped against the bulkhead. "I'm over here, sir, sitting this round out."

"I'm not asking you to take a side, Ike. But since we're talking about time, I need your professional estimate: How long would it take to reanimate everyone in cryogenic sleep?"

Ike pushed off the wall and stood. "Hell, Captain, we *could* just hit the buttons, stand back, and hope for the best. But not everyone would survive, particularly the ones who are in compromised units."

Trevor nodded. "And if we take a responsible approach?"

"Once you start the reanimation cycle, you need a doctor or physician's assistant on call for a day, because if it goes bad, it can go real bad, real fast. Currently, we have six people with qualifications, but only four of them have been hands-on, and you need to keep one of them free to help if the sleeper goes into cardiac arrest.

"So we can reanimate three people a day, safely. We have over three hundred people still in cryounits. Bottom line: full reanimation requires well over three months. If everything goes right. Which it never does." Ike sat against the wall again.

Trevor turned back to Purcett and the Lost Soldiers. "Three months. Just so everyone can wake up and choose whether they'd rather die in human space or travel beyond it in cold storage and *live*." Trevor evidently saw the same puzzled frowns Downing did. "Yes, any that want to leave would have to *go back* in their cryocells."

Purcett's face became a mass of frustrated creases. "But, damn it all, Cap'n, why?"

Downing cleared his throat. "Seaman, back when you were serving aboard *Swordfish*, how many did you have in your crew?"

"Oh, 'round about fifty-five, Mr. Downing."

"Sixty," corrected Hansell, the sub's craggy and taciturn CO. "Maximum complement is sixty-four. You might take on twenty more during short-duration rescue operations."

Downing nodded his thanks, looked back at Purcett. "Alnduul's ship resembles your old submarine in one way, Seaman: it hasn't the space, sustenance, or life support for many extra people." He folded his arms. "If all the Lost Soldiers remained awake, they would exceed the *Olsloov*'s capacity by two hundred percent. Consequently, we would have to put at least two thirds back into cryogenic stasis, a process almost as involved as reviving them. And even then, we'd soon be desperately short of food and water for the rest."

Trevor leaned toward Purcett. "Except, long before then, we'll have been found and slaughtered by the bastards hunting us."

Purcett's voice was pained. "But we hid out for almost four years and no one found us. Maybe we've got four more good years of stayin' hid."

Larry Southard shook his head. "That fuse has burned way down. Started burning lots faster when we came with Mr. Downing to find you." He glanced at Trevor. "No criticism of Captain Corcoran—he did what he had to—but that put the nail in the coffin. To catch up with us, he chose speed over caution. If we were still back on Dustbelt, they'd have found us in another three months, four at the outside. So we had to go over the border."

Trevor nodded at the gathered faces. "That's why we need you to represent the other Lost Soldiers in the decisions to come. It isn't fair. It isn't right. But it's the only option that doesn't kill us all."

Purcett had compressed his cap into an invisible ball, clenched within his meaty fist. "It's a turrible thing, makin' such choices fer others. I reckon it's a worse thing to risk all our lives to wake 'em up. But durned if'n I know what I'll say to thems what come outta those refrigerators and tell us we got it wrong, that they'd a' rather stayed behind."

Vincent Rodriguez shook his head, folded his muscular arms. "I'm sorry to say it, Preacher, but if they really feel that way, it's easy for them to fix the mistake we made. They can just stroll out an air lock. Because that's pretty much the same end they'd have come to by staying behind."

"You need to understand something else," Ike said loudly, standing. "Look at the cryocell grid. See all those yellow lights mixed in, now? Those indicate malfunctions. If we try to restore people from those cells, we could kill them. Problem is, we don't know how to fix them. Those are all Ktor coldcells. About a dozen different types. Not even the Dornaani have seen them before. We've just started trying to figure them out, but it's slow going."

Downing suppressed a sigh of relief when Franklin did not go on to mention the failing symbiopods: with the exception of their controls, they were xenobiological and utterly mysterious.

Ike shrugged into his conclusion. "Opening any of those cold-cells is like playing Russian roulette with an unknown number of loaded chambers. Do you think they'd be willing to take that risk? Would you? Particularly if a few more weeks or months of research could improve, or even eliminate, the odds of death?"

The Lost Soldiers were muttering among themselves again, but not grumbles of dissent; it was a dull murmur of grudging acceptance.

However, a new figure had stepped from the group: Missy Katano. "Director Downing."

He managed to keep a frown off his face. Katano was a steady, level-headed team player. *She's not in league with* Purcett *now, is she?* "Yes, Ms. Katano?"

She smiled. "No need to look at me that way, Mr. Downing. I'm not going to make any trouble."

Richard tried very hard not to show his relief. "I'm sure you are not, Ms. Katano. But I am at a loss to understand why you're concerned with the issues surrounding reanimation."

She shrugged. "My concerns are only with selective reanimation. Which needs to happen if I am to carry out my orders as head of training."

Richard frowned. "Do explain."

"Yes, sir. One day, we're going to be reviving significant numbers of people. But I won't be able to bring them up to speed quickly unless we start preparing for that now. I'm not worried about the situational and social acclimation; I can handle that myself. But courses on new technology and operational procedures? Since we don't have trainers, that will have to come from specialists who've not only learned how to provide advanced, hands-on training, but who'll be able to train others to assist and eventually replace them. Which means that I need to start teaching our first echelon of new teachers. Right now."

*Bollocks: she's dead right.* Downing stole a glance at Trevor, who appeared surprised, attentive, and impressed.

"That is very prudent and capital thinking, Ms. Katano," his nephew said warmly. "Do you have suggestions regarding those instructors?"

"Got the list right here, sir."

Downing suppressed a smile. *Of course you do.*

At a nod from Trevor, Katano started rattling off the names.

"Captain Hailey and Sergeant de los Reyes are probably the best when it comes to infantry weapons and operations, with Captain Hasseler as the final word on the most modern systems. Looks like we're short of pilots, so I'd suggest we rouse Donna Gaudet. She's the most patient shuttle jockey we've got and did a stint as an instructor in Jamaica. There are two crucial skill areas that are out of my depth, though, so I'll let the experts talk."

Larry Southard smiled at the cue. "Mr. Downing, I think Captain Philips and I would make a pretty good team teaching both humint and elint. I can also handle big-data analysis, and she's wrangled folks learning tactical-level field craft."

"That's excellent, Mr. Southard, but we need both of you in operations. I don't see how you can also provide intel training to dozens or even scores of our personnel."

"Spot on our own thinking, sir," Philips said brightly. "We only propose to educate a handful of particularly promising candidates: just enough to provide you with staff officers. It will necessarily be gradual, because it requires close instruction in small classes."

Trevor muttered sideways at Downing. "She's got a point, about those staff officers, you know."

Richard nodded. "Point and match, Captain Philips. Who else?"

Vincent Rodriguez put up his hand. "Sir, I've spent the past few weeks working almost daily alongside Angus Smith and Ryan Zimmerman. Mostly as combined troubleshooters and repair techs. What we've realized is that without all our three skill sets—mechanical, electrical, and computer—pulling together, we wouldn't have been able to repair half of the breakdowns we've tackled. And that's in a period where there have been almost zero active operations. So we need to train up some folks to at least journeyman status. In case, ya know, we run into trouble."

"What kind of trouble are you anticipating, Mr. Rodriguez?"

Before he could answer, Zimmerman interrupted; his tone was as flat as a door slam. "The kind where one or more of us get blown to atoms. Sir."

Downing winced. "We *are* very shorthanded when it comes to personnel with special skills such as yours, so yes, you'll train your own, er, alternates. Not to add to your labors, Ms. Katano, but I believe you may have overlooked one of our largest training needs."

Katano frowned. "Sir?"

"English instruction for our Russian contingent."

Zhigarev crossed his arms. "*Da.* About time."

Downing sent a placating nod in his direction. "That will require waking Lieutenant Shvartsman, who"—he glanced at Larry and Susan—"will also be able to assist you two, I'll wager. He's quite skilled at reading photographic reconnaissance, I understand." Downing glanced back at Missy. "Anything else, Ms. Katano?"

"Well, sir, I could use a hand with acclimation, sir. Particularly from a soldier's perspective. They're only going to trust one of their own. That means tapping someone who they'll know from Turkh'saar."

"Any ideas, Ms. Katano?"

"Chucky Martell is a private—'scuse me; now a corporal—from the Cold Guard, so he grew up in this time. And all the Lost Soldiers took to him like ducks to water."

"Granted, Ms. Katano." Downing turned toward the Three Colonels. "Gentlemen, I must prevail upon you to assist Ms. Katano in these endeavors, particularly the social dimensions of them."

Rodermund frowned as if he'd bitten into a rotten lemon. "All due respect, Mr. Downing, I visited USO clubs; I didn't run them."

"If I understand that reference, Colonel Rodermund, I am not asking that you regularly socialize with the troops. I am asking that you be available to them and actively encourage their acclimation, to both this time and this mission. You are the authority figures that bridge their time to this one, so you are the best people to explain, and answer questions about, why we had to leave human space. Which means you'll also need to help them understand why, in the eyes of some of the people back on Earth, we are renegades. Criminals, even."

Paulsen smiled. "In other words, we have to break it to them that they are now members of the most truly foreign legion in the history of humanity."

Downing paused, considering. "Colonel Paulsen, I could foresee that phrase becoming an unofficial unit motto."

Paulsen offered one of his easygoing smiles. "Consider it done. Units stick together because of shared wisecracks and grousing almost as much as shared battles, Director Downing."

Zhigarev nodded vigorously. "I agree. And no one gripes as well as Russians, you know! So, how do we start?"

Downing allowed his smile to be rueful. "By leaving this barge. It's going to start getting quite chilly in here."

# PART FOUR

# A Course and a Purpose

*"Bactradgaria"*
*April–May 2125*

# Chapter Thirty-Three

Riordan let the crossbow sag in one hand as the dustkine herd moved off into the trackless western waste. The sighting had excited the trogs, who anticipated that, after four days, they might finally get a taste of something other than lichen.

Not that anyone considered fresh dustkine a delicacy. It was hard on most palates and even harder on the human gut without special preparation. But neither of those factors entered into the consideration of whether or not they should bring one down. There was only one variable that mattered: how long it would take.

According to Bey, who'd had far more experience hunting dustkine than any of the city-born trogs, they would be fortunate to run one to ground within half a day. On the flat expanses of the wastes, pursuit was difficult and cutting out even the weakest member of a herd was harder still. Then there was the matter of hitting it with enough arrows and quarrels to cripple it, all while chasing off any others that might double back to defend it.

Assuming it could be finished off quickly with axes, there was still the matter of butchering the kill, probably in the dark. And the smell of fresh blood had a way of bringing all sorts of unwanted and dangerous visitors from all points of the compass. All in all, they'd encountered this herd too late in the day and the need was simply not great enough, yet. They still had at least fifteen days of food remaining.

What could not be calculated was the likelihood they were

being followed, but the unspoken consensus was to assume that they were. When their notional pursuers had started after them and how fast they were moving were unknowable, but Ulchakh and Bey offered similar counsel: the distance of the pursuit was less important than the weather. Specifically, would the spring rains wipe away their tracks? They could only hope so.

That was why, on the third day of their northward trek, they actually welcomed the gale force winds and battering sheets of rain that the locals considered typical of vernal storms. However, if trackers were persistent, that might only mean a delay until they ranged outward and found where the trail began again.

Which was the other reason why they had to forego pursuing the dustkine: the spoor of the kill and butchery. Had the game been smaller, the bones and remains could have been carried to the river and swiftly consigned to its depths. But the sheer mass of slain dustkine didn't merely produce a far-reaching scent, but left behind massive amounts of bone, fibrous hide, and slimy viscera that only x'qao seemed capable of digesting. Even if a group spent the hours required to haul that revolting mess to the river, there was no way to disguise the death-reeking furrows left by dragging it. In short, one could not remove all the spoor, and not all of it would be eaten or carried off by the creatures of the wastes.

"Hard to see all that meat walking off over the horizon," Bannor muttered from over Caine's shoulder.

Riordan nodded. It seemed that the Green Beret was never too far away, these days. *Probably watching to see if I go nuts after the hovel.*

Which was, to be fair, a reasonable concern. And it would be just as reasonable for Bannor to deny why he was keeping close tabs on Caine's emotional and mental state. But each episode of worried attention was another reminder of why the Crewe was so concerned and careful.

*Because I'm not like them. I'm not a soldier. I'm just a civilian who's learned to act like one. Sort of.* And it hardly mattered that Tagawa and Veriden were technically covert operatives. From what Caine had gleaned, their training and missions had been every bit as grueling and bloody as that of the soldiers.

Riordan removed the quarrel and eased the string forward on his crossbow: at least out on the wastes, you saw your enemies coming way ahead of time. "Another week, and we'll know if we can try our hand at hunting. Assuming that Ulchakh stops being cagey about who or what might be behind us."

Bannor nodded. "Yes, his enigmatic act is getting a little bit tiresome. Think he knows something we don't?"

Caine shrugged. "He might. Or just suspects something very strongly. But if it has any bearing on how long we can go without getting more food, I wish he'd share it sooner rather than later."

Rulaine's eyes pinched tight. Caine couldn't tell if he was squinting against the bright dust-glare or the contingency plan they'd settled upon in the event of insufficient rations. "Having second thoughts about running out of rations before we get to Khorkrag?"

Riordan shook his head. "It's a hell of a lot easier than the decision that had to be made in Forkus." Which was objectively true. After having to order executions in that blood-drenched charnel house, planning for a terminal food shortage was almost easy. If they ever got to the point where they only had three days of local rations left, they'd cut the trogs loose. Some of them might survive, particularly if they kept following Bey. Although, truth be told, Caine would have preferred including Ulchakh and Bey in the second part of the plan: to dip into the Dornaani rations in an effort to push on to Khorkrag and into the eastern wadi country that lay south of Achgabab. Not revealing that second food supply to the trogs had meant entering an ethical grey zone, but it was nothing like the infernal moral blackness of the executions—*no, the massacre*—he'd ordered in Forkus.

As if to make matters worse, after just four days of traveling and living alongside trogs, Riordan had come to realize that they weren't the abject brutes that the h'achgai liked to claim and Tasvar had occasionally suggested. Caine admitted that they'd probably never shed the cardinal lesson of life they'd learned among the x'qao in Forkus: that kindness is weakness. However, they already responded to firm, fair leadership as well or better than they had to the rageful threats of predatory overlords.

Yaargraukh, at the head of their formation, raised one massive arm and waved it forward; he and the advance element had resumed moving north along the river's high-water bank. That term had taken a little getting used to, but it was decidedly more accurate than high-water *mark*, because the riverine dynamics actually cut separate tiers into the land that adjoined them.

As Riordan ambled back into the van, Bannor hung back, glancing back at the rearguard. "Will Eku be all right, back there?"

Caine shrugged. "He has to be."

"How's he holding up?"

"Better today. Or so he says."

Bannor nodded. "Well, at least he's doing better than that kajh with the infected leg wound. He's costing us five klicks a day. At least."

Riordan sighed. "Might not be costing us any time at all, soon."

"Newton thinks it's that serious?"

"Yes, and he was only confirming what Ta'rel predicted two days ago."

"Do we spend the antibiotics to save the kajh or roll the dice?"

Caine shook his head. "Newton ran a chemical assay on the wound drainage. Not exactly like our bacteria, and it reproduces even more quickly. According to Ta'rel, either the kajh will fight it off by tomorrow morning or he's not going to make it. From what the grat'r could communicate, the healing paste he gave Yaargraukh would probably beat the infection easily." Riordan glanced at his friend. "You and Yaargraukh came to know each other pretty well during your contract in EpsIndi. Do you think there's any chance he might be, well, mistaken about how fast that unguent worked?"

Bannor shook his head. "One thing I know about that Hkh'Rkh is that he won't lie, or even exaggerate. Which you know, too."

Riordan nodded. "I do...but I'm as baffled as he is. Nothing should heal a wound *that* quickly."

Bannor nodded. "Nothing we know about, anyway." He spat in the dust. "More ignorance. Hell, maybe wounds here are as different as the infections. About which: I take it that Eku's wounds *didn't* infect?"

"They did, but not with the same germ. And one of the trogs knew how to clean and sterilize it."

Bannor looked over. "Let me guess: Bey, again?"

Riordan shrugged. "Eku says she probably saved his life. By the time the ones who took him captive handed him off, he was feeling pretty miserable."

"Could he be exaggerating? His remote biosigns never looked that bad."

Caine considered. "It's possible. But it may also be how the infections in this place kill. According to Newton, the one that the kajh is fighting is from a variety of strains that don't even cause fevers or septicemia. They go directly after the nervous system."

"Hence, little warning and fewer biosigns until the very sudden bitter end?"

"That's the current guess."

"Eku tell you anything else about his trip to Forkus?"

"Wasn't a lot to tell. They saw his 'chute, chased him for days. After they caught him, they didn't realize he was signaling to us, but beat him pretty savagely when they discovered that he'd been doing something behind their back. They tried to take the suit off as well, but he screamed when they tried to yank the sleeve off his broken arm and found they couldn't."

"Why?"

"He'd tasked the Dornaani reactive hardening to work as a splint, but they never gave him the chance to reverse it."

"My God! So they were trying to yank his arm out of the equivalent of a soft-cast?"

Riordan nodded. "Which is how his arm was broken again and why he's in such pain."

Bannor shook his head. "Poor guy. I hate to ask, but did he let anything sensitive slip out? Such as where we're from?"

"No. Probably because they couldn't communicate enough to question him. And because they'd probably never have thought to ask a question like that."

Rulaine expelled his breath as a low, grateful whistle. "Thank God they didn't, because if he had given that up, we'd have been in real trouble."

"We may still be. I doubt Hwe'tsara, or whoever was coming to scoop him up, is going to let this go with a shrug."

Bannor sighed. "Yeah, we've got to assume that they weren't just interested in his gear, or even his technical knowledge. A real power player is going to want to know where he came from. And his rescue, which was a case of massive overkill, is going to be very interesting to anyone whose primary job is intelligence gathering. They are going to ask why we went to such extreme lengths and expended so many assets to retrieve him before he could fall into their hands. Which will only confirm them in their determination to learn where he's from and what he knows."

Riordan nodded. "And they won't rest easy until they know how to keep his world from coming to this one, and how they can get to and plunder his." He sighed. "I guess we'd better get used to sleeping with one eye open and looking over our shoulder with the other."

Bannor smiled. "You mean, assuming we don't want to wind up with bags over our heads and spend the rest of our lives in the local equivalent of a subterranean 'debriefing facility'? Because we're prime targets now. Probably will be for the rest of our lives."

"You know that sounds paranoid, right?"

"Yeah. But maybe it's like some of the Lost Soldiers say: It's not paranoia if they really *are* out to get you." Rulaine's sardonic smile faded. "I was also wondering if Eku said anything about Hsontlosh's files?"

Caine nodded. "Yes. He's finished. He'll tell us what he found tonight."

Rulaine was watching him from the corner of his eye. "Are you ready for that?"

Riordan made sure his voice was quiet and level. "I'm ready for it to be over."

Bannor looked north, changed to a matter-of-fact tone that indicated he was leaving the unspoken topic—Elena's fate—behind. "Best we start looking for a defensible campsite."

Riordan pointed. "Up ahead, north-by-northeast. Scoped it earlier. High ground, near a dry wadi. I figure we set our watch on the crest, everyone sleeps in the lee."

Bannor glanced at him. "See, you're *already* better than a freshly minted second lieutenant."

"Huh. That's not saying much."

"And you're even getting the hang of the trademark sarcasm. I'll go forward and have Yaargraukh pick up the pace."

Eku struggled to finish reporting what he'd found among Hsontlosh's hidden and encrypted files, but his words were already slurring. He'd had difficulty adjusting to the hard marching that began well before dawn and pressed well past dusk.

Craig Girten reached out a hand to steady him. "About done with the Fireside, yeah, Eku?"

The factotum nodded, glanced over at Riordan. "I am sorry, Commodore. There is not much more to tell, but I must leave it until tomorrow's... er, chat." It still took Eku a moment to remember the nickname Girten had given their private after-dinner jawboning sessions: Fireside Chats. Initially, no one had picked up on its reference to the second Roosevelt's wartime radio messages, but it seemed apt enough. The greatest benefit of both was not the information shared, but the daily contact that fostered a sense of community.

Riordan nodded. "Get some rest, Eku. I'll be over to stand the first watch for you."

Murmuring thanks, the factotum rose with Craig's aid and made off for the campsite in the lee of the small, knob-shaped rise that was the night's watch post.

Riordan made himself smile. "So, we're going to run this like any other strategy session. We all heard the same things. What were your thoughts? Floor is open."

Uncomfortable glances went around the group. Even the typically unflappable Yaargraukh's eyes tucked in slightly. Craig returned, took one look at their faces, and sat quickly.

Dora started the conversation with a sigh. "Boss, granted that you're, well, the boss... but is this really a strategy matter?"

Riordan nodded. "Absolutely."

"But, this is about Elena," Bannor said quietly. He was one of the few people in the Crewe who'd actually met her.

"All the more reason to treat this as a strategy session," Riordan countered. "Look: why do we have these conversations?"

Tagawa bowed her head slightly. "Because you value us and our opinions. And because, as you have said, no single perspective can escape the subjectivity of the one who holds it. So, as a group, our many perspectives ensure greater objectivity."

He felt his smile become genuine; his intents almost sounded spiritual when Ayana expressed them. "So it is *because* this matter is personal for me that I've never had greater need of your viewpoints to check against my own. It's too likely I heard what I wanted to, or what I feared most, because I'm so invested in the outcome. So: Eku's report. What did you hear?"

Ayana looked Riordan in the eyes. "I shall start with the most obvious. Hsontlosh knew that Elena herself would not have been of interest to the Ktor once the various Dornaani specialists proclaimed her medical condition irreversible. That is why, in his later exchanges with other black-market entities in the

Collective's fringe and border systems, he explicitly states that she is now simply a lure."

"You mean, to keep drawing us toward Ktor space."

"More specifically, into the Scatters. His entries indicate that he was convinced that if he delivered you to the Ktor, his dubious reputation among other lojis as a willing tool of the Collective would have inverted. He had good reason to expect that he would be transformed from a near pariah to an object of admiration, even envy."

Riordan nodded. "Could some of his files be deliberate forgeries, meant to mislead any unauthorized readers?"

Duncan shook his head. "I think Eku established their provenance, Commodore. Particularly regarding the way the entries reveal gradual changes in Hsontlosh's own thinking. A grifter won't create a long, nuanced, written charade unless it's necessary to his con. And it's clear Hsontlosh never meant those documents to be seen."

Craig frowned. "Hsontlosh seemed to change his mind about a lot of things, along the way. Which do you mean?"

Duncan shrugged. "He started out believing she was still alive, because the first Collective documentation he got hold of asserted that Elena had not yet, er, passed. But they never again mentioned her, or the status of her medical coldcell, after Kutkh inserted her into Virtua.

"So when Hsontlosh learned that Kutkh no longer had her medcell, he tried to find it. Which went nowhere fast. And his black-market pals confirmed that she hadn't been reconnected to a Virtua node. Without that, her chances of survival were, well...zero."

Ayana nodded. "His coconspirators among the Arbiters communicated that they had come to the same conclusions."

Dora sighed. "Which Hsontlosh later confirmed by tracking down her medical cell through its registration code. That's why he made that one detour while he was dragging us through the border worlds: to visit its last known location." She shook her head. "Sold for parts, no questions asked."

Duncan shrugged. "At each of those dead ends, his doubt increased, step by deductive step, until he couldn't even imagine a scenario in which she was still alive."

Riordan had promised himself that he wouldn't ask questions

which were partial to the outcome he desperately wanted, but he couldn't hold back. "But then how did she speak to me in Virtua when Kutkh linked us, put us in the same place?"

Ayana's eyes were sad as she asked, "But Commodore, *were* you in the same place? As you explained it, Kutkh claimed that you had to speak to Elena while she was dreaming, that anything more direct would rouse her out of Virtua and so, cause her death."

Riordan nodded, his mouth very dry.

"So I must ask," Tagawa continued almost reluctantly, "if consciousness can be coded into terms that Virtua recognizes, is it not also likely that samples from a consciousness could be saved, compiled, and edited?"

Riordan nodded again, tried to swallow, couldn't. He'd wondered, and feared, the same thing: that his fog-shrouded conversation with Elena was just a cunning use of Virtua's smoke and mirrors. Speaking to her as she dreamed, avoiding mention of specific memories for fear of throwing her out of Virtua: the contact was so tightly constrained that later, he wondered if he'd spoken not to her, but a construct. Which Eku's report made that conclusion far more likely.

*Or... inescapable?*

Caine pulled himself back from that brink. "Which puts us face-to-face with the real elephant in the room: is recarnation even possible? Can a person's mind be transferred into a clone that's been brought to maturity without awakening it?"

Newton shook his head sharply. "Let us leave aside whether such an empty vessel can be created at all. The most pertinent of Dornaani experts—those deeply versed in Virtua—have invariably concluded that it cannot be done. Although the activity and memories of a living being may be coded for projection into Virtua, there is no evidence for the reverse: using data from Virtua to transfer a consciousness into an un-patterned brain. Eku's metaphor was as apt as it was elegant: one can capture a grainy image of a painting and it will be recognizable. But there is no way to recapture the lost detail if one tries to convert that grainy image back into an exacting recreation of the canvas.

"This was yet another significant change in Hsontlosh' thinking. In the course of his researches, he became familiar with both sides of the machine-mind transfer debate and increasingly aligned himself with its skeptics. By the end, he expressed deep contempt for its proponents, referring to their theories as, as... I cannot recall the passage Eku quoted."

Peter recited it: "'A myth worshipped by those who cling to the futile hope that they might cheat death.'"

Newton nodded. "And Eku's own practical summation proves as much; specifically, that if such a procedure existed, dying Dornaani would have used it frequently. But instead, there is no indication that it has ever been attempted."

Riordan's anticipation of an answer in the negative hadn't made it any easier to hear. But it made his last, inevitable question even harder to ask. "So now that we've finished reviewing Eku's evidence, can any of *you* imagine a scenario in which Elena isn't dead?"

Yaargraukh shifted slightly. "Caine Riordan, from the beginning, Hsontlosh's scheme never depended upon Elena Corcoran being alive. And as it progressed, he discerned that its only weakness was that she might actually be found alive." The big Hkh'Rkh's neck-and-head hung in a slight curve. "Hsontlosh would surely have taken steps to...to remove that risk."

Dora wrung her hands as she added to Yaargraukh's conclusion. "Elena was more than a risk, Caine; she was evidence. *State's* evidence. And not just enough to hang that bastard loji, but all his coconspirators. Some of whom are Arbiters of the whole damn Collective." She shook her head. "And you know what happens to evidence like that. Particularly in outer space where there are plenty of planets where things burn up on reentry. Real easily."

Several faces showed shock at Veriden's frankness, but Riordan was oddly relieved by it. He turned to the one person who hadn't responded to Eku's report. "Craig, what do you think?"

Girten stared at his calloused hands. "When I was growing up, mobsters threw guns in rivers because even the dumbest of them knew that if there was no murder weapon, they couldn't be tied to a crime. But they also knew that it was even better if there was no *body* to find." He waved at the unfamiliar stars overhead. "So I was thinking the same thing as Dora: that it's almost too easy to get rid of evidence, here. Every star and every planet is like an incinerator that can burn up damn near anything without leaving a trace...just like poor Liebman.

"I have one other thought, sir. But it isn't easy to say. And I'm sure it's harder to hear."

"Still, I'll hear it."

"Well, in a universe where anything can be incinerated almost anywhere you go, how far do you chase after something that *might* be hidden, but is more likely to have been, well, burnt right out of existence? A person could search forever and never know for sure." He snuffled a bit. "Two of my high school pals were aboard a ship that went down just a few weeks after the Nip—er, Japanese attacked Pearl Harbor. Never learned what happened, because they were never found. Sometimes, that's just the way it is. And you've got no choice but to get on with your life, despite the hole in your heart."

Caine didn't remember standing, but he was nodding at the group and turning to leave when he said, "I'm going to swap into first watch. Thank you, everyone."

Riordan concentrated on the sparse nighttime sounds and maintaining an even pace as he walked back to camp.

Without making a noise, Bannor was walking alongside him. "How are you doing?"

Caine couldn't force a smile to his face. "Second time you've asked today."

"Sometimes friends do that."

Riordan nodded, looked straight ahead. "So what do you think?"

Bannor sighed. "Caine, you had two questions to ask tonight, but only asked us one: Is it reasonable to think Elena's alive? And you got your answer: No, not really. No one could even imagine a scenario in which it was possible. All you can say is that no one has seen her body.

"Maybe you need to hang on to that. Maybe it keeps you going. Or maybe it could prove a dangerous distraction." Bannor shrugged. "Only you can know that. And only time will tell."

"And my second, unasked question?"

Rulaine shrugged. "It's the one Craig brought up: Is it reasonable to act as if she's still out there? I'll answer with a question of my own: What could we do if she is?"

He gestured upward as Girten had. "Caine, look at that sky: thousands upon thousands of stars, not one of which we recognize.

With a real computer, the right sensors, and enough time, we might figure out where we are. But even then, there's no guarantee that we could get home. And if we did, we still wouldn't have come one millimeter closer to knowing what happened to Elena...and the odds say we never would."

"So I just can't see how believing she's alive will achieve anything except reliving the misery of reopening that wound every single day."

They'd arrived at the campsite. Up on the small knob of rock sheltering it, Katie Somers and Bey surveyed the surrounding darkness. "I can take Katie's spot for you," Bannor muttered.

"No," Caine said, "I told Craig I'd do it. I'm fine."

Bannor raised a dubious eyebrow, then nodded and headed toward his place in the sleeping circle.

Riordan stared up at the watch post, wished he was already there.

Wished he could stay up there all night long.

That way, he wouldn't have to close his eyes on the last day he'd believed that Elena Corcoran was still alive somewhere, looking up at the same stars he was.

# Chapter Thirty-Four

The morning after the wounded kajh succumbed to his infection, Riordan discovered that city praakht had no rites for the dead. The only acknowledgement of his passing took the form of a debate over how best to dispose of his corpse before it attracted carrion creatures, yet in such a way that it would not leave any sign that might be useful to pursuers.

Ultimately, the dispute served no real purpose. First, Bey consulted with Newton about how best to reduce the body's buoyance and then Duncan about the resources available to bind rocks to it. Since she would oversee the urldi as they sent the body on its way, Bey insisted on personally confirming that Caine approved of the method, even though the two IRIS professionals had final authority. He asked her why she felt the need to get his approval.

"Because you will rightly place the blame on me if the method fails. So if you deem the solution unsound, I wish to know before carrying it out."

Riordan shook his head, assured her she had his trust in the matter, and then asked if the trogs had been too uncomfortable to reveal their burial rights to humans.

The look on her face was something between pity and distaste. "Trogs from cities are permitted no such rites and haven't enough interest to risk conducting any in secret."

"And trogs from the Free Tribes?"

"We are different," she said proudly and held her head high. She seemed ready to hold it there until he responded.

"I see. You have my permission then. Carry on."

She nodded, but as she turned to complete the task, he saw her expression change to one of perplexity.

Before he could join Yaargraukh to review the formation and its readiness for the day's march, Bannor approached. "Something you'll want to see, CO. Seven o'clock. Range about twelve hundred. Altitude four hundred."

Riordan sealed his visor as he turned to face south-southwest and activated the HUD's motion detector. Four guidons appeared where Bannor had indicated; whatever was there, it was too small to be reliably seen at this distance. Caine pushed the zoom to ten times as he finger-blinked for both thermal imaging and target lock.

Four shapes that resembled improbably large dragonflies appeared at the center of the magnification field, which shifted slightly to remain at the approximate center of the creatures. "Let me guess: those resemble the ones that appeared along with the x'qao you and Duncan engaged near Newton's base camp."

"And like the one that Ayana and Dora dealt with while they were paralleling the tributary running from Gurmugdu down to Forkus."

"They don't seem to be approaching, though."

"Just like the ones Duncan and I saw."

"Who's talking shit about me?" Solsohn asked loudly, coming up the low slope behind them. "I hate it when you guys—oh! Morning, sir! Hey, what are you two looking at?" Before Riordan could answer, Duncan had found the insects. "Well, I'll be damned. Haven't seen those for a while."

Insects had been the most frequent form of life they'd encountered marching beside the river, and the trogs proved adept at catching some of the bigger ones, particularly the type that had crawled across Caine's visor the first morning on Bactradgaria. While they complained that the creatures were much better when roasted, they still consumed the viscous innards, albeit with resigned disgust. But these were not merely larger; their behavior was different. Unsettling, even.

Solsohn remarked on exactly that feature. "Just like the last time, not moving."

"You seemed in a hurry to find me," Riordan prompted, "or Bannor."

"Wha—? Oh, yeah. Ulchakh said he had some business to attend to. Said it concerned you, Commodore. Have you seen him?"

"No. How long ago did he ask?"

"Almost half an hour, now."

Riordan frowned...then recalled the h'achgan trader's enigmatic and increasing fixation upon the wastes to the south. He turned back in that direction, wiped away the HUD's current settings—target lock, thermal imaging, and magnification—and called up the motion sensor at maximum intensity.

Sure enough, despite the static-haze of wind-lifted debris, flying or crawling insects, and a myriad of other small movements that the naked eye could not see, there was a cluster of guidons approximately a kilometer to the south, close to the river.

"Gentlemen," Riordan muttered as he zoomed in on that area, "I think we have visitors."

"Friend or foe?" Duncan asked.

"Not entirely sure," Caine replied as the clustered objects reappeared at the magnified equivalent of fifty meters. Then, with a smile: "Friends. Most definitely friends."

Before he could explain, Bannor's voice announced, "Good to hear it, particularly since I just found the foes. Almost directly under the insects, coming out of a wadi. I'll be damned that I couldn't see them before."

Duncan was focused on the same area. "X'qai. Two are pretty big. Who are the friends, Commodore?"

"Ulchakh and the guests he was expecting: Arashk's group. With an extra hand, I think."

"And the X'qai are heading in their direction," Bannor added.

Riordan had activated comms and was moving before realizing he was already formulating a response from pieces of different contingency plans. "Newton: report to OP. Bannor, you get Bey and bring her with all the trog archers. Follow me down to Ulchakh. Duncan—"

"Already on it, sir," the IRIS sniper answered, unlimbering the Dornaani hand cannon.

Riordan saw Newton sprinting closer. "O'Garran!"

"Here, sir!" answered the chief, who was already charging the slope.

"Set a defensive perimeter. Wu in charge, Tagawa as his adjutant. Everybody with a firearm is your base of fire. Crossbows for those who don't have a gun. Pair a loader with each."

"Just like we trained it, sir!" howled Miles as he charged back down the slope as fast as he'd been charging up.

Newton arrived, not even winded, the heavy crossbow in one hand, grapple gun in the other. "Sir?"

"You're with me. Everyone: switch to the day's freekset. Duncan, tell me when you have a target you like and are locked."

"Roger that, sir."

"Commodore, aren't you forgetting something?"

Caine couldn't help smiling as he turned at the sound of Yaargraukh's voice. Holding a battle-ax in one hand as if it were a hatchet and gripping the longsword in the other, the Hkh'Rkh looked every bit as intimidating as the x'qai. "No, friend, I haven't forgotten. You're in charge of skirmishers supporting the perimeter. They don't dare flee if you're behind them."

Yaargraukh's rounded but massive shoulders may have slumped. "They shall fight well."

Riordan nodded at him, jerked his head at Newton, saw Bannor coming up behind with Bey, the other female kajh Sho, and one of the males.

"Follow me!" Caine shouted.

But even as he led them in a sprint toward Ulchakh, he still saw Elena's face.

Halfway to the h'achgai, who were just realizing that something was amiss, Riordan stopped and raised his hand. "Newton, ready your crossbow. And. Do. Nothing."

"Sir? I—"

"I need your heart rate low enough to fire accurately. No exertion. Bannor?" Riordan called into his mic.

"Coming up behind you."

"Fan out to my right, behind the low rise forty meters inland. Stay low, set up for flanking fire, and don't be seen until I call for it. Duncan?"

"Still holding lock, sir."

"Keep holding," Riordan replied as he pulled one of the stun grenades, set it for maximum volume, and hurled it in the direction of the x'qai, still several hundred meters away from the h'achgai.

The small, light sphere landed about fifty meters away and, still rolling toward the creatures, unleashed its electronic caterwauling.

All three broke stride, then swerved toward it, yowling and snarling, apparently as eager to eat the newcomers as the h'achgai.

Arashk started to lead his group to link up with the humans, but Riordan waved for them to stop and stand. It took a few moments for that surprising order to be recognized and followed. But they did.

In doing so, their ragged group became the left flank, which put Newton and him in the center, and Bannor's team forward deployed to the right. He trusted that despite their initial perplexity, the h'achgai would understand the plan soon enough. *I hope. And now to spin the axle on which that plan turns.* "Duncan, do you have target lock?"

"Same as twenty seconds ago, sir. Why are you waiting?"

"Because we need to take them *all*. No survivors." Riordan ran a range estimate: three hundred meters to the lead x'qa, who also happened to be the smallest. "Count out the shots as you go. Fire on target one."

"Firing…" The lightning-crack report of the hand cannon clattered across the dust flats.

The rearmost and largest of the x'qa went down. The other two broke stride again as they profitlessly sought the source of the new sound. However, within a second, the smallest one—a q'akh—swerved toward Caine and Newton, probably because they were the proximate source of the infuriatingly loud grenade.

The second x'qao's next several strides were slower, as if it was awakening to the other changes that had occurred. In addition to the unfamiliar sounds, it seemed to notice that new figures had appeared and in numbers that might change their classification from easy prey to dangerous adversaries.

From the corner of his eye, Riordan detected movement. The h'achgai's two bowmen were in the act of drawing their composite bows. Caine shouted Ulchakh's name as he flung up his left arm and held it there: *An inconvenient posture, if I have to use my survival rifle.* "Duncan, time remaining for recharge?" The h'achgai archers had relaxed their draw, watching Arashk. Who was watching Caine.

"Ready to fire, Commodore," Duncan replied, "but target one is up again. Slow but still moving."

"Did you reduce the standard charge setting?"

"Sir, I nudged it *higher* for today's fun and games. Currently comparable to an old-fashioned antitank rifle. Do I reengage target one or—?"

"Negative. Engage target two and advise."

"Roger. Engaging." The hand cannon report was like razor-sharp thunder.

The second x'qao—the one that had paused for a moment—came apart in mid-stride. Hit just above center of mass, its extremities and head were flung away from the abrupt midair splatter that had been its torso.

The third was, as Riordan had gambled, less easily distracted, or alarmed, than its larger, more intelligent cousins. Fixated by ferocity, hunger, or both, it sprinted through the one-hundred-meter mark, still gathering speed.

"Status, Duncan?"

"Still charging, sir."

Riordan waggled his upraised arm to ensure Arashk was still watching it. Riordan's eyes were on the closest adversary. The q'akh was not merely speedy; the movement of its arms and head were arrestingly quick, like a moving image that skipped every other frame. As it came through the sixty-meter mark, Caine turned his head slightly toward Newton. "I will call for your fire separately."

"Understood, Commodore."

But Riordan was already back on the tactical channel. "Duncan?"

"Recharged, sir."

"Do not—I repeat, *do not*—engage target three. Finish target one. On my order."

"Roger that, sir. Reacquiring target one."

Riordan began a slow wave toward Arashk as he muttered. "Bannor?"

"Standing by. Target three now at twenty meters, sir."

"Fire, all," Riordan ordered, slashing his left arm down.

What hit target three wasn't a true volley: more a quick peppering of arrows and quarrels from Bannor's team on the right and Arashk's on the left. Approximately half the shots feathered the 'qo, staggering it. But instead of falling, it kept running unevenly, now at a human pace.

"Sir?" Newton asked as the Dornaani hand cannon cracked again.

"Fire," Riordan replied as the q'akh loped over the seven-meter mark.

Baruch's big crossbow discharged with a shuddering *thwack-k-k*—and the q'akh pitched backward heavily, limp in death.

Duncan reported a moment later. "Target one is down. And staying that way."

"Well done, all. One last job for you, Duncan."

"Sir?"

"Provide overwatch as we retrieve bolts and arrows and then assess enemy casualties. Miles?

"On the channel, sir."

"Keep an eye on those insects. Let me know what they're doing at two-minute intervals. If they leave, track them as long, and as accurately, as you can."

At Bey's whispered suggestion, Ulchakh, Arashk, and the rest of the h'achgai were formally requested to march mingled with the humans in the van. Riordan had already planned on that: they were known, reliable, and seemed well on the way to becoming actual friends.

But she obviously had a deep understanding of their ways and traditions. When Caine asked them to travel along with the command staff, Ulchakh and Arashk put their long, simian hands over their hearts and accepted with what was clearly a ritual response.

But that was not the end of the exchange. Ulchakh waved forward the new addition to their group: the second bowman, who was approximately Arashk's age. "This is my kinsman, Yidreg, who was waiting at Vranadoc's fortress for Arashk, that they might make their journey to Achgabab together."

Riordan didn't need Bannor's glance to understand the implicit request. He turned to Yidreg. "It would be an added honor if you would walk with us. We hope you will share your tales and your counsel, also."

Yidreg's response was a deep nod *and* the hand-on-heart gesture.

*The nod probably completed the formal introduction,* Caine told himself, trying to commit it to memory as they began moving.

*And the second gesture was his appreciation and acceptance of my invitation that he walk with us.*

Arashk smiled, but waited a few steps before observing, "You grow in knowledge of our ways, Caine-Riordan."

"Well," Ulchakh broke in, "he has had the benefit of *my* acquaintance, you see." The trader's quip felt like the verbal equivalent of a friendly poke in the ribs.

Yidreg masked a hint of surprise, followed by pleasure, at the exchange and Riordan's response: a good-natured grin.

*Looks like we* are *becoming friends, then.* Riordan could not recall a human culture that did not use gentle ribbing as the first step from acceptance and alliance toward genuine amity. "However it occurs, I am glad to learn more of your people, just as I am glad that we shall now travel together. But I must ask"—he turned toward Arashk—"why you did not join us sooner, or"—he glanced at Ulchakh—"why you did not apprise us that they were following."

Riordan recognized Arashk's exaggerated blink at Ulchakh: a h'achgan expression that roughly translated as, *It was your idea, so you* tell *him.*

The h'achgan trader flapped his suddenly sagging jowls: a resigned shrug. "Separate travel was necessary if we did not wish to leave an easy path for pursuers to follow. But also, by beginning his journey later and following within sight of our path, Arashk was able to watch for pursuers. Of which there are none."

"None that we can *see*," Yidreg added.

*And what does* that *mean?* But that question would have to wait for a quiet environment where Riordan could craft the inquiry so that it did not reveal yet another huge gap in the Crewe's knowledge. "As always," Caine replied, "your wisdom is a great gift to us, Ulchakh. But why did you not tell us they were following?"

Arashk reprised his bug-eyed glare at the elder h'achga.

His reply was less facile than the first. "I shall not dissemble, Caine-Riordan. Arashk and Tasvar separately assured me that you and your companions could be trusted. And so I did . . . to a point. But understand: one does not travel the wastes and grow as old as I without reserving judgment for what my own experience shows me.

"Our travels have shown that you and your companions are

who they claimed you to be, and fast friends besides...as you proved beyond doubt just an hour ago."

Bannor leaned forward to face the h'achga. "It was an honor to be of assistance." He smiled toward Arashk. "But next time, try not to bring such rude visitors along with you."

Rather than responding to Rulaine's jocular irony, the h'achgai were surprised. "But they did not follow us. We presumed they were preparing to ambush *you*, but saw us as easier prey."

Bannor glanced at Caine. "This was the first we saw of them."

"X'qao can be cunning," Arashk said with a sympathetic frown.

"Very cunning, indeed," Riordan replied, but understood his friend's concern. Rulaine was, by a comfortable margin, the group's recon expert. But after surveying the battlefield and the bodies, Bannor couldn't explain why he, or anyone else, hadn't seen them during the day-start sensor sweep. "It's as if they appeared out of nowhere," he'd muttered with a worried frown. The unspoken consensus—that no amount of "cunning" could render x'qao invisible to Dornaani sensors—was yet another conversation that had to await another time.

Riordan shifted to a related topic. "We also saw large insects nearby. Is that typical, with x'qai?"

Yidreg's eyes hardened. "Very typical. Killspawn of all kinds, from the greatest M'qrugth pureblood to the lowly 'qo, are often followed by carrion. Sometimes close, more often at a discreet distance."

"Jackals or vultures shadowing lions," Veriden muttered from the rank just behind.

"I do not know these words," Yidreg said apologetically.

Bannor explained. "She refers to carrion-seekers on Ea—from our homeland. Many fly, as did these, following carnivores at a distance and watching for signs of a chase."

Yidreg nodded. "To feed upon what is left of the kill or fly close to lamed prey that escapes and dies later."

Arashk's tone combined disgust with grim satisfaction. "They are parasites, unwilling to risk killing their own food. So you can find them following almost every predator. Except for those of us who use tools."

"Why?

Arashk bared his teeth in a savage rictus. "Because if they get too close to us, they become *our* food."

"Yes," Ulchakh agreed in a tone that seemed to invite Arashk to shed some of his sudden ferocity, "but today, the insects may do us a favor by attracting larger scavengers. I agree with Yidreg and Bannor that, if we are being followed—which is still quite possible—there will be little left of the carcasses by the time they arrive."

Caine nodded. *And, just as importantly, not enough to determine the means by which they were killed.*

But Ulchakh was frowning and shaking his head. "It is a pity we had to leave their remains, though."

"Why?" asked Solsohn from where he marched alongside Dora.

Yidreg shrugged. "X'qao bones are much stronger than those of humans, or even ours and trogs'. They are as steel is to bronze."

"And," Ulchakh added, "they are valuable, even if they are very costly to shape."

"Is it costly because they're so hard?" Duncan asked casually. But Caine knew what was behind the question: finding more ways to generate value on Bactradgaria.

Ulchakh shrugged. "I do not know if the difficulty lies in hardness of x'qai bones or in the different matter from which they are made. But it requires more shaping brew, more heat, and far more time."

Newton, who was marching just in front of the group, turned his head. "Is the chemic—eh, 'different matter' also present in their flesh and their hide?"

"It is throughout them, I would say." Ulchakh glanced at Yidreg.

He nodded. "Their flesh is not like ours. It is thick, stringy, as if shot through with small tendons."

"The trogs claim it cannot be eaten."

*Good God, they would try? The x'qai are monsters, yes, but still, they're intelligent creatures!*

Ulchakh saw the look on Caine's face. "You have questions about trogs, I think."

Riordan nodded, glanced at the nearest ones only two ranks back.

Ulchakh smiled. "When we stop for the mid-march meal, we shall walk together."

# Chapter Thirty-Five

"So," Ulchakh sighed, closing his eyes as the river-following breeze blew across their perch atop the high-water bank. "You have questions about trogs."

"Yes," Riordan answered.

"Evidently, ones that Arashk did not answer."

"Or that I didn't think to ask when we were traveling together."

"Very well, Caine Riordan. And you may rest assured that there is one question which I shall not ask *you*."

Caine smiled. "Why I need to ask *any* of these questions?"

Ulchakh opened his eyes and grinned. The sudden proliferation of creases and wrinkles revealed him to be even older than Riordan had expected. "It is always agreeable to speak with you. Ask your questions."

"One of the trogs we took from the hovel, Bey, claims to be a truthteller."

"She is," Ulchakh said with certainty. "The tattoo on her forehead is not a forgery. If it was, she would be dead by now."

"Which touches on the heart of my question: If an oathkeeper is a witness to transactions, what is a truthteller?"

"A witness to everything *except* contracts. That requires training. A truthteller need only stake their life upon bearing faithful witness to whatever they have seen."

Riordan nodded. *So they're essentially a 24/7 legal observer at large.* "What happens if a truthteller lies?"

Ulchakh shrugged. "What would happen to anyone who breaks an oath: punishment. Usually death. But for those who wear one of the Four Marks upon their forehead, death is the least of the penalties they would suffer."

Caine was fairly sure he was perfectly happy *not* asking about what those greater punishments might be. "And is it common for women...eh, females to be truthtellers?"

Ulchakh's shelflike brow rose slightly. "No. But they wear that Mark more often than they wear the others." He smiled again. "You ask general questions, but you wish to ask if you can trust Bey. You can."

"You know her?"

"Before this journey, I only knew *of* her. But from what I have seen, she is all that I heard. And do not ask me *how* I heard. The less you know about the black market, the better. So, before you begin the questions that you are struggling to keep behind your teeth, tell me: what do *you* observe of her?"

It was Riordan's turn to shrug. "She is very competent but does not brag about it. She thinks quickly, is skilled with a number of weapons, both gives and takes orders easily, and seems to be familiar with many skills." He frowned. "I am also impressed with how easily she adapts to rapid—and harsh—changes, without any real knowledge of what might come next."

Ulchakh nodded. "All true, but it is the last trait—that she bends rather than breaks when the winds of fortune change quickly—that seems to puzzle you the most." He continued before Caine was done nodding. "As with her other abilities, Bey's gifts in this regard are greater than most, but that is not peculiar. It is a trait present in, or forced upon, all trog females. And those who would be warriors must possess a great deal of it."

"Why is it so strong in the women?"

Ulchakh looked out over the river. "Because the filth-dwelling killspawn require it. Partly because they understand the world in their own brutish terms: that those above give orders and those below obey. Without question. Without self-respect. They expect this obedience from both males and females.

"But the x'qai expect the same division of power to be observed *among* the praakht. Specifically, that those who choose to be kajh hold power, and those who choose to be urldi submit to it.

"That more trog females choose to be urldi is hardly their

fault. The ones with the most promise to be kajh are usually removed. Those who may grow too large? They are rarely given enough food to survive. Those who are too strong? They come to the same end. And those who remain? They are fed less, sleep in the coldest spots, and are kept busy, even when there is no needful task to be performed." Ulchakh's expression was not as fierce as Arashk's had been, but it was even more disgusted.

Riordan nodded. "So it is not the same among the h'achgai."

Ulchakh glanced sideways at him. "Can you even wonder this? Every one of us must be as strong, as swift, as clever as they may be. Any less, and we all die. So how can one be prized above any other?

"We live a hard life, and hard decisions are all too common. It is also in the nature of things that some have greater gifts than others. But we are a People, and our strength is grounded in the knowledge that every one of us is not only needful to our survival, but a child of the same mothers and fathers that bore us all."

Riordan swallowed, wondered when more of his species would learn that lesson with the same admirable clarity. But questions remained—

Ulchakh anticipated them. "So, you understand Bey a little more, or at least, the many ways in which she and other female kajh are so very different from the urldi of their sex. Now you wonder, 'How do they thrive?'" He shrugged. "Females that choose the way of the kajh rarely best the males in size or strength, but they often have far greater agility and stamina. And because every band gang of praakht hopes to become greater, it also needs those patient enough to become great artisans or brave enough to become truthtellers. Female warriors often serve in several of these roles. That is Bey, although she commands unusual respect among her gang."

Ulchakh sighed. "And she knows beauty, as well; she is a fire-twirler. Her mother Qua taught her." He studied Riordan. "Why do you frown, friend? You dislike fire art?"

Riordan shook his head. "No. I mean, I wasn't smiling about fire art." *Whatever the heck* that *is.* "I was noticing that even the names of the Free Tribe praakht are different. Bey, Qua, the other archer is Sho. Do they have their own language?"

"Not an entirely different language, but trogs of the city may only speak Low Praakht, which is mostly Deviltongue. And yes, the short names are from the Free Tribes and risky to keep in the city, since that calls attention to them even if their appearance does not. Anything that reminds x'qai of independent humans and their influence can result in death.

"But if a female kajh is skilled enough, an x'qai liege is likely to take them as artisans or Marks or plan-makers. And so, many female kajh thrive by serving the very being that would have killed them earlier in their lives."

Riordan pursued the topic eagerly. "Does that mean that female kajh usually learn more about the x'qao, either to avoid or impress them?"

Ulchakh waved a long, flat hand at the midday sky. "I cannot say, but I suspect that living in Forkus, or *any* city, makes it unavoidable." He turned to face Caine directly. "It is you who are the great mystery, though."

"Me?"

"All of you who seem as harrows but are not. Even among humans, we feel your greater respect for us. You do not *act* as though you see us as equals. You actually *do* see us as equals."

"I am sorry to hear that my species ever does otherwise." *Although I'm hardly surprised.*

Ulchakh's nod was not just serious but somber. "Give me your hands"—he paused, smiled—"your tiny human hands." They laughed as Caine's hands disappeared within Ulchakh's.

The h'achga became serious again. "I could not do this in front of your companions, for I may only do this for one of your number. There are those in Achgabab that will wish I did not do it at all, but I will convince them otherwise." He shook his head. "Actually, I suspect *you* will convince them otherwise simply by being as you are.

"Caine-Riordan, I give you my *chogruk*. You shall walk among us as one of our own kind might. My life stands as bond to your remaining worthy of that brotherhood with the h'achgai of Achgabab. Will you accept my chogruk?"

"I am honored to do so, friend Ulchakh."

The old trader smiled. "That is well. Now let us return before the more nervous among our companions begin to fear we have been swept downriver."

Halfway to the thoroughly intermingled humans and h'achgai, they heard laughter and lively conversation.

"Well," Riordan observed, "at least it doesn't sound like they're killing each other."

"Yet," Ulchakh aemended with a guttering chuckle.

They were greeted with smiles, waves, and salutations. Amidst the high spirits, Yaargraukh sat impassive, looking on.

Arashk jumped to his feet as they approached. "It is decided! Yidreg shall also give of his stock of drink."

"Also?" repeated Ulchakh.

Riordan sighed, glanced at O'Garran, who shook his head with a chortle and pointed at a different human.

Bannor rubbed the back of his head. "I might have volunteered one of the bottles of alcohol we took from the hovel."

"You *might* have?"

"Didn't want to bother the XO with minor requisitioning."

Riordan smiled. "I see. Very thoughtful."

Ulchakh shrugged and patted Caine on the shoulder. "And I have one measure stashed, waiting upon an occasion such as this. So there will be enough for all to celebrate our reuniting."

"And our victory today!" Arashk cried.

Riordan worked to keep the smile on his face. "Yes, and our . . . victory."


Bannor Rulaine imbibed very little during the celebration with the h'achgai. He was set to stand the first watch and was not about to be sloppy about it, either in terms of his own readiness or the example he set.

Miles, however, had the last watch and had given himself over to the festivities. He'd become the life of the party with strange ease, probably because he always found common threads with warriors and soldiers, regardless of their origins. Between his acid wit and larger-than-life storytelling, he'd transformed the gathering into the biggest, happiest, most raucous gripe fest Bannor could remember. Well, not counting his pre-mustang days as a sergeant.

About midway through, the chief even roped in the kajh, sidestepping the routine social boundaries by pouring out small drinks for them from his strategically overfilled cup . . . well, skull. Rulaine dispelled the uncomfortable associations by refocusing on the growing camaraderie around the circle. The enthusiasm of the h'achgai had infected most of the Crewe, and the trogs' discomfort was offset by their pleased surprise at having been included. And by one of the most redoubtable human warriors, no less.

But with dusk darkening into night, the impromptu party broke up and Newton solemnly advised they should conclude the day as they always did: with a meeting among themselves.

Eku was, once again, the first to leave the circle. He was recovering, but the pain from marching with a twice-broken arm left him spent by nighttime.

O'Garran leaned back in fine spirits. "I do think that trog rotgut was even more powerful than meemaw's moonshine. Tasted worse, too."

Craig Girten looked from face to face, nodding and happy. "A very different Fireside Chat tonight, heh?"

"It is," Yaargraukh agreed, glancing at Caine. Riordan simply nodded.

Bannor suppressed a frown. Command image notwithstanding, his friend had been unusually quiet, even reserved this evening. No, not just reserved: somber.

"I think we just turned a corner," Duncan commented a little more loudly than he had to. "These h'achgai are pretty damned clever. Shrewd merchants, too. A partnership with them could help build up our resource base."

Katie snickered. "And they *are* a bit like orangs, aren't they? I mean, the way they act. They're, well, calmer than the trogs... and some of us, too." She grinned sideways at Miles.

His blink was pure histrionics. "You must be talking about that wild-woman Aya—er, Officer Tagawa, I mean!"

Who may have rolled her eyes. "It will be very interesting, and pivotal, to see how we are received at Achgabab: if the fellowship of a shared battle will become the welcome of a community."

"And if it does," O'Garran exclaimed, swaying to his feet, "then it's high time for us to take the rest of the planet, I say! Claim it for Earth—well, the Republic. And of course," he added, turning and bowing toward Yaargraukh, "we'll set aside a continent for any friends we have in the Patrijuridicate."

Bannor's loud correction was made in the same instant that he sent an apologetic glance toward Yaargraukh. "I believe you mean, for the New Families."

"Ah … yeah, sure. Them, too! Why not?"

Riordan stood slowly: an oddly deliberate motion that caused the group to go silent. "This has been a good end to an eventful day. You have every right to be proud. And you have every right to be relieved. But when it comes to talk of being a force to be reckoned with, even as a joke, I want you to stop and remember something."

Once again, Riordan fell quiet and looked slowly around the group. "I want you to think back to the last fight we had. In Forkus. Against some of the very people we're traveling with now. Put those pictures in your mind. Now I want you to change those images in just one way.

"I want you to add the three x'qao we defeated today. But not the way we encountered them today: on a natural rifle range that plays to all our strengths. I want you to imagine those x'qai coming at you from inside that hovel, without warning and at close range. At the range where their claws and fangs will get to you in the first few seconds. Play that out."

He paused. "Now tell me: do we all walk away? Do half of us? And of those who do, how many are so wounded they can't move fast enough to get clear of the pursuit?"

Riordan's stare became very hard. "When we can all walk away from *that* scenario, then you go right ahead and thump your chest. But not before."

He dumped the dregs of water from his "cup." "We march hard, tomorrow. Square your gear and stand to your watches." Riordan turned and walked toward the center of the camp, where the trogs were already in their several piles, huddled beneath shared furs and hair blankets.

When he was safely out of earshot, Miles rolled his eyes. "Jeeezus! What a killjoy!"

Yaargraukh's eyes rotated to fix on the chief. "You disagree with what the commodore said?"

"Well, no, but—"

"Then I suggest you consider it at greater length before complaining, Chief O'Garran. After all, he is striving to achieve what any good commander should: keep us all alive. Even you. I retire." The Hkh'Rkh rose smoothly into his first step and was at his kit in five long strides.

Miles sputtered when the Hkh'Rkh's silhouette became one

with the ground. "He really *is* an officer, ain't he? Ruining a good party like that. Why? Because he means to 'keep us alive'?"

Bannor rose and patted his even shorter friend on the shoulder. "Yes, if you'll let him."

"What?" O'Garran stared. "So it's fine that he pissed on our party? Is that why you're all staring at me?" He turned to Bannor. "Even you, this time?"

"Even me—*every* time," Bannor answered, staring. "You heard the CO, Chief O'Garran. Party's over. Square yourself away. You need to be sharp for the last watch."

# Chapter Thirty-Six

Caine frowned at the looming storm heads to the southwest. "So this is not uncommon?"

To his right, Bey shook her head. "No, Leader Caine. This is quite common in spring, although it is rare that the sea rains come so far north."

To his left, Ulchakh grunted agreement. "That is true. These great storms come up along the river. I have been caught in two, both times in a caravan moving between Forkus and the port known as Atagurkhu. Usually they bend west just before or after Forkus itself."

Riordan glanced at Bannor and Newton: both shrugged. Dornaani sensors were excellent for gathering nearby details, but in this case, the best they could give was the range to the clouds and confirmation that they were moving quickly: *too* quickly. "If you're wrong, and we hard march north, that puts us in what Ta'rel calls the western wadi country when it hits."

The mangle, standing slightly lower on the slope from which they were surveying the approaching storm, nodded. "That is correct, Caine-Riordan. That country's wadis are fewer but deeper. They could become unfordable for many days."

"And we'd be bogged down in mud," Bannor muttered. "Which, being mostly dust on this side of the river, would get in everything. O'Garran says he can't guarantee the effect it might have on the Dornaani gear."

Riordan folded his arms. "So the choice is bunkering in here, where there's almost no cover and hoping that we don't get washed or blown away. Or, we try to get north of the usual path of such storms and hope that we don't get locked into wadi country."

Bey frowned. "There is another reason not to remain here, Leader."

"Yes?"

She pointed west. "That higher ground may seem reassuring. Specifically, if we are stuck here, it is logical to travel there and skirt the heads of the wadis flooding this plain. But those lands are much more dangerous than these."

"More x'qai?"

She shook her head; her thin, tight braids swung as if to amplify her argument. "They are greater in hunger, not number. Prey is scarce upon the slopes." Her eyes hardened against the fear that tried rising into them. "And there are...larger creatures. They do not rouse often. But when they do...Leader Caine, those slopes are more likely to kill us than save us."

Ulchakh sighed. "I have never ventured there, in part because of tales which match her own."

Riordan nodded toward the soft-spoken mangle. "Ta'rel, what would you do?"

He shrugged. "Move north as quickly as I could. But whatever you choose, heed Bey's warnings about the west. Every few years, one of my people's portage trains are chased up into those slopes. Most do not return."

Riordan nodded. "Well, if going to the west isn't safe, we can't just sit around hoping that the storm doesn't come this far north. Because if it does, we'd be trapped until the water recedes and the mud hardens. So we march north. Now."

At almost the same time two days later, Caine was racing to catch the shelter halves that the suddenly spiking winds tore apart with a warbling howl. Again, Bactradgaria was teaching them the danger of their ignorance. Because the energy in the planet's storm systems was greater and because there was so little to slow down the movement of their fronts, hurricanes like this one not only held their speed longer, but rotated far more rapidly. As a result, although the eye was still forty klicks south, the wind arrived with an abruptness that none of them had ever experienced. As

Craig put it, whereas terrestrial hurricanes rotated at the speed of a clock's minute hand, the ones on Bactradgaria raced along like the second hand.

The rain was so hard and thick that they were effectively blind, except for the modest improvement provided by their helmet's thermal imaging: they could still see each other's blurry silhouettes. The winds peaked at just under one hundred ten kilometers per hour and what little shelter they found became indistinguishable from grey quagmire that soon surrounded them.

It was two more days before they could move. Only two days after that, a following gale drowned the land again, just before they arrived at a swollen tributary.

With the regular crossings washed out, the only way to traverse this smaller river was a ford ten klicks inland: which was to say, ten klicks closer to the dread western uplands. After trudging through muck to reach it, they discovered that it was almost as drowned as the downstream crossings. The local experts—Ulchakh, Bey, and Ta'rel—pronounced it uncrossable, and it would have been, but for the training of the IRIS and military veterans.

They didn't try to get directly across at the ford itself, but started almost half a kilometer upstream. Anticipating the push of the agitated current, they moved carefully, being pushed a meter downstream for every one they advanced toward the other side. By the time they reached the ford itself, they were close enough to fire line-grapples into a nearby sandstone formation. Riordan was certain that one or another of the team might have been lost on two separate occasions. But, sealed in the Dornaani suits, drowning was never one of their worries, which allowed them to focus on the other dangers they encountered.

Throughout these tribulations, Riordan and the Crewe discovered a new level of appreciation not only for the sealed environment of the Dornaani vacc suits but the smart fabrics of their garments. They had a feature that Eku called variable permissibility; it altered the weave and microstructures so that the material resisted water and wind to different degrees, as well as retaining or shedding heat.

In contrast, the locals endured miserable conditions of constant wet and cold. Even in spring, and even as they approached the punishing equatorial line they simply called Hotside, the nights were still brutally cold; they were three hours longer and in a desert. Fires, while already rare, became impossible and food was often too sodden to eat until it eventually dried. The h'achgai had good sleeping furs, at least: the hide of some creature that was as water repellent as a seal's. But the trogs, being city dwellers, only had a few blankets suitable for overland travel and so, sharing body heat became all important. More than once, Bey had to intervene when fights erupted over who slept at the colder margins of their claustrophobic piles.

What the Crewe marveled at, however, was the sheer toughness of both species, particularly the trogs. History and practical experience of human formations predicted that, under similar conditions, they'd be struck down by diseases that were perennial among campaign troops. Among the trogs, three came down with head colds.

As their extended immobility came to an end, Caine and the others were able to observe yet another Bactradgarian phenomenon in action: the cycles of tidal backwash thousands of kilometers from the coast. Predicting it seemed far more of an art than a science, much the same way Micronesians in proas had navigated their way across the vast expanses of the Pacific. The locals who were native to Forkus had little skill in the matter. However, as they resumed travel, the others were able to make reasonable guesses based on the surges and currents of the water assessed in conjunction with not only the moon's phases but its elliptical orbit.

With the ground finally favorable again, Riordan had walked along the column, issuing a few last orders that would put several skirmishers and scouts further out on the formation's landward flanks. As he waited for the formation leaders to report in on their readiness, he weighed the good and bad results of their long, wet, and mostly immobile sojourn.

For five days, they made slow progress, but that didn't mean they ate any less. That was not just bad; it was very bad. They would now run out of food before reaching Khorkrag. Also, even though the nights were becoming warmer and drier nights, the trogs were in particular need of ample food in order to recover from wearying effects of the punishing cold and wet. And there was only one answer to both needs: a hunt. And that was, itself, a bad answer.

Caine and his command staff had wrestled with the implicit risks before: that the time lost and spoor left by a hunt was a gift to any pursuers. But perhaps their path had been so obliterated by the weather that, if they kept the kill well inland from the bank, it would not be found. Or at least, it would require a wide, time-consuming search pattern. But there were only two people who apparently knew the land and prey well enough to counsel him on how to get the meat they needed in the shortest time and away from their line of march.

As Riordan walked down from the small rock outcropping that protruded into a swamp-bottomed wadi, Dora saw him and chuckled. "There's a man with a mission, if I ever saw one! Who you lookin' for, boss?"

"Bey and Yidreg."

"Saw them just a few minutes ago."

"Good. Show me."

Bey found Zaatkhur repointing several of the arrows that had been used to bring down the q'akh during the x'qao attack. He looked up as she approached and smiled, probably because he knew her well enough to almost see the words trying to burst out of her. "Now what?"

"We are to hunt!"

Zaatkhur shrugged. "This is good news. But that is not the news you most want to shout at me."

"I do not shout!" Bey almost shouted. "Leader Caine has assigned me to lead one of the three coursing teams."

"You are surprised?"

Bey frowned. "Of course I am. He has not even asked for my—for *any* of our—fealty."

"True." Zaatkhur waited. "There is something else."

Bey resisted the urge to sit and frown a mighty frown. "Ugrekh and Fwerk have been placed under me in that team."

"Ah," her friend exhaled. "I am sure those two young kajh rejoice in that honor."

Bey grumbled. "Joke if you like, but it is no laughing matter. Besides, they are not so young." She allowed herself the luxury of a small smile. "Except when their years are compared to yours, I suppose."

"You have always been a hurtful whelp. All the more because you speak the truth. Tell me: do those two refuse to be led by you?"

"No, but they could hardly do so."

"Why?"

"They were present when Leader Caine told me."

"Ah. And what of Sho? Is she also in the hunt?"

"Yes, but along with Leader Craig and Leader Newton."

"Do you envy her?"

Bey frowned. "No. It would be easier, but it bodes well that they trust me to lead."

Zaatkhur nodded. "And they know that although Sho's mother was of the Tribes, she has only known the city. Even if only as a whelp, you have been on hunts. And as far as those two young brutes are concerned, it serves them right!" He snorted. "As if anything should matter in a leader other than sharpness of mind, swiftness of foot, and keenness of eye!"

"They might not think so."

He nodded. "I am sure that they do not. Be at ease, Bey: I shall watch them. Carefully."

Bey moved to stand closer to him. "Thank you, old friend."

He shrugged, pretending not to notice her fond tone. "You are the child of the one I loved. No matter that she chose he who was our leader, back then. You are as my own."

She squatted down and hugged him gently. "I am quite sure she would have chosen you, Zaatkhur."

His body relaxed into her hug, even though he did not return it. "I was not in favor with that leader, so she had no choice in the matter. Not if she meant to protect you."

Bey sighed. "Yet it did not protect *her*, in the end."

"Our fates are never in our own hands. For me, it is enough that you survived."

"I would *not* have, if you had failed to shelter me in your shadow. Then and later." Bey moved so that she was looking directly into his crow-footed eyes. "You risked much. Even the ire of the next leader: Jzhadakh's dislike of me turned into his dislike of you."

Zaatkhur released a long-suffering sigh. "Let us speak plainly. He did not dislike you; he *feared* you because he saw, from the first, that your wit was far greater than his. And even before you chose the way of a kajh, he knew you would not submit to his, or anyone else's, will."

Bey stood, frowning. "Which is why I find these new humans so puzzling. None of them fear my mind or my will."

Zaatkhur shrugged "Why should they? They are humans."

Ignoring the galling suggestion that no human would ever deem her mind the equal of theirs, she kept after the true source of her perplexity. "Yes, but even so, they do not behave as other humans. They set no tasks to remind us that their superiority or authority is absolute. Nor have they tasked us to swear fealty to them. Yet they *did* bring us over to join them in celebrating the defeat of the x'qao."

"Their ways are strange," Zaatkhur agreed. "And yet, recall what we saw in Forkus: whatever his reasons, Leader Caine insisted upon being the first to kill one of the oathbreakers."

She frowned. "But why? I have found no answer to that mystery. Clearly he did not revel in the act."

Zaatkhur considered, then shrugged. "No, but there is still no reason why he should have performed a task that is rightly left for underlings who must still prove themselves. Unless, of course, he believes what cavers do: that he takes the power of any foe slain according to ritual." He studied her deepening frown. "You saw something different." He smiled. "As usual."

She shook her head. "All I know is that those reasons are at odds with all his other actions and speech."

"Then why would he lessen himself by executing prisoners?"

"I don't think he *was* lessening himself, not in his or his companions' eyes."

"But he did. That is the custom, everyplace x'qai hold sway."

"I'm not sure he is from such a place."

"Well, he is certainly not from Zrik Whir, if that is what you mean. With the exception of the big, quiet one called Newton, the strange humans are all burntskins."

She nodded, knowing the truth of Zaatkhur's words far better than he did. "I agree; they are not from Zrik Whir. But who knows what other places exist across the seas? I am only certain that he did not wish to execute the oathbreaker."

Zaatkhur's nod was slower, as memory rebuilt the scene. "Yes. He looked as sick as a first-day tannery slave."

Bey raised an eyebrow. "Many of the others looked as bad or worse."

Zaatkhur threw up his hands, as was his wont. "So what does it mean?"

"It means that although the deed sickened him, Leader Caine

saw it through. The way a leader does when he must encourage others to do likewise."

Zaatkhur shrugged. "Or if he believes his followers might doubt he is just as capable of a task as they are." He considered. "So, you see him as a strong leader, not a weak one?"

She frowned again. "It feels strange to say it, but yes. It reminds me what my mother told me, and I remember, of the chiefs of the Free Tribes. But even that does not answer all the mysteries of these humans' behavior."

"That is a large understatement, little one."

She scoffed. "I'm still 'little one'?" Bey stood straight and looked down at Zaatkhur with a smile. Half a head taller, she had neither his short limbs nor thick, sloped shoulders, despite being sturdily built.

He chortled. "As tall as your whakt blood makes you, you shall always be 'little one' to me."

Bey bent down quickly and gave him a faster, harder hug, in part so he would not see the tears in her eyes.

"*Grouvg!*" Zaatkhur exclaimed in mock revulsion. "Get away and be moonish somewhere else. I have work to do if we are to go hunting, and it's harder now that I'm missing half of my best fingers!"

After two blissfully dry days, Caine stood atop a small rise to observe the hunt through the HUD. Only three of the Crewe had been assigned to it: Newton with the heavy-draw crossbow; Craig as his reloader and personal security; and Bannor with the Dornaani hand cannon. He was there primarily to protect the three teams. The greatest danger was that the herd might suddenly turn on the hunters, but it was impossible to rule out attacks by chance-met x'qai.

Bannor's team were essentially drivers: a large group that advanced slowly toward the dustkine to get them moving further away from the river. The two smaller teams had already moved well out to either flank, ready to chase, withdraw, or harry as required. The HUDs could measure target speed with great accuracy, which made it fairly simple to analyze the movement of each creature in the thirteen-head herd. It quickly revealed the two best targets.

One was the youngest, which naturally lacked the speed and

endurance of mature dustkine. The second was the oldest, which had the same mobility limits but was not constantly guarded by protective females. It would be harder to bring down, but Yidreg and Bey agreed that, once cut out from the herd, it would not excite the same defense that the young one would. And of course, it had at least three times the food value.

The hunt evolved much as the two experienced coursers predicted. The dustkine saw the approach of a sizable number of humanoids and began moving in the opposite direction: westward into a small network of wadis. Already there, the two smaller teams emerged and the already nervous kine veered away at their every approach. Though they could have easily slain or stampeded those few, small harriers, their flight reflex had already been excited. At this point, they would only turn about and attack if they lacked a clear path away from the threats.

It was not long before the oldest dustkine began falling behind. Bannor's large group adjusted its pressure on the herd so that the others were gradually forced farther away from the target in order to keep retreating from the threat. Bey's group ultimately crossed that axis of advance to begin firing at the target, which caused it to veer more sharply away from the rest of the dustkine and toward Newton's team.

The hardest part of the hunt was now behind them. The two teams would parallel the target while sending occasional bolts or shafts into it, thereby bleeding and tiring it as they closed to effective range. And if it tried to break away too early, the tangle of partial wadis would bring it up short.

At least, that was the plan.

Caine wasn't aware anything was amiss until a great cloud of dust rose up from the fleeing dustkine: the kind that would indicate it was no longer simply avoiding its pursuers, but charging. Usually, it would reserve such speed to escape the pursuit teams, but as Riordan increased the magnification of his HUD, he discovered that something had spooked the old kine away from Bey's team on the right . . . and sent it charging directly toward Newton and Sho's on the left.

*Shit!* "Bannor," Riordan snapped toward the helmet mic, "do you have an angle on—?"

"Negative. My own team is in the way. Can't get lock yet."

Before Caine could connect to Newton, the old dustkine was

upon his team. More dust flew high just as two wildly flashing lights appeared in its midst: Dornaani stun grenades. Their yowling reaching him a long moment later.

The dust swirled as if it had become a dust devil and then... stillness. Over almost as soon as it had begun.

"Newton—" Caine began.

It was Craig who answered. "He—we're all right, sir. Well, most of us."

"What do you mean, Sergeant?"

"Sho is... well, sir: she didn't have a stun grenade."

Although the locals didn't even have a special term for an "after-action report," they had the concept. And, as was usually the case when things had not gone well, the faces in that circle were grave.

Riordan was sure to keep his spine very straight. "So, Lieutenant Baruch, you hit but did not kill the dustkine."

Newton nodded. "That is correct, sir. Sho did the same at about the same moment that Sergeant Girten and I deployed our grenades. Startled, it swerved. Directly toward Sho. She could not avoid it in time. It was already quite close."

Riordan suppressed a sigh. "Was there any chance at resuscitation?"

Newton's sideways stare explained before his words did. "Sir, there was... there was no longer sufficient anatomical integrity to make such an attempt."

Arashk frowned at several unfamiliar words which had no equivalents in Low Praakht.

Riordan turned toward him. "The dustkine broke her body apart. She could not be saved."

He nodded, his jowls hanging limp in his species' expression of bitter acceptance.

"Do you have any idea why it spooked away from your team, Bey?"

The hollow-eyed kajh shook her head slowly. "There was much confusion just before it did. One of my coursers slipped into a wadi, came out in such a way, and at a place, that neither we nor it expected." Her chest heaved as she drew in a ragged breath. "It was startled. An arrow was loosed at it and it fled."

Riordan raised an eyebrow. "Had you given the command to fire, Bey?"

Her eyes hardened into a blank stare at nothing. "I had not, Leader Caine. My group...*I* was surprised by the events. I did not immediately see what was occurring, nor what orders would be best to give. The fault was mine, Leader Caine."

Riordan nodded but thought, *I know the sound of someone falling on their own sword, Bey.* But that was a conversation requiring more time and a private place. Just like another matter that needed settling and which, after weeks, he couldn't put off any longer. "Are there any other questions?" There weren't. He rose. "Then we are finished. First watch in an hour."

Once the sun had set, Riordan walked down to the river to stand his watch. It was one of the rare times the shape of the high-water bank made it prudent to lay a good part of their perimeter along its lip.

When Caine was sure he was unobserved, he unsealed the chest pocket of the Dornaani suit and removed the small sheet of paper he'd kept in his pack until today. Until it was time to send it on its way. He removed the ignitor he'd carried alongside it and stood looking up at the stars across the river.

He had resolved to get it over with quickly, but found he couldn't. Because he was not parting with just one thing, but a whole host of related fantasies and hopes that he'd stacked one upon the other, like a house of cards that swayed between the extremes of its own implausible geometries.

Not that any individual card in the tilting construct defied reason. It was possible that they might somehow find a way to get to the ship. That they would discover where Bactradgaria was in relation to Earth. Or anything. That they would be able to repair it and return to the Accord. That they would bring the evidence of the conspiracy that Dornaani Arbiters had hatched with Hsontlosh. And that, in a final moment of bliss and triumph, they would be able to find some way to rejuvenate or recarnate Elena.

Except that Elena was dead. Caine had said it out loud often enough since Eku shared his report; he certainly didn't need to again. And if, in defiance of all evidence and common sense, there was some way to restore her to this life, he still had to admit that it was no more likely than discovering that Santa Claus really did exist.

Riordan looked at the paper in his hand. It had to stop. The tilting tower of fantastic hopes had to be jettisoned: all of them, all at once. It was absurd enough to hope and strive for just the first leaning card, the first impossible item, on his list: for them to find some way back to the ship. But beyond that? Well, any of the other wild hopes were like unbuilt bridges: they'd cross them when they came to them.

*"They." The ones I call my friends. That takes real nerve. Or maybe selfishness. They wouldn't even be here if it hadn't been for my growing collection of fantasies. If I had taken this simple step sooner, they'd be back on Earth right now, living their lives in safe, familiar places. But they were as true as friends can be—and so they paid the price for me to chase my fantasies right into hell. No more.*

Riordan unfolded the paper and lit the igniter. He glanced over the words of the poem one last time. There were a few others he'd kept, but he'd left those on the ship, as if that would somehow preserve Elena and her reaction to them during the very few hours they'd had together.

His eyes lingered on the title and he almost laughed. Until this very moment, he hadn't realized it was just another term for what he'd been doing for years, every time he thought of her, every time he looked at her picture, every time he read this too-aptly-titled poem:

Baggage Check

Leaving,
I fold the shirt in which you slept
within the shirt that I wore,
packing up
all our brief days
    Together, * * *
the shirts are almost
Fully entwined,
as we were almost
Fully entwined.

They recall our scents, mingled
as I recall us, senses mingled,
inseparable as
    Our eyes * * *

don't lie, nor do
   our bodies,
which fit snug along every seam of
   each Other * * *
worlds call us away.

I fold the shirts close together,
mine within yours,
inseparable,
   unlike us.

As he tilted the flame toward the words, he couldn't smile,
couldn't cry, couldn't do anything except think:
*I'd have made a lousy poet.*

# Chapter Thirty-Seven

The hunt had been costly, not just in terms of time and life lost, but to the plans for leaving as faint a trail as possible.

The next two days, the skies threatened rain that never fell. Initial gratitude for the dry conditions soured; yes, the formation was moving more quickly, but the site of the kill, and the tracks leading away, would still be there like signposts.

As if that wasn't bad enough, the grey skies meant the sun never shone and the raw dustkine could not be dried: the only means of preserving it while moving. But even if they had been stationary, smoking was all but unknown on Bactradgaria: a relief since almost all fires were fueled by dung. And although salt curing was common, it was only done along the coasts.

As a result, whereas two days of sun-drying would have certainly attracted carnivores, it could then have been wrapped and the tantalizing scent largely smothered. But with grey skies, the kill scent kept following them. And if it went on a day or two more, there was an excellent chance that, despite the freezing nighttime temperatures, their hard-won meat would begin to spoil.

Fortunately, the third day dawned clear. The F-class star that kept Bactradgaria a desert in the wake of the apocalypse that had denuded it now helped dry the meat. The smell was not pleasant to nostrils accustomed to meat on Earth; Miles insisted that it made roast possum smell like prime rib. But on several occasions, Caine saw locals literally drooling in response to the scent.

Unfortunately, they were not alone. Carnivores and scavengers made several appearances, each requiring the persuasion of the group's seven crossbows and four bows to drive them off. By the time the shafts had been retrieved, more hours had been lost and it wasn't long before the next group of uninvited diners arrived. When the locals and even some of the Crewe obliquely suggested that this might be an excellent time to put the Dornaani weapons to use, Caine and Duncan pointed out that until they could forge iron with sufficient precision and purity, they were limited to the magnetically refined projectiles that had come with the weapons. If used for routine hunting, they would soon regret having been so profligate with resources that could turn the tide of a battle.

When the column finally made camp at the end of the second day, the meat had dried enough that it could be swaddled in multiple layers of permanent wrapping. However, before the job could be completed, predators began loping closer: quadrupeds that several of the Crewe had seen before.

"Entelodonts," Newton grumbled.

"Hell pigs," Miles translated for the locals, who shared their own, very similar label for the beasts. The Crewe feared that they might be non-bipedal x'qai but the locals convinced them otherwise. One look through a "magic" monoscope at ten-times magnification confirmed their opinion: these were not x'qao, merely the animals which gave rise to x'qiigh when infested with their spores.

The entelodonts proved as stubborn as most porcine breeds. The stun grenades were simply annoyances they punted aside. Yaargraukh suggested that they might be more easily dealt with if given a few kilos of the dried meat. Despite dubious glances, Caine authorized the attempt.

He didn't realize it would involve the Hkh'Rkh snatching up his battle-ax in one hand, the meat in the other, and charging directly at the lead entelodont. He stopped one hundred meters from the big leader, roared at it, and then turned about to race back for the group. The entelodont, challenged by a now-fleeing adversary, responded predictably: spirited and thunderous pursuit.

Until, that is, Yaargraukh dropped the meat only fifty meters from the formation. He kept running, but the creature, now far ahead of its companions, once again reacted as its breed usually did: it stopped long enough to snatch up the easy meal.

That was also long enough for the gathered bows and cross-bows of the formation to aim carefully and unleash a murderous volley of poison-tipped projectiles into it.

The entelodont jumped, squealed in rage, started charging the group, then began tilting sideways: the poison was taking effect. Discretion rapidly became the greater part of its valor and it swerved away, stumbling. It collapsed approximately seventy meters away.

Also, in keeping with the breed, the remaining pair of entelodonts slowed when they reached the point where their two choices were as stark as they were equidistant: charge the numerous beings with their backs securely to the river, or make a meal of their former leader. They chose the latter. Of course.

Caine turned away from the grisly scene, nodded toward Yaargraukh who looked on, impassive as ever, battle-ax hanging in his hand. "Watch them until they're done. Hopefully, their leader's carcass should be enough. If they start acting like we might be the next item on the menu, scare them off with a few bolts."

"Yes, Commodore. But if they do not respond to that persuasion?"

Riordan glanced at the axe and Yaargraukh's clearly eager posture. "More volleys and then lead in the warriors."

"As you wish, sir. Where will you be?"

"Getting more information about x'qai."

"Very good, sir." The Hkh'Rkh turned and, grat'r eagerly in tow, gathered those waiting with melee weapons.

Riordan had walked about twenty meters when the slap of bowstrings told him that the entelodonts were either unsatisfied with the poison-fouled carcass of their leader, or preferred the more enticing smell of the sun-dried dustkine. Grunting and guttering snarls were their reply to the shafts and bolts that had struck home.

Twenty meters further on, Caine heard Yaargraukh's roar joined by the chorus of his combat team. Moments later, the grunting was replaced by roars and shrill squeals of desperation.

Riordan sighed. *Guess the leader wasn't enough after all.*

Caine found Bey where the sole male urldi told him she'd be: crouched down among the packed meat, checking that the wrappings were as scent-proofed as possible.

She stood when she heard Riordan approach. "Leader Caine, what do you wish?"

He waved them toward a cluster of low rocks that had already become the de facto "sitting room" for the formation. "Some time ago, Ulchakh told me that you might know more about x'qai than anyone else."

She was shaking her head even as she lowered herself to one of the rocks. "I understand why he might expect I do. Living in Forkus and having a reputation for being observant, it is a logical guess. But unfortunately, I saw less of Forkus than most of my peers. When my mother arrived there, the leader of the gang at that time was careful to keep her from being seen by x'qai or their agents. He was even more careful to hide me."

Riordan frowned. *Okay, so I'm not going to get any additional data about x'qai, but maybe I'll learn something almost as valuable.* "Why did he hide you both?"

Bey shrugged. "Our kind is deemed risky to keep in thrall. We are too likely to seek out contacts among humans. And nothing worries x'qai, or a slow-witted city trog, so much as that."

"Because your mother and you were both clever enough to make your own plans and agreements? And possibly use contacts with humans to threaten his leadership of the gang?"

The way she tilted her head indicated Riordan had been only half correct. "I was no danger to him, for neither I nor my mother could ever replace him. Females are almost never allowed to be leaders."

It was a logical extension of what Ulchakh had said, but another source always meant another perspective. "Why?"

Bey looked at him as if a second head was beginning to sprout from his shoulders. "To answer such an...unusual question would require much more time. However, you are correct that the leader you slew in Forkus—Jzhadakh—had concerns about the speed with which I learn and think. But not as a threat to his leadership; none of his gang cared that his ideas and plans mostly came from me. I was his counselor; it was expected. His worry was that an x'qao liege might learn."

"And, er, remove you?"

"If by 'remove' you mean 'kill,' then no, Leader Caine; that was not the risk. But if any x'qao learned how much of his success had come from my counsel, they might have taken me to serve them directly. This was why I was never allowed to be part of the negotiations, but was always in a place where I might hear and later advise."

Hoping it wasn't another inquiry into the obvious, Riordan asked, "But if the x'qai fear that you are more likely and able to seek alliances with humans, why would they risk bringing you into their seats of power and making you aware of their plans?"

Even before he finished the question, Bey was smiling. "Leader Caine, you are a warrior. You wish to wield as keen a blade as you can find, yes?"

Riordan simply nodded.

"But such blades are rarely without risk to their owners, if they are wielded carelessly. The x'qai see those of my background as just such a blade. They keep us as war planners and furnish us with much wealth and many privileges: more than humans can usually afford. But that wealth is not merely payment; it is to ensure that other praakht are envious and come to hate us almost as much as our masters."

"But if they are so confident that they can maintain control over you, why would they fear your contact with humans?"

Her smile became crafty. "Because no matter their background, the more clever praakht often come to realize that there is a still greater treasure to be had: freedom and respect. Even though few humans consider us their equals, they do not require that we grovel at their feet. That Jzhadakh used Sho as his courier when dealing with humans."

"But didn't that risk losing her to them?"

"Yes, but he had to choose between that risk—"

"Or risk losing his best counselor," Riordan finished, nodding meaningfully at her. And reminding himself for the hundredth time that though x'qai kept trogs ignorant, they remained quite shrewd.

Bey was smiling at him again. "His fear of losing me to a human liege was almost as great as his fear that an x'qao liege would take me to serve directly under his banner. Still, it was a hard choice for Jzhadakh to make."

"Why?"

Bey shrugged. "He was...fond of Sho." She frowned. "Too much, perhaps." Her expression almost became sad. "She could have been very happy among you, I think."

The comment was so unexpected, and yet so vague, that all he could do was ask, "Happy in what way?"

Bey looked sideways at him. "Sho became very interested in one of your number."

*What? One of us?* "Who?"

"Leader Miles. But she saw no way to act upon her attraction."

Riordan was surprised enough that trogs were sexually attracted to humans, but Miles "Little Guy" O'Garran? "I—he did not know of Sho's interest. I am sure of that."

Bey nodded, her frown deepening. "I must tell you, Leader Caine, that your group's mating behavior—I should say, your lack of it—has concerned your praakht captives. Despite your kind treatment, none of you have shown the least interest in any of our kind. Considering that most humans do not, eh, avoid us, many fear that you do not consider them worthy to swear an oath of fealty."

*Well, this just keeps getting stranger and stranger.*

"It might be helpful if I knew the reasons for this avoidance, either to reassure them or tell them what will happen to us once we reach Khorkrag."

"These matters require, and deserve, careful consideration," Riordan replied, trying not to appear as disoriented as he felt. "Understand that we have very different traditions and rules that guide our behavior."

"Ah!" Bey said brightly, but with less enthusiasm in her eyes than her voice. "So it is as two of the urldi guessed: that you are a league of warriors that have foresworn mating as part of your oaths to each other! Such bands are said to exist, but before now, none of us had met—"

Riordan held up his hand. "And you still *haven't* met such a group. We take no such oaths to each other."

Bey was frowning again. "So is it that you find all praakht repulsive? That your kindness is...is pity?" A hint of simmering anger began to creep into her tone.

This time Caine did shake his head. Emphatically. "No. Pity is not involved." *Well, I don't think so.* "As I said: we have traditions and rules about, er, intimacy. Particularly with captives."

Bey spent several seconds pondering this. "Your ways are very strange. I will try to allay the urldi's fears, but without details, I do not know how convincing I can be."

Riordan finally found enough presence of mind to smile. "Perhaps if I understood more of *your* ways and, er, expectations, I could provide a better explanation."

She nodded. "I agree. But—meaning no disrespect, Leader Caine—it might be best if I describe the ways of city-praakht as if you were a complete stranger to them."

*How ironically apt.* "I believe that is wise."

"Sho's attraction to a human such as Leader Miles is not at all unusual, particularly among female kajh. It is prudent and wise. Whereas x'qai do whatever they can to remove clever praakht from the common gangs, they prefer and favor humans of greater intelligence. So, smarter praakht, but particularly female kajh, appreciate that with humans, they will not have to conceal or deny their intelligence and will probably live longer, safer lives.

"The reverse is often true, among human warriors. The greater spirit, intelligence, or both of female kajh is of interest to them. However, this mostly occurs among the less well-bred human troops, the ones the x'qai do not so carefully pair with chosen mates. But even if these humans are of lesser size and wit, they are still attractive mates for female kajh, at least those who are able to overlook—" Bey stopped so abruptly it was as if she'd swallowed back a word that had half emerged from her mouth.

Riordan raised an eyebrow. *Now comes the* really *interesting part.* "Go on. This is very helpful."

"Leader Caine, I . . ." She mastered what appeared to be a mix of fear, dread, and embarrassment before starting again. "Most praakht females must learn to overlook the . . . the frail bodies of humans in pursuing such mates. That may be why it is female kajh who are most likely to seek human males. They more completely perceive the species' other values: their unity, their talent for amassing wealth, their knowledge, their skill and cunning as warriors. This does much to offset any disappointment in their lighter bodies, which do not quicken a breeding response as strongly and readily as do the sturdier shapes of male praakht."

She stopped when she saw that Caine's initially amused smile had become a wide grin. Her tone was a mix of caution and disbelief. "You find such words . . . amusing?"

Caine almost laughed out loud. "I consider them a fine lesson in humility." He forced the smile off his face. "I also consider it a fine proof of your truthfulness, Bey. Clearly, that was not easy to say to a human. Particularly a male."

Bey's long, steady exhalation was almost certainly a means of covering a deep sigh of relief. "You are correct, Leader Caine: it was not easy."

He began to stand. "You are an excellent leader for your people. I will speak with the other leaders about asking for their fealty. If you will serve as the leader for those of your species."

She stared at him. "When you say 'those of your species'... what do you mean?"

Another moment of abject confusion. "Why, all the praakht who are with us."

She blinked, looked more insulted than confused. "Can you not see that I am different? That I do not look like the others?"

"Well, yes, I do. But among my people, it would be...well, rude to inquire why."

"Here, you will find such 'rudeness' is a way of life! I look different because I am. I am only part praakht. I am whakt. I am from a Free Tribe, not a 'Wild Tribe' as many resentful praakht name us. That is why the city-praakht do not trust me." She stared at him, openly incredulous. "Do I truly not look different to you?"

*As if we've had the time or opportunity to make a study of how speciate variations might be distinct from hybridity?* "Well, yes, you do look different, but we just presumed that was common among the Free Tribes. And because you grow up, eh, healthier, not being slaves to the x'qai."

"That is part of it: we are our own tribes. We have families. We are not broken to the brutish ways the x'qai insist upon our kin in the cities. Mind you: I am not saying that the true praakht, whether from cities or otherwise, are lesser, but their masters punish everything other than victory and ruthlessness."

Riordan realized he'd sat down again. "You do not seem particularly ruthless."

She huffed over her shoulder: southward, toward Forkus. "You are not the first to say so, but you are one of the first to mean it as a compliment." She tossed her head, tightly woven braids flying to underscore her rejection of the city behind her. "Besides, even the praakht that chided me for it knew I had skills which offset that 'failing.'"

Riordan nodded. "Your skills, as a leader and a warrior, are obvious to all."

She glanced sideways at him. "I have less obvious skills that I could not frequently use in Forkus."

Riordan shrugged. "Then I have that much more to learn."

She nodded somberly. "Leader Caine, I am a good teacher of the skills I have, of passing on the knowledge I possess." She paused, lowered her chin very, very slightly. "Even to those above me."

He nodded. "I am not surprised to learn that." *Considering you've been doing it for me since we met.* "And although you are my subordinate, I am not 'above' you. Those are not the same things, in our language."

"No?" Bey's brief expression of intrigued curiosity was pushed aside by hard-jawed practicality. "Leader Caine, that is another thing you—all of you—must learn. My people do not understand the way you lead. Even I do not fully grasp it, yet. You most resemble the Mangled, who like to say they make a strength of their weakness. But from what I have seen, your people possess both kinds of strength. It is very strange." She smiled. "I, also, have a lot to learn."

"Then we can teach each other."

Bey's smile had started widening before she firmly inverted it into a serious frown. "Yes. That is what we shall do. I wish to become a better leader for those who depend upon me."

Riordan smiled. "That is excellent common ground from which to start. Now, tell me what you know of Khorkrag."

# Chapter Thirty-Eight

From Riordan's vantage point, the town across the river was barely four hundred meters across and had no ancient ruins, tall or otherwise. It was a flat sprawl of adobe hovels centered on a handful of buildings fashioned from fitted stone or better adobe: a kind that included lime, according to Ulchakh.

The h'achgan trader stared at the place with a deep frown. "I am always uneasy before entering Khorkrag."

"Because there are so few of your kind there?" Caine asked.

"Strangely, it is because there are none of *your* kind there," he answered with a shake of his head. "Here, no liege keeps humans in his thrall. They are too expensive, considering that none of what makes them valuable is found or made in so small a place."

Riordan nodded, grateful for Bey's accumulated lessons on how the town differed from Forkus. "No tracts of lichen. That changes almost everything."

Ulchakh glanced at him. "You are learning, Friend Caine. This is well. And you touch on the root of the difference. Without tracts to tend, there is less food and so, fewer mouths: barely five thousand. Fewer mouths means less power to accrue. Less power means that only disgraced or weak x'qao will create a fastness here. And with so little to gain or lose, they have no need of humans' abilities to travel widely and attack with great effect while few in number. And that is just as well, because the tools that make such things possible—rads, guns, and the substances they require—cannot be crafted or maintained here."

Riordan suppressed a smile at the slang for vehicles: "rads." It was one of the few points of overlap in every language on Bactradgaria. Even among independent humans, reportedly. "You are sure you must visit it?"

Yidreg answered from over Ulchakh's shoulder. "We cannot know it is safe for us all to use the ferry until we have measured the mood of the place. On rare occasion, it is hostile to h'achgai."

"But you're more worried it is hostile to us," Bannor added from alongside the broad-shouldered hunter.

Yidreg shrugged. "We would be foolish not to. Humans only rarely come here and then only on the business of lieges."

Ulchakh nodded. "Besides, merely seeing you—and all burnt-skins, no less!—is a subtle reminder of how very unimportant this place and its leaders are to the world beyond. No being, no matter how rude, welcomes such comparisons."

He pushed away from the low rock lip that overlooked the high-water bank. "Besides, if your rescue of Leader Eku earned the notice of lieges in Forkus, some may have reached across the miles to alert their lesser cousins to be alert for a band of humans, or rogue harrows, who might be fleeing the site of their effrontery."

"And how would they reach across the miles?" Solsohn asked, joining the group.

Ulchakh shrugged. "Mindspeaking. How else?"

Riordan and his friends remained quiet. Any honest comment or question about the power imputed to more powerful x'qai— a kind of telepathy—was too likely to be heard as an insult. Because whenever the Crewe attempted to ask questions about "mindspeaking," their tones almost always betrayed the actual word they equated with it: "superstition."

Ulchakh did not leave the topic, however. "Two lieges from Forkus are said to extend their rivalry to Khorkrag, at the orders of their suzerains: Brazhglu'u and Ormalg. The latter's proxies now control the majority of Khorkrag and have been particularly aggressive in recent years."

Yidreg nodded. "Of those two camps, those who are sworn to Ormalg are far more hostile toward humans, particularly those not safely in the stables of x'qai. When we visit Ulchakh's kins-men in their trade station, we shall learn if it is safe for all of us to pass through. Hastily."

Duncan's voice revealed his sudden curiosity. "If Khorkrag is even dangerous to h'achgai, why do any of you stay here?"

Ulchakh shrugged. "Since there is no vansary or regular place to trade here, we must keep our own. Otherwise, we would be forced to make exchanges in a place held by a third party. That is not only expensive, but very unreliable. In Forkus, there is enough value being exchanged that any liege who dared violate the rules of the vansary would no longer be able to trade. Here?" He shrugged expressively. "Trade is so rare and our anger so unimportant that, if a liege stood to gain enough, he would betray us as readily as he breathes."

"And have you decided which of our goods you'll offer alongside your own?"

Ulchakh's smile was pinched. "If only you were willing to part with some of the bronze weapons and better armor you took from the praakht's hovel in Forkus." He rolled his eyes at Duncan. "The hide-wrapped hafts you offered are hardly a rarity, up here. Are you sure you will not part with any of the salt cakes?"

Riordan glanced at Solsohn. His eager and intense expression was the one that Pandora had understandably nicknamed "merchant mode." "No, we might need the salt. But won't they be interested in the silver and the gems?"

Ulchakh gave him a long-suffering look. "A handful of uncut garnets are not gems any more than the mostly copper coins are 'silver.' And they do not have the value here that they would in a city."

"Sure," Duncan nodded, understanding. "Here, trade means barter in essential goods." He smiled ruefully. "Unfortunately, we need almost all those goods ourselves."

Ulchakh shrugged. "Then we shall see what the garnets and the hide sandals and scraps bring. After all, the trade is merely camouflage for our visit." He glanced at the sun and at the two stone stelae half a kilometer further north on their side of the river. "We must go. It is likely to be some time before they see us raise the flag at the stanchions. And some time after that before they make their way across."

Riordan raised a hand to delay him a moment more. "And if a day has passed and you have not returned?"

Ulchakh nodded slowly. "Then wait another day."

"And after that?"

"Leave. Go north, cross wherever you can using the methods you claim to have and strike overland to Achgabab as fast as you may travel. Arashk knows the best ways through the wadi country."

"But you might need—"

"Friend Caine: if I have not returned by the end of tomorrow, I will be beyond all needs. Now, I must go."

Riordan and Bey watched the praakht-crewed ferry being lashed to the mooring at Khorkrag's natural-rock jetty, the three h'achgai already waiting to debark.

She pointed at the apparent captain of the craft. "He is a whakt, like me."

Riordan could see the difference clearly now, particularly since as a male, this whakt was almost a head and a half taller than any of his trog crew. "I am finding it easier to note the distinctions."

She shook her head. "You are only seeing size. Attend, Leader Caine. Compare your skin to mine. Yours is very smooth, yes, but it is thin and burns easily. A praakh's skin is more like mine, but is thicker, even rough. The same is true for the differences in our hair. You seem to have very little except on your head, and the strands are very thin. A true praakh's hair covers more of their body and is thick, giving better protection against the sun and cold. Mine is somewhere between."

She paused, looked at Riordan's Dornaani vacc suit as if she were seeing it for the first time. "Is this why you wear armor that covers your entire body? Not just to protect you from weapons, but from the world around you?"

He shrugged. "I never thought of it that way before, but, in a manner of speaking, yes. Although 'world around us' includes places where no praakht could survive without such, er, armor." He smiled. "Nor could the most resourceful whakt kajh, for that matter."

She rolled her eyes but did not manage to keep a small grin from bending her mouth. "Do not underestimate my kind, Leader Caine! We often surprise those who do!"

"I have already learned that, Bey. Surprising me is one of the things you seem to do best."

She glanced at him. "I cannot tell if you mean that as praise or criticism."

"Well, not exactly either. I am mostly thinking how every time we speak, I not only learn something new. I learn something about which I was too ignorant to ask."

She smiled, then studied his face. "You have such a question now, do you not?"

*I may be getting too easy to read, but that's just a risk I'll have to take.* "I do have a question, but there is no polite way to ask it."

She chuckled. "As I have said before, being 'polite' has little use upon the wastes. And less still when peoples are trying to learn about each other. Ask your question, Leader Caine."

"You spoke of mates across the different species. Are all the species—I mean, well, can *all* of them breed with each other?"

"No. And before you ask which ones can, and how well each pairing breeds, understand that there are no swift answers to these questions. But here are some useful truths that apply to all of them.

"Some kinds of praakht may breed more easily with other kinds. All praakht *can* breed with humans, but for some it is difficult and even dangerous, whereas with others it is little different from humans breeding with humans. My people, for instance, breed with humans so easily because so much of their blood is in our veins."

"And this shared blood comes from more frequent pairings?"

"Yes, but also from long before. It dates to the time when the great towers stood unbroken, invisible pictures were in the wind, ships flew higher than the clouds, and finally, the skies burned and left the world as you see it." She frowned. "I should like to have seen the before-world."

Riordan had to hold back his reflex to say, "Perhaps one day you will visit worlds like that." In part he had no business suggesting such a thing when he couldn't even see a way of getting to orbit, but mostly because it was necessary to carefully manage such wild hopes and dreams. Both his and hers.

Bey had not stopped her speculations upon the connections between their species. "Whakt still see much that is familiar in humans, and it is said the reverse is true. That is why such mixed pairings are so common. Still, the breeding is never so certain and effortless that it can go untracked."

"Untracked? By whom? Humans or whakt?"

She grimaced. "No, by x'qai. Neither of our breeds bothers to keep track of how much of which blood is in our veins, other than that there is both. But the x'qao see both of us as tools, and they are determined to ensure that we stay *different* tools, according to their needs and wishes."

*Good God, they breed us like dogs. Some to be kept as pure-breed lines, some as new breeds to mix for desired traits. They buy and sell us the same way, too.* "So what were they trying to achieve in mixing us?"

"That is not a concern of theirs; they have long had all the mixes they desire. What they track is how any pair's ancestors make it more or less likely that they will whelp successfully."

"*Whelp?*" *Yet . . . of course they'd call it that.*

"Humans are—forgive me—the weakest of all breedstock. So the x'qai keep careful records on the degree to which human blood is present in any mixed whelp. Praakht females are able to carry human young without any additional risk. Also, the weight of mixed whelps is lower than that of true praakht, who typically carry their own offspring longer.

"It is the opposite with human females. For them, it is difficult and sometimes dangerous to carry mixed children. The more praakht blood is in the child, the more this is true. Breach births are not uncommon, and since the time in the womb is longer, it can overtax a human female, sometimes fatally." She paused. "Leader Caine, you grow pale. Well, more pale. Have I said something that alarms you?"

"No, Bey: your words have shown me many new things, but they all have one thing in common."

"Which is?"

"That I must learn everything I can about the x'qai. Everything."

"To what end?"

"Do you have the saying that, to defeat an enemy, you must first come to know it very well?"

"No, but it is quite sensible."

Riordan was fairly sure his smile was mirthless. "Yes, and I mean to prove that to you: you and all your kind."

# Chapter Thirty-Nine

When everyone but the first watch had gathered round, Ulchakh began without preamble. "We cannot enter Khorkrag. The streets are loud with mutters about humans in the area, even a caravan of them. Some say it is the Legate's, others swear that they are rogues, independents. But whether this is chance or connected to your activities in Forkus, the town is too excited. There are rumors that the Ormalg liege may soon announce a bounty on humans and all found with them."

"Then how shall we cross the river?" Arashk grumbled.

"Let's leave that aside for a second," Riordan said quietly. "First, should we still go to Achgabab?"

Arashk sputtered. "B-but we are from Achgabab. We must return there."

"Eventually," Caine amended.

Ulchakh nodded. "I see. Yes. It may be wise to change our destination... for now."

"Where to?"

Ulchakh looked toward Ta'rel, who was already smiling.

He extended his arms in a wide gesture. "Ebrekka would welcome its old friends Ulchakh and Yidreg, and its new friends Leaders Caine and Peter and all those humans who travel with them." Riordan noticed, but did not elect to mention, that he had not made any mention of trogs. At least, not yet.

"I think it would be a wise detour," the mangle added. "Ulchakh is well known in the streets of Khorkrag. He is also known to

397

trade with Kosvak of Forkus, who is sworn to the human liege Vranadoc." Ta'rel shrugged. "Since Ulchakh is now known to have arrived from Forkus, and might likely have humans in tow or at least word of their doings and intents, I fear that the tempers in the town might lead some to waylay him on the path back to his home in Achgabab."

Ulchakh nodded vigorously. "Friend Ta'rel speaks truth. Even if they do not suspect that I travel with you and yours, Friend Caine, I may seem a likely source of information about that which has them enraged: your kind. So we shall not head in the direction they suspect."

Yidreg nodded. "If we head due east, our course will allow us to slip beneath the southern limit of the wadi country the praakht call the Orokrosir. And I am sure that Ta'rel is familiar with all the hidden paths we might travel from there to Ebrekka."

"Not just hidden paths," the mangle added, "but hidden refuges." He turned toward Peter. "As you saw, we have concealed places—small caves, mostly—spread across the entirety of Brazhgarag. But whereas they are thinly scattered around the continent, they are thicker in the region of our largest communities, of which Ebrekka is one of the greatest."

"It sounds as though that's both the carrot and the stick, then," Craig Girten said amiably. When the nonhumans stared at him, Peter explained the saying in Ta'rel's own language.

"Ah," the mangle said, "Leader Craig says that our choice of path is simple, since there are jaws behind us and a meal before us." Approving mutters arose.

Arashk went so far as to pat a very gratified Girten on the shoulder. "It is past time a trade band journeyed to Ebrekka. When I left Achgabab, there were already careful countings of how many packets of moss remained. We shall not only elude whatever angry warriors and scouts stream outward from Khorkrag, but secure needed supplies for our home."

Ulchakh nodded. "I agree. Clan arguments prevented us from sending a timely porter caravan to our friends among the Mangled. With our growing numbers, we consume more moss... and there will have been no trade over the winter."

Peter looked from Ta'rel toward Ulchakh and back again. "I understand that the moss is an important curative, but everyone is speaking as if h'achgai will perish without it."

Ta'rel looked at his friend in genial but utter bafflement. "Of course."

Riordan frowned, glanced at Ulchakh. "Does your kind have a special medical need that only the moss can answer?"

Now Ulchakh stared at Riordan as Ta'rel had stared at Peter. "No more than yours. Or theirs." He gestured to the praakht sitting in the circle, who murmured grave assent.

"I have not had any since leaving Forkus," Arashk growled as if to emphasize the severity of their need. "And I will take any death before a descent into *s'rillor.*"

Ayana frowned. "That word seems a combination of several others. What does it mean?"

"You are correct, Leader Ayana," Ta'rel said. "They are Deviltongue words run together: 'to make ash of the mind.'"

"So... 'mindless'?"

Ulchakh's expression was one of horrible awakening as he leaned forward toward Caine and his companions. "Yes. It means the descent into mindlessness that occurs if one does not consume the moss. Were none of you aware?"

Riordan felt a cool chill as he realized that concealing their ignorance might wind up killing them.

Dora had leaned forward also. "And this is... what? A disease? That affects all species?"

"Yes," Bey said quietly, "as soon as one arrives at the age of bearing or siring young. Thinking creatures or not; it makes no difference."

"Even x'qai?"

Ulchakh shook his head sharply, surprised. "What? Of course not: not *x'qai!*"

"Of course," a new voice said—and it took Riordan a moment to realize that it was his own. "That's the x'qai's *real* power, their *real* advantage!"

"What do you mean, Commodore?" Duncan asked, eyes narrowing.

"The x'qai don't reproduce sexually. They spawn. They're asexual."

Newton sucked in a deep, daunted breath. "Of course."

"What are all of you going on about?" Miles griped, but with a hint of unease.

"It's been there all around us. From the start," Caine said, not caring about how much ignorance it revealed because this cat was not merely out of the bag; it had left the planet. "Camphor trees—all cedars—are parthenogenetic. So are all the tubers we've been eating. So is a lot of seaweed. And fungi. And moss itself. Everything here that goes through puberty, or any sexual matura-tion phase, becomes susceptible to something in the environment. Something lethal. But all x'qa are *immune.*"

Newton nodded. "Yes, and this explains the rarity of indi-viduals past early middle age."

"Except those with wealth or connections," added Katie, steal-ing a glance at Ulchakh.

"It is why," Bey added quietly, "no matter how hardy a spe-cies, we die sooner than we should...unless we eat the moss from youth onward. When we stop, the s'rillor takes hold and increasingly impairs us. Finally, we become the mindless, which the x'qai call deadskins."

*Mindless.* Riordan heard the word echo as he recalled his first thoughts upon entering the streets of Forkus. Of seeing the haggard inhabitants, some of whom were so blank-eyed and dirty that they hardly seemed aware of putting one foot in front of the other. *Because that's all they could do. Because they really* were *mindless.*

Dora was having a very similar flashback, apparently. "*Madre de Dios,* I thought what I saw in Forkus was what I saw growing up, just much worse."

Newton's voice had shifted to that of a doctor in a terminal ward. "How much moss is required?"

Ta'rel held up a small hide pouch, showed what was inside.

"Hmm. Small. What is the interval of dosing and adjustment for body mass?"

"Our healer wishes to know," Ayana translated, "how often one must eat the moss and if they must eat more if they are larger?"

Ta'rel considered the question carefully, looking a bit like a physician himself. "Every thirty to forty days. I have never seen nor heard that larger persons suffered from taking the same amount."

Duncan raised an eyebrow. "Which could mean that smaller persons might need less."

Newton almost spat his negation. "Inconclusive. Logically, onset and progression are most intense as the organism enters sexual maturity. More moss might be required at that time, but less once the progression is established. If so, observers might conclude that efficacious dosing was independent of patient mass. Without rigorous multi-phased double-blind testing, it is impossible to assert a proportional efficacy ratio supporting a 'smaller dose for smaller patient' thesis."

When the locals, and several of the Crewe, simply gaped at the stream of unfamiliar words, Newton's eyes dropped. "We can't be sure about dosing," he summarized.

Riordan noticed that while Ta'rel struggled with the vocabulary, he eagerly followed Newton's statements and seemed to have kept up with the general logic of them. "Ta'rel, these hidden caves throughout Brazhgarag: are there similar networks on other continents, as well?"

He nodded readily; no one seemed surprised, so that too was common knowledge evidently.

"And is that where you grow the moss?"

This time his nod was slower. No one was surprised, but the locals almost leaned away from the conversation.

Riordan waved as if to acknowledge that, although there were far more queries to pose, the time had come to relent. For now.

But Ta'rel leaned forward, not ready to leave the topic. "We all wondered, I think, if among your other magics, you had a mystic remedy for s'rillor." Although he phrased it as a statement, it was clearly a question.

Caine tried to keep his bounding thoughts in check. Might their precautionary battery of inoculations prove effective against the underlying microbe? What about the Slaasriithi theriac in his bloodstream: would that work like an inoculation? Why hadn't the Dornaani samplers detected the microbe? And what if there was a low-tech way to combat it? But that was an even deeper and more labyrinthine rabbit hole of possibilities and dangers. "I do not know, Ta'rel. None of our devices told us we were in danger. They still haven't."

The mangle nodded. "Perhaps when we reach Ebrekka, you will allow us to test you." He waved a reassuring hand. "It is painless and it never fails to detect the animalcule that causes the decline, no matter the species."

*If we test negative, then we have some time to decide what to do. But if positive—well, traveling to Ebrekka puts us at one of*

*Bactradgaria's major moss markets.* "I'm sure I speak for everyone when I say we accept your kind offer to be tested. But for now, we have a more pressing problem."

Arashk nodded irritably. "Getting across the river."

Caine glanced at Yidreg. "You said that it grows deeper north of here, without growing wider?"

"That is correct. The water often calms there."

Riordan nodded. *And if it's calmer at the surface, the odds are that it's even calmer toward that deeper bottom.* "That is where we must go."

"And do what?" one of the kajh exclaimed, adding the honorific far too late, "Leader Caine?"

Riordan met the praakh's eyes until he looked uneasily away. "You shall see when we get there." He turned to Bannor. "Colonel Rulaine has consulted with Yidreg and Ulchakh on how the river flows here and further upstream and believes he has a solution." Caine turned to his friend. "Colonel, how do we cross the river?"

Bannor sighed, smiled crookedly. "You're not going to like it, Commodore."

Caine simply smiled. "I suspected as much. Lay it out for us."

Riordan and his ad hoc command staff surveyed the river from the tallest of several rocky molars that pushed up from the dusty gums of the western river bank. Almost two hundred meters away on the far side, more stony teeth continued to march away into the east, albeit more rounded and worn. Starting almost a kilometer upstream, and continuing for another two downstream, the river was darker and ran slower than they'd seen elsewhere.

Yidreg pointed to the inkiest spot, just beyond their vantage point. "It is as I said: the slowest current between Khorkrag and Fragkork. But it can be treacherous."

"Because the current can grow very strong?" Craig asked. He had once again been assigned to shadow Riordan as combination guard and runner.

"More because it is harder to predict the equiflow," Bannor answered from where he was bent over one of the tallest, yet thinnest, of the basalt outcroppings.

Even with the Dornaani translator brought out of storage to help, building the necessary vocabulary had been a challenge. The terms and situation were so atypical that most of the Crewe, including Caine, didn't even know them in English. "Equiflow" had been one such: the period where flow and contraflow were in a state of comparative equilibrium.

"Hell, how do ocean tides affect rivers this far upstream anyhow?" Craig sighed, scratching his head. "It's over two thirds the distance across the United St—"

"It has to do with the moon, Sergeant," Ayana interrupted hastily. "Although it appears distant, it exerts a much stronger gra—er, pull on the oceans. This is complicated by its elliptical orbit."

"So, more, er, pull on the ocean at some times, less at others."

"Well put, Sergeant Girten," Tagawa said, trying to move the conversation away from planetary mechanics and into the less revealing realm of riverine dynamics. "Between these two factors, the oceans are subjected to unceasing yet rarely repeated oscillatory forces. Occasionally, when the patterns resulting from them align in certain patterns, a self-amplifying feedback loop is generated."

"Ma'am," Craig muttered, indicating their local audience, but including himself as one of the baffled listeners.

Ayana closed her eyes for a moment. "Because of these factors, there comes a time where the backflow—the return of all the water that has been pushed up the river—cannot fully clear, cannot equalize, over several cycles. The more of these cycles that accumulate without being able to equalize, the closer the river comes to reaching the high-water bank and the more it resists the current carrying the normal flow downstream. When that resistance and flow are almost equal, the river is said to be at equiflow."

"Must make it damn near impossible to have any kind of reliable port, around here."

"It's difficult," Bannor called from where he was performing what, to Caine's eyes, was rope-wizardry around the natural stanchion they'd selected. "A boat floating level with the high-water bank could be stranded on the low-water bank twenty meters below just two hours later."

"So that's why we couldn't start crossing right away. We had to wait for the time when the water going downstream and the water that's been forced upstream are canceling each other out."

"Actually, that's still about two hours away, Craig. We need to have our lines ready before the equiflow starts or we'll never get everyone across."

"Got it, sir." Girten turned to the onlookers: most of the senior h'achgai and trogs. About half of them nodded back; the rest seemed uncomfortable or, in a few cases, bored. But even they blinked in surprise and interest when Miles came marching out from the cluster of Crewe members who'd been prepping and checking his gear.

In addition to a Dornaani vacc suit, he had coiled lines carefully hung in containers fashioned from sections of the Dornaani 'chutes. Their smart fabric was bound together by the even more magical Dornaani tape, which could only be undone by "unzipping" the molecular bonds with the spatulalike device hanging from his utility belt. In addition to hand lights, a telescoping gaff, a grapple gun and Dornaani multitools, the life-support unit on his back had two of the Dornaani "pony tanks" mounted on either side.

Looking more otherworldly than he had for any spacewalk, he strode toward Riordan, stopped, and snapped a salute. "Ready to heroically save everyone here, sir!"

Caine couldn't help laughing as he met the salute. "Get on with it, Chief. And in advance, Bravo Zulu."

"Damn it, sir! Don't jinx me!"

Riordan casually let his answering salute fall. "I thought you weren't superstitious."

"And you believe me? A known liar? Sheesh." O'Garran smiled and dropped his hand. "Hey, Colonel?"

"Chief?"

"You done messing up—I mean, messing around—with that anchor knot?"

"Just about. You impatient and want to help?"

"What, sir? Me, sir? I'm just a SEAL. Don't know squat 'bout tyin' no knots, sir!"

"Can you just go and be a frogman, Chief?"

"Hey, that's why they pay me the big bucks!" he replied, swaggering past Rulaine but sparing a moment to look over his shoulder. He nodded approvingly at the tensionless knot the colonel was completing for the anchor line: the first one they'd require for the crossing. O'Garran gave a similar once-over to the simpler fastening of his own shore-attachment line: five linked space tethers secured around a further rock and with Eku manning the already tested hardwire comms. But since some of the Dornaani tethers had been degraded by the CME, Miles, like Caine, would be restricted to Morse code rather than voice communications.

As O'Garran resumed his approach to the water's edge, Bey's constant companion, Zaatkhur, stared as Solsohn first fixed a bag of pebbles on one side of the SEAL's belt, then a bag of small rocks on the other. "I know little of swimming," the wounded kajh muttered, "but do you mean to do it carrying *rocks*?"

The little SEAL grinned. "I'm not swimming; I'm walking. But I've gotta get to the bottom to do that." He patted one of the bags. "These will help me do it."

Bey frowned. "Then why not simply use one large rock?"

"Now that, Miss Archer-Trog, is a very good question. Because until I'm down there, I won't know how much weight I need to shed in order to maintain neutral buoyancy." Bey stared at the words. "Umm...so I don't sink lower or float up, but stay right where I want to."

Bey's frown did not fade, but she was also nodding now. So was Ta'rel. The rest of the locals wore expressions of resigned perplexity or continuing boredom.

Craig leaned toward Riordan and whispered, "But I thought the suit works like a...a BCV?"

"BCD," Caine corrected gently. "Buoyancy Control Device. It does, but only to an extent. The chief wants the mass as a backup in case the suit's system isn't sufficient or it fails. And to control his ascent, he needs to be able to shed it in small increments."

"Because otherwise he might get, uh, nitric-...nitro-...the bends?"

Riordan nodded. "Time for you to lend a hand with the tether line, Sergeant."

"But sir, I'm your guard, too. I can't—"

"Sergeant," Riordan said, facing him directly, "I gave you an order. Besides"—he gestured behind at Arashk and two of his group—"I have all the protection I need."

The h'achga stood a little straighter and nodded respectfully toward Girten, who saluted Caine. "Yes, sir."

Craig got to the line just as Miles flung a saucy wave at the gathered company and began wading down into the water. The bank was so steep that three steps in, the water was up to his

waist. Three more, and his head disappeared beneath the indo-
lent current.

Miles O'Garran had done his share of river dives, but never
one like this. After reaching the low-water point of the submerged
bank, the angle of its slope did not decrease but, contrary to his
prior riverine experience, dove even more sharply. Five meters
further down, he could no longer walk at all; it resembled the
step-off of a tidal shelf. Resigned, he signaled the shore team to
stand ready to give him a lot more slack . . . and took the plunge.

The HUD's light intensification was more helpful than the
thermal imaging for a few dozen meters, but after that, neither
one was particularly useful, in part because there was very little to
see. But as he passed the one-hundred-fifty-meter mark, O'Garran
realized why the flow slowed at this point: the depth and width
of the channel retained so much water that it became an inertial
impediment to rapid changes in either direction.

At one hundred and eighty meters, the suit's crude sonar setting pinged: he was approaching the bottom. Time to risk using
the hand light. Miles had decided against it for the descent, just in
case the locals were wrong about the lack of animals in the river.
The helmet lights were better, of course, but running them would
be the equivalent of attaching a "free meal here" sign to his head.

Happily, the light did not reveal a set of dinosaur jaws widening to greet him. It only showed the bottom rising up . . . but also,
sloping away again. The chief touched down carefully, discovered
that the surface was more solid than he'd expected. It was more
like stepping on fine clay, than sediment. He walked downward,
as if descending into a dell or a small valley.

Fifty meters further on, the slope became increasingly less
acute until, finally, he was on the surprisingly level bottom. About
time. He started forward, sending the signal that he was about
to begin walking across the river bed.

Ten steps into that underwater stroll, his lights picked something out of the darkness. A strange, still shape. He watched for
the faintest sign of movement, checked the HUD for body heat:
nothing. He took five more steps—and stopped. He only realized
his jaw had dropped open when he voiced his reaction to what
lay before him:

"Holy shit."

# Chapter Forty

Riordan glanced at Pandora Veriden, who'd been pacing for the past half hour, the length and speed of her strides constantly increasing. "This is taking too long. O'Garran is in trouble. We have to—"

"It's longer than we thought," Caine interrupted, "but his last check-in was on time, and his biosigns are good."

"He slowed down for a long time, though!"

Riordan glanced toward Bannor, who was in charge of the dive-support team. The Green Beret shook his head and shrugged. "Yes, but he's always been moving and the tether keeps playing out just fine."

"But his air—?"

Bannor called up. "Biosigns show no unexpected exertion, which means he won't even have tapped the pony tanks, yet." The Green Beret looked away as Ayana sent a hand signal. "He's beginning his ascent."

"*Gracias a Dios!* Never thought I'd be glad to see that little *pendejo* again!"

Riordan smiled. "Well, you'll have enough time to get back to the point where you're just annoyed at him."

"What? Why?"

"Because even though he's in a pressure suit, he's not going to come shooting up like a cork. There could be problems or dangers here that don't exist back home."

"Like what?"

Duncan called up to her. "That's the hell of the unknown: not knowing anything about it!"

She responded with an ancient and unmistakable gesture and stalked off.

Although fairly certain that nothing had gone wrong, Riordan still exhaled a suppressed sigh of relief when Chief O'Garran trudged up the opposite bank, trailing both the tether and the crossing line behind him. After hauling in enough slack so that he could move easily, he spared a few seconds to respond to Eku's various Morse code inquiries about what had detained him. His reply was markedly terse: "Later."

After setting up a security perimeter—four Dornaani stun grenades remote-controlled from the HUD screen that scanned for approaching objects—O'Garran secured a knot like Bannor's to one of the rocks. Then he set about reeling in both the tether and the extremely fine Dornaani cable: almost four hundred meters worth of each. It was not a swift process.

Once the line was above water, Bannor secured the loose end of a secured composite line—three linked one-hundred-fifty-meter Dornaani cables—to a grapple and, after several seconds of assessing the muzzle's elevation, launched it across the river toward Miles.

At least that was the intent: it fell short. Bannor and his team towed the grapple back to the west bank where he and Duncan reran the ballistics, tweaked the elevation again, increased the charge, and fired a second time. The grapple and line went arcing well past O'Garran. After securing the line's midpoint to another rock, the chief used his own grapple gun to send the remaining slack curving across the river, back toward the west bank.

In minutes, Bannor's team had fashioned the four-hundred-fifty-meter line into an endless loop that spanned the river with about twenty meters to spare on either bank, even accounting for midspan sag. Hauling on the loop to cycle it, the first items they towed over the river were the loose ends of four more lines. According to the crossing team, it would take every single one of those Dornaani cables to provide the necessary support and redundancy to get everyone and all the goods safely across.

Riordan glanced back at the team leader: Ayana, whose long

years overseeing cargo transfers and port-to-hold lading made her the natural choice for the job. "Officer Tagawa, if you please."

In fact, the actual technique they used was a collaborative mix between her experience with moving objects and Bannor's training for complex river crossings. The only awkwardness was personal: both were trying so hard not to notice the other or seem otherwise infatuated that their interactions were stiff, even obstructive.

Still, they finished their joint tasks within half an hour. By then, everyone was briefed—again—on the manner of crossing and had their gear double-checked; anything that shook loose into the river was gone for good. Including them. When Ayana had asked the locals how many knew how to swim, only Yidreg and Bey raised their hands. Hesitantly. And in the case of the grat'r, Yaargraukh had already explained that he would need to manage the being himself; whether modern or primordial, the physiology of Hkh'Rkh made water an unnatural, and very dangerous, medium for them.

When Bannor and Ayana had joined him, Riordan nodded toward Bey and the h'achgai leaders to gather around with their groups. He adopted the severe, unblinking gaze that seemed to bring them to silence more quickly than anything else. "Pay close attention. It is the last time you shall hear these instructions.

"We shall soon cross the river. I shall go first with Ulchakh, so that you shall know that the method is sound and that you shall be safe.

"We are using something called the 'buddy system.' Nine of my team's 'Leaders' have fully sealed suits. They shall be your 'buddies,' and will ensure that you get to the other bank safely. When these suits are sealed, we cannot drown. Also, we have done this before." *Well,* most *of us.*

"The other eighteen of you are passengers. Each of you will travel across with one of those buddies. In addition to being attached to them, you will be attached to one of these inflated suits as you cross." Riordan held up one of the two Terran duty suits; it was so inflated that it looked like the body of an over-stuffed scarecrow. "If you hold on to it, you will float.

"Your buddy will be heavier than you. This is because they can carry more cargo safely, but also because, if an unexpected current sweeps across you, it is they who will roll down toward"—*or into*—"the water. Remember: neither you nor your buddy need to do anything except stay attached to the towline. The shore groups will be pulling you across.

"Each buddy must make two round trips in order to carry all eighteen passengers across. After they are done, Colonel Rulaine will return here. He will unfasten all the lines, clamp himself to them, and be towed back through the water to the eastern bank." He let his gaze travel across the faces, noticed several that were terrified: mostly trogs. "Any questions?"

Arashk glanced at Yaargraukh. "But what of the grat'r lord and his follower? They have no such gear as you . . . and, with respect, it is well known that their kind drowns very easily."

"They will take their turn, although toward the end. You are correct that Leader Yaargraukh does not have a full suit, but we have provided additional gear that shall help him."

All the locals' eyes had opened very wide. Arashk's question was almost a whisper. "Do you mean to say that . . . that Leader Yaargraukh can *swim*?

"He can."

Arashk threw a fist in the air. "Surely, he is a great lord!"

As loud acclamations answered Arashk's bold assertion, Riordan leaned toward Yaargraukh. "Have you been in the water since Turkh'saar?"

The Hkh'Rkh's eyes rotated slowly toward Bannor, who had to stifle a laugh. "Once. During the Epsilon Indi campaign."

"And has it become easier?"

"I would say I am simply more accustomed to it."

Dora leaned over. "Enough to help your mascot across the river, Grendel?"

"The grat'r is not my 'mascot,' Ms. Veriden, any more than the 'trogs' are *your* mascots."

She swallowed as she met his stare. "So touchy! Still . . . point taken."

Ulchakh stepped forward. "Friend Caine, when should we begin?" His voice and eyes were firm, but Riordan noticed a slight trembling in his upper legs.

Caine smiled as reassuringly as he could. "Let us begin now."

Bannor and Craig—whose old paratrooper training made him well suited for final harnessing and checks—settled Caine into the makeshift rappel seat and then c-clamped him to the double anchor line that was slightly upstream of the towline. As Rulaine leaned over to check the clips, he murmured too low for anyone else to hear. "If something goes sideways, hang on to the anchor line. It's got no weight on it and we can keep it more taut than an endless tow loop."

"That's my safety line," Caine replied, mouth suddenly dry. "Got it."

"Get a little more air in your suit as soon as we shut the visor. Keep your hands on the towline to keep you and Ulchakh steady, but *don't* tow yourself. Like you told the locals, that's the shore teams' jobs." He smiled. "This is too easy. Particularly compared to deorbiting on the back of a foam shield."

Riordan smiled. There was no gainsaying that.

Bannor helped Craig do much the same for Ulchakh. He had a Dornaani strap lashed around his waist like a belt: whatever else happened, that was certainly *not* going to break. He, too, was clamped to both the tow and the anchor lines, but the cable by which he was attached to them was almost half a meter shorter than Riordan's: that way, the h'achga was certain to stay above, rather than roll beneath, him.

Craig stepped back, patted the top of Ulchakh's helmet—who flinched, startled. "Uh, that means 'good to go'!"

Ulchakh nodded dubiously and licked his almost nonexistent lips.

"Ready?" Bannor asked.

"Let's get going," Riordan answered.

The movement was gentle as they moved beyond the bank and over the water. As they continued and their weight moved more to the center of the towline, they dipped from about three meters above the water to slightly less than one.

"How are you doing?" Riordan called up at Ulchakh through the visor.

"If I do not soil myself, I shall brag of this to all my clan. And I shall do so until they wish me dead so that they need no longer endure the tale." At the midpoint, when Riordan felt spray hit his back from a few colliding swells, the h'achga asked, "How do you fashion such tools, so light and small yet so strong? I had thought your weapons and magic helmets the greatest of your artifacts. But now that I am being held to a tiny line that bears us both, and by another from which I alone dangle, I see the subtler miracles of your arts. I would know more of this, Friend Caine."

"And one day, I hope I may explain. But for now, do not look down. It will be easier if you do not."

Ulchakh made a choking sound. "You are right. We are more than halfway to the eastern shore. But Friend Caine?"

"Yes?"

"Next time, I hope we shall be able to take the ferry."

Riordan laughed but also had a nagging doubt that Khorkrag would ever become a safer town for them.

In fact, he suspected it was going to become much, much worse.

As Miles helped Ulchakh out of his crossing rig while checking for signs of wear or loose connections and knots, Riordan stepped beyond his own straps and rappel seat to inspect the duty suit's pressurization. It was still good: not bubbling at any seams.

Miles took it out of his hands with a grin. "Back it goes," he almost chirped. Connecting it to the return line, he tugged the main. The shore crew finished attaching the next buddy-passenger pair—Newton and Arashk—and then started towing again. The duty suit went back toward the river, sealed sleeves flailing as if raging against its departure.

Riordan followed him. "Chief, why were you down so—?"

"Commodore," he muttered back in abysmal German. "Not now. Besides, I gotta get hooked up and towed back for buddy-duty. See you on the other side."

Hanging onto the lines that he'd freed from their moorings on the west shore, Bannor got his feet under him and moved up the eastern bank, both walking and being reeled in. He staggered a little bit as he came over the rocky lip and released the lines. "Been a long day," he explained.

Indeed it had. Although they'd had barely enough pulleys to keep things moving smoothly, it wasn't as if they had the leverage of a block and tackle. Every person who could wear the Dornaani or Terran gloves had worked themselves to near exhaustion on the narrow, hard-to-grasp towlines. There were also just enough minor malfunctions—wet lines snagging on each other, loops slipping out of the tiny pulleys, retightening the towline as successive loads loosened it—to ensure that no one got any rest.

Even now, as Riordan stood panting as he looked down at the river, the current was beginning to pick up; equiflow was coming to an end. And they still needed to grab a fast meal, finish respooling the lines, packing the other gear, and then find a defensible campsite.

Caine scanned the weary bodies. One of the h'achgai and two of the trogs looked a bit less exhausted. They'd been the next in line to return to the towline crew, which meant they'd been the ones who'd been off it the longest. And, fortunately, Riordan could count on one of those two trogs: Bey.

She saw his glance and before he could even gesture, trotted over. "Yes, Leader Caine?"

"Bey, go among the h'achgai. See if any are familiar with the east bank this far above Khorkrag. We need to find a safe place to make camp. If they have no suggestions, go inland and look for high ground. Take one of your kajh and Hresh with you. If you encounter any creatures, do not fight but flee back here. And before you go, alert Leader Bannor; he will have someone keep watch over you with our helmets."

She nodded and ran off; her legs were not exactly long, but her bounds were so forceful that they made up in power what they lacked in reach.

A mutter at his shoulder: "Hsst, Commodore?" It was O'Garran. "A word?"

"Just one?"

"You're killing me, here, sir. How about you stroll with me while I gather in my stun grenade pickets?"

"Fine with me." When they were far enough beyond the tight defensive ring of the exhausted formation, Riordan asked, "I don't suppose this is about what caused you to be at the bottom of the river so long?"

O'Garran nodded, glancing around.

"And what would that be?"

"Traffic jam, sir."

"Traffic jam?"

O'Garran was about to reply, when they heard someone approaching behind them. He hastily bent over and deactivated the first of the Dornaani grenades.

Bey loped past with Zaatkhur and one of the young kajhs in tow. Clearly the h'achgai weren't that familiar with this part of the river, after all. As he watched, she pointed ahead and led them down into a dry wadi that paralleled the river just beyond the high-water lip. In a moment, the three bobbing heads dropped beneath its rim, heading north.

Riordan sighed. "So: you were held up by *traffic*?"

"Well, sir, isn't that what they call it when a street is jammed with vehicles?"

Riordan frowned, then stopped in mid-stride. "There's a city on the riverbed?"

Retrieving yet another grenade, O'Garran answered without looking up. "A big one, sir. My guess? This whole area was a low-lying river valley of some kind, judging from the topography down there."

"And the buildings? And cars?"

O'Garran straightened up, storing the last of the grenades, before looking at Caine directly. "It's like an . . . an underwater junkyard, Commodore. Cars, trains, parts of bridges: you could find a lot of places just like it if you went to the backward countries on Earth. But that wasn't the creepy part."

"There's more?"

Miles nodded and looked up again slowly. "Sir, that's only the *upper* city. I think there was another one beneath it, maybe at the bottom of a lake or river that went through it. And that one is—" The chief closed his eyes. "All the stuff in the upper city is rusted, sagging, rotting away. But the lower one? Metal frames still intact, vehicles—I couldn't tell what kind—poking up through the silt. And almost nothing rusted, sir. Couldn't be sure until I got close, but even before I shone a light on it . . . Well, it just didn't have that mossy silhouette that old junk gets from being underwater."

Riordan tried to rein in the raging speculation Miles' report had spawned. "So, you were delayed because you were exploring this site, Chief?"

He shrugged one shoulder. "Not so much that as navigating it, sir. I didn't go down deep into the lower ruins. Just enough to see the difference between them and the upper ones. Most of my time was spent laying out my lines carefully. I had to be sure that when it came time to reel in both the tether and the anchor line that they wouldn't snag on something."

Riordan nodded. "Make a complete report at the next Fireside Chat. We can't be sure if—"

O'Garran's head turned away slightly. Riordan heard the sound a moment later.

Something was coming back down the wadi.

O'Garran shook his head when Riordan started forward, gestured back toward the group, and began closing his helmet.

"Leaders," Bey's voice called from around the nearest corner of the wadi, "there is a problem."

Riordan gestured that O'Garran should complete closing his helmet and send a warning, then answered, "Bey? Why don't you step out where I can see you?"

"I shall." She did.

A tall, powerful man stepped out with her. He was wearing what looked like steel chain mail, had a very long sword in one hand, and what appeared to be a crude flintlock pistol in the other. It was snugged against Bey's right temple.

Before Riordan could react, two other dim figures, cloaked and shadowy, rose further up the wadi, just enough to reveal that they were hunched over ready crossbows.

Both aimed at Caine and O'Garran.

"Well," Riordan sighed, "this is awkward."

INTERLUDE FOUR

# A Course for Survival

*The Dornaani Collective*
*April–May 2125*

# Interlude Four

Alnduul surveyed *Olsloov*'s bridge crew. The new members he'd picked up since leaving the near-disastrous board of inquiry on Glamqoozht had all settled in quite acceptably. Hardly a surprise: they were all seasoned and disgruntled Custodians, or younglings whose aspirations to become such had been frustrated by the increasingly intrusive Senior Assembly.

The Dornaani's command circlet sent a tone that manifested inside his ear: Richard Downing was nearing the bridge. *Amongst the most punctual of humans, as well as perceptive.* The more time spent with him, the more it was obvious why Nolan Corcoran had recruited him as his most trusted adjutant.

The bridge's main iris valve opened; Alnduul stood, gesturing that the human should join him. "It is good that you came with such alacrity, Mr. Downing. I wished to share this information with you first, that you may consider how best to convey it to your personnel."

The tall, lean human nodded slowly. "Very well."

Alnduul led him to the astrographic hologram showing their general region of space. He reached a finger up to touch a small scarlet speck. "Today's shift has brought us into the system you designate Groombridge 1618. As this is a system that is patrolled by the Collective, *Olsloov* has received communication updates from the local network. Within that data, we discovered that the beacon I entrusted to Caine Riordan has in fact been activated here." He touched a tiny stellar dot the color of blood. "This red dwarf star is the one you label as L 1815-5 A. We call it Ygzhush, or 'Depot.'"

Downing scanned the slowly rotating spray of stars. "Getting there will require quite a long set of transits." He glanced sideways at Alnduul. "Unless we use a deep-space shift."

"This is correct."

"So we could be there in eighteen days? Less?"

"We could and we shall. But we will no longer discover Caine Riordan at that location."

"What? Why?"

"Because he deployed the beacon four and a half months ago."

"Is there any indication why he activated the beacon?"

"No, but the data string from the ship he was on is most disturbing."

The human's distressingly flexible face formed into what their species called a frown. "Is the ship unsafe?"

"Not structurally. But among the registry and origination codes embedded in its transponder data string, I found an entry I recognize. It could signify that the ship is hazardous. To Caine and his companions, specifically."

"What do you mean?"

"Each ship's code includes a unique alphanumeric reference string that indicates all travel and transactions it has undertaken. In this case, the authorization and comm codes of the agent who oversaw the ship's release, reactivation, readying, and conveyed its provisional title to Hsontlosh matches those of the loji who arranged for Third Arbiter Glayaazh's new navigator. Just before her vessel was lost."

Downing's frown deepened. "You suspect a link? A conspiracy of some kind?"

"I cannot be certain, but I would be foolish to ignore such a strange coincidence."

"So this Hsontlosh is a probable conspirator?"

"Possibly, but there is no way to know if anyone on the ship itself is an actual source of danger. Rather, the craft itself may be marked for elimination, or has had a latent failure programmed into its shift software. It is just such a failure that led to the mis-shift that killed Glayaazh, according to the preliminary research.

"However, Caine Riordan and his companions are now threatened by an additional, more tangible peril: the region of space into which they now travel."

"Is system L 1815-5 A dangerous?"

"It is quite safe, but what lies beyond is an entirely different matter. They have almost certainly ventured into the Border Worlds, which are only nominal members of the Collective. We do occasionally patrol them, though."

"Patrol for what?"

"For loji felons. And Ktor incursions."

Downing's brow rose precipitously.

Alnduul waved at the holosphere. "That is why the facility we label Depot was placed in L 1815-5 A." He extended a long finger into the dance of stars, touching the one in question. "That is the system where this thin, twisting chain of worlds from the Sphere comes into contact with the Collective. If a Ktoran advance is detected along that corridor, the ships at Depot can be manned and sent to intercept. That was, at least, its purpose."

"That doesn't explain Caine's entry into these Border Worlds. Might he be a captive?"

"I doubt it. There is no indication that the beacon was deployed in haste or under adverse conditions. I think this theory is far more likely: the Border Worlds hold clues to Elena Corcoran's location. She might even have been relocated there, where the black market and lojis have far greater sway."

Downing shook his head. "Something's missing. If there's some conspiracy underlying all this, what is the motivation? What does anyone stand to gain by keeping Caine from reaching Elena?"

"I believe that may be entirely irrelevant to them. Rather, if conspirators are involved, I suspect they are using her to lure Caine Riordan into an area where he can be approached, captured, or eliminated without any trace." He saw that Downing still did not understand. "Caine Riordan's actions have made him the epicenter of the Lost Soldiers crisis. When he proved uncooperative, the Arbiters who fear Earth's potential for rash action may have coalesced into a conspiracy to independently 'resolve' that controversy.

"Logically, they would start by gaining the upper hand in the Senior Assembly and the Collective's other high offices. From that position, they could anonymously aid the political and megacorporate entities within the CTR which mean to destroy the Lost Soldiers and also eliminate Caine, their most knowledgeable and vocal advocate."

Downing looked skeptical. "That's a rather tortuous chain of connections and hypotheses."

"Not when they are considered in the context of what has occurred since Caine Riordan left Glamqoozht. Glayaazh, my dear friend and Caine's best and most influential advocate, was killed, the timing of which also prevented her from supporting me when I appeared before the board of inquiry. The crisis that prevented the attendance of my ally Elder Custodian Vruthvur seems to have been fabricated. Glayaazh's death also left the Custodial seat on the Senior Assembly vacant. It is now occupied by the most isolationist of my colleagues, who was formerly the Custodians' Senior Auditor. That post is now in the hands of Menrelm: a bitter careerist who blames his failure on Earth's actions and, by association, me and the rest of the interventionist elements of the Custodians."

Downing was nodding now. "That does sound like the maneuvering that precedes a coup, bloodless or otherwise."

"I believe it is. Which makes our mission that much more urgent."

"Because we are running out of time?"

"No. Because in attempting to rescue Elena Corcoran and Caine Riordan, I suspect that we are also seizing the last opportunity to rescue the Collective itself."


Alnduul rose from the couch in which he'd experienced the shift out of Groombridge 1618. "Status?" he asked the bridge crew.

"Nominal," reported Ssaodralth, the pilot. "Commencing pre-acceleration toward next shift."

Alnduul let his fingers tumble in the slow sequence of casual acknowledgement, turned as the entry dilated. Trevor Corcoran strode through it, raising his foot high to clear the segments of the iris valve as it was still opening.

Even before Alnduul gestured for the human to join him next to the stellar holosphere, Corcoran's movements—gait, hands, facial—were characteristic of extreme impatience. They were also quite reminiscent of his father's.

"We'd save a lot of time if we just shifted from a standing

start again," he complained, arms crossing as he glared at the stars turning slowly in the plot before him.

"At first," Alnduul agreed, "but if we do so too frequently, we will disable the drive long before we reach our destination."

"Wherever the hell *that* is," Trevor grumbled, looking into the holographic litter of small, distant stars. His expression had become equal parts frustration and worry.

Alnduul looked up at the tall human. "Trevor Corcoran, I understand your desire to make all possible speed. Your family has suffered many losses, and Caine Riordan is now part of it."

"Well, sort of. Although it's pretty clear that if fate had allowed him and Elena to be in the same place at the same time for even a few days, he'd be my brother-in-law now."

"Still, he is the father of your nephew, Connor. And with Elena unlocated and your father's passing"—Alnduul respectfully allowed his inner lids to close slowly and remain so—"your family is not only scattered but much reduced."

Corcoran glanced down at Alnduul. "The way you say that... it's as if such feelings are, well, alien to you. Don't Dornaani have families?"

"Not such as you think of them." Alnduul waved away the stellar regional view; an almost empty system plot replaced it. Being in deep space, there were only a few rogue planetoids in the display, *Olsloov's* unobstructed pre-acceleration path marked by a shining silver line. "We Dornaani experience powerful pairing affinities, as do humans. However, they do not arise from the same relationships or instincts as yours." He waved his hand listlessly. "I felt a measure of this for your father... which is remarkable, since I never met him."

The human's eyes had become shiny with emotion. "Well, that stands to reason: my dad was a pretty remarkable man."

"This I know well." *So very, very well.* Alnduul gestured to one of the acceleration couches; its smart surfaces changed into a shape suitable for a human. "Please, secure yourself. We shall begin pre-acceleration within the minute."

Trevor Corcoran helped Colonel Zhigarev into a seat in what passed for *Olsloov's* ready room: it was like sitting inside a slightly flattened, oversized egg with furniture that could change shape and lighting that came from, well, nowhere that he could see.

"*Spaseebo*," Zhigarev said through a grunt. The Russian colonel had become quite adept getting around with only one full leg, but in barely enough centripetal force to keep their magnetic soles close to the deck, sustained movement became difficult for him.

To either side of his chair, the other two of the Three Colonels—Steve Rodermund and Pat Paulsen—made sure he got himself secured properly.

Trevor took a seat next to Commander Carlisle Hansell, who nodded curtly. From the salty old submariner, that was a markedly warm welcome. "Anyone know why Alnduul asked us to meet him here, rather than the bridge?"

"Probably too many of us," answered Richard Downing as he glide-stepped into the compartment.

Trevor raised an eyebrow that his "uncle" pointedly failed to notice. "*Too many of us,*" my ass. Probably because of their twenty-second-century familiarity with starship operations, he and Richard had noticed subtle differences prior to and after the shift to L 1815-5 A, or "Depot." There had been an early call to secure for shift; decompression of all non-habitation spaces; and now the request for the polyglot leadership of the renegade Terrans to report to the ready room. But they still hadn't deployed the hab pods for rotation at a half-gee equivalent. Nope, something was definitely different about this shift.

The iris valve cycled and Alnduul "skipped" gracefully toward and into the saddle-shaped seat just beyond the threshold. Once settled, he nodded at each human. "Our shift was nominal. We are at the heliopause of the main system and have begun receiving data from the Depot's control station. It includes all traffic updates from the entire Collective that have been received and recorded here within the last six months.

"I am gratified to report that there are several recent reports of Caine Riordan's control fob signaling its presence in other star systems. In no case was it activated as an alarm. More troublesome, the systems are quite scattered. They do not constitute a path which we may follow."

Paulsen held up a hand. "Wait: I thought we had the number for this Hsontlosh's ship. Why can't we just follow that?"

Alnduul folded his fingers carefully. "We did find one traffic record for his ship: its departure for BD +52 857. From here, that system is well within its maximum shift range. However, it has been over four months and it was never recorded as arriving there."

Trevor felt his shoulders tighten. "Do you mean it's been destroyed?" *Christ, no: not Caine, too!*

But Alnduul's hands expanded into a pair of bony-fingered starbursts. "No, that has not occurred. Or at least not during that shift. The ship has been reported in several further systems within those four months, but there is no clear shift-track which links them into a logical progression."

Downing's voice was grim and focused. "So: the loji bastard has gone off the grid. How would he do that?"

"We are not certain, but preliminary study of administrative records generated within this system suggest that an unspecified party requested and was granted access to a restricted code that can, among other things, temporarily suspend the function of a special operation ship's entangled transponder locator."

"Special operations?" Rodermund muttered. "Doesn't sound like we're talking about a civilian ship, anymore."

"In fact, we are not. Apparently, Hsontlosh either discovered, or knew in advance, that the ship he acquired had originally been a courier. A very old model, of course, and largely considered obsolete. But its transponder is the kind typically reserved for military and covert vessels. And, inasmuch as Depot is the Collective's primary repository and processing site for such craft, this was a logical place for him to secure the code that allows him to travel with the ship's transponder silent, except when he initiates communications or conducts transactions."

"So many parts of his trail are 'cut out' from the record," Downing summarized grimly.

"Yes, but that is only half the difficulty. All those systems which do show him either arriving or departing within the last four months are precisely where we conjectured he was heading: into the Border Worlds and beyond." He refolded his hands. "There are comparatively few 'keyholes' for supraluminal communication in the Border Worlds. There are almost none known in the systems beyond them. So it is entirely possible that he is charting courses to and from systems from which there will be no report of his presence. Not through the Collective's data network, at least."

Paulsen sighed. "So, how do we follow him?"

"Given the nature of the worlds in the region to which he has traveled, local cooperation is even more unlikely than timely relays of port traffic or resource exchanges. And given what he may be trying to learn or achieve as he travels, his contacts may actively conceal them."

"However, if the fob's alert mode is activated by Caine Riordan, it will attempt to put that signal into the transmission logs of any nearby Dornaani ships. Embedded in the initial exchange of comm protocols—what I believe you call the 'handshake'—it will be secretly passed along the Collective's network any place that the first, or any other 'seeded,' ship arrives. The fob will also detect the presence of a keyhole and send the alert through that medium as well. So we may eventually compile a fairly complete record of Hsontlosh's shifts, but they are likely to be reported out of sequence, with alerts from more distant systems arriving before nearer ones."

Trevor didn't bother trying to hide his frown. "Just to be clear: this signaling device you gave to Caine: you're saying it's about the size of a pocket fob?"

"Yes."

"Okay, so leaving aside a fistful of other technical challenges, how does something that small have enough energy to transmit information over such great distances, to say nothing of how it learns there's a keyhole in the system?"

Alnduul's eyelids nictated slowly. "We shall speak of that another time."

Trevor leaned over to press him on the technology of the fob—just as *Olsloov*'s emergency klaxon began hoot-moaning.

The report from the bridge came to Alnduul's control circlet, but he put it on the room's speakers: "—new location report of Hsontlosh's ship, Mentor! But it was sent directly to us! We cannot—!"

"Immediate shift to deep space," Alnduul interrupted firmly. "Send emergency shift warning to all decks. Contingency destination three." To those in the room, he added, "Secure yourselves. Now."

Before any of the humans had a chance to ask what was occurring and why it was so dire, *Olsloov* shuddered and—

—Trevor's consciousness returned with a jolt so abrupt and fierce that, despite his teeth locked together in a rictus, he nearly vomited. Zhigarev and Rodermund did, in fact, succumb to the savage vertigo and shock.

"Worst damn shift I've ever felt," Trevor gritted out, "and I've been on a few really lousy ones. What the hell happened, Alnduul?"

The Dornaani looked unusually pale and mottled. "This was one of the reasons I directed our navigator to re-express near the edge of Depot's heliopause. As we were talking, a new location report arrived through Depot's keyhole. Normally, as I was explaining, it would simply be passed along as a hidden message in the normal comms stream. But since our transponder was detected in-system, it was sent directly to us. Via tightbeam."

"Bloody hell," Downing muttered. "So not only does the Collective know we're here, but the lascom that sent us the message was also a finger pointed straight at us."

"Correct. But that is not all. Until now, we have transited Collective systems safely. Eventually, of course, the transponder records would show that we had traversed many systems without reporting our presence, and the Assembly and Arbiters from my board of inquiry would have realized that I had long since departed Terran space, and logically, had no intention of conveying the Lost Soldiers to them. But now, the data network automatically detailed a tightbeam array to send us the embedded report. And *that* will come under immediate review."

Trevor frowned. "And I'm sure the standing shift you just engaged without any warning will have shown up on Depot's sensors like a nuclear-weapon discharge."

"That is true, but the damage was already done. We had to shift before their computers could attempt to interrogate *Olsloov*'s."

"Where did the new report come from?" Downing asked, wiping his mouth.

"The system you call Psi Tauri."

"Hang on," Downing muttered, dribbled bile forgotten, "that's not even in the Border Worlds, anymore. That's—"

"We call them the cordoned worlds. They are in a buffer zone."

"Buffer between what and what?" Commander Hansell snapped.

"The Collective and the Ktoran Sphere. Or, more precisely, the worlds the Ktor do not claim but are known to travel through."

"That sounds about as serious as serious can get," Paulsen drawled sardonically.

"I wish that was correct, Colonel," Alnduul said. Most of his color had yet to return. "But it is far more serious than you know. Or even I, until I saw the identifier string on Hsontlosh's ship."

Trevor leaned forward. "What's on it?"

"What we often put on craft that must work as couriers: navigational enablers for deep-space shift."

"Wait," Corcoran snapped, "are you saying it has that technology aboard?"

Downing's eyes opened wide. "If the Ktor get their hands on that—"

"They could bypass Depot and reach the heart of the Collective in four or five shifts," Alnduul confirmed, "most of which would never be detected because they would begin and end in deep space."

"Same with Earth." Even in his own ears, Trevor's voice sounded hollow. "The balance of power—and terror—would shift overnight."

"Yes," Downing followed, already more thoughtful, "but does Hsontlosh know the ship has deep-space shift capability? Has he used it?"

"He has not had a reason to, but no, we have no evidence that he has," Alnduul agreed. "Unfortunately, because the record of his shifts is fragmentary, we have no way of knowing if that is because he has disabled his transponder or shifted to deep space. Which, of course, would mean he is not leaving any record of his passage even as he shortens the time it takes to reach Ktor space. Because now, we must assume that to be his destination. Indeed, we dare not assume otherwise."

"Not given what's at stake," Paulsen sighed. Of all the Colonels, he seemed to be the one who'd followed the strategic implications most clearly. "How fast can we get after him?"

"We already have," Alnduul said in a low, almost dangerous tone. "The destination you heard me give—Contingency Three— puts us on the most direct course for the cordoned worlds. There is, however, a further complication."

Trevor leaned his forehead into his broad hand. "Damn it. The failing coldcells."

Alnduul's fingers drooped slightly: regret and resignation. "Have you had the opportunity to study the report from Thlunroolt and Dr. Franklin?"

Hansell and Paulsen nodded. The remaining two Colonels looked sheepish. Trevor and Downing had nearly memorized the data within the same hour Alnduul had shared it.

"To summarize," the Dornaani continued, "our researchers have learned enough to detect early signs of impending failures, even before the warning light illuminates. However, this does not tell us much about when they might fail, merely that there are worrisome weaknesses in the system. Not knowing the durability of the components or the redundancy design features, all we know is that they may fail in a day or a decade.

"However, any units which *do* show warning lights will almost certainly malfunction within four to six months."

Downing was the first to venture into the cold waters of lifeboat ethics. "What's the latest tally on cryocells showing warning lights?"

"Just over half of the Ktor units."

"Good God," breathed Rodermund.

"I suspect God is going to have very little to do with what comes next," Hansell muttered bitterly.

"What do you mean?"

"I mean that we are now faced with the grimmest choice a commander ever has to make. Who lives and who dies."

"Lisle, I hate to admit you're right, particularly this time, but I can't see any choice but to give it over to chance. Given *Olsloov*'s limited capacity and stores, what else can we do? Sure, we can try to save those with busted cells, but after we reach the ship's limit, what do we do? Just let them die, or save them and accelerate the speed at which we burn through food and life support?"

Paulsen shook his head. "That's a hell of a debate, right there."

"We are not going to have *that* debate," Downing said firmly. "There is another option. I don't know if it will be better or worse, but at least it gives those who survive reanimation a chance to live."

Zhigarev leaned forward. "And what would that be, Downing?"

Trevor, understanding his uncle's intent, glanced at Alnduul. "We need to find a world where they could survive. Someplace along our route."

Alnduul folded his hands. "Understand that beyond the border worlds, the Collective has very little information about individual stellar systems. Also, bear this in mind: the path of Hsontlosh's ship, fragmentary though it is, points directly toward what the Ktor call the Scatters."

"The Scatters?" Paulsen echoed.

Downing frowned. "According to the debrief of First Officer Ayana Tagawa, late of the *Arbitrage*, the Scatters are an area where outcast Ktor are exiled."

Hansell folded his arms, scowling. "How many exiles have been sent there?"

"Enough so that they have laws and traditions governing when and how it is done," Downing replied with a similar scowl. "When one of their, er, 'Houses' is about to lose a war against its peers, but could still inflict catastrophic devastation upon them, that House is given the option to leave the Ktoran Sphere voluntarily.

"It does not get to carry away its wealth, and wherever it chooses to settle in the Sphere's outback—the Scatters—it has to follow two prohibitions: it may not create supraluminal drives or long-range radios. If it does, the Ktor will reputedly detect that colony and send bloodthirsty volunteers to lay waste to it. No questions asked, no quarter given, no innocents spared."

Trevor shook his head against the horror Downing had laid out. "Alnduul, you said you had very little information about the worlds in the Scatters. Just *how* little?"

Alnduul's fingers swayed listlessly downward. "The only surveys of that region have been automated, and the last was performed five millennia ago, long after the Elders passed. Not all probes returned. Beyond two hundred and fifty light-years from the center of the Collective, the data is quite incomplete and what exists is almost as uncertain.

"Most survey entries only indicate the star's characteristics, the orbitals of confirmed planets, and whether any are located in what you call the habitable zone. Unfortunately, our surveys were not focused on habitability, but rather on detecting potentially dangerous remains of the war that consumed the Elders and their adversaries."

"And who were these adversaries?" Rodermund asked.

"That too is a question which must be answered at another time," Alnduul muttered as he scrolled through the data in question. "No probes were sent beyond four hundred and fifty light-years, so we have no true knowledge of those expanses. However, the stellar compendium still includes data for some systems found in records that predate the Collective. There is one relatively proximal to our probable route. It is just beyond the two-hundred-fifty-light-year limit and still has an intact data string. However, it lacks any code that establishes its origins and provenance."

"And what does that signify?" Downing asked.

"It could mean that the entire data string is corrupt. Or that it predates the passing of the Elders."

"Which would make it how old?" Paulsen asked quietly.

"*Very* old," Alnduul answered.

Trevor was analyzing the roster of the Lost Soldiers whose cryocells were deemed closest to failure. "Which system is it?"

"You call it 55 Tauri," replied Alnduul. "It is a binary system and has a notation indicating it has *at least* one planet that, to use your term, has a shirt-sleeve environment. But I must point out that any subsequent sightings of Hsontlosh's ship could put it much further off our path."

"A bridge we shall cross when we come to it," Downing said.

Trevor nodded in agreement. "But there's at least one bridge that we should probably cross now."

"Which is?"

"Well, even if it's a shirt-sleeve world, whoever gets dropped there may discover they're trying to survive in a very unfriendly environment. That means—God help me—any group left there has to include as many rank and file infantry as you can find."

"Yeah, that's pretty much the situation we were in on Turkh'saar," Paulsen agreed with a nod. "And I think the Ktor made the same decision, because they left a lot of technical specialists in their cryocells. And they passed that rule along to the Nazis." He tried to smile. "A lot of the guys still in personal freezers are like the techs who maintained my Phantom: they never had reason to go into the jungle or lived more than a jog away from the PX. Hell, I'm not sure any of them did any field training at all, after basic."

Zhigarev cleared his throat. "Which is why, as on Turkh'saar, there must also be enough field grade officers."

Rodermund leaned forward. "He's right. Otherwise, they could start feeling like they're being left behind because they're 'only' grunts and shavetails. Gonna need one who's clearly senior, though. And has the right qualifications." He glanced at Trevor. "See any likely candidates on that list of imminent cell failures?"

"Yeah, I think I found one," Trevor said with a sigh. "And damn, he's gonna think it's some kind of sick joke. I know I would."

"What do you mean?"

"Well, he's the right guy for the job: major in an airborne infantry unit, has all the right scores and all the right assignments. He's also part of the last group the Ktor hijacked, so he's at the upper end of the technological familiarity spectrum. And, yes, he's in a cryocell that's already in final failure mode. The only real question is if it will work long enough for us to get him to 55 Tauri."

"What's his name?" Paulsen asked with a sad smile on his face.

"That's where the lousy joke comes in. His last name is Murphy." Trevor shook his head. "Can you believe it?"

All the Americans shook their heads. The others in the room exchanged uncertain glances.

It was Zhigarev who observed, "This name that you say is funny; it does not make you laugh. Or even smile. Why?"

Trevor sighed. "There's a joke about bad luck. It's called Murphy's Law. It means that no matter what you do, you're going to get the worst possible outcome."

Zhigarev nodded. "*Da*, so this is funny like Russian joke: bitter and dark." He shook his head in genuine sympathy. "I am sorry for this Major Murphy. But I would not want to travel with him. Ever."

"Why?" Alnduul wondered innocently.

"Because his name predicts his fate." The Russian shrugged. "And it will probably continue doing so."

# PART FIVE

# Ambushes and Rumors of Ambushes

*"Bactradgaria"*
*May 2125*

# Chapter Forty-One

Caine resisted the urge to roll his eyes when Pandora Veriden glanced over at the tall swordsman and complained, "You could have just told us your name, you know?"

"And how was I to know the name 'Tirolane' would mean anything to you? Did I have suspicions that you might prove to be friends rather than a rogue band of harrows and scythes? Certainly. Your means of crossing the river required discipline they lack. And the concern you have for your followers marks you as their antithesis. But that did not lead me to conclude that you must therefore be friends of the Legate in general, Tasvar in particular, or that my name had ever come up in your conversations."

He shrugged. "Besides, first meetings are not the time for further conjectures. I had to determine if my initial impressions were correct. And I perceived that I would be able to speak directly with your leadership, inasmuch as your whakt lieutenant did not resist taking us to you."

Dora turned dead eyes back toward Bey, who was following the lead group.

Bey raised her chin and her voice. "Leader Veriden, please ask before you judge." Though phrased as a request, Bey's tone was much closer to an ultimatum. "Given what I have seen your armor suits withstand, I did not deem the weapons of Tirolane or his men dangerous to Leaders Caine and Miles." She shrugged.

435

"Besides, I not only saw the newcomers' rad in the distance, but the pennant it was flying: the Legate's crossed sword and pen."

As Miles chuckled, Dora grew annoyed: whether at him or Bey was unclear. "Then why didn't you just say that when you returned with them?"

Bey shook her head sharply. "Although I deemed it unlikely, it could have been enemies traveling under a false flag. And since our Leaders were far more likely to kill than be killed, and would surely summon aid with their magic helmets, I chose not to reveal that I had seen and recognized the newcomers' symbol. Doing so might have emboldened them, if they were impostors."

Tirolane, who was as tall as Newton but as smooth and heavily muscled as a tiger, tilted his head and nodded appreciatively. "I see why you have her as your lieutenant, Lord Riordan."

Caine waved a hand at the honorific. "We are not your, or anyone's, lords."

"No? That is unusual. Welcome, but unusual. So you have heard my name. Did Tasvar share any details in connection with it?"

"Only that you are from Zrik Whir, that you and the caravan with which you traveled were ambushed upon the wastes, and that you left in search of two friends who were taken captive. But we would never have guessed that you and he were the same person."

"Indeed? Why not?"

"Because we have been told that the natives of Zrik Whir are very dark of skin. And you are, well, anything but."

"Pinker than most of *us*," Dora groused.

Tirolane nodded. "Your confusion is understandable. Zrik Whir is the land of my birth, but it is not the land of my ancestors."

Riordan and the others waited for him to say more, but he did not do so. "You mentioned seeing us cross the river."

"I did not see the entire process, but what little I witnessed convinced me you were extremely methodical in your use of tools. Very advanced tools. I heard what sounded like boomings—"

"Boomings are gunfire?" Craig ventured.

"That is an interesting word for it; more precise. At any rate, yes, but it was both deeper and less sharp. That is when I saw what appeared to be a heavy quarrel completing its arc just above the high-water bank, trailing a shiny cord in its wake.

"I led these scouts toward what we hoped would be an upstream vantage point. However, most of your position was concealed by low rises, and we dared not ascend for fear of being spotted. What we did see was a very complicated crossing using impossibly fine yet strong tackle and an uncommonly disciplined formation."

He glanced sideways. "Harrows and scythes are dangerous, but they resist taking orders and are impatient when giving them. You were neither. Your pickets were attentive and their placement was very thoughtful."

"Yet they could still have been troops of a hostile liege," Arashk pointed out.

Tirolane nodded. "Whether or not their liege was hostile, my expectations were as you suggest, Friend Arashk: that they were part of an x'qao's human stable, or the forces of a liege that is not sworn to one of their *M'qrugth* suzerains."

The Dornaani translator, which Riordan had activated before he'd known the newcomers were friends, gave him the English equivalent in his earbud: "M'qrugth. Meaning: Great or Evolved Lord of killspawn. Accuracy: low to average."

"However," Tirolane continued, "I have never seen any liege with so many humans uniformly equipped in what are clearly pristine ancient artifacts. And whereas humans are rarely more than twenty percent of any force they send forth, you are almost twice that portion." He shook his head; his very straight and very black bangs swayed slightly. "I have seen much in my travels, but never anything like you. I should be interested to see the land, or secret holding, that gave rise to a group such as yours. It must be quite different."

*You have no idea.* But Riordan only nodded and said, "That might be possible, one day. In the meantime, though, it is our intent to visit Zrik Whir."

Tirolane's expression slipped back into a stern mask. "Zrik Whir does not welcome visitors."

Caine could almost hear the slight bow in Ayana's reply. "We hope it will make an exception for us."

"Why should it?"

"We have a piece of knowledge that will be of keen interest to its leaders."

"Having never been there, you seem strangely certain of this. Why do you think Zrik Whir would be so interested in this knowledge?"

Duncan's offhand comment could not have been better if

Riordan had scripted it. "Well, Tasvar was interested. He not only found it very useful, but very, *very* valuable."

"Oh? And why did *he* find it so 'valuable'?"

Riordan shrugged. "You are familiar with the ancient guns that fire without stopping? The ones that do not require so much as a touch to reload them and will fire until they have no more shells?"

Tirolane frowned. "I know the guns you mean, but unless found along with the ancient shells they fired, they no longer work as you say. Now, the gunner must ready each new shell by hand."

"The knowledge we have would allow those weapons to function as they did originally."

Tirolane's eyes widened slightly before he mastered his reaction. "Perhaps you may be welcome in Zrik Whir after all." His voice became a low murmur. "Speak this to no one you meet here. Such knowledge is dangerous to those who have it. Particularly when they or their companions walk on paths that may lead to capture by x'qai. We shall talk at length when time permits, but not in haste."

"Agreed." As Riordan nodded, they topped a small rise. Several hundred meters ahead and further inland, a cluster of large rocks protruded from the sand and dust. Nestled in among them were figures and two large, boxy silhouettes.

"Are those . . . rads?" Peter asked eagerly. When asked what his favorite role had been when on IRIS operations, he'd always admitted, "wheelman" with a slow, sly smile. Then he usually had to explain what that almost-forgotten term meant.

"They are indeed rads," Tirolane replied, waving one of his men forward to report their return and that their visitors were friendly.

One of the two rads was the kind they'd glimpsed in Tasvar's fortress. Little more than stripped chassis with engines and seats, they had honeycomb rather than inflatable tires and rear sections that could carry cargo or personnel.

However, the other rad looked like a cross between a vehicle framework and a skeleton. It was made of varnished bone and had a tall drum rising up from its center. Pointing at the stubby vertical column, Riordan asked, "A windrad?"

Tirolane glanced sideways. "You have not seen one before?"

"I have only heard of them."

"How the hell does that thing even go?" Dora muttered.

Newton cleared his throat. "It is equipped with a rotary sail."

"You mean, like a windmill?" Girten sounded more amazed than confused.

"Er, yes, if you built one sideways. Imagine an anemometer, but with tall vanes instead of cups to capture the wind."

"I don't see any vanes," Dora complained.

Tirolane nodded. "That is because their housing—the short column at its center—has its sealed part facing us. When in operation, the guide vent, which is approximately a third of its circumference, is turned toward the wind to capture it. That not only focuses the force of the breeze but protects the rotary mechanism."

"Must be a bitch when the wind don't blow," O'Garran laughed.

Tirolane nodded. "They are not vehicles that one can ride into an attack. However, they still carry light loads, consume no fuel, and move much more swiftly than dustkine when the wind is sufficient. But when the air is still, it is as you say: they must be concealed until the breeze returns."

"Just like most logistical vehicles," Bannor sighed. "Really vulnerable but really useful...so long as the conditions are right."

"You sound like a soldier, rather than a warrior," Tirolane observed, glancing at him.

"At last!" Duncan exclaimed, "Someone else who understands the difference!"

Tirolane could not suppress a small smile. "There are more of us than you might think. Come: let us meet Sharat. He is one of Tasvar's most reliable field commanders. He will wish to hear your story."


The meeting of the two groups very nearly resulted in a friendly-fire event.

At one hundred fifty meters range, Ta'rel cried out in surprised joy and ran toward Sharat's encampment. The defenders raised their weapons instantly...but reluctantly lowered them when a vastly different mangle—Riordan saw tufted ears and large lambent eyes—came running out toward him. The humans that had bent meaningfully over guns and the humanoids hunched behind crossbows didn't relent in their intent so much as they no longer had a clear line of fire to Ta'rel.

In the end, though, it was probably a fine way for the two

groups to meet: bonding over shared frustrations with the impulsively sociable mangles. Even as the first tentative handshakes were exchanged, the soldiers on both sides were shaking their heads over how the otherwise clever species never quite got the hang of what they should and shouldn't do when traveling with war parties.

Sharat himself hung back with a lieutenant and two large humanoids until Tirolane approached and apparently conveyed some particularly reassuring details about the much larger party of visitors. Smiling, Tasvar's field commander came out in place of Tirolane and extended an open hand toward Caine.

The formal introductions took a few minutes, since Caine's group was comprised of a dozen equally important human "leaders" in addition to four locals of similar stature. In that time, Riordan and Bannor were able to get a head count of Sharat's unit. The four other humans bore no insignia, but their equipment was familiar: a match for what they'd seen on Tasvar's retainers. The same was largely true regarding the four whakt, half of whom seemed to be capable archers as well as axemen. Of the three h'achgai, Arashk recognized two: their reunion was loud enough that leaders from both groups had to bend warning glances in that direction.

Of the other three significantly larger beings, both were of species that none of the Crewe had encountered personally. Two were prakhbrai: outsized trogs with markedly smaller skulls but longer limbs. But the third was completely unknown to them. Slow and oddly thick, the being's genetic roots might have arisen from trogs, but it was almost well over two meters tall, with profoundly stunted toes and fingers. Two of the whakt seemed to be its handlers, and their exchanges with it were always in simple words, often repeated several times.

Caine gestured toward the closest of the trogs—Bey's old friend Zaatkhur—who approached warily. "That large being," Riordan muttered, "what is it?"

Zaatkhur, a paragon of subtlety, turned directly toward the creature, stared at it intently, turned back to Caine and shrugged. "I have not seen its like. Well, not exactly."

As Riordan braced himself to extract the additional information Zaatkhur clearly had but hadn't thought to include, Bannor forged ahead: "What does it remind you of?"

Zaatkhur shuddered. "Cave things." He made a warding sign.

"The Great Tunnels; that's what gives rise to 'em what looks like that. I've only seen one or two with those stumpy toes and fingers. Though now, I'm one to talk, hey?" He held up his half-fingered hand, apparently oblivious to the fact that the humans to whom he was speaking had led the attack which had cost him the other half. "They're not natural, though. At least, that's what folk say."

Riordan nodded at him. "Your information is helpful, Zaat-khur. You are no longer needed."

The maimed kajh nodded and moved away as quickly as he could.

"Great Tunnels?" Bannor repeated with interest.

Riordan sighed. "Yep. Another thread that we should pull on. But some other time: Sharat is gesturing toward the space between the rads."

Bannor nodded. "A community mixer, or council of war?"

"I think we both know which is more likely, but let's go find out."

When Tirolane had returned, Sharat looked around the leaders of the two groups. "All our guests are very welcome, and well met, indeed."

Riordan knew a leading tone when he heard one. "It sounds like we have arrived at an opportune moment."

"You have indeed. Tirolane was not at liberty to disclose this until he conferred with me, but we are here to settle a few accounts with a mutual foe."

"We do not have any foes."

"Hmmm . . . you made a very fast, hard march north from Forkus through some awful weather. I take it you had a compelling reason to do so. And, from what I intuit, it probably involved upsetting one or more x'qai vassals, maybe even lieges."

The Crewe's eyes rotated from Sharat's face to Caine's. "Actually," he answered easily, "that may be correct, but we deemed it unwise to remain there to investigate that possibility." The smiles and isolated chuckles that answered his reply were genuine. *So far, so good.* "But if we have angered one or more x'qao lords, it would be unwise to make a habit out of it; we wouldn't want to annoy those not already angry at us!" Riordan's tone of honest jocularity apparently had the desired effect; his reply landed not as a veiled rebuttal to Sharat, but an ironic commiseration over the challenges of being a human leader on Bactradgaria.

Sharat's grin was easy. "All excellent points, all of which invite further details from me. As you may know, there are x'qai leaders in Forkus which are part of a larger faction which we independent humans dub 'the Rustics.' They're seeking strategies to diminish and eventually eliminate their human stables, particularly the troops."

Riordan nodded, suppressed the anger and revulsion that rose up every time a local referred to human "stables" as if such thralldom was simply an accepted fact of existence. Which it had apparently been for a very long time.

"For a variety of reasons, Tasvar believes that your activity in Forkus frustrated the plans of one of those Rustic x'qai. Others, who translate their faction as 'the Erudite' are often willing to pay handsomely for the most promising 'breed stock'"—Sharat's eyes narrowed—"from these discontinued stables. It's one of their caravans that we've come here to intercept. Tasvar wishes to send a message to a liege in Forkus—Suradán, sworn to the Erudite suzerain Zhyombphal—that the Legate will not let his maneuvering there go unaddressed. But we also have word that this caravan may have a source of information regarding the location of Tirolane's missing friends."

Riordan nodded. "Those are both compelling reasons for considering a cooperative action, but I have one concern."

Sharat nodded. "Share it, that we may set it aside."

"You had no idea who we were when we arrived, correct?"

"Correct."

"Then how could you know what Tasvar does or doesn't believe in regard to 'our activity' in Forkus?"

# Chapter Forty-Two

As he uttered the words which told Sharat he'd been caught in a lie, Riordan's hand was poised near his visor. He'd almost decided upon the few orders he hoped to give before the Crewe had to fight its way out of an impossibly sophisticated and cunning trap.

But Sharat just raised an eyebrow. "How do I know what Tasvar thinks? Mindspeaking. How else?"

*Of course: how else?*

Sharat hadn't finished. "I would not have invited you into sword range without his assurance that you are who you say you are."

*Which makes* this *claim of mindspeaking different. But... no: you have to leave that for later.* Riordan nodded. "It takes some getting used to, the extent to which you rely on mindspeaking in these regions."

Sharat's other eyebrow rose briefly, but then they both descended and he shrugged. "No matter. With luck, we will have time enough to learn more of each other. But for now, be assured, this caravan is not a mere target of opportunity. It was Tirolane himself who brought word of its additional significance when he arrived. In addition to warning Suradán from ceasing his provocations in Forkus, it is a statement that the Legate will not tolerate his cooperation with the Rustics by offering coin for their humans."

"Yet," Newton said carefully, "they remain slaves, either way."

"Yes," Sharat agreed, "but the Legate's deeper objective is to hamper or intercept efforts to diminish human stables. There is no way to stop it, but the longer it takes, the more we might be able to free. If Tirolane's information is correct, the approaching Zhyombphal caravan is delivering two such humans to Suradán. That would be enough reason to attack, but Tirolane tells us that, in addition to having word of his friends, they possess knowledge that would enable us to free even more. Many more."

Riordan glanced around the Crewe. He read the answer in their eyes, but was unwilling to presume their unanimous approval.

Not even when Sharat added, "And of course, your share of what we gain would be commensurate with your numbers: two thirds of our combined force."

Actually, that was slightly more than their share. And he no longer needed to assume he was reading the Crewe's eyes correctly; they were wide with eagerness.

But Sharat was rattled when Riordan didn't leap at his first offer. "We cannot offer more than a three-quarter share. That will barely repay the costs and risks of mounting this operation, regardless of how strategically important it is."

"Then let us leave that offer as it is, for now," Riordan said with a slow nod. "I shall discuss it, and our participation in this noble mission, with my fellow leaders. We take such decisions in council. It is our way."

Sharat nodded at Riordan's need to consult his companions. "That is very fair. But before you decide, you should be aware of what we have heard on our journey here. After we met with our mangle healer, Ne'sar, to guide us through the Orokrosir, I wished to learn of any hunters or raiders that might already be in that wadi country. So I sent our three h'achgai hunters into Khorkrag to sell meat and buy arrowpoints...and to listen."

Ulchakh nodded. "We did the same. It was...not welcoming to humans."

Sharat leaned forward. "They reported that also, but heard something more worrisome. More specifically, the town's Ormalg liege was soon to announce a general bounty on humans, but had already promised it to several established groups he encouraged to comb the Orokrosir for 'a group of ten humans or slightly more' who might be moving north."

"That is much more specific," Yidreg agreed.

Sharat shrugged. "Seeing your group, I realize it could describe either one of us. You're a much larger party, but there are about ten humans. On the other hand, anyone who saw my force from a distance would likely assume that our four whakt are humans, based on their equipment and height alone. Of course, as Ormalg is a Rustic, it might have been his liege you aggravated in Forkus. Or word may have leaked that the Legate sent me north to cripple a caravan bringing human slaves to Suradán." He smiled ruefully. "Or they might be after both of us."

He rose. "I don't want to delay your decision on joining with us for the coming ambush. Our best information suggests that they're following the river along this bank and will pass near here either tomorrow or the day after. That won't leave us a lot of time to prepare."

Riordan rose as well. "Even if we do not join you, we might be able to give you a more precise estimate of their arrival." At a glance, the Crewe rose. "We will make our decision shortly. Thank you for your candor."

Since no one else at the Fireside Chat had said it, the role of devil's advocate fell to Riordan. "Does anyone have reservations about attacking a caravan that doesn't belong to a current enemy?"

Dora looked around the group as if she didn't want to be the first one to speak yet again, but she shrugged and pointed out, "Boss, given how humans are treated here, I gotta say that this seems to be our fight whether we want it or not. I know it might not be the smartest move toward getting us off this planet as quickly as possible...but *merde*! The killspawn are treating all of us like cattle! Worse!"

Duncan nodded. "I agree one hundred and ten percent, but with one exception: I think this might accelerate, rather than slow, our efforts to boost up out of this sewer."

Ayana leaned her gracefully pointed chin on her palm. "Please explain, Major."

"Look, if there is any way off Bactradgaria, we're not going to find it lying around in plain sight, in perfect condition, just waiting for us. It's likely to be buried or remote, in a place that's probably exposed to hostiles, and will need a huge amount of restoration and modification. That's about the most optimistic scenario I can foresee. Sound about right?"

The Crewe nodded, even Yaargraukh who'd learned to ape the human motion.

"Okay, so how do just *thirteen* people make that happen? How do we feed ourselves? How do we take the site? Or maybe several sites? How do we stay safe while we're busy putting our heads—and Dornaani suit computers—together to come up with a way to get to orbit?"

His eyes became both crafty and hopeful. "But if we help out on this ambush, we become not just a valuable 'information ally' for the Legate, but one that can make a difference on a battlefield, too. And while we do it, we'll be showing the same thing to all our logical allies: the h'achgai, the mangled, and the trogs. Particularly the, uh, crogs, as Miles calls them."

"The what?"

"Crogs," O'Garran supplied, "the ones that are mostly *Cro-Magnon*? Like Bey?"

Duncan nodded. "If they see us dominate a battlefield, word will get around: the kind of word, and reputation, that we can parlay into formal alliances with the groups which *can* provide the support we need to find and build a way back to orbit."

Ayana nodded. "It is rare and valuable when fate so clearly makes the right thing to do also the wise thing to do." She smiled toward Bannor, who, too surprised to hide his infatuation, grinned broadly, even as she was turning toward Riordan. "I think fate is offering us such a moment."

Riordan checked the other faces in the circle: there wasn't even a hint of reluctance. "Very well, he said. "Then we just have two matters to settle before telling Sharat. First, we have to make sure the h'achgai and Ta'rel agree. And secondly"—Caine drew in a deep breath—"we need to invite the trogs to take an oath of fealty.

"Right now, they're POWs. To become part of our force, we have to take their oaths—and be prepared to live up to our responsibilities as the holders of them." He rose, gestured to the others. "We *all* have to be the holders of their oaths."

Yaargraukh nodded. "Yes. If a single holder were to die, they might rightly deem the oath undone." He stood. "If any have reservations, speak them now. Once they are your vassals, you become responsible for them in many ways."

Eku raised his hand. "I do not know the Collective's policy on such a matter. I cannot, in good conscience, participate."

Riordan nodded. "I understand and agree. You remain here,

Eku." He aimed a smile up at his Hkh'Rkh friend before turning it toward the rest of the Crewe. "Let's get this done."

"This all seems a bit *too* easy, don't you think?" Bannor wondered aloud as he joined Caine on the walk back from the trogs' sleeping piles.

Ta'rel, on Riordan's other side, leaned forward to answer. "Since meeting Peter and Craig, I have noted that, even more than your technology, it is your caution that makes you so different. You take decisions very slowly and carefully"—his smile revealed large, almost fused teeth—"even more than my people do. And we are famous for being cautious and prudent. Annoyingly so, to others."

"That's one of the reasons I asked you to join us when we went to take the trogs' oaths. We want your counsel particularly now that we've committed our forces to the attack."

Ta'rel seemed surprised. "Why not seek the wisdom of Ulchakh? Or Bey? They are far more knowledgeable in the ways of war."

Bannor's answer was the one that had been on Caine's lips. "We have plenty of war knowledge. But you and your people seem to have more information on this, eh, region than most. And you think further ahead."

"So," Ta'rel said lightly, "you wish my counsel because I make decisions in the same boring ways that you do?"

Riordan chuckled. "I am quite happy to be bored now if it helps me live to complain about it later."

Ta'rel's laugh was very human. "Yes, that describes my people, too. But I think we come to this from different experiences."

Ayana, who drew close to Bannor—closer than usual—asked, "What difference do you perceive, Ta'rel?"

He shrugged as they found their seats in the same circle they'd left half an hour earlier. "My people consider decisions in great detail long before they are needed because that is the best way to avoid having to make them in terrible haste later on." Despite his less flexible face, he appeared melancholy. "We fight only when we must, for it is in the chaos of battle that our planning avails the least. Careful decision-making is the best way to keep the greatest number of our people from harm or death.

"But your people? I think you decide carefully because that is how you *control* events and outcomes. It is evident in all your devices, both in their power and the care with which you plan their use. Whereas we of the wastes must accept that most plans will only lessen what we must suffer, you have learned that, properly applied, your tools and skills allow you to control *outcomes*. Including inflicting far more injury than you receive."

He shrugged. "It is why you feel so much fear, even at the responsibility of holding oaths of fealty. You are accustomed to having the luxury of inspecting every choice down to details that my people would never consider."

Peter sat with a smile. "So is my friend Ta'rel chiding you about our excessive caution?"

"If it is chiding, Friend Wu, it is done in admiration."

"Speaking of admiration," Craig drawled, "you seem to admire Ne'sar. Quite a bit."

Ayana may have inched away from Bannor; her cheeks darkened and her eyes lowered to focus someplace beneath the planet's core.

"I admire Ne'sar a great deal," the mangle said without any hint of embarrassment. "She is a healer and a person of great inner strength. As you may judge from her presence with Sharat. It is not many, male or female, who make such a daring First Journey."

Riordan managed not to let on that, until this moment, he had not even realized that Ne'sar was a female.

Katie's voice suggested that she sensed a cozy story lurking behind Ta'rel's warm compliments for his "friend." "So, how did you come to meet Ne'sar?"

"On my own First Journey two years ago—Peter calls it a 'walkabout'—I chose to travel alone. I was foolish. 'Qo caught my scent and chased me for days. In fleeing them, I became lost. I had not eaten in some time, and was almost out of water when I discovered hidden signs used by my people's traders. I followed them to their camp, and from there, was brought to Ebrekka, our greatest community on this continent. I was introduced to its *durus'maan* Raam'tu and in due course, his eldest daughter Ne'sar. I think it likely that she will rise to take his place, one day."

Katie's voice had the faintest undercurrent of salacious curiosity. "So, Ne'sar's connected to an important family, is she?"

Ta'rel tilted his head. "We do not measure importance as do other peoples. The durus'maan, which means 'senior worrier,' is not so much a chief as a clever person and clear thinker. He or she has no more property or rights than anyone else. But they are revered and whereas everyone's words are listened to once, the durus'maan's words are listened to thrice."

Riordan leaned forward. "We also prize wise words, which is one of the reasons we've wanted you at all the meetings tonight. Because we think you are the only person who can answer this question: if Ne'sar felt that Sharat was exaggerating the danger to us or the general attitude toward humans in Khorkrag, would she tell us?"

Ta'rel shrugged. "Yes, but more to the point, she would not have sat idly by if his representation of either had been different from her own perception of them. She would have asked to make comment, or, if she deemed it too sensitive to do in a group meeting, she would have absented herself. This is our honor code."

Miles sighed. "Makes me wonder if we need to change our destination again, as nice as Ebrekka sounds."

Ta'rel nodded... regretfully, Caine thought. "If there are trog bands already searching through the Orokrosir, it is quite possible we would encounter them before reaching Ebrekka. She knows how to reach it by special paths, but those ways are not concealed: simply distant from the most common locations of water or prey."

*Which gets to my second concern.* "So would you agree with Chief O'Garran, that perhaps we need to shift our destination back to Achgabab?"

"It is certainly worth considering," Ta'rel agreed.

Riordan felt his lips straighten: that wasn't the clear recommendation he'd been looking for. "If you now have concerns about the hazards of traveling to Ebrekka, why do you not recommend against it?"

Ta'rel shrugged. "I might yet do so, but not until we have spoken to any captives that might be taken from the caravan. Although they have come far from Fragkork, some may be privy to mindspoken instructions or information passed between the x'qao commander and his liege. That may tell us how best to avoid both the groups from Khorkrag. Also, they may know whether we have been pursued from Forkus and if so, where those forces mean to intercept us."

"No matter where one is," Newton opined darkly, "the wastes are not a good place for travelers."

"No," Miles quipped, "but they seem to be a good place to get eaten!"

Ta'rel smiled ruefully, but glanced at Caine. "Do you have other questions for me, Caine Riordan?"

"No, Ta'rel, and thank you for helping us."

The mangle stood. "Certainly. Please excuse me, now. Ne'sar asked if I might share a reunion meal with her. She is waiting."

"Of course," Caine assured Ta'rel with a smile.

When he was gone, Bannor sighed. "If you don't like the plans on Bactradgaria, just wait a minute: they'll change. Again."

"Ain't that the truth," O'Garran agreed as he looked around the group. "Where's Eku?"

Caine nodded toward their sleeping cluster. "Grabbing some kip. The crossing was hard on his arm."

Newton nodded. "Yes. The pain exhausts him."

"Convenient, too," Dora murmured. "Look: we're talking about fighting tomorrow or the day after. But if Eku's arm is still so weak, so fragile—?"

Riordan held up a hand. "He won't be on the line. As it is, we're going to need someone running comms, particularly sensor relays. So he's going to be with Sharat back near what they call the 'real rad': the one with the internal combustion engine. That's going to the combination CP and OP for the operation, as well as a fast relocation platform."

"Is that just a fancy way of saying a 'bug-out bus'?" Miles drawled.

"Or fire brigade, or mobile weapon, platform or a bunch of other things, Chief O'Garran. So no, it's not a euphemism for a hot exfil option, although that's part of the job description. And that's where we're keeping Eku. Who, oddly enough, claims to have reasonable skill with a sword." Riordan held up a hand against the disbelieving stares. "Apparently, one of his times on Earth, he had to fit in as a proper gentleman of the period. So he learned to fence with a sword called a 'hanger': a short, cutting blade."

Newton shook his head. "The Dornaani factotum's break will not withstand the impact of striking targets, let alone parrying heavier weapons."

"He means to use it in his left hand, if he must. He was trained to use it along with a main gauche for parrying. So just give him the shortsword with the longest quillons. But frankly, if he's in a position where he'd actually have to use it, we'll have a lot bigger problems to worry about than his broken arm. Duncan, do you have Eku's assessments on our suits?"

Solsohn cleared his throat. "Sir, Eku's own suit is still intact, but its processing systems are a total write-off. The first set of trogs banged him around so much that they broke relays and the data weave of the smart materials, including its reactive hardening system. It still has pressure integrity, but no control interfaces that work with a HUD. So everything would need to be adjusted or run manually.

"Now here's the part no one is going to like, including me. He's run a close diagnostic on all our suits on the march north. The good news is that all the systems are still functioning."

Peter sighed. "And the bad news?"

Duncan shrugged. "Wherever they stopped a blow from a sword or an axe, there are ruptures in the smart fabrics. He calls these 'de-meshings" and if we keep taking those kinds of hits, they're going to lose pressure integrity, sooner rather than later. And we have to be extra careful with the Terran suits because they're just not as tough."

Katie scowled. "So what're ye sayin' then, Duncan? That we're to attack this caravan in the nude?" Miles and Dora nodded vigorous support of her question.

"No, I'm saying that if we don't set some suits aside—and right now—we might not have any EVA capacity left by the time we get to orbit. And without it, we can't get aboard the damned ship."

As the Crewe was absorbing that, Riordan added, "That's only part of it. The suits, particularly the Dornaani ones, have been responsible for almost all our advantages in every combat. Think it's the hand cannon? Think again: How many hits would it have scored—and at the ranges and in the conditions it was used—without the smart interface of the HUDs? Now take a moment thinking of all the other ways they've been absolutely crucial: early warning in day or night, remote relay of visuals, sensor assessments of damn near everything. It's a very long list and you don't need me to recite it because you've used them all countless times. And you're probably alive because of one or more of them."

"Can't save our lives if we're not wearing them," Dora groused.

"Actually, they can and they will, as long as enough are

functioning. But if they're being worn on the front line, they won't. Not for long."

"So what do we do when the caravan gets here?" Miles asked.

"We do what we've done every time so far: we wear the suits and try to keep from getting hit. But after this engagement, we've got to find the best local armor we can and stay out of melee range whenever possible. And if you're one of the combat controllers, fire directors, or sensor operators—because that's who'll be wearing the Dornaani suits—then you shouldn't even be in bow range, if you can help it. Any questions?"

After a few uneasy looks made their way around the Crewe, O'Garran sighed and asked, "Sir: *mindspeaking*? Really?"

Riordan shook his head. "I can't believe it either, Chief...but—"

*—But we can't get into that: not now, not here. Because the longer we've been on this insane planet, the more it seems there must be something to it. Tasvar trusted Yasla's "mystic" approval of us. Sharat and Tirolane, who are as skeptical as any soldiers I've known, put as much faith in it as they do in their swords or guns. A brief bit of mindspeaking with someone at Tasvar's fortress and we're fully trusted. And all done in the few minutes between our arrival at camp and Sharat's overview of the local situation—*

As Riordan let those thoughts flit past, he nodded, swallowed, and croaked, "Right now, we have to follow Tasvar's advice and not dismiss the possibility of it."

Ayana answered her nod with one of her own. "It is often postulated that there remain forces which science has not discovered or does not recognize as such."

"Yet," Newton added.

Riordan waved away the debate. "We can't settle this now. And what's more important: we don't need to. What we do need is to be up and moving before first light; we can't tell how much time we'll have to plan. So set the watches and get some sleep."

# Chapter Forty-Three

Sharat removed the HUD, which was still slaved to Riordan's suit. "And this is...is a device?"

Caine nodded. "Yes."

"And it is connected to that little telescope up there? By natural, eh, waves in the air?" He pointed at the monoscope which Eku and Katie had attached to the top of a long pole made of two bone weapon hafts lashed together.

"Yes."

It was a pretty neat trick, Riordan allowed, disappointed that he hadn't thought of it himself. Together, the two strengthened hafts made a length of five meters. Held by Tirolane while standing atop the windrad's rotary sail drum added another four meters. Parking the windrad atop a low slope added another two. With the monoscope thus elevated eleven meters above the surrounding flatlands, the horizon line jumped back from a distance of five kilometers to twelve. And with the scope's magnification set to 10X, the apparent distance from the objects rising into view was only twelve hundred meters.

The objects were the dustkine of the approaching Zhyombphal caravan. The howdahs on two of their backs had come into view much earlier, cresting the horizon before any other element of the strange procession. The rough column was approximately fifty meters in width and at least four times that in length. The two ranks of dustkine were preceded and followed by what might have been porters or skirmishers, small parties of which were also visible screening the caravan's front, rear and flanks.

Sharat handed the HUD back to Riordan with ill-concealed regret. "I have never heard of, let alone seen such an artif—device. But it would be the envy of the most lavishly equipped senior harrow." He shook his head. "The possibilities are...are endless."

Riordan smiled. "Not quite, but they are plentiful. And very useful."

Sharat cocked an eyebrow. "If understatement had a patron god, I would suspect you of being a high acolyte."

Caine chuckled. "I suppose that is your way of telling me that you feel we have sufficient information to finalize our plans?"

Sharat smiled. "To worship at your patron's altar, yes, quite sufficient. And the sooner we have done so, the sooner we can make our preparations."

Using two tall shields to work as a windbreak in the lee of the "real" rad, Bannor had outlined a sand table where he'd placed objects corresponding to the different elements of the enemy formation.

Sharat was nodding approval. "This is quite accurate, but I suspect what you see as porters and skirmishers both in front of and behind the dustkine are mostly pawns and deadskins, working as porters."

Newton crossed his arms. "'Pawns': I take it that is the Deviltongue word for those whose s'rillor has not yet progressed to full mindlessness?"

Sharat had adapted to the strange gaps in the Crewe's knowledge. "Yes. The pawns require some guidance, whereas the deadskins are completely dependent upon it."

Duncan's eyes were dissecting the makeshift diorama of the caravan. "Guidance from whom? X'qai?"

"Not directly." Tirolane pointed to the three stones representing the lead rank of dustkine and then the bone in front of them: pawns and deadskins. "There will be a mix of urldi and young kajh scattered throughout this area. It is their job to keep the porters moving in the right direction and ensure that their small travois do not become snagged on obstructions. If their instructions are not followed promptly, the closest x'qao—there are always several near the center of the formation—will punish any laggards. And naturally, the advance of the dustkine means that any who fall behind will be trampled."

O'Garran was taking in the whole formation. "This column has got to be really, really slow. It makes, what? A dozen kilometers a day, max?"

"That or a little more," Sharat confirmed with a nod. "And even if it was possible for the porters to move more rapidly, it could go no faster because of the large travois attached to the dustkine. If one of those comes undone or is broken, that often causes a long delay. Caravans without deadskins or travois can move half again as swiftly, but those are comparatively expensive for traders to assemble. This one appears to have at least a third of its cargo carried by those afflicted with s'rillor. And even close to the river, the dustkine must be allowed to filter-feed in the dust for the first and last two hours of the day."

"So when do you estimate they will arrive?" Ayana was eyeing a skullcup that had been placed at the center of the formation, between the front and rear ranks of dustkine.

"No earlier than six hours after dawn tomorrow. No later than twelve. This assumes they are not delayed by attacks or mishaps."

"And what is this element at the center of the formation?" Ayana asked, pointing at the skullcup.

Tirolane folded his arms. "That and the dustkines with howdahs are the command group. It is also their reaction force, as it includes the most dangerous x'qao and other troops. It is also where the humans will be, probably in the howdahs with x'qai."

"As officers of those troops or advisors to the x'qao?"

"Both, as circumstances dictate. But they will be kept on short leashes, particularly since they could learn that they are being transferred to a Rustic stable in Forkus. The x'qao will be the only ones entrusted with that information, but even the most carefully monitored human stable receives information through other channels."

Bannor crossed his arms. "Given all the noise and dust this column generates, it seems that only the lead element would have any chance of spotting us in advance. And if they're relying on unaided eyes and ears, I doubt they'd see us before they got inside a hundred meters."

Sharat shook his head. "As fine as your monoscope is, it could not show us any *kiktzo* at that range. We must be watchful for them. They are far more likely to detect us than the caravan's advance guard."

"*Kiktzo?*" Katie repeated. "What are those?"

Sharat did look slightly surprised this time. "Insects."

Peter shook his head. "But we were told that the word for insects is merely *kik*." He looked at Arashk ... who was looking away. Whether he was embarrassed on Peter's behalf or for himself was not clear.

It was Ne'sar who kept the moment from extending into an awkward silence. "No, Peter. Kik are just regular insects. Kiktzo are those that have not only been blood bound to a x'qao, but whose senses are as the killspawn's own."

O'Garran's voice was both angry and surprised. "You mean these kiktzo are mindspeaking sights and sounds back to the damn monster they serve?"

Ne'sar simply nodded. "It is how many true x'qao control the lessers: their kiktzo detect prey and threats at great distances."

Bannor sighed and glanced at Arashk. "The insects above the x'qao that attacked right as you caught up to us: kiktzo?"

"Almost assuredly," Yidreg answered. "Apologies. This, too, we thought you knew."

Caine managed not to smile. *Of course. Because we're ignorant. When are we* not? "Then we must hide our positions so they are difficult to detect from the air. And our scent must be concealed."

"The scent is fairly simple; we cover ourselves with dust and distract them with rotting bait. But to avoid the eyes of the kiktzo"—Sharat sighed—"that is easier said than done."

"I can think of some ways," Bannor said with a sideways glance at Caine.

"Me, too," Tirolane added.

Caine nodded his gratitude before gesturing to the sand table. "How likely is it that the caravan's master might change its traveling formation before it arrives tomorrow?"

Sharat shook his head. "The organization and size of this caravan are both quite conventional. They do not change their marching order unless attacked by a large force." Sharat's smile was wolfish. "It is difficult enough to keep the 'qo and pawns following one pattern reliably. Altering it ensures total chaos."

Riordan nodded. "Good. Now, you have referred to the 'qo but I do not see them represented on the sand table."

Tirolane smiled, picked up a handful of the pebbles to be used as markers. He tossed them in a slow underhand so they scattered among the objects at the rough center of the forma- tion. "There they are," he almost laughed. "And if you wait a few minutes, not one of them will be in the same place."

Riordan smiled back. "I see. So they cannot be kept together as a unit."

Sharat nodded. "The most powerful x'qao can rarely do more than keep them near the center of the caravan. And in this case, I expect it will prove more difficult."

"Why?"

"Because even from this distance, it is obvious that the six animals are not domesticated dirtkine. They are truly *dust*kine, recently broken to their yokes. They will be restive and their scent will be feral. That will keep the 'qo in an elevated state of 'excite- ment.' Which the senior x'qao will no doubt use to control the kine."

"As threats, you mean?"

Tirolane nodded. "And if one does not respond to the threat, the 'qo will be used to make an example of it."

Pandora sounded surprised. "You mean, by letting them attack the kine?"

"I mean by letting them devour it. Which they will do quite rapidly."

"Not a great way to make a profit," Duncan muttered.

"Understand, Lord Duncan: x'qao consider profit secondary. Obedience through fear is not only their first priority; it is their most basic instinct. Even the most avaricious liege will forgive a loss if that is the price of maintaining unchallenged control and authority."

Riordan crossed his arms. "Sharat, there is one thing you have not mentioned: the speed of the x'qao. Even if they do not see us until they are quite close, they are so swift that I am uncertain we can keep them under fire long enough. We have thirteen warriors equipped with missile weapons. Most will fire fairly quickly. You have almost the same number. Yet still, if the x'qai charge to the attack, we will be lucky if each of those weapons discharge twice before the x'qai close to contact. Do you have a strategy for slowing them?"

Sharat shrugged. "Generally, they only charge to close with prey: a target they consider harmless or a negligible threat."

Miles snickered. "Well then, the time we met them, they got a hell of a rude surprise!"

Tirolane frowned. "If you encountered x'qai hunting without guidance in the wastes, they were unlikely to be very perceptive." He pointed at the sand table. "This group will not make such errors, nor will they be motivated by urgent hunger. Indeed, even if the senior x'qao ordered them to charge into battle, they would resist that order. More strongly than any other."

"Why?" Ayana asked.

Sharat seemed to struggle to find adequately tactful words. "Perhaps the x'qai you know are unlike those of Brazhgarag. But here, whether the greatest or least, the first concern of an x'qa is to survive. So they reserve their greatest speed for flight, not attack. Unless their opponent is so obviously inferior that they feel no need for that caution."

Caine nodded. Other than the kiktzo, there had been few outright surprises about their opponents. But there was one question that was too important not to ask, even though everything he'd heard suggested the likely answer. "How rigid is their command structure?"

Sharat frowned. "If I understand your question—and I am not sure I do—it is as you surely expect: the most powerful direct the lesser ones. Like descending the steps of a ziggurat, authority moves from the top to the bottom."

Riordan nodded. "And if one or more of the higher steps were to be removed? How do the lower ones react?"

Sharat nodded vigorously. "In the case of 'qo, they will do one of two things: run or chase down the most promising prey. In the case of praakht and others, it depends. If clear orders were already given, they will be followed. If not—"

*—Or if the tactical situation changes abruptly—*

"—then all the lower tiers will be uncertain and often fail to act at all. In some cases, and particularly if there are humans present to command them, they will go into a defensive crouch and await clearer or new orders."

"And for those that do, how strong is their morale?"

"It depends upon the troops. Prakhwai and h'achgai will usually do *something*. There's no telling in the case of praakht. It depends on whether there is a strong leader in each separate group. If not, they are most likely to huddle in place or withdraw."

Pushing aside the tactical possibilities of such a fragile command structure, Riordan asked, "So, Sharat, if we had not arrived, how would you have laid the ambush?"

The Legate's officer indicated the ground on which they stood: a low rise, to which the camp had been relocated. "We would have waited here and sheltered behind this blind." He gestured to the northern side, which was partially shielded by a talus of weathered basalt. "We would have driven out in the rad as they finished passing, fallen upon their rear, doing what damage we could to their porters, and if the opportunity arose, the dustkine carrying the humans. Then we would have fled: first east, to get on the far side of the small wadi that parallels our intended battleground, and then north, back along their line of approach."

He shrugged. "Our objective was to inflict enough casualties among their kine and porters that they would have had to abandon the humans and some of their goods. The observers that would have hidden here with the windrad were to summon us when they were sure that none of the caravan's forces were doubling back. Then we would have collected what the caravan abandoned and headed northeast to avoid the Orokrosir and approach Ebrekka from the south."

Ne'sar smiled. "In addition to gladly trading with the Legate's captains, my family will be glad to have me back home."

Sharat was frowning at the sand table. "I wonder if we almost have too many warriors for such a plan, now. Or perhaps we should just shoot several volleys, retire, and wait. They would achieve the same result, I think." When Riordan did not reply, he glanced at him. "Do you have a different plan?"

Caine suppressed a grin. "I do."

"How does it unfold?"

Riordan pointed at their present location on the sand table. "Starting from your hidden position here on the slope"—he moved his finger to the open ground fifty meters to the west—"you drive the, uh, real rad, down and deposit your force across the enemy's route of advance."

Riordan then indicated the line marking the wadi that ran northward along the eastern side of the sand table, paralleling the clear ground. "This is where most of my force will be hiding, including most of its marksmen. They will wait until the column has moved abreast of them before firing, using the wadi for cover as they do."

A frown started bending Sharat's thin lips. "Granted, that will be a great storm of fire, but will it be enough? You have seen the enemy's numbers: two score kajh and drivers and just as many pawns and deadskins. And you know the hardiness of the 'qo."

Riordan nodded. "Even so, I think our firepower will be sufficient, mostly because I doubt we will need to inflict as many casualties as you believe we must. With our urldi working as loaders for the crossbows and the steady fire from our own rifles, the enemy is likely to overestimate the number of missile troops that are attacking them. Also, our best marksmen will be concentrating on eliminating the enemy's leadership. And if any attackers do reach the wadi, our melee troops will be standing ready to repel them." He leaned back. "Where I am from, this is called an 'L' ambush."

Sharat shook his head. "An 'ell'? What is an ell?"

"It is a name for a letter, one which has this same shape." Riordan let his finger follow the long eastern flank of the wadi, then turned it at a right angle when it reached the position of Sharat's blocking force.

But Sharat's frown had deepened into a dark furrow of worry. "This plan is fraught with danger. If the enemy presses forward, my force will be overrun. We might escape if we run for our vehicles, but unless the wind is favorable, we will surely lose the windrad. And how will your own forces withdraw if the enemy presses a charge through to your positions in the wadi? I...I do not understand how we may retire swiftly enough, Lord Caine."

"That is because this plan is not predicated on the presumption that we must retreat. Our objective is to force the *caravan* to retreat. Or, better still, to break it."

"*Break* the caravan?" Despite his very dark complexion, Sharat had grown pale.

But Tirolane was bent over the sand table as if seeing it anew. His bright blue eyes stabbed at its elements so intently that it was easy to imagine him as a hawk, circling an anticipated hunting ground. "You have not presented everything yet, have you Lord Caine?"

*Glad you're on our side.* "You are correct, Tirolane. I have not." Riordan moved his finger to a much shorter stretch of wadi that paralleled the northern half of the battlefield on the west, or left, side. "By the time the enemy has drawn abreast of the missile troops in the wadi on the east, they will have passed this smaller one to the northwest. We shall have a special team concealed there. It will wait until the enemy is engaged with the other two elements of our force before attacking the enemy from the rear."

Caine leaned back. "And Sharat, your forces need not hold their position across the open ground here in the south. Yours is only a delaying action."

"Delaying for what?"

But Tirolane had already seen it. "Lord Caine means to make the enemy flee south, further along their line of advance. He does not want you to stand your ground; he just needs the caravan held long enough to—?" The tall, broad warrior glanced curiously at Riordan, inviting him to fill in the blank.

Caine nodded and smiled. "We'll get to that soon enough."

Tirolane's wolfish grin almost became impish. "I do see a problem, though."

"Which is?"

"Our forces are no longer in the shape of your letter 'L.'"

Bannor smiled as he traced all three sides of the box with his finger. "It's more like a 'C' ambush, now, I think."

Riordan chuckled. "Indeed it is. Now, let's get down to the details..."

# Chapter Forty-Four

The sun was striking final flickers from the river's one visible stretch as Riordan and Ta'rel walked back to camp. Once the plan had been finalized, the leaders led their respective forces to those parts of the battlefield where preparations were required. Once completed, they'd spent two more hours dusting away the footprints they'd left in the process.

Ta'rel glanced over at Caine as Bey approached from his opposite side. The mangle's eyes were larger than a human's and a rich teal. "Caine Riordan, I am grateful that you wish me to be part of the special group that will attack the rear of the caravan, but I am baffled. You surely know that I am not a warrior." He smiled meaningfully at Bey.

Riordan shrugged. "You may not be a warrior, but you have better nerve and a cooler head than most I know. But I am not asking you to fight, except in your own defense. I want you near me tomorrow because I need the counsel of someone who has lived their whole lives in these wastes, who survives by seeing dangers *before* they arise: someone who will notice what I might miss."

Bey's voice was measured, possibly... offended? "I, too, know the wastes, Leader Caine."

Caine kept his voice gentle. "As well as him?"

Bey looked away. "No. No one knows the wastes as well as mangles."

Riordan nodded. "Besides, you have an equally important, and unique, ability: to lead your people. You make up a third of our group's number. If the battle shifts quickly, they must respond quickly. That is your task tomorrow: to see that they do. And no one can do it so well."

She had turned back toward him, eyes eager. "I shall not fail you."

"I know you won't fail *us*," Riordan emphasized: other than her, the trogs had taken an oath of fealty to all the humans as a group. "We have all seen your skills and intelligence. That is why we had your people make their oaths through *you*: so that they would know beyond doubt that you are their leader and our voice to them."

"Caine Riordan," Ta'rel murmured, gesturing toward Sharat's camp circle, "I promised Ne'sar I would join her for this supper."

*Hmmm ... maybe Katie's right about those two.* "Be assured that, if it proves more convenient, Ne'sar is always welcome in our camp circle, too."

He nodded gratitude. "That is very kind, but we shall not be in any camp as we take our meal. We have sworn that, if either of us does not see the sunset tomorrow, the other will bear our last thoughts to our families. We mean to share those thoughts as we eat."

Riordan's stomach no longer felt empty so much as hollow. "I shall make sure you have the last watch. Take all the time you need."

Ta'rel's chin dipped in thanks and he started toward Sharat's circle.

Caine looked after him a moment, then asked Bey, "Do praakht have a similar tradition?"

Bey shook her head. "But I wish we did." Her tone shifted from melancholy to practical. "Leader Caine, I came to tell you something. It will take but a moment of your time."

He smiled. "It can take as many as it needs."

She smiled back but then pushed it aside to remain serious. "I have spoken with my people and it is decided: we do not wish to be known as praakht. We wish to be called trogs."

Riordan almost blinked. "I am ... surprised." *"Trogs"? Really?*

"And," Bey continued, "I wish to be known as a ... a ... What is Leader Miles' word for a whakt?"

"A crog. But, Bey, you do know these are not, eh, respectful nicknames, right?"

"We are aware. But they were not made out of hate. Leader Miles makes jests of everything, but he is a good and fair leader."

*Although people who don't know him better might suspect him of being an old-school bigot.*

Bey wasn't done. "More importantly, though, trog is *not* what the x'qai call us."

"I assumed praakht was your name for yourselves." *Stupid me. Again.*

She shook her head. "Before the world became as it is, legends tell that we were a people of many nations and languages. So we had many names for ourselves. It is the x'qai who called us praakht. And no doubt, that shall continue to be our name in the world for many years to come. Maybe forever. But with you, we choose to be called trogs and crogs in the hope that those with us, and those who hear of us, will know that by choosing those names, we stand against the x'qai."

Riordan glanced sideways at her. "And the two young kajh feel the same way?"

Bey shrugged. "They were not as enthusiastic as Zaatkhur and the urldi, but they have no love for x'qai. They agreed happily, although I suspect that was because they are pleased that the oath of fealty you asked of them was so, well, gentle."

"'Gentle'?"

"You allowed any trog who did not wish to swear the oath to depart before the battle. That is very unusual. Most captives who have not taken or been offered an oath of fealty remain in constant danger. Or they are kept as the lowest of thralls."

She frowned. "My only fear is that some will not understand that such gentleness is not a sign of weakness." She banished the frown. "But any who think that? Well, in the long run, I do not think they will deserve to be called trogs. And who knows? Once they taste victory beneath your standard, many may begin to feel differently." Bey paused. "You *do* have a standard, Leader Caine . . . do you not?"

"Not one that we may show just yet." She'd probably seen the CTR symbol a few times soon after the fight in Forkus. The Crewe had covered the insignia on the standard-issue suits, but checking for damage and conducting maintenance had probably afforded her sharp eyes a glimpse or three.

Bey simply nodded. "It shall be a fine day when we may have it over us."

"I agree, Bey. Now, if there's nothing else, we should finish the duties of the day and then get as much sleep as possible."

"Leader Caine, do *you* sleep well on the eve of battle?"

"No," he replied with a small grin, "if I get any sleep at all."

"Another way in which we are alike," she nodded, returning his smile. "I shall go to my fur and hope for easy dreams."

Bey was the last to approach her sleeping pile, the taste of the unusually flavorful kinestew still on her lips. Prepared by one of Sharat's humans, it confirmed the rumors that the Legate's food always tasted better, in large part because his troops always had ample salt.

After readying herself to sleep, she stood before her snoring fur-mate with her hands upon her hips. As ever, Zaatkhur was sprawled across half the heap, heavy arms wide. With a roll of her eyes, she wrapped her fur tight around her and pushed against his body until, with a few twists and turns, it had shifted to make room for her. "Move over, you old kine." She sniffed. "Faugh! Did you not wash *once* while we followed the river?"

The voice that answered was thick with sleep. "I saw no need."

"Nor smelled one either, I suppose."

"I am my musk and it is me."

"And *I* have to live with it."

"Have to?" Zaatkhur was more alert, now. "I suspect you could have chosen many different fur-mates, over the years."

"But I didn't. Out of pity for your odorous self," she lied. *Who else could I have trusted as I slept among so many who hated me, dearest friend?* Which, of course, he knew perfectly well. So, if Zaatkhur stank, it was also the smell of safety... and comfort.

But despite that, sleep would not come. Bey turned; Zaatkhur's bulk was barely softened by the two furs—his and hers—between them. The change in position did not help, so she rolled back to the first.

After half a dozen such futile attempts, Zaatkhur released a sigh and spoke in the dialect she had taught him: that of the Free Tribes. "It is not the coming battle that troubles you." His mutter was almost inaudible beneath the sonorous snores of the others in the sleeping pile.

"And are you a mindwatcher, now?"

"No. I am the unfortunate creature that must sleep next to you every night. What is bothering you, Little Bey?"

"Nothing." Even she could hear the sulky undertone in her reply.

"Ah," Zaatkhur sighed, "the human. You like him."

"Who do you mean?"

"Hmmm. Now *that* is a bad sign."

"What is?"

"That you deny knowing who I am plainly speaking about: Leader Caine."

"Of course, I like him. He leads well, fairly, and honorably." Zaatkhur's only reply was one of his cackling whisper-giggles: the only sound more annoying than his snoring. "Is that so funny?"

"No, but *you* are. Now you are pretending that you like him only as a leader." Another smothered chortle.

"You are an ignorant old boor."

"And you like him because he is weak."

"What?"

"Quiet: you will wake the others. Or do you wish to share your emotions with the whole camp?"

Bey bit her lip. "He is not weak. He is certainly not mighty like the one called Tirolane, but hardly weak. In fact—"

Zaatkhur released a long-suffering sigh. "I do not mean his *body* is weak: well, not entirely. I mean that when he is outside his magic armor, he is as smooth and soft as a sprat. He is a typical burntskin: little hair, thin skin. Not at all rounded and sturdy like us."

"You mean, 'like *you*.'"

Zaatkhur ignored her jibe. "His callouses hardly deserve the name...except his feet, I allow. But those tear so easily! Halfway to Khorkrag and almost all of the humans were trying to hide the blood in their boots." He paused. "It is no great surprise, Little Bey; we are often attracted to those in whom we see parts of ourself."

"What nonsense!"

"Is it? He is as you were when the leader dragged you into Forkus behind your mother's, er, tunic."

Bey bit her lip again, this time at the kindness of Zaatkhur's reworking of the truth. Her mother had been brought through the streets and put before the gang naked. That was not a great shame in itself, but it was a message to Bey as well as all who saw: her mother may have come from a Free Tribe, but no longer had a right to pride in her origins.

As if he truly was a mindwatcher, Zaatkhur explained, "You were so very young, but you remembered that day. Which is why you've always looked after the weak, the wounded, the females with difficult whelping."

"That has been a stratagem," she retorted, almost convincing herself. "Those who survived were always devoted to me... and they were so numerous that if a leader mistreated me, they courted lasting resentment."

"Oh, I saw that, but it was not the reason you *did* it; the protection you gained was merely a happy product of your kindness.

"Now, I will allow that this burntskin is different. He has much power. You offer him good counsel." He stopped. "But are you truly attracted to him, or is he just the newest weakling you wish to save? I grant you, this one has made you a leader, and as his power and trust grow, he will make you a greater leader still.

"But Little Bey: you are a female and chose the way of a kajh. And no matter how great you become, no matter how many swear fealty to you, a kajh is all you can ever be to him. For in that one way, even these strange humans are no different than the most common praakht gang leader."

She sighed. "As if I could ever forget the consequences of my choice. So you need not remind me. And especially not in such blunt and harsh words. I shall sleep now."

But before she did, she spent many long minutes staring up at the stars and the great moon Garthyawan, wondering what heavenly mechanism spun fates such as hers.

And why it wove patterns of such intricate irony.

# Chapter Forty-Five

Riordan lifted his visor. The others with him in the small wadi—Ta'rel, Solsohn, O'Garran, and Yaargraukh—were waiting expectantly. "All observers have confirmed what the pole-cam shows: the last of the 'qo stragglers are at least twenty meters past us and continuing south."

"Did Bannor see any of those damned kiktzo?" Miles had run a full scan himself, but he admitted that Rulaine had better recon skills—even if he wasn't a SEAL.

Riordan shook his head. "None. So we can shake off most of this dust now."

"And careful of your gear as you do it," O'Garran reminded. "This isn't the time for malfunctions."

Riordan lowered his visor again and skipped quickly through the visual feeds. The master view was from the monoscope that was still mounted on the windrad, left where they'd hidden it behind the stony teeth that ringed the lip of the rise. Positioned so that it just barely peeped up into a notch between two of the screening rocks, it looked out over the length of the caravan, from the front left flank all the way back to the right rear.

The formation was, as Sharat had predicted, unchanged from the day before. Small clusters of trogs—lightly armed skirmishers who were just more aggressive urldi—were set about forty meters away from each of the caravan's four compass points. Behind the one at the front was the first mass of pawns and deadskins, either dragging travois or fitted with bone-framed portage sacks. After them was the first rank of three dustkine, the middle one fitted with a howdah and lagging purposely behind the other two.

Everything beyond them was hazy, owing to the dust raised by their broad, half-hoofed feet. It was also more difficult to get a fix on any individual creatures in the central group, since they had far greater freedom. Small teams of trogs, or possibly trogans, were in constant movement as they made sure the four flanking patrols were doing their job, that the drivers of the pawns and deadskins were keeping up the pace, and that the 'qo were not roving too far from the van.

The latter was the greatest challenge. The two dozen 'qo didn't so much move with the column as they flitted around its approximate center like a loose swarm of hyperactive gnats. Most of the actual x'qai remained close to the center, a constant reminder of its actual purpose: a flexible pool of the caravan's most effective combat power.

What followed after the center was essentially the reverse of what had come before: another rank of three dustkine, then more pawns and deadskins, and finally a trog rearguard. The only difference was that the second howdah held two humans, busily directing the actions of the central kajh as a single x'qai looked on indifferently.

The two other views of the caravan were closer views from sand-concealed monoscopes. Bannor's showed the left side of the long, ragged parade as seen from the slope behind the eastern wadi, while Riordan's own viewed it from the right rear, where they had discovered that the column trailed a stench even thicker than the dust it raised in passing.

Riordan toggled the open channel. "All units: report status." He waited through the various "go's" and dropped into the command channel. "Eku, tell Sharat we're ready. Report his movement on this channel."

"Commodore, he heard and is moving already."

"All units: stick to the plan if you can. Report if you go off-script. Unit leaders: set and send your priority target lists. Hold fire until Bannor's signal."

Bannor, Newton, and their combination bodyguard and runner Zaatkhur, rose just enough to peek over the lip of the rise that backed the eastern wadi. The three largest fighters in Sharat's band—the two prakhbra and the tunnel-being—raced down the slope and arrived at the far set of range marks. As they did, and as the caravan's lead scouts drew up short in surprise, a loud metal roaring announced the downhill sprint of Sharat's realrad, packed with almost every other member of his team.

It swerved to the left as it reached the near range marks, located twenty meters behind the other set. It slowed and rolled along an east-to-west line as the troops on its running boards hopped off at assigned intervals. In thirty seconds it had deployed the Legate-trained missile troops behind the skirmish line at the far range marks. Sharat's base of fire across the caravan's route of advance was in place.

Bannor checked his buried monoscope for the caravan's reaction. It slowed as the report from the point element made its way back to the first howdah. Bannor watched the shouted exchange carefully. The larger of the two x'qai riders was the one who received the report and roared back a terse set of orders, but only after listening attentively to a few words from the comparatively motionless and smaller x'qao beside him.

Bannor nodded to himself. "That's our boy," he muttered. "Leaders on this channel, pass the word: prepare to fire. Craig, you ready to make history?"

"Yes, sir!"

"Stand by for number two target on the priority list. Dora, tell me what you're seeing: who else do we want to take out of the command chain?"

"Checking the feeds. Pretty much what we expected; the x'qao, whether on the ground or in the howdahs, are calling the shots."

"Roger that." Rulaine switched to the open channel. "Bowmen, your targets are any x'qao on the ground. Riflemen, I am relaying the target list. Charge your shots to kill. Trust the HUD targeting if it tells you to wait a moment; it's usually right. Stand by."

Yelling arose at the head of the column. A flight of arrows and bolts from Sharat's team cut down almost half of the lead patrol element and sent them scurrying back toward the van. As they did, the pawns were slowly shrugging off their packs and harnesses as the trog handlers pulled the loads from the barely responsive deadskins. *Yep, forming them up to engage, just like Sharat said.*

The junior x'qao in the lead howdah was roaring at the kine handlers to further close ranks. In the middle of a particularly detailed rant, it grabbed at its left arm and the dustkine reared as a bloody splotch appeared on its flank. An instant later, the report of several flintlocks came rolling down the column; Sharat's riflemen had joined the fight.

One unforeseen problem, though: the rearing dustkine made anything in its howdah an erratically moving object. *And if they don't get it under control, I can't engage our priority targets on its back.*

It was the senior x'qao who provided a mysterious solution to the problem; it extended a clawed hand toward the dustkine's tossing head—and the creature's motions became less sudden, less violent. Bannor almost toggled the Crewe's private channel to say, "Are you seeing what I see?" but there wasn't a second to spare: the dustkine had calmed. A moment later, the howdah stopped gyrating. Both x'qao had crouched low against the gunfire from the front, but were still amply large targets from the flank.

Bannor rose up from behind the lip of the slope, swung his survival rifle toward the howdah, toggled the open channel, and yelled, "Fire all!" As he did, the HUD's targeting guidons showed a target lock on the smaller x'qao and he fired twice, draining the rifle's battery.

Riordan had ambushed more than a few Hkh'Rkh units while leading insurgents in Indonesia, but he still had not grown accustomed to the speed with which relative order descended into utter chaos. Often on both sides.

In the first instant, the caravan went through the equivalent of a spasm. As the central dustkine in the first rank suddenly became calm, the one immediately to its left almost leaped into the air. Halted with its left flank facing the eastern wadi, only one of the ten arrows and bolts fired by the troops who rose up failed to hit. Mortally wounded but far too large to be killed outright, the dustkine's panic caused it to wheel away from the source of pain—which brought it into contact with the recently calmed one. Its travois tilted as it turned sharply to the right and ran directly away from the source of fire—in front of the one with the howdah and directly into the pawns and deadskins massed there.

It was impossible to track everything that happened in the next second: the smaller x'qao slumped limply over the left side of the howdah; the larger one flinched a second time as it leaped clear to the right; the fleeing dustkine's travois seemed to explode as it heeled over and became a cartwheeling shower of drag poles, lashings, and cargo. As it fled, haggard, dust-covered deadskins and pawns were tossed about or crushed in its wake like bloodied toothpick dolls.

But the caravan was far from finished: only one of the x'qao among the central reaction force had gone down. Another was wounded but that only seemed to make it more fixated and ferocious as it waved a few 'qo forward toward Sharat's delaying force... only to see half of them chase after the blood-streaming dustkine instead. The kajhs at the center held their ground, crouching, waiting for orders—and only then saw what had happened to the two x'qai they expected to issue them. One was lolling dead over the side of the howdah; the other one had jumped out and was fleeing.

Riordan scanned all the views and detected the greatest immediate threat in his own camera: the 'qo from the rear half of the caravan were already starting to move forward, sensing battle. However, they were torn between heading east toward sounds they associated with plentiful corpses, or racing after the scent of a dying dustkine heading west. But as he watched, their indecision began to fade; the kill scent was becoming too faint and the lively sights and sounds of trogs being marshaled toward the wadi was exciting them. Most began trotting east, their strides extending—

"Duncan," Riordan muttered behind him. "You see that?"

"Affirmative. Take out priority target?"

"Immediately."

Bannor had just revised the target list: there were only two x'qai left at the center of the column and one at either end. But instead of engaging the closest enemy, the enemy had begun to shepherd their pawns and deadskins toward the wadi. At the same time, the dustkine were beginning to move again, ranks tightening as they started forward briskly.

"Are the kine going to *charge*, sir?" Girten wondered aloud.

Rulaine didn't have time to answer. If all the remaining

pawns and deadskins and 'qo attacked the wadi, he might not have enough skirmishers to hold that position. In which case—

A sharp crack of familiar thunder leaped from the smaller wadi at the caravan's rear right flank, its source marked by a flittering tail of flame. Duncan Solsohn had stood and fired the Dornaani hand cannon at the right-hand dustkine in the rear rank.

Bannor wasn't sure if it had been the sniper's intent, but the frangible warhead entered the creature just forward of its right haunches and exited directly underneath its lower jaw. With the weapon charged at what Duncan liked to call "light antitank setting," the round had started to come apart about a meter along its shallow trajectory inside the animal. The entirety of its higher digestive track erupted outward an instant before its right lung literally exploded.

The creature ceased moving, swayed to the opposite side, and fell, presenting a ragged bloody trough that ran two thirds the length of its body.

Without exception, every 'qo at the rear of the caravan suddenly stopped, stared...and then caught the scent. With a ghastly mix of ecstatic shrieks and eager chitterings, they swarmed over the carcass like a school of frenzied piranha.

Bannor exhaled: the most dangerous part of the gathering counterattack had been effectively eliminated. Just as planned. *So I guess I should say—*

"You're welcome," said Duncan.

Riordan immediately checked the feeds for the caravan's reactions to the rear attack. Much of the column hardly seemed aware. The 'qo that had been sent forward were entirely focused on their maniacal attempts to kill at least one of the troops on Sharat's skirmish line: about a half dozen trogs supported by the two prakhbrai and the tunnel creature. They were becoming quite frustrated.

The remaining x'qao on the ground were gathering the trog handlers and drivers to assist in massing the remaining pawns and deadskins to assault the wadi. If any registered the attack, they were not distracted by it.

Or, Riordan realized, it might be because they still had a more capable x'qao nearby: the one in the second howdah with the humans. Who had turned to the rear and was looking almost directly at Caine's buried monoscope.

"Next target, Commodore?" Solsohn said almost cheerfully. "I've got a clear shot at—"

The x'qao raised its hand, eyes almost looking directly into the lens.

Which was right beside Solsohn.

"Duncan! Get dow—!"

But the IRIS sniper slumped down heavily in the small wadi. Miles started to pop up, weapon ready.

"Get down!" Riordan barked. "Duncan, are you—?"

Newton's voice came in on the command channel. "Commodore, is Duncan wounded? Some of his biosigns spiked."

Duncan cleared his throat; it sounded dry as leather. "I . . . I can't see."

"What?" Miles almost shouted.

"Maybe I'm having a stroke?" Duncan wondered, starting to chortle.

"Negative," Newton snapped. Even though he was on the other side of the battlefield, his sharp tone cut through Solsohn's distraction. "There are no major changes in brain baselines. The physical spikes are fading, consistent with a brief pulse of panic."

O'Garran sounded angry at the whole world. "What the hell just happ—?"

"Chief," Riordan said sharply, "swap weapons. You take the hand cannon."

"Sir, you asked me to watch your back. I can't do that and be the gunner. Sir."

Before Riordan could think of an alternative, Miles continued with one of his own. "But I can still guard you if *you* equip the cannon, sir. You've drilled on it, and the HUD will make you a perfect marksman."

Riordan considered a flurry of options; he chose the simplest and fastest. "Negative. Duncan, you're keeping the weapon. Stay down. The rest of you as well. Eku?"

"Sir?"

"I need you to stream the targeting feed from Duncan's helmet to the chief's. Just in case."

"Sir, I—"

"Just do it, Eku. Chief, I may hold the weapon up and have you talk me onto the target so you can fire by remote."

"But sir, why—?"

"That's an order, O'Garran; no questions." *Because how do I explain that it's a little too strange that the moment after the x'qao gestured, Duncan went blind. And if any of us take his place, we might be next. Which would be an especially bad choice for a CO.* "Dr. Baruch, you heard?"

"Yes, sir. I do not—"

"Not now. You are Chief O'Garran's backup for remote fire. Do you copy?"

"Sir, I acknowledge, but I may not be able to carry out your order."

"Why the hell not?" Miles yelled.

"Because, Chief O'Garran, I might be dead or unconscious. The enemy is about to charge the wadi."

# Chapter Forty-Six

An enemy assault on the wadi had been baked into the battle plan from the start. But what Bannor and the other leaders had not foreseen was that the attack might come from both ends of the column, rather than the middle. Because who would have guessed that it would be carried out by s'rillor-ravaged trog porters?

"Leaders," Rulaine called over the command channel, "can you sustain rate of fire?" He received unanimous confirmations, but saw that the survival rifles on the line were not hitting as hard. Crewe was cutting back on charges since they still had to lay down fire but no longer had the time to swap in an Eku-created external power supply. And the crossbows were slowing as the urldi reloaders increasingly measured the distance from the approaching attackers to the relative safety of the slope at the rear of the wadi.

*No,* Bannor decided, *we can't hold under these conditions.* "Newton," he said without bothering to turn around, "I want you to back off the lip twenty meters. No argument. You don't have a rifle and you can't defend and treat casualties at the same time. Besides, if it all goes to shit, we need someone who can make a report that informs either a counterattack or withdrawal."

"As you wish, Colonel."

"Leaders, take your final shots at the x'qao herding the attackers."

"Wish we knew how they were doing it," Katie muttered.

476

"Me, too. But right now, last shots. Then everyone out of the wadi. Shooters shift to secondary weapons. Loaders are to carry the crossbows. Crewe, make sure the locals understand what's happening. Use external speakers if you have to. But keep your visors closed."

One of the x'qao in the center was hit near the eye; distracted, it fell back. A few last bowshots took down the one 'qo who'd shown up among the deadskins, and then the troops started pulling out of the wadi.

Most followed the so-called ramps that the locals had found the day before. They were nothing more than narrow veins of rock-muddled clay; however, that firmness was vastly better than the soft, crumbling sides of the wadi. The warriors and missile troops remembered their instructions and headed directly for those higher-traction parts of the back slope; their boots got them up the side easily enough.

The urldi quickly proved to be a very different story, however.

Already rattled by the approaching enemies, their incipient panic kept them from remembering the same simple instructions. So they turned and tried to get up the closest part of the wadi, wearing the equivalent of crude, soft-soled brogans. The typical result: sliding back down, even as their hands-and-feet scrambling dug more sand and dust out of the side.

Rulaine saw all the ingredients for a massacre beginning to coalesce. "Leaders! Grenades out to twenty meters! Buy 'em time!"

But it wasn't clear that the time bought by the grenades would be enough. Most of the urldi had already made two attempts. Now knee-deep in the dust and sand they'd clawed from the wadi, they were so terrified that they couldn't hear the instructions being shouted down by those who had already made it over the lip.

Five grenades arced out over the wadi. Bannor adding a sixth to the spot where the coverage seemed weakest. The ear-and-eye-gouging strobing, howling, and cross-frequency warbling forced two of the remaining x'qao to shy back. So too did the pawns, but the deadskins kept pressing forward like cadaverous automatons.

As if shamed by their effortless advance through the grenades, the x'qao forced themselves to advance again. And, seeing one of the deadskins bump into a grenade that went rolling away, they began to compel the pawns to do the same. *Well, that's a nasty surprise.*

Newton's voice came in on a private channel. "Sir, I am following the feeds. I will likely need another pair of capable hands."

*What?* "Can't spare any."

"Not from the line, sir."

"Then whose?" The first of the local h'achgai archers had sorted himself out atop the slope and was firing at the approaching deadskins, the pawns surging behind them now that the grenades were out of the way.

"I need Ne'sar for casualty management," Newton explained. "I have observed her. She is adequate. Without her to stabilize the wounded, I will lose many."

Bannor watched the urldi screaming as they ran up and down the wadi, unable to see and too panicked to remember where the ramps were, because they were almost buried under the dirt they themselves had torn from the back wall. "Ne'sar wasn't out here yesterday. She'll likely eat an arrow if she's not shown the way."

Zaatkhur's voice startled him: "Leader Bannor." He'd forgotten the trog was guarding him, who now suggested, "I will go fetch Ne'sar. If you wish."

Bannor nodded. "Go. And thanks for thinking of it."

The older trog looked pleasantly surprised at the human's response and then ran off on his errand.

The x'qao who was still in the howdah spent almost half a minute observing the battlefield before turning to the caravan's two humans and ordering them down the ropes he cast over the dustkine's side.

"What the hell is he doing?" O'Garran muttered.

Ta'rel confirmed Caine's guess. "They will rally the praa—trogs still sheltering around the dustkine. The kajh are in threes, a bowman in each. The humans will reorganize them to help attack the wadi."

Riordan nodded. "They'll combine the archers for supporting fire. Then have the warriors form up the remaining handlers and drivers. Use that force to follow up and exploit any breach in the line."

"That won't win the battle," O'Garran pointed out.

"Not on its own, no. But while that's going on, the bastard in the howdah could pull the other x'qao back and kick some of the 'qo loose to join them. That might carry the assault." He shook his head. "Our people's suits should keep them safe long enough to be rescued, but—" He stopped himself.

Ta'rel completed his sentence. "—but the h'achgai and the praakht shall not survive."

Riordan nodded as the x'qai commander leaned toward two of the 'qo that had eaten their fill from the dustkine. If it spoke, Caine didn't see it, but at a gesture, the 'qo began trotting lazily to the rear.

To the spot where Duncan had emerged.

"Company coming," Miles muttered.

Yaargraukh hefted his weapons and stretched his arms.

But instead of watching the 'qo, Riordan kept his focus on the x'qai. He wasn't even bothering to watch them. *Because they're just a pinning attack, a sideshow to keep us busy.*

The x'qai's next actions made his intent clear. Alternately rallying and threatening the remaining handlers, he ordered them to drive the dustkine into a trot. Surprisingly, the remaining two in the first rank began moving similarly.

Riordan nodded. *Sure: he knows he's in a box. It's what we planned on: that they'd realize their formation is too slow and stiff to reverse or turn out of. So they'd have to charge through to the south. But now, if he gets free, he'll be able to double back, gather enough of the 'qo and routed x'qai, and overrun the eastern wadi.*

The leading dustkine began running toward Sharat's line. The Legate captain had done a fine job. His skirmishers had slain or run off all the 'qo while keeping the leading forces of the caravan under constant fire. They hadn't inflicted many casualties, but that hadn't been the mission; the enemy had been suppressed and unable to reorganize. But now, the delaying force couldn't just withdraw, it had to—"Eku, Sharat has to pull out! Immediately! They mean to destroy him with a stampede."

"Yes, sir!" Eku replied. In the background, Riordan heard the factotum anxiously speaking to whoever was listening through one of the Terran duty-suit helmets down near the rad.

Within seconds, the vehicle belched smoke and raced toward the near markers. As the two lines collapsed back upon it, only one figure remained behind: the large, ogrish tunnel creature.

"What's happening, Eku?"

"I am uncertain, but two of the dustkine bellowed at the tunnel thing. It sounded like a challenge."

*Goddammit.* And Sharat was still trying to get the immense humanoid to withdraw. His rad couldn't carry it, but those hanging on the running boards were yelling at it to follow them. Riordan counted to three, then said: "Eku, my orders: Sharat has to leave it there. If he doesn't, his entire force is going to be crushed."

Bannor gave the order he had prayed he would not have to give. "Skirmish teams one and two: deploy to cover the urldi."

Two responses came back: neither were simple acknowledgements.

"Bannor," shouted Dora, "where are the two kajhs? They're not here on the left."

And:

"Colonel," Girten said, "right flank is no longer a threat. The x'qao at the rear is down and its pawns are wandering off. The deadskins are just standing around."

Katie cut in. "Craig's becoming a reasonable shot with his Dornaani popgun."

Bannor used the good news to offset the bad news. "Skirmish team two: leave Bey behind as security for our two sharpshooters, then follow Skirmish Team One to the left flank."

"Acknowledged."

"Nice to have more help," Dora shouted between breaths. She was clearly running, but when Bannor looked up and spotted her, he started: she wasn't heading to engage the haggard, oncoming trogs but had jumped down into the wadi itself, calling the urldi over toward her at the base of the northernmost ramp.

But urldi, seeing the half dozen warriors of Skirmish Teams One and Two running down into the wadi to the south, stumbled that way in desperation...only to cry out when their six presumed saviors charged up the other, lower side to close with the enemy.

Bannor forced himself not to watch the small form leading that charge: Ayana. She brought the others in close, and instead of engaging the dozens of slow-moving pawns immediately in front of them, formed a wedge to cut a path toward the x'qao controlling their movements.

Because that was what had to be occurring. Even as Ayana's warriors closed on their target, it gestured and half a dozen pawns flocked to it in a protective cluster, with more on the way. Swords and axes flashed as Arashk, Peter, Yidreg and two other h'achgai struggled to cut the enemies down faster than they could accumulate. One of the h'achgai fell...

"Bannor!" Dora cried. "Support the wadi!"

Rulaine cursed because he'd done exactly what he had told himself he mustn't, mustn't, *mustn't* do: let his eyes linger on Ayana. Let himself get distracted. And get someone dead because of it. He stood straight, scanned the wadi.

Well south of Dora, a handful of deadskins had clambered down into the wadi. Undeterred by fear, they kept stumbling and shambling forward until they were among the urldi. Screams arose. Veriden seemed to be shouting back in enraged frustration as she struggled through knee-topping pools of sand and dust. Which is why she did not see the three deadskins crawling down into the wadi just behind her—

Bannor snapped up his still-loaded crossbow, yelled, "Dora! Down!" and fired at the closest of the wraithlike trogs.

It toppled slowly backward, club still raised as it stared at the quarrel protruding from its chest. Screaming in rage, Veriden spun about. Her shortswords made quick work of the other two. She turned back toward the urldi—

But was too late. Although they had brought down half of the deadskins, none of the trog loaders were moving.

Riordan swallowed sharply as one of Sharat's men jumped down from the idling rad's running board and shouted toward his charge, the immense tunnel-bred being, as it took a step *forward*. The creature either ignored or missed the desperate entreaty; it began trotting toward the oncoming dustkine.

"Eku! Sharat has got to—!"

"Sir, they are not responding. I cannot tell if—"

*Shit.* Caine glanced at the hand cannon in Duncan's loose grip. *No time to line up a remote shot. But I could take down the x'qao's mount. Or one near it. Anything to break up the charge, give Sharat another half minute to pull his people out.*

He edged toward the weapon.

*If Sharat gets clear, we can reform in time to repel the x'qao, keep him from getting the 'qo back into the fight. Just one, quick pop-up shot, and we'll be—*

Miles' voice was as flat and hard as an anvil. "What are you doing, sir?"

Riordan ignored it. "Chief, prepare to cover me while—"

Yaargraukh came forward, hunched over to stay beneath the

upper edge of the wadi. "Please, Caine Riordan, I do not wish my only conflict this day to be with you."

Riordan shook his head. "In a second, I can—"

In the main view, snugged into the upper-right corner of the HUD, a figure detached itself from Sharat's rad: Tirolane.

*No!*

The big swordsman took two steps toward the now-charging dustkine and raised his hand as if he was ordering them to stop—

In his own monoscope's feed, Caine saw the x'qao commander collapse nervelessly over the front rim of its howdah, bounce off the kine's head, and fall to the ground.

The thundering charge of the dustkine dispersed into a wild stampede of animals that were no longer attacking, but fleeing.

O'Garran's voice was hushed. "What the hell did he—?"

"Doesn't matter!" Caine cried as the x'qao swayed to its feet. *My God, they're tough!* "Target is up! All available: fire!"

Miles jumped erect, just able to aim over the edge of the wadi. As he squeezed his weapon's trigger, Bannor's voice was loud on the tactical channel: "Craig! Take the shot!"

The x'qao convulsed as if hit by two invisible fists in a fast combination. It fell again.

Riordan snatched up the hand cannon, rose, but discovered he no longer had a target. The HUD showed the x'qao's body heat fading. The lead rank of dustkine were avoiding Sharat's force, which was finally back on the rad and speeding out of their path.

Riordan peered through the haze swirling between him and the other side of the battlefield, but the second rank of dustkine stormed across his field of vision, raising a sandy smokescreen in their wake.

"No shot," Riordan muttered bitterly. He handed the hand cannon back to the silent Solsohn, ducked back down into the small wadi, and waved for O'Garran to do the same.

As Arashk went down under a storm of clubs and emaciated fists, Ayana leaped into the gap he'd opened in front of the x'qao. She blended her motion into her attack: a long, body-powered slice down at the creature's neck.

Its head moved so quickly that Ayana thought she had blinked— and the instant before her katana made contact, a hapless pawn stumbled against her.

The shining arc of Ayana's blade did not slice into the x'qao's neck, but cut a deep groove into its shoulder. The monster howled, stumbled back a step, but recovered—just as Yidreg charged in, both sturdy arms driving his bastard sword straight at it.

The point bit and the blade followed, sinking two hand-widths into the x'qao's lower chest. It raked its claws at Yidreg as it fell; they sliced through his cured hide armor and found flesh underneath. The power of the blow flung the wounded h'achga sideways.

But before Yidreg could even begin to rise, the x'qao was already up, wobbling but wild with rage. As Ayana regained her feet, Peter on one side, a h'achgan axeman on the other, it started forward, claws outstretched—

—just as Dora's voice screamed from behind them: "Down!"

They ducked.

Dora's nine-millimeter cracked four times, just behind and above their heads.

Two rounds hit the onrushing x'qao in its face, one in its throat. Gargling ichor, the creature almost fell, but began righting itself.

Ayana was beside it in two long leaps, the second concluding in a coup de grace into its neck. As it fell, Yidreg rushed past her, the point of his bastard sword driving through its left eye and emerging from the back of its vaguely ursine head. A pool of its thick blood began widening and caking the dust beneath it.

"Bastard," Dora panted, blowing dark bangs away from her face, "eating four of my rounds."

"Three," Ayana gasped. "You only hit with three."

"Shut up," Dora smiled.

As Riordan surveyed the field, he discovered that, despite the extraordinary climate control of the Dornaani suit, he could feel still feel individual beads of sweat running the length of his torso. He had grown used to the seesaw uncertainty of battle, but nothing had prepared him for the wild swings of this one. *But maybe, if I'd listened to Tasvar about inexplicable phenomena, they might have been less extreme.*

Craig Girten's voice was eager on the open channel. "Guys, the trogs at the center are moving in pretty good order. I've got a clear shot at—"

"Negative, Sergeant. They are no longer an operational threat."

"But, Commodore, they're uh, kinda headed your way."

Riordan checked his feeds. *So they are. Hmmm...* "Keep them in your sights, Sergeant, but do not engage until and unless I instruct. Which I am not inclined to do: they're being led by the two humans. Hardly makes sense shooting toward the people we're here to rescue. Colonel Rulaine will set any further target priorities and call your shots."

"I don't foresee either, CO," Bannor chimed in. "The only s'rillor cases we've had to kill are the deadskins that were, well, eating the dead. No real preference for ours or theirs. The rest of them are just standing around. The pawns are wandering back out to the field on their own. Got a lot of trog drivers and handlers that are waiting out there, too, faces in the dust. Bey tells me it's not just a surrender gesture; it's a request for protection. As in, they're volunteering to switch to our side."

Riordan nodded absently, exhaled into a moment of relaxation as he scanned the feeds, committing the end of the battle to memory. The last of the dustkine were scattering south as if released from an invisible yoke, their travois upending and littering the battlefield with the cargo they'd dragged all the way from Fragkork. The last two wounded x'qai were racing after them with the same insane speed the Crewe had noted in the 'qo. Riordan wondered at that, switched the main monoscope view to thermal imaging, set his HUD to process it at the highest level of discrimination. The fleeing x'qai stood out like neon signs on a dark night, body temperatures at almost two times human norm. More mysteries to solve...eventually.

"Sir," Miles muttered, "we've got visitors."

Riordan switched to his own monoscope; a pair of trogs dropped out of the right hand of the frame. They'd hopped down into the wadi, probably just around the little bend to the south. "Calm, now," he said on his group's command channel.

A moment later, one of the kajh from the central reaction force came rolling around the corner—and froze when he found himself staring down two strange-looking barrels, backed by the largest, best armored grat'r he'd ever seen.

"Have your leader come forward," Riordan instructed, using the external speakers at nearly full volume.

Still not daring to move, the trog made nervous waving-forward gestures behind him.

A human in well-made armor and a metal helmet came around the corner, one of the trog archers at his side. His eyes widened. "Harrows!" he cried.

Mistaking it as a command to attack, the archer drew—

Riordan jogged the survival rifle to the side and fired three fast rounds. Three geysers of dust erupted sideways from the wall of the wadi. The archer had frozen even before his commander waved for him to desist.

"Don't do that again," said Riordan, triggering the visor release. As it sighed open, he met the human's eyes. "We are not harrows. Or scythes."

The human gaped. "Then what . . . what are you?"

"That," Riordan said, allowing his rifle's muzzle to dip slightly, "is a longer conversation. But first, put down your weapons. Slowly."

# Chapter Forty-Seven

Riordan and Bannor sprinted toward the yelling that had erupted not from the mass of trog prisoners sitting on the battlefield under the watchful eyes of the h'achgai, but in what Miles sardonically referred to as the "terminal debriefing area": a spot just beneath the stone-capped rise where potentially friendly captives were answering questions.

As they arrived, the human that Caine had believed to be the leader of the two, a warrior named Orsost, was shouting at one of the archers he'd commanded while the actual leader Enoran—a "technicker"—watched coolly, arms folded.

Orsost waved his knife under the nose of the oldest bowman, who, like all the others, were trogans. "You lie!" the human shouted. "You *must* have known!"

"As if lieges tell us anything we do not need to know?" the other protested, not quite cowering but shrinking back from the knife.

"What's going on here?" Bannor asked, adopting the same role as Orsost: asking the questions so that the leader could stand back and observe.

Sharat shrugged. "Old business from their liege's stable, it seems."

Orsost turned to Riordan. "Leader Caine, this prakhwa received aid from our war leader. He was honor bound to tell us if we were to be sold, as the Legate captain claims."

Bannor looked sideways at Sharat. "And how certain was your information?"

486

"It was more than adequate," Tirolane answered. "I have contacts in Fragkork. They would not lie. I shall prove it."

"How?" Enoran asked calmly.

Tirolane turned and went to what was clearly the most valuable of the cargo frames that had been recovered from the field: it was heavily bound and secured with unusually thick straps. He loosed one, tossed aside several larger sacks, and revealed a smaller one made of x'qao hide.

A hiss went up from the group that could see: a reaction to both the value of the pouch and the detested source of its material.

Tirolane opened it and pulled out two smaller pouches. He opened one that was of fine manufacture. Ne'sar sighed. "That is handiwork from Lessíb, one of the outlying communities of Ebrekka."

Tirolane tilted its contents into his hand. A small amount of moss fell out, followed by several bound clusters of lichen.

Enoran spat. "Barely enough to get us to Forkus. Our liege broke his oath. Clearly, he meant us to be passed into the claws of another. Or knew we were to be killed."

The trogan archer stared at it. "And certainly none for us! Despite our liege's promises!" He turned toward Orsost. "Do you believe us now? That is our death warrant as well, or at least a further slip into s'rillor."

Before the human warrior could answer, Tirolane opened the other pouch, trickled a few grains of the contents onto his palm.

"Gunpowder," Sharat said, crossing his arms. "Not unusual for them to hold back anything more than a single shot for each gun in the caravan."

Tirolane nodded, held the bag out to Enoran. "Test it."

The technicker took the pouch, trickled a measure into his own palm, sniffed and then tasted it. He spat it out: not in response to the taste, but disgust. "At least half of the charcoal is ash. It would be almost useless in a gun."

Orsost sheathed his knife and reached that hand down to the archer. "Apologies. Rise and know I believe your oath was not broken." The archer allowed the human to bring him to his feet. "I am baffled."

"At the duplicity of your liege?" Bannor asked.

"No, that he managed to make such preparations without our friends among the prakhwa learning and informing us. They find it easy to keep many secrets from us, but not those involving our tech. They do not understand it well enough."

Enoran nodded, turned to face Sharat, and gestured to his fellow humans and the trogans seated nearby. "We would swear allegiance to the Legate, if he will have us."

Sharat shook his head in obvious regret. "If we were bound for one of our enclaves, I would do so. But we are not, so it could be a season or more before I could bring you before either one of our mindwatchers or oathkeepers to receive your fealty."

"We would follow on our own," Orsost said... impulsively, judging from Enoran's expression.

Sharat kept shaking his head. "Our orders forbid long travel with those who cannot be adequately vetted."

Enoran nodded but was already staring at Tirolane. "Lord Tirolane, I would offer our oaths to you, then."

Tirolane bowed. "Let us travel as comrades, instead. My path is too uncertain to take the oaths of others. I may have to travel alone, as I already have. And then, where would you be?"

Orsost turned to Caine and Bannor. "Then what of you, lords? Surely you have taken oaths of those who serve you?"

Riordan and Bannor exchanged glances. The hard fact of the matter was that over half of those who had taken oaths the night before were dead or soon would be. "We must consider this before we agree. Our path is—"

From the other side of the slope, troggish voices began screaming: some in pain, some in fury.

One of the voices was Bey's.

Riordan and his small group slowed as they approached the grim tableau: Zaatkhur lying atop a brown, baked disk of his own blood, the two missing kajh lying beside him, one with an arrow in his back, the other with one in his leg. And Bey, with shortswords out, half bent over her friend, tears falling into his gaping wounds.

"What happened here?" Caine asked, keeping his voice neutral.

Bey pointed at a spot behind her. Riordan waved the h'achga who'd accompanied them—Hresh—toward the place she'd indicated.

"They killed him?" Riordan asked.

Bey nodded, shoulders quivering.

"Why?" Bannor asked.

Hresh stood. "Zaatkhur discovered their treachery." He pointed at the spot Bey had indicated. "I do not know the meaning of this sign, but they left a marker: a pattern of stones that looks random but is not."

"They must have followed Zaatkhur when I sent him to get Ne'sar," Bannor muttered. "He probably didn't know about the concealed route back to the camp, either."

Riordan nodded, glancing at the sequence of low rises that, followed with care, hid crouched figures from most of the battlefield. "And they were worried that he'd see this marker." Caine felt a chill run down his body. "Which means we're being followed."

Bey looked up, eyes red, tear-carved spiderwebs cut into the dust caked on her cheeks. "I will learn who, how, and when," she muttered hollowly.

Riordan glanced at the rest of the group who'd come with him. "Stay here. Watch them. Bey, come with me."

He led her over the rise that screened the scene of treachery from the battlefield.

Before he could speak, she was looking up into his eyes, hers unblinking and almost devoid of emotion. "This is my failure. Whatever punishment there must be, must fall upon me, and me alone. I have failed you."

Riordan crossed his arms, responded carefully, calmly. "Tell me: how is this *your* failure, Bey?"

Her eyes stared through him. "How is it not, Leader Caine? It was I who suggested to Leader Bannor that Zaatkhur would be an able guard and runner. It was I who failed to see the blackness in the hearts of these two honorless kajh, even as they took an oath of fealty. And above all, it was I whom you asked to lead and protect my people. And see what has come of that. Zaatkhur here. And Sho, at the hunt. They thought she might have seen the marker they left and so they..." She tucked her face down and shut her eyes very hard.

She opened them, startled, when Caine touched her chin and lifted her head to look at him again. "You are a fine leader, Bey, but no one—*no one*—can see into the hearts of clever traitors. That is why they are so dangerous. Now, what do you plan to do?"

"I plan to learn all that these two beasts know about those who paid them to betray us. Then I will see to those of my people who remain. And finally"—her eyes started to glimmer, but she forced the tears back—"I shall take my friend to the river, that nothing may feed upon his remains."

Only then did Riordan realize he'd left his hand on her chin. He removed it briskly and nodded. "You have much to do. And I know that you shall do all of it well. Be careful in your questioning of these two. If Duncan were not... afflicted, I would send him here to—"

She shook her head. "That is not necessary, Leader Caine, I know best how to unfold the lies these two have been telling. If you leave one of the h'achgai, that will be sufficient. They will not think of trying to overpower me, that way."

Riordan agreed and sent her back over the rise. She met Bannor coming over the crest, nodded respectfully at him, and marched down to begin her tasks.

"I don't like this at all," the Green Beret muttered as he drew near.

"Neither do I. It must go all the way back to Forkus, since the two kajh weren't in the group that Ulchakh took to Khorkrag."

"Which means that these two were on somebody's payroll before we hit the hovel."

Riordan nodded, started down toward the debriefing area. "What do you think about Enoran's and Orsost's request?"

Bannor drew in a sharp breath. "Mixed feelings. On the one hand, I wish we knew them better, but on the other, they're a really timely replacement for the casualties we took today."

"Which are?"

"Four of the urldi, including the male, killed outright. Another wounded. A lot of light wounds among the rest of us. Yidreg will be okay, but one of the h'achgai that was in Ayana's flying wedge is going to be touch and go."

"And Duncan's blindness?"

"Gone. When his sight came back, it was just as quick as he lost it."

Riordan let out a sigh of relief. "And what about Sharat's people? Did they all get out of the way in time?"

Bannor nodded hesitantly. "All except for that big humanoid from the 'Great Tunnels.' Seems that once the dustkine roared a challenge, there was no controlling him. Charged them all and damn near killed one before they rolled over him."

"Speaking of control; has anyone in Sharat's group said anything about whatever it was that Tirolane did?"

"Not a word. Seems like it didn't surprise them. I get the feeling it was part of the reason Sharat didn't pull everyone off the line right away. They were counting on an opportunity like that, and didn't want to withdraw until they'd had a chance to capitalize on it."

"Yeah, without telling us they had it up their sleeve."

Bannor shrugged. "Not sure Tirolane shared a lot of details with them. Also, given our skepticism every time they start mentioning effects and powers that they know we doubt, I suspect they wouldn't have read us in even if they had known what he could do."

Riordan nodded as they arrived in the debriefing area, where Katie's sunburned face had become alarmingly red. "They do *what*?" she shouted at Enoran. "That's a bowfin' outrage!"

"Corporal," Riordan said in his command voice, "is there an argument, here?"

"No, sir!" she said, still shouting. "B-but these poor scaffies just told me what happens if they don't give over to these manky x'qao lieges."

"'Give over'?" Bannor repeated, perplexed.

Enoran's gaze was frankly curious as he supplied the answer. "Leader Katie is, eh, surprised at the realities of life in an x'qao liege's stable."

"Such as?"

"Well, that we have no choice in regard to our mates, that all our newborns are immediately taken from their mothers and put into nurseries, and that neither parent ever learns the child's identity."

"Feck!" Katie shouted even louder. "Better to fight and die!"

Enoran shrugged. "Yes, and many of us might...if the worst that happened was that we died."

She stopped. "What do you mean?"

"He refers to the moss." It was Tirolane who answered. "It is withheld if there is the faintest hint of resistance or disobedience." Katie went very pale, as did most of the Crewe.

"Our greatest fear," Enoran explained. "is not in that we shall die, but in what manner."

Sharat nodded. "If we lose our lives through bold deeds, in possession of our faculties, and tenacious in our resistance?" He shrugged. "It is not particularly uncommon among our species to be able to gird our loins to end our lives that way.

"But to slowly lose the ability to think, to maintain our resolve, to keep in mind and memory those we've loved, why we lived, or even the act of defiance that earned such an end?" Sharat shook his head.

Tirolane's jaw was rigid as he spoke, looking into the distance as if he was seeing some other place and time. "It is one thing to have your life torn away by an enemy, but quite another to feel yourself slowly erased by the frailty of your own body. And to know that the husk of what you were will be paraded about to terrify others into obedience."

As if punctuating the silence that followed, shrill screams once again rose up from over the rise.

By the time Caine and Bannor cleared the crest, they knew what was happening.

Bey was poised over one of the kajh, a dripping knife in one hand, the other close to a leg wound that had not been there before. One h'achga was holding the trog down, the other—Hresh—was wide-eyed and grey-faced. He swallowed as four members of the Crew rose into view.

Riordan forgot not to shout. "Stop! We don't do that! What are you *thinking*?"

Bey rounded on him, eyes fierce, wild. "*I think* we need information. Just as you said!"

Riordan strode down and knocked the knife out of her hand. "We do! But that's not how we get it!"

"You said I am good at what I do, yes? Well, then leave me to it." She moved toward the knife.

Riordan stepped into her path. "I can't let you do it this way."

"Why not? They murdered and lied and will do so again. They deserve worse than what I'm doing!"

Riordan did not move. "Bey, this is not about them; this is about *us*. What we do, and how the tools and methods we use define who and what we are. And what we will become." She looked aside, shaking. "Do you understand?"

She dashed her hand at his words. "Of course I understand. I am not a fool." She looked back up at him. "The better question is, do *you* understand?" She looked past him at the rest of the

Crewe. "Do any of you *truly* understand? Your—*our*—enemies count such scruples as weakness, as an assurance that we shall never use all the weapons against them that they use against us."

Riordan nodded. "We know. But there is benefit in refusing to use certain weapons. Savagery aimed at enemies ultimately becomes so familiar that you begin using it on your own people. It is like any other thing that becomes a habit; you cease to notice when you're doing it." She looked away and nodded; it was not agreement, just a sign that she would follow his orders. "Tell me what you've learned."

"They were each promised five years of moss. They never met the factor who hired them. And they do not know if that factor or intermediaries have followed us. Their instructions were simply to observe Eku and his equipment until they were delivered to the liege that purchased them."

Bannor walked to the h'achga holding the traitor's legs, urged him to move away. "So they were leaving these marks on their own initiative? No one told them to expect that the hovel was going to be attacked, that Eku and his gear might be removed?"

"Not specifically, no. Rather, the factor was concerned that many parties might be willing to seize those prizes either before, during, or after the exchange. Most of their concern seems to have been with rival lieges. Or the Legate."

Dora frowned. "Why would these two idiots even trust such a deal?" she said sourly. "They've got to know that most betrayers wind up being betrayed themselves."

Bey nodded. "True, but the factor arranged payment through a bondward who had first witnessed the factor's promise, so they knew the deal was in earnest. Upon conclusion of their service, it would once again be the bondward who would have conveyed the moss to them."

Riordan nodded. "And that way, they never see who they're dealing with."

Dora nodded along with him. "Because if they did, that would be the last thing they ever saw."

"Which they knew," Bey sighed. "I do not believe they know more. I am sorry to have failed yet again."

Riordan sighed. "You did not fail, Bey. Duncan is recovering, and he will ask them more questions. In *our* way. You may watch him, if you wish."

She shrugged. "Perhaps. Am I dismissed, Leader Caine?"

He nodded. "You are free to see to your friend. If you require any assistance—"

"No. I shall do it myself." She strode stiff-legged past the four Crewe members without glancing at them.

Riordan nodded for Hresh to approach. He did, trembling slightly. "You are blameless in this. Go to Ta'rel. Ask him to watch over Bey as she finishes honoring Zaatkhur. Just to be sure that none of the x'qa from the caravan return and discover her alone."

Hresh nodded and was gone, passing Ulchakh at the top of the slope as he did. The h'achgan trader walked slowly down to Riordan. "I wonder if we might walk together," he murmured.

Riordan nodded, glanced at Dora; she settled into the stance of a sentinel.

After they had walked ten meters beyond the marker that had become Zaatkhur's death warrant, Ulchakh said, "Bey is being far too hard on herself."

"Torture is not something we can tolerate."

"I am not speaking of that, Friend Caine. I am speaking of whatever plot has been uncovered here."

Riordan nodded. "I agree. I said as much and will continue to tell her so."

They walked further. Ulchakh sighed. "This scheme, whatever it might be, is more subtle than anything I have ever seen."

Riordan replied with a h'achgan idiom. "You are saying something between your words, Ulchakh. Sadly, I cannot hear it."

The h'achga's long orang face became even longer. "This is not the work of any x'qao. Oh, the lieges are certainly crafty enough to conceive of such a plot, but they are also clear-sighted enough to know that none of their typical servitors have the patience and concentration to carry it out. No, there is someone or something else at work here. And I would give much to know who, or what, that is."

"Me, too," Riordan said, fighting back a deep frown. "Me, too."

# Chapter Forty-Eight

Fezhmorbal rarely had a private audience with Liege Hwe'tsara. And although there were two of the x'qao's senior harrows present—although neither of which were deciqadi like himself—it was a sign of great trust, great secrecy, or both.

The Hwe'tsara gestured for him to stand before his rough-hewn granite throne . . . but not to sit. "So, where is your assistant? The one named, er, . . . Gasdashrag?"

Fezhmorbal concealed his surprise; it was noteworthy when Hwe'tsara simply remembered what he'd had for breakfast. Not because his mind was weak; he just didn't trouble it to retain information that was not of immediate import. "Your Horror's memory is as the keenest obsidian. Gasdashrag is presently embarked upon a mission in the service of your interests." *Which is to say,* my *schemes.*

"Where is he?"

"It would be better to end with that information, Liege Hwe'tsara."

The x'qao glanced at the "great hall's" one obvious addition: a large urn of water. "I do not ask questions a second time, *stoop.*"

Fezhmorbal ignored the slur used to insult his race. "Gasdashrag is presently very near Khorkrag, Your Horror."

"What? So far? What new madness is this, counselor?"

"It is not madness, nor is it any further than he must be in order to pursue your interests assiduously, Your Horror. But as I observed, his location is best understood once the whole story of his journey there is told."

"Very well. It and your other reports are long overdue, you know. I have not heard results since the start of spring."

It was a gross exaggeration, but what was the good of pointing that out? "It has been challenging gathering forces sufficient to do your bidding, Liege Hwe'tsara."

"You anticipate having to launch large attacks?"

"No, Liege, but there are many threads that need to be traced with careful fingers in order to perceive the full tapestry of recent events."

"And that tapestry is—?"

"—is but half-completed, Your Horror."

"What? After all this time?"

"The progress may seem slow, but that is required if we are not to give away more information than we gather."

The x'qao was becoming cross. "Speak in plain language."

*I am, you insufferable fly-wit!* "It is in the nature of gathering hidden information that one encounters trip wires designed to detect anyone who attempts to access it."

"Hmmph. If one must go to such trouble, then better a trap to slay them!"

*Yes, you* would *think that.* "Certainly that would be most satisfying, but once the trap is sprung and the intruder is killed, they cannot be interrogated or followed. But our adversaries are careful and wily: had we been incautious, our agents would have been detected and scrutinized. And so, were likely to be trailed back to this very stronghold, and your interest and objectives revealed. Or at least implied."

"So, to protect me, you moved slowly so you would not be caught as you crept in to get the information."

"Precisely." *So simple for you to understand, when you reduce all the nuanced principles to the only one with which you are concerned: your interests and safety.*

"Very well. So in the course of these slow movements, what did you uncover?"

"The connections between the theft of the arcane artifacts, the person discovered with them, and the Legate caravan we struck shortly afterward."

"And what was revealed?"

"That the goods stolen from you were not in that caravan at all. It was a ruse."

"Well," Hwe'tsara moped, "at least it cost them a caravan."

"True, but it cost us one of the few sets of eyes and ears we had within the Legate's fortress, and by far the best."

"What? How so?"

"Your Horror, do you recall how I asked your express permission to contact your best agent within Tasvar's fortress to determine the nature of the caravan?"

"I do. How else were we to learn if they had stolen my goods and sent them away?"

"Quite so. But by attacking the caravan, we confirmed what Tasvar himself had been unable to: that he had a spy high enough in his command ranks to pass such information to us. Including the misinformation with which that agent had been furnished: that your goods were being carried by that caravan, when in fact they were not."

Fezhmorbal saw the cruel truth slowly dawning in Hwe'tsara's almost pupilless eyes. "So when we attacked it—"

"—we not only missed the actual target but revealed to Tasvar which of the three persons he misinformed passed the news of the caravan to us."

"That agent is also the one who poisoned Tasvar's mindspeaker, is it not?"

"Yes," Fezhmorbal replied, hiding his irritation. Grooming that agent within Tasvar's fortress had been his first task for Hwe'tsara. "Most unfortunate, it took two seasons of work to get an agent close enough."

"Was it really so hard to find someone who would infiltrate his organization?"

"No: it was so hard to contact and suborn someone who was *already inside*. Fortunately, prakhwai have families."

Hwe'tsara shook his head. "It is an endless puzzlement to me."

"That prakhwai have families?"

"No, that any of these breeds are willing to die for each other. Not merely risk their lives, you understand, but die."

Fezhmorbal shrugged. "It was thus with our agent. To protect one he loved, he poisoned the mindspeaker. Once he'd thus broken his oath of service, he was our creature. This time, he never had a chance of escape, since it was a trap specially set for an informer. All Tasvar lacked was his identity."

"And he was tortured?"

"If so, it would not matter. We are not implicated. The one we used as his contact was a kajh without a gang."

"And our agent was willing to trust so humble a source?"

"Not since we had the kajh represent himself as an agent of your archrival Shvarkh'khag. Our agent had no reason to suspect that the source of the very generous bribes was other than the one credited with them. Indeed, the kajh we used as a go-between never knew any different, either."

"'Knew'?" Hwe'tsara repeated, emphasizing the past tense.

"Your Horror, certainly you do not believe me so stupid that I would allow such a trivial catspaw to live, do you?"

The x'qao shifted in his seat, glanced down at his "throne room's" immense new urn, vapor drifting up in lazy wisps. Fezhmorbal had never heard the liege was fond of bathing, but then, he had little interest in Hwe'tsara's personal habits or preferences. "So," the monster said, face folding into a terrible frown, "there was nothing of value in the caravan at all?"

"Other than a smattering of routine trade goods, no."

"Very well, but...where are *my* goods?" the x'qao roared suddenly, as if the latch on the gate of his rage had finally broken.

"North of Khorkrag. As I said at the outset, Your Horror."

"Very well...but how did they get *there*?"

"Do you remember the strange humans who appeared shortly after the splitting star?"

Hwe'tsara shook his head, as if dizzied by a sudden change of direction. "Er, what? Well, yes, I do."

Fezhmorbal thought it possible that he might actually have remembered. "What you may not recall is that, other than their visit to the vansary, there was no further report of them here in Forkus."

"They housed with the Legate. Did they not take service there?"

"Unfortunately, the loss of our informer in Tasvar's hierarchy occurred before we had reason to inquire." *Probably the crafty waterbag's intent.* "But it appears that the humans left Forkus shortly before his treachery was discovered." *And I must pause, so that I can remember the look on your hideous face as I add—*"In fact, it seems the humans left Forkus the very same night that your goods were stolen."

Hwe'tsara blinked, then jerked upright. "Them? *They* stole my goods?"

"It is almost certain. I believe I apprised you of the strange nature of the attack on the hovel where the trade was to be conducted."

"Yes," snapped Hwe'tsara.

*Which actually means, "no" given the asperity of your reply.* "There is evidence that some of the devices they used were artifacts, including their armor...which reportedly bore a strong resemblance to that which you had agreed to purchase." Fezhmorbal shrugged. "Typically, I do not trust reports of brief sightings by hungry wretches who may or may not have been present to see what they claim, but the similarity among the descriptions of the armor the humans were wearing as they left Forkus is striking."

"But how do you know they are in Khorkrag?"

"*Near* Khorkrag, Your Horror," corrected Fezhmorbal, buying time to make sure his next words did not betray him. *If he learns that I employed my own watchers because of his own refusal to take adequate precautions...well, that will not end well.* "To answer your question. You are naturally aware that I maintain many informers in the city, both to keep track of developing frictions among the lieges and to note any unusual activities that might lead to opportunities."

"Yes, yes: you are well informed. Go on."

Fezhmorbal mentally breathed a sigh of relief which he dared not show physically. "Two such informers reported that those who attacked the hovel hastily departed north into the wastes that same night. Those two informers have since remained quite close to the humans." *True enough.*

"And how do they report to you? Are they mindspeakers?"

"No, Your Horror. But this is why you have not seen Gasdashrag. He set out north along the river, just as we suspected the thieves had. They had all but given up hope of finding their trail until they discovered a marker some four days north of Forkus: it was in the form of the secret sigil I had given the two informers to alert me when they had news."

Hwe'tsara's brow descended. "They are suspiciously loyal, these informers, to venture into the wastes alone."

"Not so much loyal as very eager to get the rest of their pay, Your Horror. Each received a season's worth of moss for their trouble, but we had a further understanding that they could expect up to four years' more if their news was worthy of that price." *Every word, technically true.*

Hwe'tsara's eyes widened at the extravagance of the reward, but he simply said, "Go on."

"Many of their marks were washed away by weather, but Gasdashrag's group was persistent and always found another mark further along the river's course. The humans were clearly concerned with getting as much distance from Forkus as possible, so remained on the swiftest path. That made it relatively easy to rediscover their trail when it was lost."

"And where are they now?"

"Gasdashrag has reached Khorkrag. His reports are as yet inconclusive, but the humans are not far off. My informers left a marker near the river ferry, but no humans entered the town. So it is almost certain that they remained on the western bank, quite possibly because Khorkrag's sentiment against humans was already rising. He stoked the fire of that irritation by visiting your cousin, Suzerain Ormalg's liege in that place, and funding a bounty upon any humans found in the wadi country, particularly those which might be headed to Ebrekka."

"Why there?"

"Although my informer's sigils are general, the humans seem to have several races with them. One of them is a mangle, and Your Horror hardly needs me recount the vile cooperation between that species and humans."

Hwe'tsara nodded slowly. "This Gasdashrag of yours has done well. And with a quarter the number of the words you require."

"Your Horror is the very embodiment of wit. At the risk of taxing your patience, Liege Hwe'tsara, I wish to return to the decoy caravan that Tasvar dispatched eastward the night your goods were stolen."

"Is the matter important?"

"It is often difficult to know if peculiar events are important or not, but this is so singular that I feel I should share it, so that your superior mind might detect meaning or guile that I have missed."

"Yes, yes, Fezhmorbal, I am delighted to help you do *your* job for me! Be quick, though!"

"I shall be the soul of brevity, Your Horror. When the caravan was intercepted three days east of Forkus, our forces quite nearly fully destroyed it. Several praakht, and their more human prakhwai kin, fled. They were not tracked; there was neither time nor need. Unfortunately, all the humans were slain. However, one of them—a female scribe whose origins were likely from Beyond—did not join in the defense of the caravan, but rather, freed a well-secured pack from the best cargo frame and dashed it to the ground. It began fuming immediately and was consumed by the time the attack had concluded."

Hwe'tsara became interested despite himself. "So: bottles of acid that vaporized everything else in the pack?"

"Your Horror's perspicacity remains unmatched. Yes."

"Do you have any clues as to what it contained?"

"There were no residues that the attackers could detect, which would be peculiar if any metals were present. So I presume it was a repository for secure messages."

"Is that so odd?"

"It is, if the caravan's only purpose was to serve as a decoy. And it is an extraordinary level of precaution to take if the communications were of only a routine nature."

"Yes, I agree, but what is to be done about it? What is the profit of your telling me this?"

*Asking that tells me how you shall die: on the claws of a reasonably clever opponent.* "The profit is in knowing that such a strange thing occurred in such unlikely circumstances. One can never tell beforehand when just such a detail will prove the key to unlocking a much greater puzzle box later on."

"Fauughh! You and your puzzles, Fezhmorbal. You are still entirely too like the humans you wish to replace, I tell you." He stared. "Well, is there something else?" There was a taunting relish in his query.

Fezhmorbal cleared his throat. "I have noticed that there is a heated urn of water just beside your throne."

Hwe'tsara almost smiled. "And?"

"And I have it on good authority that one of Ormalg's own viziers, the renowned keeper of knowledge, W'sazz-Ozura, arrived in Forkus but two days ago. So I cannot but wonder: has she brought news of the splitting star?"

Hwe'tsara did not seem to mind that Fezhmorbal had solved the rather obvious puzzle. "Indeed! You are correct. And here is my esteemed guest!"

Without warning, the waters in the immense urn frothed and the mostly serpentine form of W'sazz-Ozura broke the surface. Her six arms dripped and rivulets paralleled the ancient wrinkles and folds running down her torso, which resembled a human female as much as an asp.

"He is an interesting deciqad, is he not?" Hwe'tsara asked his guest before turning back to Fezhmorbal. "Great W'sazz-Ozura has *illijor* Talents, you know!"

Fezhmorbal tried not to swallow or blink. *Which means she could be a mindwatcher.*

"He isss a sstoop, like any other," she said dismissively, every sibilant sound louder and longer than usual.

Fezhmorbal slowly released his breath.

Hwe'tsara, oblivious to his counselor's momentary panic, eagerly asked his august visitor, "And what of his foolish projection about the equally foolish star?"

"It isss as the sstoop foretold."

Hwe'tsara's smile fell away. "What?"

"You were foolishhh to disregard his perceptionsss, Hwe'tsara. The splitting star has indeed changed its path through the heavensss. What this portends is unknown. But it is unlikely to be a star, which are fixed in their placesss. It is more akin to Garthyawan, which moves around us. Thisss does the same. It iss more swift. But it iss also lesss stable."

"What do you mean?"

"The star-splinter's period has shortened. The best eyess of our breed assert that it glows slightly brighter. Logically, this occurs because it comes closer. This is all I know or wish to discusss. Your failure to pay heed to the sstoop shall be brought to Ormalg's attention. Do not make such a mistake again." She sank back into the urn with a long, relieved hiss.

Hwe'tsara turned amazed and angered eyes upon Fezhmorbal. "How did you know?"

"I did not know," Fezhmorbal said truthfully, struggling not to gloat. "But its timing, arriving only ten or so days before the humans, seemed too unusual to be a coincidence."

"And you think that they somehow created this splitting star? Or summoned it? How would they so confound the normal order of things?"

Fezhmorbal simply stared at Hwe'tsara before asking, "They *are* humans are they not?"

The x'qao half rose from his throne. "Do not take that tone with me, stoop!"

"I did not mean to insult Your Horror," Fezhmorbal assured him. Which was true: he had actually hoped to keep his contempt out of both his voice and his gaze. "I merely underscore that if humans were to be described with only a single term, it would be 'surprising'—and usually, in the most worrisome and inconvenient sense of that word."

"Well," Hwe'tsara sulked, "that much is certainly true. Now get Gasdashrag more resources; he seems to be achieving far more than you!"

# Chapter Forty-Nine

The sun was striking day-end sparks from the river when the battlefield was finally cleared and the Crewe met with the two humans and fifteen kajh—both trogs and trogans—who had sworn to follow them. One part of Riordan wanted to urge them all to make their own choices, but then shrugged and admitted that he wasn't here as a union organizer and that this was Bactradgaria. As Bey had repeatedly pointed out, such ideas and gestures would simply not be understood. Not yet, at least.

What none of the Crewe had been prepared for were the additional twenty-three trogs—scouts, porters, artificers, handlers—who'd decided to follow the lead of the warriors. They were the majority of the survivors and, like their leaders, shifted their interest to the Crewe when Sharat turned away the humans and trogans.

The trogans had then approached Bey, and were, by turns, stunned to learn of the strangely reasonable terms of the Crewe's oath of fealty they would take with and through her, as well as the unusual equity in the distribution of food, water, and routine duties. She recounted with a mix of amusement and worry how they had reacted to the strangest of its arrangements: that she was the leader of all the trogs who joined.

This had sent the captive kajh of all races into a huddle. There, it turned out that several of the trogans had roots in the Free Tribes and reminded—or in some cases, informed—the others that

504

female leaders were known among those peoples. They explained that while it was uncommon, it was not unusual, particularly when a female was extremely clever and skilled. And if there were a few who had not been completely swayed by these assertions, they decided that inasmuch as Bey was the trusted friend of a small band of harrows who had utterly shattered a much larger caravan, they would gladly follow her.

Hresh stood as oathkeeper when they swore fealty, but was surprised by some of the changes the Crewe made to the typical terms. He stared when Caine concluded by telling Orsost and Enoran, "For now, we take your fealty, so that you, and those sworn to you, know yourselves to be an honored part of us. However, when we come to a safe place, we shall release you from this oath, so that you may choose your path—with us or not—unpressed by the desperate circumstances of this moment."

After Caine turned and began walking away from the wondering trogs and the two somberly nodding humans, several others caught up to him, Miles in the lead. "Damn, sir," he asked, "were you quoting Shakespeare or something?"

"Shut up, you little *pendejo*," Dora whispered sideways in Spanglish. She jerked her thumb back over her shoulder. "Look at them; they're *loving* it."

"In both our cultures," Yaargraukh nodded sagely, "great warriors are often depicted as admiring poetic words that give voice to the honor in their hearts."

"Well, this warrior could use a drink!" O'Garran proclaimed.

"Right after we decide where we're heading," Bannor announced, remaining close to Ayana as she limped along with the group.

Girten frowned. "But...we're going to Ebrekka, right?"

"We may still go there," Riordan replied doubtfully. "But now that we know the two kajh from Forkus were leaving a trail of breadcrumbs behind us, we have to ask if that's still the best path."

"Besides," added Duncan, "there are a lot of different groups here and they don't all want to go to the same place. The h'achgai would all rather go to Achgabab, as long as it's safe to do so. Sharat just wants to break trail and lose whoever's tailing us—and now, him. The mangles want to go to Ebrekka. And although we need to go to Achgabab *eventually*, that doesn't mean it has to be our first stop. What do you think, Commodore? Should we—hey! Where are you going?"

Riordan had veered off, heading toward his place in the camp circle. "Mission of mercy," he called over his shoulder. "I'll catch up with you at the meeting."

Bey jumped to her feet when she heard Caine approaching. Since their disagreement over her means of interrogation, she had been respectful and amiable, but remained withdrawn. She eyed the large, heavy hide sack slung around his neck but said nothing.

Riordan considered and rejected what would have been his natural greeting: "Mind if I sit down?" Like almost every other polite nicety he'd been taught on Earth, it just wouldn't be heard the way he meant it here. She'd most likely reply that, since he was "Leader Caine," he could sit wherever he damn well pleased.

So instead, he stopped a few meters away and glanced at the empty space around her gear and sleeping fur. "Looks like you've moved away from the others." *Not like there are many "others" left from Forkus, anymore.*

She shrugged. "I had to."

He walked closer, sat well over a meter away from her. "I'd like to understand why."

She sighed. "Losing Zaatkhur today means I am without a fur-mate. So I had to move to a place away from all others."

"Fur-mate," Riordan repeated, nodding. "I've heard that term and wondered about it. What does it mean, exactly?"

She still did not meet his eyes. "We sleep in groups. But our places in them are not random. They are determined by many things, but the most important is that we have a fur-mate who is always next to us. You have felt the nights here: even in summer, it is rare that there is no frost. To keep from becoming cold, or sometimes from freezing, you must rely on a group, or at least one other person, with whom to share your body's warmth, and they with you."

She glanced at him, but not suspiciously. "It is not—as Leader Miles jokes and seems to believe—about mating or any such nonsense. It is about trust. You will be putting your back to your fur-mate. For a long time. If you are lucky, for years." She sighed. "On the other hand, making a wrong choice when agreeing to a fur-mate could very well be your last mistake."

Riordan nodded. "So losing Zaatkhur is not just a pain to your heart. It is a danger to you, as well."

She looked straight ahead. "I trusted Zaatkhur from childhood. To him, it did not matter that I was female and kajh. He was as the father I cannot remember from the Free Tribes. And as a leader, not merely a truthteller and counselor, I cannot take a fur-mate without transferring some of that privilege to them."

"So the trogs from Forkus and the new ones could become jealous as a result of your choice."

She sighed. "If I choose a fur-mate who is from Forkus, the new trogs will presume I favor my original band and that I am likely to take their side in future disputes or sharing of goods."

"And if you chose one of those who just joined us?"

She shook her head. "Even worse. Firstly, they do not know me. Secondly, whichever one I choose will be envied by the others in their own group. Worse yet, there are very few females among those new to our ranks. So males might mistake my choice as an invitation to mating. Which would bring up greater difficulties. And those from Forkus would be sure I was abandoning them to be with a group that has crogs like myself."

She raised an exasperated hand toward the emerging stars. "But none of that truly matters because I still do not know any of them and have no way to know which ones I might trust and which not."

"It sounds like there are no easy answers," Caine agreed. "And it sounds like even if you had one, you couldn't act on it soon. Not until you found someone you trusted."

"That is true." She sighed, then glanced at him. "It was a hard day," she said quietly. "I thank you for seeking me out and trying to understand our ways."

Riordan shrugged. "I'm happy to do it. But tell me: would an extra sleeping fur help?"

She stared at him. "We do not have extras. Leader Duncan often asks me the value of things. In turn, I learn about our supplies and stores. So I know we have just enough. And I have heard that so many of the newcomers' kits were lost in the attack that there are more of them than new furs. So as I say, we have no extras."

"Well, I wasn't thinking of an extra, exactly. The fact of the matter is that I really don't need my sleeping fur. I have this suit."

She stared at what she called his magic armor. "That cannot be comfortable to sleep in."

"Actually, it's probably a lot more comfortable than you would be, sleeping with just one fur and no fur-mate." He extracted his sleeping fur from its sack and handed it to her. "Here. I know you won't accept a gift. So just keep this until you find a fur-mate. Is that acceptable?"

She took the fur from his hands very slowly, eyes on his. "You are very kind, Leader Caine."

Riordan smiled. "Kind has nothing to do with it! I need my leader of trogs to be fit and ready for each new day, no matter how cold the night is."

Bey stared sideways at him. "You are a very poor lia— eh, you are not convincing when you deny your kindness, Leader Caine."

"Okay, but"—he lowered his voice to a conspiratorial whisper— "let's keep that a secret. Just between us."

First, Caine couldn't keep a straight face. Then, when she smiled, he couldn't keep from laughing.

Bey rolled her eyes a moment before a chuckle escaped her and she punched his arm.

It was a playful blow, but Riordan figured it was even odds that he'd have a bruise there in the morning.

Without any suggestion or prompting, the h'achgai and mangles joined the Crewe for the discussion on where to head next. As soon as the last of them was settled, Yaargraukh sat very straight and said, "We must start from this proposition: that we are now the hunted, not the hunters. To assume anything else is to invite ruin."

When he did not add anything, Arashk confessed, "I suspect that many must now think we should go directly to Achgabab. But if we are being followed, I am less certain."

Ulchakh shrugged. "It is widely known that was always my final destination. Yes, I saw the value of going to Ebrekka, but between our pursuers and those seeking bounties in the wadi country, that seems a much more perilous path."

Arashk seemed to be supporting his head with one of his arms. "But if we go to Achgabab now, we might lead those pursuers to it."

Ulchakh nodded. "Yes, but it is not as though the location is unknown. Yes, it is hard to find, but anyone who wishes to do so could. And there are ways to signal our approach before we would be revealing any of the hidden ways." He glanced at Yidreg who confirmed the trader's assertion with a stately nod.

"Still," Arashk pressed, "from the oldest legends and wisdom, we are told never to go there if we are being pursued. If so, we could forever ruin one of the reasons it has always been a haven: that the x'qao cannot reach it, not without losing the element of surprise."

Yidreg and Ulchakh nodded at that, too. Riordan wished he knew what that signified, but was pretty certain—chogruk or not—that he wasn't supposed to.

Duncan put out his hands in what was almost the universal gesture of an appeal to common sense. "We have to assume that whoever is following us knows, or will soon discover, that we changed our destination to Ebrekka. We didn't keep it a secret, and the traitors had ample opportunities to leave marks at the ferry. And again when we made our way further north."

O'Garran frowned. "Yeah, but that trail ends where we crossed, which isn't too far from here."

"I would be interested in knowing how any pursuers would cross the river where we did. Or any place but the ferry at Khorkrag, for that matter," Peter pointed out quietly.

"Okay, point taken," Miles admitted. "But here's the real worry: What if one of the pursuers is a mindspeaker? Doesn't that mean they could be sending back, oh, I don't know...sitreps on the state of their pursuit? And if they've got a boss who can read minds, doesn't that mean that the two who betrayed us could have been making, well, reports? If so, then the bastards who knifed poor Zaatkhur in the liver and cut his throat have been walking, talking transponders the whole time. And their last signal was right here, damn it." He thumped the ground.

Caine shook his head as the h'achgai and mangles exchanged long glances. They could have been reacting to the dire ramifications of O'Garran's summation or at his ignorance for even thinking such things possible; there was just no way to tell. "Look," Riordan started, "if the traitors could send some kind of mental updates on our position, then they wouldn't have needed to leave markers behind. Because, as what happened to the two of them today proves, that can go seriously wrong in all sorts of ways. So let's leave that worry behind for now.

"What we can't leave behind or avoid is the simple fact that there could be an ambush waiting for us if we keep heading for Ebrekka. And until today, that's been the destination we've been talking about since we left Khorkrag."

"Could be an ambush on the way to Achgabab, too," Katie muttered.

Riordan shook his head, but Ulchakh answered first. "It is very, very unlikely, Friend Katie. To go to Achgabab we mostly travel north. This keeps us well to the west of the wadi country—the Orokrosir—where the bounty hunters from Khorkrag are said to be searching. So unless someone already knows we are headed to Achgabab, which we do not yet know ourselves, they are very unlikely to catch up to us."

"Whereas," Ne'sar added quietly, "the entire width of the Orokrosir must be crossed to reach Ebrekka. It is almost due east of this place and while it is good traveling country for small parties afoot—and especially with a mangle guide—it would be difficult for a cargo-laden group as large as ours, and the two rads would make it far more visible."

Arashk frowned but said nothing. Nor did anyone else.

Bannor sighed, leaned back. "Sounds like we have a destination."

Riordan rose. "So, if we're all in agreement, let's go tell Sharat and the others."

"Do not bother," said Tirolane, approaching out of the darkness.

"Why?"

"Because our group has arrived at the same destination. And I suspect by the same logic." He paused, looked directly—purposely—at Riordan. "I would ask a favor of you, however."

Riordan nodded. "If we can help you, we will."

"I wish to travel with you." In response to their raised eyebrows, he hastened to add, "I have nothing but admiration and gratitude for Sharat and his band, but I know my path does not lie with them. They are about the Legate's business and so, follow his orders as to what they must do and where they must go." He shook his head. "I cannot be so bound, for I know not where my duty will take me."

The others had risen as he spoke. Bannor shrugged. "Can't say our path will be any more convenient for you."

Tirolane nodded. "You are correct, it might not. And yet, I think our journeys might be bound closer than you, or even I, suspect."

Riordan watched his eyes and detected something beyond affability, something more like...pleading?

Caine put out his hand. "We are proud to have you traveling with us. Bring your kit over tonight, if you like."

Riordan drew a deep breath, much as he might have before diving from a great height or at a forking path in a forbidding forest. "Bannor, you and I need to be up earlier than usual. We're going to need to work out a formation for this crowd. Everyone else, we head for Achgabab at first light."

# Dramatis Personae

## HUMANS AND ALLIES

Alnduul: Dornaani renegade; former Senior Mentor of the Custodians of the Accord, Dornaani Collective

Ayana Tagawa: former XO of SS *Arbitrage*; former Japanese Intelligence

Bannor Rulaine: colonel, crew of UCS *Puller*; former US Special Forces/IRIS

Caine Riordan: commodore, USSF (ret.); former IRIS

Craig Girten: Lost Soldier; former US Army

Christopher "Tygg" Robin: lieutenant, SAAS/IRIS; crew of UCS *Puller*

Dora Veriden: security specialist; crew of UCS *Puller*

Duncan Solsohn: major, former CIA/IRIS; crew of UCS *Puller*

Eku: factotum in the service of Alnduul

Karam Tsaami: pilot and flight officer, CSSO; crew of UCS *Puller*

Katie Somers: corporal, UCAS Armed Forces

Melissa Sleeman: advanced science and technology expert; crew of UCS *Puller*

Miles O'Garran: master CPO, former SEAL/IRIS; crew of UCS *Puller*

Missy Katano: Lost Soldier; civilian contractor

Murray Liebman: Lost Soldier, former US Army

Newton Baruch: lieutenant, Benelux/EUAF; former IRIS; crew of UCS *Puller*

Peter Wu: captain, ROCA/UCAS; former IRIS; crew of UCS *Puller*

Richard Downing: former Director of IRIS

Susan Philips: Lost Soldier, former captain, special operations executive, UK

Trevor Corcoran: captain, USSF; SEAL/IRIS

Yaargraukh Onvaarkhayn of the moiety of Hsraluur: exile from the Hkh'Rkh Patrijuridicate, former Advocate of the Unhonored

## THE BEINGS OF BACTRADGARIA

Arashk: h'achgan band chief

Bey: whakt, kajh truthteller

Fezhmorbal: deciqadi war leader/liaison

Hresh: h'achgan oathkeeper

Hwe'tsara: x'qao Liege

Sharat: captain, forces of the Legate

Ta'rel: mangle merchant

Tasvar: station head, forces of the Legate

Tirolane: soldier from Zrik Whir

Ulchakh: h'achgan trader

Yasla: mindsenser, forces of the Legate

Yidreg: h'achgan hunter-of-clan

Zaatkhur: praakh kajh, friend of Bey